monsoonbooks

THE MALAYAN LIFE OF FERDACH O'HANEY

Frederick Lees was born in 1924. He served in the RAF during the war and afterwards studied at Liverpool and London universities. He then joined the Malayan Civil Service and held posts ranging from District Officer through State Secretariat duties to Emergency work on the Director of Operations staff. His last position was Secretary of the Election Commission. Lees' most memorable moment in Malaya was his rousing call of '*Merdeka!*' at the conclusion of Malaysia's Declaration of Independence ceremony on 31 August 1957 after Syed Jaafar Albar – who had been asked by Tunku Abdul Rahman to lead the crowd in cheers of '*Merdeka*' as the dignitaries left the stage – lost his voice after the first two proclamations. Lees, who was sitting with Syed Jaafar in the control box of the newly erected Stadium Merdeka, stepped up to the microphone to save the day.

Lees returned to Southeast Asia in the British Diplomatic Service and worked in Singapore. In the 1970s he became involved in the work of British and European non-governmental organizations concerned with Third World development. This took him to Ethiopia and the Sudan. Later he returned to diplomatic work to train the foreign service of Papua New Guinea. The last part of his career was spent in the Asian Development Bank in Manila.

His first novel, *Annals of the Purple City*, inspired by a sojourn in Macau where he studied Chinese, was published in 1995. In the following year he published a widely praised historical novel, *The Arthuriad of Catumandus*. He is married, has two sons, and now lives in England in a little Sussex town about which he recently published a novel, *The Rape of Rye*.

THE
MALAYAN LIFE
OF
FERDACH O'HANEY

FREDERICK LEES

monsoon

monsoonbooks

Published in 2009
by Monsoon Books Pte Ltd
52 Telok Blangah Road, #03-05 Telok Blangah House
Singapore 098829
www.monsoonbooks.com.sg

ISBN: 978-981-08-2382-5

Frontcover photo: Cricket pitch at Government House (1950).
Image©Hulton-Deutsch Collection/Corbis
Backcover photo: Police talk to an old Chinese man who may have
information about communist terrorists (1949). Image©Hulton
Archive/Getty Images

National Library Board Singapore Cataloguing in Publication Data
Lees, Frederick.
The Malayan life of Ferdach O'Haney / Frederick Lees. – Singapore :
Monsoon Books, 2009.
p. cm.
ISBN-13 : 978-981-08-2382-5 (pbk.)
1. Malaya – History – Malayan Emergency, 1948-1960 – Fiction. I.
Title.
PR6062.E4185
823.914 -- dc22   OCN313646903

Printed in Singapore
12 11 10 09   1 2 3 4 5 6 7 8 9

I

In spite of his father's Irish nationalism and the subversive fact that, eighty-two years earlier, his grandfather had been in a Fenian plot to blow up Chester Castle, Ferdach O'Haney joined the British Colonial Service in 1949. Like so much else in his life, the step was something of an accident. At no point before, during or after World War II – in which he had fought because he carried a British passport – had he really considered what he wanted to do in life. With no desire for power or making a lot of money, but much addicted to pleasure, he had naturally enjoyed being a student. So, once he had got his degree – a First in History – the only path that appealed to him was that of postgraduate study. He just wanted to stay put; study had never made great demands on him and was no obstacle to having a good time. At heart he was a drifter though in no feckless sense. Perhaps best described as an intellectual dilettante, he enjoyed the present, he loved the past, but he drifted into the future looking backwards.

Because of his academic results, he was cocksure that a fellowship would be offered to him, though, to encourage this, he had shamelessly ingratiated himself with members of the academic staff, both male and female, several of whom already perceived him as a desirable addition to their ranks and sometimes to their beds. The eminent historian Geoffrey Barraclough once prophesied that he would end up as an eccentric old professor of early medieval history. Ferdach could think of many a worse fate.

But one morning, at breakfast, before any firm academic offer had been received, his mother glanced at him over the top of *The Times* and said, as though talking to herself, 'I wonder how Ferdie would get on if he applied for this?'

Accustomed to his mother's third-party form of address, Ferdach immediately replied, 'Now what in the world would he be applying for?'

'His Majesty's Colonial Service,' his mother replied with a disarming smile.

'The Colonial Service,' Ferdach repeated in amazement for the idea of such a career had never entered his brain. 'Me, an Irish patriot, in the service of the Crown?'

'Yes,' said Mrs O'Haney, with reserved English calm. 'For service in Malaya.'

At this Ferdach thought his mother must, for a regular *Times* reader, be suffering from some obscure form of amnesia. Didn't she know there was a communist rebellion in Malaya – an unpleasant guerrilla war? Did she want him to risk his life again? After four years in the RAF, bombing Germans and once being obliged to crash land in flames, he wanted no more of war. She must think he was an inveterate fighter like his father who, being also a man of conflicting convictions, had contrived to serve both the Irish revolution and the Crown. But before he could dismiss the idea his mother, who in many ways knew Ferdach's needs better than he did, continued enticingly, 'And candidates who want to learn Chinese will go to Macau for language study.'

In that instant, incredible though it may seem, Ferdach's mind was made up. Europe apart, the Far East was an area of the world about which he had always indulged in the most romantic speculations, though speculations they seemed likely to remain for he had never identified any way of realising them. But in life as in love a good chance should be seized. Macau, China, journeys to marvellous cities, mountains floating above expanses of white mist, living among and learning to love fascinating people, mastery of an ancient culture through its language, quickly formed a glorious kaleidoscope of ideas in his brain. One of those irresistible impulses with which he was all too familiar was bubbling up in his mind like volcanic magma below a calm plain; one that did not require rational decision but acceptance. It was as though some inner being was compensating for his conscious lack of purpose. So it was that the following day he responded to the advert and not more than six weeks later, after a number of exams and interviews, he found himself in a long dark-panelled room in the Colonial Office nervously approaching seven elderly gentlemen seated on a raised dais behind a horseshoe table.

He was cunning enough to know that he must show this clutch of former colonial governors that he was the right material. And he was a good actor. To their initial questions, which were ordinary enough, he gave crisp and to-the-point replies, succinctly outlining his background, his interests, his conservative views on most of the important things in life, and, of course, his sporting activities, about which he lied even more for he hated physical exertions unless they were amorous. At length came the crunch when a small and rather emaciated bald gentleman, through whose features the skull seemed almost visible, asked in precise Scottish tones, 'Now what, Mr O'Haney, would you say was the primary duty of a Colonial Service officer?'

Seated at a lower level, Ferdach shot up at him a gaze that was at once sincere, piercing and, strange to relate, compounded with affection, and said in terms equally precise, though not Scottish, 'To maintain law and order, sir.'

There was an almost imperceptible, but nevertheless quite distinct, murmur of approval from the other members of the mystical panel; seven pairs of old eyes seemed to light up at the sight of this handsome, well-groomed young man, who would carry forward the imperial sword of destiny which each of them had, in his own youth, taken up. In that moment Ferdach said to himself, 'I'm in Ferdie, dear boy. I'm in.'

On the first day of the course at London University designed to familiarize recruits with their future life, their supervisor of studies, a Mr Eliot, began his welcome address by saying, 'Gentlemen, you have entered this service to work yourselves out of a job.'

This did not come as a shock to Ferdach. In the years leading up to the war, he had already been seduced by the left-wing apostles, Auden and Spender, Laski and Orwell, the gullible Hewlett Johnson and the progressive rest. He had even, when at the university, joined the Communist Party and studied the dialectics of this, that and the other in the rather dirty Liverpool branch, complete with unwashed spitoons, of the Boiler Workers Union. Although he had left the party sometime during his time in the RAF, he was still very much of the left and he knew which way the wind was blowing. And sharing the anti imperialist sentiments of his father, it didn't worry him a jot. But he was amazed that such a prescient statement should trip so lightly from the mouth of the man appointed to monitor and maybe spy on them during their year of study. However, the expressions on the faces of the thirty or so rather serious young men around him hardly suggested that the words had jolted their view of the world. They were upright, loyal to the Crown and, apparently, the epitome of Dr Arnold's Christian men, who anticipated a lifetime of undiluted colonial authority and honest work ahead of them in places ranging from deepest Africa to the far Pacific. Unlikely that they would be persuaded otherwise by some none-too-senior liberal-minded functionary – perhaps a misfit unsuited for duty overseas – from the Colonial Office.

Their studies embraced the anthropology, economics and history of the territories to which they were to be posted. There were also language studies at the School of Oriental and African Studies, where Ferdach had his introduction to the Cantonese dialect of Chinese. Unfortunately, the far from inscrutable staff in the Chinese Department seemed unable to agree on teaching methods; bitter feuds raged over varied forms of romanization, so that the instruction, using conflicting systems, was pretty useless as Ferdach discovered when he eventually reached Ipoh, a prosperous mining town in the north Malayan state of Perak. There, although Cantonese was the lingua franca among the Chinese, Ferdach's knowledge of it on arrival turned out to be less than minimal. In fact, it would have been better if all of the young men destined for Malaya had been taught some Malay, a simple version of which was commonly understood by the majority of Malaya's inhabitants, regardless of race.

Chinese apart, the other subjects to be studied were not unfamiliar to well-read Ferdach, who quickly slipped into the habit of cutting many of the lectures. This gave him the opportunity to immerse himself for a while in the world of Fitzrovia, which he soon discovered from his dingy digs in Little Russell Street. In five minutes he could be in Charlotte Street or Rathbone Place, with their exciting pubs – the Fitzroy Tavern, the Marquis of Granby, the Wheatsheaf and the Black Horse – frequented in those days by a varied assortment of artists, actors and writers, easy women, servicemen looking to be picked up, and an extraordinary variety of dropouts. Across Oxford Street were slightly, but only slightly, more salubrious haunts: the Gargoyle, Berlemont's French pub, the Mandrake Club, the Colony Room. In these places the literary and artistic company was amusing, occasionally brilliant but invariably inebriated. He had stumbled into the heyday of postwar Fitzrovia in which sexuality, a subject of great concern to lusty young Ferdach, was even freer than it had been during the war years. He threw himself into that life with gusto.

Truth to tell, Ferdach was sometimes inclined to abandon his intended career. Not just because of the temptations of London but because of the stuffiness of some of his fellow students. Could he really fit into their kind of colonial society? He could see merit in their seriousness and their honesty and he came, almost against his will, to see merit in much that he learned about British rule in the colonies. But there was his other self that stood aghast at their self-satisfied belief in the English right to rule. They gloried in the obverse side of the coin and forgot the reverse of which he, with his Irish blood, was well aware. Maybe if he had fallen in love at that time with one of the women with whom he had affairs, he would have strayed from his chosen path. But he did not; none of the women captivated him sufficiently. None held sway for more than a few weeks, some only for a night. However, in his last academic term he was taken up by a film director who, fascinated by Ferdach's melancholy good looks and that slim young body always given generously if somewhat casually, wanted him to take a substantial part in a film on Modigliani he was making provided, of course, that Ferdach moved into his Belgravia flat on a permanent basis. What young man wouldn't be tempted by a film career? Before long he too might possess just as luxurious a flat as the director's where he had begun to spend more time than he should, though so far without commitment.

Late one hot and sunny morning, Ferdach woke up there alone in bed to find his naked body being sketched by an almost legendary Fitzrovia artist, Nina Hamnett, whom his film suitor, as part of his research for his Modigliani masterpiece, was cultivating … for as long as she could come up with useful information. It being morning she was not yet sozzled on gin. He asked her what she thought of the director's offer. She went on sketching, then turned to look at him intently before saying, 'Pity you haven't got big muscles – apart from that monster. I love men with muscles. They make better models. I'm always glad when Ross brings back his guardsmen. They're his real cup of tea. Real thickheads. He must have had a brigade of them. Yes, I've always liked his guardsmen.'

Ferdach knew what she was telling him but he wanted her to be more explicit, not giving him an ambiguous warning like some ancient oracle. He had always been aware of the sadness that seemed to exude from Nina's frail body belying both her bravado and her strident contempt for convention, but he knew that the sadness was combined with wisdom born of pain. He asked her again first with his eyes, then with, 'Ross says I look like Modigliani. And I can act Nina.'

She put down her charcoal deliberately. 'Maybe so, but don't accept it. Ross is an exploiter. Don't listen to him – especially when he tells you what a fool you are to leave this country. No, get out of the bloody place while you can. I've observed you closely. You're an original, not a copy. Acting's not for you.' Her voice became unusually grave. 'I've had a good life Ferdie, no, not good, not good at all … an exciting life. Once I knew everyone who mattered.' As was her wont, she reeled off names: Sickert, Roger Fry, the Sitwells, Augustus John, as well as many people she knew in Paris for she was an ardent Francophile; Ferdach knew about Cocteau, Picasso and Gaudier-Brzeska but there were others he had never heard of. 'But look at me now. Finished, a ghastly wreck. People tell me I stink. And where are the marvellous men I put before my talent? My artists, my sailors, my boxers? Nowhere, nowhere at all. I tried to live through them. I used them as my mirror but never saw myself. No darling, you'll have a better life in the East. Get out. This country is a shithouse.'

'Well it won't be before too long. Now there's a Labour government, we'll see great changes. We'll see–'

Nina gave a peculiarly throaty snort. 'Do you know one of the very first things Clem Attlee did when he got to Number 10? He rang up his old school to tell them an Old Haileyburian was now prime minister of England. Doesn't augur well for classless education does it?'

'It's probably a fairy tale. Anyway, change takes time,' Ferdach temporized uncertainly, remembering that day when he had given an extremely left-wing speech to a hangarfull of RAF guys at a mock election organized by the commanding officer at RAF Swinderby as flying had been cancelled due to bad weather. He had won by a resounding majority. It had been a harbinger of the great Labour victory a few weeks later. No, things really were going to change. People wanted change.

Nina had come over to him and was staring down at him as if he were some sort of odd biological specimen, which of course as a human being he was. 'No, my pretty boy,' she said stroking his hair and then, more delicately, his cock, before returning to her work, 'it's no fairy tale. It's true. But you can just take it as a metaphor if you like. That way it has more meaning. Things will change for sure. There'll be more bread and lots more circuses. And they'll probably let the masses behave as wantonly as us in time. Anything to keep them in their place once religion's gone phut. But fundamentally things will be the same. The top drawer will stay in place, only the muck in it will change, for the worse. So, not being rich, if you want a good life, get out. And here's some really practical advice: always go to places where it's never cold. Oh, the cold of London and Paris in the winter! Now get up. Get dressed. Let's go to the Café Royal. You can buy me a foxy gin. I don't want to use my begging tin today.'

As usual, Ferdach was happy to go with her. She might look a sight but she was generous minded and gay in the true sense of the word; and when necessary she could talk wisely. He was influenced by her greatly both in taste and in outlook. She was a model for the sort of woman he would admire: not one concerned with money, social position or breeding, but a woman who loved passionately and with complete feedom wherever she chose. She could tell marvellous stories; she could make people laugh; she thought boldly and she could be outrageous. One night she went into the Black Horse and shouted to all the writers, artists and soldiers gathered there: 'Darlings, I've had the change of life and I can fuck and fuck and fuck.' Some wag replied: 'But Nina you always have.' Her coarseness might make her anathema to respectable men and decent women yet her sensitive intelligence helped Ferdach to understand an earlier, more brilliant, world – the London and, above all, the Paris of the first decades of the century when all that was to become fashionable and allegedly new towards its end had first been experimented with without being didactic or under the false impression that it was breaking new ground.

2

Not long after that, following a voyage to Penang aboard the P&O liner, the SS *Canton* – during which the more elderly first-class passengers, and not a few of the younger ones, seemed phrenetically and pathetically intent on reviving what they imagined to be the prewar style of life *à la* Somerset Maugham – and a rail journey south, Ferdach found himself, one Saturday just before midday, at Ipoh Railway Station on a platform occupied by a milling crowd of Malays, Chinese and Indians. Waiting to be greeted by someone unknown, he stood among a little group of other newly arrived Britons, none of them his friends but some of whom he had become acquainted with on the *Canton*: a mathematics teacher and his wife, a geologist, a police officer, and a forestry expert. Nearby, looking as though they had just returned to their kingdom, were several self-confident English men and women whose loud and imperious conversation revealed them to be in tin or rubber. Their behaviour, not just to the porters, suggested that they expected absolute obedience from mankind at large. Gradually, everyone else in Ferdach's group was greeted by future colleagues, the tin and rubber masters went off with their friends and, invariably, their well-armed security guards, and the crowd of Malayans thinned out until, at last, Ferdach found himself abandoned and almost alone on the platform.

No one had asked for him. No one had even looked at him. Something had obviously gone wrong. Never mind, a large hotel was an integral part of the station, he could get a room himself. At the reception desk, however, he learned that it was Ipoh race week meaning all the good hotels and the government rest house were booked solid. Resentment and anger at not being met or sent any instructions began to well up in him. People in the hotel lobby were scrutinising him curiously.

He was pouring with sweat. He could feel it running off the top of his head and into the corners of his eyes, down his cheeks and his neck, down his spine, his stomach, his thighs, in fact just about everywhere. Only his feet felt cool. He seized his suitcase furiously and made off. Outside the station, which faced a large well-tended formal civic garden, there were no taxis left with which to search for accommodation. He did not trust the drivers of the trishaws drawn up before the row of fan-like palm trees opposite the station to understand his absurd predicament. In any case they did nothing but stare at him, bemused. So, most unwisely, he set off on foot, with no idea how far he would have to go. It turned out to be a long way.

The roads beyond the garden seemed devoid of even a single hotel. Lugging his suitcase along under the brilliant sun he felt dazed as he trudged on and on. Why were these well-ordered streets so quiet? He was quite unable to take in his surroundings. He later found himself on a road with some traffic and a stream of people. The road crossed a long bridge over a river that flowed between wide-set grassy levees and led into a less pretentious but far more vibrant part of town, bustling with people and noisy with conflicting styles of Asian music. Sweltering in the heat, still clad in an out-of-date tropical suit purchased in Golden Square, Soho, wearing a ridiculous stetson which, he had been wrongly advised, was replacing the topee, and sweating so copiously that his clothes looked as though they had just come out of a wash tub, he no longer gave the impression of being a newly arrived colonial master. Judging by the amused glances of passersby and the squeals of laughter of the Chinese kids who had taken to following him this way and that in mimicking procession, he had only succeeded in becoming a figure of fun. When almost at the end of his tether, in a seedy narrow street down which he had darted for refuge from mocking eyes, he saw the words 'Carefree Hotel' over a doorway. On an impulse he pushed through its bamboo fly curtain and into a dark hall. A very fat Chinese lady was sitting behind a counter. He asked her for a room. Without a word she waddled up the stairs, along a narrow corridor and pointed into an empty, musty-smelling cubicle. Ah, the huge relief to escape into its obscurity.

Supine and motionless on a hard bed with his head on a smooth, well-worn wooden pillow, Ferdach stared gratefully up at the slowly rotating fans which provided a little cool relief below to ten or so cubicles whose partition walls rose only eight feet high. His thoughts went back to Nina Hamnett and her advice. Maybe he shouldn't have listened to her after all? Then he remembered how the fearless wreck of a woman had laughed scornfully in Ross's face when, furious at losing his potential Modigliani, he accused her of being an interfering old fucker.

Almost to his own bewilderment, Ferdach's innate resilience took over; this annoyance would be transitory, just another matter to be laughed to scorn. Nor would Nina have thought a toss of his present slight discomfort set against some of the problems in her own extraordinary life. And at least there was no danger of being cold in this place, that would please her. Drowsily he wondered what might have become of those few sensitive sketches of himself. Probably they had already been sold to pay for more foxy gins. Perhaps one day they would be valuable and collectors would wonder who was the slim young man sprawled so shamelessly, so priapically, on that ruffled bed. Then he fell into a very deep sleep.

3

He was awakened by the sounds of love – or rather of fucking. It was dark, save for the glow given off by a couple of small bulbs high in the rafters above the fans but he could tell that most, if not all, of the cubicles were occupied by couples hard at it. There was also a lot of loud Cantonese conversation. Though the grunting and groaning of the lovers and the creaking and thumping of beds could mean only one thing, the voices did not give much impression of tenderness. In fact there were occasional brawls, over what he could not tell. There was also much coming and going as occupants left and were replaced by other couples. Race week business must be very brisk. No one bothered to close doors or do anything else quietly.

He had obviously jumped into the Far Eastern pool at the deep end. This was a knocking shop. But, who cared, it was at least a place to rest until the morning. Anywhere was better than the street and the torment of those mocking kids. But to rest? Not likely. Ferdach O'Haney was young and lusty; he took after his frequently absent father who, he had been told, was as randy as a goat. The sounds had stirred his blood.

He had seen a tiled bathroom at the end of the corridor when shown to his cubicle. He wanted to piss and he was feeling sticky and dirty. Under the showers two Chinese men – one solid and muscular with a tough guy expression, the other athletically tall and truly an Oriental adonis – were soaping their parts and laughing uproariously as they chatted in Chinese and English about their recent sexual activities. They grinned at Ferdach – a fellow conspirator – when he stood beneath a shower faucet. The eyes of the adonis roamed over Ferdach's body before he said in a mellow voice suggestive of a high-church cleric, 'Did you have a jolly good fuck, my dear chap?'

Ferdach's face registered his surprise but he nodded with a smile and they left, still laughing.

How was he to get company for the night? His need was not just sexual, in fact it was hardly sexual at all. He felt very lonely, fed up and ill at ease. However, it turned out that getting company presented no difficulties. His cubicle bell quickly summoned a *fo gei*, a waiter, and Ferdach ordered a beer. No need to ask for anything else. The *fo gei* just said, 'You wan shor ti or all ni?'

'All night,' Ferdach replied. 'But want girl speak English.'

Miss Wong Siu Bo did speak English, and well. But this Ferdach found out only after he had made love to her somewhat mechanically and quickly, for the noises around spurred him on to a quick and decidedly unromantic release. Siu Bo was compliant though unmoved during the operation but once Ferdach had recovered from his exertions and thanked her very politely, as if he had just been given a cake, she told him about herself. She was proud to reveal that she had been educated at the Bukit Nanas Convent in Kuala Lumpur, where she had been dumped on the doorstep as an orphan. Ferdach told her that he only had one parent at home, his mother, whom he had, like his father, selfishly abandoned. He also told her about his unfortunate arrival.

She switched on a concealed reading lamp that Ferdach had not noticed. He saw that she was quite pretty with a face much broader than it was long.

'Why have you come to Malaya?' she asked, looking at him with a puzzled frown.

'Well ... to work of course.'

'Everyone must work. But why here? Why leave your mother? She must be sad.'

The thought that his mother might be sad on his account had never really struck Ferdach. He stared at Siu Bo. Questions and answers to many things seemed to lie in her eyes. 'I'm not sure. I don't really know. It was my mother's idea – I think.'

Her expression grew serious. 'You are still a boy and boys understand nothing – except this.' She gave his cock a little squeeze. 'But I tell you, Siu Bo and Ferdie same kind of people. We know where we come from but we don't know where we are going. We flow here, We flow there.

We abandon people. People abandon us – you at the station, me at the convent. Now we meet up together. This is very good omen. We shall always be good friends. I will help you.'

He was intrigued by Siu Bo's insight but not sure that the omen was so good. If it ever got out that he had spent his first night in town with a prostitute, the Establishment Office might not be too approving.

But he need not have feared. Friendships with Chinese people, he was to learn, tend to be sincere once entered into. None of that false 'do come and see us when you're in town' of the home counties. When Siu Bo said she would help, she meant it. One of her friends, most probably a client, was the owner of a small hotel, the Western Hotel – a respectable place, she emphasized. She went to see him early the following morning, came back in a taxi and conveyed Ferdach there, in a proprietorial sort of way. The owner, Mr Tan Heng Shan, seemed anxious to please her and promised to look after her friend well. Then she left after shaking Ferdach's hand rather formally. He only saw her once more in Ipoh, a few days later, when she visited him in the District Office to tell him, very quietly, that she was going to Penang as a secondary wife. As several pairs of clerical eyes were on them, he too spoke quietly, thanking her for what she had done. He felt a sense of real loss when she said she had to go, and so, anxious to keep a potentially useful path open, he made her promise that they would keep in contact.

4

Ferdach's room in the Western Hotel was high ceilinged and, after the cubicle in the Carefree, spacious. It was simply furnished but spotlessly clean with a black-and-white chequered marble floor that suggested the building had known better days. Beyond its two French windows there was a tiled patio extending to a white-washed wall, which contained great pots full of luxuriant plants with huge leaves. The overhanging branches of trees on the other side of the wall shaded the patio from the glare of the sun. Across the open windows, a reminder of the ever-present communist menace, stretched wire netting – strong enough to stop a grenade from being lobbed in from over the wall by a hostile passer-by. Presumably the idea was that it would bounce back and explode in the garden but it struck Ferdach that he could still be hurt by the blast. When he was checking in, Mr Tan had told him that there had been a number of grenade attacks in town but that he must not worry: they had ceased after it was forbidden to ride a bicycle at night in the town centre. Yet after the colonial splendour of the E&O Hotel in Penang and the comfort of the air-conditioned railcoach to Ipoh, the dangers of the Emergency still seemed unreal to Ferdach. By the time he had unpacked his clothes and arranged his few books and photographs he felt quite recovered from his dismal previous day, and went into the bathroom to wash and immerse himself in an enormous bluish green Chinese water pot decorated inside and out with pop-eyed goldfish. When he got out he noticed a stout frog about nine inches tall sitting next to the water outlet in the corner of the room watching him seriously like an aged gentleman at a strip show. The sight disturbed him more than the thought of a hand grenade.

In the dining room over breakfast he sat alone. Nearby were the mathematics teacher and his wife from the railway station. Ferdach now recalled they were the Sweinsnoeps. Were they of Dutch origin perhaps? Or Afrikaans? What a ghastly name. They were talking to a tall, red-haired clergyman who, to judge by the serious conversation about grades, algebra and calculus, must be from the Anglican school at which Sweinsnoep was to teach. What fun the pupils would have with the new teacher's name. Mrs Sweinsnoep, who looked left out and rather distracted, smiled sweetly at him and directed her eyes to the empty chair beside her. He smiled back but decided that he would not join the group or tell them that he was not safely moored like them but at present adrift and unsure whom to contact. In a way, he did not mind about this. Being adrift made him feel a bit like a tourist who could do what he wanted. It pleased him that, as yet, he was not irreversibly committed to the place and he wanted no assistance. Perhaps he would not join the government service after all. Someone's negligence might have given him a chance to opt out. Perhaps he had even disappeared from the official records. Maybe he could find some business position and make enough money to live on for the time being, repay the outward fare and get back to London, back to where he really belonged and eventually to that career in films. Mrs Sweinsnoep kept on glancing at him. She had beautiful olive skin, an oval face and regular features, set off by lustrous black hair that fell in a long sweep over her right cheek down to her elegant neck. She kept pushing it back with her hand. Ferdach found this movement, which was accompanied by a slight incline of her head, intriguing. It suggested an inner nervousness that did not quite accord with her voluptuous figure. Sweinsnoep, the husband, was pale, blond and skinny and looked very dull. Perhaps she wanted to leave him and marry someone else – that would be understandable, if only to change her name.

Ferdach went to work on a luscious mango. On a large wooden *dulang* – a wok-shaped receptacle used for gold panning – papayas, jambus, bananas, rambutans, mangosteens and a pineapple awaited his attention. So colourful, so sensual; he would never be short of vitamin C. He glanced across at Mrs Sweinsnoep and wished he knew her Christian name. She was still looking at him. He allowed a rambutan to wink at her from between his lips, white framed by red, before swallowing it. Their eyes met and they both smiled, she very broadly. The association of the sound Sweinsnoep with such beauty seemed absurd. Perhaps when her husband was teaching the Pythagoras' theorem he, handsome and irresistible young Ferdie, would call on her, bored and lonely during the heat of a tropical afternoon, and she would open up to him as unresistingly as his ripe mango. Ferdach's libidinous reverie was abruptly shattered by an Australian voice speaking his name.

'O'Haney. It is you, isn't it? Sorry to disturb your tucker. Yes. You must be Ferdach O'Haney.'

Before him stood a white man; that is to say a man clad entirely, or almost entirely, in white: a stiff starch-rich white shirt, brillian white drill trousers, equally starched, tight at the waist and ballooning below, and to complete the impression of purity, white socks and surprisingly elegant pointed white shoes. The only exception to this white get-up was a clip-on bow tie in garish green and red culminating in two bright orange dots at each of its pointed extremities.

Ferdach stared up at the newcomer then half rose for an instant to greet him. How was his presence here known?

The man said, 'Mr Tan phoned me this morning. I'm really sorry; I should have–'

'You are?' interrupted Ferdach.

'Waite, Jimmy Waite. I'm the ADO, the Assistant District Officer. You're supposed to join my office. Well, you see … I always try to get away when it's race week and the telegram about you arrived after I'd left for Penang so–'

'I wasn't met,' said Ferdach, with a chuckle intended to relieve Waite's obvious embarrassment. 'Well I guess I did feel a bit unwelcome but in the end it was no problem. I found a place to sleep quite easily.'

'Sleep easily! In the Carefree? I do apologize.' Waite then gave a broad grin and put on a slightly interrogative look.

'I said I found a place easily not that I slept easily. But once I finally fell asleep I was out all night,' said Ferdach censoring the events between his two sentences though he felt sure the circumstances would not have bothered this oddity. 'And this morning someone directed me here. Anyway, join me.'

Waite sat down and set about the rambutans. 'I like your linguistic precision O'Haney, very necessary in government. Now you know we have this Communist Emergency, silly bloody name. Lack of precision again. Emergencies should be temporary things. This one will go on for years. Well, it's not the only emergency. We've got all sorts of emergencies – in health, education, transport, you name it. And we've got a housing emergency. Which is where you come in – or rather don't, if you see what I mean. You're a bachelor, so you're only entitled to a hotel room or a room in the rest house. And as the rest house is full, it means you'll have to stay here. Unless,' Waite paused, 'you'd like a room in my place, the house I share with Lars Gunnar Ericson.' That was the first and last time Ferdach heard Waite using Ericson's Christian names.

Ferdach assumed that Ericson was a Swede, at least in origin, but asked no more about him. Instead he took another of his impulsive decisions. Whatever Waite and Ericson were like, he would need company if not friends and, in his first job in life, he would certainly need advice. So, 'Yes,' he answered enthusiastically, 'I'm most grateful. I'd be glad to move to your place as soon as you can have me.'

5

Some people found Waite's withdrawn manner intimidating; those better acquainted with him said that he was very modest. Both views, skimming the surface, had failed to apprehend the unusual intelligence and the rich interior life before them. But how could the average man judge otherwise? Manner apart, people might also be put off by Waite's facial features, which were large and not particularly attractive; his nose was too protuberant, his mouth too small when set below such a great conk, his eyes deep set with perpetually half-closed lids, and his head, like his body, big and fleshy. Yet Ferdach had already sensed, emenating from beneath this unsatisfactory agglomeration of discrete elements, kindliness, serenity and good humour, which must surely well up from a profoundly calm source deep within him.

Indeed, Ferdach had taken to him instinctively, sure that he had encountered a genuine human being, but on reaching Waite's house in Sturrock Road near to the racecourse the first thing he was asked to do seemed odd. They had just dumped Ferdach's luggage in the hall, outside the room he was to occupy, when Waite barked: 'Come upstairs. Now.' They went up to a very long sitting room, extending from the staircase, which was well inside the house, out over the whole of the large carport. Waite sat Ferdach opposite him at a round coffee table on which stood an abundance of tumblers and beer bottles. Ferdach also noted whiskey, brandy, crème de menthe and three bottles of pernod. There were also blowpipes, one long and one half its size, together with a bamboo quiver containing darts. Under the table Ferdach's feet connected with an airgun. Waite picked up a deck of cards, shuffled them, took a card at random, it's back to Ferdach, stared at it, then closed his eyes with an expression of deep, almost pained concentration.

'Right, Ferdie. Don't think too hard. Just tell me quickly; is this a heart, a diamond, a spade or a club? If you feel like it, specify the card.'

'It's a diamond,' said Ferdach without hesitation. 'Jack of diamonds.'

Waite made a note on a piece of paper and took another card, again concealing it's face from Ferdach.

' A diamond,' said Ferdach. 'Not sure, but it's a picture.'

Waite made another note, took another card, and Ferdach said what came into his head. This was repeated another eighteen times before Waite stopped abruptly. 'Eleven out of twenty,' he said quietly, 'And two cards spot on: the jack of diamonds and the joker. Well above mathematical probability.'

Ferdach said nothing; not because his telepathic success had struck him dumb but because a single question was exercising his mind: Was this how everyone carried on here? Had he dropped into some universe in which a completely different form of behaviour prevailed, one in which telepathic questioning of new acquaintances was quite ordinary? The novelty of everything he had encountered since arriving in Malaya, coupled with his own uncertainty about himself, had disoriented Ferdach. And since he had no desire to appear odd, or unable to cope, he was by now determined to take everything that came his way without comment – until he had got the lie of the land.

'Didn't that surprise you?' asked Waite.

'Why should it?' Ferdach replied, waving his hand airily.

'Eleven out of twenty – and two spot on?' For a moment Waite looked surprised himself, even excited, as though he had discovered someone quite out of the ordinary. Then he saw the grin flickering around Ferdach's mouth. 'Oh you clever bastard,' he said. 'Well, let me tell you, it won't happen again. It's only when people aren't prepared, aren't even remotely thinking about it, that telepathy succeeds. See, I'll try you again.' And Waite went once more through the procedure of holding up cards for Ferdach to scry. The result was abysmal, not even one out of twenty.

'It's like not being able to remember a word when one tries too hard,' observed Waite. 'When one is too aware, a little door closes in the brain and the message can't get from one cell to another. See what I mean?'

'Yes Jimmy. Now can I unpack my bags? By the way, where's

Ericson? What's he like? Does he go in for this sort of thing? Telepathy and stuff?'

'You won't like Ericson,' said Waite. 'I don't like him much myself. He's out tonight. You'll meet him tomorrow morning at breakfast I guess. Let's go down for tucker. Cookie always makes us eat at eight. And no, Ericson doesn't go in for telepathy and stuff. The two pleasures of his life are hard work and screwing.'

6

Ericson *was* at breakfast – deep into the *Malay Mail* which was spread over the table covering the cereal, the fruit, the toast, the marmalade and the butter. Had it not been for a tall milk jug, the paper would have dipped into the dish of hot bacon, sausages and fried eggs that Cookie had placed on the table. He barely grunted when Waite announced 'This is Ferdach', continued reading about the most recent ambush while the others did their best to get their breakfast from under the newspaper. When he stood up to leave he stretched and bent his arms, flexing his muscles; it was clear that he was proud of his body which was tall, slimly athletic, bronzed and also handsome in a Duke of Edinburgh sort of way. He was only wearing very short shorts that exposed an expanse of magnificently tanned thigh and emphasised a phallic bulge more or less at a quarter to nine while higher up a tight sweat shirt rode up to reveal his flat muscular stomach. The display complete, he belched and looked down saying, 'Ferdach? Funny bloody name that. Your first day on the job isn't it? Remember to duck the bullets.' Then he was off shouting, 'Some people have to start work early, you know,' as he went through the front door to the Public Works Department landrover waiting for him in the car port.

As though Ericson and all he said and did was nothing but insubstantial air, Waite looked under the table at Ferdach's feet. 'Those won't do at all,' he remarked casually.

'What won't do?'

'Those shoes. I'll lend you some jungle boots.'

'To wear in the office?'

'You won't be in the office. You're starting on resettlement today.'

Though not in the least sure what his job entailed, Ferdach had certainly heard about resettlement, so he realised that Ericson's remarks about bullets was no joke. Was he about to be chucked into the deep end? He knew that during the Japanese occupation half a million Chinese, and many Malays, had fled the towns to squat on small clearings in the jungle. There they grew tapioca and kept pigs and chickens to stave off starvation and to escape the hated invaders. But there too they fell under the influence of the Malayan People's Anti-Japanese Army (MPAJA), whose redoubts were in the jungle. The squatters were not dominated by the largely communist MPAJA unwillingly; most of them believed they were doing their duty to China and Malaya by helping the MPAJA with supplies and recruits.

Despite the wartime role of the MPAJA, the British, on their return, refused to devolve power to any government in which the communists had a say. However, thinking to give the Chinese a more equitable role in public affairs, the Attlee Government dreamed up a centralized constitution, the Malayan Union, which transferred powers from the Malay States to the Crown. It seemed crass to Ferdach that this had ever been tried for it should have been clear that the Malays would never submit to a system which they rightly considered to be a humiliation. Their inevitable resistance, led by Dato' Onn bin Ja'afar, obliged the British to back down and set up the Federation of Malaya which preserved the power of the Malay States. And just in time: for when the communists failed to foment social and industrial unrest and opted for an armed liberation struggle, the Malays were prepared to support the British who told them that independence would follow a communist defeat. Neverthless, before victory could be achieved, the problem of the Chinese squatters had to be solved for they were a sea in which the communist fish swam freely. And so, not long before Ferdach's arrival, a plan was devised to gather all the scattered squatters into Resettlement Areas in which there would be effective civil administration. Though named after General Briggs, the Director of Operations, the plan was really the brainchild of Tan Cheng Lok, the Malayan Chinese leader. Since the squatters must first be found, young men like Ferdach were to move around the countryside to plot their houses and record details of the occupants' numbers, sex, age, occupations, dialects, livestock and so forth in a sort of twentieth-century tropical Domesday survey.

Out of pride, reserve, or foolishness – it was difficult to say which – Ferdach did not ask Waite precisely what his duties might be, nor did Waite give him any inkling of them. But the necessity of wearing jungle boots implied that he would be in the jungle and this did worry him as he had never been in anything resembling a jungle in his life, apart from the conservatories at Kew. And Waite's insistence that he should also borrow a jungle-green shirt and trousers as 'white would make him too conspicuous', made him feel a bit like a man preparing for execution.

Thus clad he went with Waite to the garage behind the house where a white Jaguar was being lovingly polished by a slim and extremely beautiful young Malay named Yusuf whose equally beautiful wife stood modestly in the doorway of the driver's house nearby. Yusuf must have been married very young for his wife had a little child on her hip and was attended by two small shy boys each of them, as the Arabian Nights might say, more exquisite than the next. Ferdach was very conscious of lustrous brown eyes staring, quite pityingly, at him from round serious faces and this heightened his foreboding of doom.

On the way into Ipoh, Ferdach sat in the rear seat while Waite sat next to the driver, Yusuf. Both of them talked softly to each other in Malay which seemed to flow from Waite's mouth as easily as it glided from Yusuf's finely shaped lips. Ferdach decided to interrupt sarcastically: 'Ericson's a charming man isn't he?'

Ferdach heard the word 'Ericson' in the Malay translation that Waite gave to Yusuf, then both of them laughed out loud, Waite explosively and Yusuf in a musical giggle.

Ferdach thought he must try another conversational tack. 'Shouldn't I be signing various documents today – to say that I've assumed duty and things like that? I need to be paid you know.'

'All taken care of by Mr Suppiah, the chief clerk. He'll just ask for your signature at the office.'

'Well, won't I have to open a bank account?'

'I've already spoken to the manager of the Hong Kong and Shanghai. You can go in any time to sign the documents.'

'Well, won't I need a car? I can't depend on you for transport all the time.'

'Best car for you is a Morris Minor. I've already arranged it with the manager of Wearne's Motors. Suppiah will ask you to sign the government car loan agreement.'

Ferdach sank back without a word. It seemed he had been taken over completely by Jimmy Waite who, though kindness and consideration itself, and thereby saving him much trouble, had done everything without a word of consultation. This was outside Ferdach's experience. Maybe Waite was trying to make up for his dereliction of duty when Ferdach had first arrived. Anyway, like it or not, it was done. The image of the Red Queen seizing Alice's hand and charging ahead with her willy-nilly crossed his mind. 'Faster, faster,' he said to himself. 'Don't try to talk.'

As they approached the rickety wooden District Office, Ferdach noticed that Jimmy's hand was playing with the wavy black locks that fell onto Yusuf's neck. It was not the sort of thing that anyone would do to a chauffeur either in England or Australia but it seemed an entirely natural gesture here. Ferdach's memory suddenly went back, as it often did, to his distant grammar school and to a Greek class. They were reading the end of *Phaedo*. Socrates had been playing with his disciple's hair and had said, 'Tomorrow maybe you'll cut off this beautiful hair, Phaedo.' Ferdach hoped that Yusuf would do no such thing.

7

When they got out of the car a gaggle of white-robed Indians surrounded Waite, all arguing in excited voices with many gestures and much head wagging, each one doing his level best to gain the ADO's attention. They continued as he moved with them towards the office like the stamen at the centre of an exotic white flower. He shouted towards Ferdach, 'Report to the chief clerk. Report to Mr Suppiah.'

'Ah, Mr Ferdach O'Haney, sir. You must be an Irishman. I know that because my last boss in KL was Mr O'Rourke, Mr Kevin O'Rourke,' said Mr Suppiah, who was a small white-haired gentleman, a little podgy but with an expression that contrived to be at once worried yet benevolent. 'He told me so much about your beautiful green Ireland and so I knew you must be of the male sex even before I met you because in the Gaelic tongue, a woman is prefixed by 'Ni' and a man by 'O'. We have many such subtleties of expression in our own language, you know.'

Ferdach had no desire to lose Mr Suppiah's obviously great goodwill towards Mr O'Rourke's homeland by telling him that he himself had been brought up in Chester in a very English environment. He even affected a slightly stagey Irish accent when he replied, 'Ah yes, Mr Suppiah. Sure and I'm pleased to meet you, I am. Yes Ireland is a lovely green place, a lovely green place, but Malaya is lovely too, now isn't it?'

Mr Suppiah's voice fell a little as he answered, 'Oh yes, Mr O'Haney. But you should visit Ceylon – we say Sri Lanka. That is the most beautiful green island in the world – I mean except Ireland. And like Ireland it has so many historic places. Have you never been there then?'

'Yes indeed. But only for a couple of days. We stopped in Colombo on the way to Malaya. I thought it was very beautiful even though we only went some thirty miles out of the capital. And the people are beautiful too.' His brogue had slipped so he added, 'Sure and one day I'll be going there again.'

Mr Suppiah beamed mightily but fluttered his hands deprecatingly. 'Now Mr O'Haney you need worry about nothing. I've prepared all the assumption of duty and car loan documents for you. Here they are. You only need to sign them.' His voice fell again. 'You will be requiring a salary advance quickly no doubt. I will speak to my good friend Mr K. M. Milvaganam in the financial department. He will take action at once.' Mr Suppiah glanced over Ferdach's shoulder towards the end of the large barnlike office. 'Ah, Mr Waite is wanting you. He has got rid of those dreadful Tamil fellows. They are constantly desiring him to settle their domestic problems. That is how they pester the district commissioners in India you know. Tchek. Tchek.'

Ferdach went off to see Waite, comforted by Mr Suppiah's final precise, lilting, reassuring words: 'Any problems Mr O'Haney, sir, just come to me. I am here to help you. And top of the morning to you dear sir, as Mr Kevin used to say.'

Waite's huge desk, which looked as if it was a survivor from the earliest days of British colonialism, was strewn with large black-and-white maps on a scale of six inches to a mile. That is to say, the limited number of features – roads, rivers, contour lines and spot heights – were in black while the rest of the paper on which they were printed was a large expanse of white. Without more ado Waite gestured to the topmost map and said, 'Now Ferdie, this is your area. We know that there are a lot of squatters to the northeast of the main road south, just a few miles out of town near Gunung Rapat. I want you to chart the positions of each house as accurately as possible.'

Ferdach apprehensively asked one of the many questions jostling in his mind. 'How do I get there?'

'By lorry.'

'Lorry?'

'Of course. You'll have a platoon of special constables and an ARO – an assistant resettlement officer – an excellent translator. Ah, there he is. Come over here Mr Choo.'

There emerged from among the numerous people who were milling around the office a youth, no, more like a boy, for he looked about fifteen years old. Short but well built with broad shoulders and a round smiling face his head seemed somewhat large for his body. Ferdach noted that his hair was thick and wavy – more like a Malay's, but his skin was the ivory white much admired, so he had heard, by the Chinese. Mr Choo and Mr O'Haney smiled at one another nervously, each sensing the other's lack of experience.

'Well, you've got one thing in common,' said Waite reflectively and as though something had only just struck him, 'It's the first day for both of you. So keep a sharp lookout. There was an ambush just south of Gunung Rapat five days ago.'

Then followed the distribution of census forms with instructions on what to ask for and how to behave. They were rudimentary and obvious. Neither Ferdach nor Choo spoke about the ambush but they did want to be told exactly where the lorry would drop them off and what sort of terrain they would encounter. Unfortunately the expanses of white on the map told them virtually nothing. Waite did say, after talking across the office to a superior-looking Malay *penghulu*, or headman, that the dropping point was adjacent to jungle or was it *belukar* – secondary jungle? Nobody seemed too clear. The *penghulu*, who was responsible for the Malay population in an entirely different *mukim* or parish of the district then made off without offering further information. 'You'll be fine,' said Waite reassuringly. 'Your platoon will be composed of Malays – mainly *kampung*, village, boys. They're used to that kind of country.'

After rolling up the map and receiving some rations and a metal box of first aid equipment from a cunning-looking office boy, who introduced himself as Jamal, Ferdach and Choo left Waite who had swung round to survey the tall stacks of sawdust-coloured files on the long table behind his rotating chair. But before he could pick up a single one the Tamils were back in force, led by the same crafty office boy, to besiege him again. Choo whispered to Ferdach, 'They've paid Jamal to put their files on the top of the in-tray.'

Outside the office, sitting near a lorry under the canopy of a rain tree, were twelve young men in jungle green each armed with a rifle. They were under the command of a corporal who jumped up and saluted Ferdach smartly. He then said something in Malay.

'What did he say?' Ferdach asked Choo.

'Don't you speak Malay?'

'No.'

'Oh.' Choo's eyes widened in amazement and concern.

'I've only been in Malaya for four days. No. Less than that. Well, what do you speak?

'English, Malay, Cantonese, Hokkien, a little Hakka. Oh, and some Mandarin.'

I'm in at the deep end again, thought Ferdach. Obviously he had to form the closest alliance with his new ARO. 'Well Choo. Your many tongues will have to get us by. My French, Latin and Greek won't help me very much here. But as we go along, do your best to teach me a bit of Malay. Anyway, what did the corporal say?'

'I've forgotten now,' said Choo who had not got over the shock of Ferdach's linguistic ignorance. He turned to the corporal and started a conversation that resulted in him looking even more anxious than before. Ferdach heard both of them saying '*yang pertama*', Choo saying it several times.

'What does *yang pertama* mean?' asked Ferdagh.

'It means "the first". It's the first time this patrol's been on an operation. They're all recent recruits. Corporal Tahir says that all but him have only just finished their training.'

'This can't be true,' sighed Ferdach. 'Why didn't Waite ask us to make our last wills and testaments before we set out. Come on Choo. Tell Corporal Tahir to get his blokes moving. If we're all heading for doom, let's get it over with quickly.'

8

The lorry stopped beside the tiny village of Gunung Rapat. This consisted of a coffeeshop and a number of wooden houses inhabited by Chinese; some of their children came out to stare at Ferdach and his little band of warriors. The police lorry driver shouted that he'd be back in the evening, without saying exactly when, reversed his vehicle and roared off to Ipoh at top speed as though an ambush was imminent.

Ferdach was bewildered. He hardly knew where he was; he had no idea where to start, and he could not guess how he would get on with a group of men he had only just met and whose experience and way of life were very different to his own. But he was sure of one thing and one thing only: not an iota of his misgivings should be visible externally. While the Specials were sorting out some rations which they had heaved from the back of the lorry, he looked up and down the road as though making some important assessment, then at the village behind which lay his area of operations.

Further away to the south, and east of the main road, he could see great limestone bluffs capped with a mantle of jungle. Could guerrillas be observing them from up there? Choo saw which way his new boss was looking and told him that penetrating the near vertical cliffs were deep caves, several of which housed Chinese temples. The most famous of the temples was high in the rock face and difficult to access. As though he had forgotten the dangerous mission ahead, Choo rattled on about these wonderful places explaining that the larger shrines possessed gardens lying between their facades and the main road. They were fantastical and beautiful with small lakes and streams crossed by crooked bridges and mossy stepping stones. His voice now became suffused with enthusiasm. In hidden corners there were ornamental pagodas to which couples liked to retreat for privacy after their fortunes had been told by the Taoist priests. The couples would eat rice cakes and fruit, admire the gawping goldfish in the pools and, here his face was wreathed in the most joyful of smiles, would court one another, sometimes with poems. When Choo said he had been there himself only last weekend to celebrate his eighteenth birthday with his friend Agnes Chan, all was clear. Ferdach realized that his ARO was more mature than the lad of fifteen who had seemingly appeared before him only an hour ago. Love could drive even the danger of death from a young man's mind.

While Choo wittered on, the Malay special constables lounged around or bought soft drinks in the coffeeshop. Ferdach suspected, nay hoped, that they were under the impression that he and Choo were discussing their tactics for the day. This belief he sought to heighten by unrolling the six-inch map and studying it before calling Choo back to the present by saying, 'Do you think we should ask in the coffeeshop whether there are any squatters in the area behind the village?'

'No. Oh no. No, Mr O'Haney.' The sweet memory of Agnes Chan had evidently sped from Choo's mind. His voice fell almost to a whisper, even though no one within earshot was likely to understand much English. 'Many of the people around here support the CTs.'

'The what?'

'The Communists … the terrorists. The CTs,' said Choo, repeating the term that had received a semi-official kind of acceptance.

Ah yes, thought Celtic Ferdach; the enemies of the British, whether Afrikaners, Indian or Irish, are always terrorists. 'Well Choo, if we can't ask, we'd better plunge into the area assigned to us and hope for the best. But first I'm going to look in the coffeeshop – show the flag as it were. Ask Corporal Tahir to come with us.'

In the shop four Chinese men of different ages, but all quite robust, were sitting around a table playing mahjong. Ferdach drew on the few words he remembered from Mrs Chin's Cantonese lessons in London. '*Zou san.* Good morning. *Sik jor faan mei ah*? Have you eaten rice today?' which more or less meant, 'How are things?'

All four jumped up, one knocking his stool over, and grinned while at the same time breathing throaty noises of appreciation, mainly '*Ho ah, ho ah*. Good, good' to which newly linguistically proficient Ferdach replied. '*chor lah, chor lah*. Sit down, sit down.' Stooping he picked up and replaced the fallen stool. One of the men courteously offered him a cigarette, which Ferdach, with an equally courteous gesture, declined. He then said, '*Zoi gin*. Au revoir.'

Choo and Tahir watched with interest, not having seen Ferdach in action before. Choo whispered, 'I thought you could only speak English Mr O'Haney.'

'You heard almost a hundred percent of my Cantonese vocabulary Choo. By the way, do you have to keep on calling me Mr O'Haney?'

'I'm sorry. I meant Tuan.'

'Not Tuan either. My name is Ferdach.'

'Fer– what?'

'My friends call me Ferdie, Mr Choo. So Ferdie will do for you too.'

'But why then do you keep on calling me Mr Choo? I am Choo Wu Yung.' He paused thoughtfully. 'Agnes has an English name. I should like one too.' Then he chortled like a schoolboy. 'Choose one for me. Christen me. Will you?' He repeated his request in Malay to Tahir who nodded his approval.

Ferdach glanced back into the interior of the coffeeshop. Behind the counter there were rows of alcoholic drinks including gin. 'What about Gordon? It's a good strong name!' Having received Choo's assent, like the Queen launching a liner, Ferdach said, 'I name this ARO: Gordon Choo. May God speed him wherever he goes – on land, sea or in the air but especially with Corporal Tahir and me – and occasionally, but only with our permission, with Agnes Chan.'

Ferdach then strode behind the shophouse and through the village accompanied by Corporal Tahir and Gordon, the three of them in a very good humour. The Specials spread out to right and left to provide cover, as they had no doubt been instructed at the police training school. The houses quickly gave way to vegetable gardens, and then to an area of sprawling fruit trees which was soon limited by a long barrier of scrubby undergrowth pierced, so it seemed, by a single narrow path right in front of them. Well, thought Ferdach, a path must lead somewhere; he hoped to a squatter house – perhaps to several of them.

'*Mahu ke mana?*' asked Tahir.

'Where do you want to go?' translated Gordon.

'Straight ahead,' stated Ferdach.

'*Jalan terus*,' translated Gordon.

This was not possible with the platoon spread out either side. So, led by Corporal Tahir then Ferdach and Choo, the whole party went forward in single file. Even Ferdach, with no military training, apart from the drill that the RAF considered adequate for aircrew, could see that this made them vulnerable to attack.

Tahir issued an order barely audible to Ferdach, who glancing around, saw that the constables were now bearing their weapons at the ready. Instinctively everyone had started to move as quietly as possible. Their caution seemed ominous; Ferdach did not like the feeling at all. Things had started to resemble a film about jungle warfare in Burma, but Ferdach did not believe himself capable of confronting any calamity with the aplomb of John Mills or Jack Hawkins.

Ahead of him Tahir had produced a long-bladed chopper, a *parang*, with which he hacked at branches blocking the way. This was so effective that their penetration of the undergrowth proceeded quite quickly until the foliage either side of them became more dense and the path was like the soft floor of a green chasm.

'I think this is just a wild pig track,' grumbled Gordon. 'Do you think we're going the right way?'

'There is no right way,' replied Ferdach in the same tones. 'We have to go on. Waite said there are squatters in there. We have to find them – a few at least. We don't want to look stupid.'

They pressed on. The trees and bushes around them were getting taller. Everything was gloomy and before long little sunlight reached down to them. It surprised Ferdach that it was not particularly hot. In fact the further they went, the cooler it became. It was eerily quiet. Not a sign of animal life but a few insects could sometimes be seen on dark stems or on the carpet of matted leaves and moss underfoot.

They were supposed to be looking for squatters but, on either side, it was difficult to see anything but leaves and creepers. Everything was so dense that had some living thing been just a few feet away it would have been invisible. Were the alleged settlers an illusion, an error founded on false information? Moreover, was the platoon in the jungle at all? That was where most squatters were said to have made their clearings.

Yet surely, Ferdach thought, the true jungle was far more majestic than this? Wasn't it, according to those LSE cultural anthropologists, a place held in awe by the Malays who, despite Islam, revered it as the dwelling place of jins and *hantu hutan*, spirits of the forest? Wasn't it an ominous place into which the Malays would not venture without repeating some charm to assure the spirits that they came in friendship? And wasn't it a strangely shadowed place typified by magnificent tall trees with immense trunks, high canopies and trailing lianas, a sombre place into which the rays of the sun never penetrated? There was nothing so mysterious here. Only very thick foliage of medium height on a terrain likely to discourage the most intrepid settler and be shunned by any self-respecting jin.

As he walked on, still trying to look purposeful, Ferdach began to find the silence around them, especially when they stopped for a few minutes to take stock of exactly what he could not say, peculiarly soothing. Surely there was no danger lurking in all this still vegetation that exuded such a lulling fragrance. Everything about them was quietly beautiful, slumbering in remoteness from the rest of the world, an Eden not to be disturbed, a place in which to day dream. He remembered a science fiction story in which some time travellers were walking, as he was now walking, along a forest track in a remote past time through such a place as this. They were not allowed to step off the track because if they did, even by a hair's breadth, something in the future would be changed. Perhaps if I go a few feet off this path, Ferdach kidded himself, when I come out I'll be back in London drinking foxy gins with Nina in the French pub, listening to her telling Gaston Berlemont her life story for the umpteenth time or maybe celebrating my first successful film role; it will all depend on how many twigs I have broken. Then all at once there was a sharp crack and he was struck by Gordon Choo who fell against his back with a yelp.

The platoon all faced outward thinking Choo had been hit by a bullet. But only silence followed; nothing unusual to be seen. Choo's foot had snapped a low rotten branch that had tripped him. He giggled and shrugged his shoulders apologetically. Everyone looked at Ferdach who gave the signal to continue. After half an hour or so, the path opened out and they emerged into an open space with a shallow stream on the far side.

Above them a menacing sky had become visible through a gap in the tree cover. It was like being beneath a partly finished dome that let in more light than before but not much. No longer was there any leaf or moss cover on the ground, only friable reddish soil and pale yellow sand over which the stream ran swiftly dispersing itself in shallow runnels. Ferdach remembered a story about some children lost in the Amazon jungle; they had got home by following a rivulet that in turn reached a stream leading to a river and then their village. Squatters must surely build their houses near streams; they needed water.

'Follow the stream,' he said to Choo who repeated the order in Malay, '*Mengikut anak sungei.*' This was reasonable enough at first but before long the stream, instead of flowing into a larger course, was joined either side by other indeterminate surface waters – scarcely streams – to form a broad morass into which their jungle boots sank from view, maybe dangerously for in some deep hollow the friable soil might form quicksand. Soon they were obstructed by scrubby bushes growing in the water as though the area had only recently been flooded. While floundering in this sloshy terrain Ferdach realized he had no idea which direction they had come from. Before he could think about the problem this posed they had to get out of this mess. The solution came from example: Corporal Tahir, afraid of getting stuck, began to struggle up an incline on the far side of the waters. Others followed. But none of them climbed up easily for the slope was wet and the plants growing on it simply uprooted when grasped.

'There isn't any jungle round here,' Choo gasped as he struggled upwards beside Ferdach. 'Just *belukar*. And we're on very old tin tailings.'

They had got into one of the nastiest environments imaginable. For these old tailings, the detritus left after some early mining operation, were uneven and crumbling. What was worse they had been abandoned for so long that secondary jungle had had time to form the thickest possible cover so obscuring the effects of decades of erosion by streams and rain that had sculpted the ground into weird shapes: here a miniature peak, there a plateau and now a shallow vertically walled ravine. By the time the whole platoon had helped one another to clamber their way up and join Tahir on top of the steep mound, everyone knew they were lost. All around the growth was high and thick. Tailings like this could go on for miles. And there was no way back.

How ludicrous, thought Ferdach. *A week ago I was dressed to the nines for dinner on the* SS *Canton and six weeks ago I was gadding around pubs in Soho. What a marvellous preparation for war. If we were attacked now, we'd be picked off one by one on this hillock. But what to do? We have to rest a while. Anyway how can I tell them to move on when I don't know which way to go?* Ferdach could scarcely contain his anxiety. So he let his mind stray, irritably and jealously, to the other men who had come out with him from England. Gilbert de Guise would be making his number with the chief secretary or 'signing the book' at King's House while the others would be comfortably ensconced in offices in KL or one of the state capitals. Was this peculiar experience some sort of a test devised for him alone by the Colonial Office or a divine joke thought up by the Almighty or was it all just a nasty accident? He plumped for the last explanation. But to be angered by it could be just as dangerous as being fatalistic. He had to stay calm and get everyone out safely. By now his thoughts had gone round in a useless circle and shamefully he had to admit to himself once more that he hadn't a clue what to do.

For a while they all squatted on their haunches atop their vulnerable perch smoking cigarettes and eating some of the rations. Most of the constables had leeches on their skin and were getting rid of them with lit cigarettes. Ferdach felt something like a sting on his leg. How the hell had anything got up there when his boots were tightly fastened. Then he noticed that one lace was not so tight after all; he loosened it further, rolled up his trouser leg and saw two leeches gorging themselves on his calf. A constable – Ferdach had heard him called Mat Noor – leaned over with a cigarette to scorch the leeches, which immediately gave up their feast. '*Terima kasih*,' said Ferdach, who was already picking up necessary phrases like 'thank you'. Mat Noor then gave his cigarette to Ferdach who returned the service where a leech had fastened itself to the small of the constable's back. Mat Noor's eyes suggested that Ferdach now had a friend for life. Gordon Choo watched the anti-leech drive with a smug grin.

'Why aren't there any on you?' asked Ferdach in an accusing tone.

'Chinese ointment,' replied Choo. 'I thought you'd all know about it. But I left the jar at home.'

At one point or another everyone stood up, faced away modestly from their companions and had a piss. Ferdach was glad he did not need a crap. Since the Malays sometimes glanced at him as if studying a strange animal he unrolled his useless map and stared down at it, overcome with embarrassment. Soft Malay conversation was murmured from one to another around him.

'Are they angry with me?' Ferdach whispered to Gordon. 'Are they blaming me?'

'Oh no Ferdie,' said Choo quite gently using his nickname for the first time. 'For Malays everything is the will of Allah. It's not your fault. We shouldn't have been sent here.'

Choo's words seemed to lighten the burden on Ferdach's mind. He looked up suddenly at those around him. Detecting not a sign of hostility or anger, he flashed a smile at their pleasant faces – for at that moment they all seemed uniformly handsome. It was returned abundantly. The gloomy spell had been broken, psychologically that is, for the dark clouds in the heavens had become ominous and rain had started to fall.

It was Tahir, for a second time, who decided what they should do, telling everyone they must push on regardless of difficulties, away from the stream but keeping fairly close together and on their guard. He said that no CTs could possibly be in such a foul hole because they had too much sense. Thus reassured and under Tahir's watchful eye they slid off the hillock and moved on, battling their way over rough ground through thick clinging foliage and helping one another every inch of the way. Ferdach was strangely pleased that he had virtually ceded command to the corporal; it gave him the feeling that he was now on the same level as these raw Malays recruits and Gordon Choo.

Mat Noor produced a spare *parang* from his backpack and handed it to Ferdach who took to slashing roughly at the undergrowth. '*Begitu tentu ta' jadi*,' chided Noor, which Ferdach took to mean 'you can't do it like that'. Then Noor taught him to wield the *parang* more skilfully with, '*Eh, buat macam 'ni*' clearly meaning 'this is the way to do it', which Ferdach copied as best he could. When necessary, some of them formed a human ladder so that others could more easily climb or scuttle over the unpredictable contours they encountered. This physical grasping exhilarated Ferdach who needed contact with human bodies as much as

Antaeus needed it with the earth. Despair had now been replaced in his mind by the warm glow that radiates from comradeship. In adversity a happy equality had developed; Ferdach hoped that he was accepted as one of them and that he no longer had to pretend to be a colonial master.

They fought on. The rain was persistent but now of little account; in fact it helped to cool their heads and faces during the next couple of hours. It was a hard and exhausting struggle, a true test of stamina. Yet no one complained, not because complaint would have been useless but because a singular friendship was growing between them. They could take whatever was going to happen. Once they thought they could hear the sound of automatic gunfire but though they stopped and listened hard, the thick vegetation muffled distant sounds and they heard nothing but the constant spattering of rain on the leaves and on themselves. Probably some practice fire, Tahir told them confidently. They gladly accepted his word and, without further ado, resumed their progress.

At long last, and quite unexpectedly, they reached the edge of yet another minor escarpment from which they saw an expanse of thunderous sky hovering over yet another darkly wooded landscape. Below, right in front of them, however, was a clearing in which stood a wooden house with a corrugated iron roof surrounded by a vegetable garden and fruit trees. Just here, it seemed, the tailings had come to an end. Surely the squatter area had begun.

They descended cautiously, the platoon fanning out around the perimeter of the clearing while Ferdach and Gordon approached the house. Tahir and Mat Noor went with them, their guns at the ready. There was something eerie about the place. The garden that from above had appeared tended was sadly neglected. The whole place was unkempt nor was there any sign of goats or chickens. The house was silent yet a thin column of smoke rose from a metal chimney. Could they be walking into a trap?

It was Mat Noor, over zealous and anxious to please, who went through the open door first. Almost at once he ran out gesturing to them to retreat. '*Jangan masuk!* Don't go in!' he cried, betraying for the first time a knowledge of English. '*Orang kusta*. A leper's house.'

'No, Ferdie,' cried Choo. 'Don't go in.'

Only Ferdach and Noor entered the house. A strangely sweet smell gave the impression the dwelling was abandoned but huddled in a chair was an old woman almost entirely swathed in black clothes. Her face was hideous for her nose had all but vanished. Both her hands, assuming she had hands, were covered in bandages. When she tried to stand Ferdach beckoned her to remain seated. But leprosy or not her eyes still seemed very much alive. She looked right at him and greeted him in Malay with 'Selamat, Tuan,' even though the household altar and the paper gods on the doorway told that this had once been an active Chinese household. Tears welled up in Ferdach's eyes for beneath his defensive cynicism his emotions ran close to the surface. Not surprisingly, Nina Hamnett, so pathetic, so frail, so defenceless, came to mind. He turned and saw Choo and Tahir still hovering at the doorway.

'Ask her who she is,' Ferdach told Choo who, from a safe distance, soon discovered that the old lady spoke Hakka, a Chinese dialect.

'Write down all her details on the census form,' Ferdach instructed. 'And make a note that she's a leper. Leave her some food. What else can we do?'

'We must report her to the leper hospital in Tanjong Malim,' replied Choo. 'They'll take her in. Food's not a problem. She says her relatives come and leave her food. But she shouldn't be alone outside of the leprosarium. It's against the law.'

To the consternation of those watching, Ferdach stepped forward and put his hand on the old lady's head. As he touched her, he wondered how anyone could believe in a compassionate deity; if it existed at all, it should be bloody well ashamed of itself. One of those stupid hymns he had once been obliged to sing, 'God moves in a mysterious way his wonders to perform', sprang to mind. Why did people make children sing such rubbish? Of course he pitied the woman greatly but what was the use of pity if he could do nothing to help her. But maybe God was in the same position? Having started the whole peculiar business off, perhaps the deity could do nothing now but sit back and watch. Ferdach stroked the woman's cheek gently. She looked up at him. Their eyes met again but he was unable to do more.

When he left the house everyone recoiled except for Mat Noor, who unexpectedly took hold of Ferdach's hand and whispered, 'Tuan very good, very good, *baik sekali*.'

Ivory-skinned Choo still looked anxious. 'Come on Gordon,' mocked Ferdach as he gently freed himself from Noor's grasp, 'You can't get leprosy that easily.'

'I know that,' said Choo shuddering. 'But I'm terrified of *ma fung* – leprosy.'

'Well let's go on, down that path. If the old lady's relatives bring her food they must be living nearby.'

The rain had finally stopped and during the next hour or so they found three squatter houses. Ferdach and Choo agreed on their rough location in relation to a nearby stream that, incredibly, was marked on the map. They also enumerated the inhabitants, recorded their ages, their occupations and the fact that they were all Cantonese. At each house, all went smoothly. The platoon fanned out. Tahir told his men not to steal any fruit or vegetables, and the Chinese inhabitants, though apprehensive over what was afoot, were co-operative enough.

It was now time to make for the main road. The squatters had told them how to get there. Soon it would be dark but all the same they delayed along the way to visit three more houses where they noted down all the required particulars 'Seven hits,' said Ferdach to Choo a bit too self confidently. 'Waite will say, "Is that all?" But you and I and the whole platoon know that we've done bloody well. By the way, why wasn't Mat Noor afraid of leprosy like you and Tahir? And why didn't he let on earlier he can speak English?'

Choo looked embarrassed but replied diffidently, 'He didn't want to stand out from the others. He's shy. But Ferdie, haven't you noticed how he hangs around you? Can't you tell how much he likes you? Maybe fear for you made him break into English – to protect you. Don't you see that if you aren't afraid of leprosy, how can he be?' Choo fell silent for a moment and then said, 'Tuan Ferdie, I watched you with the leper woman. I am glad to be working with you too.'

Tuan Ferdie was gratified by such trust but feared it might be sadly misplaced. Despite Choo's admiration he believed it was Tahir's example rather than his own, that had helped them to avoid disaster. He knew he had a lot to learn.

9

Declining Waite's offer of Sunday curry tiffin at the Ipoh Club, the nerve centre of expatriate social existence, Ferdach decided to spend the rest of the day by himself. He felt the need to recover from his baptism of fire, or so it might easily have been. After such an experience he needed a change of company and to relax. Still, his idea of opting out of the service had weakened. Here he was and here he must stay even though a fish out of water was better off; he wasn't just out of his tank, ready to be chucked back by any kind passer-by, he was on a different planet where all the life forms were alien. It was abundantly clear that he did not know why he was here at all: his ill-considered response to his mother's suggestion, an easy acceptance of Nina Hamnett's sibylline utterances, provided no explanation. His own commitment seemed curiously absent. Yet was it all chance or had he unconsciously glimpsed in this outworn colonial life a challenge to be something different? His first day at work had certainly provided one kind of challenge; it had been unexpected and exciting but was it what he had come for? He needed to take stock of himself and while doing so what better than to explore the town, to see what sort of a place he had washed up in.

He had not yet taken delivery of his new car so he set out in a taxi for the Western, where he hoped to encounter the Sweinsnoeps, especially Laura, and ask them out for a drink but as they had already been taken to the Swimming Club he decided to go for a walk. Outside the Western, in Hugh Low Street, rows of two-storey terraced shophouses reflected the light from their cream- and ochre-plastered walls. On the ground floor, shops lined an arcaded five-foot way, above were the owners' dwellings. Though most of the shops were closed many people were about. On the upper floors, pale green window shutters were closed to shade their interiors. The shutters did not, however, contain the shrill sounds of Cantonese opera for this part of the town, laid out on a gridiron pattern, was essentially Chinese. Across the river, Ferdach found himself once again near the railway station and where Waite's office stood amidst more sedate buildings: banks, commercial houses, a few European-style shops and the elegant Town Hall – now the State Police Headquarters, a result, no doubt, of the Emergency. Further wandering brought him to tree-lined roads leading to suburbs too distant to explore. But the most distinct impression that Ipoh left on him that day was that of its surrounding hills and those distant mountains always visible from the centre of the town. Especially to the east towards the central spine of the Malay peninsula, deep green, then darkest purple, they rose in waves, until, finally floating above low-lying banks of unmoving clouds, they were silhouetted by a peerlessly blue sky. For a while he felt that he had entered a beautiful warm dream world, a paradise where everyone must be content.

Then, quite unexpectedly, as he rounded a corner, he came across an idyllic English spectacle: white-clothed men engrossed in a cricket match on the town *padang*, the familiar crack of bat on ball, the triumphant shout when someone was caught out, and the ripple of languid applause from the British men and women up on the verandah of the Ipoh Club where he might have had tiffin with Waite. On the opposite side of the *padang* to the club, appropriately seated at a lower level on deck chairs or on the grass, was a group of Asians similarly engrossed in the game and ready with slightly more fervent applause. All was in its right place, well ordered and serene, but to Ferdach it was also a disturbing sight. At school he had been good at cricket but always hated the game or rather the people who liked it. He drew in his breath and held it a little before letting out a long sigh. The nauseating feeling of being out of place re-asserted itself; this was no paradise after all. How often he had felt like this on the SS *Canton* when obliged to dress for dinner, to sit at a table with people dedicated to status, with the placement of the exalted ones on the captain's table, or with who was invited to Lord Cockahoop's drinks party. He had not wanted to be there at all and now he felt just as ill at ease here in this unfamiliar land, this enigmatic Malaya. Almost involuntarily he cupped his hands over his eyes as though wanting to obliterate the world around him. He was a man outside, a mere observer.

But at that moment he himself was being observed, quite closely, through a pair of borrowed binoculars. As he was about to turn away from the cricket match someone rose from among the Asian spectators, handed the binoculars to a friend and began to saunter across a corner of the *padang* towards him. His movement was so purposeful that Ferdach looked about him to see if anyone else was the object of the man's trajectory. No. Nobody else was nearby. Whoever it might be was aiming for him.

Ferdach was unsure whether to stay or make off. In all the ports at which the *Canton* had called, no sooner had he gone ashore than some character would sidle up with an offer to take him around, be a cut-price shopping guide or show him the best brothel. The approaches were always tedious and cost money, if only to get rid of the tout. But the person approaching him did not look the usual type. He was obviously a Malay for he was smartly dressed in a beige *baju* and trousers, a patterned batik sarong and a velvety purple *songkok* pushed well back on his head. By the time he was nearby, Ferdach saw that he was a clean-shaven young man with a broadly smiling face that made him look almost boyish.

A velvety voice said, 'Good afternoon Tuan. I am Mizan bin Abdul Rahman, Tengku Mizan. Are you a tourist? No. Not many tourists come to Malaya nowadays. May I be of assistance?'

The English was perfect, the accent impeccable but the words were spoken slowly as though the speaker found life a little boring. He might have been to a good school in England, perhaps one in which an upper-class drawl was regulatory. For some reason Ferdach still did not introduce himself – perhaps out of caution. Who could say what strange dangers the Emergency held? He stared hard, maybe a bit rudely, at Mizan, taking in the contours of a sensitive face, admiring the wide, welcoming eyes, the sensual lips and breathing in the delicate scent of some oil which, emanating from a lithesome body, made the man's hair, where it escaped in tiny quiffs from the edge of that jaunty *songkok*, lustrously black. When he offered his hand Mizan took it lightly and briefly after which he touched his chest for an instant.

Some reply now being necessary Ferdach offered: 'Well, I am a visitor. I'm just going for a walk round Ipoh – to gain impression, I guess.'

'Then maybe you're a journalist, or a writer or an artist? Or all three?' continued Mizan with a little laugh that seemed to signal that he would not press for any more information for it could not possibly be of interest to him. However, he now turned his radiant smile on Ferdach and said, 'How extremely nice to meet an educated Englishman of my own age. Well, maybe I'm a bit younger than you. But not so handsome.'

Ferdach smiled affably but asked, 'How do you know I'm educated. I could be a British soldier.'

Mizan laughed as though surprised. 'Oh, by your bearing, by your accent. You could never be a British tommy. They walk like this.' And he gave a little demonstration of a walk that was half slouch, half aggressive and wholly apelike.

'You don't seem to like them?'

'Oh but I do. But they're not so easy to meet, as a Muslim I can't go drinking in bars. In fact, I feel sorry for those national service guys, poor British working men's sons; they belong to a class that's been put down for so long that they must show their strength some way or other. So they get drunk and fight; they have to walk tough and speak tough. They musn't show affection to each other or else they're called queers. Now we Malays, however humble, walk upright. We can wear flowers in our hair and still be great lovers of women. And the poorest Malay, the *kampung* Malay – the 'village' Malay – speaks the best Malay, as good as in the Sultan's Istana. In Britain it's the other way round, working men speak bad English, just like Mr Shaw says in *Pygmalion*.'

'Well, you're certainly a master of the language and you know a lot about us. Obviously you've lived in England.' Ferdach paused suspecting that the Tengku's observations concealed a degree of contempt for the British. Yet a lot could be learned from him about the Malays. 'Are you staying to watch the cricket?' he asked tentatively.

'Of course not. I don't come to the *padang* to watch games. I prefer observing people. So I'm going to walk around the town with you. I know you want me to. Then I'll get some impressions of an Englishman getting impressions of the barbaric East.'

They sauntered into a tree-lined street in the commercial quarter with Ferdach asking ignoramus questions about the state of Perak. For instance: why wasn't Ipoh the capital when it was the biggest town?

'Because the Sultan has always lived in Kuala Kangsar. Anyway this place is too Chinese' was the answer. Then, since Ferdach knew that *tengku* was a royal title, he asked, 'Are you one of the Sultan's sons?'

'No. Sorry to disappoint you. In Perak the title also belongs to more lowly princes. I am a very lowly prince as you can see.'

'No, I can't see. And why should that disappoint me? You're very distinguished as you are – especially in those beautiful clothes.'

'Ah, I'm wearing them because this morning I had to visit the *mentri besar*, the chief minister – my uncle – to pay my respects on his birthday. Do you like my sarong? It's very old. English people always like old things: old churches, old furniture. We value old kris, old *kain sarung*, old titles, especially old titles – just like the English. Yes, we have one thing in common: Malays and British are snobs. That's why we get on well together. Just look at this state. There are two social pyramids: the Malay one with the sultan on top and the British one with the British adviser on top. Of course the British adviser is half an inch lower than the sultan – socially though not in power.'

This made Ferdach laugh. His new acquaintance was a real card, a sophisticate very different from Mat Noor and those special constables, all of them mere *kampung* lads. As he turned to reply he noticed that they were both reflected in the large display window of Whiteway Laidlaw's department store. Mizan's gaze met his in a long mirror between an array of jackets. Liquid brown eyes seemed to be staring right into his head and he heard the words, 'Something is troubling you Tuan. I was watching you on the *padang*. I'm sure that something is making you unhappy.'

Ferdach's attempts at reserve were weakening. A drowning man floundering in the deep grasps at any hand stretched out towards him. Nevertheless he did hesitate, if only for a few moments, before saying, 'Just now, on the *padang*, watching the cricket, I realised I'd made a mistake coming here. To Malaya. You see Mizan, I'm not a colonial type. I'm post war. I voted for a socialist Britain. That will never extend as far as here. I'm out of place. I don't know what to do.'

Mizan took Ferdach's arm and led him to one of the benches beneath the sprawling trees lining the road. 'Tell me about it Tuan,' he said. 'Tell me and I'll advise you. I'm very good at giving advice … though not many people take it.'

The truth was that Ferdach's experience since leaving England had left him pent up with anger. Until now he had found no one he felt he could talk to. So responding, perhaps over readily, to Mizan's seductive sympathy he started to pour out his grievances. 'Well Tengku, I was already feeling like this when the *Canton* arrived in Penang; social life on board was prewar ... and I mean pre-1914! In the E&O Hotel, seven of us, all new officers, were greeted by a man from the secretariat, Aynsford-Ellis. He told us about our postings. They were all good except mine. Ellis just eyed me coldly and said, "Oh yes, there's some modest sort of job for you in the ADO's ofice in Ipoh." You see Tengku, although I got the highest results on the colonial training course, I'm not from the top drawer, and I'm Irish, well, half Irish but wholly Irish in sympathy. The postings showed me how the old boy network could bring people from Oxford colleges or good regiments cosily together with their cronies in different government departments. Please dont get me wrong, I'm not saying that the other cadets aren't good chaps. That's exactly what they are: fearfully good chaps. I guess that's why the system feels justified. One of us, a Tibetan-language expert, Gilbert de Guise, even became private secretary to the chief secretary, Del Boca, probably because their names go well together. Ah well, Del Boca must have a sense of humour. But, my god Mizan, when I listened to Aynsford-Ellis all I could think was, What a mistake to come here. And to make matters worse there was a balls-up over my arrival in Ipoh.'

'Ah yes, I heard about that. You see I work in the district office. I am a *penghulu*, a headman. So you are Tuan F. O'Haney, the new recruit. You and I will be working in different sub-districts. But I wish I was working with you – under Tuan Waite.'

'I'm sorry I didn't introduce myself. That was rude.'

'Not at all. But really, you're not unlucky at all. Tuan Waite is a fine man, very fair to everyone. This posting could be good for you. Is that all that's upset you?'

'If that was all Tengku, it wouldn't matter. The trouble is that the outlook of the English people here, the sort of people who are up in the club, is very different from my own. Maybe I'm not even on their side against this Communist menace. I don't care a tinker's cuss for their empire or the British way of life. What the hell am I going to do here then? Even my hope that I might soon be able to learn Chinese in Macau vanished when Aynsford-Ellis told me in his dry clipped voice, "Oh that's what we were hoping for eh? Well Haney, the Chinese training scheme in Macau has been put on ice – probably for good."'

Mizan fell silent. He turned as though only intent on searching into Ferdach's eyes silently but at length seemed to take command with, 'We'll walk back to the *padang* and talk some more. The match will be over by now. I've got things to tell you too.'

The match was indeed over. Up on the club verandah a fearfully jolly party was in progress. The hearty voices of the tuans and the shrill laughter of the mems carried right across the broad green *padang* to where Mizan and Ferdach sat in two of the vacated deck chairs. Mizan was the first to speak.

'You're much too concerned with your own feelings, Tuan. If you feel out of place in all this,' he gestured towards the club, 'then how do you think we feel when we see it in our own land? An Irishman is less alien to that lot over there than me. But if you knew for certain that you were unable to fit in with them, what made you join the Service? No. There's some part of you that relishes the idea of authority, British authority, and you don't want to admit it. What was your father like? Was he a disciplinarian, a soldier maybe?'

The memory of his Janus-headed father surged into Ferdach's mind but he held it at bay, reluctant to describe a man who was perpetually at war with himself, who could be both harsh and indulgent to his own son, and who had confused his young head with his own contradictory beliefs. Mizan might find it difficult to digest yet how could he, as a stranger, have the power to see into him so clearly? Drawing back under the calm gaze fixed on him Ferdach replied, 'Oh, he was nothing special, but yes, a military man. And what is your father like, Tengku?'

'I've nothing to hide about my father. He's an intellectual. He studied in Cairo and Mecca and he's a very wise man. Not that study alone makes a man wise. My father is a Sufi, a mystic. But there's no point in my telling you about that because you wouldn't believe in such unscientific stuff. Would you?'

'How do you know what I believe in? Anyway I do know an old, well, not-so-old, very unscientific wise woman,' said Ferdach thinking immediately of Nina Hamnett. But probably you wouldn't believe in her kind of wisdom either. Or would you?'

Mizan grasped Ferdach's hand, long enough to ask earnestly, 'The way we speak – we're mirrors to one another. Shall we be friends then? Able to trust each other?'

Yes, we are like twin mirrors, Ferdach thought. He had spoken to no one so freely for too long and so, although an inner voice did warn him that Mizan was too easily forthcoming, he refused to see any reason why they shouldn't open up to one another straightaway. He wanted to respond positively and so with every appearance of sincerity, he replied, 'Yes, I do trust you. And you can trust me.'

'Then let me tell you something which I don't talk about more than is necessary. When Malaya was occupied my family was stranded in Cairo. My father decided to continue his studies in Mecca but he sent me with my mother to England, where I went to Dulwich College. I bet I've been to more Anglican services in my life than you have, Tuan. After the war I went to Indonesia, to Java. I witnessed the liberation struggle. I was with a group of young Malays, some of them keen nationalists, some of them Marxists who had studied in Moscow. They all believed that the future of this country lies with Indonesia. Since coming back I've changed my views on that. The Dutch wanted to hang on forever. The British are not so stupid; they will leave - the sooner the better as far as I'm concerned. But Englishmen don't like to leave a mess behind. They're very responsible. Do you know that when the Japs got to Kuala Lumpur the chief secretary had prepared handing-over notes for their civil administrators? So I work on the British side because the quicker the communists are finished off the quicker we'll get *merdeka*, our freedom. But not with Indonesia because Indonesia will still be in chaos. So maybe you and I have things in common. If I can work with the British, so can you.'

Everything Fergus had just been told fascinated him. For the first time he had been given an inkling of a modern Malay intellectual world –of nationalists, Marxists, and Sufis who studied in the Middle East. And there must be many other strands. He was an awe-struck Drake catching a glimpse of an unfamiliar ocean. Of such fermenting contemporary matters little had been said on the Colonial Office course packed, no doubt laudably, as it was with a wealth of history and cultural information on Malay customs, law and art. Where religion was concerned the special position of Islam in Malay society had naturally been emphasised but apart from making reference to Winstedt's *Cultural History of the Malays* with its not entirely correct decription of Malay mysticism, the subject of religion, still less of political activists, was largely avoided. Nevertheless, Ferdach recognised the relevance of this sort of knowledge to his work. However he felt he must probe Mizan. 'How could a Muslim Sufi let his son attend Christian services?'

'Oh there was no problem in that for him. The Sufis hold that the universal spirit expresses itself through all religions. My father likes to quote this poem of Shabistari:

> I and thou are a veil
> Between earth and heaven.
> Lift it and you will see
> The restraints of creeds, of sects are gone
> And I and thou are no more.

Well, to me that's always seemed too facile, an easy way out of the problem, but maybe it makes sense to you Tuan O'Haney?'

Though surprised at Mizan's rejection of his father's wisdom, Ferdach nodded sagely then, without venturing to ask who Shabistari was, replied, 'I get the point,' leaving it at that. In fact the poem's overtones were not unfamiliar to him for, as a student, he had had more than a passing interest in mysticism ranging from the serious to the meretricious doctrines of the Hollywood mystics. Indeed he had been accused in his student days of being a trifler who went through and discarded the latest intellectual enthusiasms like a fashion-conscious woman with her clothes. But maybe his undergraduate vanity had concealed a morsel of wisdom for just as the tide leaves deposits on the shore so in the mental detritus of Ferdach's fluctuating interests lay many a jewel which he could still use – as, for instance, just now. In time his Marxism had passed, and his mysticism, not to mention the existentialism of the post war years, so that he was finally left with no respect for anything but what scientific research could prove and what his own experience of human beings taught him. He was thus determined not to lose the clever, though possibly vain, young man now before him and decided, after all, to feed him some paternal bait. 'I don't think you'd like my father in the least,' he said with a wistful look into Mizan's eyes. 'I didn't think you'd even like to hear about him.'

'Oh but I would. I would. For then I'd understand you better.'

'Well Tengku, he was a weird bastard,' said Ferdach, with emphasis on the last word. 'When I was a child he never did much more than pat me on my head or give me a sixpence when I really wanted to be picked up and cuddled by him. I grew into adolescence feeling rejected. He loved cricket, rugby, horse racing, all manly sports but not me it seemed. His coldness was worse than the strictest discipline. As I grew older I began to wonder whether my problem with him might have some other cause. Had I inherited some crazy Irish gene from a man who was first of all a British military hero on the Somme – double Military Cross would you believe – then a Royal Flying Corps dog fighter – one of the first DFCs – before he saw the light of freedom and joined the Irish revolutionary fighters. Yes, he did speak to me about Ireland and about its brave rebels, praising them to the skies and I adored them for his sake but before long he went and severed his relationship with my Irish heroes. With him all human relationships are trifles to be broken, including his relationship with my mother. I'm afraid that even though my mother advised me to join the colonial service, I reacted to her idea more like my father, making a snap decision that's got me to Malaya, where I feel totally out of place.'

This diatribe must have contrasted with Mizan's view of his own father. He put his arm around Ferdach's shoulders as though to suggest that male affection was not so difficult to find. 'I think your mother was cleverer than you think,' he said. 'As for fathers, they needn't be that important if there are other men in the family to help you. And what about your teachers? When I felt all alone at Dulwich my teachers helped me a lot.'

'Most of my teachers had been in the First World War, in the trenches, and they believed that trenches lay ahead for us too,' Ferdach said dismally. 'They never talked about the War but they remembered it all right and we felt their fear – the fear of the haunted room that no one's allowed to enter. Perhaps they felt sorry for us – poor kids in the shadow of a nightmare, mere cannonfodder. They should have shown their feelings but proper Englishmen don't open up as easily as half-breed Celts like me. All the same, the thought of war never frightened me; it just made me unwilling to think about careers or the future. Only the pleasures of the moment mattered to me.'

An echoing Mizan: 'Ah yes, the pleasures of the moment.'

It was now late afternoon, the sky was darkening and odd spots of rain were falling. Soon there would be a heavy downpour for huge black clouds were billowing in from the eastern mountains, themselves silhouetted by great flashes of lightening. They would have to find shelter.

'There's no time to go to my house or your hotel,' said Mizan as though those two alternatives had been uppermost in his mind. 'But I know a place nearby. Come on.' He led the way into a wooded garden beside the *padang*, before breaking into a run for the heavens had opened suddenly and with a vengeance. Thunder rolled and rolled as if it would never find satisfaction in silence. Ferdach drew level with Mizan and ahead through the swirling wind-blown rain he saw a long two-storied cream building that could only be a school. Mizan called Ferdach to follow him onto its covered verandah along which a row of rattan settees and armchairs were ready for the staff when not teaching. By now the intensity of the storm had so increased that the rain and water from overflowing gutters had become a shimmering liquid wall obscuring their view outside. Their shirts were soaked through so they removed them, wrung them out and spread them over some chairs. Then they sat together on a settee, hardly looking at one another. Ferdach had an inkling that some significant association between them lay ahead but whether for good or for ill, he was not sure.

When the fury of the storm began to abate and they could hear themselves speak, their talk turned inevitably, since they were young men, to sex. Mizan said, 'You're not married are you?'

'The absence of a wedding ring mightn't mean a thing, but no, I'm not.'

'What will you do then for ...?' But Mizan did not complete his question.

'Are you married Tengku?'

'Yes and I have two children – both boys. My wife is pretty and a good mother but she does not stimulate my mind. I think I need ...' and again Mizan fell silent.

'So young to have a family.'

But domestic matters were not high on Mizan's agenda and he said, in a world weary way, 'I suppose before long you'll be sleeping with another officer's wife or you'll have found some girlfriend or other – maybe one of those serious Red Cross women who are all over the place. Or you could just visit the brothels. That's what some Englishmen do.'

An alarm bell sounded in Ferdach's brain. Mizan was fishing. He might intend well but even the best of friends gossip and as they were both to work in the district office any slip about one's personal inclinations might soon become common knowledge. It was, of course, inevitable that his night at the Carefree would become widely known so he remarked disingenuously, 'Oh yes, I tried choice number three – at the Carefree, a Chinese girl. She was very nice.'

Mizan glanced at him sharply. 'Is that why you're so keen to go to Macau? You like the Chinese.'

Ferdach knew of this danger. British officers who learned Chinese were often accused of being indifferent to the Malays. 'Oh no Mizan, not that please. Liking one thing doesn't imply disliking another. I want to learn everything I can about the Malays. And I'd like to learn about the Sufis, and about you. Yes, especially about you. And maybe you could introduce me to your father. No. Sorry. I don't want to push myself. Your father is a scholar. He mightn't think as much of me as you do.'

Mizan was silent. His hand began to stroke Ferdach's neck very gently. It felt like the beginning of an embrace but went no further. 'Yes, we're going to be good friends,' he said. 'Before long I'll introduce you to my own circle, men who think like us. You can learn a lot about our politics from them. Will you come home with me now – to meet my family, as a beginning to our friendship?'

Ferdach was unsure whether Mizan's touch was sensual or just gentle. He was in deeper water than he cared for. The signs here might be different from those in England. It would be gross to ask Mizan precisely what he did want. Nothing here was very precise. Nor could he respond with any physical gesture. Just now Mizan had said that tough English soldiers did not touch one another without being thought queer. Asians, on the other hand, like Italians could touch each other affectionately without more being implied. But Mizan obviously knew the two worlds so his intention remained obscure. And what was his 'own circle'? Something political that a new recruit should steer clear of? All that was sure was that he and this personable young man would soon be working in the same set-up, even if separately. He did not want a false move to wreck his job in advance. He leant forward to separate himself from Mizan's hand and said, 'Our friendship has already begun Tengku. We are good friends. But how can I visit your family just now, looking like this – wet and bedraggled. They might think you'd picked up a British other rank. Wait until I've got my car. Give me time to settle in properly.'

Neither of them had said anything about leaving for the rain was still falling though lightly, but quite abruptly Mizan pulled on his damp shirt, adjusted his sarong and bid Ferdach goodbye with, '*Selamat tinggal* Tuan,' in a glum sort of way. Then he added in a neutral voice into which it was difficult to read anything, 'I don't pick up British other ranks.' He looked so stonyfaced that Ferdach was inclined to say, 'OK. I'm sorry. I'll come with you and do as you say.' But he dared not. Offence had obviously been taken but why, he could not tell. All the thoughts mystifying him about Mizan, whether amorous, political, both or neither, might be entirely on the wrong track. With prickly people it was best to step back so he confined himself to wishing him well on his way: '*Selamat jalan* Tengku,' he said, in as gentle a voice as he could muster.

10

When Mizan had disappeared between the trees Ferdach stood up and recovered his shirt. It was damp and cold and not to be put on. He found himself shivering, which seemed odd in a tropical climate but nothing had turned out for him as expected since he had set foot in the country. The encounter with Mizan that had started off well had left him more disturbed than ever. Not just the communists, it seemed, were threatening the stability of Malaya. Many subtle political and religious undercurrents were towing this way and that. And the different races; how easy it must be to offend their susceptibilities. Working here would be like finding a submerged track across Morecambe Bay with its shifting quicksands. Was he up to it? Finding out. That was the problem, finding out. Could he learn quickly about Malaya through Mizan's subtle friendship – it was impossible to deny that there had been some sort of a current between them – or would he find out about the Malays much better through contact with simpler people, like the men in his platoon. However it went, as with Ross and his promise of a film career, he wanted nothing to bind him. Maybe, without intending, he had made this clear. That must explain Mizan's touchiness. He did not pick up servicemen; he wanted something serious.

Ambling along the verandah he halted from time to time to peer through the windows into the classrooms. In the first a prayer book on a desk bore the words 'St Luke's Grammar School for Boys, C of E'. The blackboard, like the Thirty-Nine Articles, bore traces of unresolved equations. In another classroom they were studying *Hamlet* under a photo of a brooding Laurence Olivier in the role. In the next there was information about the Commonwealth with large wall maps of Canada, Australia and, much smaller, India and Pakistan. In the adjacent room, where the desks were tightly packed as though to encourage intensity of concentration, the blackboard was devoted to English grammar, in particular the parsing of sentences. Was this school preparing Malayan youth for the country's future as an independent country Ferdach wondered? But did education anywhere ever fit the young for life as it really was?

A wicker chair at the end of the verandah drew him to sprawl comfortably on its form-fitting surface. From it he could look across to the school chapel which must double as the local Anglican church for behind its narrow lancet windows soft golden light had suddenly glowed. The arrival of some cars and the sound of an organ suggested that Evensong was imminent. It was eerily familiar to Ferdach and he lay back and let his mind drift, fishing up memories in the hope … in the hope of what? Not surely that he would find his way back to some early halcyon days of faith. Even when fascinated by mystical teachings he had known that never would a shred of belief lodge in his mind. Nor would he ever find a spiritual home in Islam, however his friendship with Mizan might develop, not even in the deeper Sufi form the Tengku had spoken of, though possibly not agreed with. He, Ferdie, was a man without religion and he was glad of it. So if he was to have memories of any guru let it be of the man who had been pivotal during his school days in shattering all his early superstitions. Gratefully he remembered Hiram Jones, the history master who, against his will, had been railroaded into teaching scripture and ended up by freeing a generation of boys from Christianity convincing them, rationally and analytically, that it was nothing but mythic history. For Hiram held that the imposition of religious beliefs on children should be made a crime, the only need of the young being, in his very Confucian view, good character training. A statue, Ferdach thought, should be raised to such a man.

Just then the sound of the *Magnificat* came sweetly over the grass from the chapel. Ferdach loved the sound. Indeed he regarded the preservation of ancient music, beautiful buildings and ceremonial as the only justification for the existence of the C of E. It also stirred something deeper in his pool of his memories and he recognised that the first grain of his disbelief lay further back in time than his schooldays in a layer that was more emotional for it was infantile. It was sown when he was only five and in St Bede's Parish Church with just his cousin Stephen who had been told by his mother that if anyone but a priest dared to cross the chancel rails, he would be struck down by the Lord. Stephen dared it first and Ferdach followed. The Lord hid his face. They were both amazed that grown ups could practice such deception on them. That was Ferdach's first true dash for freedom. Now too he must find his own way without external props.

Tired after walking in the heat he drowsed off until a great gush of wind began to shake the trees again and he awoke, thinking sensually of Wong Siu Bo, and of Tengku Mizan. Over in the chapel the final hymn was being sung, very loudly. 'Pleasant are thy courts above, In the land of life and love'. Not wanting to be seen he got up, put his shirt on and made his way towards the town centre.

There he encountered something ghastly. In front of a coffeeshop stood a circle of people, mainly men. They were hysterical with laughter, pointing down at something and shouting. As he got near Ferdach could hear an unearthly screeching. Being taller than most of the crowd he was able to look into the circle from the pavement. On the road was a squashed cat, at least the hind part of it was squashed; the fore half was twisting and writhing in a terrible way, its wide open mouth was squealing and croaking, its claws were flailing and scratching. It showed no sign of dying quickly yet it had no chance of life for some vehicle had caused it too much harm. More dreadful to Ferdach were the delighted expressions on the faces that gloated and gestured at it. No one thought to lift a finger to put the creature out of its misery. He looked around desperately for a stick or a stone but could see none He must go into the circle and kill the animal himself. But he couldn't do it. Reluctant to face the derision of the crowd he ran off unable to stand the sight of such agony any more. Trembling with shame he staggered along the river bank and then stopped at the middle point of the bridge that linked the two sections of the town. He hardly noticed that the oncoming dusk had drained the world of its colour for no light was left in his own world.

Disconsolately he stared into the fast flowing water of the silty river Kinta. Was it his upbringing alone that had so enervated him, or was there something else? Could it be the ingredient of war? Maybe he had only come to Malaya with its Emergency because a part of him desired another war of the comradely kind he had once experienced. Perhaps his years in Bomber Command had inured him to war as something simple and beautiful in which all that mattered was to live until the next day together with his aircrew? It made him happy yet sad to recall how, in the crucible of war, when not on operations, he had passed his off-duty hours almost exclusively with his pilot, his bomb-aimer, his wireless operator and his gunners. He had depended on them, as they on him, their navigator, to get their Lancaster in and out of danger in one piece. Yet until they were shot down – and they never wanted to think about that at all – they felt themselves to be entirely detached from what they were doing to others. Oh so happily they lived and slept together. They might have had girlfriends and parents at home but their closest emotional bonds were with one another. They ate together, played together, drank together, fucked women together and the pleasure of taking part with his mates in such innocent orgies had meant much more to Ferdach than any of the discardable women who were the objects of their joint lust. In those heroic days, which were to brood like huge peaks over the flat lives of future generations, he had only felt truly alive when he had been at one with his comrades in the shadow of death. Yet here, years later and many miles away, he found himself unexpectedly thinking of how he had dropped bombs on Germans without ever witnessing, even imagining, their agony. He had no more faced up to it than he had to the agony of that cat. When the furnace of war had been quenched the irresponsible years of study had been no more than an anodyne period of guiltless convalescence. But now he had emerged from the academic chrysalis and had to take part in another war, Ferdach felt unable to face the horrors it might bring for he was no longer able to fly, and no longer capable of his former detachment.

He leant heavily against a pillar of the five-foot way where he found himself, exhausted and despondent. His introspection had produced no answers. Dusk had given way to tropical night. Yellow streetlights had come on and just above him he saw the words 'Carefree Hotel'. What strange chance had brought him back here? Or was it chance? Perhaps he had hoped that Wong Siu Bo would be here to help him through his loneliness but if so he was disillusioned by the *fo gei* who had brought him his beer on that first night. Poking his head through the fly curtain the lad said, 'Siu Bo no here. You wan fuck nudder nicey lady?'

Ferdach smiled, shook his head and said, 'Thank you,' following it with the same in Cantonese, '*M goi nei.*' To himself he added, 'And thank God I know about this bolthole. It helped me once, it might help me again.' Then he made his way back to the Western. Outside stood a familiar white Jaguar with Waite at the wheel just on the point of driving off. Waite looked at him oddly, for quite a long time it seemed to Ferdach, before saying, 'Someone said you'd been seen round here so I came looking. Sure you're all right, mate?'

'Of course I am. Why do you ask?'

There was another strange silence. 'You looked stonkered – whacked.'

'I've been walking a lot. And thinking a lot.'

Waite went on staring at him quizzically for a while, then said, 'You're different Ferdie. You don't fit the usual Pommy pattern. And I guess I've been feeling guilty about you too. Your average kipper would have been in a towering rage not to be met and properly looked after.'

'Pommy! Kipper! Any more such flattery and I'll puke. Your average Aussie would be much less tolerant than me. Anyway I'm only half a Pommy. And never call me average'

'Well Mr Cut-above-the-rest old bean, let's get home. Your eyes tell me you need sleep. They look like piss holes in the snow.' Then Waite's voice fell as though he was about to give the gravest of admonitions. 'And by the bye there are times for thinking and times for action. To think too much when it's time for action can be dangerous – especially in Malaya just now. I'm being serious.'

'Why are you telling me this Waite?'

'What was it people used to be told in Britain when they asked for something they couldn't have. You remember: "don't you know there's a war on?" Do you get me, matey?'

'Yeah cobber, oi shua do,' replied Ferdach in his best strine.

II

For Ferdach's band of untried warriors that first day of census could well have been the last and a bloody last at that. At the very time when they had been stumbling around in the *belukar*, there had been a massive attack on a military convoy only a couple of miles away. Three British Other Ranks had been killed and several wounded. The level of communist activity throughout Perak, explained Waite as they drove to Wearne's to pick up Ferdach's car, was rising. Ambushes were to be expected on minor roads and even main arteries.

From the newspapers and the radio it was clear to Ferdach that the situation was deteriorating throughout the Federation. Raids on the homes of European tin-mining and rubber-estate managers were a common occurrence. Of course such attacks were not entirely new. On a smaller scale they had occured even before the Emergency began in 1948. Until then the government had not taken the communist danger very seriously. It was only after some merciless killings had taken place in the Sungei Siput area of Perak in June of that year that the High Commissioner, Sir Edward Gent, declared a state of emergency. In the following period it was the fortitude of those engaged in the tin and rubber industries that kept the country going economically. Mine managers and rubber planters were living a life under siege, with their homes and their labour lines surrounded by barbed wire defences manned by Malay Specials most of whom had as little experience of war as Mat Noor. Unfortunately the outbreak of the Emergency had caught the security forces shorthanded and this situation had yet to be fully remedied. When managers travelled outside their perimeters they did so in cars whose windows had been replaced by steel sheets with only a small aperture to see through. If Ferdach had at first found these Europeans arrogant, after a few days at work he recognised that, in one respect, they could be proud of themselves. They held the front line. Defiantly their social life proceeded as furiously as ever. Their families still visited each other to play tennis or bridge, or to drink and eat enormous curry tiffins. Wild horses could not keep them from visiting the Ipoh Club; armoured cars disgorged hearty men bearing arms and gay, sallow women wearing evening dress, ready to drink and dance the night away. Wild horses were no less absent from the Turf Club, espcially during Race Week, which had been the cause of Ferdach's own initial discomfort on arrival. It was on Jalan Sturrock, the road leading to the Turf Club, that he was now living with Waite and Ericson, within earshot of the club's loudspeakers and in sight of the coming and going of a multitude of punters.

During his first week at Jalan Sturrock, Ferdach felt he had fallen into limbo or become an automaton. His old self, the self he knew so well from his student days, seemed in abeyance. Early in the morning, the three housemates enjoyed an almost wordless breakfast. Alsway finishing first, Ericson would flex his muscles then tear off in his mud-spattered Vauxhall. Yusuf, of the beautiful locks, would drive Waite to the District Office in his white Jaguar. Had Waite lounged in the rear seat instead of sitting in front enjoying the sight of Yusuf's profile, his progress would have seemed quite magisterial. Ferdach would then follow in his newly acquired green Morris Minor to meet up with his team and get on with his census work. The house was left in the efficient care of Cookie – a large self-confident Hakka Chinese, whose real name he never learned – and the garden in that of Yusuf's wraithlike younger brother Subian, who was to be seen each morning gracefully tending the haphazard plots of hibiscus, frangipani and canna lilies clad only in a sarong, or cutting the grass around them in an abstracted sort of way as though he was a celestial gardener tending the lawns of paradise.

In the evening all three housemates returned in the same order: Ericson first, sweeping up the drive and parking under the car porch in such a way that no other car could share the space, then Waite, whose car was carefully parked in the garage to receive Yusuf's loving ministrations, and finally Ferdach, who put his car anywhere he could find – generally alongside the house in case he had to run for it in a heavy downpour.

As often as not, after showering they would sit around the coffee table boozing until dinner. Ericson was invariably on Scotch and soda, Waite on Pernod and little else, and Ferdach on brandy and dry ginger. This greatly simplified accounting. Again, conversation was minimal. One of the favourite occupations of both Waite and Ericson between drinks was to blow darts or shoot airgun pellets at the *cicak* that scurried over the ceiling in search of insects. In consequence the walls and the ceiling were pockmarked with little holes. Ferdach never saw one of the tiny lizards receive a direct hit but sometimes they fell to the floor in shock, or just their tails would drop off and continue wriggling on the floor for a some minutes. *Cicak* could soon grow another tail.

Now this was precisely the sort of matter that could lead to a more protracted conversation, especially with Waite who adored anything out of the ordinary. Supposing, he asked one evening, part of a lizard's leg was grafted onto the tail stump. Would it grow into a leg or a tail? The answer was that it would grow into another leg and this had in fact been done. So there must be some chemical that allowed regeneration to take place. Could it be isolated and used on humans to grow new limbs? Under Waite's enthusiastic direction the topic took wings with all sorts of strange combinations of bodies and limbs suggested. For once Ericson took part heartily, making suggestions as to where male genitals might be grafted, as on fingers, toes or nipples. He then sketched a head where the tongue was replaced by a one-eyed cock protruding savagely from between its lips while the ears were the seat of two erect cocks with flapping foreskins imparting to the head the look of a fabulous beast that was about to become airborne. Ferdach fancied that Ericson might see himself in that way. But the fact that conversation around the table, if it developed at all, tended towards the bizarre, the occult, the fantastical, or, in the case of Ericson, the aggressive, made Ferdach feel even more isolated than ever. There was practically no normal – let alone civilised – talk at all. He felt like the only sane man in a lunatic asylum, pandering to the inmates. Or was he the lunatic and they the sane ones?

The issue of leg regeneration apart, Ericson was reluctant to be drawn into discussions either fantastic, political or anything else. What he said was brief and generally related to such things as road-, bridge- or office-construction, matters on which he and Waite had to liaise. However, though he clearly enjoyed being uncouth, he was always most polite to Asians, especially those working for him; Ferdach observed that Cookie and his family adored him. According to Waite, he was an efficient officer who never failed to honour his work commitments. His hostility, which was powerful, seemed reserved for male Europeans – with the exception of Waite, of whom he seemed in awe. Every man Jack who might crop up in coversation when the three of them dined together in the evening – be he from the Public Works Department, the District Office, the Forestry Department, the Geological Service or wherever – would be harshly criticized in threatening tones by Ericson for his faults, real or imaginary. When deriding a seemingly innocuous officer, Ericson could even go as far as threatening to 'break his fuckin' legs'. This tended to create an atmosphere akin to that of a rough East End pub making dinner a menacing occasion that was hardly relieved by both Waite and Ericson always placing their revolvers on the table when eating. Firearms at dinner seemed not only ludicrous to Ferdach but also superflous since no government houses in Ipoh had been the object of attack. Ericson, however, never spoke ill of the officers' wives though he would sometimes say that some woman or other should leave her oaf of a British husband who didn't deserve her. There did not seem to be a single British married woman in Ipoh who, according to Ericson, did not need 'it'. From the day Ferdach took up residence in the house, Ericson would be off to no-one-knew-where shortly after dinner, returning noisily in the early hours of the morning. Ferdach felt sure that he must have been relieving the tensions of one of those ill-treated colonial wives with whom he had such sympathy, generously providing her with 'it' while her oaf of a husband was out of town.

Ferdach saw little possibility of anything resembling friendship with Ericson, but with Waite, well, that was a different matter. This man, Ferdach discerned, had a vein of genius. His judgement was acute, his capacity to pick up languages was remarkable for besides Malay he had, self-taught, become proficient in both Cantonese and Hakka. But there was also his academic background that Ferdach only learned about when he asked how it was that Waite was able to translate a Sanskrit expression in a book on Malay customs he was reading. Waite was at first reluctant to explain that he had been awarded a Double First at Oxford, where he had studied oriental philosophy under the eminent

Indian scholar Radakrishnan. Yet it puzzled Ferdach that such profound academic knowledge seemed to have been peculiarly transmuted into a predilection for the occult, or to put it baldly, for magic. One evening, when he was alone in the house, Ferdach, had gone into Waite's bedroom to borrow some book or other. On a long table, together with several phosphorescent hand grenades and a powerful .30-06 Winchester rifle with a telescopic sight, there was a great assortment of multicoloured clip-on bow ties of the kind Waite was wearing when they first met. There was also a well-thumbed Indian book that set out, with textual support from ancient Hindu writings and gaudy illustrations, the most auspicious combinations of colours that should be worn on each day of the year. The reason for the ever-changing daily neckgear was now apparent. But why ties should be mixed up with weapons was not so obvious, except that Waite did seem to have an obsession with firearms and explosives that was not exactly justified, despite the Emergency, by his civilian status in the administration. These unusual enthusiasms, and the repeated efforts at telepathy, made Ferdach believe that it might be some time before he could understand the complexities of Waite's mind.

Happily, between the morning and the evening there was work and in this, challenging though it was, Ferdach began to find both satisfaction and the beginnings of that warm emotional contact that had always been for him the wine of life whether at school, in the air force or as a student. The arduous first day with Gordon Choo and the platoon of Malay constables had been the beginning of a better life.

Waite had also observed the bond established between Ferdach and his platoon. Furthermore, he had learned, by subtle questioning of Corporal Tahir, exactly what had transpired on that first day of adversity. What had emerged from it pleased him and he was also satisfied with the way in which the census had been carried out. After a few more days in the field, Ferdach's area of responsibility was extended to take in a huge area of *belukar* as well as a strip of primary jungle, into which numerous squatter families had penetrated in their anxiety to escape the Japanese.

By now Ferdach had learned a lot about local politics from Gordon Choo. The young man was virulently hostile to communism for the most personal of reasons. His father had been tortured and executed during the unruly period following the Japanese surrender by Communist fighters who had emerged from the jungle in the semblance of victors before the establishment of the BMA, the British Military Administration, or, as it was unkindly but not too unjustifiably called by Malayans, the Black Market Administration. His father had been no collaborator but one of those who supported the Kuomintang, or Chinese Nationalist Party, in China. Gordon told him that most of the squatters they visited were under the influence of the Communists. Some of them were almost certainly active members of Min Yuen, the People's Movement. This had been established during the Occupation under a different name, the Malayan People's Anti-Japanese Union, to mobilize support for the Malayan People's Anti-Japanese Army, MPAJA. Without the supplies raised by such a mass movement, the activities of the MPAJA, and now of the Malayan Races Liberation Army, MRLA, as the military arm of the Communist movement had been renamed, would not be sustainable. In fact the Min Yuen acted as a strong protective screen around the MRLA for its membership probably ran into hundreds of thousands throughout the Federation – a substantial section of the Chinese population. Some of its support was willingly given, but often it was coerced. Moreover, many Chinese supported the Min Yuen as a sort of insurance policy for they were fence sitters, hoping for a government victory but fearful of a communist take-over. Fence sitting, so Gordon impressed on Ferdach, had become more prevalent since the British government had recognised communist China. This had put the will of the West to oppose communism in doubt with the result that many people, of all races, felt that it was only a matter of time before the giant to the north held sway over Southeast Asia.

The area in which Ferdach was operating had been one in which support for the Party had been strong during the war and there was little doubt that it was still pro-Communist. In fact, some of the most active terrorists came from that same part of Perak where Ferdach's census was being carried out. If the Communists had wanted, it would have been the easiest thing in the world for them to track the movements of his platoon and ambush it. Tahir knew this as much as Choo. In consequence he took every precaution possible, the raw constables under him swiftly became proficient and ever on their guard. He also saw to it that his men behaved with kindness to the families being questioned. On one occasion, Ferdach noticed him berating a constable who had been peeping at a Chinese girl who was bathing behind a wooden screen. This might seem a small matter but it was important. 'Respect for the People' was a political platform of the Communists. In no way could Government forces lag behind them in this respect.

Whenever Ferdach and Choo entered a house, before they began to ask their questions, Choo would make polite enquiries about the family and especially about those who were sick. He told Ferdach that the news of the old leper lady being taken into the leprosarium at his instance had got around and was appreciated.

Sometimes, however, behind the normal Chinese politeness they would encounter a reserve, indeed a coldness, and this was very noticeable when they were in the houses of people with more intellectual pretensions, in particular teachers working in Chinese-language schools. Although no Communist literature was to be seen in their houses the family's feelings for China would be evident in maps and pictures of the old country rather than of Malaya. It was in these houses that Ferdach and Choo would linger, doing their best to convey the impression that they too were human beings and that the census they were carrying out would result in the squatters being better housed and administered. Though the effect of their effort might be imperceptible Ferdach considered that it mattered. Over time the people could be won over. Like throwing mud at a wall, much would drop off, but a speck could remain and over time, if resettlement was followed by good administration, those specks could combine to give the lie to some of the beliefs held by members of the Min Yuen, long and deeply indoctrinated with Marxism.

Why then, were they not attacked? It could have been no more than a question of Communist priorities in the face of limited resources. The Party's primary objective at this time was to undermine the economy. The police and the military were attacked, naturally enough, for they were the protectors of the tin mines and the rubber estates. Also, with a varying degree of consistency, the CTs also made sadistic attacks on rubber tappers, especially on those reluctant to obey them. Sometimes rubber tappers, both male and female, young and old, would be tied to trees with wire and disembowelled with *cangkul*s – the implement, half pickaxe, half hoe, farmers used to break up the ground. Since tappers invariably worked in isolation the fear instilled in them could make them reluctant to work and thus grind the rubber industry to a halt, or so the communists hoped. But cruelty can backfire and so the communists, ever aware of the necessity to win the favour of the masses, sometimes wavered in their ferocity. Certainly they rarely went for those features of government administration considered beneficial to the people. Thus, there were no attacks on hospitals or medical facilities; there were few intentional attacks on officials of the Labour Department, the PWD and the Forestry Department. And there seemed to be no great threat to the district administration here in Ipoh. What else could explain Waite's apparent total safety when he cruised around the district, often late at night, in his highly visible white Jaguar; it was no secret that the Chinese around Ipoh saw him as a good man, sympathetic to their problems.

Another unusual being who seemed to move about unchallenged appeared one evening when Ferdach was in the house alone, taking a shower. Ferdach heard a refined English voice shouting: 'Come and look at these Waite.' Without dressing, Ferdach popped his head round the bedroom door to look into the hall. Squatting on the floor was an extremely filthy, scantily clad, bearded white man, who had spread the mouldy looking contents of several baskets all around him on Mrs Cookie's highly polished tiled floor. Instead of introducing himself he held up some pottery shards and some tiny pieces of carved wood. Then he dug out a few bones holding them up for Ferdach's ignorant perusal. Accustomed not to question anything in this house, however odd, Ferdach squatted down in the buff beside the visitor and took to examining everything that was passed to him, at the same time listening to precise explanations of their origins. This piece had come from an indigenous tribe at Sungei Woh, another was stone age and from Bersia, and so on. The man said that he had been in those areas for the past two months and was now taking his material to the Raffles Museum in Singapore. More place and tribal names followed. It was as though he believed Ferdach was quite au fait with the remotest places in the state of Perak. Perhaps he thought he was talking to Waite. To somebody who spends most of his time immersed in the jungle with aborigines, one washed white man probably smells as nasty as another. While holding forth he was perpetually scratching various parts of his anatomy until eventually he took off his battered shirt and shorts which were clearly

73

the dwelling place of a multitude of little jungle cockroaches. Thereafter the conversation about indigenous and prehistoric matters was resumed between the two naked hominids but without so much scratching. Ferdach thought that, given the subject matter, this was somehow appropriate but the visitor remarked that among indigenous people no one ever went completely naked like this for to do so would reduce his status to that of an animal not to mention attract the attention of ill-disposed demons.

Gradually Ferdach found himself taking an interest in everything he was being told and he asked what he hoped were intelligent questions. While he was listening to an account of life among a group called the Semai Senoi he suddenly realized that this man must be Major Williams-Hunt, the renowned expert on the indigenous people of Malaya.

Well before their normal dinner time, Cookie appeared, frowned at the two men and the mess on his wife's cherished black-and-white chequered floor, and told them that Ericson and Waite had gone outstation for two days. Then stating that food was ready with a challenging '*makan siap*' directed at Ferdach, he continued in rather worried tones to say that Mrs Cookie wanted to be taken to the cinema.

'That's fine,' said Ferdach, well aware that Mrs Cookie, if thwarted, could transform herself into a dragon. 'We'll eat down here straightaway.'

Cookie's teenage son soon appeared with a huge dish of fried rice, which he set down on the floor in the midst of the anthropological session. Without waiting for a bowl or chopsticks, still less washing his grubby hands, Williams–Hunt started to scoop the food up and into his mouth. Ferdach felt it would be cavalier to impose another set of manners on a guest and followed suit hoping that he would not pick up some peculiar tropical ailment. The food vanished quickly and the dish was replenished by Cookie himself who bore in an earthenware bottle of Chinese wine, some fruit and a mat on which, he said, the visitor could sleep. He then departed but not without giving a pleased nod at Ferdach.

After a further late-night tutorial on the multifarious differences between the indigenous tribes, Williams-Hunt replaced his prized finds very systematically, politely refusing any help, in the baskets. Then they both went into the adjoining bedroom. Ferdach had another shower, hoping that his guest, whose body odour was not very pleasant, would do likewise but when he emerged from the bathroom Williams-Hunt was already fast asleep on the floor with a serene smile on his face. The mat had not even been unrolled. He left early the following morning leaving Ferdach to sleep on and to marvel, when he got up, that a dedicated anthropologist could travel in and out of the jungle all alone into areas which were notoriously terrorist infested without a shred of harm ever coming to him. Obviously the communists were not stupid and Ferdach could not help feeling a grudging admiration for them.

All the same, at this stage of the game it did seem strange that the communists had not attacked the men who were preparing the work of squatter resettlement. Maybe they thought that the way in which resettlement would be carried out would further alienate the people from the government side, or maybe they calculated that they would be able to dominate people gathered inside New Villages just as effectively as in the open country. In due course their calculations would need to be revised.

12

Although Ferdach's life in Malaya represented a new beginning, it rested on the underlying continuum of his earlier life which, however deeply he might be involved in the often dangerous problems of the Emergency, demanded attention. In the days when men still travelled to Southeast Asia by liner, and overseas telephone calls were both expensive and inaudible, letter writing was indispensable for keeping in touch. Ferdach exchanged letters with his mother regularly; hers were largely concerned with the all important trivia of family life while on his part, knowing how earnestly she desired his success, Ferdach liked to speak of the satisfaction his work was giving to his superiors, in fact almost exclusively to Jimmy Waite for at this stage no one higher up took any interest in him. This was to make his mother feel that her son might well be a budding Lord Curzon. He would also tell her of any social events, few though they were, that had pleased him for he knew that she deeply desired his happiness.

Correspondence with his father was rarer and increasingly strange. No loving greetings were ever exchanged for each spoke only about politics though, as Ferdach at least knew, this was a coded form of muted affection. Ferdach wrote of the Emergency knowing that anything about guns, blood and explosions would fascinate his father, but what came back from Cork, where his father had settled after the War, was of a disturbing nature. Sean O'Haney had grown disgusted with the Irish republican leaders, especially the Taoiseach, Eamon de Valera, for O'Haney the elder was now virulently left wing. He had once served, as an adviser, in the air force of republican Spain and been more than willing to serve again in the RAF during the last war. The Taoiseach, he maintained, had betrayed Ireland by failing to show anti-fascist solidarity in the struggle against Hitler. What was worse, he had recently heard that Churchill had offered de Valera sovereignty over the North on condition that Ireland came into the war but that de Valera had turned the offer down because he feared to lose his majority in the Dail. Exactly how true this was Ferdach did not know but he was sure that his father now hated the Taoiseach on the second score of losing the opportunity to unite Ireland. Oddly enough this had led his father onto another tack. The Celts, he believed, and this was probably true, constituted the majority of the population of the two great islands. This had been masked historically by the dominance of the English language and government. The two islands, with their four countries, should now move towards reunification with a Confederate Constitution that would unite the talents of their peoples. Ferdach had no problem with the concept but it alarmed him to learn that his father was proposing to establish a Reunion Party. He warned his father that Cork did not seem the best place to do this and at the same time remain in one piece. 'I know what I am doing,' retorted Sean O'Haney in his latest letter to Ferdach. 'I am not betraying Ireland. I am working for its greater future. In fact at present I am studying Gaelkwa intensively because it will be one of the official languages of the Confederation. God Save Ireland. Your father, Sean.'

Ferdach groaned aloud and gave a deep sigh when he read this. Maybe in his father's offbeat behaviour lay implications for himself. His mother was his model in respect of common sense, concern for others and generosity but was he destined to become as unpredictable as his father for whom, it seemed, politics had beome the art of the impossible. He expressed his fear to Waite who gently advised him again not to think about it too much, or to desire too much when ahead lay dangerous work that would demand his undivided attention.

'You should be receptive to ideas but not try to winkle out the future like an oyster from its shell. Problems always work themselves out whatever we do. That's what most Oriental thinkers teach us. You have a lot to learn about them.' Waite seemed to be proved right, though it might have been fortuitous, when some months later Ferdach's father moved to Hampshire to take up farming. He was highly unsuccessful in this but at least he remained alive.

Anxious to learn about one Oriental school of thought of which Waite had spoken, Ferdach tried to cultivate the friendship of Tengku

Mizan whose father was a sheikh in a Sufi order. In this objective he did not get very far. If he visited Mizan's lovely wooden *kampung* house, with its intricately carved eaves and windows – a complexity that contrasted starkly with the simplicity of its rooms – he would certainly be made welcome and fed excellently. There would be a great deal of polite conversation with the male members of the family – the women generally kept out of sight – but whereas Mizan was able to gather a lot of information about Ferdach's past life and in particular about his political views, for having lived in England he knew what to ask, to Ferdach the young Tengku was like a tantalisingly glimpsed silver fish in a deep pool whose depths hid many secrets. In short Ferdach felt that he was being kept at arms length, as though his sincerity was doubted. Yet his desire to learn about Sufism was far from just passing curiosity. He knew from Waite that in Malaya, Sufi doctrines, which laid emphasis on non militancy and peacefulness, underlay its people's attitudes to social and political order. To be an administrator in a country without comprehending its beliefs seemed to Ferdach the height of foolishness, despite which it seemed that few British officers possessed such knowledge. However, instead of trying to remedy this deficiency in Ferdach, when questioned about Sufism, Mizan made his replies as obscure as possible. He would ramble on at length about each Tariqah or Sufi order, nine of them in number and all with long Arabic names, which Ferdach found difficult to remember and impossible to distinguish from one another. Such detail totally muddied the picture. Although Ferdach was certainly left with admiration for the intellectually rich life of the Malay sheikhs or Sufi leaders, he concluded that Mizan only knew about the subject as an outsider, like a student who had done a crash course for an examination, without real interest in, or understanding of, the subject. It might have been different had Mizan's father been present but he never appeared. A further cause for regret was that though Ferdach could chat with Mizan about many objective things, he was never given the opportunity of speaking about more personal matters, either his own or Mizan's, because there were always friends and relations in the house. At length Ferdach decided to let things develop without his own effort, as Waite said they always would, though it seemed that whatever lay in store for himself and Mizan was a long way off and might not be all plain sailing.

This was a pity but it did not get Ferdach down. His contacts were widening, he now had a home of sorts, men he enjoyed working with and a job he liked. Other recruits who had joined the various branches of the colonial service were not so lucky for many had received a shock far greater than Ferdach's first experience of Ipoh. Men trained in geology, forestry and other disciplines were told, but only on arrival, that such work had been halted by the Emergency and that, for the time being, they were to act as resettlement officers. Next door to Waite's place, in an old style wooden colonial house, lived a group of men in this category: three geologists, a meteorological officer and one rather older recruit to the education service, a portly handsome man who had trained at RADA and had a London stage background. Ferdach could not make out why an actor, who had already made some mark, should wish to serve in Malaya. The young geologists and the meteorologist seemed bemused by the hand they had been dealt and were inclined to drown their anger in drink each night. But setback was as nothing to Algernon Broadstairs, who was a more mature man accustomed to both failure and success. Even off stage he had a very grand, though somewhat fruity, speaking voice in which he delighted to retell stories of the theatrical world, especially those about the scandalous lives of his many actor friends who seemed to comprise the whole of the London stage.

Broadstairs had a tremendous enthusiasm for the Richards Wagner and Strauss. Often when the lawn between the two neighbouring houses was basking in tropical evening warmth, under a starlit sky, fragrant with bushes and sentinelled by tall palms, great waves of Teutonic music would flow from Algernon Broadstair's first-floor bedroom. Cookie would reluctantly switch off his shrill Chinese opera and Yusuf's family would sit attentively on their little verandah for Malays respond easily to different kinds of music. And if it was the great waltz from *Der Rosenkavalier*, the drunken geologists might join in raucously: 'lah lah laah, lah lah laah, lah lah laah, lah lah laah, didle dumpong dee dee didle dee' and Waite and Ferdach would respond. Just when most of the dogs in the neighbourhood had decided to join in, Waite would pick up his airgun and fire through Algernon's window until, with a ping, a pellet hit one of the hideous German beer steins that stood in a row on a desk. This was the signal for Algernon to come across for a drink.

Ferdach enjoyed his company for it enlivened the rather barren evenings he had become used to. Conversation would soon grow more amusing even if Broadstair's remarks about the Europeans they knew in Ipoh were either acidic or bitchy as though each and everyone of them was a rival in his former theatrical world. Of course Broadstairs loved to be told about Ferdach's more bizarre Soho experiences, especially if they involved well-known people, since they would inevitably soon become his own. This did not worry Ferdach, indeed it amused him for such stories belonged to a world he had left behind. His new life was what mattered most and in that life he was growing in success.

For young O'Haney was now considered to be methodical and thorough in whatever he did but these characteristics were not genetic; they had been carefully imparted to him in childhood by his mother as an antidote to the instability she expected him to inherit from his father. They were characteristics that had developed during his time as a bomber squadron navigator and they had stood him in good stead as a student both in research and in passing examinations. They were now useful in ferreting out squatter houses, plotting them accurately on his maps, carrying out the census in scrupulous detail, and calmly persisting in his inquiries when often surrounded by garrulous people. At the District Office it was becoming recognized that, where census was concerned, O'Haney was 'the tops'. But he never took credit for this himself. In Gordon Choo and Corporal Tahir he had fortuitously encountered two people of equal efficiency so that with the platoon of Malays, who were both fearless and fighters by nature, an effective little instrument had been forged. They had even begun to build up a special mixed language among themselves. Choo helped everyone to remember a few important ice-breakers in Cantonese. Ferdach encouraged the men to build on their scant knowledge of English while Mat Noor was always ready to teach Ferdach more Malay, this to the gleeful amusement of the other Specials, who could see that their boss and Mat Noor had begun to form a mutual attachment which it was neither easy to conceal nor possible to pursue. But all that took place in the field. Once work was over, it was back to Sturrock Road. He did not know where Gordon went to, still less into which barracks Tahir and Mat Noor disappeared. For Ferdach being at work represented sanity; Sturrock Road the abnormal – even if sometimes tempered by the presence of Broadstairs.

In his way Waite made an effort to help Ferdach feel at home. However, when Ericson was in the vicinity his observations tended to be brief, almost monosyllabic. Nevertheless, once God's gift to unsatisfied expatriate women was out, Waite would start up long conversations. Naturally enough these could be about Ferdach's work, in which Waite took the greatest interest but also, less comfortably, about Oriental religions, especially their mystical doctrines. It was difficult to understand what mysticism meant to Waite. Although an array of esoteric Oriental volumes was on his bookshelves, the *Bhagavad Gita*, treatises on Thai Buddhism, Tibetan Tantric doctrines, books on Zen in its Chinese and Japanese forms and so forth, Ferdach found it hard to accept that an educated Australian – good lord, an Oxford man – actually believed that the *I Ching* and geomancy, not to mention manuals prescribing daily auspicious colours, could have any validity at all. Yet Waite most clearly did.

Perhaps it was the nearby presence of the Ipoh Race Course, or a greed for money – even though his family in Melbourne was well off – that now impelled Waite to devise another transcendental experiment in which Ferdach was to be involved. This was a method of predicting the results of the Ipoh races. It was typical of Waite's clever brain. He was much taken by J.W. Dunne's book *An Experiment with Time* in which it was suggested that the unconscious, unlike the conscious, mind was capable of projection into the future. The analogy of the escalator was used: man is ascending the escalator of time but he has to stand looking backward, down into the past. Experimentally, however, he might be enabled to turn around so as to look into the future. But how? Here Waite brought in another of his influences: Jung with his concept of the collective unconscious and his word association tests.

Someone, unaware of the experiment, would be given a number of words to which he had to react by saying whatever idea came to mind. After the horse race, Ferdach had to surprise this person with a telegram in which the name of the winning horse was associated with a word used during the word association test. If the unconscious mind did work in a continuum with the future the unexpected telegram might startle the person questioned before the race to come out with the name of the winning horse – or something like it.

What then happened was that Waite arranged for a word association test to be given to a Mr Aske in the Public Works Department. This man, in response to test word 'skin' at once said 'smooth'. As one of the horses running in a particular race was called Smooch, Waite decided that it must be the winner, bet on it and won.

Ferdach, out of an impish desire to see whether the past could be changed – to Waite's loss – never sent Waite's telegram connecting the winning horse with 'skin'. But the past stayed unchanged and Waite kept his winnings. Ferdach did not confess his treachery but perhaps Aske revealed that he had not received a telegram. In any event, Waite never repeated the experiment – at least with Ferdach. But his success at the races continued so perhaps he did possess psychic powers as he claimed.

In another effort to be friendly with Ferdach, Waite took him to the Ipoh Club, not fully realising that it was not the new cadet's cup of tea. He even suggested introducing him as a member. This was not really possible for by the time Ferdach had paid his rent, contributed to the overheads and food expenditure, and had deductions made from his salary to pay for his new car and his pension fund, there was not enough left for an even moderately expensive social life. Salaries in the Colonial Service, contrary to what future generations were to imagine, were not high – in no way comparable to that earned by men in commerce.

Waite himself was not a popular member of the club. In fact on the night he took Ferdach along he had not been there for several weeks. During his last visit he had vastly annoyed other members by taking a harmless snake, which nevertheless looked like a krait, out of his jacket pocket and letting it loose along the top of the bar at which both men and women were sitting. 'The man's cracked' and 'A bloody fool!' were the politer remarks hurled at him amidst the hysterical uproar. Maybe they were justified. But Waite enjoyed cocking a snoot at some of the stuffy snobs who frequented the place. Perhaps too his joke was intended to show that he believed, in a derisive sort of way, in female equality. Anyway, as he pointed out, the snake wasn't as unpleasant as some of the humans who struck out at it before it got away.

The night of Ferdach's visit, the same bar was occupied by men only and Waite and Ferdach joined them in drinking and talking about horses. Ferdach did his best to look interested though all white male company of this sort bored him. Not many women were present in the other rooms but one of them happened to be the beautiful Mrs Sweinsnoep whom Ferdach had not seen since leaving the Western Hotel. Coming back from the men's room he encountered her in a long corridor lined with club photos of past officials and sporting teams – rather as in a minor public school the names of otherwise unmemorable people are vainly perpetuated.

She walked at him as if daring him not to give way. They came together face to face. She gave a sweet smile.

'Remember me?' she asked.

'Mrs Sweinsnoep. Elegant as ever, I see. Black becomes you.'

'Flatterer. Black becomes every woman. Yes, I've an awful name. So don't dare to grin. Call me Laura. And I'll say Ferdie. See. I found out your pet name.'

'My pet name? Oh, I like the idea of being a pet. Well Laura, how is Mr Sweinsnoep? Settled down in his job, I hope. Where are you both sitting?'

'Alfred isn't here. I dropped in out of boredom.' She swept her hand over her hair, the nervous gesture that Ferdach had found attractive in the Western, then said sarcastically, 'No, I'm lying. How could anyone be bored in Ipoh? I came for a women's get-together … the women's tennis committee. They've made me a member. The meeting's over now. So I'm free to do anything I want.' The sweet smile returned. 'Absolutely anything.'

There was an undercurrent in the way she spoke, an invitation. Ferdach wanted to respond to it but he was also on guard. Getting one's rocks off in a brothel was one thing; making love – for that might be how she would see it – to another officer's wife was another. He said, 'I always thought you might be athletic. Your figure you know.'

'Flatterer a second time Anyway either you know nothing about women or nothing about tennis. By the way, do you play?'

On an impulse Ferdach gave her doe-eyed look and said, 'When I'm in the mood.'

She turned away as if to look at a photo of one of the club's past presidents. Ferdach noted the curve of her neck and the dark hair caressing it. He was again aware of that delicate perfume which he had first noticed aboard the *Canton*. The lustful stirring when he had glanced at her across the dining room of the Western was rising again. He heard her asking, rather softly. 'And are you? A handsome young man shouldn't be alone if he is.'

Not much had really been said but the atmosphere was fully charged. Ferdach replied, 'I'm not alone. I'm with Jimmy Waite, the ADO. Just with Jimmy.'

'Jimmy the snake charmer. I've heard you live together?' Her eyebrows arched quizzically. Her gaze sauntered over him, up and down, up and especially down, taking in everything except his face, it seemed, rather as a man might look at a tart.

Ferdach laughed. 'Not exactly. I live in the same house as him.' Then boldness seized him. 'It's not the sort of place I'd take anyone back to.' But perhaps he had misread her expression and gone too far. 'Sorry. There's another guy in the house, the uncouth Ericson, I never know how he'll speak to my friends. Well Laura it was nice to see you again. Maybe I could call on you and your husband one evening.'

'The uncouth Ericson.' Laura repeated with a tinkly laugh. 'How apt. I know him. Yes, most apt.' She glanced over Ferdach's shoulder. 'And talk of the devil; there he is talking to Waite. Drinking away. They won't miss you in the least.'

Ferdach was still unsure whether she was entirely on her own in the club so he said, 'I'll come and join you then – if your lady tennis friends don't mind.'

Laura stared at him full in the face. 'Look Ferdie, I saw the way you were looking at me in the Western – as if I was just another mango to be devoured. You're a real dog aren't you? But I like you – instinctively.' Everything was out in the open now. She said, 'The coast's clear. Alfred's gone to Singapore. He's trying to get a transfer there. He hates Ipoh. So–'

'I came in Waite's car. He'll expect me to go back with him.'

'Well, I'll run you home instead – eventually.'

So began Ferdach's tempestuous affair with Laura Sweinsnoep.

13

'I think you should get a gun,' said Waite over breakfast.

His remark produced a spasm of alarm in Ferdach's mind. He thought at once of Alfred Sweinsnoep. What sort of man was he? Jealous? Obsessive? Likely to fly into a rage if he found out about his wife's infidelity? It was not easy to believe Laura's assertion that he couldn't care less what she got up to. Recently married people, most men, faithful or otherwise, weren't like that when their pride was at stake. 'Oh I don't know,' he replied too quickly. 'I don't think it'll come to anything. No one cares what we've been doing. There'll be no problem.'

Smarter than Waite in certain ways, the ever-observant Ericson looked up and said, 'Been up to something O'Haney? Putting your hand in the cash box – or someone's knickers?'

'Drop dead Ericson. I mean I don't think I'll run into any problems in the census.' Ferdach picked up the *Malay Mail* to hide his slightly flushed cheeks then put it down and began to elaborate in an effort to deflect Ericson's suspicions. 'Choo believes we're being left alone. Observed of course. The CTs observe everything. They probably even know where you go every night Ericson.'

'Choo? Choo?' reflected Ericson. 'Sounds like a train. Oh I know, he's the fat bottomed boy who translates for you. Does he bend over for you as well?'

Waite frowned at Ericson but as quickly shrugged his shoulders indifferently as if to say an oaf is an oaf and that's it. But Ferdach threw Ericson a supercilious grin. The reason for the insult was obvious – envy. For last night he had learned not only that Mr Muscleman had been one of Laura's lovers but, to put it mildly, was no great shakes in the role either with her, or she guessed, with any women. To put it politely, it was almost over before it began. Ericson must have seen him leaving the club with Laura and just now he had understood what was behind Ferdach's grin. Both of them knew everything and Ericson was worried. His reputation was at stake. However, Ferdach was not without pity and so, after breakfast, he followed Ericson out and surprised him by asking for a lift into town giving some trivial reason for not using his own car.

'Get in,' said Ericson a little less abruptly than usual. He revved up the car noisily and roared down the drive. His usual crude conversation followed. 'Did you have a good shag with Laura Swinesnogger?' to which Ferdach said, 'So so.' There was a silence for a while as the car hurtled on, well over the speed limit. Then Ericson could not help blurting out, 'Did she say anything about me?'

'About you? Why you?'

'Well then – about Waite and me. You live with us. Women always want to know other people's business.'

'She didn't talk about anyone but herself – and her husband. And I don't believe in talking about my friends.' Ferdach paused and added, 'Of whom I hope you are one Ericson.'

Ericson's face relaxed and they drove the rest of the way to the government offices under thirty miles an hour.

14

Ipoh, into which they were driving, was in those days a boomtown. Its wealth depended on tin mining which, despite the presence of some big European companies using enormous tin dredges, was very much in the hands of Chinese miners. Their methods had been brought from China during the nineteenth century and were well tried: powerful jets washed out the tin-bearing shale into a slurry which was pumped up to a tower whence it flowed downwards over a series of catchments in which the tin ore was deposited by gravity. These bamboo structures, or *palong*, scattered about the landscape around Ipoh, stood amidst creamy expanses of deposited sand and shale, variegated by man-made lakes serenely blue or vermilion in the bright sun and given variety by sporadic vegetation. Artificial the landscape might be but Ferdach, who in his search for squatter houses had by now wandered across it many times, thought it was strangely beautiful.

The workforce on both the European and the Chinese mines was largely Chinese. Pay was good and there were not as many labour problems as there had been in the years following liberation, certainly few that the communists could easily exploit. This did not mean that none of the workers were in the Min Yuen; some of the good money they earned could be as useful as any other source to the communist cause. But the Chinese middle class in Ipoh was too intent on getting rich from mining or the commerce and industry dependent on it to waste time supporting either the Communist Insurgency or the government's efforts to suppress it. As for the Chinese capitalists, the *towkays*, they were well organized in the Malayan Chinese Association; this was generally supportive of the government which hoped it would be able to rally the Chinese as a whole to its side. Unfortunately there was much dissent in the MCA which was

87

only held together by the skilled leadership of Tan Cheng Lok, a Straits Chinese of great acumen. At the same time membership of the MCA did not prevent some rich Chinese from maintaining hidden contacts with the Communists for, given the renewed might of China, who could tell what the future held.

It was a situation fraught with difficulties but Ferdach was rapidly learning about it sometimes from the mouths of the *towkays* themselves for it was their custom to invite anyone they believed to be of influence, which included most British officials, to sumptuous and extremely boozy Chinese dinners. These were generally held in large restaurants adjacent to the Happy World amusement park, the lively centre of Ipoh's popular nightlife though the wilder ones, that is those at which all the diners were male, took place in more discrete places.

Ferdach was invited to several of these dinner parties during his first month in Ipoh. The third was one he was never to forget. It was the only time in his life, until then, that he had disappeared under the table. Someone had to take him home, strip him and put him under the shower where, after vomiting, he had lain for several hours with a head riven, as it were, by a red hot axe. That party had been one of the wilder kind and Ferdach had been invited by a mining manager he had met when passing a tin mine with his platoon.

A voice had shouted, 'Hi, Mr O'Haney,' from a works building and was followed by the emergence of a muscular vaguely familiar looking man who had, in rather posh English, said, 'Last time we met, dear chap, was in the shower and in the nude – at the Carefree. Now let's have a proper introduction. My name is Kuok Lai Kuan.'

Ferdach remembered him at once. He was also able to connect him just as rapidly with everything he had heard about him and his family which was a very important one in Perak. There was no escaping such information when talking to Gordon Choo and other Chinese. For Kuok Lai Kuan was a son of the richest tin miner in Perak, a man who had come from China as a coolie some forty years earlier and risen through hard work to become a multi-millionaire. Ferdach already knew that Lai Kuan's elder half brothers had all gone into mining after leaving Chinese middle school. People said that they had inherited their father's toughness and business acumen and relished the hard physical work involved in mining. Not everyone believed this but it was common knowledge that they were big spenders and famed for their womanising throughout the Kinta Valley. Lai Kuan's mother was a younger wife and there was a twenty-year age gap between him and his next elder brother. By the time he was born his father, on account of his wealth, had joined a more educated level of society and decided that his youngest son should have the benefit of an English education: at Gresham's. Fortunately Lai Kuan was a brilliant student and, on the eve of the Japanese attack on Southeast Asia, was able to get to Cambridge where he obtained an excellent degree. It would have surprised no one if he had married his English girlfriend, become an academic and settled in Britain. None of this happened; for some reason known best to himself he decided that he too would learn everything about the tin industry and returned to Malaya to do so as soon when the war was over.

One late afternoon a few days after their encounter on the mine, Lai Kuan asked Ferdach for a drink in a clan association building in Ipoh. Much of the conversation was political and eventually turned to Ireland on which subject Ferdach always liked to adopt a nationalist stance, not so much out of conviction but to draw a line between himself and the run-of-the-mill Englishman. Maybe Lai Kuan failed to recognize that this was, to a certain extent, a pose. But he must have felt that he and Ferdach were on the same wave length for drinks led to a dinner with just the two of them at the Station Hotel. This was not a place much favoured by Chinese or by anyone wanting good food but it was suitable for a private tête-à-tête. Lai Kuan wanted to talk about British policy in the East and was very interested in the content of the colonial training course in London. When Ferdach told him that the first words he had heard on starting the course were none other than, 'Gentlemen, you have entered this Service to work yourselves out of a job,' he seemed full of disbelief stating that, in his view, the British had no intention of relinquishing their hold on the country. For some reason, probably a desire to tease, Ferdach lowered his voice conspiratorially and said, 'So you think you're right to follow our example?'

'Your example?'

'The example of Pearse and Connelly. Dublin 1916. The British only give in to force.'

Lai Kuan looked at Ferdach seriously, obviously beset by a multitude of thoughts. He replied, somewhat nervously, 'I met some very interesting people at Cambridge. Some of them thought like that too. Why on earth did a guy like you go to Liverpool?'

'Because my father isn't the head of the rich Kuok dynasty.'

Again Lai Kuan stared thoughtfully at Ferdach. He said, speaking softly, 'You're carrying out the census. I've seen you at it, as you know. But you're not involved in actually moving the squatters are you?'

'Not yet.'

'Stick to the census work Ferdie. Stick to the census.'

The rest of their conversation contained nothing unusual, that is to say they talked about brothel sex in Ipoh and more recondite forms of sex at Kings. Before they parted Ferdach had accepted an invitation to the dinner party at which he nearly brought up his guts. That party started in a little room just below the rooftop Jubilee Cabaret, the hangout for young Chinese bloods with money to burn. There Ferdach found himself the only European in a room of eight Chinese mine owners. They were all hard men, strongly built and distinctly fearsome; Ferdach thought there was something of the frontier mining camp in the air. They mainly spoke Cantonese and Ferdach did not get far with his attempts in that direction. However, two of the eight, besides Lai Kuan, spoke some English. After an hour of stiff drinking Lai Kuan asked Ferdach for his car keys, telling him that his Morris Minor would be taken back to Sturrock Road while he would be transported in Lai Kuan's Studebaker for the rest of the night. This worried Ferdach somewhat but he was by now so full of liquor that he didn't argue about it. To tell the truth he was not a little besotted by Lai Kuan's warmth towards him; it was as though he was being wooed and the overtures seemed to be encouraged by the other men. Everyone then drove in large American cars to a mansion in the suburbs, full of black mother-of-pearl-studded furniture, huge silken lanterns and Chinese décor at its gaudiest. Ferdach was conscious of the mansion being hidden on all sides by tall trees.

Into an air-conditioned upstairs room pretty girls served up a surfeit of dishes. All the usual Chinese delicacies were there – some Ferdach loved, others, such as sea slug, he forced himself to swallow quickly. Unfortunately his speed in disposing of the latter gave Lai Kuan the impression that he liked them and his bowl was recharged with more of the obnoxious creature, which he felt obliged to eat. Meanwhile the company grew rowdier and noisier. This was less an assemblage of Confucian scholars, more a party of barbarians. There were no sad poems about long-lost friends and past pleasures but a lot of what were, Ferdach deduced from certain oft repeated scatological words, dirty stories which Lai Kuan made no attempt to translate. The drinking got heavier; every time someone yelled '*yam seng!*', 'bottoms up!', the glasses were refilled to the brim. Ferdach was vaguely aware that he was drinking brandy, then whisky, or was it a mixture of the two? Before long, the girls – hired for more than just their waitressing skills – were being mauled and fondled, their cheongsams and then everything else pulled off. Two of the men took one of them off to a side room and came back later to great cheers and hysterical laughter. Others were not so modest. Then followed a game in which all the men sat around a circular table while a girl called Plum Blossom dived beneath it. Ferdach felt his flies being opened and lips embrace his cock. His face showed obvious surprise and the others all shouted '*Kui! Kui!* Him! Him!' pointing at Ferdach. Plum Blossom struck at random beneath the tablecloth. A game point was won if the accusation of '*Kui! Kui!*' proved wrong. The fun lay in the grotesque faces that could be pulled to delude the other players. Deep inside Ferdach's reeling brain, in that little centre which is ever observing, the certainty grew that in some way or other he was being deliberately debauched for a purpose. It was then that he realised that before something occurred that would irretrievably compromise him, his one escape lay in getting so drunk that he would pass out.

There was a round hole at the centre of the dining table with a little oil heater in its depths. Ferdach looked at it doubtfully. 'No, not live monkey brains tonight,' Lai Kuan mocked. 'Just a live fish.' The hole was covered by a large dish on which suspired a flat plaice-like fish which had been lightly fried and was far from dead. Ferdach was sure that its glinting eyes were taking in its surroundings. Lai Kuan, as host, began to shred the fish's scales and used his chopsticks to put some of the living flesh in Ferdach's mouth. When he had gulped it down Ferdach, without considering the implications of the question he was about to ask, said, 'Where's your friend and comrade?'

'You are my friend, Ferdie.' Lai Kuan hesitated then added, 'And comrade.'

'Yes. I am. But that other friend. He's always stayed in my mind. I wish he was here. The good-looking guy who was in the shower with you? The guy who asked me whether I'd had a jolly good fuck.'

Lai Kuan leaned towards Ferdie and spoke quietly amidst the Cantonese din, 'Why do you want to know? You liked him? You wanted to have him? Or – ah ha – you wanted him to have you? Ah yes, I see, you still do. Harry told me he saw your eyes devouring every bit of him. I didn't believe him but now I see he was right. Lust at first sight – on both sides, I'd say. Nevermind, we'll keep it a secret.'

'Just conversation Lai Kuan, to stop you putting more of that wretched fish in my mouth.'

Lai Kuan pulled over Plum Blossom, who was naked except for a diaphanous silk stole draped prettily around her shoulders. She opened up Ferdach's trousers and wriggled naughtily on his, to her already familiar, jade stem, kissing him as though overcome with desire, which was most unlikely. Meanwhile his host had brought his mouth right up to Ferdach's ear. His breath was like a caress as he whispered, 'Wong Chooi Fong, alias Henry Wong, but handsome Harry to his best friends, decided last week to go into the jungle, Ferdie.' Then, more surprisingly, he murmured, 'And maybe that's where you and I should be, together with him, my friend.' Except that he did not say 'friend' in English. He said it in Cantonese, '*pang yao*', or did he? Had Ferdach heard '*tung bao*', 'comrade'? He wasn't sure. So drunk was Ferdach by now that he was never to be certain what words had been spoken or whether he was about to be seduced politically or photographed naked amidst a bevy of girls. It was all immaterial for soon afterwards he had to be retrieved from beneath the table where he had drunkenly vomited up a brown mess of sea slugs onto Plum Blossom's dainty little feet.

15

The work of resettling the squatters of central Perak now began in earnest. It was not the first resettlement to take place in Malaya; the process had started in Johore and had gradually moved northward though Negri Sembilan and Selangor with the intention of covering the Chinese squatters in the entire peninsula in the protective blanket of government administration. The earliest resettlements had often been done hurriedly without adequate planning but as time went by the huge task of resettling half a million people required a more ordered approach in which the state governments, which had responsibility for land matters, were required to play an important role. The governments of the Malay states were, however, understandably apprehensive since resettlement could lead to permanent titles to land being acquired by a huge section of the Chinese population. Their caution meant that they did not always move quickly – even though General Briggs emphasised to them that as long as the squatters were uncontrolled and largely supportive of the Min Yuen, it would be impossible to defeat the well organized, highly efficient Communist military machine.

From the outset Ferdach had understood that his own census work formed but a small part of a much larger operation. But only gradually, as he learned about the various departments of government, did he perceive the magnitude of the task ahead. The Perak State Government had to provide suitable locations for the New Villages; sometimes the RAF carried out aerial surveys; the Town Planning Department had to draw up settlement plans which would determine the layout of the roads and the individual house plots. It was especially important that space should be provided for village council offices, schools, shops, clinics, mosques, temples, churches, community centres and so forth, for in the long run the social facilities envisaged were to be a significant ingredient in winning the hearts and minds of the people to the government side.

All the villages were to be surrounded by two high concentric chainlink perimeter fences punctuated by gates and watchtowers. Between the fences and also in a zone outside it, land would be provided for the resettled people to cultivate. The villages had to be sited so that there was an adequate water supply and no danger of flooding and this was the responsibility of the Drainage and Irrigation Department. But an extremely significant role would be played by the Public Works Department for in the first instance trees had to be felled, roads laid down, and fences erected before any movement of people could take place. Finally, when resettlement began, fleets of lorries would be needed to transport the squatters to their newly allocated lots and building materials provided for them to erect their houses. Ferdach began to look forward to the great operation with excitement. He liked action. It gave him a lift and he wanted anything he did to be done with excellence. With the starry eyes of youth he saw the New Villages as being a social experiment that would provide the people with a better life.

Nevertheless, his personal knowledge of the Communists warned him that they and their left-wing supporters the world over would depict these places as concentration camps, akin to the hellholes of the Boer War or even of the Nazis. But the care with which he observed the villages being planned belied that for him. He was sure they could be viable settlements within which people could live without fear of communist depredations, running their own affairs under the provisions of a new local council act that was already being discussed. Indeed, Ferdach saw the process as a brilliant way of bringing peace to the country and so making possible its independence. His enthusiasm for what was afoot now impelled him to press Waite to make sure that he was given a more active part to play – despite what Lai Kuan had advised about sticking to the census. After all, wasn't he here to work himself out of a job?

16

'Oh no,' said Laura. 'Keep out of it as much as possible. I just don't want anything to happen to you. If Lai Kuan warned you, take his advice. He obviously likes you. Remember he's a member of the Kuok family and they know everything. They'll have a foot in both camps.'

'A whole leg I should imagine,' Ferdach replied. 'But what do you think I'm here for? I'm a government officer. I must do my best whatever job I'm given. No one can pick and choose to play safe.'

'Yes. But you've been pressing Waite for a change just when he's pleased with the work you're doing. Stupid Ferdie, he knows best what you're here for … better than you do.'

Ferdach suspected that Laura's view of what he was here for, that is to say here on earth for, was quite simple: he was here to make love to her. Whenever she told him that her husband had gone away, he would always try to comply with her demand for his presence in her bed. But he was not in love with her – or at least he did not feel he was in love with her, just yet. When a woman gave herself so easily love might, or might not, come along; for now, he just wanted to enjoy her voluptuous body and her enthusiastic love making as well as the quite frivolous relief from the spartan atmosphere of Waite's household and the daily hardship of toiling under the sun. It was worth more than a visit to the Carefree.

Yet sex alone would not have been enough to sustain the affair between them. Ferdach was quick to see that Laura was in some ways the female equivalent of himself, or to put it another way, her attitude to sexual relationships was similar to that of his much admired Nina Hamnett. It was obvious that Laura would never make friends among the other expatriate wives. Most of them were concerned with their homes, their clothes, their husbands' careers and above all else with their children. It was unlikely that many of them would take to her either, for Laura's attitude to children was like that of the Welsh woman in an Emlyn Williams play who, when asked why she had given up her new-born baby, replied, 'Well dearie, as soon as I saw it I said to myself – naw.'

More important than that, Laura was an intelligent, one might say an intellectual woman though she never represented herself as such. She often liked to talk about books and new ideas but more especially about music though these were hardly in the forefront of her mind when it came to personal relationships. Ferdach had been surprised as he approached the Sweinsnoep's house for his second evening visit there to hear the sound of a skilfully played Mozart sonata, or at least he thought it was so played. Laura had not mentioned that a piano had been on its way from Penang or that she could play. Ferdach was not without interest in music though of a different kind from Laura's. He had become quite friendly with Jack Moeran, a composer friend of Nina Hamnett in London, to some extent because E. J. Moeran had the same Anglo-Irish background as himself but more particularly because Jack was one of the few people who were still kind to the dreadfully impoverished Nina. However, when he tried to interest Laura in Moeran's music she showed little interest in it or in that of his mentor, Vaughan Williams, firmly disparaging the folksy side of their music as belonging to the 'cowpat school'. She was a firm classicist but if music had to be modern, then it must be Bartok whose chamber music she greatly admired. Ferdach's musical taste developed under her guidance but her enthusiasm left him wondering why she had never taken up music as a career.

Declaring herself to be extremely self critical, Laura stated that she was just not good enough to become a professional but Ferdach was unconvinced. There must have been some other reason that had impelled her to marry a dullard like Alfred. Conversation with her led him to conclude that she had wanted quite desperately to get away from two not particularly well-educated parents and a couple of unaspiring siblings. All the same, he suspected that she was holding something back from him. Clearly she longed for the good life without having to work for years to get it and even though conditions in Malaya were not luxurious they were a damn sight better than living in postwar Bethnal Green from which she had only partly escaped by studying at Bedford College. That was where she had met Alfred who unfortunately had never lived up to her even mildly romantic expectations. And so whenever she got around to talking about her life after a bout of extended love play with Ferdach, she portrayed herself as a once dormant volcano that was at last fully aroused by her darling Ferdach. Flattering it is to any young man to hear such rubbish and he naturally enjoyed it even though he did not believe it. She always graced their inventive amorous sessions with the word 'love', never 'sex' which rarely crossed her lips. It was, of course, foolish, if understandable, of Ferdach to accept this self-deception without protest. With her husband, she emphasised, in case Ferdach had some residual stirrings of guilt, love was a dead letter if, indeed, it had ever been written nor had she been truly aroused by any of the three other young men, one of them Ericson, she had slept with since arriving in Ipoh. But occasionally she would look sadly at Ferdach as though thinking of an immense lost chance which he himself must surely have witnessed on the voyage out and she would confess to him, yet again, and once with tears, how much she regretted the loss of that clever forestry officer, Ambrose Heath, from Sarawak, to whose cabin she had stolen, well not exactly stolen since everyone aboard seemed to know about it, on the three nights between Colombo and Penang. He could have been the answer to her fierce need for Life with a capital L, but his ailing wife awaited him in Kuching. And he was too decent, too loyal, to abandon someone who was an invalid. If only he could have recognised that Laura was capable of returning such loyalty in abundance.

On the *Canton* Ferdach had learned a lot about who was sleeping with who from his own cabin steward, the lustful raven-haired young Kevin O'Malley from Knotty Ash, with whom he had forged a happy, albeit only voyage-long, relationship. But he said nothing to disillusion Laura about her paragon for Ambrose Heath had made at least four other conquests of women on their way out to join their husbands. They, with the cool discretion born of greater ocean liner experience, had insisted on doe-eyed Ambrose being the one who discreetly visited their cabins after the passengers, but not the all-observing stewards, had retired for the night. But what happens on a ship is dead wood the moment it berths. Only the present mattered and so, 'What about Ericson?' Ferdach demanded for he foresaw difficulties if he and the Swede were to continue sharing Laura's embraces.

'Oh, don't worry, I've told Ericson I can't see him again because of his reputation. It's become a joke which house his car's parked outside each night.' But in regard to the other two men she was dismissive. Ferdach was sure that she still received them if he himself couldn't get around even though she mocked them; they were just a couple of young British Army lieutenants, one named 'Blondie' Phelps, the other 'Starkers' Mason, mere boys who drank like idiots and wanted nothing but a quick screw. On one matter she was, however, adamant: her darling Ferdach was different. He cared, he understood, he was gentle, he knew how to arouse her feelings. If only she had met him earlier, before Alfred had appeared on the scene. But was it too late? After all, she had only married Alfred to get away from home, or from an earlier lover or from some other threatening entity that she could never quite identify. Ferdach began to feel that the nameless horror she sought to escape was none other than some dreadful gloom within herself. However, for all he knew of her at present, a greater cause of gloom, but not for her, might well be her divorce from Alfred and remarriage to himself. Maybe that was what she hoped for.

Nevertheless, what disturbed Ferdach most about Laura was not the inner sadness that gave rise to her constant complaints that life had passed her by. After all, in a happy relationship that could change. She could easily become a most desirable companion for besides being very good in bed and intelligent, she was obviously an efficient manager. Nor was it any reluctance on Ferdach's part to marry when his career was at the formative stage. Many young recruits were already married and a man with a sensible wife was regarded as an asset in the service. Nor was it even any fear on his part that, once married, he would be prevented from having a fling with other guys, a pleasure he had no intention of giving up. Laura was sophisticated; when talking about this subject she had told him categorically, and probably with the intention of clearing away any obstacle in his mind, that she believed, as Proust had written, that most sensible women always married men who were ambidextrous because they were less likely to lose them to female rivals. No, what put Ferdach off was the way Laura behaved to her husband.

One Saturday evening she invited Ferdach to dinner. As her house was not far away and the evening was balmy he decided to walk there. He thought it would be just the two of them but when he approached the Sweinsnoep's front door, there was Alfred to greet him most affably. Obviously, thought Ferdach, there had been some change in the man's schedule so it would be necessary to play along in a social sort of way. For a while he sat chatting inconsequentially with Alfred who was generous with the *stengah*s, in this case mainly whiskey with a very small dash of water, indeed the ice apart it was difficult to believe there was any water in their drinks at all. They talked, or rather Ferdach talked, while Alfred gazed at him with blue unblinking eyes, about the emergency situation which seemed to be deteriorating. There had, within the last few days, been several ambushes on police convoys in the north of Perak and a protracted attack on a rubber estate athwart the main road south which had resulted in the death of an estate manager and his wife. Ferdach said he believed that when resettlement was underway, such attacks would intensify as the CTs knew that once the squatters were outside their control their supplies would gradually dwindle. And so, Ferdach concluded, with the confidence of a propaganda chief, the government would most certainly win but not quickly. His entire monologue was delivered with never a sight of Laura.

When she did appear she was wearing a beautiful Indian sari, a garment Ferdach loved to see her in; its green silk was edged with gold and it set off the olive skin of her bare midriff to great advantage. There was a slight tinkling sound as she came towards them and Ferdach knew she was wearing his own gift, delicate anklets with tiny bells on them, the sort Indian dancers often wore. In other words she had dressed in the provocative way which she favoured when Ferdach was with her alone, not in the sort of sensible dress English women wore to entertain their husband's associates. Alfred hardly looked at her nor said a word.

Towards Ferdach she behaved in an openly affectionate way – again as though they were alone. It embarrassed him. It was not that she was actually rude to Alfred – that came later; it was as though he wasn't there. But when she did take to addressing him it was invariably to complain petulantly that something was wrong: the fan was on too strongly, he should slow it down. Then, 'No, that's too weak, a little stronger,' and not a 'thank you' when he had adjusted it just as she wanted. He had opened the wine for dinner; she noticed a tiny bit of cork in the bottle. 'Oh God Alfred, can't you open a wine bottle now?' The rain began to fall. 'Oh God Alfred, can't you see the rain's coming onto the balcony. Why didn't you tell the boy to roll down the blinds?'

To all of which Alfred complied in a heavy drawl, 'Yes, Laura' or 'No, Laura' though once, when his wife went to the bathroom, a sardonic grin appeared on his face and he said, *sotto voce*, to Ferdach, 'She who must never be disobeyed but better still, never listened to.'

Ferdach, to Laura's clear irritation, tried to interest Alfred in another conversation, this time about Chinese education. Unfortunately Alfred's opinions on the subject were dismissive, even hostile; he saw no need for higher education other than in English, so that instead of finding himself in any way drawn towards Laura's husband, Ferdach soon came to the conclusion that Alfred was an unimaginative bore who thought himself more intelligent than he was. Nevertheless, when the topic changed again it transpired that Alfred knew some of the people Ferdach had met in Soho where, instead of indulging in the Bohemian life, he had been involved in an effort to establish an intellectual magazine in which he would write, or edit, articles on philosophy. Ferdach wondered how this could possibly be. To be a philosopher one had to be intelligent, or how could one formulate rational concepts. Alfred was as dull as dishwater but filled to the full with a sense of his own importance and a false certainty that he had something significant to tell the world. Far from offsetting Laura's coldness towards Alfred with his own warmth, Ferdach found himself sharing her obvious contempt for him and the despised man undoubtedly felt it.

Dinner was excellent having been prepared under Laura's expert supervision by a Chinese girl she was training. Ferdach told his hosts that it was a cut far above what Cookie produced in Sturrock Road and that Alfred was lucky to have such food each day. At that Alfred came to life. Getting up briskly he gave Laura a cold smile, no, more a grimace, that suggested inner loathing and said loudly, 'Well, that's one way in which she could always make a living, ain't it luv.' The last words were spoken as if she was just a clippie on a bus. 'Despite which, none of your delicious coffee for me tonight; I'm off to see a dear friend. So I'll leave you two love birds together to shag yourselves silly.' This crude statement shook Ferdach. It was his first intimation that Alfred knew about his affair with Laura and that he did not care a tinker's cuss. Alfred had relished turning the tables.

The moment he was gone Laura said, 'You heard that Ferdie? He wants to get rid of me. He wants to be free. And by God, so do I. Freedom! I long for it, you long for it, he longs for it. We long for it. We do, don't we Ferdie? See, I've already conjugated our happiness into existence. We'll have such a good life together. We're meant for each other.' She rattled on about how easy it would be. She would file for a divorce on the grounds of Alfred's admitted infidelity with a mousy little Chinese teacher, Mona Wee. There'd be no problem. He wouldn't contest. In any case, very soon he'd be off to Singapore on his new posting. She and Ferdach could take up together even before the divorce was through. So much happiness lay ahead for them.

Ferdach didn't say much, just 'yes' and 'no' and 'hum' and 'haw', but he was thinking how this woman might behave to him once she was fed up with him. How could he be sure that there had never been passion between her and the now despised Alfred. When they got to bed soon after Laura's impassioned description of their new life together, the love making didn't do much for him because his brain was full of disturbing thoughts and no one can make love well when thinking too much. During their fourth round in the early hours of the morning it seemed to Ferdach that he was just acting like a steam piston, in and out, in and out. But strangely enough Laura didn't seem to notice or to care. In fact she started to cry out Alfred's contemptuous words, 'Shag me silly, shag me silly,' followed by 'Woofy' which was her pet name, not for her current ravisher, but for Starkers Mason. Had she cried the name of Phelps, he might have thought he was hearing wrongly, but Woofy could not be mistaken for Ferdie. Then, to crown it all Laura insisted that it had been the best fuck she had ever had.

Ferdach did not go to sleep. He cradled Laura in his arms for a while feeling a strange pity for her. Her behaviour to Alfred had been unpardonable but misery can make people do horrid things. As he stroked her hair he was close to tears. A world disparaged might be a world lost. He had not wanted to make love as they had done. It had left him with a feeling of emptiness. He did not want to be devoured by a woman. In memory, the single act of sex with Wong Siu Bo in the dingy Carefree Hotel and her subsequent uncalled for kindness seemed nearer to his needs from a woman than what Laura had given him. And yet he was also disturbed to feel, for the first time, a singular affection for her; the more he knew of her unhappy character the stronger his attachment to her might easily grow. His feelings for her seemed more akin to what he had felt for poor decrepit Nina Hamnett than to anything flowing from the well springs of passion. He was still grappling with this enigma when, not long before dawn, he heard Alfred return home and go into his bedroom. Ferdach rose quietly, tiptoed downstairs so as not to disturb Laura's black dog Barty and started to walk to Sturrock Road.

It was quite cool with a soft wind blowing from the mountains. An almost full moon that looked as if it was made of silver paper hung low in a sky brilliant with stars and not a trace of cloud. The delicious fragrance of tropical flowers and vegetation came variously to his nostrils as he strolled along and the air was quietly noisy with the sounds of cicadas. No one was around apart from the occasional cyclist who would greet him with '*selamat pagi, Tuan,*' as he pedalled by at a leisurely pace. What a relief it was to be alone and free amidst such peaceful serenity after letting his body tangle too long with Laura in her overly decorated bedroom.

Then unexpectedly, and almost at once, he was surrounded on all sides by loud croaking. Bloated frogs from the storm drains were hopping all around him. There seemed to be scores of them on the road ahead as if it had developed big black pustules. He thought to walk faster and then, squelch, he stepped right onto a large frog which wriggled in its death throes around his sandal-clad foot. He shouted aloud in disgust and ran ahead with his feet sometimes coming down on more of the creatures that were out in some froggy mating activity. All he wanted was to get home as fast as possible and into the shower to wash off the disgusting mess.

17

The State Secretary, Tuan Haji Mustapha Albakri, who took a close interest in everything concerned with resettlement, decided to invite a number of officers engaged in the process to a reception at which the guest of honour would be General Briggs, currently on a fact-finding tour of north Malaya. The occasion was to be informal, in keeping with the tenor of the times, and Tuan Haji's secretary had requested the District Office to provide some suitable names for invitation.

The administrative situation in Ipoh was unusual. It was the largest town in the state, its economic hub and, though not the seat of the Sultan, the location of the State Secretariat. However, the administrative district in which Ipoh was situated was at the small town of Batu Gajah situated a few miles away. There, in an unusual cream-plastered Jacobean District Office, replete with obelisks and delicate strapwork – the brainchild of some brilliant but now forgotten PWD architect – reigned the imperious Mr Harmsworth Bertelli from whom Jimmy Waite took his orders. Mr Bertelli – whose ancestor Luigi Massimo had followed the Corsican patriot General Pasquale Paoli into exile in the eighteenth century, settled in England and prospered – had definite ideas about status. Accordingly he told Waite that only officers of a certain rank would be put on the invitation list. This did not of course include Ferdach who was only a lowly cadet.

Waite was determined that Ferdach should go to the reception not just because his work had been good but because he believed that, circulating among the squatters, Ferdach must have picked up a lot about their reactions and fears which would be of interest to both Albakri and the General. Waite also had a hidden agenda. He was often critical of Bertelli but could not always express some of his own views on the Chinese that he knew Ferdach shared with him. If Ferdach blurted them out like an innocent, Albakri would hear them and maybe take them to heart for he was a shrewd man, subtle and intelligent. All this had to be kept quiet from Bertelli who, once he had uttered an opinion, rarely changed his mind except on matters concerning his own advancement when he could be remarkably flexible. And so Waite seized the opportunity presented by the inauguration by Tuan Haji Mustapha Albakri of a new Muslim religious school, or Madrasah, in a Malay *kampung*, to take Ferdach along with him to the modest opening ceremony. By judiciously ascertaining Bertelli's movements in the weeks ahead through a friend, none other than Tengku Mizan in the District Headquarters, Waite had ensured that the opening would take place when Harmsworth Bertelli was away in Kuala Lumpur.

Ferdach had met Albakri soon after his arrival in Malaya but only briefly. It was usual for new government officers to 'sign the book' at the Secretariat on their arrival. Somewhat unusually on that occasion Ferdach had been ushered into the State Secretary's office for a personal audience. He saw before him a rather handsome greying middle-aged man with a courteously gentle manner and twinkling eyes that seemed to have settled on him with some degree of amusement. After a few enquiries about his voyage out and where he was living Albakri did not, to Ferdach's relief, ask why he had joined the Malayan Civil Service but said, out of the blue, 'Now, what do you think of Everton's chances on Saturday?'

For an instant Ferdach felt he was taking part in one of Waite's telepathy tests until, glancing down at a form on Albakri's extremely large desk, he read, upside down, the word, Littlewood's. He knew nothing about football. In fact it bored him to the back teeth to hear people blathering on about it, but he said very firmly, 'Lose'.

Tuan Haji made a cross on the form and then gave Ferdach a broad smile. 'Nice to have you working with us Mr O'Haney. I hope you will be very happy in my country.'

Ferdach rose to go and then he remembered Mr Eliot's words about joining the service to work himself out of a job. His ultimate boss in Perak was already a Malay and he was glad of it. Why shouldn't he say so. At the door he hesitated an instant then turned and said, 'It's an honour Tuan Haji to be serving under a Malay officer.' Albakri's eyes lit up as if he had just witnessed something new, which maybe he had. For although Ferdach was no fool he was no balls carrier either and Albakri must have sensed his sincerity.

Now about the Malays, Ferdach still felt ill at ease. Having opted to learn Chinese, he had, so Mizan had pointed out, suggested a preference. This was untrue but he must rectify the balance and get to know more about the Malays. Since his hope that Mizan might help him in this seemed unlikely, his visits to the Tengku's *kampung* became less frequent. Moreover, since Mizan's *mukim*, or parish, was on the other side of Batu Gajah their paths rarely crossed at work. On the couple of occasions when they had seen one another in Ipoh, Mizan's greeting had been so peremptory that Ferdach felt he was now being given the cold shoulder. Was Mizan annoyed not to be visited so often or did he still suspect Ferdach of being over partial to the Chinese? The difficulty was that Ferdach's work mainly took him among Chinese squatters. The *towkay*s who invited him to social functions were Chinese. The only Malays he mixed with were in his platoon of special constables, with Tahir and Mat Noor foremost among them and contact was largely related to their duties in the field. True, in Waite's office there were some Malay clerks and office boys who seemed well disposed towards him. There were also in Waite's sub-district three other *penghulu*s but they seemed distant towards him as though suspecting, probably with justification, his ability to do anything better than they could. In any case their work lay in different directions from his own.

He was doing his best to learn Malay but he was conscious of the fact that the little he had learned was a crude version of the language and quite different from the courtly Malay Tuan Haji Albakri used when talking to his staff or from what Waite used when talking to Yusuf. Indeed the language between Waite and Yusuf sounded light and fanciful; it was enriched sometimes by an exchange of *pantun*s, the poetic quatrains composed by the Malays to heighten the expression of feelings and it was often punctuated by laughter. When he heard their exchanges Ferdach felt envious, left out of a hidden, seemingly magical, world of ancient provenance. The grammar books he used did not seem to provide a key to this language so rich in idiom.

One Saturday he had driven with Laura, when all had been glowing between them, to Kuala Kangsar. There, they had admired the beautiful Ubudiah Mosque and the Sultan's Istana, though from a distance. They had also been struck by the grace of the Malay youths playing on the fields of the Malay Boys College and both of them had sensed the distance between themselves and a seemingly serene culture marked by a delicacy quite absent from the crude business world of Ipoh. The visit left Ferdach feeling ill at ease.

At the religious ceremony marking the opening of Waite's Madrasah, Ferdach had done as Waite told him, taking off his shoes, bathing his feet and opening his hands when the prayers were recited. Afterwards they had gone to the Imam's house for food and soft drinks and there Tuan Haji Albakri singled him out. Ferdach felt that this was particularly kind of him because everyone but himself was talking away in Malay.

'Did you read the football results, Mr O'Haney?'

'Yes I did. I don't usually do so Tuan Haji, but I felt that I had to. I'm sorry Everton won. It must have affected your betting results.'

'Oh no it didn't. All my results were bang on. I won quite a bit. I was just testing you. You're obviously not one of the herd if you know so little about English football.'

Ferdach smiled. He had taken instinctively to this man who seemed to be both cunning and wise, the sort of man anyone would wish to have as a father. He really felt like opening his heart to him and telling him about his difficulties making contact with the Malay world. Hesitantly he blurted out, 'You're very understanding Tuan Haji. Sometimes I feel at a loss here. I've only been in Malaya for a few months and I'm still a stranger in a strange land.'

Albakri took Ferdach by the arm. 'Take your time. I hear from my nephew Mizan that you're doing well. I've told him that the two of you should come to my home one evening and we can settle the state of the world together. Mizan talks well and he's clever though not as clever as his father. When they're together it's a case of "*anak harimau menjadi kuching*" – "the tiger cub becomes a kitten". One day you'll see for yourself. But that can wait. Mizan tells me that you sympathise with the squatters. A lot of people don't. So you must come to my party. Maybe you'll be able to give some of your ideas to General Briggs. He's an open-minded man.' He glanced across at two disputing Imams and sighed. 'I hope not one of a dying breed.' Before turning away he added, 'Oh, by the way, watch your Ps and Qs if Bertelli's around. But speak the truth to the General.'

The conversation cheered Ferdach up immensely, mainly because Albakri had heard about him from Tengku Mizan who had obviously not forgotten or turned against him. Friendship between them might still be possible.

'How is your nephew, Tuan,' he managed to ask later, before the State Secretary went off. 'I haven't seen much of him.'

Albakri replied, 'The remedy for that will be at my reception.'

Naturally enough Ferdach's name was put on the guest list with a note indicating that it was the State Secretary's wish to have it there. No objection came from the office of Mr Bertelli.

18

Only in novels does a young man, newly posted to a country, meet one of its highest officers, impress him with his originality and so have a decisive influence on events. This did not happen to Ferdach, except in a negative sort of way, when he came face to face with General Briggs at Albakri's reception.

Ferdach accompanied Waite in his gleaming Jaguar. He sat in the front seat next to Yusuf but did not think to play with the latter's hair. In the rear with Waite was Algernon Broadstairs who had been invited to join them. Earlier on Waite had told Ferdach, as he had also advised Albakri, that he considered the ex-actor an excellent raconteur capable of keeping any party alive particularly when it was inclined to become heavy going, or dull, a likely occurrence when a lot of military men were expected to jell with 'colonials'. But another reason for his presence was that Waite, reluctant to defend the indefensible, wanted Ferdach to learn for the first time, from the horse's own mouth, that Broadstairs had been given responsibility for a substantial resettlement operation due to start the following day in an area to the north of Ipoh. As this was a job that Ferdach had coveted he felt extremely resentful when Broadstairs boasted about it the moment he turned up at Waite's house.

They left Sturrock Road late in the afternoon for Waite wanted to make a final inspection of the resettlement arrangements which involved considerable numbers of District Office staff, police and military. Broadstairs was insistent that all the logistics had been carefully prepared. Everyone had been briefed on his duties and knew exactly what his role was. The families to be moved had been given warning that resettlement was imminent – no inhumane turning up early in the morning to evict helpless people, he emphasised. This operation would provide a model of how things should be done. As was standard practice, in addition to being transported by lorry with all their chattels each family would be given seventy Malayan dollars in cash and a free supply of building material to construct a new house on an alloted site. The Resettlement Area had already been surveyed and provided with rudimentary access roads by the Public Works Department. All was in order and 'Really, Waite,' Broadstairs chided, 'no final inspection is necessary.'

Of course the overall planning of the operation had been done at a higher level. Waite had been involved in it, at least as an observer for Bertelli was not keen on his subordinates putting their faces up, as he put it, when decisions were to be taken. Broadstairs was no more than a field officer carrying out a single item in a huge human movement. Yet as he lolled back comfortably in his seat, holding forth with great confidence on the work ahead, he conveyed the impression that he had planned it all. He was now acting the part of generalissimo of the entire operation and an arrogant generalissimo at that.

In an attempt to show interest, Ferdach asked him the names of the Chinese Assistant Resettlement Officers who were working under him as he knew, from his experience with Gordon Choo, how very important it was to have an excellent interlocutor between himself and the Chinese population. Broadstairs was dismissive of the question. 'My God, don't ask me the names of these Chinese Johnies,' he said. 'Wong, Pong, Tong, it's all the same to me. All I care is that they should do exactly what I tell them. I give the orders, they carry them out – to the letter.'

'But they're very important to your work,' put in Waite mildly. 'You should get to know them as individuals. They're important for your success.'

'Not at all, my dear Waite. Success lies in absolute obedience to commands. Little personalities don't matter unless someone fails to carry out instructions. Then that personality may have to be squashed, which is why it's dangerous to get too involved with any of them. And I don't want any subordinate staff coming up with their own ideas. If they are Chinese staff they are probably wrong, and not to be trusted. No. I believe in total obedience to me in every detail,' Broadstairs pontificated. 'If the detail has been properly thought out, nothing can go wrong. You know my dear Waite, it's no different really from directing a play. If everyone knows his part, no, not just his part but how his part fits into the totality of the drama, the unexpected can be surmounted. I grant you that each subordinate must be trained – no, empowered is the right word – to fill in any gaps in the defences by playing another role. But he is empowered as part of a machine, in this case my machine, not as individual Mr Wong. Let the enemy break through, and he will then be quickly encircled.'

My dear Waite flinched but said nothing. He was an excellent listener, especially when he was unsure of something. For it was not him but Bertelli who had made the decision to assign Broadstairs to this exercise, a decision only taken, Waite knew, after an agreeable lunch in the club at which Broadstairs had put everyone, but especially Bertelli and his wife, into stitches with his camp impersonation of Johnnie and Larry having an argument during a rehearsal at the Old Vic. In fact, even without Waite's intervention, Broadstairs was now assured of a place at any important social gathering in Bertelli's district.

They stopped at the small town of Chemor where they visited the Resettlement Office and spoke to some police officers and several army officers, one of whom happened to be Lieutenant Starkers Mason – he who, as Woofy played by Ferdach, had given Laura the best fuck of her life. Woofy gave a knowing wink at Ferdach, who stared back blankly as though he had met his doppelganger. Then they moved on, for more important to Waite was a brief visit to the site of the intended New Village which was in a hilly area east of Chemor where many squatters had occupied rubber estates abandoned during the Japanese occupation. They passed through a number of road checkpoints efficiently manned, so it seemed, by special constables and noted the presence of a small military camp less than a mile before reaching the site which had been cleared and surrounded by a barbed wire perimeter fence. Everywhere looked calm and well ordered. Neatly drawn up along the roadside were some thirty or so lorries intended to transport the squatters. Ferdach was surprised to see that, apart from a few drivers, eating and smoking by the roadside, there were no guards. The lorries were not even inside the new perimeter fence

'All ship-shape and ready to go at the crack of dawn,' said Broadstairs proudly. 'I've made sure that every vehicle has been serviced and has a full tank. We don't want any breakdowns.'

'I don't think they should be here at all,' said Ferdach, very firmly addressing Waite rather than Broadstairs.

'Does Bertelli know they're here?' asked Waite. 'I thought they were to be parked securely.'

'Of course he does. I've cleared it with the old man.' Broadstairs replied irately. 'I'm on the blower to him every day you know, Waite.'

'But I thought we were all supposed to work through Mr Assistant District Officer James Waite,' Ferdach observed tartly.

'God, you'll go a long way as a bureaucrat,' said Broadstairs, seemingly from some twenty feet in the air. 'Let me explain young man. We'll have a lot to do tomorrow, hundreds of people to move. In the afternoon there could be a downpour. We have to start *de trés bonne heure. Savez?* It was my idea to have the lorries drawn up here. I don't believe in wasting time "working through" anyone.'

'Yes but ... where are the guards?' Ferdach, now a bad tempered terrier, insisted. He knew Waite was on his side.

'Guards? Who wants guards? Use your bloody eyes boy. You saw the drivers. You saw the military camp. This area is safe. We'll have police and soldiers enough tomorrow but only to give the squatters reassurance.' Broadstairs' confidence was overwhelming; easy to see how he got his way with Bertelli, in fact with anybody. Only a full-blown row could change things now and it would be wrong to countermand the orders of a man who had just been given authority by the District Officer. And maybe the risk was acceptable; despatch would be all important.

'Come on then,' said Waite, now an unhappy conciliator. 'We don't want to be late for the State Secretary.'

They drove off. Ferdach kept quiet. To himself he said that he didn't care a fuck what happened to the lorries; he even obeyed meekly when Broadstairs ordered him, as though he were the assistant chauffeur, to press the cigarette lighter and pass him a light. Waite said little but Broadstairs, undeterred, was soon into a tale of what he had done at Bristol when the Old Vic was evacuated there during the war. It sounded as if he had been responsible for the survival of British Theatre when its very existence hung in the balance.

19

Parties at Albakri's beautiful official residence invariably turned out to be larger than expected for some people gatecrashed them while others, not on the original guest list, were invited by Tuan Haji himself at the last minute. Success was always assured by copious supplies of three alcoholic refreshments: brandy ginger ales or BGAs, whisky and water or *stengah*s, and gin and lime or gimlets. Muslim guests were provided with soft drinks if they insisted on them. Not all did. Tray after tray of delicious Malay small eats were always served by handsome sarong-clad Malay boys gliding silently and smiling among the gabbling guests. When Waite and his companions ascended the steps from the carport they joined a little queue of guests being received in the hall by Tuan Albakri who said '*Selamat datang*' to each and every one of them but to Ferdach added, *sotto voce*, 'Now, how about giving me a few wins for next Saturday so I can put them down as losers.'

'What was that about?' quizzed Broadstairs, but Ferdach did not reply for now they were assailed by a torrent of chatter from a mixed throng, mainly male but with a fair scattering of women, slowly moving in accordance with the inexorable law of cocktail party circulation soon to be formulated by C. Northcote Parkinson who, it so happened, was among the first people Ferdach saw as he entered the glittering reception hall. Their eyes lit up as though they were Livingstone and Stanley and they made for one another forgetful of their companions.

'What on earth are you doing here sir?' Ferdach asked. 'I never expected you to leave Liverpool. When we last met you were up to your neck in some huge naval history project. Why should that bring you out here.'

'Well I've got a Chair at Singapore and I'm involved in Malayan

Historical Studies. I'm lucky to be where the best source material is –the Straits Settlements records, you know. Well probably you don't. Why should you? I remember that in Liverpool you were more interested in having a good time than in research. That's why we never offered you a fellowship – despite your amorous cajoling of staff members.' It was clear that Parkinson had not lost his habit of smiling kindly while injecting the acid.

Ferdach hid his irritation. Had his mother missed that advert in *The Times* he would have hung on – and been disappointed. Coolly he replied, 'Oh what luck! I would have lost out on all this. But what brings you among soldiers rather than historians?'

'My dear boy, a party like this, with so many top military and colonial types, is living history: the last of the dinosaurs. No, I'm being snide.' As so often, thought Ferdach. 'I'm travelling round Malaya to get the feel of the place. To talk to people like Tuan Haji Albakri; people who know it well. I paid my respects to him this afternoon and he told me to come along tonight – as I'm on my own in the Station Hotel. But what are you doing here? I knew you'd joined the Colonial Service but I thought you were the lotus-eater type who'd opt for some South Seas paradise.'

Knowing from experience that Parkinson's shafts were best ducked, Ferdach briefed him quickly about his Emergency work before moving on to chat about people and things familiar to them both in Liverpool; this was a pleasant respite from the odd conversations of Sturrock Road. At the same time he was wary. Besides his reputation for being acerbic and ambitious, Parkinson was no great respecter of confidences. Though they had moved in the same circles in Liverpool, even paying court together at the salon of Mrs Melly, the rendezvous of the brightest people in town, they had never been close, always treating each other with reserve. But since it would be useful to have a port of call if ever he went to Singapore, as a friendly gesture he invited Parkinson to join him the next day for a tour of Ipoh. Then he introduced him to Algernon Broadstairs who was hovering nearby. Algernon expressed fulsome pleasure at meeting someone from the University of Malaya in Singapore and, after knitting his brows in furrowed thought, said he was sure he had heard of Parkinson's work.

'In maritime history perhaps?' asked Parkinson, pleased that his modest fame should have spread so far. 'Perhaps some naval monograph? On the Far East Fleet maybe?'

'It could be,' boomed Broadstairs very deliberately. 'Yes. It could well be. Probably from my father.' Then he spoke briskly. 'He has strong naval interests, but only academic. He couldn't enter the Senior Service. The great disappointment of his life. Poor health, you know. His heart. You see his father served on the Iron Duke under Vice Admiral Shadwell, C. in C. of the China Station in the 1870s.'

'Really?' exclaimed Parkinson warming to Broadstairs. Intent on talking to one another they turned sidewards on Ferdach, who was glad enough to escape from the two egocentrics, though wondering, as he made off, how the hell it was that Broadstairs was always able to pluck important connections out of the air whenever he talked to anyone of any consequence.

He felt a hand on his arm and a familiar voice saying his name. It was Mizan dressed this evening in very fine Malay clothes. His *baju* and trousers were pale blue and his short sarong was black embroidered with gold thread in an intricate pattern. 'I'm helping my uncle to entertain,' he said. 'I have to mingle and see that no one is left out. I really would like to speak to you – on our own. I hope you haven't forgotten our vows of friendship.' Though Ferdach could not remember taking any such vow he was happy to learn that, as Albakri had hinted, there was no rift between them. Then Mizan whispered, 'Promise you'll meet me at your place tomorrow afternoon,' and hovered just long enough to hear Ferdach reply, 'Yes. I Promise,' before he disappeared among the guests.

Under an oil painting of the Sultan of Perak in his ceremonial clothes, General Briggs and Tuan Haji Mustapha Albakri were evidently enjoying one another's company. Ferdach stationed himself nearby and began a desultory conversation with a brigadier who had a moustache of such thickness that it looked like a brush. He expressed admiration for it, which on consideration might have seemed an odd thing to do – after all this wasn't the Fitzroy – but the Brigadier, who introduced himself as Teddy O'Malley-Frigg, was not in the least taken aback but launched into a monologue on moustaches which clearly would go on for some time. He expressed admiration for waxed moustaches, regretting that the style had fallen into desuetude in Britain, though not in France. Ferdach asked him about the cultivation and care of the waxed moustache. Teddy's exposition, when underway, allowed Ferdach to appear interested while really catching the conversation between the General and the State Secretary. It was not about the Emergency. It was about the orangutan.

'So you've seen some of them in their natural habitat, Tuan Haji?'

'Certainly, General. I was travelling up the Kuching River and on to Kalimantan – on the Indonesian side of the border – to a densely forested area. We had some Iban guides. One needs great patience. The animals are shy. Do you know the Malays say that women should be careful when they go to bathe in a river if there are orangutan about because their males like our women? Some women have given birth to hybrids – so they say.' Ferdach was sure that the last sentence was slyly intended by Albakri to test whether Briggs thought him a credulous primitive.

But Briggs passed the test by laughing and saying he could believe the story as he was sure that a number of such hybrids had found their way into the British other ranks.

Then Ferdach could follow no more of this significant exchange as the ebb and flow of guests had borne a posse of guffawing officers adjacent to them and O'Malley-Frigg's discourse was brought to an end by another brigadier saying loudly in Ferdach's ear, 'Boring you about moustaches is he, eh? Waxed moustaches, I'll be bound. I think he could qualify for a job in Madame Tussauds.'

All the conversations around him seemed to be of a similar sort. Here something about golf, there a bit of scandal about unfaithful wives or some cad of an officer; information about holiday resorts was being exchanged but the women were mainly interested in what was new in fashion and what could be bought in Whiteway Laidlaws in Penang. The item nearest to military matters that Ferdach heard was about a drunken British private who had staggered alone across the golf course after leaving a bar late at night and fallen asleep beside a storm drain. A couple of days after his disappearance the wretched man was found dead covered with leeches – 'even up his arsehole' averred an officer in a lugubrious but satisfied voice to Mrs Bertelli, whose smooth black dress made her look like a long leech herself. She grimaced and exhaled wearily, 'Really Clifford. Not while I'm eating caviar.' At which everyone who heard her hooted with laughter.

Mrs Thelma Bertelli was one of those women who, after toadying for years to persons of greater social significance than herself, blossom into a great 'character' when their spouse achieves seniority. Whereas her husband was short, florid and gruff, Thelma was tall, pallid and thin with an extremely narrow face and a voice that was so languid that it seemed that she was dying of consumption. Reluctant to make a virtue of necessity she did not try to make either her body or her face look any broader but wore clothes, and dressed her hair, in a manner that accentuated her narrowness. Tonight, for instance, her far-from-luxuriant hair was drawn back tightly in a bun at the back of her head, her eyebrows were thinly etched to curve upwards at their outer extremities, and her tight sheath of a dress was relieved by two glistening lines of black costume jewellery that started at her waist and flared out, over her flat chest, towards her shoulders. She looked like a human arrow speeding earthwards. Ferdach was reminded of illustrations of women on remote planets in science fiction magazines. Her appearance certainly made her the cynosure, albeit discreetly so, of all eyes. Her own keen eyes took in Ferdach who was staring at her in a bemused sort of way. She bore down on him. 'Everyone else laughed,' she said. 'Why not you?'

'I didn't find it funny. I was thinking of that young man – dead by a storm drain.'

'If we mourned every death we learned of, life would be unbearable. It's better to laugh at death. Then life can go on.'

Ferdach looked full into Thelma Bertelli's face. 'Am I supposed to find that witty too?' he asked, impertinently. 'Do you want me to laugh?'

'Some idiots laugh at whatever the DO's wife says, funny or not. But I prefer people who don't. What's your name young man? I haven't seen you around before. Are you a journalist rooting out the imperfections of colonialism?'

'Unfortunately not. I work under your husband. At least under Waite who is under your husband.'

'What do you think of Jimmy Waite? Oh I know I shouldn't ask you but–'

'I don't mind telling you in the least. He's brilliant, but unusual.'

'You mean a bit mad.'

'It's the world that's mad. Waite is unusual in that he's sane.'

'I like loyalty. Your name is?'

'Ferdach O'Haney. Ferdie if you want.'

'Ah yes. I have heard of you. Waite let you down on your arrival and you spent your first night in the Carefree – screwing, I expect?'

'Lordie me, how news travels.'

'In Malaya, yes. So let that be a lesson. Discretion is quite useless here. So there's no harm in my telling you that my husband can't stand Waite. He suspects him of being too pro-Chinese. Are you in that camp as well?'

At this point the circulatory tide had borne Waite within their ken and Ferdach, irritated by Mrs Bertelli's indiscretions replied, 'Here's the traitor himself. I think you should have this conversation with him.'

'Oh but I have.' Thelma said. 'On several occasions. Because I'm very much on his side Mr O'Haney.' She smiled at Waite and said, 'You've got a difficult young beast on your hands here Jimmy.' Then she gave Ferdach's hand a friendly squeeze, turned away and took up with others she knew better.

'I won't ask what she was talking about,' said Waite. 'The subject doesn't matter so long as she can play her role. A few years ago the poor thing was a mousy little nothing. Amazing how a man's rank can go to his wife's head. But she's kind at heart.'

Ferdach looked at Waite as though he was an exhibit in a glass case. How could this man be so composed, so calm under all circumstances? He never got angry. He never lost his nerve. He was always forgiving. Maybe it was the yoga exercises he allegedly performed.

'Aren't you a bit worried?'

'Worried?' Waite's eyebrows were raised interrogatively. 'About what?'

'About tomorrow. Aren't you worried about that pompous ass Broadstairs? He'll alienate everyone he comes across. And what about those lorries? Standing there without a guard.'

'I shouldn't be in the least surprised if the CTs attack the lorries. They may be doing so at this very moment. As for Broadstairs he'll go his own way whatever I say. He isn't interested in what we are doing. He only wants to express his personality. A bit like Thelma, I guess. No, I'm wrong. He only wants to express personality. Anyone's will do providing he can do the expressing.'

'OK, you're right about Broadstairs,' said Ferdach. 'But the lorries. That's a different matter. An immediate matter. Are you going to do nothing?'

Waite turned full face towards Ferdach and grasped both of his arms. They stood there like a couple of dancers waiting for the music to begin. Ferdach thought that they must look odd but nobody seemed to remark on it. Then Waite looked into Ferdach's eyes and spoke quietly and seriously, 'The trouble with you Ferdie is that you haven't learned the difference between "do nothing" and "not do anything". You think in terms of the former, I think in terms of the latter. "Not do anything" – "*wu wei*" as the Taoists put it – is all-important. Things will happen whether you will them to take place or not. It's like the flow of a river. If you go with it you will experience the movement; and the strength of the movement will become part of you. And so you may be able to influence the flow just a little. A little to the left or a little to the right. Nothing more. To "do nothing" implies activity regardless of the flow. It also implies impossibility both grammatically and in reality.'

Listening to this little exposition at the centre of a noisily gossiping, decidedly unmystical throng, Ferdach experienced a sense of unreality. Was this what it was like in the eye of a storm when a hurricane swept across the land? Everyone else in the room was talking banalities while at this still point, surrounded by gossiping people, Waite was, Ferdach felt sure without knowing exactly why, telling him something profound about life. Or maybe not, perhaps Waite was pulling his leg? Yet his simple but not-so-simple words were not uttered facetiously like those of Mrs Bertelli. They had an air of certainty, they demanded attention. Despite which he had felt embarrassed to be addressed like that in public, whereas for all Waite seemed to care they might have been totally alone. He felt he should say, 'Well Jimmy, if that's so, why are you here at all? Why aren't you on a mountain sitting beneath a tree or meditating in a shrine beside a frozen lake. That's how all the Taoist seers seem to be "not doing anything" in the Chinese pictures I've seen.' What he actually asked was, 'How can you work under Bertelli? According to Thelma, he regards you as some sort of subversive. When she said you are pro-

Chinese she made it sound like pro-Communist.'

Waite was not going to help Ferdach out on that question. 'You will never know how I work cobber, because I don't know it myself,' he said and turned away to speak to someone else leaving Ferdach, who knew few people there, feeling decidedly superfluous. Just then he saw Mizan beckoning him and heard him call, 'My uncle would like to speak to you again.' Ferdach realised that this was a summons and moved towards the side of the room where Albakri and Briggs were still deep in conversation. He had never thought that he might speak to the General who, despite his quiet affable manner and his civilian suit, had about him an aura of distinction, even of remoteness, as though he really dwelt on a higher plain. Ferdach was sure that nothing he himself said could possibly be of interest to a man who had many years of experience in India, the Western Desert and Burma. And so he felt alarmed when he heard Albakri say to the General, 'Oh this is O'Haney, the young man I spoke to you about. He's one of the new intake of Colonial Service cadets. They tell me he's built up a good rapport with the squatters he's been working with.'

Sir Harold Rawdon Briggs, CBE DSO, looked at Ferdach with an avuncular eye. He was far from overbearing which put Ferdach more at ease. When Albakri was speaking Briggs gave him complete attention. He was obviously a good listener and, his expression suggested, a shrewd thinker. Like Albakri he was also very courteous, not at all Ferdach's idea, at that time, of a military man, and with a few questions he drew Ferdach into the conversation: how did the squatters react to the idea of moving; were they pro-CT or just fence-sitters; had Ferdach met any Chinese in the mining community who seemed critical of government policies? Ferdach at once thought of Kuok Lai Kuan and handsome Harry Wong but confined himself to bland answers though he did say how much he admired the skill and hard work of the squatters who had often brought very inhospitable land into cultivation; then, growing more confident, he expressed the hope that when resettled they would be given reasonably good soil to work on and that there should be as little delay as possible in issuing land titles to them.

The general nodded approvingly. 'So you expect the resettlement exercise at Chemor to go smoothly tomorrow, O'Haney?' he asked, no doubt expecting another of Ferdach's anodyne replies.

And then it popped out. The reply that he had never intended to make, the impulsive reply made without reckoning the consequences. 'Oh yes, sir. It could go smoothly – if there are any lorries left.'

There was a moment of silence. Albakri looked at Ferdach in amazement, 'What on earth d'you mean?'

It was too late, or rather impossible to say, 'Oh, nothing.' Within General Briggs' kindly regard a stony hardness was forming. His eyes narrowed; he wanted a reply. Ferdach was obliged to say, to his own consternation, that he had some misgivings over that long column of lorries waiting undefended out on the open road. He ended his reply by stating that he was surely worrying unnecessarily. But it was too late. Awkward questions would be asked not of Broadstairs but of Bertelli and he would not like it.

Rather as people have to size up the situation without being told when a royal audience is at an end, Ferdach knew it was best to withdraw into the crowd. Albakri and Briggs spoke briefly and then an adjutant was summoned and then Waite and then Bertelli and then the Chief Police Officer of Perak and various others. No doubt all sorts of enquiries were about to be made over the phone and over radio links. Waite soon drew away from the confabulation and sought out Ferdach.

'I think we'd better leave,' he said. 'I don't think you're going to be very popular with the DO.'

Yusuf was ready for them. Waite got in the car beside him. Ferdach sat in the back seat. He dared not say he would like to stay on to speak to Mizan or Northcote Parkinson, which was what he had wanted to do. Nothing was said about waiting for Broadstairs. They sped off into the quiet night. Waite was already fiddling with Yusuf's lovely locks. He turned and grinned broadly at Ferdach. 'Well, you've made sure that those lorries will be guarded after all – even though you're probably going to be dropped from a plane tomorrow.'

But it was not to be. It took only five minutes to reach home but hardly had they got there when the phone rang with an urgent, though no longer useful, message. The CTs had already burned every single lorry waiting to transport the squatters into Broadstairs' perfectly planned New Village.

20

General Briggs had been appointed in 1950 to pull together the disparate government forces coping with the Communist Insurgency, which by that time had attained dangerous, almost desperate, proportions. With little delay he gave practical form to Tan Cheng Lok's idea that was ultimately to defeat the communists, but he was never given the plenary powers which the situation justified and which he had hoped for. Though director of operations, he worked as a civilian under the High Commissioner, Sir Henry Gurney. This was why Ferdach had been surprised to see him wearing a floppy tropical suit at the State Secretary's party whereas the senior army officers were in uniform. It struck Ferdach that in manner and appearance the quietly spoken general looked much more the academic than rapier-tongued Northcote Parkinson; certainly he was more of a gentleman.

That sympathetic manner which had led Ferdach to speak so easily – and too frankly – had been widely experienced by people throughout the country, convincing many of them that, at last, the Federation had someone who would listen, understand the problems and put the war effort on a sounder footing. Briggs quickly recognised that the underlying problem of the Emergency concerned the squatters and the powerful Min Yuen working among them, for just as Mao Tse Tung had seen the masses as an ocean in which the Peoples Liberation Army could swim freely, so the Malayan Communists perceived the squatters as their natural habitat. Briggs summed up his strategy in a single sentence: 'protect the populated areas, cut the enemy lines of communication, and force him out to battle'. Yet this was easier said than done. To execute it under a federal system of nine State and two Settlement Governments each with reserve powers and not always in accord with the Federal Government, would be an art in itself. Not possessing overall powers, everything Briggs intended had to be done by skilful negotiation and diplomatic persuasion.

Fortunately the General had the full support of the High Commissioner, Sir Henry Gurney, a brilliant administrator with much experience in Palestine. Whereas Briggs' duties were military, Sir Henry devoted himself to the political, social and economic problems of Malaya. But this had to be done within the confines of a rapidly changing political framework. True, the anger of the Malays against the ill-conceived Malayan Union had been calmed by the establishment of a federal system in which the Malay States retained powers over land, religion and much local administration but for the Chinese the problem of citizenship loomed large. In his Chinese contacts both in the squatter community and in business circles, Ferdach had become aware of their deep concerns: how would the Chinese fit into this federal system as democratic institutions – based on citizenship suffrage – developed? What would be the qualifications for citizenship? How many non-Malays would qualify? If these fundamental political questions were not answered satisfactorily the Emergency would continue.

The Federation was an embryonic democracy. The High Commissioner was no absolute ruler but acted with the advice of an Executive Council responsible to a Legislative Assembly containing a substantial number of non-official members. The latter, who were representative of different sections of the community, would before long be replaced by elected members. Further constitutional change would lead to the assembly become a fully elected parliament. As elsewhere under British rule, the path to independence would be evolutionary, not the revolutionary path of the communists. Ferdach hoped, when he told Malayans of all races that the insurgency was setting back the day of independence, that they would believe him. He also hoped that it was true. At the same time he realised that this was of little concern to the communists since their goal was not a free democracy but a Marxist state. It was more convenient to them to be seen fighting against British Imperialism than against an independent Malayan state.

Briggs might be able to communicate easily himself but he knew there were immense internal problems of communication to be solved. Not only was the country multi-racial, multi-lingual, and complex constitutionally, but there were problems of communication between the civilian administrators, the police and the military, which in turn was composed of Malay, British and Gurkha battalions, and before long of battalions from the African and Pacific Commonwealth countries. In fluid emergency situations it was not always easy to determine the limits of the civil, police and military responsibility. To deal with this problem Briggs set up State, District and Sub-District War Executive Committees. On each committee, beside the police, military and civil officers there were representatives of the racial communities and of business. In Batu Gajah, Harmsworth Bertelli was the chairman of the committee whereas in the Perak State Committee the chief minister or *mentri besar* presided, though as often as not his place was taken by Tuan Mustapha Albakri whom Ferdach was beginning to think of as a sort of surrogate father. Each District War Executive Committee, or DWEC, reported its activities to the State War Executive Committee or SWEC, and the SWECs were responsible to the Director of Operations War Council in Kuala Lumpur. Each committee met in its own operations room which was provided with a huge wall map on which current operations were marked. Since the committees met regularly, everyone was kept in the picture and action was supposedly coordinated. However, as Ferdach had observed in a small way at Chemor, chains of command were still not always clear.

The whole administration was thus geared up for war. However, on the communist side the organization and the will to win were no less strong. Briggs respected that; he knew the enemy's strengths but he sought its Achilles heel. He never boasted of a quick victory nor did he aim at a glamorous form of leadership. His method was more subtle. He had devised the organisation; if the people concerned ran it as intended, it would prevail. Though he would sometimes drop in quietly to SWEC or DWEC meetings if he was in the vicinity on his travels, he avoided the limelight. When Albakri suggested to him the day after the lorry fiasco that they should visit Chemor together he replied laconically, 'Generals don't like visiting the scenes of their defeats.' All he did was to phone Bertelli and say, 'Tell your DWEC that the setback will only matter if it prevents you from keeping the machine rolling.' And with that he continued his tour on of the north.

At the next meeting of the Batu Gajah DWEC, the Broadstairs affair, as it was now called, was discussed though in no great detail. Bertelli reported that, at his request and to save the man further embarrassment since he had admitted his fault, Broadstairs had already been transferred to Kuala Lumpur. And there the matter rested. Ferdach had seen Broadstairs off at the station and was glad to hear him say that he'd already been asked to play an active role in the KL Arts Theatre; indeed he was quite certain that it stood in need of his management. With a serious mien he said that, as an opener, he intended to stage Shaw's 'St Joan'. 'I played in it once with Sybil,' he said, with a sigh as if sadly recalling some past glory. Ferdach was inclined to ask, 'As a faggot?' but held his tongue.

The thought of Broadstairs having an outlet for his dramatic talents relieved Ferdach for it was through him that the incident had become known as the Broadstairs affair. He had stayed at home after returning from the State Secretary's party while Waite, who adored scenes of mayhem, had dashed off in his Jag to examine the damage at Chemor. Ferdach saw little point in staring gormlessly at thirty burned out lorries. Later, when the phone went, Ferdach answered and heard the irate voice of Mr Bertelli who was no doubt smarting in the knowledge that responsibility for the disaster could easily be laid at his doorstep for falling in with Broadstairs' suggestion.

'Where's Waite gone to?' Bertelli demanded brusquely.

It was then that Ferdach made another of his disastrously spontaneous remarks. Instead of saying, 'He's gone to Chemor to look at the burned out lorries,' he said, 'He's looking into *l'affaire* Broadstairs.'

There was a distinct silence at the other end of the line and then Bertelli asked, quite mildly, '*L'affaire* Broadstairs? So that's what they're calling it are they Ferdie?'

Ferdach had never before spoken with Bertelli yet there he was using his nickname. Had Thelma reported on him so quickly? The tone in which 'Ferdie' was uttered was not at all hostile. It was even slightly friendly. Ferdach decided that the moment was opportune to put the knife in, deliberately, 'Well, what else should it be called, sir?'

'Quite, quite,' said Bertelli. 'Damned actor. Only fit for farce.' Hearing this Ferdach felt guilty. He kept silent. But no cock crowed. Then Bertelli said, now in a really warm tone, 'You know, young man, you should have phoned me at once about your misgivings. No need to go through Waite every time. I'd have taken action. Well, no good crying over spilt milk. You must come and see us in Batu Gajah. Thelma was taken by your directness. And I like that too. Goodnight, Ferdie.'

'Goodnight, sir,' said Ferdach, putting down the phone slowly and realizing he'd better not tell anyone that Bertelli had approved the risk Broadstairs had taken. As for Waite, Ferdach knew he was far too generous a man to dig anyone's grave, even Bertelli's, while he himself must just adopt the Taoist stance: *wu wei*, 'not do anything'.

21

Ferdach clearly adopted a stance of *wu wei* the following morning, a Sunday, when declining Waite's invitation to go wild-pig shooting.

'No Jimmy, that would definitely be "to do something" I wouldn't like.' In fact he was not in the least against blood sports but his mind was full of Mizan's intended visit later that day.

Mizan had not said what time he would arrive and by seven thirty Ferdach had given up on him and sat down to dinner with Waite, who had not only been charged by a wild pig, which he had killed in the nick of time, but had also been at the receiving end of some shots fired by CTs, warning him not to advance any further when he had gone into the thick *belukar* on the far side of the aerodrome. Waite's capacity to survive amidst explosions because of some unorthodox relationship made Ferdach think of his own father who had once narrowly avoided being shot as an Irish terrorist because some British officer knew of his previous service to the Crown.

It was while he was musing about his own problematical father and the difficulty of being his son that Mizan finally roared up in a battered green MG from which he did not get out but instead shouted to Ferdach, 'Come at once Ferdie. I don't want problems with my father. We mustn't be late at his house. He can be difficult.' The concatenation of his own thoughts with some of Mizan's words made Ferdach imagine that Waite's telepathic obsessions must have created an unusual mental force field about their house. However, since Mizan's precipitation was an equally rare phenonomen among Malays, he quite rudely abandoned Waite and got in the car which sped off as swiftly as it had come.

'You've always wanted to meet my father,' shouted Mizan. 'Well, he's back from Johore. I've told him about you and he'd be happy to meet you.'

'Oh,' said Ferdach a bit crestfallen for he had been anticipating a cosy talk with an exchange of intimate ideas and who could say what else, alone with Mizan for the first time since that day on the *padang*.

'Is it far to go?'

'Only to Tambun. You should have a great talk together. I've told him you're a scientific atheist.'

'You've what ...' began Ferdach but then he realised he had fallen victim to some puckish joke. Maybe something worse was to follow. He recalled the words 'too facile' that Mizan had applied to that poem beloved of his father. Was he about to be used in some skirmish, set up by a son against his father? Determined not to cooperate if this were so, Ferdach talked about *l'affaire* Broadstairs all the way to Tambun where they went to meet Mizan's father in an old house that stood alone and quiet in a large garden.

Sheikh Mahmud Shah was a short, sturdily built man with a typically round Malay face made larger by a short beard and sideboards. Mizan bore no resemblance to him at all except perhaps about the eyes which, on both of them, were large and expressive. Mizan greeted his father with the usual Malay courtesy before introducing Ferdach. The three of them then sat crosslegged on a Persian rug around a low table on which stood a copper Arabic coffee pot and small cups made of blue glass. 'I became addicted to this strong coffee when I was in Egypt,' said Sheikh Mahmud as Mizan filled the cups, 'though I know that one shouldn't become an addict to anything.'

'It is written that everyone is permitted one weakness,' said Mizan.

'Where is it written?' asked Sheikh Mahmud.

'I don't know. I just thought it must be written somewhere,' Mizan said with a broad grin directed at Ferdach.

Sheikh Mahmud laughed and slapped Mizan's leg. 'You see what sort of a son I have. He respects nothing at all.'

'He obviously respects you – and loves you, Sheikh,' said Ferdach.

The Sheikh liked hearing this. He beamed at Ferdach and began to ask him questions about his home, his parents, and his reasons for coming to Malaya, to all of which Ferdach gave the answers he had given to Mizan when they had first met. This went on for quite a time during which Mizan said little except to chime in with some bit of information that Ferdach had omitted but which proved that he had stored in his brain everything Ferdach had told him. There was a lull when a servant brought in some Malay cakes and fruit after which Sheikh Mahmud took to asking about the Emergency and especially whether General Briggs would defeat the CTs for the subject weighed on the minds of even the holy men. But eventually the matter of Sufism arose when the Sheikh asked Ferdach very directly, 'Are you thinking of embracing Islam? Or has Mizan given me the wrong impression – which wouldn't be so strange?'

'I never said Ferdach was thinking of any such thing. I said he's been asking me about Sufism,' Mizan stated, a little crossly.

'But Sufism is part of Islam so could he be a Sufi if he wasn't a Muslim? That's an important question.' Sheikh Mahmud's eyes twinkled with amusement as though he enjoyed catching his son out.

Ferdach thought it best to state his position. 'Well, at present I don't intend to embrace Islam nor did I ever imagine that I might become a Sufi. I said I was interested in learning about Sufism.'

'But why?' asked the Sheikh. 'What's the point of hearing about something if one's mind isn't open to the possibility of being affected by it? It would be like learning to ride a horse from a book without ever intending to sit on a saddle.'

'Mizan told me that you once lived in Egypt, Sheikh Mahmud. You must have heard about the ancient Egyptian religion without being open to the possibility of worshipping Amon Ra.'

'Not in the least. The possibility was there. I liked some of the Egyptian concepts, their ideas on balance and harmony for instance, but I couldn't stand gods with human bodies and animal heads. Conversation with them might be a problem. Would one snort, bellow or miaow?'

So the lighthearted talk continued until Sheikh Mahmud said quite abruptly. 'Of course Tuan O'Haney, I quite understand your need to know about every aspect of Malay thought if you are going to have a position of authority here. Quite a reasonable point of view; indeed far more reasonable than that of Mizan who would like to change the Malay way of thought for some foreign ideology – nationalism, Marxism or maybe something worse. My son is a man who doesn't believe in building on what's already there.'

Mizan rose to the bait. 'Bapa, you can't build a new house on old foundations. The ground must be cleared completely for a new building.' He was silent for a moment and then added, 'I never suggested that we should discard Islam.'

Ferdach sensed a rise in tension between father and son as the sheikh replied, 'But why not? To refuse even to envisage some course of action is intellectual cowardice. Why wouldn't you discard Islam? Ah I know why: merely because you see in it a vehicle for your new brand of nationalism. Maybe you don't even believe in it at all, but you know you'd never be in power without Islam because the people would disown you.'

'We seem to be getting away from Sufism,' Ferdach interrupted mildly. 'Clever young men often question what their parents have taught them and Mizan is still young. But he's also honest and kind; so indulge him a little Sheikh Mahmud. Let go of the leash. Whatever you say, he'll find his own way. In the end it might well be Sufism.'

'I pray that it may be so, Tuan O'Haney, for Sufism, which you say you want to learn about, is the finest flower of Islam.' The sheikh suddenly looked at Ferdach intently, right into his eyes, right into his head Ferdach imagined, and then said, 'I suppose you know next to nothing about Sufism. After all, why should you as an atheist?'

Somewhat indignant at being thought an ignoramus Ferdach decided to demonstrate his knowledge by pontificating quite confidently that the word 'Sufi' must derive from the Greek 'sophist', the name given to teachers of philosophy in the later Roman Empire, men whose knowledge of neo-Platonism, must have been transmitted to their Arabic conquerors, for did not Sufism have much in common with early Christian gnosticism? As he held forth Ferdach felt that he was back in a history tutorial.

Sheikh Mahmud's eyebrows were raised. This Englishman knew more than he had expected; perhaps he was worth talking to after all. Ferdach then found himself at the receiving end of a scholarly rejection of what he had just said: the word 'Sufi' was derived either from the Arabic 'safa' meaning purity, or from the Persian word for wool, 'suf', which the Sufis wore. But Sufi mysticism owed its true origins to the Qur'an itself which, Sheikh Mahmud averred, had an exoteric sense, meant for the ordinary believer, and an esoteric mystical sense, intended for the elect. Twice, as though to prove his point, he quoted from the Holy Qur'an:

> God is the Light
> Of Heaven and Earth.
> This is the parable of His Light:
> It is as if there is a Niche
> With inside it a Lamp:
> The Lamp is enclosed in Glass:
> The Glass is, as it were,
> A Brilliant Star.

Although Ferdach suspected that his own opinion on the origin of the word Sufi might still be right, he held his peace. It was more important to listen to Sheikh Mahmud talking about the religious beliefs of the Malays which had made them a tolerant and peaceful people and which were of greater intellectual complexity than he had ever realised. As he listened he wondered how many of those industrious planters, tin-mine managers, important civil servants and captains of industry who lorded it over the country had any idea of the profound philosophical life, of the spiritual depth, of the land in which they made their living. It also struck him that this hidden life was why the Malays were able to be forbearing before the behaviour of their colonial masters. Perhaps the English were to be laughed at and pitied rather than attacked.

The Sheikh's voice then fell, almost to a whisper, so that both Ferdach and Mizan had to strain their ears to hear him. He gave the impression of a man telling a dangerous secret. 'First let me speak frankly about my own convictions on Sufism even though some might think them heretical: just as a fruit can be taken from a tree, so can the wisdom of the Sufi be appreciated by a man of another faith. That is the meaning of, "the restraints of creeds, of sects are gone" in the poem by Shabistari which Mizan, with greater insight than he knew, once quoted to you. That being so, you Tuan, could hear the wisdom of the Sufi without becoming a Muslim even though Islam is the perfect faith. Now you must know that to the Sufi, love is the central mystery and a wisdom that does not require dogma; words are unnecessary for the Sufi who

130

has lost himself in love of God. When it started Sufism was a method to aid those who had a mystical bent. The Orders only started up when the wisdom began to be poured into doctrinal bottles. There were once many Orders but today, in Malaya, only three are significant. I am a sheikh in the Quadiriyyah Order founded long ago in Baghdad. Not only do we assert, in accordance with the words of the Holy Qur'an, that there is no God but God but that the only existence is God. Our way is not militant but our mystic path, through which we aspire to knowledge of the Divine Presence, is far from easy. We must pass through a number of ascending stages before we achieve "*baqa*", consciousness of survival in God. Forgive me if I do not name these stages or try to describe them for they are only understood through devotion and self control.'

Mizan was shifting uncomfortably. Perhaps he felt that his father was about to embark on too erudite a sermon. He asked dubiously, '*Bapak* – Father – how could a man ever know for sure that he has reached these ascending stations and how would he know when he has reached *baqa*, the highest station of all?'

'*Anak saya* – my son – to answer that I'll use the words of my good friend, Haji Mohhamed Shah. When he was the Chief Qadi of Johore, a man put your very question to him and he replied, "Only the fisherman holding a rod knows when he has caught a fish."'

Mizan found not a word to say as his father continued to expound his ideas at great length while the evening passed into deep night. Ferdach wanted no more than to listen. What the Sheikh told them was involved and subtle for the Malay Sufi, following the example of his predecessors in other parts of the Islamic world, was ever keen to speculate on the nature of the deity and of the universe. Some Sufis had strayed beyond the orthodox view that God is omniscient into holding that God contains all being, a belief bordering on pantheism. One of the greatest Malay mystics, Hamzah Fansuri, had held that Allah was identical with the spiritual essence of man and with the universe. Though Sheikh Mahmud admitted that Hamzah had been condemned for this, it struck Ferdach that the Sheikh might be sympathetic to such a view himself. Other mystics had concealed their concept of the immanence of God in all things in the symbols of earthly love which, in reality, they saw only as a stage in the progress to divine love. At this point Sheikh Mahmud paused and thereafter seemed to be oppressed by some inner sadness.

'Unfortunately the intentions of the Sufis are not always understood and some Malays, unversed in our doctrines, take the concept of mystic love not as a symbol but in a purely physical sense. Because of this unscrupulous religious leaders are sometimes able to mislead *kampung* people into unorthodix practices. Even today, such a deviation, the Taslim, the Safe Message, is at large. It is led by a man with hypnotic powers called Syed Ali. He claims to be Muhammed on earth and that his teachings replace the Holy Qur'an. Many *kampung* people have submitted themselves and their families to him. High on ganja, and convinced that God is in their bodies, they take part in orgiastic rituals. Ah Tuan O'Haney, ah my son Mizan, uneducated people can so easily be mislead.' Sheikh Mahmud fell silent and shook his head. 'How can we ever teach the world that there is love of such a nature that, for the mystic who has reached *baqa*, the veil between the lover and Absolute Being ceases to exist?'

All these subtleties and their inherent dangers reminded Ferdach of the theological disputes of the Christian sects in the Eastern Roman Empire or of the convolutions of medieval scholastic philosophy. Both of them had exercised the ingenuity of the most brilliant minds of their time yet today they seemed strangely irrelevant to the modern scientific outlook. Nevertheless Ferdach was not without some apprehension of what the Sheikh said, for though he was, as Mizan had told his father, a scientific atheist, the possibility of a transcendence that sustained mankind's experience of the world made him nod appreciatively when Sheikh Mahmud ended by quoting again from his favourite Arabian poet, Mahmud Sa'udu'l-Din Shabistari:

> I and thou are only crystals
> In the wall of a lamp
> Through which the Divine Light blazes.

For a little while no one spoke at all. The reiterated image of that lamp, that Brilliant Star, glowed in their minds. Ferdach found himself wondering whether such a pregnant silence had arisen, like perfume from a rose, from the image, or was it perhaps emenating from the Sheikh who was smiling gently first at him and then upon his own son as though bestowing a quiet benediction on their friendship. Yet Mizan's eyes were questioning Ferdach as though he wanted to hear something he himself dared not say – perhaps a specific acceptance or refutal of his father's words. At length his eyes faltered and it could have been that Ferdach's expression of gratitude to Sheikh Mahmud made him feel that this alien British officer was more open to his father's wisdom than he could ever be.

There was a different sort of silence, as they drove back to Ipoh. Ferdach suspected that Mizan still wanted him to express an opinion on his father's views for he remained withdrawn until Ferdach asked how influential the Sufi orders were in the *kampung*s. 'Their influence on the people is immense throughout the country,' Mizan replied confidently. 'Control the Orders, make them militant, and you could raise a whirlwind.'

It was past three in the morning and Ferdach, not wanting the noisy MG to disturb Waite or Ericson, asked to be dropped at the end of Sturrock Road, but before he could budge he was taken aback to hear Mizan blurt out, 'Ferdie, I'm surprised my father didn't ask you to dissuade me from my plans. He must have taken your words about letting go of the leash very seriously. Well, you might as well know my ambitions: first to get into Special Branch and gather all the information about people I can, and second, to use it when I enter politics – in fact I've already got all the contacts I need to do so. Ferdie, I am your friend but I still want to be part of the whirlwind that will sweep away the British.'

Ferdach got out of the car to walk home but first he lent down towards Mizan and said gently, 'My friend Mizan, a whirlwind won't be necessary. A slight breeze will suffice.'

22

In the days following his transcendental instruction, Ferdach resumed his census duties to the east of Ipoh. By now he and Tahir with his Malay Specials and Gordon Choo had become an enthusiastic and efficient group with a strong esprit de corps. Their weakness, of which they were not really aware, was that they had become over confident. Ambushes, attacks and skirmishes were reported from all over the district although nothing had happened to them. It was as though the platoon had a charmed life. Tahir and Choo attributed their safety to the fact that they behaved so well towards the squatters that the communists would not risk alienating the people by harming them. Ferdach imagined, as a result of his conversation with Kuok Lai Kuan, that for some unknown reason it was not general CT policy to attack census teams. They were all living in cloud-cuckoo-land.

As attacks on its camps intensified, the MRLA was beginning to face a shortage of supplies, in particular of food. The jungle does not easily support large bodies of men. To hunt animals or gather fruits and berries is a fulltime occupation requiring skills which the indigenous people have developed over centuries. Not much time is left for war.

The area in which Ferdach was operating produced a great quantity of vegetables, some rice, as well as pigs and poultry. Many members of farming families could easily get work on rubber estates or tin mines for at that time world prices of both commodities were booming. The squatter families could therefore quite easily supply the CTs either with their own produce or with canned food and medicines bought in town. Another reason why they did not feel economically under threat was that they had been told by AROs like Choo that, if possible, they would only be moved when their rice was harvested, and also that when they had to be moved, they would be financially compensated for any losses either of crops or animals. This information must have reached the CTs who would see that no benefit would accrue to them by ambushing Ferdach's team. An ambush would certainly lead to counter measures and probably quicker resettlement; the area would be awash with troops and it would be difficult to milk the people as before.

So Ferdach and his merry men pressed on, plotting house after house with ever-increasing accuracy on the once unmarked six-inch maps. They became a familiar sight to the squatters who greeted them warmly enough and often asked for assistance in dealing with permits and licenses from government departments or on medical matters. But at night when they had vanished the CTs would come in and be given an equally friendly reception. In fact there were two governments and the squatters were past masters at maintaining equilibrium between the two.

Ferdach often came across Lai Kuan when traversing the Kuok tin mines. He was always welcomed and, to onlookers, they must have seemed like old friends. But one day an unexpected meeting occurred between them in an area where the plain gave way to rising ground covered by a zone of abandoned rubber trees cut into by outliers of primary jungle on hill spurs linked to the mountains. It was a controlled area to which access was forbidden without a police permit. As his platoon toiled up a track which ran beside a fast-running stream whose source was in the mountains, Ferdach caught sight, just a little ahead of him, of Lai Kuan and another man coming down towards them. Tahir and his Specials were alert the moment the two came into view.

'They shouldn't be here,' said Choo, 'without a permit.'

'They'll have one for sure,' replied Ferdach. 'The Kuok family always operates within the law.'

'I don't like it anyway,' said Choo. 'And I don't like him.'

Of course Lai Kuan did have a police permit giving him and an engineer leave to inspect a small dam, marked on an attached map, further up the river. Ferdach made a point of asking, sternly but politely, to see the permit before starting up a conversation.

'I'm glad you take your duties seriously,' said Lai Kuan. 'After all, I might be a CT. But if I were you, I wouldn't walk up so boldly.'

Ferdach laughed, 'Lai Kuan, that's exactly what a man like you would do. Well then, how about your dam? Is it in order? What's it for? The map shows a water catchment area but I don't see a pipeline leading down this way.'

'To you I'll confess all. It has no commercial use. I built it with a few friends, just after the war ended – before this bloody Emergency. We used it as a swimming pool. It was our secret place then. Oh the water's so fresh and clear, Ferdie, and if you go higher up the river you can let it swirl you down over the smooth rocks until you reach the pool. If I had time I'd go with you now and we could all have a swim.'

'And get our heads blown off,' exclaimed Choo, possessed, it seemed, by a sudden fury. 'Is that what you want? Like my father was ...' He stopped and turned away. There was clearly some unpleasant history in the background.

'I knew Choo when he was a little boy, before I was sent to England. I was much older than him,' said Lai Kuan pensively as though he was addressing only the rubber trees. Then he looked Choo straight in the face and asked, 'Did I ever bully you my friend?' As if only something like that could explain his present hostility. 'Funny how childhood likes and dislikes can persist. Well Choo I like your white colonial master too much to want him dead. But I can tell you there are no CTs up there. And no squatter houses by the way. So don't waste your time looking for them.' With that he shook Ferdach's hand and proceeded down the track.

They stood in silence watching the two men walk away. Everyone was in doubt about them, wondering whether they might be Min Yuen members who had just had a rendezvous with the terrorists? And Ferdach had other suspicions. Perhaps there really were CTs further up the track, maybe in one of their camps and Lai Kuan wanted to save him from attack. But he could hardly just accept Lai Kuan's word and tell his men to go back since the same suspicion might be in their minds as well. That would suggest his own subservience to Lai Kuan.

Choo approached Ferdach and said quietly, 'After the war when the MPAJA came out and terrorized everyone, his brothers supported them. His family could have protected my father. I'm sure he's on the other side.'

'Be careful not to accuse people, Gordon. He's not responsible for what his brothers did. There's no evidence against him.' Ferdach could say this because he had already asked Special Branch whether Lai Kuan was a suspect but Choo was not to know that. 'Lots of people did things in the past that they regret now. Sometimes hatred just has to stop.'

Choo was adamant. His ivory skin seemed to have gone a shade paler, if that was possible; there was a tautness about his mouth and his eyes seemed to have grown much bigger. He stared into Ferdach's face as if questioning his boss's integrity. 'Surely you don't believe him?' he demanded angrily.

The Specials were looking perturbed and instead of standing with their weapons pointing at the ready had gathered around Ferdach and Choo as if they expected to hear something interesting.

'Believe him about what Gordon?'

'About anything he says. That there are no squatter houses up there for instance. Even that there's a swimming pool. Rubbish.' Choo gestured with his thumb up the track.

'There's only one way to find out isn't there? Let's go and look for ourselves. After all I promised Waite to investigate this valley carefully.'

Choo seized Ferdach's arm. 'So you do believe what he said then?'

Ferdach turned in amazement to face the young man who was no longer angry but clearly worried. 'What's got into you Choo? I let you see that I don't take Lai Kuan's word about the squatter houses but now you say I believe him?'

'No. No. Not about that. He said there are no CTs up here. We may be walking right into them.'

Tahir joined it, 'Yes Tuan. Where was Lai Kuan coming from? Looking at a dam? Shit.'

'Yes. Shit,' said Mat Noor, who had followed the whole argument closely.

'By Jaysus and his Holy Saints,' said Ferdach resorting to an expression he had heard his lapsed-Catholic father use in moments of stress. 'Why do people always pick up the nastiest words in other people's languages? So what do you want me to do? Go back and tell Waite we didn't complete today's assignment because we were afraid there might be some CTs around. If we said that he'd say we should never go anywhere. Look. We've got a job to do. We'll go at least as far as the dam – to see it's there. OK, Gordon?'

Choo had suddenly become contrite. Not only did it show in his face, it showed in his eyes where little tears, as delicate as tiny pearls had formed. 'Tuan. I'm sorry.'

'No *tuan*-ing and no sorries, Gordon. We're buddies and that's the end of it.'

They began the ascent again. Tahir ordered the platoon to divide and walk some distance either side of the path. A close ambush in this comparatively open rubber estate was not likely even though a certain amount of undergrowth had started up. Choo, lugging his bag of census materials, kept to the track some way behind Ferdach while Mat Noor, also on Tahir's orders, led the way just in front of Ferdach. It seemed to be generally accepted by Tahir and everyone else that Mat Noor was Ferdach's familiar, or at the least his personal bodyguard. Certainly no other Special was ever assigned that role.

Ferdach was obscurely conscious of the reason for this. In fact he was obscurely conscious of all sorts of undercurrents in the platoon. Smiles, greetings, farewells, thanks, other forms of politeness – the lighting of a cigarette, the sharing of food or drink – all seemed to acquire a heightened quality, a subtly emotional quality, among these Malays and this one Chinese. No doubt among British soldiers there were also strong emotions, but among them there was greater reticence and certainly a much lower level of courtesy or, to put it bluntly, no courtesy at all. Ferdach knew that since their visit to the house of the old leper lady, Mat Noor had become possessive about him. In a way it was flattering though he would have put an end to it long ago had it caused any trouble among the other men. But it had not. The fragile bond between them seemed to be accepted, and not just because Mat Noor could speak English and was better educated than the others. To Ferdach, Mat Noor's behaviour seemed no more than the sort of crush that can spring up in children and soon dies away. But how did his own behaviour seem to Mat Noor, or to all the others who so easily deferred to Mat Noor's wishes.

For once, as they walked ahead, Ferdach and Mat Noor were out of earshot of the others. The only sound was that of their own footsteps on the dry ground and even those were almost obscured by the gurgling river. After only a few yards Mat Noor said, 'Tuan.'

'Yes, Mat Noor.'

'Lai Kuan is your close friend?' There was more than a hint of incredulity in the words.

Ferdach was regretting the encounter with Lai Kuan. It seemed to have annoyed first Choo, even Tahir and now Mat Noor. He could not make out whether the three of them really disliked the man or whether they resented their boss's friendship with someone outside their tight little band, someone made alien to them by virtue of his wealth. 'No,' he said as blandly as he could considering he was talking to the back of Mat Noor's head. 'No. Just a friend. Not close at all.'

'But you went to the Carefree together.'

Ferdach turned around to take a look at Choo. Too far off for him to hear these irritating questions. 'Why do you ask – if you know so much about me, Noor?'

'So you do go to the Carefree. With Chinese.'

'Noor. You're on duty. You're supposed to *jaga baik baik*.'

'Please speak in English, Tuan. You're Malay isn't very good.'

Repressing a desire to thump Noor for his unusual rudeness, Ferdach said, 'A thousand apologies, *Encik*. English version – you're supposed to keep a good look out.'

'I do that with my eyes Tuan, not my mouth.'

It occurred to Ferdach that Mat Noor's unpleasantness might be an extension of his possessiveness – or even jealousy. Perhaps it was time for Tahir to choose a replacement. Yet another part of Ferdach was intrigued. If Noor was jealous, jealous over what?'

'So I musn't go to the Carefree?'

Mat Noor was not keeping a look out now. He shrugged his shoulders, stared at the rotten rubber trees and then, a little in front of him, into a little pool fringed with bushes and at the waterfall cascading down into it. 'If you wish Tuan. It's not my business.'

'Then why ask?' Ferdach said loud enough to be heard above the surge of the water.

'I am sorry, Tuan. Please do not shout at me.'

They were right beside the fall now. To be heard Ferdach had to yell, 'I'm not shouting at – oh drop dead. Let's go on.'

Mat Noor walked ahead, now a little faster than before, so that the gap between them widened. Ferdach felt worsted by the exchange. He was a little dog scurrying after its master and like a little dog he started to yap angrily. 'No, I do not go to the Carefree with Lai Kuan. I met him there. By accident. Just once.'

'It is not my business, Tuan.'

'Isn't it? But you asked me, Noor. You must have made it your business.'

Noor stopped in his tracks and turned. Ferdach walked straight into him. A calm smooth face was close to his own, gazing up at him. Skin not brown like the average Malay but almost golden, lips sensual but small, the wide set brown eyes deeply searching. There was a smell of fresh sweat, of a desirable young body. How sweet and soft his breath. Ferdach heard Noor whisper: 'Everything that happens to Tuan is my business. *Betul-lah hal saya.* I am not afraid to die with you.' Then he turned and walked on. Ferdach stood quietly for a few moments, before following but keeping his distance. Only then did he fathom what Mat Noor had said. It was a declaration outside his experience.

At such uncertain moments as this Ferdach felt that he was a variety of species vainly trying to survive in an environment to which he was not at all adapted, a sea creature left under the hot sun by the retreating tide, crawling from pool to pool hoping that the water would last long enough to provide it with sanctuary. This was an unsatisfactory life. For the present his future path had no clear markers on it. Certainly the civil service rules and regulations could tell him all about promotion, the various grades, salary levels and conditions of service but they seemed unreal. The present was war. He could easily be killed or wounded on duty and his career would be a blank page. Living with Waite and Ericson was like living in a mental barracks. Their house was comfortable enough but there was an absence of normal human responses. The two men were, like him, oddities. He might, so easily, escape into marriage with Laura but that would not remove the perils of war; moreover, the possibility would then arise that she could be bereaved. And what if there were children? No, that course was out of the question. Life had torn him up by the roots from family and friends in England and now he was floating without meaning, a weed in a stagnant sea. Despite being in the midst of many people and enjoying exciting work, his loneliness was absolute. He craved contact; not the sterile contact of someone who just wanted physical pleasure with him. With Laura, or any of the women he was likely to meet around Ipoh, which largely meant other men's dissatisfied wives or prostitutes, sex would always be the main activity. He wanted love, a reciprocal love within the boundaries of his present dangerous situation. Neither Laura nor any woman could provide that. He wanted a comrade who felt he was their possession, someone who could share death with him if necessary. He had feared that he was seeking an impossible exotic flower yet, just now, he had heard a man willing to share death on such terms.

As they ascended the track, they saw scrappy uncontrolled undergrowth encroaching on the old rubber trees which were dying and almost leafless. Some still had cracked latex cups attached to them as if the whole place had been abandoned in a hurry. To the left the river ran more deeply in a little gorge either side of which bushes and small trees were well established. Ahead of them was a narrow but powerful waterfall plunging like a dagger over a V-shaped depression in a wall that had been built across the narrowest part of a hanging valley some thirty feet above them. Coming from either side through the rubber the platoon had already reached each side of the wall or rather the dam for that was what it was. Mat Noor led Ferdach and Choo up some steep steps, half cut in the rock, half made of mouldering logs, to the top and there they saw a beautiful green girt reservoir. The water was crystal clear revealing grey and blue and black rocks distorted in its depths. Opposite them another cascade, broad and foaming, splashed into the pool from higher up the valley. Up there in its rushing course must be the smooth rocks over which Lai Kuan had said it was possible to slide down into this, his hidden pool .

'For once he wasn't lying,' said Choo. 'Look, an old diving board. I'd like to swim.'

'No,' said Tahir firmly. 'We've got here. We've seen the pool. There are no squatter houses. We must go back We must not go into the jungle.'

Ferdach knew he was right. Maybe they had already gone too far. Above the lake real jungle with its high canopy of great trees reared up darkly. Ferdach had already picked up from the Malays some of their awe of it. And what man-made dangers might also lurk up there? His men were only armed with rifles. Not an automatic between them. In a fight,

141

they would be finished. After a brief rest Tahir ordered the withdrawal and his men filed off but Mat Noor and Choo lingered with Ferdach to gaze at the swirling water. Choo was still annoyed that he had not been able to swim. Noor began writing something in a notebook taken from his pocket. Then he blurted out, 'Above my father's land there's a lake, bigger than this and deeper. A spirit lives there. Oh, don't smile Tuan. There is a spirit there. One day we'll all visit my lake and swim there together.'

There was no longer any anger in his voice, nor in Choo's, as they went back to the road where their truck was waiting. Serenity had been restored by those hidden waters. Just as they reached the District Office Mat Noor pressed a piece of paper into Ferdach's hand. It was obviously not to be looked at straightaway. When he got home he saw that it was a four-line poem, a *pantun*. He quickly got its gist with the help of his Malay dictionary:

> *Kalau padi, kata padi*
> *Jangan sahaya tetampi tampi*
> *Kalau jadi, kata jadi*
> *Jangan sahaya ternanti nanti.*

> If it's grain, say it's grain
> Don't let me go on winnowing
> If you want me, say you want me
> Don't let me go on waiting.

23

By the time he had translated the *pantun* Ferdach's mind was vacillating between serenity and perplexity. He took a shower, put on a fresh sarong, drank too much of Waite's Pernod and went to bed. But he did not sleep easily. Had Mat Noor's *pantun* dimly revealed a light ahead, a solution to his emotional isolation? He wanted to be involved with a Malay but exactly how? It was a byword that single English officers often fell in love with the Malays, not necessarily in a sexual sense, but emotionally or, as some even claimed, spiritually. The hardest Anglo-Saxon shell could dissolve in this country's gentle culture. Of course Ferdach knew that such romantic predilections might be codswallop for without doubt, when circumstances required, the Malays could be as tough and unyielding and as nasty as anyone else. But as things stood Mat Noor seemed to be offering something he needed. Ferdach had no doubts about his friendship with Gordon Choo; the young man was reliability itself. He understood the mental toughness of Lai Kuan, and also his deviousness, both characteristics which would set firm boundaries to their friendship. The only Chinese man about whom he had ever had sensual reveries was the mysterious Wong Chooi Fong, handsome Harry, the sophisticated intellectual who had, to everyone's amazement, gone into the jungle and so rendered any further contact an impossibility. Things Chinese seemed to reflect a rational mirror image to everything in western culture – even if left was right and right left, so to speak. But the Malays possessed a quality Ferdach knew little of. It was fleeting like starlight on water, insubstantial like the shadow of a tree rustled by the wind; he wanted to capture it, to reach like Narcissus into its depths hoping that what he touched would reveal to him how he appeared to Malay eyes, yet apprehensive that he might be engulfed by its mystery.

No doubt he needed some one other than a professional teacher, who would give him a grammatical understanding of Malay but no more. Only through close friendship with Malays could he learn not just the language but also something of how they saw life. He envied Waite and wished that he too could exchange delicate *pantun*s with someone who would respond. This desire made him wonder exactly what was implied by the word '*jadi*' in Noor's *pantun*? The dictionary said, 'to come into being,' 'to turn out satisfactorily'. Neither helped. How easy to take a wrong step and open himself to ridicule. Better instead to give up any idea of a close relationship with Noor as he had now given up all thought of Mizan. He must just be self-controlled with both of them. His whole approach to the problem must be unemotional. So thinking he quite relished the prospects of the new directions he had determined and so eased himself into a profound sleep.

But the next morning he had to face up to a problem: learning two languages at the same time while working in the field would be too much for him. However, a knowledge of Malay was essential whereas his apprenticeship to the Chinese language was more long term and probably dependent on whether he would ever get to Macau. Waite had found him a Chinese teacher but the man's instruction was not what Ferdach required. Lessons with the overbearing Mr Wong Sing Nam, who came to the house three evenings a week and just when Ferdach returned dog-tired from work, had turned into a nightmare.

Wong Sing Nam, a robustly built man of about seventy, was taller than the average Chinese person in Ipoh. Unlike most Chinese men, he never wore western clothes but always arrived in a trishaw wearing a long purple, or sometimes black, cheongsam made of the finest silk. His socks were of the purest white cotton and his embroidered black slippers made his feet look small and incongruously dainty. Sometimes his shiny bald head was covered by a Chinese skullcap, but more often he turned up wearing a broad brimmed black fedora which gave him a Dr Fu Manchu look. Invariably he carried a tasselled fan which he would open with a snap to cool his proud face which was clean shaven apart from an auspicious wisp of hair growing from a mole on his right cheek.

He had been highly recommended by Waite who had learned the written language from him with the speed of which only a genius was capable. But before trying to emulate Waite, Ferdach felt that it would be more useful to learn some ordinary, common-or-garden expressions to enable him to speak to the people he met in the field. Wong Sing Nam would have none of that however. His family had once been rich and powerful in Guangzhou province from which it had fled before the war. He despised the people in the field, he despised the people in the town, indeed he despised the majority, if not all, of the Malayan Chinese whom he regarded with contempt as some low form of life. And so, before he would allow Ferdach to learn how to say 'the cat sat on the mat', he subjected him to hours of gruelling drill in the nine tones and two variants which the Cantonese dialect used. What made it even more annoying was that while Ferdach was endlessly intoning '*sing*' (falling), '*sing*' (rising) and '*sing*' (even), at the high, the medium and the low pitches, followed by '*sit*' (expletive) and '*sing*' (in the variant tone which started low falling and curved up to the high pitch) until he felt totally ridiculous, he could often hear Waite in his bedroom hooting with laughter at the whole procedure.

Nor was that the end of the torture. Wong Sing Nam was not going to have any pupil of his using a mere biro. A gentleman must write with a brush; this at least appealed to Ferdach's artistic nature. At the same time, instead of teaching him to read sentences of graduated difficulty, Wong Sing Nam introduced Ferdach at once to ancient Chinese literature by making him study the *Liao Chai*, a collection of Taoist tales of magic written in the old literary style. Thus, before he could recognise the characters for 'lavatory' or 'District Office', Ferdach was obliged to master esoteric characters such as '*hsien*' meaning 'a genii who by a process of physical and mental refinement has succeeded in deferring death or become exempt from dissolution'. Even if he had not intended to switch to learning Malay, such torment could not go on much longer.

Ferdach decided that the only way to dispense with Wong Sing Nam's services without making him lose face would be to invent a government directive instructing all officers engaged in the field to master Malay before any other language. Waite said he would give the game away but he was joking. Together they bemoaned the government's short-sighted policy to Wong Sing Nam; Ferdach gave him an extra month's salary and promised that once he had passed his Malay examinations he would at

145

once request his honourable mentor to resume his instruction. He quietly prayed that either he or Wong Sing Nam might be dead before this could happen.

With Wong Sing Nam out of the way, Ferdach was ready to proceed with his re-orientation towards the Malay world. But how exactly? It was on a Sunday evening during the late hours, which Ferdach liked to reserve for quiet reading and planning for the coming week, that he decided how he might draw Mat Noor apart from the other Specials on the following afternoon just as they were going off duty, to broach the question of their getting together … for informal Malay lessons. That was how he would put his intentions and it must be kept that way. Yet the certainty that Noor would respond favourably inevitably revived in Ferdach's mind the seductive hope of happiness he had glimpsed amidst the serenity of the hidden pool. In his mind's eye, he was contemplating drives to the coast, or to Noor's *kampung*, even taking Choo along. Unfortunately all this was shattered by a phone call bearing the voice of a distraught Laura.

Ferdach was, by nature, compassionate; poverty or illness moved him quickly to sorrow and easily to charity but he liked to act on his own terms. He could give generously if it came to his possessions, but there was a limit to what he could provide emotionally for personal involvement disturbed him. So he tended to avoid confrontations and emotional outbursts that could lead to ruptures. He liked to leave things vague, to let relationships wither on the vine rather than cut them off. Because of this he had never done anything to clarify his intentions towards Laura for the simple reason that he did not know them himself. She was left in the air, wondering whether his absence was due to a busy period of work – quite feasible given the conditions of the Emergency – and anticipating his next visit with no idea of when it would happen. Whenever she phoned him, which was often, she would complain about his absence. This was a mistake for bitter complaints made him forget the more rewarding side of her character and made him hope that in his absence the visits of Starkers Mason would be redoubled, or reinforced by other officers. He had even begun to think, crudely perhaps but crudity can be nearer the truth than the romantic, that one cock was much the same as another to Laura if it worked well. Maybe she was just a bored wife who hid her need for sex under shallow sentimental rot.

Yet this telephone call sounded different from Laura's usual complaint. There were no reproaches, no accusations, no declarations of love, not even weeping, just a statement that she was desperate, no longer able to live and that she had to see him to get through the night. The message was simplicity itself and he could not slither out of responding. Clad only in his sarong he jumped into his car and drove to her house. All was quiet, the servants were in their quarters and the lights were on in the hall but not in Laura's bedroom. The front door was not locked and Ferdach went straight upstairs.

Once in her room the moonlight was sufficient for him to see Laura naked and supine on the bed staring, open eyed like a corpse, at the ceiling. On a side table were a lot of pills, a half decanter of brandy and an empty glass. Ferdach thought the worst had already happened and threw himself down beside her, grappling her to him and calling her name. She was far from dead. Wearing a sarong had been a mistake; his precipitation had made it slip off. Laura's hand shot as quickly as a cobra down to his cock. The next moment she went down on him sucking him to a quick erection. That accomplished, almost before he could say Jack Robinson, not that those words were uppermost in his mind, he found himself beneath her with her arse bouncing up and down athwart his prick. She kept moaning how much she needed him. It was all over in a minute, probably less. He gushed in her like an Icelandic geyser. They lay in a sweaty mess in one another's arms for a minute or so and then, on the pretext of getting a drink, he detached himself from her. Until then, he had not believed in male rape by a woman and he was intrigued, rather than irritated, by her trickery. He had never been taught to admire sexual control by his own promiscuous father nor had he ever felt any desire to practice it, either at school or in the RAF or the academic world. Indeed, he had observed that sex drive when subjected to rules of continency tended to come out in other far less pleasant ways. Yet like many, if not most, males, he had tended to believe that his pattern of easy behaviour was not shared by the opposite sex. Nina Hamnett had of course been as free as the wind, but he had always thought of her as a man's brain in a woman's body and, in any case, he took it for granted that no artist should be bound by the conventions of ordinary mortals. Now, taken

147

by design by the entirely feminine Laura, he recognised that women in general, given their freedom, might behave no differently than men.

He sat on the edge of the bed and looked at her. She was far from distraught and the alleged desire to be rid of life had been discarded. Plumping up a couple of pillows she lay back on them, quite naked and legs apart, with her hands behind her head. An amused smile played on her face as she looked at him in silence.

'What was all that about,' he demanded. 'You could have used a dill doll or phoned the barracks for Starkers Mason – or a replacement.'

'Didn't you enjoy it then, you silly boy? Can't you take a joke?'

'There was hardly time for me to enjoy anything.'

'Well that's your fault. You got over excited. Or maybe you've not had it for a long time and it's been on your mind. Thinking not acting. That dams up the vital juices in a young man's loins – so I'm told. No wonder you exploded like that.' She put her hand on his thigh lightly. 'At least I'm honest about my needs.'

'No you're not. You tricked me into coming here.' Ferdach had gone into a sulk and stood up to put on his sarong.

'Oh for goodness sake. Do grow up. I wanted to see you. You mean a lot to me. Yes, I wanted you to make love to me but I also wanted to tell you something.'

'There's always the phone.' Ferdach could not help feeling amused by Laura's childlike directness and he was curious. He let the sarong fall to the floor and lay beside her.

'That's better. You look much better in the nude. And you're comfortable again. Now Ferdach, just relax. I'm not going to ask you to do it again – just yet. I really want to apologise for putting pressure on you. I shouldn't have done it. You're not ready for marriage. Maybe you never will be. What did our parents say about men who never married? "He's not the marrying sort".'

'What are you implying? That I'm not capable of taking responsibility? That I'm one hundred percent queer?' Ferdach was unwilling to accept any such verdicts and grew vehement. 'I would marry – if I met the right person. Someone I could love and who loved me. You must be annoyed because I'm not sure you're the person.'

'Love is so easy for people who love like us Ferdie. You'll always take your pleasure where you find it, easily and with no attachments. I know about you because I'm like you. Listen then. Next week I'm following Alfred to Singapore. He's already taken up his job in the Department of Education. And the two of us have come to a civilised agreement. We're going to stick to the outward forms. But he can visit his floozies and I can find my lover boys. There are lots of soldiers and sailors in Singapore so I won't go thirsty.' She sat up and kissed Ferdach on the lips, neither a deep kiss nor a lingering kiss but somehow a loving kiss. She repeated it holding his head between her hands and then stroking his hair. 'You can visit us there – when you go down to see that old devil Northcote Parkinson. So you'll have two places to stay and no hotel bills at all. Who knows, you might even fall for someone wonderful in Singapore.'

Ferdach was cautious; Laura still hoped to hook him. Alfred might be complaisant for the moment but he was capable of turning nasty. The ideal for Laura would be the sort of arrangement she had apparently settled for with Alfred but with someone who provided her with good companionship, as well as some sex – in other words himself. It was time to get out of this situation with the most absolute lie he could command but one which could not possibly make Laura feel rejected.

'I have found someone I can love Laura. I have found someone but marriage is out of the question.'

Laura did not seem a bit jealous. On the contrary she replied in a blasé manner, 'Oh, another married woman. But next time you may have to look over your shoulder all the time. Not all husbands are like Alfred.'

'No, not a woman. A bloke and not one of your officer types.'

Laura took that in her stride too. 'That's better, less risky. I always thought you might go for a brawny British soldier. They're exciting – once you get over the language barrier. But darling, you can't have a love affair here with a bloke in the army – it will just be sex. Who is it? One of Starkers' Guardsmen?'

'Well, military in a way Laura. But not British.'

This did seem to affect Laura, who sat up to look down at Ferdach. She even switched on the table light to see him more closely. 'Go on darling. You're not going native?'

The sudden brightness startled Ferdach. He wanted neither his face nor his hidden thoughts to be lit up. But one hidden thought declined

149

any longer to be held in check either from Laura or from himself. 'He's a Malay. One of my special constables,' he said, immediately wondering why he had said it.

'Oh dear, oh dear. You're in for a rough ride or a big let down. And for chrisakes be careful. You're not in Soho now. A Guardsman would have been better. They know the score. They know what's wanted and they've generally got it. A Malay! I've never thought about them in that way. Oh Ferdie, careful, careful, careful. Not with someone you're working with.' Then Laura shook her head. 'But knowing you, nothing I say will stop you. You'll just have to tell me all about it when you come to Singapore. That will be fun, if you haven't suffered – or been chucked out of the service.'

She embraced him passionately, impressing on him once more the need to be careful and as she whispered her advice in his ear, tantalising it the while with her tongue, her gentle hands took to exploring his body again, stroking him in her usual skilful way, arousing him. No, arousing not him, not Ferdach, but his cock. Male genitals have a life of their own. They cannot be denied. They have to have their daily canter. Laura was one of those truly rare English women who could accept what men were really like, so different from the majority of her kind who, once married, seemed to believe that men could or should remain faithful to a single one of them till death did them part. Few women, it seemed to Ferdach, had the slightest notion of what an unremitting tyrant a man's cock was. Laura did and she deserved her reward for having broken the mould. The memory of Mason and all the other men who had ploughed her so easily increased Ferdach's lust making it simple to give what she and that unruly prick of his were both demanding. But once the kissing, the biting, the mauling, the moaning, the groaning, the scratching, the stroking, the greedy play of lips, the fucking, the final thrusting and the last sad gasps of pleasure had come to an end, he knew that something was wrong. All the time his mind had been detached from what his body had been up to. As he withdrew slowly and gently from Laura the thought of a different love, a more consuming passion, began to stir in a deep cavern of his mind. He lay back, closed his eyes, began to breathe deeply and, quite unmindful of Laura, let his brain become receptive to an undeniable image. It was concerned with love, not in a physical sense but with love encapsulating an ideal; it was like a vision seeping into his consciousness from some place where it had existed timelessly. Slowly, uncertainly he could see it taking shape until at last it took the form of a youth, who else could it be but Mat Noor, rising from the water, his golden skin dappled by sunlight filtered through a canopy of trees. It was so vivid that Ferdach was scared. You are losing the plot, he told himself. Then, 'I must be losing it!' he shouted. In a sort of panic he seized Laura and held her close to him. His next sentences sounded incoherent but there were two strands: 'Must you go to Singapore?' and, ' I was just kidding you.' Then he calmed down and said very deliberately, 'There's no one really. I just wanted to put you off.'

Ferdach loosened his grip but they still held each other, tenderly now. Their faces were close together and she whispered, 'Did you Ferdie? I don't think so. And there's no need to put me off in any case. No, it was more than that. Maybe you've been working too hard. Been out in the sun too long. Walking around in the heat day after day with only a few young men as company. It's natural you should hit on one of them to relieve your frustration. But if there is some guy, then just treat him like the others. Don't give yourself away. Remember, he'd probably laugh at you or exploit you if you told him your inner feelings. And maybe he'd tell the other men too. Then where would you be?'

'You're right Laura. I've been stupid. Nothing has happened so far but I'm sure the men can see what's on my mind.' Then Ferdach sighed deeply and let out a little moan for there was a part of him that wanted his feelings neither for Laura nor for Mat Noor to be a mirage. 'Ah, I've made a big mistake coming to Malaya.'

'Ferdie, you're already a success. I've heard people talk about you. You've just not adjusted yet. But you certainly don't need me to help you to do that. And I do have to go to Singapore. I've promised Alfred. You and I still have time to think things over. Maybe when you come to visit me we'll be able to reach a conclusion. At the very worst we'll remain good friends for the rest of our lives. Everything is so unnatural here – especially for you. This terrible Emergency. The weird life you have with Waite and Ericson. Singapore is a big city; we can be anonymous there, be ourselves at least for while, and work things out.' Ferdach thought it best to agree. Yes, the door between them must be left wide open, just as

24

The following day, even though it was one of Malaya's many public holidays, Choo, Tahir and the platoon were raring to go when Ferdach met them outside Waite's office. Unusually for him, Ferdach had come to work late but he was determined that today the last sector of his allotted area – a remote sector that was little more than a clearing, well inside thick jungle – should be thoroughly investigated and censored. When that was done all would be ready for the first phase of resettlement. A scheme for the relocation of the population of Ferdach's census area had already been planned and the Public Works Department would be starting work on the roads, the wells and the perimeter defences within the week. Very soon the population would be obliged to move into the new settlement. The first chapter of Ferdach's job was nearing completion. He looked forward to being in charge of the resettlement operation and ensuring that his squatters – for he now took a proprietorial interest in them – should be moved humanely and with every consideration. He also believed, he hoped not vainly, that the people had confidence in him and would come to him if they wanted assistance.

While they were waiting for their lorry Ferdach chatted with the men, taking care to say no more to Mat Noor than to anyone else. He remembered Laura's words of caution that he might be laughed at if he showed his feelings for a subordinate, but she could be wrong. What could she know of Malays or of Mat Noor?

The lorry drove up and the men had already piled in when Ferdach heard his name called by Waite who was standing at the District Office door. Ferdach had already grasped a hand rail to pull himself inside after the others. 'Can't you tell me later?' he shouted. We're already behind schedule.'

'Afraid not. In you come.'

Once inside the office Ferdach was given the news. He was to hand over his work to one of those young geologists, a black-haired frowning young Scot named Hamish Kinloch, who had, to his extreme annoyance, been drafted into resettlement activity.

'Sorry, Ferdie,' said Waite. 'I know you're at the end of the Gunung Rapat census but someone with experience is wanted urgently at Chemor. The man chosen to replace Broadstairs was shot up last night and the resettlement operation starts today. New lorries are available. We've held things up there too long. There's a police car waiting to take you right away.' Waite then introduced Ferdach to a police lieutenant, Sam Ongley, who was standing by waiting with an impatient expression on his face.

'But this young chap, Kinloch,' Ferdach protested. 'He's only just arrived. How will he cope?'

'He's luckier than you were Ferdie – and, by the way, he's a bit older. He's got your experienced men to rely on. Choo and Tahir can do the job with their eyes closed. They'll train him.'

Ferdach couldn't deny that, but he was shocked all the same. He was to be abruptly estranged from his team. It would be like losing his family. And there was to be no way of softening the blow. No party. No photos. No fond reminiscences. None of the sentimental farewells that make losing comrades easier. He was speechless.

Ongley glanced at his watch. 'Come on, O'Haney. We're late. The CPO Perak is going to Chemor to see things get underway. He's not the sort of man who takes kindly to being kept waiting.'

Ferdach exploded. 'Bloody hell, Waite. If anyone thinks I'm going without saying goodbye to my men they're mistaken.' He rounded on Ongley. 'You can wait and the CPO can take it as kindly as he wants.' Then he noticed Kinloch standing behind Waite. 'Come on Kinloch. I'll introduce you to all the boys in my platoon. The best bunch you'll ever have the luck to work with.'

With that he walked over to the lorry followed by Kinloch and watched sympathetically not only by Waite but by many of the District Office staff.

The men climbed out of the lorry and Ferdach briefly explained what had happened. They did not look at all happy. Choo's mouth was screwed up as though he was about to roar some defiance of authority but he thought better of it. Tahir's face wore a frown but he too said nothing. Noor's eyes were just staring. Ferdach introduced every man to Kinloch, then urged them to look after one another. His voice became hoarse when he said that he would never forget their days together. Finally he shook hands with each of them. Somehow Mat Noor contrived to be last. But maybe contrivance was not necessary as the other men seemed to know how it should be. He held Ferdach's hand longer than the rest had done. Their eyes searched each other but neither could be absolutely sure that what they saw held the answer to his own question and they were each left with a feeling of loneliness. Ferdach turned quickly and strode off to Ongley's car.

Over the next ten days Ferdach worked harder than he had ever done in his life. As soon as he arrived at Chemor he was shown the operational plan that had been drawn up a long time before the burning of the lorries. It had of course involved the civil, the police and the military authorities. The Resettlement Area had been surveyed, the land made available by the state government while the Town Planning and the Public Works Departments had already carried out much of the preparatory work so that in addition to the defences, a police post, an office and a basic network of roads had been laid out and the dwelling lots demarcated. Indeed, in Perak the planning of the Resettlement Areas was, in many respects, superior to the way in which it had been done further south in Malaya where the Briggs Plan was first implemented, often in a rushed manner. However, the final stage, the procedures for the actual movement of the squatter families, had been planned more recently, much of it by the unhappily maligned Broadstairs. Once he had examined them Ferdach could not help admiring his predecessor's competence and his attention to detail. The order in which the families were to be moved, the assignment of lots within the perimeter, the grouping of people of the same dialect group had been given careful attention. Though the majority of those to be moved were Chinese, there was also a considerable number of Malay and a few Indian families who would be placed in discrete sections of the new settlement. The allocation of staff and of lorries to execute the operation was admirable. Broadstairs had even indicated on an elaborate map the routes to be followed, from the widely dispersed squatter areas to the new dwelling lots. Ferdach felt that his predecessor must have seen it all as a huge dramatic pageant – something like the Oberammagau *tableaux vivants*. What had not been foreseen was the extent to which the communists would work to frustrate the operation.

Ferdach could see that he would have to live on site so on the afternoon of his new posting he hastened back to Ipoh, picked up some clothes and supplies, and moved into a police mess near to Chemor. For the first time he drew a revolver, a Browning automatic, from the police armoury as he did not want to be defenseless when on duty – not that he had great faith in his expertise as a marksman. Strangely enough he felt more at ease in the mess than in the comparative comfort of the house in Ipoh. There was no need to go through the evening charade of formal dining with Waite and Ericson or socialising with any visitors, mainly male, who dropped in for a drink later in the evening. With the exception of Williams Hunt, Ferdach had rarely found that he had anything in common with those people; they tended to be commercial or banking types who considered it useful to cultivate Waite because of his position. On that account they sometimes found themselves, to Ferdach's secret delight, subjected to extrasensory perception tests whether they liked them or not. It was never clear whether Waite's persecution of his visitors was intentional or not.

In the Chemor mess it was not necessary to make conversation about anything except the work in hand. His new companions there were a couple of police officers, Lieutenants Lionel Smithers and Colin Blakeley, together with another of the reluctant geologists, Simon Jenkins, who were all in their mid-twenties. There was also an older man of about fifty, a Chinese-speaking Resettlement Officer who had been an Anglican missionary in Fukien province in China. Mr Masters, or to give him his full name the Reverend Peter Wentworth-Masters, was not only completely fluent in Hokkien but also proficient in written Chinese. Unfortunately most of the squatters to be resettled were Cantonese or Hakka.

On the basis of his experience in resettlement work at Gunung Rapat and, of course, of being on the District Office staff, Ferdach became the Chief Resettlement Officer with Masters and Jenkins as his number two and number three. It was agreed by the three of them that they would each be responsible for a third of the area in which the squatters were currently living. In this way, Ferdach reckoned, no one would tread on anyone else's toes. However he and his staff, together with police and military officers met each morning for 'morning prayers' to ensure that proper liaison was maintained.

However, there were potentially many toes to be trodden on. Even apart from the military and the police flooding the area, large numbers of civil staff were engaged in the operation. For some time stockpiles of building material had been readied by the Public Works Department and by some half dozen Chinese contractors in its employ, to enable the squatters to erect new homes once they had been moved inside the perimeter. The new houses, like their old ones, would be constructed of wood and attap but well aligned and separated from one another within each building lot. Walls would be made of wood and roofs of attap though owing to the shortage of the latter material, stocks of aluminium sheeting and corrugated iron had also been brought in. Beyond these, great quantities of nails, screws, drainage pipes, water butts, wire and tools of all sorts were in a temporary store within the perimeter. A number of wells and latrines had already been drilled; more would be necessary and for this reason supplies of concrete were in readiness together with concrete paving slabs to make surrounds for the well heads.

Of great importance even before resettlement began was the work of the Health Department and the Red Cross. The affected areas must be sprayed as an anti-malarial measure and preparations must be made to look after any one, particularly the old, the infirm and the young, who might be taken ill once the movement had started. Moreover, the squatters had been promised medical examinations for anyone who wanted them. The Red Cross was represented by three young, very dedicated women, two English – Patricia Mellors and Wendy Tollet – and one Irish – Sinead O'Rourke – who lived together in a caravan on site. They brought to their work the sort of disciplined fervour that Ferdach remembered of such women during the blitz on Merseyside when he was at school.

Ferdach anticipated difficulties in regard to finance. All the squatters were entitled to a resettlement grant as well as compensation for lost crops or livestock. Moreover many small jobs would have to be performed quickly, on the spot, by local contractors who were not always honest. All these payments would be made in cash. Easy enough to keep thousands of dollars in a police station but once payments started, they would be made in the field by Assistant Resettlement Officers or seconded District Office staff. Effective control of claims and disbursements would be well nigh impossible. The best Ferdach could do was to make the Rev Peter Masters into an ad hoc financial controller. He assumed that the man was honest. Most of the staff knew his background and must believe this to be the case. In any case Masters had a somewhat eagle-like face, sharp and, Ferdach suspected, a bit cruel which accorded well with his new role.

Like other young men newly arrived in Malaya and faced by similar circumstances, Ferdach had to develop administrative skills quickly to deal with the men, the equipment and the logistical dispositions which had to be made. He did this on the basis of honesty and common sense, virtues emphasised to him on the Colonial Office training course but which were entirely natural to his own disposition. With so many people involved, each with their individual responsibilities, it was inevitable that disputes would arise. Ferdach knew he had to be the just regulator of these issues and to that end made a great effort to be open to all who approached him and to listen in an affable manner to what he was told.

Inevitably the memory of his attachments in Ipoh took a back seat. He received a long farewell letter from Laura written on the day she boarded the train for Singapore. It was loving enough but her indiscreet references to certain idiosyncratic details of their love-play made him suspect that she was really wondering whether similar pleasures awaited her in the big city. He regretted that he had not seen her off; he would miss her, even if the missing resided to some degree in his own reluctance to go to her whenever she commanded. As for Mat Noor he felt that his feeling for him must have disappeared into some kind of mental cold storage though he knew it was still there.

However another earlier attachment resurrected itself in the form of a letter from Wong Siu Bo in Penang. She was moderately happy, she claimed, with her Hokkien husband who gave her considerable freedom in exchange for hard work supervising a little hotel – read brothel – which he owned. Yet she really longed to see her heaven-ordained soulmate

Ferdach again and hinted that his earthy needs would be fully satisfied at her establishment in Lebuh Armenian should he ever visit Penang. Naturally enough he soon took to driving there for the occasional weekend and Siu Bo made him most welcome. Although he always had a lot of fun with her pretty girls or, at Siu Bo's insistence, 'test flying', as she put it, any new ones, he enjoyed their mistress' company more for they both found it easy to relax with one another, gossiping about her clients, assessing the varying skills of her young ladies or doing nothing in particular. In the fleshpots of Penang the Emergency seemed a thousand miles away and the brief escapes gave him as much sex as a young man needed, without fear of attachments. Even when later it became difficult for him to get away to Penang, he and Siu Bo continued to exchange letters which were largely concerned with her problems running the brothel and with wife Number One, who did not like her. Ferdach was an expert advisor on the former which, given the nature of the male, he considered an admirable and socially desirable business, though not so in regard to her domestic problems for the internal arrangements of a traditional Chinese family were pretty well impervious to outside interference.

The breaks certainly helped him to face the harsh realities that were a daily occurrence at Chemor during resettlement. By the time he and his staff met for morning prayers, information, sometimes horrible, had come in overnight about the depradations of the communists who were exerting great pressure on the squatters not to cooperate with the authorities. Not only was the Min Yuen doing its utmost to oppose government efforts but at night armed communist bands would enter the area to cow the population. Not infrequently, *pour encourager les autres*, a character suspected by the CTs of being pro-government would be eliminated by being roasted or disembowelled or, if he was lucky, just shot. Ferdach knew that the squatters were between the devil and the deep blue sea and their distress, especially that of the elderly, troubled him greatly.

By now the communists had fully grasped the dangers to them of the Briggs Plan. Though it would not starve them into submission, experience in parts of Malaya where it had been implemented showed that their fighting effectiveness was radically weakened because of their reduced ability to collect or extort supplies. The squatters were therefore told to raise every possible objection to being moved, perhaps on the grounds of crops not being ready for harvest or of illness or of some superstition or of any excuse they could think of. Many squatters did this willingly, wanting to prove to the CTs that they were obeying orders. However most of them were secretly hoping to be moved quickly within the new settlement where their protection by the police and military would become possible.

When that move would take place, no one in the Chemor area knew and certainly not Ferdach; he was only a cog in a great administrative operation, important only in that when resettlement began he would be a significant link between those making the strategic decisions and the people to be moved. It was at the level of the State War Executive Committee and lower down, the District War Executive Committee, that vital decisions were taken on the basis of situation reports built up from police and military intelligence. All Ferdach was sure of was that when the resettlement operation began, it would take place at very short notice in the early hours of the morning. But which morning was anyone's guess. In the event, an unusual increase in patrolling and the sudden deployment of lorries lasting a couple of days suggested that a certain sector south of Chemor had been chosen for the first phase of the operation. This, of course, was sheer bluff. When resettlement actually began it was to a sector to the north and east of Chemor that a large mixed force of police and soldiers was swiftly deployed. Nor did Ferdach know what was in the offing until a security cordon had already been thrown around the sector making it difficult for anyone, whether squatters or CTs, to get out without being stopped and searched. Only when the cordon had been established was the civil arm, of which Ferdach was the field respresentative, told to send out its lorries, and its resettlement and medical staff to the various squatter houses identified for first removal. Ferdach first knew that the operation was underway when he was awakened by Waite at three thirty one morning with a thump on his shoulder and the words, 'Come on Ferdie, it's all systems go.'

'Couldn't you think of a more original expression?' Ferdach grumbled for he was not at all pleased by Waite's arrival. Moreover, he had always hoped that he might have been involved with the military in the first stages of the operation and he said as much, whilst pulling on his clothes. But Waite was firm. 'You weren't told because you didn't need to know. Everything has to be on a need to know basis. Now let's get going. You and your teams have to be in the field with the lorries before daybreak.'

'And why are you here at all? The arrangement was that I would be woken up by the police. You should be at the District Office with Signor Bertelli. Surveying everything from an Olympian height.'

'Because I like giving you my personalised attention dear boy,' said Waite in a posh English accent. 'And I need to know from personal observation that you are doing your duty to the Crown to the best of your ability.' Then seeing that Ferdach was not sufficiently awake to take a joke he smiled disarmingly and, reverting to broad strine, said, 'No matey, I know you'll be on top of it but if it gets curly you may need more help than you think. We've got some newspaper men here. They'll be watching us like hawks, especially Harry Miller from *The Straits Times*. He's a top-rate man, beavering into every bloody thing. But there are also a couple of Chinese reporters with lines to Hong Kong – and further afield. So I want to make absolutely sure that our military treat their fellow Chinese, every man Jack of them, with respect. We know we want to win the squatters over but we want everyone else to know it too. So don't let's give our enemies in the outside world any opportunity to criticize us. Got it?'

Ferdach had indeed got it and once he had watched the departure of the AROs, the lorries and their escorts, some of them Malay police, others British Guardsmen, he was careful to invite the two Chinese correspondents, one of whom took photographs incessantly, together with the perspicacious Harry Miller, to join him in his jeep. As it turned out Waite's concern over the behaviour of the military seemed, on this occasion, to be groundless. Moving from house to house, Ferdach was repeatedly struck by the humane way in which the soldiers, both Malay and British, behaved. As a part Irishman with memories of his father's stories about the 1917 Rising he was not expecting this of British soldiers. True, when the men first mounted guard around any house while the Assistant Resettlement Officer told the family that the time had come to gather up their possessions and load it on the waiting lorry, they looked menacing enough as they waited at the ready for any sign of resistance but once the family had shown that it was prepared to move a perceptible change occurred. Never was there an occasion when all the soldiers just stood by and watched. Whenever possible they helped with the loading, they lifted heavy boxes, they played with the children and helped them into the lorries; they were kindly to old men and women and assisted those who were too infirm to move on their own; they helped to crate poultry and, if not Malay, pigs both large and small, the latter not always too efficiently but often in a way that made everyone laugh. In short, their presence was reassuring and not threatening and both the squatters and the correspondents could see that clearly enough. It went without saying that the soldiers had been well briefed by their officers on how to behave, but everyone could see that they were acting willingly and not because they were under orders.

Harry Miller seemed as anxious as Ferdach to convince the two Chinese that the ordinary British soldier was the very epitome of humanity, the everlasting protector of the poor and the scourge of tyranny but they were both young men who had, in their short lives, already been subjected to a great deal of propaganda, nationalist and Communist no doubt, but all propaganda has the same stink about it. Before long their faces showed that they thought they were travelling in some sort of brain washing set-up. So, quite sharply, Ferdach told them as they arrived at the third family they had seen receiving its notice to quit, 'Why don't you two stay here and question anyone you want – especially the Chinese in their own dialect. No need to listen to what we are telling you. You can get in the lorry with this family when they move to the Resettlement Area. That should give you a good story.'

As soon as Ferdach drove on, Miller chuckled. 'Why didn't you just tell me to belt up. I was speaking like a government information officer, wasn't I? But you're taking a risk. They only have to speak to some Min Yuen member and the wrong story will appear in every Chinese paper around the Pacific.'

'It's a risk I'll have to take.'

'Ah, a young man who isn't afraid to displease his masters.'

Ferdach stopped the jeep at a junction on the track. Before looking at his planning map and deciding which way to go, he turned to Miller and said, 'Frankly Harry, I don't care a tinker's cuss about my masters. What does it matter? No one in my service is going to be in this country for long. There's no career in it for me is there? But I reckon that if I'm going to do anything useful here, it must be on the basis of what I, yes I myself, think is right. I've read your stuff in the *Times* and I admire you. So let's just rely on those two guys to do as well as you without feeding them a word.'

Harry Miller looked at Ferdach seriously and then shook his hand with an almost painfully tight grip. 'I'm impressed. I stand, sorry I sit, corrected. I had quite forgotten the distiction between a mere journalist and a good administrator.' For the rest of the time he was at Chemor, unfortunately only a couple more days, a firm friendship developed between them. This was no great gain to Miller once he had left, but it was beneficial to Ferdach for Harry Miller was in the confidence of some important federal government officers and especially of Commissioner of Police William Nicol Gray, to whom he made confidential reports. Moreover, within the week articles began to appear in *The Straits Times* and *Sin Chew Jit Poh* about squatter resettlement in Perak. In the former, the work of young expatriate Resettlement Officers in the state was singled out for praise as successors in spirit to the early British pioneers in Malaya such as Hugh Clifford and Frank Swettenham who had worked tirelessly for the people. One of those officers, a certain F. O'Haney, was referred to by name. The Chinese paper's article was shorter, concentrated on the squatters' hardships and said hardly a word about the benefits of resettlement; O'Haney was again referred to – in a photograph that made him look dark-jowled, sallow and rather unsavoury.

25

Ferdach had often wondered why his treatment on arrival in Malaya had been so cavalier. He learned the reason for this during his visit to Ipoh a couple of weeks after Miller's departure courtesy of a Mr I. K. Furnivall who, until recently, had been a senior Establishment Officer; it amazed him on account of its stupidity. Furnivall, who had recently been appointed to the post of Chief Registration Officer, was not overtly apologetic about what had happened but he let Ferdach read a letter written by a certain Mr Miles Jowitt. This man, a former Colonial Governor, had been asked by the Colonial Office to visit the recruits in Ferdach's Colonial Service training course while they attended an agricultural short course at Wye College in Kent, a course of limited relevance to the agriculture of the countries for which they were destined.

Ferdach remembered Jowitt well: a short pompous man, with an accent so far back that at times he was incomprehensible, a snob who liked name dropping particularly if the name had an HH or, better, an HRH in front of it. In the college common room he mainly spoke to those men whose relatives he knew to have held high colonial posts. Some of them were a bit dim. There was one, a Mr Wilmington Pessey, who, when asked by Jowitt why he had joined the Colonial Service, replied in a blasé manner, 'Oh, Pesseys have been governing subject peoples for generations.' Jowitt had laughed immoderately at this in that loud hee-hawing way that made Philip of Spain's observation that Englishmen sounded like horses entirely comprehensible.

Jowitt had also listened in to some of the course discussions. In these Ferdach was always active and invariably had something to say, not always of a conventional nature and invariably, if he could help it, controversial. Jowitt would stare, with the eyes of a dead fish, at Ferdach whenever he was speaking, obviously resenting the fact that a man who was not 'one of us' should have the nerve to outshine those members of the course who most distinctly were. Unfortunately Ferdach was not always able, when emotionally aroused, to oblige his discretion to suppress his feelings. Aware of Jowitt's silent hostility he refrained from making any attempt either to approach him or pay him the least respect.

However, Ferdach had made another error. In that immediate postwar world, people were beginning to strike out where fashion was concerned and one of the new fashions was, for men, the French crew cut hairstyle. Ferdach had adopted it a few weeks before going to Wye. Admittedly it didn't suit him and he had decided to let his hair grow until it resumed its more conventional look. Jowitt had seized on this. His letter, forwarded from his private address to his contact in the Malayan Establishment Office, stated that:

> O'Haney, a grammar school boy who has received some sort of 'education' at a northern university, is not, in my opinion the right type for the Colonial Service. Not only is he unduly opinionated and not aware of his place, he has made himself look bizarre with a ghastly haircut. *I cannot see him in Colonial Service dress uniform*. I am utterly convinced that he lacks all respect for traditional British values. This may not be unconnected with his *Irish* background. However, since he has already been accepted for service in Malaya and has done well enough on the Colonial Service course, not that this says much in my opinion for it is character and class rather than bookish learning that count in a man, perhaps he could, on arrival in Malaya, be quietly transferred to some other branch of government. In this regard I would mention the contractual resettlement posts now necessary on account of the Emergency, or possibly, if he learns more self-discipline, the police.

'Do you mean,' asked Ferdach after a long pause, during which he stared right into Furnivall's eyes, ' do you mean that account was actually taken of this tripe?'

Perhaps, momentarily, Furnivall recalled Jowitt's stricture that

Ferdach did not know his place but if so he mastered it. 'The letter was written to my predecessor – a friend of Jowitt. I believe it was most irregular. I have withdrawn it from the file.'

Ferdach did not observe that such a withdrawal was probably irregular. He felt furious not just with Jowitt but with all Jowitt stood for. Conservative men like him sincerely believed themselves to be above the law because only their outlook was held to be valid. They were entitled to use their old-boy systems to benefit themselves and to derogate outsiders. Of course, if anyone complained they had a phrase ready for them: 'Oh, he's got a chip on his shoulder'. But before he could even think of expressing his anger or his thanks Furnivall recommenced: 'If it had not been for Harry Miller you could easily have been sidelined as Jowitt suggested, even though Waite has reported well on you.' Yes, Ferdach thought, I can imagine that; Waite's well-known unconventionality isn't likely to endear him to the Establishment Office either.

'I would suggest O'Haney that we put all this behind us. Miller thinks highly of you and, though you mightn't believe this, so does Mr Gray, the Commissioner of Police who saw Miller's reports. He has suggested to the Establishment Office that you be appointed to a special post to deal with the identity card crisis and we intend following his advice. You would be responsible to me.'

Ferdach fell silent. He had heard that William Nicol Gray was a brilliant but ruthless man not well disposed to idiots. His reputation was enormous for he had reorganized the entire police force, increased its efficiency and above all hugely expanded its size so that it was now developing a capacity that extended to the smallest *kampung*s throughout the country. Ferdach had also heard about the identity card problem for it was starting to arise in the Chemor area.

The identity card represented a relationship between the individual and the government. That it was a symbol went without saying, but it was also a necessity to a population in the clutch of the Emergency. Without such a card anyone's movement about the country, and safety if arrested, could be at risk. The CTs had started to confiscate identity cards whenever possible in order to break the link between the people and the state.

'What we want,' Furnivall continued, sensing that he had Ferdach's attention, 'is to establish a system which will make it possible to issue some form of identification to any member of the public almost immediately after an identity card has been stolen. If what is devised in Perak is satisfactory, it can be used all over the country. Well O'Haney, I know that it's not a very glamorous sort of job but it's an important one, a difficult administrative exercise that has to be done well. So what about it. Are you up to it?'

Ferdach pondered for only a little while. He could not help saying, 'Ah, so you're offering me an eraser to rub out Jowitt's bad report.' But he went on, 'No. I'm just joking. Of course I'll do it. I'll do it to the best of my ability.' Then feeling that ungraciousness could be carried a bit too far, he added. 'Thank you Mr Furnivall for all you have done. Truly I am grateful.'

By the time Furnivall had left for Kuala Lumpur, Ferdach knew that in two or three weeks time he would be out of Chemor. In a way he was sorry to be leaving. It was fascinating to watch the speed with which the newly settled people were building their houses. Of greater significance was the fact that many squatter families still living outside the perimeter were complaining that their resettlement was too slow. They wanted to come in, to build a new house, to claim their allotted piece of land and their agricultural plot either just outside the settlement or between its two perimeter fences. Their enthusiasm to move was increased rather than discouraged by the mounting level of CT attacks and ambushes several of which had been very serious resulting in loss of life both of Malay and British soldiers as well as of two brave Chinese Assistant Resettlement Officers. Even shots fired at random into the village at night by CT snipers did not deter the squatters' wish to come in. But despite this success, or perhaps because of it, Ferdach knew that his presence was no longer necessary for Wentworth-Masters and Jenkins were every bit as resourceful as he was in dealing fairly with the squatters and the problems that arose from their orderly settlement. At the time of Furnivall's visit, some of the most difficult issues still related to the construction of village infrastructure by Chinese contractors; roads were still being spread with laterite, wells still being bored, latrines still being constructed. The whole site, what with these activities and the erection of houses, looked a confused mess. But it was a purposeful mess and order was gradually emerging. Unfortunately the contractors could not always be effectively supervised by the PWD and though hard working, they could also be rapacious when money was at issue. The sharp eyed Masters was much better at dealing with these matters than Ferdach would ever have been. As for young Simon Jenkins, being a physical training enthusiast he was popular with the Chinese boys for whom he quickly organized such sports as badminton and soccer. In short, morale in the village had risen from low to good and was still rising. One of the lessons that Ferdach learned from all this was that, contrary to many a man's self-satisfied belief, no one is ever indispensable. This was a conclusion that he liked to emphasise to those Britons who sometimes scoffed that Malaya would fall apart when they and their ilk had departed. Another thought that inevitably occurred to him was that the success achieved had depended to a considerable extent on the efforts of bachelors who were prepared to give all their day to work among the people in the field. Men encumbered by women would not have been able to do this. Likewise the work of the three unmarried Red Cross women, Patricia, Wendy and Sinead, would not have been so effective had they been burdened with families. The unmarried status of all these people had happily not entailed celibacy. Indeed, the lovely raven-haired Sinead was particularly inclined to spread goodwill to men of all races. But that was a matter that Ferdach held to be none of his or anyone else's business.

Most important of all Ferdach felt happy over the way in which his resettlement office staff were being supported by the police and the military. Nevertheless a lengthy struggle lay ahead to win over the settlers' hearts and minds and a long period of good administration would be needed to achieve this. The resettled areas – *Xin Chun* or New Villages – as the Chinese were already calling them would eventually have to be run by the villagers themselves. Although there was no legislation or government policy as yet to effect this, he had gathered together a number of men who seemed to be respected by the other squatters to form a liaison committee at which problems could be discussed and then brought to the attention of his own resettlement staff. Until other quarters could be provided, this committee was given at first just a table but later, once it was built, a room in his own office building. One of the first matters which the Chinese committee members wanted to pursue was the erection of a school, promising to pay half its cost if the government would match their contributions. Ferdach saw that the process of dealing with the village people's problems on a mutual basis was acting as a sort of psychological glue which would slowly but surely bind them ever more closely to the government.

On the last weekend of his stay in Chemor he was promised a big party in a local hall by many of the people with whom he had been working, for short though his time there had been they were reluctant to see him go. There would be Malay *joget* girls for the Malays and anyone who wanted to join them in their dancing, booze of course for the British soldiery and large quantities of Chinese, Malay and Indian food for everyone. The party never took place because on the day before the party, a Friday that would long be remembered by Ferdach, a dreadful ambush took place in his old stomping ground of Gunung Rapat.

26

Ferdagh had never told Waite or Ericson, much about his personal life, nor they him. The three of them, though living in close proximity with one another, led isolated lives. It had only been accidental that something of Ericson had become briefly apparent to Ferdagh through their joint knowledge of Laura. But once that matter had been resolved their mutual indifference towards one another had returned without, however, Ericson's former antipathy. With Waite there had never been a Laura to enable Ferdach to fathom the depths of that strange esoteric obsessed mind, despite which Ferdach was sure that in some obscure way Waite felt for him and probably understood his loneliness which was perhaps mirrored in his own mind.

Ferdach was surprised when Waite turned up very late one evening; he sensed from his expression that something was wrong and that it concerned him.

'Why are you here?' Ferdach demanded. 'So late. Your face so tense.' And almost at once, before Waite could say a word, the figure of Mat Noor, frozen deep in his mind soared up. But that was foolish. Waite could know nothing about his feelings for Noor. Then it must be the platoon – of which Noor was a part. 'My men,' he said. 'My men. Are they all right?'

'No Ferdie,' Waite said softly. 'They're not alright. They were about to come back to town late this afternoon as usual. They'd gathered near a temple about fifty yards off the main road, around one of those little pavilions beside the goldfish ponds. All at once they were surprised by automatic fire from the cliffs and from close by. They hadn't walked into an ambush. They were sitting ducks. I don't know why they'd relaxed their guard. Maybe they'd grown over confident.'

Ferdagh could not ask who was killed, who was wounded; he just stood and listened for he knew Waite would spare him nothing. 'Hamish Kinloch was killed straight off. He was sitting at one of the tables beside the pavilion, looking at his maps. The platoon did return fire but no one could pinpoint where it was coming from. They were trapped between different lines of attack. Tahir thought Kinloch was only wounded and went to pull him into the pavilion but he was shot as he lent over Kinloch's body. None of your platoon ran. They took up positions around the dead men and fired but it was hopeless. Six of them were killed and the rest were wounded, including Gordon Choo. When the firing stopped it was Choo who staggered to the road to flag down a lorry and ask for help.' Waite saw that Ferdach was going to ask for more details, for names no doubt, so he said, 'No Ferdie. I don't know any more than that. Best if we leave for Ipoh at once.'

In Waite's office Ferdach saw the familiar maps which he had helped to fill in, the marks representing the positions of houses, of tracks, of formerly unmarked streams and pools, the work of himself and of Choo so ably supported by the platoon of Malay Specials. Now those once white expanses of paper were also stained with the mingled blood of Tahir and Kinloch. When Waite had told him of the casualties, strangely enough the thought of Mat Noor had receded again. He had not said to himself, 'Let Noor be alive. Let him only be among the wounded.' The names of all the men, of Ismail, of Harun, of Abdul Ghani and all the others whom he had got to know so well, were equally uppermost in his mind. Apart from Tahir and Mat Noor none of them had had much of an education; they were *kampung* boys, rural boys who had become Specials not just because it was a job, important though that was to them, but because they wanted to serve. None of them was reluctant to risk his life. They had an inkling that they were working for their own people and country even if it was not yet independent. Without the large numbers of such young men, limited though their training was, the protection of the mines, the rubber estates, the industries and the villages all over Malaya would have been impossible. In Ferdach's mind the bravery of the men in his platoon had never been in doubt; he grieved for them deeply but his grief was underscored by a feeling of guilt. Kinloch had been new

171

to the job. A greater burden had been thrown upon Tahir and Choo. Under such circumstances how could either of them have been certain that they were doing the right thing, whatever precautions they took? Had he still been with the platoon perhaps he and Tahir together would have been able to avoid what had happened. But who could say? Ferdach remembered that fearful first day when they had all stumbled about in the *belukar*. They had certainly been sitting or rather walking ducks the whole day long. They were just lucky not to have encountered the CTs then and been completely wiped out.

There was no casualty list in Waite's office and, knowing the administrative complexity of police headquarters, Ferdach was not inclined to ask for it there. Fortunately Chief Clerk Mr Suppiah who had been fulsome in telling anyone who cared to listen that he never let a day go by without praying for Ferdach's safety, knew that Choo's wounds were slight and that he was resting at home. Ferdach went there straightaway to find Gordon being pampered by a tearful Agnes Chan who stared sourly at this visitor from the District Office which she seem to regard as the source of her boyfriend's woes.

'Go and order tea for Ferdie,' said Gordon in a peremptory manner. 'And some biscuits.' As Agnes made off pouting a little, he added, 'And I'd like some ice cream. Ice cream for both of us.' Both obviously did not comprise Agnes.

Ferdie took a chair and looked down at Choo who was lying on the bed naked save for a pair of bright red shorts bespeckled with Micky Mouses. He might have thought that before him was a large smooth-skinned chubby baby had not Choo's left upper arm been swathed in bandages on which a red patch indicated that a wound had not entirely closed. As soon as their eyes met Choo's commanding air dissipated and tears seemed to be in the offing. Ferdach thought, this isn't a good sign at all. Choo knows all about my feelings for Mat Noor. He doesn't want to tell me the bad news.

In reality Choo was savouring Ferdach's anxiety. Almost since the day they first met he had enjoyed tantalising his young boss, sometimes tricking him a bit, sometimes telling him tall stories about Chinese customs, but always worshipping him. He had a great desire to know how Ferdach's mind worked and the little puzzles he put up were artificial markers intended to help him in that pursuit. He had half intended to beat about the bush regarding the casualty list so as to string Ferdach out as he recounted the names of those killed or wounded one by one. But that would be disrespectful to the dead and bring him bad luck.

'Mat Noor,' he began nervously, before falling silent for so long that Ferdach thought his own heartbeat must be audible throughout the house. 'Mat Noor,' Choo repeated, 'is alive. He's slightly wounded.' His face took on a broad smile as he stared intently at his victim.

Ferdach made no effort to conceal his feelings. He let out a deep sigh of relief and then asked, 'Slightly wounded. What does that mean?'

Choo looked down at his navel. Agnes came in with the tea. Choo then waved her off with, 'We're discussing office matters,' before whispering, 'Can't tell you in front of a woman.'

With Agnes gone, Choo gazed at Ferdach with a most sympathetic expression. 'Ferdie my friend. I'm sorry to tell you that Noor has lost his testicles.' But the last word was no sooner out of his mouth than Choo was convulsed with mirth. He would have gone on rolling about the bed had not sudden pain in his arm which had struck the mattress too hard stopped him.

But for that wounded shoulder Ferdach would certainly have jumped on Choo and enjoyed pummelling him. 'Is that a Chinese joke?' he asked sarcastically.

'Of course, Ferdie. But not a Chinese joke, just a joke. I made you suffer a bit more just to enjoy your happiness when you learned the truth. It's so good to see your face bright as the sun now.' He seized both of Ferdach's hands and whispered, 'After all what good would Noor be without his balls?'

This over familiarity irritated Ferdach. What's more it did not seem very Chinese. 'That's too much Choo. What are you dreaming up about me? You've gone too far.'

Choo looked puzzled. 'But we're friends, Ferdie. Comrades. We'd die for each other wouldn't we? Surely we can say anything we want to each other – especially if it's true. There's no harm in your feelings for Noor. He's very lucky. And so are you.'

Ferdach fell silent. It struck him that in Malaya everyone he had met apparently knew everything about everybody else without passing judgement on them. Or at least, so it seemed among his Asian friends; the English, he suspected, were more censorious. Then he felt guilty. They had only been talking about himself and Noor. It was time for Choo to tell him exactly who had died and who was hurt and how badly. In doing so Choo was serious and sorrowful, particularly about Tahir who had tried to save Kinloch's life and for whom he had a very high regard. Neither Ferdach nor Choo talked about funerals or the men's families. Instead their talk dwelt gaily on the days when they had all roved around the countryside together as a team, and especially of the days when working had been, if not an unmitigated pleasure, always full of the profound joy that springs from comradeship heightened by danger. Agnes put in another appearance, drawn no doubt by their laughter, only to be dismissed. Such treatment embarrassed Ferdach but he could say nothing especially as he and Choo were intent on making their dead friends live again in their common memory. It was a way of mourning.

From Choo's house, Ferdach went at once to the hospital where his wounded men were being treated. There were four of them in adjacent beds, each suffering from wounds to their arms or legs or, in the case of Abdul Ghani, his right buttock, which made him laugh uproariously when he explained where he had taken his bullet. They were in good spirits and keen to tell Ferdach that their wounds were not serious. Within a day or so they expected to be discharged and before long they hoped to be back on duty. All that is except for Mat Noor who had stayed quiet until he said that his foot had been hurt badly. It was the worst wound suffered by any of the four men. Choo had been ignorant of its severity. Ferdach realised at once that Noor's police days were over. The flesh wound in his thigh was nothing in comparison but it seemed to be worrying Mat Noor more than his foot. 'There'll be an ugly mark on my thigh,' he said gazing miserably up at Ferdach.

'It will go after a while. You'll see.'

'I'll be leaving the police Tuan Ferdach. My foot will be useless.'

'We'll see about that, Noor. You don't know for sure.'

'Yes I do.' Suddenly Mat Noor seemed to be convulsed with grief. He did not cry out or weep. He just trembled violently and turned away from Ferdach who heard him say. 'Tuan, please go. You'll not want to see me again.'

Ferdach moved towards Mat Noor but as he did so he saw the other men shake their heads in warning at him. Again he heard Mat Noor speaking. 'You won't see me again.'

Ferdach stood motionless for a while. But when he turned to leave, he said firmly, 'You're wrong Noor. I promise you that you're wrong.'

27

The pressure of Emergency work under Waite, who was a hard taskmaster, had prevented Ferdach from really getting to know other members of the Malayan Civil Service in Ipoh – Tuan Haji Mustapha Albakri was a distinguished exception to this. Nor had he got to know members of the local European commercial, mining or rubber estate fraternities except by hearsay. He had, in the course of duty, developed transitory working relationships with various police and military officers but those men he inevitably judged on the basis of the efficiency of their co-operation and their usefulness to him. Whereas his association with Kuok Lai Kuan had resulted in invitations to Chinese banquets, some dubiously intimate, some huge and noisy, but all with superb food, he was not at all sure whether Lai Kuan wanted to be his friend or just to use him. By now, Ferdach had become just another familiar European face about town and his failure to mix had resulted in him being labelled a peculiar loner, a reputation enhanced by the fact that he did not play golf, rarely went to the swimming club, and was never seen at the big social events in the Ipoh Club. He certainly never attended the Turf Club meetings despite their proximity to Waite's house. Only because his affair with Laura had become widely known, thanks to the underground channels of communication provided by everybody's servants, was he not labelled a queer. Had he lived with Waite alone, that too might have been considered a pointer, but Ericson's womanizing was enough to dispel any idea that the Sturrock Road house, to which he had now returned, was a den of unnatural vice. Ferdach's closest relationships, apart from that with Laura, had from the beginning been with Gordon Choo and the Malay Specials. Laura maintained that such limited contacts were not teaching him much about Malaya but he was sure that he must be picking up more about the country and the people from his workmates than he would by socialising with even the most liberal expatriates in their homes or their clubs.

One Englishman who was interested in him, though from afar, was the Secretary for Chinese Affairs, Mr Noel Aspinall, who was considered to be something of an eccentric by most Europeans. For one thing he was a bachelor, always a suspicious status in British Asian colonial society. Since the Indian Mutiny, a monstrous regiment of wives had stood, like Hadrian's wall, between their husbands and the wicked, tempting, sensual brown-skinned barbarians. For another, he was an excellent Chinese speaker as befitted his job. This made him suspect among the British who maintained that they loved, and more important, were loved by the Malays whose interests they were doing their best to protect. And thirdly, Noel Aspinall was an intellectual who had achieved a slight degree of fame on account of several books of long poems addressed to him in the somewhat antique form of heroic couplets by a friend of his youth, Mark Shiner. To write poems was bad enough, to be addressed admiringly in them by a poet looked exceedingly odd.

Ferdach had encountered Aspinall at a number of Chinese celebratory dinners. With his portly body clad in a scholar's cheongsam and his bald pink head glistening with sweat, Aspinall would deliver a speech in Cantonese enriched with clever couplets from the Chinese classics which everyone applauded but few could understand. Ferdach and Aspinall often acknowledged one another's presence with a nod and would liked to have talked but not once were they seated together, and following each dinner Ferdach would be invited elsewhere by a drunken crowd of Kuok Lai Kuan's friends and Noel Aspinall by a few of the older rich *towkay*s who ruled the Chinese business world. But a week before he actively started his new job of combating the CTs' identity card stealing propensities, Ferdach received a letter by hand from the office of the Secretary for Chinese Affairs which read:

Dear Mr O'Haney,

Interested to hear of your new job from one of my Chinese Affairs officers. I would be glad to meet up with you to discuss how my staff can be of help. What about my office at 10.30 tomorrow. Phone to confirm.

Yours ever,

Noel Aspinall

Ferdach could not see what Aspinall's staff, which numbered but a few, admittedly extremely talented, Chinese Affairs officers, could do to help apart from giving advice but he decided to accept the invitation.

Aspinall's office was in the same compound as the State Secretariat and like it was set amidst neat lawns, which strayed amidst colourful stands of bougainvillea, hibiscus and frangipani. The warm air was fragrant with the scent of flowers, and the Malay peons dressed in the Secretariat's rich black-and-gold uniform lolling gracefully at the doorways or staring listlessly out from the windows only added to the somnolent atmosphere. At the main entrance of the Secretariat stood two highly polished Rolls Royces, one yellow and slightly antique, the other black with a Union Jack on the bonnet. Clearly there was some important meeting in the Secretariat necessitating the presence of both the Sultan of Perak and the British Adviser – or was Albakri just entertaining the two dignitaries to lunch before attending them at the races? Ferdach made no effort to find out but walked from his car, which he parked at a discrete distance from the other vehicles, towards Aspinall's office.

'I was sorry to hear about your friend,' said Noel, blinking at Ferdach interrogatively through a pair of wire-ringed spectacles. 'Do you smoke?' He pushed forward a round air-tight tin of State Express cigarettes across his unencumbered desk.

'Thank you. No. Who do you mean by "my friend"?'

'Why, your Mat Noor.' Noel's expression was now benign and half-smiling.

Ferdach felt his face flushing, not with embarrassment but anger. Were his hidden feelings so widely bruited abroad in this place?

'Several of my men were killed,' he said heavily. 'And several wounded. Mat Noor was one of the latter. Fortunately for him only in the leg.'

'Yes. His thigh and his foot. He won't be able to stay in the police, you know.'

'Mr Aspinall. I don't get it. What's this to do with my new job. What's Mat Noor to me? Or to you? Or is everything about my life in Ipoh common knowledge?'

'What's Hecuba to him or he to Hecuba, that he should weep for her?'

'Mr Aspinall, I'm weeping for no one. Mat Noor is alive.'

'Exactly so Ferdie. May I call you that? I wonder if you'd like to join me this weekend on a trip to Pangkor Island. You've been all work and no play for too long. By the way, this is Tuan Haji Albakri's suggestion – though I fully agree with it. And by the way, your friendship with Mat Noor isn't common knowledge. One of my Chinese Affairs officers, Choo Ban Yit is the elder brother of your Gordon Choo. That's how I know so much.'

Ferdach limited himself to asking, rather coldly, 'And my new job. Your help?'

'Oh I know nothing about that sort of thing. I'm an ideas man not a practical geyser. But you're very clever – so I'm told; you'll find a way of dealing with the problem. Then, when everything's running like clockwork you'll have enough free time to enjoy yourself. Now I hope you realise that you'll have to travel all over Perak. That will be tiring. You'll need a driver. Have you thought about Mat Noor? Now that he's out of a job?'

Ferdach gazed at Aspinall as if hoping to get a clue to the man's inconsequential questioning from his appearance which, however, told him nothing. Noel just stayed a pink, round-faced Buddha with strands of gingery hair. Perhaps he was plain stupid, tactless as an undeveloped schoolboy, but more likely he had some hidden agenda. It was as if he was playing that children's game, magnetic fishing, in which each player's line can bring up an unfamiliar marine object from inside an aquatically painted cardboard box. Ferdach did not know precisely what the prey was, except that it involved male friendships, but he decided to play the game himself. 'D'you know Kuok Lai Kuan well?' he asked. 'Or his friend – handsome Harry Wong?'

Noel glanced quickly at the office doorway and then back at Ferdach. 'I met Lai Kuan at Cambridge; Wong Chooi Fong, I think in London. I think it best, by the way, for us both to say "knew" Chooi Fong since he's now in the jungle though God knows why. Neither of them were my contemporaries of course; both were much younger. It was before the war. But we had academic and other friends in common. Why are you interested in him?'

'This Wong Chooi Fong, why did you say "God knows why"? Isn't he a communist?'

'What Harry Wong is, only heaven knows. He's rich, he's clever, he could have any career he wanted but he's unbalanced, too swayed by his emotions. Very un-Chinese. Not at all like Lai Kuan, who's the soul of good sense. About two years ago there was a scandal when Harry started an affair with the wife of a senior police officer in KL, threats of violence between them, public quarrels, once even a fight in the Selangor Club. And it was all a waste of time because as soon as it was clear that the woman wanted to stay with Harry, he gave her up, left her stranded. I don't know why but I do know he's the last person I can imagine being a loyal communist.' Although Noel enjoyed retailing gossip his curiosity about Ferdach was sufficient for him to halt his flow and ask for a second time, 'Why are you so interested in him?'

'I'm just curious about people. Probing, Noel, like you. Who knows what both of us may find out? OK then, I'll go to Pangkor with you. This weekend? Yes, a change will do me a lot of good.'

28

The route to Pangkor led Ferdach west from Ipoh across the Sungei Perak by ferry, on to the small town of Bruas, then south through the monotonously flat swampland known as the Dindings. At last, near the coast the party approached a rocky outcrop: Bukit Ungku Busu, a small mountain overlooking the settlement of Lumut. There Ferdach and Noel, accompanied by another officer, Richard Barnett, the State Commissioner for Labour, stopped for the night in the government rest house.

Their journey had been nerve racking, for Noel had driven them erratically all the way in his antique Citroen, delivering, as they sped along, monologues on a variety of subjects: the poems of his friend Mark Shiner, life in Macau where he had studied Chinese, and the private lives of the rich Chinese of Perak. The last subject was clearly dear to him and neither Ferdach nor Barnett could say that it did not interest them but as Noel had the habit of constantly turning his head to address either Barnett sitting next to him, or Ferdach in the back seat, their attention would dissipate as they approached another vehicle, passed a bullock cart or, most dangerous of all, went by a crowd of Malay schoolchildren. Pouring with sweat caused by this ordeal rather than the heat, it was well into the evening when they arrived. Ferdach and Barnett retreated at once to their rooms to shower. Noel, unwashed and somewhat malodorous, took a seat on the rest house verandah where he drank gin until the other two joined him for dinner.

'Well, how are you going to deal with this identity card problem,' Noel asked airily, turning towards Ferdach as though examining him for a job. 'Have you given any thought to it?'

'I've worked out a system which I won't bother you with now because you told me you're really an ideas man not interested in practical solutions,' said Ferdach.

'True. But we have to start a conversation somewhere. And you're both obviously tired of listening to me speak about Shiner and the like. Neither of you said much in the car.'

'We were frightened out of our wits by your driving ... as usual,' Barnett replied. 'As well you know it. Do you terrify us like that for some reason, Noel?'

'Ferdie. You should have brought your wounded boy Mat Noor down here. He probably needs a good rest,' said Noel, once again showing his propensity for changing the subject abruptly. This really annoyed Ferdach for he had only just met Barnett and had no idea what sort of a man he was: liberal minded or an old colonial buffer who would be outraged at the kind of friendship Noel's use of 'your' hinted at.

'It must be quite a problem for a *kampung* boy who has been wounded on active service to settle down at home – especially if he's not capable of working any more,' Barnett said in a sympathetic sort of way. 'Has he any sort of education? Perhaps he could be found a clerical job somewhere. Do you know anything about his background? Maybe we could help in the Labour Department. I have many contacts, you know.'

Ferdach was relieved by Barnett's easy acceptance – of anything it seemed. But why on earth should these two experienced colonial hands be so interested in a wounded special constable or his own relationship with him. There was no sense to it – unless they were just a couple of old women who made everyone's business their own. He was prepared to believe that Barnett was just a very kind man, maybe quite innocent of the undercurrents stirred up by Noel who now seemed to have forgotten what he had just been talking about and had blithely drifted on to some topic concerning the Emergency. That did not last long however and soon he was back to conversation about his own interests or the foibles of the people he knew both at the present time or before the war – what he did during the war was never mentioned. He was a master of trivia. Maybe, therefore, an imagined liaison between a fellow officer and a Malay youth was just another item to be added to his store of gossip. And yet Ferdach could not help suspecting that there was more to it than that. The memory of that slight embarrassment when he had mentioned Kuok Lai Kuan and Harry Wong lingered at the back of his mind.

Then, all at once, Ferdach thought of something about Mat Noor that he had never inquired into. He remembered Gordon Choo telling him that Noor's father was a *pawang*. He should have asked what that was. But when traipsing around in the *belukar* seeking out Chinese squatter families, so much new information, so many new words, had kept on coming his way that it was not possible to follow up on everything, particularly on matters not directly related to work.

'Noor's father is a *pawang*,' Ferdach said, addressing Barnett who seemed to be better informed than Noel about the Malays and whose language he spoke to perfection. 'And I believe that on his father's side he's part Thai. That's all I know about his background.'

'A *pawang*,' said Barnett. 'Most interesting. If you could get to know his family you'd learn a lot about Malaya.'

'Yes, but what is a *pawang*?' demanded Ferdach. 'You haven't told me.'

Noel widened his eyes and in a lugubrious voice said, 'A *pawang*, Ferdie, is a sorcerer. So you'd best beware.'

'And some of the most powerful *pawang*s are partly Thai,' Barnett added.

All of this made quite an impression on Ferdach. It added a rather fascinating dimension to Mat Noor, a dimension not related to Noel's concern with him. But he pretended to be uninterested in the matter and, like Noel, decided to change the subject abruptly. 'When are we going to Pangkor?' he asked, and on being told early the next morning bade goodnight as he had had enough of Noel for one day.

29

The voyage from Lumut to Pangkor Island was exhilarating and not without risk. The rows of benches athwart the wooden boat were overcrowded with men, women and children, both Malay and Chinese, together with a few Tamils and, of course, Ferdach and his two companions. Everyone had miscellaneous pieces of baggage and a few had baskets in which hens and geese kept up a discontented racket. Noel blamed Barnett for not arranging to use the District Officer's launch, especially when the outboard motor started up with a roar and the wash at the bow looked fair fit to spill into the boat. Richard Barnett chortled at Noel's and everyone else's alarm but quickly took control telling the ferryman to reverse and let a couple of families off to wait for another vessel. When everyone had rearranged themselves so that the bow was higher in the water, the ferryman started up the engine again and off they went. However, rounding the headland where the River Dindings enters the Dindings Channel was like entering the open sea so choppy was it. The boat pitched violently and Ferdach found himself wondering about sharks and sea snakes. However, as everyone whooped and laughed each time the boat smacked over a particularly boisterous wave, he too took to enjoying the sight of the rocky shoreline vibrant in the sunlight and the jungle-covered slopes rising to Bukit Ungku Busu, the hill of Prince Busu, whoever he might have been, not far off on the port side.

They docked on the leeward side of Pangkor at a Chinese fishing village which was separated from the waterfront by dramatically tall wooden frames on which hung nets, drying or waiting for repair. Small Chinese fishing craft were moored alongside the rickety jetties and the bustling activity, involving large baskets of fish, suggested that the village was doing well out of the sea.

Barnett, who had taken command of all practical arrangements, went off to arrange transport, leaving Ferdach to saunter up and down the plank walkways raised on stilts over the water, and to have a good look at the fishing tackle and the fishermen. Noel sat on a bench outside a coffeeshop smoking a cigar and staring up in the air as if deep in thought, which possibly he was though Ferdach doubted it. Before long, down the village street came a snorting old Morris driven by a white-bearded Haji puffing at a thick disintegrating cigar; the seat he was on was so low, or possibly the man's back was so short, that he was hardly able to peer over the steering wheel. Barnett leaned out of the window to announce that this was Pangkor's sole taxi; in fact it was the island's only vehicle.

They bumped over the track across the island between sad looking rubber trees which were still being tapped by a few graceful Tamil ladies who paused in their work to stare at the newcomers or to adjust the babies that some of them bore on their backs. Seated on the rear seat Ferdach glanced down to see, through a gap between his feet, the laterite surface over which they were speeding. Very soon they reached the rest house on the westward side of the island. Ah, what a fine place to relax in after all that resettlement work, thought Ferdach, for they saw before them a most beautiful bay bordered by a creamy strand between the foaming sea and a line of shady trees.

After being shown to their rooms by the Hainanese manager all social intercourse between them ceased. Barnett sat on the verandah and proceeded to analyse pages of statistics related to labour conditions on mines and estates that he had brought from his office. Noel put on a truly voluminous pair of lime green shorts but left the upper part of his body naked to sunbathe on the beach. When Barnett looked up for an instant from his work and shouted a single warning that pink people like Noel did not get brown but only developed freckles or moles that turned cancerous, Noel bellowed back, rather like a Biblical prophet, 'He that would save his life shall lose it.'

Ferdach went off to play. Soon his eye was taken by a couple of Malay fishermen throwing circular glistening nets out to catch the fish that swam adjacent to the steep rocky pillar on which they were standing. This action looked beautiful but it never seemed to result in much of a catch. Obviously they were fishing for themselves and not commercially

185

30

Away from the money grubbing and the fleshpots of Ipoh, Lai Kuan was a man transformed. He no longer spoke in the staccato English of the Malayan Chinese, with its inserts of Cantonese and Malay and its discourse particles '*lah*', '*meh*', '*mah*', etc, at the end of sentences. His manners were less rough, indeed not rough at all, his voice was no longer harsh and not once did he perform that long clearing of every gobbet of phlegm from his throat which is the majestic prelude to a real man's full-blown expectoration. If, for a moment, Ferdach closed his eyes, the voice was that of a mellifluously spoken Cambridge don and when he opened them, the behaviour of this muscular, hard-faced Chinese was equally academic. All this became quite apparent to him when he joined Lai Kuan and Noel and walked back with them to relax on the rest house verandah, which Barnett had vacated together with his homework.

Apart from greeting Lai Kuan and giving him a quizzical stare Ferdach kept silent, intrigued by the recollections of prewar and wartime England he was hearing. Where Noel was concerned, the reminiscences stretched back to the late Twenties, when he was at Trinity College. Lai Kuan's memories of Cambridge started just before the war and went on throughout it, but both of them seemed to know a lot of people in common. It was the sort of brittle chat which the outsider may resent or wonder at but can never enter, concerning amusing parties and balls, shows in London, and the foibles – sexual and otherwise – of eccentric dons and other more socially prominent people. The gossip flowed as freely as the Scotch and soon the tropical night was upon them, the stars glistened and the thin moon was reflected in a long line across the sobbing water. Occasionally the people they talked of seemed half familiar to Ferdach from his conversations with Nina Hamnett, for instance Dady

Rylands, Anthony Blunt, Tom Driberg and Morgan Forster, all referred to by their Christian names. Such a degree of familiarity amazed him. How could these two men have got to know such distinguished people? But there were others too. Ferdach could not make out the connections between them. Some were literary while others had, so it seemed, become civil servants. All were alleged to be brilliant or if not brilliant, terribly amusing. One person who seemed very familiar to both Noel and Lai Kuan was a certain Andy Cohen with whom both had apparently been very close and about whom they found much to reminisce. It was all remote to Ferdach, but since he remembered Nina contrasting such English intellectual life adversely with that of the Paris she had known in the Twenties, he refused to be intimidated by it.

'Ah, we're leaving our dear Ferdie out,' remarked Noel condescendingly. 'Were there any clever people at Liverpool?'

'Well let me see Noel, there must have been a few. But they were difficult to identify because we didn't keep on telling ourselves that we were all terribly brilliant.'

'There are brilliant people everywhere … even in slums and *kampung*s,' said Lai Kuan, sensing Ferdach's irritation. 'I bet Pangkor has its share.'

'No doubt about it,' said Ferdach. 'But the brilliance you've been talking about is a reflection of social status – which is why you were all so clever at Cambridge. Wealth and background are the brasso that make the dullest metal shine.'

'Miaow, get you Mavis,' Noel blurted out a little too quickly with a mincing gesture that quite belied his normally manly behaviour. This surprised Ferdach but not as much as the remark that next dropped from Lai Kuan's lips, 'Oh Ferdie, now you've really upset Madame.'

The penny dropped: the easy acquaintance with the lives of men across the lines of race and class ranging, as it were, from the royal duke to the telegraph boy, the cosy familiarity with men who had become important later in life, the partiality to certain types of theatre and literature. Why hadn't it struck him before? They must feel very certain about his sexual tastes – not only because of Mat Noor; Lai Kuan still liked to make pointed remarks about his alleged partiality for Harry Wong. As the conversation went on Ferdach drifted in and out of it but preferred to task his brain with the question: what is this all about? They couldn't imagine that he could be seduced. In any case he had never felt that Lai Kuan, though maybe capable of anything if it profited him, was anything other than a keen womaniser. Then why were they all here? What was it they wanted?

In the evening, when Barnett announced that work unexpectedly obliged him to return to Ipoh the next day, Noel said, 'Oh it's always the same with you Richard, but never mind; we won't let you spoil our weekend. You can take my car when you get over to Lumut. Ferdie and I will come back with Lai Kuan in his ugly, big but very comfortable Studebaker. I'll enjoy that immensely.' It was clear that Lai Kuan was to stay on Pangkor as long as Noel and Ferdach.

31

Ferdach rose with the sun and went for a swim, to be joined before long by Barnett. Neither had drunk as much the previous evening as Noel and Lai Kuan, who continued talking and hitting the Scotch well into the small hours. As these two were unlikely to emerge for some time, after breakfast Ferdach accompanied Barnett in the perforated-bottomed taxi back to the fishing village where they parted. It was clear that Barnett was the sort of man who hated to be away from duty any longer than necessary. Although it was already hot and humid Ferdach decided to walk back through the rubber estate where the Tamil ladies had been up since before dawn tapping the latex. Barnett had told him a lot about life on the rubber estates, about the hard work involved and about the medical needs of the workers. It struck Ferdach that Barnett lived up to the highest traditions of the Colonial Service. He was a prewar type, a survivor of the Japanese horrors of Changi Prison and his life had been spent mainly in the Labour Department where he had worked assiduously, inspecting labour lines to ensure that they were up to standard and to see that employers complied with the legislation passed by government in regard to wages, hours and health. The truth was, Barnett said, that those conditions were more likely to be adhered to faithfully by the big European companies than by Chinese or Indian employers who were often under-capitalised and naturally wanted to maximise their small profit margins. Barnett had also worked enthusiastically with the trade union advisers whom the British Labour government had posted to Malaya. He was particularly keen on the workers learning to bargain collectively with the employers rather than being manipulated for political ends by the communists. Direct action motivated by revolutionary ideals rarely resulted in improved labour conditions.

During breakfast, Ferdach asked Barnett whether he had enjoyed the previous evening's dinnertime conversation which had been much the same as it had been before Barnett emerged from his statistical analyses though without so much sexual innuendo. Barnett had merely shrugged his shoulders and said, 'Dear old Noel, he's one of those oddities the Service has always managed to pick up. But he's a kind man. He humanises the Service. And the Chinese love him for his weaknesses. As for Lai Kuan. Well now, there's a deep one for you.' And having, with a slight frown, spoken thus, Barnett resumed his discourse on his experiences as a magistrate in the Labour Courts. Ferdach never questioned him on the nature of Noel's weaknesses or of Lai Kuan's mysterious depths.

He was glad he had resisted the temptation to go back to Ipoh with Barnett as a sort of rebuff to his two mental suitors, if one could so describe them. It would have been childish and Ferdach was intrigued to find out exactly what they were up to. When he got back to the bay he came across Lai Kuan and Noel, who greeted him impatiently with, 'Look. The boat's here. We've been ready for half an hour, you know.'

'Ready for what?'

'For our trip to Pulau Pangkor Laut – for our picnic. What's got into you?' Noel was quite red – with anger or sunburn it was difficult to say.

From behind him Lai Kuan winked at Ferdach suggesting that Noel's perception of reality did not always concur with fact, so Ferdach smiled sweetly as though indulging a badly behaved child and said, 'So sorry Noel but Barnett forgot the keys to your car and I had to race after him with them.'

'Well I left them out in the middle of the dining table for him. He's getting too absent minded by far,' said a slightly mollified Noel. 'They do have some oddities in the Labour Department. Not surprising considering many of them have to learn Tamil. Enough to drive anyone mad. Come on then. Get aboard.'

Lai Kuan grasped the tiller of the small boat, Ferdach sat in the bow, and Noel took his position amidships soon to be joined by a lithesome Malay boatman called Samad who, having cast off the little boat, jumped in to raise its dark brown sail. The journey to the island across the bay was slow, the sail was often limp, and Samad tacked this way and that so much that sometimes it looked as though they were going back to the rest house. The gentle sea swell, the strangely still atmosphere and the heat made Ferdach so drowsy that by the time they reached the palm fringed shore of the almost uninhabited little island he was lain back fast asleep. But once they had struck camp and Samad had made a fire to prepare a meal, Ferdach had every reason to keep awake. A most intense political discussion had begun.

To Ferdach's surprise it did not concern the situation in Malaya but encompassed world politics concentrating largely on what position the West should adopt in regard to Communist China. Lai Kuan, it seemed, believed that the swiftest way in which China could become a great power was through an accommodation with the West at the expense of detaching itself from the Soviet Union. Noel was adamant that this was an impossibility, that Marxist doctrine required that the two huge land powers should march in step, thus manifesting their total solidarity. What was unusual in the discussion was not its content but the heat which both Lai Kuan and Noel brought to it. Ferdach knew that had he said something like 'Oh stuff it. What the hell does it matter? We can't influence things from this little island,' his intervention would have been unwelcome. There was an intensity about both men's attitude which suggested that they themselves were in some way deeply committed to an important ideological position. Obscurely Ferdach suspected that there was a history to all this, going back in time and well away from Malaya. Maybe it had run parallel to the social butterfly life of Cambridge. Had they, when there, participated in similar discussions in some milieu in which political ideology really mattered?

Then Ferdach remembered his own brief foray into Communist Party life in Liverpool before he had joined the RAF. Those serious occasions in the Boiler Makers Union building where he had been obliged to attend a series of meetings on the 'Dialectics of the Nineteenth Century French Novel' and 'Class Struggle during the Weimar Republic' as well as one particularly long and dreary seminar on the significance of the Marxist *Die heilige Familie oder Kritik der kritischen Kritik*, a title which had at least provided him thereafter with material for considerable ribaldry. This conversation was every bit as ponderous as the discussions at those meetings. Absolute truth was the issue. A correct line had to be established and deviation was unacceptable. When no line had already been laid down for everyone to accept whether they liked it or not, the discussion was always more vitriolic for what was at issue with the sort of people who had become Party members was power, the capacity of one group to achieve domination. Under such circumstances the mild could become fearsome, the vague mutate into rapiers of precision, and the bumbling Noels of the world fierce tigers. The debate was furious because Noel's objective was clearly the subjection of Lai Kuan to his point of view.

Indifferent to the argument Samad cooked some fish and set before them a passable meal of curried chicken and vegetables, some rice and a delicious peanut sauce all of which he had brought along with him in a tiffin carrier. Bottles of Tiger beer which had been kept cool trailing in the water were opened and a tray of fruit completed the spread. Lai Kuan and Noel fell to with a will, their appetites no doubt stimulated by their crossfire. Samad wandered off along the strand to a small headland to do a bit of line fishing from a massive red rock around which the water sobbed and heaved deeply. Ferdach didn't feel very hungry, in fact he had a slight feeling of nausea which he was sure arose not from any physical illness but from a certain nervousness, a feeling of unease that he was on the verge of some development that he would not enjoy. Nevertheless he felt that it was at least incumbent upon him now to make some sort of a contribution to the argument that had just ranged, and so he said mildly, 'Well, your disagreement seems at bit academic to me, at least in the sense that whatever I think about it, I can have no possible influence on the outcome. But it does seem to me that whichever way the penny drops there'd be implications here where the Emergency is concerned.'

No one responded but Ferdach felt sure that he was expected to go on. But to go on why? He took the plunge: if something was expected of him, best to give it to them good and proper. 'If I had to give an opinion I'd say I support Lai Kuan. Two huge adjacent land powers like the Soviets and China, are bound to clash in the end. Both of them occupy territory the other once ruled. The Soviets will only support the Chinese Communists as long as they can control them. On both sides the basic fears remain – rivalry is unavoidable. Clearly neither of them is creating a really socialist society. If they were, they would be able to work together – as Noel imagines. But they are just creating a Slav empire and a Chinese empire. So the right road for China is to dispense with Soviet aid and control as soon as possible. Then it can go on to modernise far more quickly with the help of the West. After all what has the West to fear from China? Between China and Europe lies half a continent, and between China and America the Pacific Basin. In the end it's geopolitics that count.' In full spate now and to Lai Kuan's evident satisfaction Ferdach concluded by stating, 'So in fact this Malayan Emergency is a total waste of time. Both from the point of view of China and from the point of view of the West, the West being in this case Britain.'

'Oh marvellous,' sneered Noel 'Well, let's not be unduly influenced by mere facts. People in Malaya don't see themselves as pawns in a great power game. You assume, for instance, that the Chinese communists in Malaya are no more than the pawns of Beijing. Well they're not – any more than the Federal Government here is the pawn of the Americans. In politics it's very often the tail that wags the dog you know, Ferdie. Or maybe you're too young to have learned that yet.'

Although Ferdach recognised the truth of what Noel was saying, being sneered at angered him. He also thought that Noel was insensitive; hadn't the silly queen seen that his own support for Lai Kuan was no more than a *jeu d'esprit*. He could just as easily have argued the opposite way. And that being the case, why not annoy the old ass a bit more? 'Oh no my dear Noel. It's you who fail to see that there's more to Lai Kuan's viewpoint than stinking politics. He's right in a deeply moral sense too. Right thinking people should do everything in their power to bring an end to this ghastly Emergency and all the suffering it's causing. Make peace and Malaya will quickly become independent.'

'Exactly,' cried Lai Kuan.

'Bollocks,' shouted Noel whose face had become scarlet. 'What sort of an independence do you want Ferdach O'Bloody Irish Haney. Any one that will bring discredit to the British oppressors I suppose.'

A dour silence descended on everyone around the dying campfire. The argument had become unpleasantly personal with the foolish impugning of Ferdach's loyalty. The fact that Noel soon mumbled an apology and that Ferdach said it didn't matter failed to restore a friendly atmosphere. Ferdach decided to go for a swim in the nude partly to tantalise Madame Noel and partly to declare that he was who he was and didn't care a damn about anyone else's opinion. Before long he was joined by Samad who kept his sarong on but enjoyed the two of them sporting together in the water. This meant that Lai Kuan and Noel had to wait on the shore sitting glumly on the sand talking *sotto voce* to one another until the two mermen agreed that it was time to leave. The voyage back to the rest house was mercifully much quicker than the journey out. Great black clouds were mushrooming to the west over the Strait of Malacca obscuring the setting sun save for a faint red glow that seeped like blood oozing slowly from a deep wound through a peculiarly shattered bit of cumulus just above the horizon. The wind blew this way and that for a little while until, quite suddenly, it bore the rain down in a squawl that grew successively more violent scudding the little boat like a fragile leaf across the bay.

The three of them rested in their rooms whilst the wild storm raged all about; the endless grind of heavy rain on the corrugated iron roof of the rest house and the surge of water down its pipes and drains would alone have made conversation impossible. But within the hour the violence had passed, the air was cool, the vegetation refreshed and fragrant. Above, the black velvet dome of the tropical sky pierced with silver stars had reappeared only lightly veiled here and there by skimpy clouds let free by the cumbersome black giants that had now vanished. Human beings felt that some heavy weight had been lifted off their brains. Ferdach felt sure that when the elements raged so wildly electronic discharges distorted people's minds; no wonder Lear was at his maddest during a storm. But now he felt entirely at ease again; it was time to make up to his two companions, but especially to poor old Noel.

Dinner passed lightly. Noel was in excellent form discussing now the foibles of his own junior officers, pecking order struggles in Kuala Lumpur which he affected to despise, and finally some gossip about the Sultan's Court in Kuala Kangsar. Lai Kuan kept Noel's glass topped up consistently and laughed when it was appropriate for everyone to laugh, but Ferdach sensed that beneath Lai Kuan's affability was a mind set on something serious. And so it was not at all surprising that towards midnight, instead of turning in, Lai Kuan said he was going to play mahjong with some of his clansmen in the Chinese fishing village where they could join him at midday tomorrow for the return journey to Ipoh.

32

'I suppose,' said Noel, over breakfast, 'You've been wondering what this has all been about.'

'Tell me,' replied Ferdach indifferently.

'You don't seem very interested.'

'Well just now, looking beyond you at that marvellous bay and the sparkling waves and the fishermen going about their work, whatever you might be about to tell me seems quite unimportant. It seems to me that in government and politics we rabbit on about this and that and down below, the real business of life goes on – with fishermen and farmers and the like.'

'A philosophic notion without much basis in fact. Unfortunately people like us do affect those down below quite a lot.'

'Allow me my philosophic delusions, Noel. You have a lot of them yourself. All the same, let's hear it. You clearly have something to tell me.'

'I do indeed. I suspect that you're about to be drawn into an area you may not like.'

'Ah, I'm sure it concerns our absent friend Lai Kuan. Do you really think he went off to play mahjong?'

'Oh I'm sure of it. Chinese play mahjong all night long if they feel like it. But they don't play alone. It's who they play with that often matters.'

'And so you think he's probably been meeting up with local members of the Min Yuen – or even with terrorists.'

'I didn't realise you had the slightest inkling about it,' Noel said sharply, scrying Ferdach intently as though seeing him in a new light.

'I haven't. I know nothing at all of his activities. But I've had my suspicions. As a matter of fact Noel, since coming to Malaya, I've learned to suspect a lot of people – including you. That conversation yesterday on the beach. It reminded me of one of those tedious Leninist papers on Inner Party Struggle. I know the jargon, Noel. I've been there myself but only briefly. The party thought I was too superficial, too much the dilettante, to be a reliable member. So they chucked me out. But don't think I was disappointed. I knew their weaknesses too. I deliberately courted expulsion.'

'So they thought you a dilettante, did they? Perhaps they were right and saw through you – despite your own deception. But many far from superficial young men were attracted to the left when I was young.'

'Like you and Lai Kuan, and the man we mustn't mention, 'ansome 'arry. Interesting isn't it that some of the "comrades" you mentioned have now become quite important in the world. Now dear oh dear, what am I to make of that?'

Noel remained silent and got on with his toast and marmalade. Ferdach went over to the balustrade of the verandah where he returned the friendly wave of Samad who was about to push out his boat. He was tempted to join him but didn't. He believed now that everything Noel did was pure theatre: the alternating pomposity and prissiness, the concern with upper-class gossip, the attempt sometimes to give the impression of a man on the threshold of senility, not to mention the more public demonstrations of unconventionality like the mauling in the street of Chinese miners' unresponsive bottoms after he had just given a brilliant speech in Chinese replete with quotations from the Great Learning at some boozy dinner party in Ipoh. It was a terrific act and now, Ferdach felt sure, he was going to be given a glimpse of the reality that lay beneath. He heard Noel push back his chair and pad over to him bare footed. Then there was a deep sigh.

'How exciting it was then,' Noel half whispered. 'So exciting Ferdie. We believed it all so sincerely. It wasn't so much Marx as Blake; to build Jerusalem in England's green and pleasant–'

'Then why the blazes did you come to Malaya? Why join the Colonial Service of all things?'

'I suppose that I shouldn't tell you this. But I will since soon you're going to be involved.'

'For Christ's sake Noel, involved in what?'

Of course there could be no direct reply. But Noel did explain that after his left wing enthusiasms had cooled he had decided to 'change sides'. He did not specify what this had involved but proceeded to tell Ferdach that even in the distant 1920s certain people in government were well aware of communist plans in the Far East and, indeed, elsewhere. Even then, these experts – Noel mentioned no names – foresaw that the independence of the colonial territories was inevitable and had determined that when it came, the nationalist leaders who surfaced should be men who had been recruited and trained to that end by clever British agents, of whom, Ferdach suspected, Noel must be one.

'Our long-term objective is the establishment of independent states that look to Britain and not to the Comintern,' Noel affirmed, before adding *sotto voce*, as though the world was listening, 'Now in regard to Lai Kuan, I don't know whether he is still one of them or favours us. You see their Intelligence is every bit as far sighted as ours.'

'I see, Noel. And if he is "one of them" you think he may be trying to recruit me – for some reason I can't fathom.'

'We'll have to wait and see Ferdie. Or as our dear friend Jimmy Waite would put it, we mustn't "do anything", our posture must be that of "not doing anything".'

It was only gradually that Ferdach was to learn that one of the greatest problems in the world of Intelligence was not whether a person was serving 'them' or 'us' but whether 'them' and 'us' within themselves were speaking with a single voice or were utterly fissured, and sometimes even whether 'them' and 'us' meant anything at all. Further that where individual members of Intelligence networks were concerned, their minds had been so laundered and relaundered and then stained with the myriad possibilities open before them, they could, as often as not, end up unsure which side they were loyal to or, still less, believed in. What he was experiencing with Noel was his first eye opener into this complex world which at one and the same time fascinated yet appalled him. It was now clear to him that at some stage in their lives Lai Kuan and Noel had thought along the same lines and that a long standing, maybe comradely, friendship still bound them together personally even though they were now, it seemed, diverging in their allegiances.

Inevitably Ferdach had to put the obvious question to Noel, 'If you think that Lai Kuan may be targeting me, why do you have to come along with us. Ah no. Don't tell me. He thinks you are still on his side. Or no I'm wrong again. Noel, please make things clear – if your capable of it.'

'I'll make it as clear as I can which won't help you very much. Some people in the Malayan Communist Party want to do a deal with the government. They think that the present military struggle will run them into the sand. They also think that as long as the Emergency continues the British will have every excuse to stay on. As you know from the support he gave you yesterday, Lai Kuan holds this view. By the way there's no evidence that he's been involved in any terrorist activities. Others in the Central Committee think quite the opposite. Now my dear O'Haney, just as the communists are not united on the issue, so on our side there are conflicting views. You might say that the Intelligence people in Singapore take the "world view": they'd like the Emergency to end and to have a rapprochement with China. And Britain being in decline – economically, militarily, in every God damn way – they'd like an early British withdrawal from Southeast Asia, provided that whatever new governments emerge keep opportunities open for British trade and investment. Of course the Korean War will bugger up their viewpoint if it goes on too long. Still, those are their long term objectives. In consequence they were in favour of the Labour Government's recognition of Communist China. But our Federal Intelligence people in Kuala Lumpur don't want any deal with the Malayan communists. They want them eliminated. They hated the Labour government's recognition of Communist China. They're convinced that it sent the wrong message to the Malayan Chinese. And they think primarily in terms of the interests of the Malays.'

'Most interesting. In fact fascinating,' said Ferdach. 'But there's nothing you or I can do about all this.'

Noel ignored this comment and concluded with the air of a judge delivering a long delayed verdict, 'It's my considered opinion that there are sections of the Communist Party that want to open up a channel of communication with the British government – without involving Kuala Lumpur. I suspect that Lai Kuan represents this faction. But in view of the variety of conflicting interests, they may just now be finding this very difficult to do securely.' At this point Noel's voice fell to become very slow and precise as though he was resolved that Ferdach should digest his words completely. 'I also suspect my dear Ferdie that he may think you could be useful to him in this matter.'

Ferdach stared at Noel still unwilling to accept that he himself could be involved in whatever it was Noel foresaw. He now suspected, in fact he felt sure, that this weekend visit to Pangkor had been set up by Noel to probe Lai Kuan's mind as much as his own.

'And which side do you support, Noel?' he asked at last. 'The Singapore world view or Kuala Lumpur's concern for the Malays?'

Noel smiled. 'Yesterday you said that every right-thinking man must want to end the Emergency and the suffering it brings. So in that sense I support the Singapore, or you could say the Lai Kuan, viewpoint. On the other hand, I may be Secretary for Chinese Affairs in Perak but I don't want to feed the Malays to the crocodiles. So, as I have to come down on one side or the other, I'm a KL man.'

'I once knew a circus lady in Liverpool who could do the splits on a tight rope,' said Ferdach.

'And what became of her?'

'Far too nasty to talk about; I don't want to spoil your tiffin. But right now I'm off for a swim before we leave,' Ferdach said abruptly, for he wanted to get away from this man whose mind and whose business constituted a morass which he did not want to be sucked into. He had also begun to experience revulsion from the brittle male companionship into which he had fallen over the weekend. It was not the simple masculine comradeship he had so loved when on duty with his platoon. Noel Aspinall had not been good company when he needed a respite from work. He should have gone to see Laura in Singapore, or asked Wong Siu Bo to arrange a sex party for him in Penang with her most dissolute girls and some randy sailors. Pangkor had not been a proper holiday at all.

Nor was the journey back to Ipoh at all pleasant for most of the way it rained and rained with that unremitting intensity peculiar to the tropics. It was well into the afternoon before they had crossed to Lumut and got into Lai Kuan's car. Then, after leaving Sitiawan and taking the long straight road over the swampland the tense leaden sky exploded. The thunder rolled with hardly a break and great sheets of lightening swathed around them turning the flat landscape eerily grey and white like a vision of an underworld. Before long, on either side of the road, the

Dindings had become a shoreless lake. Not that it was much visible for water was streaming down the car windows. Fortunately the powerful windscreen wipers on Lai Kuan's large American car were just about able to provide a view of the road ahead but the going was slow. For a while Lai Kuan and his driver kept up a querelous argument in Cantonese the gist of which, so Noel whispered, centred on the driver's reluctance to drive on in such conditions. But Lai Kuan's imperative to get back to town won the day. At long slow length they reached Sungei Perak where, being the only vehicle, they drove straight on to the ferry. Then they sped across the river far more quickly than they had moved in the car for the ferry depended on the force of the current, the vessel itself being attached to a cross-river cable upstream by two hawsers whose length could be varied to present the vessel at the appropriate angle to the current. In fact they were fortunate to get over at all; just after their disembarkation the ferrymen decided that the river had become too dangerously swollen for further transit.

By now the rain had abated a little which led Noel to exclaim rashly, 'Ah, the worst is over,' thereby irritating the gods who, however, took a little time before inflicting their punishment. As they passed through little towns and *kampung*s they were reminded of the ever present Emergency by the number of roadblocks manned by suspicious looking policemen all sweaty because of the weight of their raincapes, and then, just a few miles south of Lahat, on a curve of the road where not a single friendly *kampung* house could be seen, there was a loud bang. The car jolted.

'Ambush!' cried Noel, throwing himself across Ferdach's lap.

But Lai Kuan yelled back at them over his shoulder, just as loudly, 'It's a bloody puncture.'

As they had slid off the road a little way onto the soft shoulder it took an age for Lai Kuan, Ferdach and the driver to edge the car back onto the road. Fortunately they had a flashlight so were able to find the car jack and set about changing the wheel. But this took an age because the jack started to sink into the badly surfaced road and they had to bolster it with stones before starting all over again. When at last they were nearly done it took to raining as heavily as before. On reaching Ipoh Noel had to be dropped off at his comfortable home before Lai Kuan could drive Ferdach on to Sturrock Road. It was half past four in the morning and the morale of both them had fallen to a low ebb. Yet instead of driving straight off Lai Kuan started to laugh. 'That lazy bugger hasn't changed since Cambridge,' he said. 'No one but him would have stayed high and dry in the car all the time we were struggling to change the wheel.'

Ferdach opened his eyes in mock surprise. 'But Lai Kuan, how could he have done anything else. He is a colonial master but you and I are mere peasants, an Irish peasant and a Chinese peasant.'

Lai Kuan quite unnecessarily jumped out of the car and seized both of Ferdach's hands. 'You know Ferdie, I only went to Pangkor because Noel said you would be there. Just be careful of that man. He's devious as a snake.' He paused and Ferdach got the impression that he was going to say more but Lai Kuan only added, 'Good luck in your new job and keep out of danger. You and I may have work to do together before very long.' And with that he was off into the darkness.

Ferdach took off his wet clothes and threw himself on his bed. Though deeply tired he was unable to sleep. In Pangkor he had not really discovered much except that he was likely, before long, to be approached by a left-wing certainly pro-communist Chinese man for purposes unknown. The thought made him increasingly restless for, despite the political analysis Noel had given to him he could not believe that Lai Kuan would want his assistance. In the meantime, within a few hours, he was starting his new job as identity card tsar. He had been provided with his own office in one of the old municipal buildings and a small staff. This would be an improvement on being a mere cog in the District Office. All he wanted to do at present was to have a couple of hour's sleep before appearing there at eight thirty as a fresh and enthusiastic new boss. After tossing about trying in vain to sleep for almost an hour he decided to spruce himself up before phoning Laura in Singapore at seven o'clock in the morning.

33

'Oh God,' drawn out with great emphasis on the deity, was Laura's usual greeting when something, albeit slight, irritated her. Her own convenience invariably surmounted all other considerations – at least initially. Ferdach was sure that even if someone had phoned in the sombre tones people use when announcing sad news – say the death of her mother, the reply would be the same before she brought herself to find out the actual cause of the phone call. So he said nothing, waiting for her anger to rise. 'God, who is this? Can't you reply? Oh God, don't you know what time it is? God it's five o'clock in the morning and I'm still half asleep.'

Since there were a few crackling sounds on the line Ferdach took the opportunity to answer in a high-pitched Indian voice, 'Long distance call from the United Kingdom for Mrs Laura Swine Shop.'

'God. Can't you bloody people get anything right?' Laura was now fully awake and shouted 'Sweinsnoep' three times.

'That is what I said, Swine Shop.'

Laura came out with a few fearful expletives. Ferdach found it difficult to restrain his mirth so he made some atmospheric noises ending up with his operator's voice again saying, 'Sorry Mrs Swine Shop. The line to London has been cut.'

Laura put down the phone after yelling 'Bugger you' in a very loud voice.

A few minutes later Ferdach phoned again. Laura snatched up the phone and shouted, 'Is that the bloody international operator again? I'm going to report you for–'

'Hello Laura dear,' said Ferdach softly. 'Are you all right? You sound upset.'

'Oh God. This telephone system is ghastly. There's a call for me from

London and they haven't put it through. Oh God, perhaps there's some bad news. Perhaps something's happened to Alfred.'

'To Alfred? He's in London?'

'You know he is. I wrote to tell you. Why didn't you come down here? I really want to see you.'

Ferdach remembered that pile of unopened letters in Sturrock Road. The work at Chemor, the ambush, so much to occupy him. He'd put all the letters on one side, even letters from his parents.

'I'm sorry Laura. I never received it. I'd have visited you straightaway had I known. In fact this last weekend I've just been wasting my time on the coast, basking in the sun. Why has Alfred gone to London?'

'Oh for some Colonial Office conference on education. I don't mind him being away but I don't want him being ill or anything. It would be just like him to kick the bucket or something in England and leave me with all the trouble of getting home on my own.'

It was not for nothing that in his childhood Ferdach had been known within his family as TM, for trouble maker. It was also a regrettable fact that he had discovered from bitter experience that forgiveness for making trouble was rarely ensured by a frank confession. So true to acquired form he soothed Laura by saying, 'If anything serious has happened the call will come through very soon. In any case Alfred – if it is Alfred – may only be asking you what you'd like him to bring from home.' Ferdach also knew that, Laura's main preoccupation being her own activities, her anger could easily be dissipated by a few questions about how she was liking Singapore, had she met any one interesting and so forth. This had the desired effect of opening up Laura's floodgates.

'Oh God, Ferdie. You should get a transfer here. Ipoh's so dull. There are so many interesting people here – poets like Beda Lim and Gung-Wu, and …' Laura rattled off other unfamiliar names. 'And there are clever people like Patrick Anderson and your dear friend Northcote Parkinson. I was talking about you with him only last night. If you and I were together here Ferdie darling, life would be perfect.' On and on she went about the fascinating personalities, and the terrific time to be had, in the greatest city in southeast Asia where, apparently, everything was happening and everything was possible.

'Well Laura, maybe I could come down soon and see it all for myself.

And how about men? Have you been playing the field?'

'You know me, Ferdie. What a pity you're not here while Alfred's away. I could give a terrific party and introduce you to everyone I know. And we could get up to all sorts of fun, just the two of us together or with some of the marvellous guys I've met in HM Forces. You could swing both ways if you wanted dear. You know I'd never mind.'

Not much you wouldn't, thought Ferdach, but all the same he promised that he would visit the Sweinsnoeps over Christmas. Alfred would be home by then but, according to Laura, this wouldn't matter in the least since he was still spending most of his spare time 'with the short-arsed Mona Wee'. Before they ended their chat Laura said, 'Ferdie darling, I've been thinking about that phone call from London. I've just realised that the operator sounded remarkably like you putting on an Indian accent.' Then after peeling with laughter she said, 'I'm putting the phone down now,' normally her signal that she was angry but now as a joke against herself, and rang off.

Despite her multifarious imperfections Laura was a warm-hearted person with a sense of humour, even if often delayed, and though she was also both self-willed and self-centred these foibles often amused rather than irritated Ferdach. His light-hearted conversation with her had, therefore, done much more to repair his spirits after the arduous night than some extra hours of sleep could have done and he left for the office in a good mood.

He had in fact already worked out what had to be done in his new job and started to lay his plans. The work did not require a great deal of intelligence but it did require meticulous organisation. The objective of the communists, when they came in the night to a Chinese village or a Malay *kampung* to force every person, male and female, to hand over their identity card was quite simple, namely: to break the connection between government and the people and thereby put the people into a sort of legal limbo, in particular making it impossible for any villager to move around freely in a land where roadblocks and police checks were everywhere. What had to be done, therefore, was to organize teams of clerical officers, drawn from District Office staff, to descend on any village or *kampung* the day after the theft had taken place, to re-register the villagers. This involved questioning them carefully but sympathetically, and providing them with temporary Local Registration Forms, complete with a finger print. The duplicates of these forms were then used to check the fingerprints on the documentation at Registration Headquarters and so enable the issuing of a new permanent identity card. The last step would take place as quickly as possible. The organisation of the syetem was done at breakneck speed necessitating staff training, the production of supplies of documents, and the provision of transport. In any *kampung* affected the *penghulu* became the officer in charge of the operation, while in any New Village affected, the function was borne by the Chinese Affairs Officer. Within a few weeks the system was up and running. Basically, Ferdach's staff had to repair every depredation of the communists quicker than it had been committed. One of the beauties of the job was that Ferdach was no longer tied to the Ipoh area but was obliged to travel over the whole of Perak to ensure that the teams were in place and equipped. But once the system was established and shown to be working well he would be able to go here, there and everywhere on rather pleasant tours of inspection. As Perak was a very large state, he decided to employ a driver.

34

About a month later Ferdach was on his way to Grik, a small town not far from the Thai border. For a while after leaving Kuala Kangsar, Mat Noor was at the wheel but before they had gone ten miles Ferdach could stand it no longer, and making the excuse that Noor's foot was not sufficiently healed to deal with the clutch, he took to driving himself. Noor was the most terrible syce he had ever come across. He had caused a cyclist to fall into a ditch, he had almost run into a bullock cart and several times he had put the lives of some schoolchildren strolling innocently along the road at risk. Noor had found the sight of the cyclist diving into the watery ditch side-splitting especially as the man yelled imprecations after them in Tamil, a language that Noor found hilarious, but the thought of knocking down some Malay kids sobered him up for everyone knew that to be involved in such an accident near to a *kampung* would lead to an eye-for-an-eye retaliation by the villagers.

The road to Grik was long and winding leading, on the western side of the upper reaches of the Sungei Perak, past the extensive Chenderoh Lake towards a sparsely inhabited mountainous area covered with thick jungle. The further north they went the fewer the people and the more widely spaced the *kampung*s. Ferdach was conscious of danger as they journeyed on for this was an area in which the communists had carried out numerous ambushes.

Mat Noor did not feel that he had lost face by being relieved of his duties. On the contrary he was pleased to be able to sit back, look at the sights and talk to Ferdach whom he seemed to regard as a new possession. Ferdach was aware of his benign expression beaming across at him almost patronisingly as he drove along. It was almost embarrasing or it might be if it was noticed by people they met. 'When your foot is

207

better, you will have to do most of the driving,' he said to emphasise the fact that Noor was his employee.

This concept was at once neutralised by Noor who said, 'Ah yes, Tuan. But more important, we are good friends now. We can talk together without other people hearing us. We can say what we are thinking.' In fact it was only since leaving Kuala Kangsar that they had had this freedom for they had given a lift that far to Gordon Choo and his girlfriend Agnes Chan who was going to visit a relative in the town.

Unfortunately Ferdach was not at all clear in his mind what he was now thinking about Mat Noor. Yes, the young man was attractive and had an appealing manner but since they were no longer slogging around in the heat censusing squatters under very dangerous circumstances, the emotional tension between them seemed to have evaporated. Ferdach's present line of thought was more to elaborate an excuse for Noor's presence: yes, he truly did need a driver in order to roam over the entire state in pursuance of his new duties and he really did need a companion who could translate adequately since his own knowledge of Malay, though developing, was still inadequate.

Travelling about Perak Ferdach had observed that the re-registration system was working well. The quick response of his staff to the identity card thefts that continued to take place proved that his procedures were efficient. All the same, whenever a really bad incident took place, he liked to dash to the scene himself to make sure that the staff for whom he was responsible felt his eyes upon them and to praise them in person when their work was speedy and efficient. Such a large-scale theft of identity cards had taken place in the Grik District just two days ago. Hence his current journey, the first that he had made with his ill-trained driver.

What Mat Noor was thinking of his new boss was a mystery. He had accepted the offer of the job without any thanks, indeed as if it was decreed, and as they drove along he preserved that expression of superior calm, sometimes subtly mutating into an enigmatic smile, which is often to be seen on the faces of Oriental deities. Ferdach had come to the conclusion that the Malays were an emotionally complex people whose sensitivities could easily be upset if they were offended. The problem was that he was not sure precisely what might offend them. That some strong bond had been established between Mat Noor and himself was not in doubt, but what was its nature? That he found Noor as serene as one of those superb pages in a Gozzoli mural or that Noor had remarked to Gordon Choo that Ferdach was *kacak sekali*, very handsome, could mean no more than what was said. It might easily be that if he were to express his friendship physically to Noor, beyond the hand holding which was not uncommon among Malay friends, he might be making an unhappy error. On the other hand, what had Noor implied in that *pantun* he had written by the hidden swimming pool? It had suggested desire. But for what? Maybe some sort of romantic affection like that of the medieval knight for his lady with the eternal sword ever between them. Therefore Ferdach felt ill at ease. This was totally different from meeting a woman or a guy in Soho, totally different from going to the Carefree, and totally different from the no-holds-barred sexuality of Laura. This was a situation in which to do something might cause offence but to do nothing might be found even more objectionable. And so, since Ferdach dared not broach the matter of what might be going on in the recesses of their two minds, he embarked on a discussion of practically anything he could think of which did not involve his own feelings.

'Have you ever been to Grik, Mat Noor?'

'Of course, Tuan Ferdie'

'Just Ferdie now, please.'

'Of course, Ferdie. I thought I told you. My *kampung* is near to Bukit Kelah in Upper Perak.'

'I guess I did hear you say so Noor. But I never asked exactly where Bukit Kelah is.'

'Well, it's east of the road to Grik. When we get to Kampung Kuala Kenering you'll see the Sungei Perak coming in from the mountains on the right of the road. To get to my place you have to walk up beside the river. There's no road. But all the same we're going there on our way back from Grik.'

'Are we Noor?' Ferdach asked, wondering whether he had a say in the matter.

'Of course. Didn't I promise you and Gordon Choo that we'd all bathe in my swimming pool?'

'You did indeed but Gordon isn't with us.'

'Oh, he'll be there. We're all meeting the day after tomorrow at

Kuala Kenering. Agnes Chan won't be with him. She's staying with her Auntie in Kuala Kangsar.'

Small though this incident was, Ferdach had the feeling, which he was often to experience in Malaya, that somehow or other he was superfluous; that the real life of the people was something going on quite independently of the Anglo-Saxon superstructure arrogantly, or absent-mindedly, thrown over the country; that whatever he took part in, was as a matter of grace on the part of those to whom the land belonged. He decided to assert some very English ingredient about the place they were visiting. 'Have you ever heard of a District Officer called Berkeley?' he asked, ready to give Noor a lesson in his own history.

Noor gave a short staccato laugh. 'The king of Upper Perak. Who hasn't heard of him? Some Malay people in Grik are descended from him too. He had a harem of girls. He even took some from an orphanage. He was a real man Ferdie. The British sent out real men in those days – so my father told me.'

Ferdach at once felt miffed. The implication that officers of his generation, himself in particular, were not real men hovered in the air. 'So tell me, what else did this real man do to make himself so admired?'

'Well Ferdie, let me see. I know he made Malaya bigger.'

'How?' asked Ferdach mystified.

'When the border was being settled between Thailand and Malaya, Tuan Berkeley and a Thai officer had to fix the boundary stones. My grandfather was working in the District Office then. When night came Berkeley told him and some labourers to move the stones further back onto the Thai side of the boundary – so you see Berkeley made Malaya bigger. Yes, he was a real man. No one bothered about his women. In fact it's said that they liked him very much.'

'So to be a real man I'd have to build up a harem and make Malaya bigger. Quite difficult to do these days Noor. If I stole a girl from an orphanage I'd land up in jail and if I pushed into Thailand we'd have the United Nations on us. What a pity. I've come here too late. Yes, District Officers were kings in those days.'

'But there were other things, Ferdie. Berekeley was a Perak man – loyal to the Sultan. He didn't care what the British officers in Kuala Lumpur thought and he didn't always do what they ordered. But the *kampung* people say he was a just man. When he held his magistrate's court it was often under a big tree in the open air. Everyone could see what was done.' Noor paused for a while and then added, 'The people loved Tuan Berkeley, Ferdie. Not every British officer is loved by the people.'

This again set Ferdach wondering. So many British officers, civilian and police, harboured the notion that they were well liked. No doubt some of them were. But how to tell? Work assessments, promotions, leave, a variety of benefits depended on the boss and if the boss was an Englishman, Malayans – like the Irish in the old days – were not so foolish as to tell him what they really thought about him to his face. In reality many expatriates were living in an illusory world. It seemed that they were in control, that important decisions were made by them and them only, that they were the ones who mattered. But in the *kampung*s, in the coffeeshops, in the mosques, in the Chinese clan associations, in the Indian labour lines, in sports clubs, at work, and above all else in the burgeoning political movements, all sorts of new ideas were stirring, things being done, and plans being laid of which the British had not got a clue. Ferdach had the feeling that his life, and the lives of his fellow British officers, was something of an aimless progress over the ice of a frozen river whose current was running strongly but invisibly below. When a crack appeared or the ice became too thin, what would happen to the whole lot of them, from the newest recruit like himself, up to the High Commissioner?

Then out of the blue Noor asked, 'Why aren't you married Ferdie? Don't you want to have children to carry on your name?'

It was Ferdach's instinct to reply to the second question first, to say that he was not particularly interested in having children since, from his own experience of being a child, there was not much to be said for the institution of childhood but he felt that this viewpoint would not be appreciated by many people in Asia who apparently regarded fecundity as the *sine qua non* of human existence. So he replied casually, 'Probably I would be married by now if it hadn't been for the war. And the woman I really like here is already married.'

'You mean Mrs Sweinsnoep, the schoolmaster's wife.'

Ferdach stopped the car on the grassy verge between the road and the edge of the jungle. All around he could hear the high insistent whirr of insects and somewhere beyond the road the rush of the Sungei Perak, eddying and swirling for it was in full spate. He stared hard at Noor and asked, 'How the hell do you know that?'

'Tuan Ferdie, everyone in Ipoh knows about it. I was told by Yusuf, Tuan Waite's driver.'

'In that case why do you ask why I'm not married.'

'Shall I drive again Tuan Ferdie?'

'Yes. I suppose so. But try not to kill anyone.'

They got out of the car, pissed into the jungle and then stood looking down at the surging river making its way into Chenderoh Lake. Noor suddenly rested his hand on Ferdach's shoulder. 'But I thought that maybe there's some other reason.'

'So why aren't you married, Mat Noor? Twenty-one years old and not married. That's old for a Malay, isn't it? But maybe there's some reason for it also.'

'Oh but I'm getting married next month,' Noor replied abruptly. 'It's all arranged. Do you understand? Arranged. A beautiful girl from my *kampung*. Very beautiful, Ferdie. I'll point her out to you when we go up there with Gordon. Come on. Let's go.'

Noor crossed the road, hardly waited for Ferdach to get in the car before starting up, and released the clutch too quickly. The car shot across the road and Ferdach feared they would go over the cliff into the valley. Then, with a rough jerk on the wheel Noor regained control and drove forward. His laughter sounded a bit crazed.

Why worry, thought Ferdach, who was now exhausted by the heat and the strain of driving, not to mention irritated by Noor's capacity to baffle him whenever they got into conversation. He said, 'I think I'll climb into the back and sleep for a while. Wake me up if we ever get to Grik in one piece.' Once settled he added, 'Anyway, I like to be free to do what I like. That's the best reason for being single.'

'*Betul lah* – very true. But I shall always do what I want Ferdie – married or not.'

35

Ferdach woke with a start. He was still sprawled uncomfortably on the back seat of his car, his mouth fetid as a parched drain, his sweaty clothes sticking to him uncomfortably, his head aching. A lean, bronzed-faced man with a sharp nose, thin lips and slitty eyes was peering in at him intently. The strongest of Australian voices greeted him with, 'Wike up, mitey. Yer look as if yer in need of a scrub dauwn.'

'Where's Mat? Where's my driver?'

'Gone to stay with rabbit's friends and relations I guess. He'll be back tomorrow.'

Half alseep and dopey, Ferdach said as he got out of the car, 'So you're the great Berkeley's successor, I suppose. You're Mr Carling.'

'The one and only. I know about you from Jimmy Waite. He said you were coming and you're staying here with me. But I'm not that old. There've been a lot of good men between Berkeley and me – though I can't vouch for the Japs.'

No sooner had Carling delivered Ferdach over to the care of his house boy who was a very reserved old Hakka Chinese, than he announced that he would be back later that night because, 'I have to go and find out what's happened to me bloody elephants.'

When Carling did return, Ferdach was asleep – following a shower and an excellent *mee goreng* – and he was not inclined to get up. However, Carling was insistent. 'The District Office has three elephants, or rather had,' he said. 'They're for transport where there are no roads. I don't think the CTs meant to harm them but the animals got in the way when your identity card theft was underway a couple of days back. One of them was killed outright. No almost outright. The police had to put her out of her misery. But as soon as the others saw her dead they went berserk and rushed off into the jungle trumpeting like mad. Well one of them has come back tonight and maybe the other one will follow. They don't like living in the jungle when they're used to being well fed by us.'

'I'm very sorry,' said Ferdach sincerely for he had great sympathy for animals and did not see why elephants should have to carry anyone, still less work pushing huge logs about for greedy timber merchants ravishing the jungle. 'Truly I'm sorry.'

'Oh I've got over it. We'll get by.'

'I don't mean sorry for you. I meant for the elephants.'

Carling gave Ferdach a peculiar sidewise stare before saying, 'Yes. Jimmy Waite told me all about you. He said you're very liberal and progressive so I guess concern for elephants fits the bill.'

'Isn't Jimmy all liberal and progressive himself? I'm glad he reported on me correctly.'

Carling's face broke into a quite charming smile, somewhat at odds with his sharp, thin-lipped features. 'Come on cobber let's get on the shicker.'

The drinking went on for a couple of hours during which Ferdach discovered that a strong camaraderie existed between Jimmy Waite, Marcus Carling and a couple of other Australian officers in the Malayan Civil Service which they had all entered by taking part in the postwar British Military Administration. In those uncertain days they had developed a deep affection for Malaya and its people and a certain contempt for the British who, they believed, had done insufficient to defend the country, or, for that matter, Australia. For the first time Ferdach heard of Waite's bravery during the retreat before the invading armies of Japan, and how he had always shown scant regard for his own safety as when he had been the last Australian out of Johore riding, under fire, across the causeway to Singapore on a motorbike with a rucksack filled with hand grenades on his back. The bond between Waite and Carling seemed to Ferdach to transcend their intellectual differences. Carling had an outback background and made no pretensions to scholarship. Nevertheless he could appreciate that Waite had some unusual inner quality that came neither from his wealthy New South Wales family, nor from Oxford. He contented himself by remarking that 'Jimmy was "something else".' The expression was not clearly defined but Ferdach felt that it was about right.

Both Waite and Carling possessed a confidence in their own judgement and a disdain for authority which Ferdach suspected was a very Australian trait. He could see that Carling suspected any interference from Kuala Lumpur, or even from the Perak Government. He was even suspicious of Ferdach's own visit. 'There's no problem in issuing the new Local Registration Forms. I don't see why you have to pay us a visit. Unless the State Secretariat has asked you to report on something or other.'

'Well if you want to know: I'm really here because I enjoy travelling around Perak. I've been stuck in the Ipoh area for months doing census work with just a few trips to Penang. Outside Ipoh I don't know what's going on. I guess I'm both sciving and learning.'

Carling relaxed and said, 'That's fine. I can't stand fact-finding missions. In any case, they're usually just scives without your honesty.'

'Sounds as if Berkeley's spirit has possessed you. I'm told that once when he knew some bigwig was coming from KL he stopped the visit with a telegram saying, 'Heavy rain. No bridge at the fifty-seventh milestone,' when there never had been a bridge there at all. You haven't done anything like that have you Marcus?'

Carling smiled but instead of answering said 'learning' rather thoughtfully before continuing, 'Then you should know that things throughout the country are moving politically much faster than it might seem. Since Dato Onn forced the British to replace the Malayan Union with the present Federal structure, the Malays have become conscious of their own power. They've got the bit between their teeth. They'll want total independence as soon as the back of the communist threat is broken. Some of the British – the planters, the estate managers, the business people – think they've got thirty years of colonial rule ahead, but I'll tell you the country will be free within this decade.'

'So fast,' said Ferdach, most surprised.

'That fast. Up here I may be away from the centre of things, but it's a good place to listen. I'm in contact with the people – especially the Malays. I speak mostly with Malays each day and they almost forget that I'm not one of them. Oh well, maybe I'm flattering myself. But at any rate I immerse myself in Malay currents.'

215

'Couldn't that be dangerous?'

'Not for me Ferdach because I don't identify myself with any one faction. Which is where you have to be on your guard. A hidden power struggle is on. Now that he's brought the Malays together Dato Onn wants to lead them forward but he'd like to bring non Malays into UMNO; he'd also like to extend citizenship to some non Malays – even before independence is achieved. Of course, he's a man of great imagination – so he'll probably be dropped in the end. Other Malay leaders, like Tengku Abdul Rahman and Khir Johari from Kedah, will never accept his ideas. They'll take his place.' Ferdach did not say that this was the first time he had heard of these names. He listened intently as Carling went on. 'Meanwhile there are Chinese around who still think that the communists could do a deal with the British. I've heard that one of them – yes, I'm talking of Kwok Lai Kuan – has become friendly with you. Be very careful Ferdach. Government officers have to keep out of politics. You might get more than your fingers burned.'

The next day Ferdach and Carling rode the remaining elephant to a remote *kampung* whose inhabitants had had their identity cards stolen. He felt curiously isolated. Mat Noor had not turned up and the entire day he heard nothing but Malay spoken swiftly and idiomatically. The District Office staff needed no instructions from him on how to proceed with their re-registration work. Nor from Carling who spoke Malay well though with an Australian accent. The number of times he used the word '*gajah*' showed that just now he was more interested in finding his lost elephant than in anything else. Ferdach felt out of place and useless. It was a relief to return to Grik where he went for a walk before going back to Carling's house. The town was small and well planned with the inevitable street of Chinese shophouses and neat government buildings widely spaced amidst expanses of open grassland. Everything looked well kept, the buildings freshly painted, the lawns trimmed, the flower beds at attention – almost as though it was an army camp. Shades of Berkeley were still apparent for the roads bore such names as Whitehall and Downing Street. This Ferdach found a little odd since Berkeley was alleged to resent control from above. But maybe the names were intended as a defiant assertion of Grik independence. When he went to the District Office – Number 10, naturally – to pick up some documents he saw a happy sight: the lost elephant had come back of her own accord and was being fed, watered and pampered by Carling and his staff. Everyone was laughing and being affectionate and the elephant stood quite still but squirted water and made modest trumpeting sounds which suggested that she was telling all her good friends how glad she was to be back from that beastly jungle.

Over dinner the conversation again turned to Jimmy Waite, this time to his differences with his superior, Mr Bertelli. 'If you want to get anywhere Ferdie, you have to be well in with the powers that be in KL,' advised Carling. 'That's Bertelli's strength and Jimmy's weakness. Jimmy will never get anywhere in government but he has the makings of a great scholar. As for you young man, I hear that your work has made an impression. If you know which strings to pull maybe you'll be able to get to Macau and learn Chinese. Isn't that what you want to do?'

Ferdach nodded and asked, 'And you?'

'Don't worry. I don't want to be up here when my wife arrives. She's not the country sort. KL for her,' replied Carling. 'I'll get there, even if I have to do what Berkeley did.'

'And what was that?'

'Well, once he sent a telegram to the Chief Secretary requesting three hundred miles of rubber tubing. When asked what it was for he said he didn't see why he should be denied the opportunity of sucking the arseholes of those on high in KL just because he was so far away. So Ferdie. Does that answer your question? Berkeley is still here. I'll act in his spirit when the time comes.'

36

Ferdach woke in alarm. Something unpleasant was moving against the sole of his foot – a snake maybe, or a centipede? He pulled his leg back sharply and sat up with a yell. A great laugh came from the end of the bed and there, inside the mosquito net, sat Mat Noor vastly amused at having woken his boss by running a hairy rambutan under his foot. The brazen intruder had switched on the bedside light; outside it was still pitch black. Ferdach pulled his sarong up over his shoulders for it was chilly.

'What the blazes? What time is it? Haven't you got a place to sleep or something?'

'It's five o'clock and time to go. We have to meet Gordon at Kuala Kenering and then the long walk up to my *kampung*. It will take all day. Have you forgotten already?' Velvety though the voice was it seemed to envelop a note of irritation, maybe of contempt, for Ferdach's allegedly lackadaisical behaviour.

Ferdach stared hard at Mat Noor who was now pushing the newly peeled rambutan between his lips. He could not remember any arrangement for their departure being made. Or had he fallen into the habit of only half listening to Noor when he gabbled on about this and that. Or had Noor told him when he was in fact asleep in the back of the car. Or, fantastic though the notion was and only entertained for a moment as a serious proposition, did Malays arrange matters between themselves in some sort of telepathic way known only to themselves and a few cognoscenti like Jimmy Waite. Well, whatever the answer he would not dispute Mat Noor's assertion.

'Do you shave every day Ferdie?'

'Why do you ask me that Noor? Yes I do.'

'I will shave you. Just lie back while you are waking up. And afterwards you can go and shit and shower. See I have brought in the shaving things. When I was a boy I worked for the *kampung* barber.'

Ferdach gave a little yawn and rested his head back on the towel that Noor put on the pillow. Why resist? He closed his eyes and submitted yet again to Noor's superior will. The shaving process was extremely slow. What he could do for himself in five minutes took Noor more than thrice the time. His cheeks, his chin, his throat were all dealt with twice, gently and thoroughly. His nose was pulled back so that the razor could get right under his nostrils, his ear lobes were similarly manipulated and finally Noor wrapped his face in a cold flannel before dowsing his skin copiously with eau de cologne taken from Ferdach's travelling case.

'Now,' said Noor, surveying his handiwork, 'You look nice. I shall tell Tuan Carling's boy to make coffee and toast and you will take your bath.'

'Don't you think it's too early to wake him up. Last night Carling and I went to bed after a very late dinner.'

'He is only a houseboy,' said Noor making off.

Ferdach thought that the young woman to whom Noor was engaged was not very lucky but he acquiesced and went to the bathroom. When he emerged expecting to dress and go down for breakfast he saw that a tray of coffee with toast thickly sprinkled with sugar, Chinese style, had already been brought up by Noor who stared at him and said, 'Did you cry when you were circumcised, Ferdie?'

Ferdach put on his underpants quickly. 'I can't remember, Noor. I was only a baby.'

'A baby? We Muslims are circumcised when we are about ten.'

'It must have been painful, Noor. Did you cry?'

'No I did not,' Noor replied with absolute certainty. 'How could I. There were more than four hundred guests at the *jamuan*, the big feast, after I had been carried round the *kampung*.'

'That wouldn't make any difference to me,' said Ferdach. 'During the war I saw wounded airmen cry. It's natural.'

Noor ignored this and continued, 'The next morning when the *mudim* cut off my foreskin it was so quick that I didn't feel it. And do you know what the live cock did when it was held before my penis?'

Ferdach was a bit perplexed by the double meaning of cock in

219

English, especially in regard to a circumcision ceremony, so very passively he asked, 'No, Noor. Please tell me.'

'Well Ferdie, the feathers round its neck puffed out. Do you know what that means?'

'Truly Noor I haven't a clue. Perhaps the bird was in a state of shock It might have been thinking, is this going to happen to me?'

'It means,' said Noor proudly. 'That I am to be highly sexed and will have several wives.'

'Is that so?'

'Yes. But I'll tell you the truth, Ferdie. After the *mudim* had dressed the wound and every one had gone I cried a lot. It was sore for days.'

Ferdach felt quite relieved that Noor should confess to a human weakness, and, as he ate his breakfast, watched him packing, thinking indulgently that the boy's bossy manner might be the result of his use of English which, though good, lacked any tendency to understatement so that opinions which an Englishman might express tactfully, became categorical imperatives. Noor took the greatest care with each item of clothes, or books, or official material, as though mentally he was making an inventory of all his employer's possessions. Sometimes he made a comment like 'I don't like the colour of this shirt, I will choose something better for you' or 'These trousers are frayed, I will throw them out when we get back to Ipoh'. And a couple of times he tut-tutted to note that some of the underwear or socks had been badly darned, actually by Ferdach who had always performed such chores when he was a student.

Ferdach left a note of thanks on Carling's breakfast table and then they set off. Or were about to set off; Ferdach had seated himself beside the driving seat in a democratic way but Noor said, 'No, you must sit in the back seat. Then Gordon will see that I am being a proper syce for you.' When Ferdach had done as he was told, Noor drove off, with a jerk to begin with because his control of the clutch was still enigmatic but after a while, not too badly.

At Kuala Kerening they found Gordon Choo who had travelled up on an early morning bus. In the short time since Ferdach had last seen him he had become even plumper and this he attributed to the fact that he was now working in the District Office without field duties as well as to his growing taste for Tiger beer. Ferdach told him to be careful as he would no longer be so handsome if he put on too much weight but Gordon equally made it clear that Agnes approved of his new shape. This caused Ferdach to wonder whether women's tastes were perhaps determined by social rather than aesthetic considerations; a fat Gordon Choo represented a prosperous man, the ephebe-like shape which he himself favoured, might well be synonymous with poverty and failure. After all wasn't that the reason why Malay and Indian male film stars were rotund, rather than like Errol Flynn, in appearance.

'Well the walk to my *kampung* will make you thinner,' observed Mat Noor, with no trace of sympathy. 'So I hope you're ready for it.'

'I am ready for it Noor,' said Gordon. 'But I'm worried about your foot. I've noticed you limping.'

'I'm not limping,' Noor said decisively and led the way towards the river from the *kampung* where they had left the car. Ferdach and Gordon followed. They were all bearing rucksacks but these gave no problems for they were light and as yet the heat was not too great. As they walked on it seemed that they were descending not into a solid landscape but into a realm of clouds for the valley was filled with fleecy white mist through which a few tall trees emerged erratically as if they were slowly drifting around. Ferdach imagined that their roots were weird blanched tendrils writhing in search of some aerial sustenance far below. Amidst spurs of higher land, in unfathomable depressions, were more vast swathes of mist, or were they clouds, that cut off the peaks from the earth and made them float on high, so many Laputas masked by ominously black and purple jungle. Above this unsubstantial watery landscape serene and peerlessly blue, pierced only by the golden morning sun, was the immense bowl of the sky whose very remoteness made the world, despite its forests, its rivers and its ranges, seem no more than the squalid abode of pygmies.

They crossed a tributary some way upstream from the *kampung*, made their way along the narrow bunds that separated the small *padi* fields where they were solemnly regarded by huge water buffaloes, crossed the foaming, winding Perak river and began their ascent along a narrow path that wended its way towards the jungle. Strangely enough Ferdach had never before given much thought to the nature of the jungle. Nearer to Ipoh whenever he had entered it, there had always been an almost imperceptible change as the vegetation mutated from the low dense semi jungle of the squatter areas into a kind of mangled jungle partly cleared in places for houses and vegetable gardens. Now there was no doubt that real jungle, silent jungle, virgin, full of mystery, darkness and delight lay ahead of them, like a vast impenetrable wall.

They had gone just a little way into its darkness when Mat Noor stopped and opened his hands in prayer. Ferdach had seen him do this before but had never asked what he was saying. He did so as soon as Noor had finished. Gordon Choo cut in to say that Noor was praying to the spirits like the Chinese did from time to time.

'Not like the Chinese at all,' Noor contradicted. 'I said "*As-salam aleikum, aku datang ini bersahabat sahaja*" which means "Peace to you, I come just as a friend".'

'You see, Ferdie, there are spirits everywhere in the forest,' said Choo didactically. 'There are giants or "*gergasi*"; invisible spirits, "*orang bunyi*"; there are jins and many more. So I've been told. The Malays believe in all this childish stuff.'

'Who's to talk,' Noor said crossly. 'You Chinese believe in a mass of nonsense: door gods, household gods, monkey gods, even lavatory gods, I've heard. Who are you to talk?'

Choo was unrepentant. 'The Malays aren't the only ones to be childish. I agree: we Chinese are just as bad – and so are the Indians. But me, I believe in science. Science has no ghosts and spirits.'

'Let's get a move on,' said Ferdach. 'How does anyone know what there is in a place like this? If there are spirits I shouldn't be at all surprised if they're annoyed if they hear any arguing about it.' To emphasise his conciliatory role he said, 'Peace to you all. We come as friends. We come in peace.'

They set off again but the riling did not stop. 'Perhaps the *hantu hutan* didn't understand your English,' jested Choo. 'What d'you think, Noor?'

'I'm sure they wouldn't even listen if you spoke to them in Chinese,' Noor replied. 'Anyway spirits don't need language.' Then turning for an instant to look straight at Ferdach he added, 'It's possible to have a conversation without words. Like I always know what's going on in Ferdie's mind.'

'Then you know more than I do. Please, both of you, let's be quiet for a while.'

They walked on without speaking and in so doing Ferdach became more aware of the deep silence enveloping them. The path was narrow and no doubt kept open merely by the passage of the *kampung* people from the settlements ahead of them down to the main sweep of the Sungei Perak from which they had just come. Their feet trod on that familiar carpet of dead leaves and moss which made the going comfortable. Either side of them there was thick undergrowth but not of the impenetrable kind found in secondary jungle. Most impressive was the enormity of the trees and the thickness of their trunks often festooned in their lower stages by lianas, ferns, brambles and a rich variety of creepers but higher up far freer until, way above, they opened up to form an enormous canopy through which little light could penetrate. Nor was it really hot as it had started to become before they entered the jungle cover. Because the air was so fresh and cool, to walk in such shade was an unexpected pleasure.

From time to time they would stop, especially if they came across a cool stream and then they might catch a glimpse of the sky. Ferdach was aware of an eerie feeling rising in him. He could well imagine the Malays believing that the place was full of strange beings other than animals which, in fact, were rarely to be seen. If a tiger or a deer or a large snake were to be quite close, no one could see it. Yet the jungle, in its entirety, seemed to be peculiarly alive. Sometimes, even though no wind penetrated its obscure depths a frond would stir as if pushed by an invisible hand or there might be some muted noise, a crackling, a rustling, a slithering nearby but never sight of whatever creature it was that had caused it.

The prevalent colour was dark green, but occasionally high above them something lighter could be seen, a spray of unusual leaves, perhaps an orchid or some fruit. Even more rarely a glimpse could be caught of a flower, a bird or a butterfly with startling colours, but it would never be more than a glimpse for almost at once Ferdach's own movement caused some leaves or branches to obscure what had been momentarily revealed.

Twice during their long walk they met some Malays coming down in the opposite direction. They all seemed to be well acquainted with

Noor and engaged him, after the courtesies of introductions to Ferdach and Gordon had been completed, in swift conversation, replete with much laughter, of which neither Gordon, and still less Ferdach, could make much sense. The encounters left Noor in a good mood. He even admitted to Gordon that he was limping, though only a bit, because his foot had not fully recovered. From time to time he gave them a little lecture about the jungle, telling them that if they knew it well, as he did, you need not starve in it: water could be extracted from rattan plants, there were many berries, though some were poisonous, and there were shoots and roots which could be eaten. What was more if you knew how, and again Noor was at pains to say that he did, you could noose birds or catch them by smearing twigs where they perched with gum, bait fish or even set a trap for a mousedeer. Sometimes he would demonstrate his knowledge by telling them the names of plants and their qualities. Once he pointed down at some marks where an animal had recently passed by. They were not the pug marks of a tiger he assured them because the smell told him otherwise. In this habitat Noor seemed to grow in stature while Ferdach and Gordon diminished. In the late afternoon when all of them were moving more slowly and longing to rest the jungle thinned out, little gardens appeared and they came across a beautiful Malay *kampung*, extremely clean and well cared for, set beside a stream and centred around a square stone mosque. Everywhere there was the sound of running water and Ferdach saw that a clever reticulation of raised bamboo pipes was conveying it to the houses and the mosque. Children came out to greet them, women peered shyly at them from verandahs set around the houses, which were all raised on stilts, and then some men appeared. Among them was a tall grey-haired man with rather severe features that suggested power. It was Mat Noor's father, the *pawang* Haji Ahmad.

37

Ferdach's good name had preceeded him, as had Gordon's. Noor's father seemed to know as many details of the trekking his son had done with Ferdach and the platoon around the squatter areas, as Ferdach did himself. In particular he knew of Ferdach's kindness to the leper woman and how he had treated all his men as equals. It was apparent to Ferdach that Mat Noor had spoken with more respect about him to others than he had ever done to his face. It was no surprise, therefore, that after the three travellers had taken showers in the coldest of water that came down to a tank behind Haji Ahmad's house, which was the largest in the *kampung*, Ferdach found that quite a feast had been prepared to which a dozen or so *kampung* people, all male of course, had been invited. It obviously pleased Mat Noor that his family was able to entertain his colleagues from the city and he was assiduous in seeing that Ferdach and Gordon were constantly plied with food, prepared by the invisible women folk of the house.

Gordon Choo could chat away quite easily with the other men at the feast, all of them seated cross-legged in the open-sided front room of the house, but Ferdach's vocabulary still limited his exchanges. Sartorially at least, he and Gordon fitted in for their host had provided them both with a sarong, a loose fitting *baju*, and a *songkok* to wear on their heads, the first two garments – if not the third – so much more comfortable to wear during a feast than European clothes. It was also a relief to Ferdach that Mat Noor's father could speak English though, on this first night, not much was spoken between them. Despite that, even in the silences, he was aware that Haji Ahmad was an unusual person. There was something about his dignified bearing and the intense way in which he looked right into people that made Ferdach treat him with reverence.

What was more, in the room in which he and Gordon were to spend the night, and from which someone else must have been temporarily evicted, there were many books not only in Malay and Arabic but in Thai and English. Among the latter Ferdach noted two books by C. F. Jung and one on the Indonesian mystic Pak Subud.

To Ferdach the meal was mainly remarkable for its spices in the harmonious compounding of which Malays are the world's experts. He had never tasted such Malay food in Ipoh for in those days there were virtually no Malay restaurants in the town. He had always been told, it being alleged that Malays were not business oriented, that the best Malay food was to be tasted in Malay homes. And it was true: here it was set before him, awaiting some genius to put it on the international culinary stage. Noor informed him that the chicken korma was cooked with coriander, cumin, anise, and a seemingly endless number of other spices, none of which Ferdach could have identified but which, so subtly combined, gave rise, when they touched his taste buds, to great reverence for the cooks. It was delicately blended with coconut milk and yoghurt and over it, to give it final zest, were sprinkled sharp chillies. The very names of all those magical spices made him think of the days of the raucous trade that had first brought European imperialism, selfishly but understandably, to the many islands and peninsulas of Southeast Asia. The beef rendang was enriched with shallots and ginger, galangal and garlic, while the onions, brinjal, beans and the green peppers in the sayur goreng were vegetables prepared as no one could ever have imagined them fried in wartime or postwar England. There were other savoury small dishes too, not to mention fluffy boiled rice, the fruits of the *kampung* gardens and cooked sago covered with coconut milk and syrup, as well as soft drinks to complete everyone's pleasure. A bottle of Tiger beer was also offered to Ferdach who at once declined it out of respect for Islam though this was no great sacrifice for he disliked beer. Gordon Choo did likewise but with a look of regret on his face.

When the business of eating was at an end and the company was engaged in conversation, Ferdach was impressed by the great respect that everyone present showed to Haji Ahmad. A silence descended on the room whenever it seemed that he was about to utter an opinion. It was as though his words were deemed to have a magical significance that must not be lost. Sometimes, so Ferdach inferred from the switch to Arabic, Haji Ahmad must be quoting a Surah from the Holy Qur'an and the men present would receive the words with due reverence but at other times his voice took on a strange hollow, sound, as if it was coming from another person. When this happened Ferdach could see that his eyes had rolled upwards as if they were off somewhere gazing at an invisible interior world. The room would go completely silent and at the end of the utterance each man would murmur some sort of prayer or the name of the Prophet on whom be praise.

Ferdach was seated between Haji Ahmad and the *ketua kampung*, the village headman, whose English, being more or less on a par with Ferdach's Malay, made possible a reasonably interesting bilingual conversation, largely about the squatter problem in the Kinta Valley. Ferdach was glad of this because he did not want to disturb the obviously oracular nature of Haji Ahmad's utterances at the feast. However, there was one matter that did disturb him. Mat Noor, sitting almost opposite his father and behaving towards him with deference, occasionally seemed to be the butt of the Haji's thunderous glances. Also, occasional quick remarks were shot at him by his father, almost *sotto voce*, which the other guests were clearly at pains to ignore. Ferdach wondered whether the father's anger in any way involved himself. But no. It could not be. Haji Ahnad had treated him with studied politeness. He was clearly a welcome guest. What could have happened to disturb the relationship between father and son? Ferdach then remembered that while he and Gordon had been alone in their own room he had glimpsed Mat Noor and his father walking towards the mosque in quiet but intense conversation. Some controversial exchange must have taken place then.

The mystery was resolved when he and Gordon turned in to sleep after thanking their host and lightly touching, rather than shaking, hands with Haji Ahmad's wife who came briefly from the back quarters of the house to receive them. Neither of them could go straight to sleep and they exchanged what information they had learned from their neighbours at the feast. It was not long before Gordon said, 'Did you notice Haji Ahmad looking angrily at Mat Noor?'

'I don't think anybody could miss it, Gordie.'

'And the remark about disrespectful children?'

'No, I didn't. But surely Mat Noor was in no way disrespectful to his father.'

'That's not what his father thinks,' replied Gordon, adopting his you-don't-know-as-much-as-I-do tone of voice. 'Tuan Haji has arranged a marriage and Mat Noor doesn't seem very happy about it.'

'Really! He boasted to me how beautiful his bride was.'

'So you knew about it? You never told me.'

'I only found out in Grik'

'I'm going to sleep now,' said Gordon, as if the explanation was insufficient excuse. But Ferdach was not taking that and asked how Gordon had found out.

'Everyone in the *kampung* knows about it. Goodnight.'

Ferdach did his best to get to sleep but without success for soon Gordon was snoring. How was it that these young men could always get the better of him – even in sleep. Perhaps it was because they all grew up in large families and became adept at winning. Yet he had to admit that in some peculiar way he liked being downed by them since he also knew how to laugh at his own irritation. At length he too relaxed into a fitful sleep but sometime during the night he was sure he could hear an argument going on either in, or in the vicinity of, this rambling building. Beautiful though the *kampung* was, idyllic even, he did not want to stay here too long. In the loveliest flower there could be a canker.

38

The next day, in the bright light of early morning, all seemed restored. A few older men were at the mosque, sitting around talking after prayers. Further away, beneath the trees, four youths were practising the Malay art of self-defence, or 'bersilat'. The only people to be seen working were women sweeping the hard soil beneath and around the houses so that all looked neat and tidy. Ferdach and Gordon sat on the house steps waiting for Noor, happily anticipating his long-promised picnic at the famous pool upriver in the mountains.

Near to the house was a group of people come to seek the help of Haji Ahmad, whose supernatural powers were renowned throughout the district and even further. It was said that he could heal mental ailments where Western doctors and psychiatrists failed and he could predict the future. Ferdach was not surprised that the house bore all the marks of prosperity.

Mat Noor seemed now to be serene in the presence of his father who wished Ferdach, Gordon and his son a pleasant day when they set out to make their way leisurely up the valley. In a couple of hours they reached the pool which was natural though substantially deepened by an earthen barrage across the river course, and took to swimming about in it and playing like schoolboys. Sometimes they showed off their diving skills to one another, sometimes they swam as deep as possible to retrieve coloured stones which glistened tantalisingly like rare jewels in the depths but looked rather drab when cast on the land. After a while they explored upriver, before the water's gushing entry over huge moss-covered rocks into the pool. They then struggled – half in the water, half on the bank – much higher still to a place where weird pitcher plants waited to devour errant insects and where, for a rare moment, they saw some living creatures: two jungle hens scratching for ants on a rotten tree trunk. Then Mat Noor made them cut some broad leaves on which to slide over the smooth rocks, down chutes and even over small waterfalls, all the way down until at last the force shot them like missiles over the mossy rocks into the pool. He told them that in Malay there was a single word for this exciting pastime: *mengeluncur*. The game was such fun that they repeated it several times before returning for their food, a rest and then a more leisurely swim.

They were shut off from the rest of human creation. Not a whiff of a breeze rustled the treetops; only their own voices played like a treble against the heavier sound of the water gushing in to, and out of, the pool. Ferdach wished that the three of them could be naked for it seemed that nakedness was an aesthetic requirement in such a sylvan place, a classical landscape with nude figures, but he never suggested it for in both Gordon and Mat Noor he detected a shy reticence that would have refused such an un-Asian idea.

Nevertheless the beauty of the scene and the joy of their own presence in it had got through to Ferdach's companions. Gordon, who was not a Christian but knew everything about Christianity from Agnes – a Seventh Day Adventist – called from the rock on which he was sitting, 'This is the Garden of Eden, Ferdie. This is the beginning of the world.'

At which Noor, who was standing waist-deep in the water, called out, 'Then we are all Adams. No Eves to make trouble. So we can stay in paradise for ever.'

Ferdach swam across to stand before Noor who was smiling broadly, perhaps at the idea of everlasting paradise, and said quietly, 'What a strange thing for someone who's getting married to say. Would you really like to play like this forever? With never an Eve to disturb you?'

Noor replied, 'Oh yes, Ferdie. I could be in a world like this with you for as long as you wanted.' As he spoke, either on purpose, or due to the force of the water, he moved close to Ferdach who, for a brief instant was aware of the sensual contact of their bodies below the surface. And then, just as quickly, it was over; it could all have been unintentional for Noor had swum away.

Though the cold of the water spread ruthlessly through Ferdach's body it did not dull his desire which was nevertheless tinged with the same uncertainty he had experienced when Noor had given him the romantic *pantun*. He asked himself why was it that Noor did not want to obey his father and get married? But now was the time to be careful; it was important to do nothing to thwart Haji Ahmad's plans. Respect for elders, for the family head was all-important and not to be upset by an outsider. So he said, loud enough now for Gordon to hear. 'I wonder if the CTs ever come near here?'

'Of course they do,' said Gordon. 'Noor knows that they've been in his *kampung* quite recently. But they don't harm anyone here. The *pawang* is too useful to– "

'Useful to whom?' Ferdach cut in sharply and Gordon, as though he had made a mistake, said quickly, 'To the people of course. The *pawang* is a healer and the CTs don't harm anyone who helps the people.'

Noor laughed at this as if it were a great joke. He swam away from Ferdach then stopped and shouted. 'If the CTs killed the three of us now, just think Gordon, just think Ferdie, our blood would mingle in the water and it would flow past the *kampung* and down through all of Perak to the sea. After a while no one would know we had ever been here. But in the sea we would be together for ever.'

It was after this that things became more sombre. Everyone fell silent, dwelling on difficult inner thoughts. Mat Noor fell into a deep reverie, sitting beside the pool and beating a leafy frond on the water's surface as though bidding some living thing to rise up from the depths. Ferdach took to swimming slowly back and forth across the round pool. Gordon Choo discovered a small boat under some overhanging bushes. It had a flat deck and he lay face down on it using his hands like paddles to navigate the waters. Soon he drew alongside Mat Noor and watched him intently. Noor's lashing of the water continued and when the boat was adjacent to the bank the branch struck Gordon's back without Noor showing any sign of realizing what had happened.

'Get on the boat, Noor,' Gordon ordered abruptly. At once Noor stood up and stepped onto the boat deck where he squatted down, trailing his branch listlessly in the water. Gordon slowly paddled out into the middle of the pool to meet Ferdach. Their faces came close to one another. 'Watch,' Gordon whispered. Then quite loudly he called, 'Drop into the pool, Noor.' Noor obeyed in a flash, coming up from the depths with a faraway look on his face. He seized Ferdach roughly and held him close. They began to sink and Ferdach had to struggle hard to undo Noor's strangely powerful grasp. Once on the surface Ferdach pushed Noor towards Gordon, who pulled him aboard. The three of them made for the bank and lay together on a smooth rock. Noor was like someone awakening from a dream. He stared up at the sky and the trees and breathed deeply. Ferdach felt sure that Noor knew what had just happened to him and that it had happened before. After a while all returned to normal and Noor, looking crestfallen, went off to swim. Gordon seized the opportunity to murmur one word in Ferdach's ear: '*latah*'. No more was necessary for Gordon had told Ferdach about the condition some time ago. *Latah* was a nervous state in which the person afflicted could become very quiet and then be open to any suggestion made to them, as when Gordon had ordered Noor to drop into the water. Apparently no one was sure why the condition existed, whether it was the result of diet, stress or whatever.

Noor swam or rather drifted towards the bank and emerged from the water a little way off. Indifferently he let the loose sarong in which he had been swimming float away, and lay naked in the sun with his eyes closed.

'He's so beautiful, like a Greek statue, isn't he Ferdie?' said Gordon, weakly articulating Ferdach's thoughts. 'I hope he's alright now. We won't disturb him though. Perhaps he'll sleep for a while.'

'I hope so too,' Ferdach replied but in his head other thoughts were struggling: I must look at him just as Gordon said, as a beautiful object , yes as a statue, and nothing more. I must not offend his father; I must not upset whatever arrangements for his future have been made. Then, most cautiously, he thought, you're just infatuated, don't be a bloody fool. nothing good can come of this; what you want and what you can have are irreconcilable. Yet ineluctably other memories from Ferdach's more academic past were welling up, including a Greek poem by Meleager thrust under his eyes by an over-discerning classics master:

> What excuse have I for not loving?
> For he is beautiful, entirely beautiful.
> And if he gives me pain,

> Isn't it the way of Eros
> To mix bitterness with honey?

As they walked back to the *kampung* it was as though Gordon Choo had become the wise guardian among them. He had wrung out the water from Noor's sarong and dressed him in it; he had put his hand on Ferdach's shoulder in such an understanding way that Ferdach imagined that Gordon must know, must be in tune with everything that was transpiring between himself and Noor. And as if to dispel his companions' gloomy thoughts Gordon took to telling them about Agnes and how much he wanted to marry her but that there was only one dark cloud on the horizon: Agnes's religion.

'I'll never become a Seventh Day Adventist,' he stated. 'but she won't leave off trying to make me go to her church. She won't give up. She thinks she owns me. Even up here I'm only given two days off. She expects me to do everything that suits her. Why have I fallen for such an unsuitable person, Ferdie?'

39

The next morning Gordon left for Kuala Kenering in the company of the *penghulu* of the *mukim* or parish. Even apart from the dictates of the dominating Agnes Chan he had to get back to work. Ferdach, on the other hand, had given no clear date to his office about his own return and decided that another day in the village would be rewarding. That morning Noor was to visit relatives to pay his respects but in the afternoon they could return together to the pool where Ferdach would be instructed in a few simple jungle arts which might one day be useful to him. More importantly they would spend the night together in a little bamboo bivouac that Noor had built and used to catch birds and spy on animals when he was younger.

For the first time Ferdach found himself alone with Haji Ahmad, sitting in a room which might best be described as a consulting room for it was there that the many people who brought their problems to the house were received and counselled – for a fee. Four people had already been in to see the *pawang* before he had time to receive Ferdach, who was still wearing Malay clothes and sat cross-legged on the mat facing the Haji. The scene was no different to the earlier consultations, save for one thing: a bottle of Cognac and two glasses stood on a floral-painted metal tray between them. Tuan Haji poured out two strong measures and passed one to Ferdach.

'I never drink in public but in private I see no harm in it – if it's done for medicinal reasons.' A thin smile crossed his lips as he said this but though his manner was affable, Ferdach was on his guard. He felt sure he was going to be grilled by this fundamentally overbearing man. To begin with, Haji Ahmad merely asked courteous questions about Ferdach's parents, about his father rather than his mother, and about his years of education. The war was then touched on but lightly, mainly with reference to Ferdach's RAF service but nothing was said about the Japanese occupation. By the time that both of them had drunk two strong brandies – with a third containing barely any water awaiting consumption – Haji Ahmad said in an offhand sort of way, 'Mat Noor admires you very much. And I think I understand why. You are a natural leader, a man of character. You are like the young officers they used to send here before the war.'

'You are flattering me, Tuan Haji. From what I've seen, you are more a natural leader than I could ever be. People have need of you. I'm told they come from all over Malaya to seek your advice. So I admire you.'

'And do you admire my son? No. You cannot. He's still a boy. What can anyone ever find to admire in a boy?' An implication seemed to lie behind his last sentence; its delivery, if not hostile, was certainly contemptuous.

'He's no longer a boy and I can tell you that he's brave and generous. I saw it in the platoon. He proved it in the ambush. Isn't that reason for admiration?'

'Young men can easily be brave – out of bravado. Yes, bravado. That is the word, isn't it?'

'Tuan Haji, it's easy to denigrate. But I like to take what seems good at its face value. To identify the good – isn't that what holy men like you teach us.'

'So you see me as a holy man? You take me at my face value?'

'Until I find reason to do otherwise, Tuan Haji. But why do you ask me about your son. You know him well enough.'

Haji Ahmad finished his brandy. It didn't seem to affect him in the least, certainly not in the way it had got to Ferdach. He filled his glass and topped up Ferdach's. Then he said very firmly. 'Nothing about him would matter Tuan O'Haney if I had other sons. I have two wives but all my children – all eight of them – are girls, except for Mat Noor. Do you know what that means to me?'

'That you are most fortunate to have a good young man as your heir. Maybe to provide you with grandchildren.'

Ferdach seemed to have struck the right note. Tuan Haji nodded his affirmation vigorously. 'Yes, if it turns out like that. But what do you know about my – how should I put it in English – my profession. You know what a *pawang* is?'

'I have some idea,' replied Ferdach, and this was true, for following Barnet's initial information he had read up what he could and also asked Waite for information. Not only was a *pawang* a sorcerer, he was alleged to be the descendant of a long line of sorcerers going back millenia, maybe in unbroken succession, to shamans in the deep recesses of Asia. Such men had existed in Malaya throughout the period in which Hinduism and Buddhism had prevailed, or half prevailed, picking up from those religions age-old rituals and the names of powerful gods like Shiva, Vishnu and Ganesa. Ferdach also knew that those deities had continued to exist under Islam, though downgraded to the status of demons or jinns, who could only be addressed in prayers tempered first with obeisance to the Holy Prophet and to Allah the Compassionate and the Merciful. Into this conflation of beliefs had also been added the more erotic utterances of the Sufis but debased to form the substance of love charms and spells. However, beneath the reverence for the so-called higher religions the ancient knowledge of the *pawang* continued unchanged. He knew how to contact the spirit world, to travel the earth in a spirit body, to learn from spirits about the future and how to cure the afflictions of the mind. He did this by incantations, by secret rites, by going into a trance. He invariably inherited his powers from his own father and he was bound to pass them on to his son. At this point of remembering the powers of the *pawang* Ferdach recalled how Haji Ahmad's eyes had sometimes rolled back, whether genuinely or to impress he did not know, when giving utterance at the feast. He also, whether rightly or wrongly, connected this with Mat Noor's retreat into a state of *latah*. Was some hereditary factor at work there? Ferdach took another swig of brandy and said boldly, for the drink had at last made him careless, 'Medicinal or not, this isn't permitted by Islam, is it Tuan Haji? You are not setting a good example.'

Tuan Haji leaned forward, angrily it seemed but maybe it was an act. 'And what do you know of Islam young man? What do you even know of your own religion? Noor tells me you have no religion. Now since he admires you, no not admires, worships you I think, maybe he'll end up the same as you. Have you thought of that?'

'I have no wish to …' Ferdach began weakly, but Haji Ahmad

continued fiercely.

'No need to apologise. You weren't in the least necessary to lead him astray. Why did he become a Special? I'll tell you. To get away from here, to get away from me. He prefered the lights of Ipoh, dancing the night away in the amusement park with *joget* girls, the cabarets, the street life and all that. But let me tell you. He doesn't just think of Ipoh. Ipoh's not exciting enough for him. I've heard him chattering about leaving Malaya – even going to America. Why do I have such a foolish boy for a son – for my only son?'

Since this was a not uncommon sort of complaint for fathers to make in changing societies all over the world, Ferdach tried to be as conciliatory as he had been between Sheikh Mahmud and Mizan. 'Oh all young men go through such a phase. They want to find something different. They want to explore. Didn't you ever want to find something different, Tuan Haji?'

There was a significant pause during which Haji Ahmad looked searchingly at Ferdach as though considering whether or not to let him into some truth. 'Of course I did,' he said eventually. 'And I found it. In Indonesia. I found it in the presence of Bapak, of Bapak Subud, the wisest of teachers. I was in Java during the war when there was so much suffering. I found it then because I was looking for hope and for wisdom, not for foolish pleasure like the youth of today. Bapak's wisdom embraces all manner of beliefs.' Haji Ahmad looked at Ferdach questioningly but seeing no response curled his lower lip: the expression this produced on his face was not too pleasant. 'No. I didn't suppose you'd know anything about him.'

'I should certainly like to know,' said Ferdach, quite sincerely.

At this Haji Ahmad returned at once to what he had found in Indonesia. Bapak, he enthused, had reconciled the teachings of the great religions into a single strand which he called Subud, a typically Indonesian acronym composed of '*susila*', the ability to live according to the will of God; '*budhi*', the existence in every man of the divine power; and '*dharma*', complete surrender to the will of God. Haji Ahmad said that he himself had found further affirmation of Bapak's teaching in the works of Jung, especially in regard to the religious symbols, all different yet all conveying the will of God, that lay in the collective unconscious. Ferdach said nothing but kept his reservations about all of this to himself. He saw at once that Subud, which united three such easily acceptable concepts, and claimed to enable mankind to follow the right way of living, was totally different from the wise acceptance by the Sufis of the co-existence of different faiths. It seemed to be vague, wishy-washy and suspect and, if not a religion, a movement capable of delving into people's pockets. Still less did he even think of saying a word about Haji Ahmad's own spiritual concoction, a brew of everything from immemorially old shamanism through every faith that had come to Malaya and on to the neurotic obsessions of Freud's Vienna, but he saw that it might easily push a sensitive youth like Mat Noor over the edge and could well deter him from following in his father's footsteps. Yet despite his misgivings Ferdach did feel a grudging admiration for a man who, though a traditional *pawang*, was endeavouring to syncretize his ancient knowldge with up-to-date concepts. Maybe his partly Thai ancestry, and the fact that he had travelled widely and read deeply had strengthened his magic art as a healer, but more relevant to his ability as a leader, Ferdach thought, must be his dominating manner and his absolute determination.

'And now,' Haji Ahmad enquired very directly, having dealt with Subud, 'isn't it reasonable that I should ask my only son to continue in my path, the ancient path of his ancestors. Otherwise the knowledge I have inherited and built on will be lost. I do not want him going off to big towns and cities, even to London – yes, maybe he'd follow you there – or to America. His place is here. He must marry; he must provide me with an heir.'

Ferdach felt great sympathy for Haji Ahmad, but greater sympathy for his son. What a dreadful burden Mat Noor would have to carry, dreadful that is if he did not want to bear it. Although he felt very ill at ease he nodded at Haji Ahmad and said, 'I fully understand, Tuan. I do understand.'

Complete silence fell between them. More brandy was consumed. Ferdach felt that he really needed it. Haji Ahmad rocked a little on his haunches as he drank and seemed lost in thought. At last his face knotted angrily and he said, as if giving an order, 'Mat Noor will get married very soon. I have arranged the wedding. I have also chosen the girl.

She is very beautiful.'

'So Noor told me,' replied Ferdach, glad to say something that might please the tyrant.

'He did? That is good. You will come? I am inviting you.'

'Of course, Tuan Haji. Of course I will come,' promised the inebriated Ferdach, who by now was only too anxious to escape from the clutches of the irascible *pawang*.

40

On the way up the narrow valley beside the noisy river, Noor told Ferdach about some of the jungle arts he knew: how to converse with various kinds of bird, how to recognise different types of fish, how to whistle with a flute to attract pigeons, but there was no time for demonstrations and when he spoke the rushing water almost drowned his voice. In any case Ferdach only half believed what he was told and promptly forgot it for he knew he could never master such skills. On both of their minds there was only the thought of getting out of the humid heat of the afternoon and into the crystal-clear pool. As though with an intentional rejection of modesty, no sooner had they arrived than their clothes were off and they dived into the pool.

They surfaced together just as the sun was shaking off the ragged clouds that had been irritating it most of the morning so that it was free to cast its rays directly down into the circle of jungle where the pool lay. The deep hollow was entirely open to the sky, the water sparkled, the rocks achieved the full potentiality of their colours and the mighty jungle trees which soared up were suffused, at different levels, with ever mutating degrees of shade. Ferdach felt sure that this was a moment of epiphany and that Mat Noor was seeing everything as he did. Together they had become free. No one was here to watch them, no one to hear them, no one to hold them back. They were the twin monarchs of this cauldron of light.

For a time they played in the water only conscious of their happiness in being together. Their pleasure was visible in their eyes when they looked at each other. It was audible in their foolish jokes, even in the silly insults they made about each other's athletic prowess. Sometimes they wrestled in the water and it was difficult to say whether they were contending or embracing. Once they held each other so tightly that each could feel the other's breath on his own lips. Perhaps both of them were on the verge of transmuting that breath into words. Neither did so for words would have been insufficient to express their joy. But at length they were tired. Clambering from the water, they spread out their sarongs and lay in the sun, eating the food they had brought. It was only then that Mat Noor asked Ferdach what he had talked about with his father.

'Subud.'

Mat Noor made a harsh noise. It sounded a bit like 'Yaaak,' but was much rougher.

'So you don't think much of it, Noor?'

'Ferdie, I hate it. I think it's mad. Especially the *latihan*.'

'The *latihan*?'

'Didn't he tell you about it? Didn't he invite you to take part in one. No I suppose he wouldn't in case you gave him away to someone in Ipoh.'

'Truly I don't know what you're talking about, Noor.'

'Followers of Subud take part in *latihan*. It's supposed to be a spiritual exercise when you surrender yourself to God and accept whatever he sends you. That's when you're introduced to your real self. Men and women are supposed to take part in *latihan* in separate groups. But it isn't so in my *kampung*, I swear it. You surrender yourself to God and wait until things come from inside you. Then you rave and shriek and dance and roll about on the floor and go into contortions. You can imagine what sort of things people shout and do, Ferdie.' Mat Noor's eyes were darting angrily. 'I have taken part in *latihan* but I never felt God coming out, I felt only madness. I hated it. I feel ashamed when I see such things. I feel ashamed of my father. I can't see any difference between what goes on in my *kampung* and what happens in the places controlled by that madman Syed Ali and his Taslim movement.'

'What do you know about Syed Ali?'

'Hah, he's a hairy little idiot with mad eyes. He came to our *kampung* with two of his followers and two of his women. My father spoke with them and even though he despises them, he let them join in the *latihan*. Oh, how they liked that. You see my father loves power. Maybe he thought he could get a hold over the Taslim by befriending them but I could see that Syed Ali is too wily for that; he would be the one to end up on top. My father will have to be careful not to be condemned like the Taslim.'

Ferdach was both interested and alarmed. 'You think that Islam is hostile to Subud?'

'Some Muslims are suspicious of it, but so far the Department of Religious Affairs hasn't taken any action. My father has been on Haj to Makkah three times; he delares he's a good Muslim, so most people ouside the *kampung* believe him. But I bet he's being watched. Not that it worries me,' Noor added as though quite indifferent to his father's fate. 'Ferdie, I'm going to tell you something I've never told to a Malay – or to anyone else in this country. I don't like religions at all. I don't believe in any of them.' He hesitated; his body and his features grew tense. 'Most of all I hate my father's sorcery and those spells and incantations he makes me learn. I'm supposed to inherit his magical power and pass it on to my own son. But I will not. I cannot. I hate it.' In full flood now Noor's voice rose. 'When those Taslim people came to the *latihan*, Syed Ali told me that my father wanted me to do it with one of their women; to test me, he said. She was pretty but I would not. I could not. Syed Ali's men laughed at me. They said it proved I am a *pondan*, not a proper man, Ferdie. I tell you, I swear it, if they come here again I will kill them.'

The fury of Noor's words had made them both sit up. A troubled silence had opened up between them but Ferdach did not want to break into it by asking for any more details. Noor's eyes were tightly closed as if he was trying to shut out a memory. Ferdach gave him a little time, then took his hand and said, 'It's all right Mat Noor. It didn't prove anything. You are a man, a fine man, a brave man. Now listen to me. I agree with you about the sorcery and about Subud and about the *latihan* but you certainly must not tell anyone else that you don't believe in Islam. You know as well as I do that by law a Malay is considered to be a Muslim. Your opinion could lead to severe punishment and, if some zealots got their way, even to–'

'Death. I know that.' Noor held on to Ferdach's hand but his grip became more of a caress when he said, 'I can tell you this Ferdie because I know you will keep it secret.' Very lightly then he touched Ferdach's lips. 'You and I can tell each other anything because we love one another.'

There it was; it almost took Ferdach's breath away. The affirmation of their love had been made so casually as if there had never been any doubt about it. He replied, 'Yes, Noor. Everything you have said is true. We are in love.' But the next instant he had a doubt. Did 'we love one another' imply the same as 'we are in love'? Best not to ask. Best to wait.

They both made themselves comfortable again on the smooth rock and thought their thoughts until Noor said, 'There's another secret I have to tell you Ferdie. You remember Gordon saying that the CTs had been in our *kampung*?'

'Yes. I wasn't sure what he really meant.'

'He almost let the pussy cat out of the bag didn't he? He meant that they came for supplies. Don't worry. The *kampung* people support the government because they're loyal to the sultan and if he supports the government that's it. But we have other loyalties too. Ferdie, don't imagine that all the CTs are Chinese.'

'I don't think that Noor.'

'Good. Some of the CT leaders in Upper Perak are men from our *kampung* – good Malays.'

'Noor, you are making things awkward for me.'

Noor sat up and looked down at Ferdach. Then he put both his hands on Ferdach's shoulders as though to hold him in place. 'I'm glad. I'm making you share a secret with me. A secret to separate you from everyone but me. I'm going to make it even worse for you. Tonight we are going to spend the night together in my bivouac. So you should know that I've often spent nights there with a Malay Communist Party member, a childhood friend. He wanted me to join the CTs. I said I'd think about it. I even said that when I became a Special I'd be an informer if I decided to be a communist. Ferdie, it was you and Tahir and Gordon who made me give up that idea.'

'Do you have to put me in this position, Noor? What's the point?'

'To disprove what you've just said – that all Malays are Muslims. My Party friend isn't Muslim. He's an atheist, a real communist. He taught me that religion is used to dope the people and I believe him. He asked me to think about this: why are Europeans Christian, Indians Hindu and Malays Muslim? The answer's clear, Ferdie. It's all an accident of where you're born. So none of those religions can be more true than the others – or true at all. Don't you see, Ferdie?'

'I've seen it for a long time Noor.' Ferdach raised his arms to embrace Noor's shoulders. For a while they must have looked like some sort of statue so unmoving were they on that warm rock. Ferdach often wondered, much later, how it was that neither of them had sought to let that still embrace mutate into passion. They knew of one another's love and it would have been easy to go as far as they wanted and yet the simple act of holding one another had been absolute. When at last they released each other they dived into the water for a last swim before settling in the bivouac for the night.

41

The bamboo floor of the little building, raised on stilts about three feet above the ground, was springy and very comfortable. Ferdach relished the close proximity of the jungle and the cool scented air and watched Noor light some joss sticks to deter mosquitoes. They lay back together, side by side on the same mat listening for a while to insects chirping and frogs croaking and sometimes speculating on what animal it was that was snuffling its way quietly beneath them. Ferdach felt very relaxed and certain that the night was going to see some sort of consummation of that mutual affection that they had both admitted as love. Noor then produced a box containing some rather badly rolled ganja cigarettes, the sort that was commonly smoked by young men in Malay *kampung*s. For an hour or so they smoked, inhaling deeply until their happiness turned into a dreamlike state of bliss in which they chatted and giggled like children. Ferdach was vaguely aware that in many of Noor's sentences there was an implicit acceptance that from now on their lives were bound together. There was talk of Noor travelling down to Singapore with him to see Laura and even questions about what it was like where Ferdach came from in England. Then for some reason or other Noor took to railing against his father and mentioned the marriage that he had so stupidly arranged without his son's consent.

'I'll never get married now,' he stated happily. 'But my father doesn't know that yet.' He chuckled gleefully, then asked, 'Did he tell you all about the wedding?'

At once Ferdach replied, 'Yes. He invited me to attend too.'

Noor, still amused by it all, said, 'And what did you say?'

Without thinking Ferdach blurted out, 'I promised to come.'

The bivouac was immediately filled with silence. Ferdach heard Noor breathe in deeply then throw his cigarette through the little peephole intended for the observation of birds. Then he heard him say, 'It's time to sleep, Tuan O'Haney. Goodnight.'

The silence grew oppressive. Noor had turned his back on him and seemed to be sleeping but Ferdach was more wide awake than he had ever been in his life. He must prove that the promise meant nothing. He must prove that he had not failed to understand the intensity of Noor's feelings. He must prove that he had not betrayed him. But how to undo his mistake? He must show his affection for Noor. He desired him. He was racked by a longing to hold him and love him. Maybe Noor was just as afraid to make the first move as he was. But there might never be another opportunity like this. Ferdach slowly slid out of his sarong and lightly at first, then more firmly, put his arm around Noor and moved his hand up to caress him over his heart. He could feel it beating strongly and this close contact with Noor's lifeblood aroused him. He pressed his body against Noor's. Perhaps the embrace lasted a minute, perhaps it was just a few seconds. Ferdach could never remember how long it was afterwards. All that remained in his mind forever after that was the mighty push that Noor gave him knocking him across the floor against the rattan wall and that wild shout, 'I'm not your *pondan*.' Then the silence of the jungle engulfed them.

Like a wounded animal Ferdach slid back to his bed space. He lay flat on his back listening to Noor's breathing. It sounded irregular but perhaps he was imagining it. He wanted to get up and return to the *kampung*, and then fly from it altogether. But that was impossible in the black night. He wasn't sure whether his feelings were of shame or pain. Did Noor so misunderstand him that he believed he was only wanted for sex? There was nothing for it now but to find refuge in sleep which at last stole mercifully upon him.

How long was his sleep or how deep he never knew. Once during the night he did wake up conscious that Noor was still beside him. But he was too despondent to stir or to worry what the next day would bring and he fell back to sleep.

Then in the stillness, perhaps during the early hours, he became conscious again and heard Noor moving roughly about the bivouac, opening the little door, doing something to disturb the peephole, making the whole place tremble. It was intended to awaken him, maybe annoy him; he feared what might follow. When he dared to open his eyes he saw Noor crouched over him.

'Are you awake Ferdie?' Noor whispered.

'Yes. Yes. Forgive me. You see I thought that – I don't know what I thought Noor. I–'

But before he could say another word Noor was upon him, hugging him, kissing him and saying, 'I wanted to hurt you Ferdie. Forgive me too.' Yet the most awful thing was to follow. Despite Noor's intimate embraces Ferdie could not respond. He willed himself to respond but he could not. It was useless to say 'It's because of what you did a couple of hours ago, of what you said. I'm in a state of shock' or something like that. What had happened had happened. Noor must think that he was false, at best shallow. For a while he simulated love but there is one thing a man cannot simulate if desire is not there. And so, after a while, they both rested silently and at length fell asleep.

At least it was good to wake in one another's arms, but after that there was nothing to say. They returned to the *kampung* uttering hardly a word to one another and it was the same as Ferdach got ready to leave. Haji Ahmad had read the pain in their faces; it must have gladdened him for he was very genial to both of them and said he looked forward to seeing Tuan O'Haney again soon at his son's wedding. Ferdach wondered whether the cunning *pawang* really could fly in spirit form and had joyfully observed the sorrow of their night together, or even caused it. There were just a few moments when he and Noor brought themselves to exchange a few words alone before Ferdach was to leave the *kampung* with a couple of Malays. Noor said he would stay at home for a while because his foot was aching but both of them knew that it was in his heart that the greatest pain was burning. Ferdach realised from the strangely distant expression in Noor's eyes that it would be useless to ask him to come back to Ipoh today; all he could do was to say softly, 'Everything you told me last night Mat Noor, everything that happened last night is a secret between us.'

Noor looked at him distrustfully with his broad set dark eyes and said, 'Yes, Ferdie. But nothing did happen, did it? That is our real secret.'

42

The end of this affair can be told briefly. It is more dreadful than anything that occurred during its course. A few weeks later, when Ferdach returned to Ipoh from spending Christmas in Singapore, there was a letter waiting for him from Upper Perak. He opened it avidly for while in Singapore he had written to Noor asking that they should try to repair the damage they had done to each other. Now he expected a reply. In fact his own letter, unopened, was contained in the outer letter that was from Gordon Choo.

Dear Ferdie

I am writing to send you sad news which I am unable to say to your face because I could not bear to see your pain. Forgive me for that.

My news is that Mat Noor is no longer on this earth. The *penghulu* of his *mukim* who is my friend told me the details. After you left, Noor became very quiet and would not speak to anyone. When your letter arrived he sat looking at it but would not open it. He hardly slept, he would not take a bath or change his clothes. Everything his father Haji Ahmad said was ignored.

Haji Ahmad's old mother asked the *kampung bomoh*, the native doctor, to prepare medicine for him, and the *pawang* himself recited prayers and carried out some sort of a ceremony. But to no real avail. After a week Mat Noor seemed to improve a little. He bathed and put on new clothes and then he went and sat by the river. At about sunset the whole *kampung* heard a terrible roar like a maddened bull. It was Mat Noor with a kris in his hand. He killed two men and wounded several others and then he rushed up the valley shouting wildly. Everyone knew he was amok. The *kampung* guards got out their shotguns and followed the stream and found him in his bivouac where they shot at him. He staggered out dying and fell into the pool where we swam together. Oh Ferdie, I can write no more because I know how you and Mat Noor loved each other.

Your sincere friend
Gordon Choo

43

Blissfully ignorant of the tragedy and the sorrow it was yet to bring him, Ferdach was inclined to minimise the seriousness of Mat Noor's dejection. What had happened was nothing more than a setback in a delicate courtship, for with Malays, it seemed to Ferdach, everything must be delicate. Before long there would be other trips outstation; Noor would still be his driver, and the damage to the heavens would quickly be repaired by the inconstant moon. In the meantime Christmas loomed and with it the prospect of a lazy holiday in Singapore, involving, in all likelihood, renewed voluptuous pleasures with Laura Sweinsnoep. Her most recent telephone call to Ferdach suggested that she and the tolerant – most likely indifferent – Alfred were perfectly happy in the big city, which she was finding sufficiently sophisticated to demand her continued presence. Perhaps like Ferdach, Laura had begun to find her place in this equatorial society.

For Ferdach now admitted to himself that many of his own misgivings about joining the Colonial Service were dissipating fast. He enjoyed his work, he was falling in love with the country and its people, and he was inclined to believe, or perhaps to convince himself, that he, and his fellow officers, were really doing something worthwhile, saving the place from communism and preparing it for independence.

It was true that his commitment to this fine cause was in no way as profound as that of Jimmy Waite who, he now knew through their evening snippets of conversation, had earlier in his life thought long and hard about a possible colonial career, actually rejecting several more remunerative prospects before joining the Malayan Civil Service. What was more, when Ferdach had gathered from fellow officers how intimately Jimmy's life had already been involved with Malaya both before and during the Japanese invasion, he felt that he must conceal the rather casual way in which he himself had drifted out here. Waite was one of Aristotle's teleological arrows winging its way purposefully to its target whilst he, Ferdach, always seemed to arrive at any place or state as haphazardly as a fragile leaf blown about by the wind.

Perhaps because he was afraid that Waite suspected his seriousness, even maybe his political commitment, Ferdach had never made much of an effort to penetrate his boss's reserve. Each of them was inclined to admit that the other had merit, and at the very least was a first-rate bloke to work with, but deeper contact between them remained elusive. What Ferdach learned of Waite was often through a throwaway remark or a brief reminiscence, as when Waite might say something about a college in Oxford, or an idiosyncrasy of the great Professor Radhakrishnan, or even, very occasionally, quote from an Indian classic. But unaccountably they always avoided long serious conversations. Nevertheless, they often knew instinctively that the one had the other's support, as for example when they were united in opposing Bertelli's intention of moving the squatters into some area forcibly and without warning. Probably each recognised the compassion in the other's personality.

Yet there were ways in which Ferdach's outlook differed profoundly from Waite's. Waite seemed to believe, with complete sincerity, that it was possible to foretell the future. Did he then conceive of the future as being preordained? He also seemed to hold that some events were providentially designed so as to advance his own life purposefully. If that were the case, Ferdach thought, then there could not, in the final analysis, be much difference between the trajectory of Waite, so consciously devoted to the fulfillment of a noble end, and his own erratic course which twisted hither and thither with no insistence on a purposeful career. Either track must lead to an inevitable and predetermined end but this Ferdach could not accept.

Ferdach's observation of Waite at work had led him to develop the greatest admiration for him as an administrator. He had seen how Waite had won over the allegiance of many of the rural Chinese by treating them fairly and by opposing the sometimes harsh treatment meted out to them by the police; he had seen how Waite's shrewd establishment of squatter committees had induced Chinese farmers to bring their problems to the

District Office for solution; he had seen him, at some risk to his own career prospects, oppose the authoritarianism of Bertelli. Every official act Waite undertook seemed to be in accord with his concept of the Colonial Service officer as an agent of enlightened change. But there were other areas in which Ferdach found himself doubtful of Waite's motivation. Was his philosophy really grounded in Oriental mystical philosophy or was it the result of an earnest Australian family background in which the old homespun nineteenth-century values of positive thinking were all important? Moreover, if Waite's concept of Oriental religion was so profound was it not in some peculiar way vitiated by those odd quirks of telepathically predicting the results of horse races, or wearing different combinations of colours each day.

There was, however, one area in which Ferdach held Waite in high esteem, and that was in the field of Malay culture, Malay language and the Malay character. It was clear that Waite moved among the Malays with ease. Everyone agreed that his proficiency in their language was absolute. He was able to match their verbal poetic sallies with couplets seemingly of equal standard to judge by the pleasure that showed in Malay faces. Nor did any Malay suspect that Waite leaned towards the Chinese side politically. They knew that he had learned Cantonese so that he could speak persuasively to his Chinese constituents; they knew that he had frequently acted in the defence of Chinese squatters, sometimes in the face of opposition from police officers who were as often as not Malay. But Waite's empathy with the Malays was sufficient to override any accusations of pro-Chinese partiality. All the same Ferdach was far from clear how Waite would react to any confession by himself of partiality of a different sort for a Malay youth, for Waite seemed to have been brewed in a Protestant Australian vat and was probably little sullied by any decadent Oxford wine. Despite these misgivings Ferdach decided, perhaps rashly, one evening, soon after his return from Grik, to tell him about himself and Mat Noor and to ask for his opinion of Noor's behaviour.

He did not succeed in doing so. Waite had never been told of Ferdach's journey to the north and was, in consequence, more interested in hearing all about fellow Aussie Carling and the affair of the three elephants than in anything this green recent recruit to the service might have done. Their conversation quickly led to exciting stories by Waite of Carling's wartime bravery and his many hair-raising escapades. Before long the presence of brave highly masculine chaps seemed to hover all around them in that airy upper floor sitting room but all the friendships Ferdach heard of were martial and completely asexual so that his intention of telling of his own romantic relationship with a probably neurotically disturbed young Malay began to recede and soon became impossible. Then Ericson came home from some obviously failed erotic expedition and took out his anger, equally unsuccessfully, with both a blow pipe and an airgun on the *cicak*s scurrying across the ceiling. There was nothing else to do but join in the banality. Ferdach had just concluded it was time to escape to bed when Waite asked, 'Did you have anything to defend yourself with in case of ambush?'

'Only the revolver you had the police issue to me,' answered Ferdach.

Waite disappeared into his bedroom and returned with two cannister-shaped objects. 'In future take these. They're phosphorescent hand grenades.'

'He'll only incinerate himself with them,' Ericson sneered.

You're probably right, thought Ferdach, who took the two weapons, excused himself and went to his room. Before he fell asleep he considered this other idiosyncrasy of Waite – a positive delight in weapons. His room was full of them: rifles, revolvers, grenades, blow pipes, bows and arrows, even thunder flashes, those big fireworks used by the army in training exercises. They all seemed a far cry from the wisdom of the *Bhagavad Gita*.

The next day Ferdach's curiosity over the contents of that room gave rise to an accident that might well have put paid to his budding colonial career. It was Saturday and a meeting was underway at the racecourse. Waite and Ericson had already made their way there. Waite no doubt intent on winning on the basis of one of his extrasensory predictions. Alone in the house Ferdach watched the throngs making their way along Sturrock Road in a continuous line of slow-moving cars and buses flanked by a tide of colourful humanity, for the whole town seemed intent on the races. Malays in smart *baju*s and sarongs, Indians in their white robes and beautiful sarees, trim Chinese men, some still in dun-coloured working clothes but others smart in white, and Chinese ladies wobbling fatly in flower-printed *samfoo*s or sprucely slim in elegant cheongsams. In the distance loudspeakers blared equestrian announcements about this, that and the other in different languages. Still thinking of Waite's oddities, Ferdach wandered from the sitting room into Waite's bedroom more rich in weapons than a warrior's tomb. Its unusual content drew him inexorably. Almost at once his eyes fell on a superbly crafted object just inside the door: Waite's pride and joy, a .306 Winchester rifle with a telescopic sight. Now the only gun that Ferdach had ever fired in his life was a shotgun when, in the RAF, he had gone clay pigeon shooting. But this was no such crude device. He held the awesome weapon in his hands. What in heaven's name did the mystic Waite see in this thing? What made anyone of sensitivity want to kill either men, or animals, with such an unfair device? What was Waite seeking in his own heart when he looked through this finely wrought instrument of death? In what did its fascination lie? As though hoping to find a clue to the mystery Ferdach determined to look through the telescopic sight himself. And so, forgetting that primary rule which the RAF had taught him – never to point a weapon, loaded or not, in anyone's direction – he returned with it to the sitting room, raised it to his shoulder and looked through the sight at the people passing down the road. Happily none of them had any idea that a rifle was trained upon them. If so, they would certainly have ceased to flow so calmly. Just then, Ferdach was surprised to see Ericson's Vauxhall creeping in fits and starts along the road against the general movement of the traffic. Why was he coming home so soon? For an instant he got Ericson's head very precisely in the sight, then suddenly he lost it, for once his car had made it into the house compound, Ericson accelerated rapidly, coursed furiously along the curved drive and stopped under the carport with a screech of brakes. At that moment, Ferdach, reluctant to be found playing with Waite's toy, lowered the weapon too quickly. Accidentally his finger touched the trigger, which patently had a light action. There was a loud explosion. A smoking hole appeared in a floor board right in front of Ferdach's left foot and a yell came from below, a mighty yell from Ericson as the bullet struck the door which he was about to open.

It had been a yell of rage, not of pain. An instant later Ericson's big feet could be heard thundering up the stairs. He was definitely alive. But in the brief time between the shot and the sound of Ericson ascending, Ferdach's imagination had ballooned like the cloud over an atomic explosion. If he had killed Ericson, some reptilian journalist would have quickly revealed a *crime passionnel* involving the two of them plus Laura. If he had killed a Chinese, the communists would have made hay of it and there would be anti-British riots throughout Malaya. But if he had killed a Malay, that would have been the worst scenario. Ferdach could only have expected a gory death at the hands of kris-wielding Malays. Yet none of these things had happened and now Ferdach stood dazed beside the coffee table on which the rifle had somehow or other come to rest. Wide-eyed and white faced he stared at Ericson who was advancing on him, surely to punch him in the face. Yet a different Ericson emerged from within that athletic frame, an Ericson who took Ferdach's arm in a kindly sort of way and told him, very gently, 'Sit down Ferdie. I'll get you some brandy.'

All at once, or so it seemed to Ferdach, the place was teeming with people. From next door came Dr Seamus O'Reilly, the generally drunk State Medical Officer, demanding in his querulous Irish voice, 'Now what the divil's goin on here? Blazes Kate, I hope no one's been hurt.' A couple of young men had appeared from the geologists' mess and were fingering the bullet hole as though it was an unusual rock formation, and of course from the back of the house came Mr and Mrs Cookie and a host of Yusuf's friends and relations. All of them milled around and stared at Ferdach who was now drinking a large brandy as if he were an exhibit. More ominously there suddenly appeared a European Police Lieutenant who had been passing by on his way to the races. He was young, pompous and menacing. 'All you people out,' he shouted at the Malays and Chinese, as if they had no right to be in the house at all. 'What's happened here?'

Ferdach could only think of his own foolishness and was on the point of confessing it when he heard Ericson say, rather condescendingly, 'Oh, it's you Blenkinsop old chap. Nothing's happened at all really. Ferdach and I were cleaning a gun and we didn't realise that there was one up the spout. Damned silly of us. But no one's hurt, Lieutenant. So do go on to the races. I'll write a brief report if you think it necessary.'

For an instant Blenkinsop looked dubious, then disappointed at the absence of death or injury, but at last mumbled, 'Don't bother. It's a minor matter and we've enough bumph floating round the office without giving us any more.'

'Very decent of you Blenkinsop,' replied Ericson. 'I'd ask you to stay for a drink if I didn't know you wanted to watch the nags.'

Only with everyone gone did Ferdach say, 'Thanks Ericson. Thanks a lot.'

Ericson flashed a magnificent smile, stretched his arms above his head as though sure that Ferdach would like to see yet another muscular display as his shirt rode up and said, 'Ferdie, one good turn deserves another. Remember?'

Ferdach was too absorbed in his recent escape to remember anything. 'If you hadn't come back just then,' he began, 'I might have–'

'But you didn't, Ferdie. That's what life's like. Everything hangs by a whisper. God, the whole universe is only a bloody accident. It's all chance. I wish Waite could see that.'

'Why were you coming back early? Didn't you win anything then?'

'No. I bloody well didn't. I've had enough.' Then Ericson burst out laughing. 'But Waite did – as usual.'

Ferdach joined in and said, 'Well then Lars, maybe everything isn't all chance after all but only Jimmy Waite has found the key.'

44

The near fatal result of pressing the trigger on Jimmy Waite's rifle had shaken Ferdach to the core. When Waite returned home from a late meeting in the District Office, Ferdach apologised profusely for even touching the gun. But Waite stayed his philosophical self and, very mildly, told Ferdach to accept the incident as a salutary lesson; guilt was not involved, only poor judgement. However, to underline the lesson, Waite insisted that Ferdach had, with no shadow of doubt, escaped disaster by a hair's breadth. Just think what would have happened had the bullet killed their housemate Ericson or, much worse, a passing Malayan civilian. In the former case, Ferdach's career would have ended, in the latter, quite possibly his life. Vainly trying to justify himself Ferdach later told their neighbour Mr O'Reilly what had actually happened in regard to the Winchester rifle; he protested that it was all an accident; he had only wanted to look through the telescopic sight; he had never imagined there was one 'up the spout', but the doctor enjoyed looking po-faced and soon, with no small degree of malice, expressed his cynicism to his wife Mavourneen. Since she was the biggest blabbermouth in town, Ferdach soon found himself at the receiving end of remarks like, 'What a bloody idiot you were ever to point a gun, loaded or not, at another human being.' Yes, it was true; an idiot he had been, yet he never thought of defending himself by saying that his boss shouldn't have left a loaded gun lying around. No, all Ferdach wanted was to get out of town as soon as possible.

So, instead of leaving Ipoh on Saturday morning which, he had told everyone, was his intention, or of asking whether anyone in the office wanted a lift to Singapore, he decided to do a flit after work on Friday evening. He gave the servants, Muslim and Buddhist alike, their

Christmas presents – money for themselves and their families – and said he was spending his entire leave in Singapore. As he was packing his bags the phone rang. Expecting to be the butt of more cutting remarks he was relieved to hear his loyal friend Lai Kuan asking him what time over the weekend he would be off.

'I'm off now.'

There was a pause before Lai Kuan said, 'A good idea. I know what almost happened. But wait a bit. I have to see you.' Ferdach had no time to object.

Within fifteen minutes an old car snorted down Sturrock Road and soon Lai Kuan was deposited at the front door by the sort of vehicle in which he hardly ever travelled, a mud-bespattered prewar Ford taxi whose driver, an antique Malay gentleman, went off the moment he was paid. 'I'm coming with you, as far as Tanjong Malim,' Lai Kuan stated with an interogative sort of frown that suggested anger if he were to be rebuffed.

It never occurred to Ferdach to ask Lai Kuan why he had not ordered a company vehicle to take him so far into Selangor. He knew that the best way of finding things out in this place was to remain dumb, to observe, to wait for hints dropped accidentally or on purpose. Hiding his surprise, he took in the appearance of Lai Kuan who was not in clothes befitting the boss of a big mining company, but in the practical garb managers wore on the mines: well-worn baggy trousers, a short-sleeved shirt and, on his feet, leather sandals, a labourer's footwear. He had no luggage, only a battered brief case that he clasped to his chest with both hands.

'Tanjong Malim,' Ferdach repeated vaguely. 'Oh yes, I have to pass through it, don't I? Get in. I want to leave now.' But Lai Kuan had already installed himself in the back of the car behind the driving seat. As Ferdach started up he glanced into the mirror expecting to see Lai Kuan's face but saw no one. His passenger had slumped down out of sight to passers-by but by the time they had got well south of Gunung Rapat, where Ferdach had first experienced the dangers of the Emergency, he had not only sat up but climbed over the front seat to sit beside Ferdach, the briefcase still grasped in his hand.

By now the tropical night had fallen and Ferdach was careering along the main road south with his headlamps undipped. Occasionally, as they turned some bend bordered by thick foliage, the eyes of an animal, a mousedeer, a wild pig or something bigger, glistened like twin jewels in the darkness or sometimes an animal would be caught in the glare darting frantically from one side of the road to the other. Ferdach was not driving slowly because an alarming number of ambushes had occurred recently on this road. His driving made Lai Kuan ask, 'Are you nervous Ferdie?'

'About what?'

'Being ambushed.'

'During the Blitz old women used to say, "If there's a bomb with your name on it, it'll get you". Maybe it's the same with ambushes.'

'I thought only Asians believed in fate, not you Augustinian Christians.'

'Fate seems impossible to me. Chance is more likely.' It struck Ferdach that he might as well have a conversation on fundamentals as anything else, to ward off sleep. 'In fact Lai Kuan, I don't believe in a thing. I don't know enough to come to any conclusions, except that I exist.'

'Then you shouldn't be here at all. Why not go back to Europe, to Paris maybe? Join up with the existentialists.'

'Much too limiting. Here anything can happen. Here things touch me, probe me, disturb me. Gassing away on the Left Bank could never equal what might happen to me in Malaya.'

On and on they bantered. It was a form of mutual reassurance in the face of danger, and to keep alert. The strain of following the winding road in the hypnotic glare of the car's headlights, could make both driver and passenger sleepy. Yet under their badinage something else was stirring. They were probing one another, not just for facts, nor to know where they stood politically, but to find out how much they trusted one another.

'If we ran into an ambush and the CTs made us get out, I wonder what you'd do?' asked Ferdach, in a jocular way. 'Would you be on my side?'

'How do I know?' retorted Lai Kuan. 'It'd depend on whether I was shitting myself with fear. If I was, I'd say you were an imperialist swine and I was an oppressed worker.' He chuckled before continuing, 'On the other hand I might say that we're great buddies and if they kill you, I want to die with you.'

'And what would the truth be?'

'What is truth, said jesting Pilate, and would not stay for an answer. Ferdie, why ask such stupid questions? Things never turn out as we expect. For instance, I can imagine a scene in which you suddenly reveal yourself as a communist agent and say that I am a running dog of the British. But is that likely?'

'You must think it's possible, or else you couldn't imagine it.'

An unwanted silence fell between them; even the drone of the car engine could not dispel it. Ferdach knew that Lai Kuan was going south for a reason that demanded secrecy. Yet he, Ferdach, had been asked to provide the transport. Since this hinted at some kind of trust Ferdach decided to cast discretion to the winds and ask Lai Kuan what he was up to. But before he could they came to a roadblock manned by three stern Malay policemen. Ferdach slowed the car but was suspicious; the communists sometimes set up roadblocks to disguise an ambush.

A corporal asked for Ferdach's identity card and took an age to read it. Now the car had stopped, Ferdach was acutely aware of the humid heat of the night, of the sounds of insects and the croaking of frogs in the side drains. Supposing these men were CTs in disguise. The corporal then shone his torch first in Ferdach's face, then in Lai Kuan's. Lai Kuan at once produced his identity card from his shirt pocket but the sergeant, instead of looking at it, asked Ferdach, '*Siapa orang Cina itu?* Who's that Chinese man?'

'He works for me in the Pegawai Jajahan Ipoh,' said Ferdach.

At the words District Office Ipoh, the corporal stepped back, saluted smartly and said, '*Jalan, Tuan.*'

Ferdach thanked the man with, '*Terima kasih*, corporal' and drove on. He was surprised to hear Lai Kuan let out a sigh of relief.

'You really don't want to be recognised do you Lai Kuan?' Ferdach said abruptly. 'You're up to something aren't you?'

Lai Kuan occupied himself by returning his identity card to his back pocket. It seemed to be a cumbersome operation. Then he said, 'Ferdie, there's one thing I swear to you: I'm not doing anything against the government, against the British. I want you to believe this. Put your mind at rest. I'm not compromising you.'

Their conversation flagged again but after a while Lai Kuan put his right hand onto the nape of Ferdach's neck to kneed it and sometimes to press his fingers onto the back of the cranium as though to relieve its inner tension. The action was gentle but intended to keep Ferdach awake. It succeeded. When Lai Kuan took his hand away to light two cigarettes, Ferdach said, 'Don't stop the massage. I need it.' He waited for the practiced hand to resume its work; then added, 'It helps me to believe what you've just said is true. Truth comes through the body better than through words.'

Deep into the night they arrived at Slim River where the road, unlike the nearby railway line that forges south over the river, turns sharply eastward towards the mountains. There they stopped after passing through yet another roadblock manned by more sleepy policemen. 'Are you fixed to put up anywhere?' Lai Kuan asked. He thought Ferdach must have contacted some European officer with whom to stay.

'No. Maybe we can find a small Chinese hotel.' Ferdach stopped, realising that Lai Kuan wanted to maintain his cover. 'So where will you stay?'

'In the car. I'll sleep in the back seat. I don't want to be seen.'

'But you'll have to get out sooner or later. Then you will be seen.'

'Just before Tanjong Malim, we get to Kampung Kereyang. A Chinese shopkeeper is expecting me there. He'll drive me on to Tras.'

Even the cleverest men can make mistakes, especially when they are tired and Lai Kuan had just done so, or it seemed to Ferdach.

'To Tras, Lai Kuan? Why, that's over the mountains, in west Pahang.'

Ferdach knew that Tras was in an area infested with communists. At briefings he had heard the town talked of as a communist lair. He knew better than to probe further but he did say quietly, 'I believe you when you say that you're not compromising me.'

Lai Kuan made a throaty sort of noise as he leaned forward and Ferdach was relieved when, instead of spitting on the floor as it seemed he might, he found his brief case, held it up and said, 'I swear I'm not compromising you. Promise not to tell anyone where I'm going and I'll tell you about the document I've got here.'

Ferdach filled his voice with curiosity as he said, almost in a stage whisper, 'Go on then. I promise.' However, his instinct told him that Lai

Kuan had intended all the time to let him know about the document.

'Let's drive on through the night Ferdie. I'll take over. You rest. See how cool and pleasant it's becoming. We'll see the sunrise together. When we get to my friend's house you can rest a while before going on to KL. Come on. Change over. I'll speak to you as we go along.'

Ferdach felt himself succumbing to Lai Kuan's will yet he liked it. By surrendering, he often got to know his captors and their friends, whether Chinese, Malay or Indian, much better. They seemed to gain confidence to speak when in the ascendant. He knew that Lai Kuan must have, beside his clutch of down-to-earth miners, a more politically active circle. Ferdach wanted to be in it. For instance, would not an anti-imperialist, emotional Irishman like himself find a true soulmate in a natural rebel like Harry Wong, Lai Kuan's far too handsome friend? How easy, with such a man, to transcend the differences of race and culture that other people thought so important. An unreal idea of course as long as Harry was a terrorist but one day the Emergency would end. As the car drove off, with Lai Kuan at the wheel, Ferdach said he was ready to listen and as an earnest of his friendship took to massaging the back of Lai Kuan's neck even though by this time, in the early hours of the morning, they had both got their second wind and were in no danger of falling asleep.

Unlike Ferdach, Lai Kuan did not drive quickly. Indeed, not only did he just drift along but from time to time he stopped if something interesting caught his eye, like an idyllic *kampung* dreaming away beneath the trees, or a stream glistening in the starlight. As dawn broke the excuses for stopping became quite frequent for more could be seen until, over the mountains, came the glow of the sun which at last appeared as liquid fire from which the huge golden orb gradually freed itself. But the stops were made not so much for aesthetic reasons, as to allow Lai Kuan to talk more easily and indeed to repeat some of the things he had said, not so audibly, when driving. For Lai Kuan's voice, when speaking English, was not loud as it was when bellowing in Cantonese at his mining workers or talking in one of those ever noisy Chinese restaurants. Instead it was velvety with a beguiling quality that strengthened what he was pouring into Ferdach's ears.

The document he was carrying had, he insisted, the support of many people in the communist movement in Perak. They came from a broad spectrum of society and included many young people. Recently many students and the more politically aware workers had shifted, quite dramatically, under the tutelage of the Party, from straightforward Chinese patriotism to an understanding of the world struggle that pitted the reactionary fascists against the toiling masses. When he began to use these terms Ferdach told him not to slip into Marxist jargon. Lai Kuan took the point and, more pragmatically, emphasised that the movement had grown stronger since the communist takeover of China. However, in Malaya certain factors made choice difficult for revolutionaries: how, for example, to decide whether British imperialism was fascist or a dying dragon whose weaknesses could be exploited to advance the liberation struggle?

Ferdach felt that this was an obvious, and rather boring exposition. What held him was the personality of Lai Kuan, this hard-headed man of evident sincerity who had turned his back on the sybaritic lifestyle which his wealth could provide him, either in England or the East, to involve himself in the politics of a country whose dominant people, the Malays, might eventually want nothing of him. Lai Kuan's analysis of what was going on, both in the community and the communist movement, might be accurate, but set against the larger scheme of things, he could be living in cloud-cuckoo-land.

Having prepared his ground, Lai Kuan went on to sow more seeds in Ferdach's brain: the more doctrinaire as well as the less educated Party members were all for intensifying military activity against the British, but there were others, those with whom Lai Kuan had most contact, who believed that a mistake had been made ever to take up arms against them. As though for Ferdach's benefit, Lai Kuan emphasised that Harry Wong, despite his absence in the jungle, was one of this faction which recognised that as the British were sticklers for the law, they would never leave Malaya if confronted with force. Even in India – chaotic though the relinquishing of power had been, largely because of the Labour government's flawed judgement – all had been done in accordance with the law.

Lai Kuan then mounted a dialogue with himself: ah, but what about Palestine, the pro-war group said. Quite another story replied the moderates: there, Britain was only a mandatory not a sovereign power and legality had been complied with when responsibility had been handed over to the United Nations. In Malaya, however, an ongoing insurgency confronted by British obduracy based on the law, would delay independence. It would also force the British to rely more and more on Malay manpower and political support to defeat the CTs. It would thus be to the Malays, once the communists had been defeated militarily, that sovereignty would be handed over. Best then, for the Party to come to terms now with the British, to work in the open and to join in a coalition of all groups, political and racial, wanting early independence. In the absence of a communist military uprising the British would have no excuse for refusing it.

Lai Kuan's words dried up just as they stopped for a rest not far from Kampung Behrang Ulu, a small village through which a limpid river ran. The place was coming to life, people were stirring, smoke was eminating from some of the houses and a few children were running down to the river. Some little ones came up to the car to stare with beautiful round eyes at the unkempt travellers. The scene made Ferdach pass some trite comment on how pretty Malay villages and Malay people always seemed to be which, in turn, made Lai Kuan pass some equally trite remark about how the British, historically, had fallen in love with the Malays because they were beautiful without posing a commercial threat to their colonial overlords. Ferdach just laughed at this and said, 'Mary Wortley Montague once stated that general notions, like the one you've just uttered, are invariably wrong. But let's not talk generalities. Cut the story short Lai Kuan and tell me where you stand. No. Don't tell me. I'll put two and two together: you're all for making peace and your journey down here is connected with that. You're going to see some important CTs in Pahang. Right?'

'You'd have no objection to that?'

'No. I think it's a great idea. I agree. Peace will speed up independence.'

'You don't worry that quick independence might be at the expense of your beautiful Malays?'

'I'm sure they'll know how to look after their own interests. But whether they can or not, I'm all in favour of ending this stupid war. I don't like people getting killed. I've seen enough of death in the Air Force. But how is the Emergency to be ended? It won't be so easy. You must know something you've not told me.'

After a moment's thought Lai Kuan said, 'There are things I can't speak about just now. I only hope I've told you enough to make you see that I'm not about to betray your confidence in me. Give me time Ferdie. Don't tell any one, any British officers in KL, about my journey.'

Ferdach knew that such a promise would compromise his integrity as a government officer, but he made it all the same. 'I believe you are working for the country's good. I won't tell a soul about our journey together.' Lai Kuan took Ferdach's hand and squeezed it hard. Then he started up the car, waved to the little girls and boys and they sped on to Kampung Kereyang where they parted company.

45

When he drove across the Causeway linking the peninsula's southernmost state of Johor to the island of Singapore, Ferdach was high on Benzedrine. It was unintentional. Exhausted after too much driving and too many late nights talking into the small hours in Kuala Lumpur, he had caught a cold. His nose was so blocked by the time he reached Senai, a village north of Johore Bahru, that he bought a nasal inhaler from a Chinese apothecary whose shop sign announced it was 'Specialist in Styes and Piles', neither of which, happily, he suffered from. Not knowing the effect of Benzedrine, which was legally sold over the counter in those days, he had sniffed it all the way to the Causeway. So as he glanced towards the west at the rippling waves in the Straits and the brooding clouds whose undersides were turned into a furnace by the setting sun, he felt he was nearing a city of boundless joy. All at once, amidst his drug fanned euphoria there arose the image of the young man who was the object of his surely unwise current passion, of Mat Noor who would no doubt be waiting for him when he returned to Ipoh. But that image was at once relegated to the back of his mind as a promised joy waiting faithfully for him in the future. Right now, in the great city ahead, lay the embraces of Laura and his own exploration of her new world.

Once through the frontier post on the Singapore side of the Causeway, where Customs controls were apparently non-existent, two white-helmeted Chinese traffic policemen sitting astride powerful motorbikes waved him on with broad smiles. Singapore seemed a welcoming place. But he had hardly driven a mile in the gathering darkness, along the strangely deserted main road to the city, when a volley of stones hit his car, one shattering the rear window and the others clattering over the roof. He glanced in his mirror and saw some men rushing into the undergrowth. The incident dissipated his thoughts of pleasures past and promised, and his feeling of security. He had heard that Singapore was in ferment over the custody of a girl, Maria Hertogh. The case had political and religious implications but he had no idea that it was resulting in violence.

Road traffic was so thin that he was able to drive quickly across the island to Orchard Road from which he turned, as directed by Laura, towards the Goodwood Park Hotel, a teutonic sort of building as befitted the home of the German Club before the First World War. Near to it was an annexe, an old colonial house where Laura and her husband lived in an apartment on the first floor, reached by an external staircase. Laura greeted him, not with any pleasantries or enquiries about his journey but, as was her wont, with a dramatic, 'God, Ferdie, you're late. I don't know how I'm going to cope with this situation. I'm too frightened to go out on my own and Alfred's gone to some bloody conference or other.'

Ferdach was at once suspicious. 'Another conference? Not long ago he was in England at a conference. Does he ever work here?'

'Well aren't you glad that we'll be on our own over Christmas?'

'Of course. But where is Alfred? Just before Chrismas isn't conference time generally speaking, except for Santa Claus.'

'He thought it best if we were left together.' Then Laura gave that derisive laugh which she often applied to anything connected with Alfred. 'No, he's not that unselfish. He's gone to Johore with his adorable Mona Wee.' Turning serious again and, looking Ferdach squarely in the face, she added, 'Perhaps we'll have enough time to work things out between us now Ferdie darling. You do want that, don't you?'

Ferdach knew that all the time in the world would not be enough for him to make up his mind about anything so fraught as a long-term relationship with Laura. He nodded delphically with mouth pursed and brow furrowed but came out with nothing connected with Laura's question. 'So what's happening here? This Hertogh case. Why is everyone so worked up?'

'Oh God,' exclaimed Laura, always ready to explode. 'It's the fault of the bloody British, the trouble I mean. The way they've handled it.' It intrigued Ferdach that Laura should disassociate herself from her fellow countrymen. Was it because she was a feminist and saw all evil as the result of male supremacy? 'Maria Hertogh was a Dutch girl given to an Indonesian family by her parents during the war to avoid her landing up with them in a Japanese prison camp. Naturally the girl was brought up as an Indonesian and a Muslim. Now the parents have reappeared and want the child back.'

'Don't they have that right?' asked Ferdach.

'Oh trust you to see things so simply, like a man. Don't you know that according to Malay *adat*, Malay law, once a child has been given, she becomes the child of the foster parents. So two sorts of law, the *adat* and British law, are in conflict.'

'Yes, I do see that Laura. I'm not thick. But what does the child want? She must be a teenager by now.'

'What she wants isn't the point either. God, Ferdie, you live in Malaya and you can't see it. No Muslim has the right to give up Islam. If Maria, or Nadya as the Malays call her, went back to her natural parents, she'd be brought up as a Christian. To a Muslim that's unacceptable. What's more, to make their case stronger, her foster parents have married her off to a Malay teacher.'

'Then why is all this the fault of the British?'

Laura looked at Ferdach with contempt. 'Don't you follow the news?'

'Laura dear, I've been on the road all day in Malaya.'

'Typical of you to find some excuse. Well, the authorities have put the girl in a Catholic convent whilst the case is being considered. A Catholic convent! That's the British for you. No concern for Muslim susceptibilities. Or maybe I should say, no commonsense, considering that the police rank and file are mostly Malays. As a result, all sorts of anti-British elements, Malay nationalists and Indonesians, have seized the opportunity to whip up the Malay population. That's why Muslim mobs are rioting. The Government will have to put the whole city under curfew, I'd say.'

Ferdach mentioned that he had been attacked on the way to the hotel but Laura didn't bother him for any details about his personal safety. 'God, so you see why I'm afraid to go anywhere. How could Alfred leave me on my own at such a time?'

'I thought you'd arranged for him to be away whilst I'm here.'

'Yes, but I didn't know there'd be riots.'

'How selfish of the mob not to consult you.'

Laura's mouth tightened. She was not going to tolerate his sarcasm. 'I'm going to take my bath,' she said archly. 'I'll see you at dinner when you've calmed down.' With that she showed Ferdach to his room and left him without a word.

His reception had not augured well. Yet maybe it was best to see people at their worst before deciding whether to live with them. But was that Laura's worst? He doubted it. In any case, unlike her, he was not in the least excited. What interested him just now was the situation in the city. Was it going to spoil his holiday? He did not relish the idea of being marooned by a curfew with Laura for a week. He took a shower which refreshed him but almost as soon as he had dried himself and dressed he felt as uncomfortable as ever in the vile Singapore climate that was eternally hot and eternally humid.

Reluctant to hang around until Laura deigned to appear, he put on a tie and strolled through the garden to the Goodwood for a drink and maybe to meet people with news about the situation. In the bar he did not have to ask anyone a thing: the place was full of expatriates exchanging the latest information about the chaos that angry Malay mobs were causing. There had been deaths, European vehicles set on fire, amazing escapes like that of a Radio Malaya producer, Derek Cooper, who had only just managed to flee his burning car. And there had been unselfish assistance rendered to Europeans not only from unlikely sources such as John Forbes-Sempill, the actor–manager of Singapore's theatre, but by ordinary Malay and Chinese folk, who had defied the mob. The authorities, it seemed, were at sixes and sevens. Initially, Malay police had been deployed near the Supreme Court where the mob had first demonstrated, only to be replaced by more dependable Gurkhas and some Eurasians; this further inflamed Muslim feelings. The bar crowd speculated on which areas were safe and which were not, though not with any certainty. Someone turned on the radio but it offered little useful information apart from announcing that a curfew had been imposed and that the situation was under control. No one in the bar seemed to believe the second statement. Thereafter dance music was played, to calm people's nerves.

The bar crowd was largely British, with a few Americans and Australians; most were male, loud and angry. Stray remarks revealed that they were businessmen. Without exception they shared Laura's view that the colonial administration had handled the crisis in a crass way and they favoured draconian steps to bring it under control.

'You can't reason with a mob,' declared a large flabby man, who was a study in red and white. His cheeks and hands were a fiery crimson, the rest of him white which rose from his corresponding brown and white shoes, along his well starched cotton trousers, over his protruberant belly and his obvious, almost feminine, breasts until it was taken up, above his collar, by a small pointed beard, thick moustache and wavy hair.

'We all know that Mansfield,' said a wiry, nervous-looking thin man, who kept on blinking and switching his glass from one hand to another, as if it was too hot to hold. 'But how would you deal with it?'

'Like Napoleon. With a whiff of grapeshot. They'd be back in their holes before you could say "Maria Hertogh".' Mansfield roared with laughter as though he had just uttered a great witticism.

An American nearby drawled, 'Oh yeah. Great. Sow the wind and reap the whirlwind, Mansfield. But a whirlwind's going to come here before long howsoever. So best we get it over quickly, I guess.'

For a while Ferdach listened in silence to the lurid tales of narrow escapes and failures to escape. 'I saw a family burned alive in a taxi, fighting to get out. Jesus, the screams. And the mob just laughing,' hissed a thin-lipped young man of sallow appearance. His eyes seemed ready to pop from his head as he spoke. Everyone was struck silent by the horror but the American shouted, 'And wow, did you enjoy it Ferguson.' This was followed by shouts of 'Shoot the bastards!' and 'Send in the Gurkhas!'.

The dangers of the Emergency around Ipoh seemed straightforward in comparison with this. The British planters and miners in the Ipoh Club confronted death on a daily basis yet they preserved their dignity when they met socially. Here hysteria was stalking abroad as though the money-making business community had unexpectedly become aware of a dreadful force bursting up from below to threaten the surface. Even the tales of bravery were told with an air of disbelief as though they had been performed by an untypical minority. Ferdach had to admit that the thought of communist terrorists waiting to ambush him in Malaya was less nerve racking than the threat of an enraged mob bent on mayhem. He almost regretted that he had not spent Christmas in Malaya, which was more like home than this Crown Colony.

At last he got his brandy dry from the hard-pressed but happy Hainanese barman, who was clearly enjoying the situation because of all the tips coming his way. Then he retreated to one side of the room to sit at a table occupied by a hatchet-faced man of intellectual appearance; at least his high forehead, intense expression and rimless spectacles gave that impression. Before him, a paperback edition of Virginia Woolf's *The Waves* lay next to a glass of red wine. The man stared at him quizzically for a little longer than seemed polite, before saying, 'If I'm not mistaken, you are Mr Ferdach O'Haney.'

Affecting complete lack of surprise Ferdach looked a little condescending and said, 'And you are?'

'Howard Walsingham.'

Ferdach had never heard the name but instinct told him the man was there to observe; perhaps he was in some organisation that liked to know what people, including government officers like himself, got up to in their spare time, so he stated, without making it sound like a question, 'And you work in Phoenix Park.' Ferdach had only a vague idea of how Phoenix Park operated but he knew it was the nerve centre of British intelligence in Southeast Asia. Quite likely his dubious friend Aspinall, back in Ipoh, was in the same net and had suggested that it might be worthwhile contacting young O'Haney who was spending Christmas in Singapore. Boldly he added, 'I suppose old Aspinall informed you, with an appropriate photograph, that I was coming to Singapore and staying with the Schweinsnoeps.'

'Well yes. But I say dear chap, you do have quite an idea of your own importance.'

'Not at all. I just know that people in intelligence are so understretched that reporting every bit of information on other people becomes a substitute for worthwhile activity. But how could you know I'd be in this particular bar?'

'I didn't, that was chance ... well, not exactly. I knew I'd be dining with you this evening. Laura invited me. She and Alfred are good friends of mine.' Walsingham's voice fell, 'Please don't think me rude but Aspinall told me that you and Laura are ...' His voice drifted off in mid air.

Ferdach decided to give Walsingham a run for his money. Why should an intelligence officer, a cheeky bastard at that, be dining with them at all? 'I'm very fond of Laura,' he replied drily, 'But, as Aspinall must have told you, I'm as queer as a coot. I couldn't touch a woman with a greasy bargepole. By the way, how about you? Are you one of us? Or just a voyeur?'

Walsingham bristled, straightened up his very long back which until then had made him sag over the table, and threw back his head. His answer was to pick up Virginia Woolf so abruptly that a bookmark fell to the floor. Ferdach picked it up and said, 'Oh dear, you'll have lost your place, in the book I mean. Are you enjoying it?'

Walsingham's own stream of consciousness flowed forth angrily as he cast his eyes contemptuously about the bar. 'This lot. These bloody expatriates. A bunch of hysterics. They are the trouble. They could represent our future, our commercial interest in the East, but they live in the past. They want us to hold on to the colonies as if there hadn't been a war, everything unchanged, all their old privileges intact. They understand nothing.'

Ferdach knew the intention behind the change in tone. The preliminary fencing had been aborted as something Walsingham had lost, or rather was no longer interested in. He wanted to draw Ferdach into a political conversation that would help him in some evaluation. By a nod of his head Ferdach showed himself willing to hear more and said, 'There are benches in the garden. Wouldn't it be better to sit out there? The babel in here mightn't be enough to stop someone from overhearing what we say.'

The garden bench they chose was at the edge of an irregularly shaped pool, almost a miniature lake, from which aristocratic lilies raised their heads between saucer-like leaves on which a few frogs were discussing the meaning of existence. A lion-headed faucet trickled water from a low wall opposite them while above rose tall fan palms that swayed in the slight breeze and provided a sense of coolness even though the air was as warm and moist as ever. The burble of conversation in the bar was thankfully masked by the splashing water. The path to the Schweinsnoep's quarters led off to the right but neither Ferdach nor Walsingham showed any inclination to take it. When a waiter slunk lazily out of the hotel obviously intent on doing no work but now obliged to ask them if they would like another drink, they both ordered, so acknowledging the probability of quite a chat together. Walsingham turned at once to Ferdach and asked him how he thought the Emergency was developing in Malaya.

Sure that he would draw Walsingham out more easily if he gave a gloomy prognostication, Ferdach said, after pausing a little to give the impression of profundity, 'I think we've only a fifty–fifty chance of winning, probably less. Oh yes, we have our successes – squatter resettlement for instance – but the truth is that the majority of the Chinese are excited by the emergence of their country as a great power. They see the future of Southeast Asia as a zone of Chinese client states, as it was in the Ming dynasty.'

'As they believe it was in the Ming dynasty,' cut in Walsingam with historical precision

'Myth or reality, the effect is the same,' Ferdach said with equal assurance.

For someone working in intelligence, Walsingham certainly exhibited an overly impulsive nature. He stood up, walked rapidly back and forth beside the pool and blurted out in a high querulous voice, 'Exactly so. That's what we keep on telling the government. The whole situation demands a radically new approach.'

'Which government?' Ferdach asked. 'London, Singapore or Kuala Lumpur?'

Walsingham stopped right in front of Ferdach and glared at this young man who was too supercilious by half. 'Oh yes, you would know the dissensions that exist. God, how can we ever formulate a coherent policy when so many people know that people in authority are pulling in different directions, especially the dunderheads in the colonial administrations.'

Ferdach felt sure that Laura's derogatory remarks about the Singapore government's handling of the Maria Hertogh crisis had emenated from Walsingham. She wasn't a politically minded woman and her view of the world, outside the parts of it that concerned her personal interests, invariably reflected the opinions of her friends. He replied airily, 'Whenever two or three are gathered together my dear Walsingham, there'll be differences of opinion. It's the way of the world.'

Walsingham sat down on the bench, a bit too close for Ferdach who found his breath rancid. 'I won't beat about the bush, O'Haney. Yes, I've been told to speak to you,' he said. 'So take it that this is a sort of official contact.'

Ferdach was easily irritated by any intrusion into his privacy. He almost said, 'You mean official interrogation' but he asked, as indifferently as he could, 'How can I help you then?'

'Well, I'd like anything you can tell me about Kuok Lai Kuan. For instance, what state of mind was he in, when you travelled down with him from Ipoh?'

'My goodness, you do know everything about me. Noel Aspinall must have written quite a letter.'

'Noel is always verbose and, not to offend you mind, he did say that you are something of a dilettante, a young man who thinks life's a great joke.' Walsingham's thin grin suggested that he enjoyed passing on Aspinall's disparaging assessment. He went on, 'But he likes you and, after all, you are still young. However, you have taken an oath of loyalty to the Crown and you have signed the Official Secrets Act. I have the right to question you if it's in the public interest.'

'I've been called a dilettante before, mostly by people who take themselves too seriously Walsingham. All the same you only have to ask me, straightforwardly, whatever you want and I'll give a straightforward reply, if it's not against my conscience. Yes I did travel, almost to Tanjong Malim with Lai Kuan.'

'To Kampung Kereyang, in fact. Do you know why he was going there?'

'No I don't. He didn't tell me. But he did assure me that he was doing nothing against the government and nothing to compromise me.'

'And you believed him?'

'Implicitly.'

'Why?'

'Because we are friends. Real friends. I'm sure of it. So I trust his word.'

'Are you …?'

'No, we're not. There's such a thing as straightforward male friendship Walsingham. And it's more important than oaths to the Crown or Official Secrets Acts.'

In that moment Ferdach felt sure that he had forfeited any chance of becoming a creature of Phoenix Park. He would be assessed as 'not one of us'. At the same time he had a feeling of resentment that he should be expected to be on any side if he did not want to be. This thought led him to say, 'In my view Lai Kuan is genuinely loyal to Malaya. He wants peace for Malaya. He wants independence for Malaya. He thinks the present Emergency is a bloody waste of time and effort, and so do I.'

'And so do many of us,' Walsingham interjected smoothly. 'But to revert to my first question: what was his state of mind when you were with him?'

Ferdach looked at Walsingham unbelievingly. What a silly question! How could anyone know anyone else's state of mind? However, it seemed that in Walsingham's world they could. So he said, 'He was his usual self, calm, assured, intelligent but if I may hazard a guess, a bit worried that he might be seen travelling south.'

'You mean travelling to Tras?'

'To Tras?' said Ferdach as if the word was new to him. 'I don't know where the blazes he was making for. All I'm sure of is that he didn't want to be seen leaving Ipoh.'

'Ah,' said Walsingham, as if he had just discovered something.

'Exactly what does "Ah" mean?'

'It could mean, my dear Haney–'

'O'Haney.'

'Sorry, my dear *O'Haney*, it could mean that he's up to something unpopular with a section of the communists in Perak. It could mean he's up to something that may be just what we want.' Walsingham gave a dry little laugh that sounded unpleasant to Ferdach's ears. 'Come on dear boy; back to Laura's. I'm sure she must have concocted one of her exciting menus by now.'

46

Laura did concoct excellent menus, though 'concoct' hardly did justice to her efforts. Cookery was her main diversion, after men. She loved to learn about different cuisines and this being Singapore with its melting pot of races and cultures she had every opportunity to acquire new culinary skills. For this dinner she had borrowed the services of a Cantonese cook from the hotel, who, in return for some generous assistance that she had provided for his ailing wife, had shown himself willing to part with a few secrets of his trade. Laura liked to participate in the preparation of the dishes if she was entertaining since she could then justifiably enjoy the praise that the food evoked from her guests. Such efforts were somewhat unusual for an English mem but they did not, of course, extend to such chores as washing up and laying the table. In regard to the latter she did, however, make it her task to embellish the setting with whatever she thought would consort well with the food. Alfred, who was well-off on his own account and from a family more distinguished than her own, had brought out an array of fine silver from which Laura might choose as a centrepiece some prowling tigers or a brace of longtailed phoenixes or an ornate Victorian candelabra. But she also made quite a thing of flower arrangements and since there was a profusion of carefully tended flowers in the garden of the hotel, her thieving forays into it could easily result, as it did tonight, in a dramatic spray of orchids, that rose from a red cloisonné vase.

Ferdach noticed that she had put aside the acerbic manner he had encountered on his arrival. She was dressed in a low-cut black gown which showed off, in her favoured candlelight, her creamy shoulders and her neck which was relieved by a gold chain with a pearl pendant and, of course, by that long black hair which hung, according to her mood, asymetrically to one side or other of her face. Tonight it was to the left. She glided, consciouly graceful as a mannequin, when she descended a few steps of the external staircase to greet her guests. Her sentences, which were uttered in an equally creamy way, were sprinkled with 'darlings' addressed without discrimination to both Ferdach and the foul-breathed Walsingham, who kissed her on both cheeks. Then she made quite a fuss over the fact that the two men had already met and that her introduction of them one to another had been superfluous.

They were late, she told them, like a mother chiding naughty children, and they must come straight to the table on which hotel waiters began to place steaming maritime dishes. Ferdach would hardly have known what they were, for each contained a mixture that was enhanced beyond recognition. Laura, however, soon told them that this one was lobster sashimi, that contained stewed abalone, the frizzled crispy looking stuff was seaweed and the huge blue and white bowl was full to the brim with bird's nest soup with quails eggs and angel hair noodles. And there were other delights including two bamboo containers of crab, twice-braised squid dumplings, an oval dish of fried rice, and a veritable long barrow of prawns. Altogether there was far too much food for just three people but Laura explained this by saying that Northcote Parkinson and a new English Literature lecturer, Patrick Anderson, whom she was certain that Ferdach would like, had both phoned to say that they and their companions could not make it because of the curfew.

Walsingham shared Laura's enthusiam for cookery to such excess that every effort Ferdach made to start some sort of intelligent conversation was at once engulfed in knowledgeable exchanges about various ingredients and the best places in Singapore, or over the Causeway, to find them. Like most of Laura's dinners this one was meant to be a voyage of discovery of hopefully new, or at least of slightly different, recipes which everyone was expected to analyse to the point of tedium. But tonight there was more to Laura's culinary chat; she loved to wind Ferdach up. She knew that talk about food left him cold; he was the sort of man who expected it to be excellent as though by magic. Not for him the boring details of how it had come about. By the time the meal was ending he had grown morose which gave Laura the oppportunity to say, 'Oh, let's talk about something else Howard. Ferdie's bored. Aren't you darling? He thinks all this talk about food is unimportant.'

'How very wrong he is. How very callow,' sneered Walsingham.

'Did I say a word?' asked Ferdach. 'No. Well I will say this: I've observed that people who go on about food and the best restaurants, and who belong to wine and food societies and the like, are generally rotten cooks. Meat and two veg types when you get into their homes. I can imagine you making a real hash of a tin of beans Maitre Walsingham.'

Laura laughed loudly. She was quite happy to see Walsingham get one in the eye. In fact, whenever men were present, particularly men who, she believed, thought her attractive, she enjoyed pitting them against one another. Ferdach remembered her telling him how she had maddened her two foolish swains Blondie Phelps and Starkers Mason in Ipoh by dropping hints to each one of them that the other was better in bed, though who came out on top was never quite clear. Her barbs had led to a brawl between the two young idiots in the Ipoh Club one night after a military stag party. All the same, even though Laura could be so unpleasant, she could also charm men and make them feel important. In a world of young males new to their careers and uncertain of themselves, this was quite an asset.

Coffee and liqueurs were brought in by a hotel waiter who left the red-haired devils sitting on three settees around a low Chinese table, an antique recently purchased by Laura, which, Ferdach thought, must have set Alfred's finances back considerably. Indeed it had already passed through his mind this evening that Laura's fine clothes, her jewellery, the sumptuous food, the hired hotel staff and the variety of drinks represented an outlay way beyond the capacity of his own modest salary which could just about support the spartan lifestyle of Sturrock Road. He gazed around the room noting what other artifacts had been acquired since the Schweinsnoeps had left Ipoh. Oblivious to his concern Laura, without asking her guests whether they wanted one, poured out three '*hijaus*'. The word just meant green and was applied to the crème de menthe fashionable then in Singapore. Unfortunately Ferdach's cost analysis had set off a little alarm bell in his brain with regard to any future with Laura so that he was somewhat po-faced when he found himself facing an equally solemn Walsingham and listening to Laura who had decided to sparkle. 'Now, we're all going to have a really interesting exchange of ideas together,' she gushed, knocking back her *hijau* and quickly refilling her glass. 'I've told Howard all about your brilliant work in the squatter areas and about the fascinating people you know, Ferdie, and I'm sure he's got some really fantastic things to tell you.'

Laura loved to employ words like fascinating or brilliant or fantastic as they seemed to add lustre to her conversation. Ferdach and Walsingham caught one another's eye and their reserve began to dissolve into a kind of mutual understanding that anything of importance that needed to be said should be held back as long as Laura was present. Yet neither underestimated her; whereas she might not be interested in the political implications of anything at all, provided she could continue to be a fascinating centre of attention, she was, like a chameleon, adept at picking up the hue of all that went on around her. When men from Phoenix Park or the Colonial Secretariat, under the impression that she was miles away, let confidences slip in her presence, she invariably cottoned on. In consequence, she was well aware of the deep internal dissensions over the formulation of British policies in the Far East and it had been child's play for her to divine that Walsingham's desire to meet her friend Ferdach must stem from consideration of some use that British intelligence could make of him as an MCS officer.

Although in this she was on track, for most of the evening there was certainly no exchange of interesting ideas for her guests concentrated on the riots and how to ensure their own safety. Both men rather enjoyed frightening Laura mildly whilst insisting that she had nothing to fear. It was thus several days before Ferdach was able to get down to business with Walsingham who had asked him to meet Colonel Adamson-Hitching, his boss in Phoenix Park.

47

The two intelligence men, seated on a leather settee with their backs to a large sealed window, affected to be relaxed as though the encounter was a friendly one in a local pub. Sitting opposite them Ferdach could see, over their shoulders, an expanse of well-trimmed lawn leading to a high bank studded with bushes. Along its crest was a thick hedge of bouganvillea whose spiky stems, he later learned, were entwined with razor wire that would make any intruder's entry extremely unpleasant. By and by he came to think of the hedge as a symbol of the intelligence operation, colourful, intellectually interesting, capable of drawing deep-veined blood yet, at the end of the day, pretty pointless. Sinking deeper into the upholstery and trying not to shiver in the excessive air conditioning, he clasped his hands together behind his head and shot a disarming smile at Adamson-Hitching, the older of his interrogators, whom he took to be in charge; inwardly he had resolved to enjoy himself by being difficult.

Refreshments were brought in by a slim well-groomed English girl in a tight cream suit. Her hair was blond and her skin very white. Even her lipstick seemed unnaturally pale. She gave the impression of being some way towards invisibility. She threw Ferdach a thin smile. He knew that her apparently menial duties concealed the fact that Asians were not trusted in such secret surroundings.

'So, you dropped Lai Kuan at Tras did you, Mr O'Haney?' was Adamson-Hitching's opener.

'No. Not Tras. Tras is over the mountains. At a small *kampung*, Kampung Kereyang.' All at once Ferdach decided to be impertinent. He raised his eyebrows at Walsingham and said, 'I'm surprised that you reported what I told you so incorrectly. Surely Mr Hitching requires accuracy.' Reluctant to use a double-barrelled name, he had wondered whether to call Walsingham's boss Adamson or Hitching. Plain Hitching seemed more appropriate for the angular looking man whose narrow eyes were scrutinising him as if trying to lacerate his skin. 'Itching' might be more appropriate.

Walsingham responded with politeness. 'I think your safety was on AH's mind. The whole area around Tras is dangerous. There have been many incidents there. But clearly, Ferdach, in the company of Lai Kuan you must have felt quite safe.'

'Not in the least. In fact Lai Kuan and I discussed how we might behave if we were ambushed.'

'Really,' said Hitching, sitting forward intently. 'And how would you have behaved?'

'Oh, we both agreed that we would die for one another,' lied Ferdach. 'We're bosom friends you know.'

Walsingham and Hitching exchanged a quick glance at the word 'bosom'. What a couple of bigots they are, thought Ferdach. The urge to take them for a ride grew in his own bosom. 'So you want to know who I met, and what I did in Kuala Lumpur,' he said gaily.

'Well, that would be interesting, I suppose,' Hitching growled, as if it was the last thing in the world he wanted to hear. 'But we're much more interested in what you made of Lai Kuan. Is he trustworthy, in your view?'

'Trustworthy to whom? I trust him implicitly. But that raises the question of whether you trust me.'

'One must assume,' said Hitching, a note of sarcasm hung in the air, 'that every member of the Malayan Civil Service is on our side. After all you yourself are deeply involved in the struggle against the communists.'

'My dear Adamson-Hitching,' Ferdach stated, in a condescending way, 'I'll tell you this: I know for certain that Lai Kuan is not doing anything to help the communists, in the sense, that is, of actively supporting their struggle. On the other hand, like most Malayans, he'd like to see the British out. I also know that he believes the British will never get out until peace has been restored, either by the elimination of the communists or by their making peace with government. I suspect he favours the last course. He definitely believes that this Emergency is a complete mistake.'

There was a silence of maybe a quarter of a minute during which Walsingham and Hitching looked at one another as though they had just heard something of extreme interest. Walsingham then asked, 'And do you believe that Lai Kuan's visit to Tras was in any way, how should I put it, to further that second course of action?'

'Lai Kuan gave no hint of what he was up to or where he was going. By the way, I wish you wouldn't harp on Tras all the time. On the basis of what he told me, or didn't tell me, I can't answer your question. However ...' and here Ferdach paused deliberately, to invest his next words with a sense of mystery, 'after what I heard in KL, from Gilbert de Guise, my friend in the Chief Secretary's office, there might be some point in your question.'

Both men then expressed fulsome interest in hearing about Ferdach's visit to Kuala Lumpur. They sensed that he was playing them along, suspected that he was vain and self centred, and felt certain that he was one of the amoral breed of youth that had resulted from the war and which would probably increase to a flood in the years to come. 'So you were quite taken by Kuala Lumpur. It reminded you of a small English county town,' said Hitching, repeating some of Ferdach's pleasantries on his first arrival. 'Well, as far as the expatriates are concerned, there's something in that I suppose. The same inbred social life, the parties, the gossip, the amateur theatricals, the sport and the snobbery. Yes, there's something in that. Though as far a I can remember neither Winchester nor Tunbridge Wells has a Malay *kampung* or a Chinese quarter.'

'No, but they have some mean streets occupied by proles who count for nothing, like the Malays and the Chinese in some British eyes.'

'Does your friend de Guise think of them like that?' sidekick Walsingham demanded.

Now for it, thought Ferdach. 'Well Walsingham. Well Hitching. De Guise is something else. You probably know that he's a Tibetan scholar. It must be on your files. He looks down on all levels of society but not because of his academic learning. He's a member of a famous French family, the de Guises, once the rulers of Lorraine and they claim descent from Charlemagne. So naturally he feels very superior to a mere high commissioner. I should imagine he probably thinks the British royals are mere parvenus. So he can mix with British officers, Chinese workers,

Malay policemen and Tamil night soil collectors with equal ease since he condescends to the lot. I guess that in a way he's extremely democratic.'

Hitching was visibly angry, especially at the mention of British royals. Scathingly he said, 'Surely he's not like that to you?' He turned towards his assistant. 'I can't see O'Haney accepting that kind of treatment, can you Walsingham?'

'Oh no, not to me. In me he sees an equal, intellectually,' replied Ferdach, helping himself to a chocolate biscuit and sipping his coffee. Both were unpleasant. As he put his cup down distastefully he was conscious of dislike flowing towards him across the table. He relished the sensation.

'Do tell us more about de Guise. He sounds an unusual man. The Chief Secretary must have chosen him as his private secretary for a good reason. Just what are the de Guise qualities?' The words were delivered from Walsingham and Hitching as a medley.

'Well, apart from the fact that he's a brilliant scholar, apart from the fact that he's thin and rather wild looking with staring eyes that bore into you even more than yours do Mr Hitching, and apart from the fact that he's a highly efficient officer, so the Chief Secretary thinks, Gilbert's deeply interested in Tibetan religion. That's what first brought him into contact with Hester, his wife. I must say that I found her more Indian, culturally that is, than English even though she went to Oxford. Perhaps she first made the acquaintance of Gilbert there, I don't know. She's an artist and also a talented dancer – Indian dancing. I found her fascinating but something of a mystery. A bit too intense for me but obviously not for Gilbert who adores her. Of course it was she who instructed Gilbert in Tantric yoga.' Ferdach hesitated, looked dubiously from one to the other of the expressionless faced men opposite him, before saying, 'As a matter of fact, one night they kept me talking into the small hours about Tibet and especially about Tantric sexual practices.'

'What exactly are those, Mr O'Haney?' A degree of sternness had entered Hitching's voice. It was obvious that he was expecting to hear something he would not approve.

Ferdach sat up, warming to a subject dear to him. 'But surely Mr Adamson-Hitching, your masters wouldn't send you to the Orient without briefing you extensively on major aspects of the cultures here.'

Ferdach shook his head as if apologising for an error. 'Well, I mustn't be churlish; the Colonial Office never told us about Tantra. I guess we all have to learn that Asia's quite different from Tunbridge Wells.' Meeting with cold stares, Ferdach began to expatiate. 'Forgive me if I bore you, but I must speak my mind: some Eastern religions see all creation as a unity whereas Christianity, Judaism and Islam believe in a dichotomy between the spiritual and the physical, light and dark, good and evil, though in those religions some mystics, like the Malay Sufis, have a vision of things that transcends the opposites. So, whilst the West sees sexuality as sin, the Hindu, the Buddhist, accepts it as part of a totality. Out here, you only have to go to Sukuh in Java to see that Shivaism, with its phallic worship, is still alive.' The thought then came into Ferdach's mind, not of the gentle Sufi mysticism that prevailed in Malaya but of those unorthodox orgiastic practices, which, Malay friends had told him, had sprung up in remote *kampung*s. However, he had no wish to reveal fields in which these men had neither the right nor the need to trespass, so he decided to betray no interest in them, merely saying, 'It's best to be open minded about all religious matters, especially where sex is involved. But believe me, many ancient ideas are far from dead hereabouts, things beyond the remit even of British intelligence.'

Walsingham looked furious; he clearly believed there were no limits to the remit of his probing. He glanced sideward at his boss who interrupted with a loud and very irritated, 'Look here, O'Haney, we're not completely ignorant. You're not here to lecture us. And as far as I'm concerned, all religion, Western and Eastern, is rubbish.'

'If you say so,' replied Ferdach with the blandest of smiles which masked his glee at narking the two conventionally minded men glaring at him. 'But you asked me a question and when I do my best to give you a proper reply, you get oddly irritated like a couple of maiden aunts. So what am I here for?'

'To brief us on what you've picked up from Lai Kuan and de Guise and in KL generally,' Walsingham stated angrily, turning to Hitching as though for approval.

'But I've just been giving you a *tour d'horizon* of Gilbert's views.'

'You mean of Hester's views,' Walsingham snorted.

'Of Gilbert and Hester's views.'

'Oh for God's sake let him get on with his lecture, Walsingham,' said Hitching. 'There'll be a needle in his haystack sooner or later.'

Ferdach laughed rudely. In fact it was a guffaw. Adamson-Hitching stood up to indicate that the interview was over. Walsingham followed suite. Ferdach remained seated and said quietly, 'Such as the very pointed fact that de Guise's wife was formerly married to Peter Molyneux.'

Adamson-Hitching sat down and gestured Walsingham to do likewise. 'Married to …' His voice died for an instant. 'But Peter's near the top in Special Branch. He's the intimate of the Commissioner of Police.' He ran his hand over his forehead. 'Is there anything to be gained from this information Ferdach?'

'Only that where there are pipes there can be a leak, Mr Adamson-Hitching.'

Walsingham was about to say something but Hitchings gestured him to silence. He was in control now. 'And what has leaked your way, Ferdach?'

Ferdach had had his bit of Irish fun tweaking the ears of these, as he saw them, stolid Englishmen but now, in a schizophrenic sort of way, he reckoned it was his duty to say what he thought as a member of HM Colonial Service. 'Well, I admit that I had heard that Tras is a communist redoubt, though not from Lai Kuan; it's common knowledge in Special Branch and beyond. If some of the top Party bosses are in its vicinity, as is rumoured, Lai Kuan is probably going to see them. At least that's what I surmise.'

'Now Ferdie, why should you so surmise?' Adamson-Hitching's voice was a study in patience.

Ferdach was amused at how he had first acquired a Christian name and now, on Adamson-Hitching's lips, its diminutive. 'May I go back to Tantric sex, sir?'

'Go back to Adam and Eve if it's going to be useful,' said Hitching. 'And do take as long as you want.'

'Hester is half Indian. She's a pacifist. At least she believes in passive resistance à la Mahatma Gandhi. Now Mr Hitching, you know that sex and politics can be both happy and unhappy bedfellows. Where Gilbert and Hester are concerned they are certainly happy. To be blunt, if you will allow me, in Tantric sex the male is not supposed to ejaculate quickly.

He has to learn how to achieve orgasm without losing sperm. The two events are made separate. In Tantra, the orgasm of a man and a woman is symbolic of union with the godhead. To enhance it, to prolong it, can become a mystical experience. Both Gilbert and Hester believe in all this very sincerely. They're undoubtedly very much in love but even in the grossest physical terms all this is bound to make Gilbert an unusual lover. Hester is besotted with him. Stolid old Peter could hardly have had a look in. He never had, I imagine. But Gilbert didn't steal Hester from Peter; Gilbert only arrived in Malaya when I did. From what Hester hinted I gather that she was in an on-and-off relationship with a Chinese man when Gilbert came onto the scene. Even so the marriage surprised many people and maybe annoyed some stuffy people in KL as well.'

'Well, all this is very interesting,' said Hitching indulgently, 'and good material for a novel, if Somerset Maugham hadn't done it all so well already. But Mr O'Haney, where's the political dimension to all this. For instance where does Hester stand?'

Ferdach was now anxious to get away from this office. The more he talked the more he would inadvertently get enmeshed in Hitching's web. He decided to give a quick resumé of his findings. 'Well, Tantra and the rest apart, Hester is, as you might expect, a committed pacifist; she believes in negotiation. So not unnaturally she rejects the hard military line being advanced by the security forces in Kuala Lumpur. Gilbert fully agrees with her. I agree with her myself and I'm sure Lai Kuan would. The truth is that the security forces are against any negotiated peace with the communists. The top Malayan brass and Special Branch, not to mention many influential Malays, are convinced that since the majority of the Chinese are communist supporters at heart, only the total elimination of communism can save the Malays from future Chinese domination. I got all this from Gilbert, who got it from Hester, who prized it out of her ex-husband. Oh, I forgot to mention that poor old Peter still wants Hester back. They still see one another, as friends of course. I'm not sure whether she rather enjoys playing with him like a fish on a line or whether she feels genuinely fond of him in some way.'

Both intelligence men looked nonplussed. Walsingham failed to glance at his watch surreptitiously and Hitching, rather wearily, asked, 'And so your final conclusion to all this fascinating information is precisely what, Mr O'Haney? For I suspect you had time to think up something or other driving all the way down to Singapore.'

'No need for much thought at all, my dear Hitching. It's obvious. I could see the answer straightaway: my good friend Lai Kuan must be up to something in Tras very much against the policies of the Special Branch people in KL.'

48

Despite their occasionally acid arguments Ferdach and Laura were held together by a strong physical attraction. With Alfred away this could be given free range and since the curfew still limited travel around the city, the heat of the afternoon generally drove them to his study, the only airconditioned room in the house, where they could let their desires rip.

In that room there was also time for confessionals. Ferdach told Laura of his visit to Mat Noor's *kampung* and of his consuming passion for him. Whereas at other times Laura would have pooh-poohed the idea of such a relationship, in that love nest her face took on a distant look when she listened to Ferdach's words as if she too longed for an affair of the heart. She recognized the delicacy of such love for Ferdach's decription of a jungle pool with the sunlight breaking through to bathe Mat Noor's body with dappled light so that it seemed insubstantial, moved her, even though she was outside the picture. Inwardly, however, she believed that Ferdach should steer clear of further involvement with Noor, not for any moral reason but because she saw that two people with such different backgrounds could never find a common space in a colonial society. Yet, since it was understanding that Ferdach sought, she muffled her feelings and accepted his statement that all would be well when he returned to Ipoh. 'I sincerely hope so,' she responded. 'I want you to be happy Ferdie.' She was less understanding, however, when he joked about his Penang escapades in the House of Everlasting Happiness, a brothel now owned, he said, by Wong Siu Bo, the first woman he had had in Ipoh. Was he not aware how disgusting it was to lure young girls into prostitution? Had he no respect for womanhood? When Ferdach responded that, like the majority of women in French brothels who gave a social worker '*le goût pour les hommes*' as their reason for becoming prostitutes, Siu Bo's Penang girls had told him they liked their profession. Even those who had doubts said they preferred it to planting rice or rearing pigs, or worse to domestic slavery as a secondary wife. Laura sneered that the social worker was probably a man with tastes like Ferdach; while restraining her feminism from erupting she still resented what he got up to.

There was also a less altruistic side to her behaviour: she knew that her marriage to Alfred was doomed. Increasingly their interests were taking different tracks. Alfred was immersed in the work of the Education Department, but in a way that seemed out of date to Laura. He might just as well have been in Bradford, which was where he came from, and he saw education as no more than a functional instrument to qualify students for jobs. Laudable enough and a goal no different to what the students and their parents wanted, but the scheme of education he supported was hardly changed from prewar days. He could not see that the boys and girls for whom he toiled were sailing into a non-colonial future. The rising wave of nationalism that was moving them had not entered his consciousness.

Laura was sensitive to the changing mood of Singapore, at least on a personal level. She moved in academic circles and was the friend of aspiring writers like Beda Lim and Gung Wu. She knew the more intellectual newcomers working in government service like Kenneth Topley, who had been on the same Colonial Service course as Ferdach in London, and his ebullient, often amusing wife Marjorie, herself a perspicacious anthropologist already probing the mysteries of Taoist cults in the island. She spent evenings talking with them and their leftwing friends like Lim Chin Siong, Jack da Silva and Devan Nair in smokey bars or at open-air food stalls in off beat parts of the city. Some of them had their first experience of an Englishwoman with Laura for, unlike Ferdach, she was no romantic where men were concerned. Ever the pragmatist she was deeply curious about human males and their motivations and this curiosity impelled her to an exploration of every aspect of their personalities; arousing their sexuality invariably led to them revealing information otherwise kept hidden. And so, within a short time, she grasped the uncomfortable fact that a volcano was stirring. The accident of the Maria Hertogh case convinced her that the hatred of the people for the colonial system, alleged by the students, was real and might get out of hand. Yet she never imagined that she herself might ever be in danger for the intellectual young men she knew all seemed so civilised and kind. She was now horrified by what the gentle Malays were doing; what could happen, she wondered, if the Chinese, the majority of the population, got going?

In another sense too, her open marriage with Albert was failing. Despite the freedom that he had to see Mona Wee, whose flat was not far away, Alfred had shown a tendency to fly into rages if Laura stayed out with any of her men friends. Whatever she did turned out to be wrong. If she went out to dine in public with, say, an army officer, she was humiliating Alfred. If she avoided public places and retreated to the anonymity of a man's apartment, then she had become sex mad. She could not win. Ferdach's transitory visit was just about tolerated because Alfred believed that he and Ferdach had, if not deeply, been friends in Ipoh. In any case he could easily refer to Ferdach as a former colleague from Ipoh if anyone asked who Laura was going about with. Even so, Alfred only came to the house briefly whilst Ferdach was there; he was fortunate that, as a responsible Singapore government officer, he had a pass that enabled him to go travel during the curfew.

Laura still cherished the idea that she might marry Ferdach. Theirs could be a real open marriage; even Ferdach's occasional half-jocular suggestions about their sharing partners seemed to accord with her ambition. The trouble was that outside the confines of the bedroom, or more likely Alfred's study, Laura was not able to convince Ferdach that she would be a reasonable person to live with on a daily basis.

Why for instance, a couple of days after his visit to Phoenix Park and just after they had made love in Alfred's study, did she have to speak so aggressively to him. 'God, Ferdie, you really made a bosh of your visit to Phoenix Park. They don't think much of you there. You don't seem to be able to make up your mind whether you're a supporter of the IRA, a liberal do-gooder or just a naughty child. And after all the work I put in for you.'

'Put in for me?'

'You do realise that Adamson-Hitching is the number two in Phoenix Park, don't you? You'd never have got anywhere near his office if I hadn't talked about you to Walsingham.' Laura's tone was withering, like that of a female army officer berating a stupid member of a platoon. 'My God, do you want to spend your life up in that boring Ipoh, that backwater?'

It was not Laura's unjustified assumption of credit that irritated Ferdach so much as her way of saying it. Her voice, always firm to put it mildly, had risen several degrees. Ferdach had heard that some women in the Ipoh Club used to avoid her solely on account of her voice and her hectoring manner. So Ferdach raised his voice to the same level when he replied, 'As a matter of fact I love Ipoh, I love Perak, I love my work there. And I don't care a toss what those wankers in Phoenix Park think.'

'Don't shout at me, please. Don't persecute me.' Laura's voice had now fallen, become dulcet, in contrast with her earlier tones. 'We won't talk about it if you're going to be so aggressive.'

'To tell the truth I don't see the need to talk about it at all.' Ferdach said quietly, though with difficulty. 'You raised the matter.'

'Oh yes, blame me. I'm sorry Walsingham isn't here to tell you how you disgusted Adamson-Hitching.'

'Disgusted?'

'Yes. With all that talk about sex, Tantric sex, not ejaculating. Hitching thinks you're some sort of degenerate.'

Ferdach, squatting gnome-like on the tatami floor mat, stared solidly at Laura's naked body sprawled voluptuously on the settee before his eyes, before saying very coldly, 'Please enlighten me. What business is it of yours to talk about me to Walsingham? I'd really like to know.'

Now Laura became strangely coy. She curled up like a cat, dropping her gaze in an affectation of embarrassment. 'Sorry Ferdie, I didn't speak to Walsingham. He spoke to me. In fact a week ago, just after you phoned to say you were coming, he sought me out. I'd never clapped eyes on him before.'

'Well then Laura, don't pretend you've been helping me. Phoenix Park was told of my visit by Noel Aspinall. After all he's the only one of them that I know.'

'One of them?' queried Laura incredulously. 'But Walsingham, Adamson-Hitching, aren't homos.'

'In this case I mean members of Her Majesty's Intelligence Service.

Though Noel falls into both categories. Did Walsingham tell you why he and Hitching wanted to see me?'

'Oh just general information gathering, he said, but I doubted it. I'm sure they want more than that.' Laura paused, stetched out again and looked contrite. 'Honestly Ferdie, I was hoping they might want to make use of you. That's why I told Walsingham what a brilliant young man you are. I thought that Phoenix Park might add you to its payroll. I thought that if that happened I'd see you more often. I thought that maybe it would lead to you changing jobs and coming to work here. Then we ...'

The unreality of Laura's plan made Ferdach experience a surge of compassion. Everything, whether espionage, politics, the riots, her husband's work or the social whirl, was merely there to be manipulated by her for her own ends. And at the present time she was deeply in need of him. She wanted him not just for sex. That was an easily available commodity for her, but because, in some strange way, they were on the same wavelength. The idea that marriage could provide him with a protective shield again crossed Ferdach's mind. But then, as usual, came the doubts: could he afford a woman with such a passion for clothes and high living? He would be impoverished. He did not take her statement that she could easily get a job seriously. Yet there was worse: why was it, when they were together, that he was always waiting upon Laura's moods? He often found himself glancing at her for she was one of those people whose inner feelings quickly found expression in her body language. Irritation would be sensed in the way she would snatch up something offered to her, or the way in which she would bang something down. Boredom would be expressed by slow movements, disappointment by sudden quick dashes if they were walking together. She was quick to anger yet at the same time easily moved to affectionate gestures. Her body was like a barometer of her mind. Ferdach himself, being sexually ambiguous, had, generally speaking, learned to hide his inner state of mind but not to modify it. In different ways they were both wilful which made him doubt her ability to accept what he had to tell her. 'Laura, doesn't it strike you that I can't be involved in what goes on at Phoenix Park. It's aims are different from those of KL. Gilbert told me that the Malayan security forces want a decisive military solution to the Emergency. Can't you see that it'd be impossible for me to link up with the likes of Walsingham. They'd want me to find out all I could about Malayan government policies, to spy for them. So please get this clear in your beautiful little head: I'm a servant of the Malayan government. My loyalties lie there and that's the way it will stay.'

'Oh they are both part of the British Raj,' Laura replied airily. 'You'd have no conflict of interest. In any case what you men do in your silly offices is all a lot of baloney. You think you're shaping the world with your committees and sub-committes and your pompous directives. Haven't you realised it yet? The world shapes itself regardless of what you all do. The only world that matters is the miniscule world, the world of personal relationships in which, in nine cases out of ten, the male of the species lacks understanding.'

'Which you do your best to remedy,' said Ferdach tartly, even though he did not entirely disagree with her.

In reply Laura leaned over towards him, took his hands and drew him up onto the settee. Then she knelt on the floor where he had just been sitting and started to move her fingers very sensuously over his body. 'You're angry with me, I can tell,' she whispered. 'You need to be soothed. Go on. Turn over, on your tummy first. Oh look, the carpet's made a pattern on your bum. Now I'm going to run my lips light as butterfly wings all over you from your head to your feet and I'm going to …'

As she made good on her promise she ceased to prattle. Ferdach lay back compliant, enjoying her ministrations until it was time to play the man's role which, so Laura always said, he did to perfection.

It all seemed so satisfying that a notion entered Ferdach's head that they really were intended for one another. It was only when he awoke from a snooze and saw Laura staring despairingly at herself in the mirror that he wondered whether his love making had been so good for her after all.

49

Once order was restored and the curfew lifted, Singapore social life resumed at a frenetic a pace as ever. When people fear that the volcano they live on is about to erupt, there is always a frisson in the air. An unusually friendly Alfred turned up and took Laura and Ferdach to a dance at the Tanglin Club where everyone recounted and embroidered upon their horrid experiences and escapes during the riots. The next night Ferdach returned Alfred's hospitality by taking them all to Princes Restaurant where the soft lighting, the food and, above all, the fine French wine induced a sense of well-being in the three of them. This was especially so in the case of Alfred who led them into an enlightened discussion of how successfully he and Laura had arranged their private lives so that nobody in Singapore government circles thought them too offbeat, his affair with Mona Wee being considered nothing more than a peccadillo to which any red-blooded expatriate was entitled.

The fragility of this enlightened régime was demonstrated on their third night on the town. Their dinner at the Raffles had ended earlier than they had anticipated on account of the stony rudeness of the Tiffin Room's Hainanese waiters, whose deadpan stares and impatient shuffling made it clear that they too had families and wanted an early night. 'So much for one of the fables of the exotic East,' fumed Laura. 'What lousy service! What rotten food!' She had slipped into an angry mood as she started ahead of them almost charging through the palm-fringed gardens to the road. There, loitering on the pavement, Ferdach was surprised to encounter someone he had last seen in the London flat of Ross, the film director who might have put his name in lights. 'Norman!' Ferdach shouted to a young man in uniform who was arguing with a comrade.

'Fuckin' hell, it's fuckin' Ferdie,' the man replied. 'Belt up, Jeff! Meet me old opo Ferdie.' He pushed his friend towards Ferdach. There was a general shaking of hands, accompanied by dubious glances on both sides, as Ferdach introduced the two Royal Marines to Laura then to Alfred. All at once Laura's mood changed; her frown turned into a radiant smile directed at the two young men, but especially at Norman who was a bit like a Nordic god, blond and tall, as Royal Marines were supposed to be. Jeff was not so sublime but much more muscular. In comparison with Siegfried he was swarthy and his heavy moustache gave him a Turkish look.

'What are you doing here?' Ferdach asked. 'I mean here, outside the Raffles? It's terribly expensive. The NAAFI isn't far down the road you know.'

In a flash the Turk sneered, 'Get back to your kennel Norm.' He looked Ferdach up and down as though sizing him up for a fight.

'Oh, I didn't mean it like that,' said Ferdach. 'I meant if you want to eat and drink cheaply, the NAAFI's very good.'

'Take no notice of that bugger,' said Norman putting his arm around Ferdach's shoulder and speaking reassuringly into his ear, at which point his breath suggested that the two marines had been drinking heavily. 'Anyway it ain't no fuckin good us goin to a fuckin' forces club. We're skint. We'll have to hitch back to the fuckin' base.'

Whereas Laura had moved next to Norman to hear the chat, Alfred had drifted away; it wasn't done to mix with other ranks. He looked at his watch and made some remark about getting home. At this Laura rounded on him, though gaily, and said, 'Oh God, come on Alfred; these two boys have a tough time in the navy. We should be hospitable. Let's take them somewhere for a drink, to Bugis Street, and later on get them back to the base.' Then she added, 'After all, Norman's an old friend of Ferdie, isn't he?' and gave Norman a sweet smile which elicited the response, 'Not arf he ain't.'

Ferdach wondered what Laura was up to. He had already made up his mind that the two marines had drifted near to the Raffles in the hope of meeting some well-heeled admirer of male physique to subsidize them. There was no other reason for their presence.

Faced with the inevitable, Alfred agreed. 'Fine then. Pile in the car. I'll drop you all at bloody Bugis Street. That should give them something to remember. But I'll have to get back; got work in the morning. It'll be easy for you all to get taxis there.'

Somehow or other Laura managed to get in the back seat squeezed between the two marines and Ferdach found himself next to Alfred. When the car started up, Alfred muttered, 'Bugis Street … buggers street more likely. Can't stand the place. You'll both be back late and Laura won't be quiet if I know her. Tell her I'm going to Miss Wee's house. I want a good night's sleep.' Laura heard nothing of this as she was engaged in nonsensical conversation with the two marines, all three of them pressed together in sweaty proximity with the two men's arms around Laura's shoulders and her hands resting on their thick thighs for 'there's nowhere else to put them,' she cried.

Alfred certainly knew his way around the backstreets of Singapore. Soon he had deposited his passengers near to a short street ablaze with bare electric lights, crowded with foodstalls and tables and thronged with people. There was also something electric in the atmosphere; people were here to enjoy their own and other people's humanity in a warm, friendly atmosphere made pungent by the smell of spicy cooking and sometimes smokey from the charcoal that glowed beneath the sticks of delicious satay. Laura barely acknowledged Alfred, with a 'See you when I see you', and went off arm-in-arm with her two newfound companions. The marines seemed cock-a-hoop at being the escorts of an attractive English woman in a multiracial sea of observers.

'I'll give the guys their taxi fare to the base,' Ferdach told Alfred, who grinned maliciously.

'You better had or else you mightn't get home in one piece.'

It was Ferdach's first visit to the street, named after the pirates who once plied the narrow straits offshore, but not, apparently, the first time Norman and Jeff had been there. They were the ones who managed to find an empty table halfway down the street, strategically placed for seeing the world. There they set up court, giving boisterous greetings to the skinny waiters, clad in singlets and shorts, and making crude remarks to the elaborately coiffed and highly rouged prostitutes lingering nearby; the latter were of both sexes but all wore female clothes, either the Malay *sarung kebaya* or the Chinese cheongsam. This was the hour when Chinese families who had been eating out were beginning to clear off, soon to be replaced by a hodgepodge of Europeans, many escaping from the stuffiness of their clubs and hotels, and by members of HM forces. Tonight, roistering RN sailors predominated, but, being sailors, they knew the limits of permissible behaviour.

The sound of Chinese, Malay and Western music blaring from numerous loudspeakers mingled with the high-pitched orders sung out by the waiters, and with the loud voices of the revellers, was truly cacophonous yet the atmosphere was in no way intimidating; this was a tolerant, happy mixture of humanity. Alcohol was being consumed, often to excess, and sexuality of every type happily flaunted. When a couple of lurching merchant sailors with Liverpool accents decided to join Ferdach's table he told a waiter to bring Tiger beers for everyone. Other waiters then descended on them from stalls arranged under awnings at the side of the road, and fried noodles, lamb and goat satay, and mutton soup were ordered very discerningly by Norman's friend Jeff. Since nothing here was too expensive Ferdach did not worry that everything would be on him.

Laura had, of course, been here before and she was blasé about it. Being quick in mind she had picked up a number of expressions in Cantonese and Hokkien and she had also made progress in the kind of market Malay spoken throughout the region as a lingua franca. In the latter she was considerably more adept than Ferdach, who always made an effort to speak good Malay but invariably stumbled. Listening to Laura anyone might think that she was a fluent Chinese speaker for she larded her sentences with long drawn-out 'lahs', 'ahs', 'mahs' and exclamatory 'aiyahs', all intended to give force or persuasiveness to whatever was being said. Only the Chinese knew that Laura's use of them was, as often as not, inappropriate and often ludicrous. But as she was only intent on impressing the men at her table this did not matter.

'Yer like slummin, don't yer mate?' When asking this Jeff shifted his rickety chair, and so himself, close to Ferdach's stool as though seeking a mate's physical support.

'Slumming?'

'You 'eard what I said. This ain't your sort of place. You belong to Raffles or the posh clubs.'

'How wrong you are,' Ferdach replied. 'This is exactly my sort of place. And I don't reckon I'm slumming.' Though reproving Jeff, Ferdach had noticed something in his cynical expression and in his derisive tone that suggested a clever brain though one much concerned with status in the world. Whether his rough manner arose from this or was an affectation, it certainly appealed to Ferdach who just then became conscious of the deliberate pressure of Jeff's limbs against him.

Jeff let out an unexpectedly gentle sigh, a sad sigh it seemed. 'I'll tell yer: this is the best bloody place in town. 'Ere, everyone's equal. See all them guys, soldiers, sailors, airmen – they're lonely and lost. They're British but the local British look down on 'em. They might as well be bloody lepers. But blokes don't want your NAAFI or your Union Jack Club, cut off from the rest of mankind. They want to be human beings. And they don't want to be looked down on by the bastards they're 'ere to defend.'

Ferdach noticed that Laura was having a discreet tête-a-tête with Norman while the two Liverpudlians were joking with a *pondan*, a transvestite Malay. Their little party seemed to have disintegrated. He turned to face Jeff closely. 'I'm not a Singapore officer. I'm from the Federation, from Malaya. And my job takes me into country areas where there are terrorists. I work intimately with soldiers. Officers of course, but also British other ranks and Malayan other ranks. I'm no different from them. I'm not your typical colonialist whatever you think. But I know what you're saying Jeff.'

Jeff looked nonplussed then, nodding across at Laura and Norman, he whispered, 'What's with 'er? Will she let 'im 'ave it?'

Ferdach almost asked 'Have what?' but fortunately thought better of it. 'Depends on her,' he answered truthfully. Then he added, 'I'm staying with her you know.'

'Does that matter?'

'Well, yes and no.'

'Come off it mate. Norm's told me what you an 'im got up to in London with that poncey film director.' Jeff was unpleasantly assertive as he spoke; indeed Ferdach was conscious of threat in the air. But, noticing Ferdach's expression, Jeff suddenly became all sweetness once more and murmured, 'Nothing against it mate. No, nothing against it with a nice bloke like you.'

298

'What are you two talking about?' Laura shouted over to them. The happiness in her voice was a silver dart piercing the din.

'Only you darling,' Ferdach called back. 'Who else but you?'

Everyone then concentrated on the food that had been plonked down on the table. Ferdach paid for everything except the satay, and also tipped the waiters. At the sight of money, beggars appeared and were given some change before being chased off by the waiters. They tucked into the food while at the same time observing the passing pageant of whores, pimps, transvestites, pretty boys, servicemen, ordinary beings of all nationalities and drunks. The two sailors asked for more beer and showed a propensity to make obscene comments about every passer-by.

'Ooh, look at 'er. Legs right up to 'er fuckin' bum.'

'Wonder if she's got a prick. D'yer think she takes it back or front?'

'Who cares? If it's wet and warm ...'

' Like fuckin' the whole world through the fuckin' kitchen window.'

Ferdach could not decide why a kitchen window was so poetically specified but did recall that at the back of some Liverpool slum houses the only window on the ground floor was in the kitchen. Anyway, this sort of banter went on throughout the meal until the Scousers began arguing over the merits of their city's two football teams. Their voices grew loud and heated. Every other word seemed to be 'fuckin'. People sitting at nearby tables began to watch out for violence. Ferdach looked anxiously at Jeff with whom he had developed a conspiratorial relationship based on both eye and thigh contact and was glad to hear him say, 'Let's clear off. I'll give the wink to Norm.'

Ferdach called the satay man; all the little kebabs had been eaten so payment could be made quickly. Jeff signalled Norman who took Laura by the arm and the four of them made off. As they did so one of the sailors laid into the other. Both tottered to their feet; dishes crashed to the floor and a fight began. Laura wanted Ferdach to go back and intervene but he pushed on through the crowd to the main road where he found a taxi. They piled in and before any argument could develop Laura said imperiously, 'Goodwood Park Hotel.'

Despite which they did not go straight there. Approaching Orchard Road, Jeff, who had taken command, announced that they had not had enough to drink. Useless for Laura to protest that there was plenty of booze at her place; she named some of the interesting alcoholic drinks in her bar. But no, they must go to a dive Jeff knew because, on a hot night like this, they really needed beer.

A muffled roar of loud voices and louder music flowed into the road from Queen's Bar. Once in its smokey depths, Ferdach saw a melée of soldiers, mostly in uniform, propping up the long counter, lounging around linoleum-covered tables, and leaning against the black walls which were adorned with huge pinups of Oriental ladies with come-and-get-it expressions on their faces and flowers hiding parts of their bodies. The pictures were not very alluring; indeed the way in which the flowers seemed to be actually growing out of their bodies was both ludicrous and obscene. A number of older Europeans of unsoldierly appearance were scattered about the place each holding court to a soldier or two. At the bar, an elderly aristocratic-looking man with a thin aesthetic face, was in the process of ordering a round of Anchor beer for his unlikely military companions from one of the three hard-faced Chinese barmaids, almost the only women present except for Laura and a few superannuated whores who were all but ignored by the men. At the centre of the room three callow soldiers were in rivalry to see who could down the most liquid. There were cheers when one of them gulped a pint without a pause and then looked fair fit to vomit. Ferdach felt sorry that young men sent out to defend Britain's interests felt obliged to come to such a lousy hole to pass their free time. Surely everyone here, himself included, would have been better off in the jollier atmosphere of Bugis Street.

At one end of the bar a diminutive lady, dressed in black Chinese clothes of an expensive material, was in urgent conversation with two corporals. Her pretty face, which bore not a trace of make-up, seemed to occupy an incongruously small part of her enormous head. 'That's Wendy Lo. She's booking 'em up for the night,' Jeff told Ferdach. 'She's got contacts in all the knocking shops. Tell her what you want – Malay, Chinese, Indian, English – and what you can afford and she'll arrange it. Some Europeans ring her up if they want a British soldier. One hundred percent reliable she is, a real businesswoman and no tricks. It's safer to let her fix you up than going to places like Lavender Street where you might pick up anything, including a knife in your back.'

Norman had already bought two beers for himself and Laura, and the two of them had gone off to a dark corner to resume their intimate chat. 'That's generous of him,' said Ferdach, but Jeff answered, 'Yes, he's a real mate. He knows we want to be together.'

This irritated Ferdach as 'being together', whatever that implied, was the last thing on his mind. It also narked him that a couple of soldiers, after greeting Jeff briefly, gave the sailor the sort of nod and wink that meant, 'Good luck to you mate for what you've landed.' In fact the Queen's had something of the atmosphere of the Pakenham pub in Knightsbridge which Ferdach had once visited with Nina Hamnett and Ross for the latter to size up the Horseguardsmen who were on offer for the night. Before he could work out how he might join Laura, assuming she would want him to, Ferdach found himself propelled into an alcove by Jeff who resumed the affectionate closeness that he had started in Bugis Street. Before either of them could say very much they were joined by Wendy Lo who sat down opposite them and gave Ferdach a piercing stare.

'You come here first time,' she asked or rather stated to Ferdach. 'Maybe my good boy Jeff showing you the town?' She half raised herself from her seat, leaned over and patted good boy Jeff's cheek.

'So the place isn't new to you?' Ferdach asked Jeff, not a little surprised.

'Oh yes. He come three four time already,' Wendy Lo answered. 'No. Maybe five time.'

A conversation then developed which showed that during a very short acquaintance Wendy and Jeff had struck up an unusual friendship that Ferdach could not fathom. It became quicker and increasingly furtive as they spoke. Only once did Ferdach hear himself referred to when Jeff said, 'He's OK. No, he's not police. He doesn't even live in Singapore.' At that Wendy glanced across at Ferdach, revealed two batteries of gold teeth in a brilliant smile, and resumed talking with Jeff, mainly about beer. Ferdach got the impression that they were engaged in some sort of a business deal, but how could that be? Then as abruptly as she had arrived Wendy went off, or rather shuffled off, for her tiny feet were clad in slippers several times too large. She was also very short legged and at each wee step her large bum swayed like a lantern in the wind. As she left she said, 'Now I go see my good fliend Miss Laula. Tonight she not alone. I see she find handsome boy aleady. Ah, she clever woman finding nice boy.'

Taken aback Ferdach asked, 'What the hell goes on here? What are you both talking about? What beer? Are you buying it cheap at the base and flogging it here? Not that I care. It's Laura that worries me. Miss Laula. She's been here before too. And on her own.' Ferdach then recalled Wendy's parting words and the penny dropped. Did Laura really go out at night, on her own, to pick up soldiers? It could mean social death for her and Alfred, and possibly the loss of Alfred's job.

When most people seemed to have decided it was time to leave the bar the four of them were pretty drunk. Laura had fallen into one of her sentimental I-love-you-all-moods and was into indiscriminate hugging, lascivious stroking and deep kissing of her three male companions which Ferdach, unlike Norman and Jeff, did not take to. Had he really heard her say in seductive tones to a totally unknown soldier who was eyeing her, 'Not tonight Joe. Next time lover boy.'

Outside on the brightly lit road the soldiers tried to restrain themselves for opposite the bar a jeepful of military police was keeping an eye out for trouble. But Laura only saw four stalwarts in bright red caps and white webbing sitting there stiffly erect and ready for action. At once she began to walk towards them calling out, 'Oh such gorgeous men, Ferdie. Just look at them.' Ferdie held her back while Jeff and Norm tried to grab a taxi. This was not easy because there was competition from soldiers who had not found a local Englishman to take them home. The taxi they finally got was old and dirty but, being American, large. Its thickset Malay driver was accompanied by a stalwart boy, his son maybe, grasping an iron bar. Taxi driving by night in a garrison city was not a safe job. Soon Laura, Ferdach and the two marines were in an indiscriminate heap on the back seat and on the floor.

By now Laura's voice had grown slurred and she was saying things like, 'I don't see why I should be the only one to love everyone. Norman go on, hold Ferdie, love my darling Ferdie, and Ferdie, I want to see you kissing Jeff.' Her strictures were pretty useless, however, as there was barely room for anyone to move a limb. Despite that, their enforced body proximity and streams of sweat created a feeling of togetherness that was absolute, uncomfortable and unpleasant.

302

Then Laura became a real pain in the neck to Ferdach when she took to saying in an extremely drunken way, 'No. No one's to have Ferdie but me. I love you Ferdie. Oh God how I love you.'

Ferdach decided to divert her stream of endearments by saying, very harshly, 'Jeff was making some agreement or other with Wendy Lo about Singapore beer. Weren't you Jeff?'

In reply, Jeff tightened the grip of his hand, which somehow or other had found its way onto Ferdach's cock, until it was quite painful. 'My own business,' he hissed angrily. 'Keep bloody shut about it.'

'*La bière de Singapour*,' shrieked Laura, her voice dissolving into laughter. 'You are a gump Ferdie. Don't you know what that is?'

'Shut your fuckin' mouth Laura.' Jeff said angrily. 'It's me own business.'

But Laura was in no mood to shut anything tonight. 'Oh don't worry,' she replied. 'None of us will say a word. Ferdie tried everything when he was living in Soho, didn't you darling? And I'm sure Norm knows the wickedness you're up to Jeff. Anyway, we'd all like to get high on whatever you've got.'

No need for further mystery then. When they got back to the Goodwood Park Hotel and had crept as quietly as their state of intoxication permitted into the annexe, Jeff produced a packet of heroin. With practised hands he and Laura rolled it into the cigarettes that Laura carefully opened up. Then they sprawled on Alfred and Laura's huge double bed passing the smokes around and talking unbridled nonsense. Almost imperceptibly they moved by gentle gradations up to a pleasantly euphoric stage that was heightened by more drink, this time Pernod. Laura insisted on calling it absinthe and burbled idiotic words about their all being marvellously decadent as if that was a state that made them in some way or other superior to the rest of mankind.

Though the neighbouring buildings were quiet and most of their lights off, Laura kept on shushing them all and insisted on candlelight, so as 'not to attract attention'. For a while Ferdach closed his eyes. Laura's voice seemed to be coming to him from far away across a broad white plain, as though from the other side of Antarctica. He had a feeling that he had entered some Neverland where nothing mattered nor would ever change. At the same time he was vaguely aware of hands removing his clothers and then embracing him intimately though hardly arousing him. Once he sighed, 'I'm sorry Mat Noor. I'm drunk. I'm too tired.' But the hands persisted. He opened his eyes and saw Jeff's lips approaching his eyes, which they kissed gently, one after another, before moving on to his mouth. How could a muscular giant be so soft, so sensuous? Ferdach did not object. It was not unpleasant to be kissed, to feel an insistent tongue probing into him. But though it made him sure that he was desired, he knew that his body, as it was now, would not be able to respond, even though his brain half wanted to. Undeterred Jeff went on with his love play, breathing amorous words like, 'You're my type Ferdie, I want you. You've got to let me have you.' But Ferdach had grown so still and heavy that all Jeff's efforts to make love were foiled by a body that was no better than a limp dummy.

Very soon he heard different sounds from nearby. Turning his head he saw Laura being fucked by Norman. The heroin and the candlelight made the sight strangely insubstantial. At one moment the coupled naked bodies looked beautiful, the next moment Norman's panting intensity and Laura's sobs and moans made the performance seem ridiculous. He heard Jeff telling him, 'Ain't they both gorgeous Ferdie? That's how we should be doing it.' In a while Norman's efforts came to an end and he lay back like an exhausted athlete breathing deeply. Ferdie was then aware of half intended words coming out of his own mouth. 'Go on Jeff. Give it to Laura. I want to watch you.' His advice must have been followed for when he awoke, much later it seemed, he found himself in Norman's arms, while Jeff and Laura were entwined together.

Ferdach got up and went to the broad verandah onto which all the rooms gave access. The day was sullen and grey but already hot and humid. During the night it had rained and he heard a rythmic dripping of water from leaves, from eaves, from gutters, and further away, in heavier antiphon, an artificial waterfall spuming into yet another ornamental pond.

Down in the garden, amidst the rich foliage, a few brown-skinned figures moved slowly and purposefully: Malay gardeners, sweeping up leaves, tieing back fronds too heavy with water or just doing nothing in particular. One of them, a heavy lipped boy with a red band twined about his head of wavy black hair, looked up with a broad smile of flashing white teeth. Ferdach smiled back, was reminded of Mat Noor and went inside to the kitchen where he made himself a coffee. Looking about him he noted the meticulous order of the shelves and the kitchen equipment. It was not the work of a tidy servant for the apartments were serviced by the hotel staff. No, everything bore the stamp of Laura: methodical, precise and rational. She seemed to be able to order everything in her life – her entertaining, her language study, her copious reading, her athletics – in a supremely sensible manner. That is everything but her love, or more exactly, her sex life. In the latter she defied all neat patterns, all conventions. And yet it was precisely her rejection of convention that Ferdach found attractive. Her behaviour could be unrestrained, but about her there was a radiance that drew people, especially men, to her. Maybe she possessed the potentiality of becoming a man-devouring goddess, a Medusa, for whom many a man would risk being turned into stone. Yet Ferdach felt sure that the failure of her marriage had nothing to do with sex but arose from Laura's inability to tolerate Alfred's pedestrian heaviness. On the other hand it was Ferdach's own refusal to be burdened with domestic responsibility and Laura's giddiness that had brought them together, making them into something like soulmates.

Barefooted Ferdach walked softly along the verandah and peeped over the swinging double half doors into the bedroom. Inside the mosquito net Laura's young stallions were making love to her again, this time simultaneously, like the erotic deities in Indian temple carvings. He felt neither jealousy nor any desire to join in, but he did feel an unlikely happiness. He was witnessing the pure pleasure, an innocent frolic that the three lovers would remember all their lives. The two boys might be killed on operations, or worse still marry two ordinary women after they were demobbed and have to spend the rest of their lives bringing up a brood of kids on insufficient wages in the dullness of working class Britain; and Laura might have to face sordid divorce proceedings from Alfred, public scandal and then a return to England and a dreary life slaving away in some London school. But for them this morning would always be a time of enchantment that might have gone on forever if only they had had the wit to live it out.

Then he became angry. Life should always be lived in full acceptance of joy like theirs: open, untrammelled by the dead conventions in whose

50

The atmosphere in Singapore was calmer now but no one could predict whether more trouble would break out; in parts of the town people were still reluctant to venture far from home. Laura decided to play a small role in returning everything to normal by throwing an afternoon drinks party for student friends from the university. Those invited were among the most intellectual and brilliant on the campus, she claimed. They were also suspect to the authorities for their left-wing views. 'You'll have some stimulating young people to talk to,' she told Ferdach when he returned, looking hot and sweaty, from dropping Norman and Jeff at the naval base. 'And by the way, I'd like you to look a bit better than that.' She frowned at his clothes before scanning the array of drinks and glasses that the hotel staff had already set out on a long sidetable. It was not surprising, given her present managerial mood that she added, 'Now run along and make yourself smart: clean slacks and a fresh shirt.'

'Yes, Miss Swineslop, but I always look smart,' Ferdach replied taking a curry puff from among the plates of small eats. 'I exude smartness from my finger tips, but I'd rather spend another day with those marines than with a lot of posturing intellectuals.'

Laura put down the bottle of gin she was holding with a smack; a tinkling of glasses and cutlery ensued. She spoke angrily, her voice rising. 'You, of course, never posture, do you. God, how you were posturing last night: in Bugis Street, in the Queen's, even in bed. You always like to give the impression of being reserved and wise, which you definitely are not, and hence superior to everyone. Why can't you let yourself go, Ferdie? Norm and Jeff let themselves go but you hovered on the verandah. Oh yes, I saw you, like a bloody dragonfly that's about to settle but never does.'

'I wanted the boys to enjoy themselves.'

'Liar,' she shouted shrilly. 'You wanted to watch them screwing because that gives you a perverted thrill. What about me though? Did it never strike you that I wanted you to join us? You only think of yourself. God, I'll be glad when you've gone back to your Mat Noor. Mat Bore, I should say.'

'Laura, you're always saying that you want me. Well, I'm sometimes tempted, a little. But does it never strike you that the way you get so ridiculously angry, just like now, puts me off. Your ups and downs are unbearable. Every day I'm here I'm wondering what sort of mood is she in today? Christ, I'd soon become a doormat if I lived with you.'

At once Laura fell silent. Ferdach knew that she was turning in on herself. She was actually trembling. Was that look of pained sadness going to be succeeded by tears or a further outburst? It was as though he had hit her. She made him sit beside her on the settee, searching his eyes, for what lay in the recesses of his skull. 'Most people get married because they think they're in love,' she said seriously. 'But it's an absurd basis on which to spend a life together, this love thing. When people used to get married at eighteen, had children and died in their forties, it was well enough. But now we might both live until we're eighty. Can you imagine half a century of having to say you're in love with the same person, my God having to sleep with the same person? Yes, women can pretend to do it, they often have to, once they've got their children and their nest. So it suits them to say the men must do the same. But I know all about that beast between a man's legs. I've made a study of it. It has to be stimulated by sight as well as by touch. It gets hot quickly but it's easily bored, even if things don't go wrong between two people. It knows nothing about any moral order. It can't resist what makes it hard. All right then, I know some people would say I'm simplifying things and that I'm crude but at heart I'm right. Yes, I swear it: saying you are in love is no basis for a life together. But similar temperament and intellectual understanding can provide the strongest foundation for a real partnership Ferdie. I can see that we could be wonderfully happy, precisely because we are not in love but know each other perfectly.'

Ferdach took both her hands and said, 'Fine. Most people wouldn't agree with your point of view but I don't object to it. All the same why are you so often angry with me?'

'Because although I'm good at seeing things, I'm not so good at getting them. It's your hesitation that maddens me. I guess I get cross like a child when I can't get what I want. I'm just a spoiled child.'

'You mean a foiled child?'

'Maybe. But I do know all about being spoiled too; so I'd know how to spoil you wouldn't I?' Now Laura had become calm and as she gazed at the recalcitrant Ferdie with loving tearful eyes, his irritation with her quite melted away. Soon they fell into one another's arms and before very long into the Schweinsnoep's bed which once again knew the action and the delight of passion. Barely had it subsided, or so it seemed to Ferdach, when his ears were assailed by the sound of laughter, chattering voices and a loud hammering on the door of the apartment as he awoke from a deep sleep.

'My God, what time is it?' Laura cried jumping up. 'They're here already. They mustn't find us like this. Get dressed Ferdie. Go into the sitting room quickly. You must receive them.'

It was indeed well past lunchtime. Ferdach pulled on his slacks – not too fast as the legs were in a tangle – put on his floral shirt and then his Japanese flip-flops and rushed from the bedroom. He brushed back his hair with his fingers but did not really succeed in hiding his dishevelment. The loud voices were still jabbering away when he opened the door. Before him stood a collection of what Ferdach took to be undergraduates. The men had the vaguely unkempt look of students the world over, not so much on account of their clothing for most young men in Singapore dressed in the same neat but unimaginative style, but in the way they postured: leaning on the balustrade, slouching on the stairs, and scowling at the world in general. On the other hand, the two Indian women students who were with them wore elegant sarees and stood demurely a little way down the stairs.

'Oh do come in,' Ferdach said, as he opened the double doors as wide as possible. 'Mrs Schweinsnoep will be out presently.'

'Out presently,' repeated a studious Chinese youth with thick wire-rimmed spectacles. 'Presently, meaning after a short time. That is how Jane Austen uses the word.' He looked appreciatively at Ferdach as though he was an archaeologist who had just come across an interesting artifact. 'Ah, do excuse me. I am Li Soon, Faculty of Arts. You must be Mrs Schweinsnoep's MCS friend Mr O'Haney. Allow me to introduce you to my fellow students.'

In they trooped, single file, Mr Martin Ayerthuray, Mr Mark Puthucheary, Mr Cuthbert Lim, Mr Gung Hoh, Mr Mohammed Kassim, Miss Iris Gunasekera and Miss Narlini Milvarganam. Each nodded politely and shook hands limply with Ferdach, who became aware, as they passed him, that their beautiful brown eyes were taking in the fact that his shirt was open down the front. When he tried nonchalantly to do up one of the buttons, he realised that he had put the damn thing on inside out. Had he, he wondered, remembered to pull up the zip on his flies? Was his recent amorous activity plain to see?

Ferdach asked everyone to sit and be at ease. This they did at once but not very easily for each student perched rather rigidly on the edge of a chair or along the settee as if they were awaiting further directions.

'Is Mrs Schweinsnoep still at her toilet?' asked Narlini with a smooth smile that revealed a row of tiny pearl like teeth between rather thin unsensual lips.

'You mean on the toilet,' said Mohammed Kassim with a saucy look that suggested he was envisaging their hostess with her knickers down.

'I mean nothing of the sort Kassim,' Narlini replied crossly. 'Why are men always so vulgar? I mean at her toilette – 'twa-*let*' – French, you silly ass, getting herself ready for her guests, making up her face and so forth.'

'Exactly so,' commented Li Soon looking over the top of his glasses. 'I have seen a French painting, "La Toilette de Venus". The goddess is very pink, with large buttocks, so I'm afraid she must be a European Venus, and she is being patted all over and caressed by little naked cherubs. Was that the general use to which cherubs were put Mr O'Haney?'

Disconcerted by the disparaging reference to large-buttocked European women, Ferdach said vaguely, 'I think that such creatures were called putti. Cherubs have a more Christian connotation.'

'Venus is the pagan goddess of love,' commented Miss Gunasekera knowlegibly, as if no one else in the room knew about the Latin classics.

Ferdach was sensing that the conversation had already degenerated into a classroom discussion when Laura walked swiftly into the room saying 'Darlings' loudly.

'You're here already. Please forgive me for being late. Ferdie, have you been looking after them properly?'

Everyone stared admiringly at Laura. She looked radiantly happy, a very picture of health and, in fact, just then in her white pleated skirt and short sleeved top, a bit like a Twenties flapper about to cry, 'who's for tennis?' All that was missing was green eyeshade.

'I cannot imagine Mr O'Haney ever doing anything improper,' said Li Soon standing up with the rest of the students but in his case simultaneously performing a polite, almost Japanese half bow, to Laura.

Had there been a slightly sarcastic smirk at the rim of Li Soon's rosebud mouth when he had spoken? Was it possible that his sarcasm was shared by his companions who were all grinning so unctuously? Then Ferdach remembered that he had not put on his underpants. Could a trickle of his natural juices, the residue of his recent love making, be visible on his slacks? He was careful to keep his hands folded on his lap when he sat next to Narlini on the settee.

A hotel waiter, booked by Laura, made an appearance asking her if he should prepare tea to which she assented with a condescending air. He was accompanied by a female member of the kitchen staff and, almost at once, noisy chatter in Hainanese flowed into the sitting room from the kitchen. Li Soon looked askance and said loftily, 'I don't know why hotels employ these Hainanese. They're so rude and noisy.'

'Come,' said Laura. 'Tell me what you've all been doing during the riots.' Ferdach thought this was a silly question as some of them might have been out watching, even participating in, things better not spoken about. But his misgivings did not seem to be shared by Mohammed Kassim who said quite perkily, 'I watched the mob in Geylang. Mobs are dreadful things Mrs Schweinsnoep. Without pity you know. I saw them laughing and dancing at the sight of a European family burning to death in their Vauxhall. The man worked at Jardine's.'

'I often saw such things in India during partition,' countered Mark Puthucheary with a weary shrug of his shoulders. 'It's just one of those things that happen when there's a liberation struggle. I suppose the car was a write off.'

Mohammed Kassim laughed. 'It didn't really matter. It was a prewar

311

model. Hardly worth scrap.'

'But, but,' began Laura with a pained expression on her face. She had just picked up a shapely knife with which to cut a rich fruit cake that had been placed on the coffee table only to put it down. It seemed to some of those present that her hand was trembling. 'Couldn't you do anything to ...'

'Laura, Laura,' Ferdach put in softly, for he sensed the indifference of the students to the fate of any well-paid, or even poorly paid, European. 'It's like a wartime situation. People get killed at the front and in air raids; not just soldiers but people like you and me sometimes. It's just like that. Ordinary behaviour goes by the board.'

The students all stared at Ferdach with interest. They must have heard Europeans going on, sometimes quite hysterically, about the awful things that had happened to their white kith and kin during the riots. It was, however, a matter of common acceptance among undergraduates that colonialism had had its day and that the security of everyone would deteriorate before it improved. They certainly no longer revered the British, as their parents had revered them before the Japanese occupation. Yet here they saw an Englishman who seemed, in this one regard at least, to think as they did. They nodded approval and began to talk animatedly to one another. Laura held her peace, abandoned the cake, asked Ferdach to pass around the delicious small eats which had been brought in from the kitchen, and assumed the position of mistress of the house by dispensing tea from a magnificent silver teapot which was a Schweinsnoep family heirloom. The important business of 'Sugar? One lump or two? No sugar at all? Really! Milk or lemon?' occupied everyone so entirely that no possibly embarrassing discussion on whether Singaporeans should go to the aid of grilled Europeans could take place.

Yet amidst the lighthearted tittle-tattle Ferdach was deliberating whether the situation here was radically different from that in the Federation. Were these young people fully aware of the divergence? Would Mohammed Kassim admit that in the Federation the Malays were largely behind the effort to eliminate the communists? Would Li Soon agree that a substantial part of the Malayan Chinese population too was either in favour of the government or fence sitting, but in fear of a communist victory rather than in hope of one. Of course slight Cuthbert Lim would

312

know that in Malaya those Chinese who were pro-communist were weakened by their dispersal around the country whereas in Singapore, communism drew unusual strength from a geographical concentration of pro-communist Chinese, especially among the enthusiastic young. But had he too been swept up in their fervour? Did he look with awe towards his resurgent Chinese motherland and with growing contempt on the British who had quit India with indecent haste and were likely to give up their possessions elsewhere in the world? Ferdach wished he could discuss their attitudes openly with them. Would dour Mark Putucheary ever tell him honestly whether there was a residue of goodwill towards Britain left over from the days when Mountbatten had freed their city from the horror of Japanese occupation, or state, without dissembling, that it had been dissipated by the corruption of the British Military Administration and the continued arrogance of British officials who still ran the place. Being so taken up, as students generally were, with their own lives in Singapore could they even begin to recognise that contrasting factors were at work in Malaya, such as the truth – unpalatable to left-wingers in general – that CT depradations had invested the European rubber estate and tin mine managers with the same aura of gallantry as surrounded the youthful Malay special constables? Probably not. The likes of pretty Narlini Milvarganam or serious Gung Hoh would only be conscious of the reality that since the communists in Singapore had concentrated on subversion among the students and trades unionists instead of becoming militant, the unscathed fat-cat Europeans really did live up to the image of capitalist exploiters that communist propaganda made them out to be. In view of these negative thoughts, Ferdach decided that it might be better to listen rather than be drawn into a discussion of the Malayan Emergency in which the students might cast him as a typical colonial master.

He was not to be left out of the conversation so easily however. The tea and the cakes and the sandwiches had all been consumed and pronounced delicious when Martin Ayerthuray said with an upward interrogative jerk of his chin, 'Mr Ferdach, which poet do you think is the greater, T. S. Eliot or W. H. Auden?'

Ferdach felt that this was some sort of test of his cultural background, and of his ability to stand up to these well-informed young intellectuals who probably believed that he had no right to be ruling in their backyard. At the same time he was not an expert in poetry and at the best of times would have been loathe to make the assessment asked of him. Everyone was awaiting his words and Laura's eyes were wide open with anxiety. 'Do you think,' Ferdach asked, with due deliberation, 'that it would be wise to make such a judgement in the lifetime of the two poets?' Just then at the back of his mind there lurked a half-remembered essay by A. A. Milne on how to be expert on something one knows nothing about. 'I like Auden,' he went on, 'because of his social conscience. But I like him even more because he seems to belong to a long poetic tradition that stretches back to Anglo-Saxon verse. Think, for example, of his alliterative creativeness, think of his lyrical power. Eliot, on the other hand, seems to me to belong to wider traditions, to the classical of course, but also to a deep mystical tradition that has its roots in the east and the west. But as Lao Tzu says, 'To say which horse is fastest is difficult when they are not in the same race'. He paused, feeling sure that he had been uttering sheer gobbledegook but the gobbledegook had been expressed with conviction and in the most thoughtful tones he could muster. The expressions on the faces of his audience suggested that he had won.

He hoped that no one present was well enough versed in Lao Tzu's philosophy to know that his quotation was a fake.

Narlini broke the brief silence, 'Ah yes Mr O'Haney, I think you have spoken very wisely. How can anyone make such a black-and-white judgement? How can a pearl be better than a ruby? But you must understand that we Asian students like to know how to formulate answers. Examination questions require clear-cut replies. Now in our English Literature department we seem to get quite brilliant Englishmen; at the moment it's Mr Patrick Anderson, who encourage us to think for ourselves.' She paused and glanced around. 'But that might get us nowhere. Success in examinations means a good job, safety. Some students fear that if they are too original, if they say what they really think, they will get into trouble with the authorities and their exam results will suffer. I guess that Martin was just following the form we are used to. His clear-cut question was of the sort that required a clear-cut answer.'

'Which Ferdie failed to deliver,' Laura commented archly, followed by a distinctly ingratiating smile at the students. This surprised Ferdach. He was under the impression that, all things considered, he had not answered so badly after all. Then it struck him that perhaps the riots had frightened Laura considerably more than she would admit and that she no longer felt entirely secure in Singapore, even in the company of these, her favourite, students.

'Oh, don't reprove him Mrs Schweinsnoep. He and his friend Lao Tzu made a very clever effort,' said Martin Ayerthuray who in an instant seemed to regain his superiority. Ferdach could see that this young man was too clever by half, especially when he went on, 'Narlini is more Westernised than most of us, despite her lovely saree. She favours Englishmen as boyfriends. So hers is the view that Westerners like Mr Anderson often have of Singapore students. But you must understand why we are as we are Mr O' Ferdach. We have been seduced by you so that now, most of the student body just want to become successful middleclass brown Englishmen.'

Ferdach smiled his most sincere smile. 'But you and all your clever friends here, do not, I take it?'

'No,' came the immediate, unanimous and decidedly forthright reply.

5I

Two days before returning to Ipoh, Ferdach received an invitation to dinner from, of all people, Lai Kuan, whom he had believed to be closeted with communist leaders in Pahang. The invitation was for himself only, for which he was thankful; Laura might prove to be an embarrassment by saying the wrong thing or by talking too much. What struck Ferdach as odd about the invitation was that it sounded more like a summons – there was no RSVP, nor was the venue specified. It was merely indicated that a car would come to collect him at 8 pm that same day.

Being picked up by a car sent by Lai Kuan would be nothing new in Ipoh and Ferdach supposed that he should not be surprised by it here, for Lai Kuan had many clan contacts. Nor was the failure to mention the venue so unusual for gourmet Lai Kuan had been known to argue with restaurants about dishes and menus before he made his choice. What did surprise Ferdach the moment he stepped into the promised car was the driver: he was not Chinese but a thick-set European who looked vaguely familiar. Only when Ferdach asked the man where they were going and heard him reply with a hint of cockney 'To a restaurant not far from the railway rtation' did Ferdach recall seeing him in Phoenix Park. Back then Ferdach had assmumed, wrongly as it turned out, that the man must be some sort of security guard, or heavy. Clearly tonight was going to be different from Lai Kuan's usual booze-up.

They swept down Orchard Road, past Raffles Museum and St Andrew's Cathedral and on to Empress Place with its grand imperial buildings, then over the perpetually smelly river and along Collyer Quay towards the railway station. But the restaurant was nowhere near the station. On they drove, far beyond Keppel harbour into an area of unimpressive buildings and open spaces until they made a sudden right turn into a laterite-surfaced lane up which, after a hundred yards or so, they entered a courtyard, or maybe a farmyard for there were chickens running about, and Ferdach was sure he heard the snuffling of pigs. Under the high-pillared portico of an historic mansion they came to a halt.

The driver introduced himself as Sam Coulthwaite before walking ahead through the open double-doors and into a large square hall two storeys high. Ferdach, following him into this atrium-like space, took in the rows of Doric pillars that were broken halfway up by the balustrade of a gallery onto which, it appeared, the first floor rooms must open. No grand staircase led up from the hall, as might be expected, but in front of Ferdach, beneath the gallery, a door was suddenly opened from within to allow them to ascend a wrought-iron spiral staircase. Ferdach was aware as he climbed the stairs that someone was behind him, presumably the person who had opened the door. Once upstairs they entered a small room, very bare and unfurnished, where Sam Coulthwaite told him to wait. Ferdach now observed that the man who had followed him was a powerfully built Eurasian, another heavy maybe, but his pleasant, rather fleshy face, smiled reassuringly when he introduced himself as James da Souza.

'What is this place?' Ferdach enquired.

'It was built in the middle of the last century by an Armenian. A millionaire.' Da Souza's voice was high and lilting, an Indian upbringing perhaps?

'Yes, but what is it now?' Ferdach demanded irritably. At that same moment he heard his name uttered in the familiar tones, not of Lai Kuan, but of Noel Aspinall who was standing in the doorway of the room into which Coulthwaite had disappeared. Aspinall's pink face was beaming and his outstretched arms resembled a bishop greeting a delegate at a diocesan conference. Ferdach declined to take either or both of Noel's hands but said 'Good evening' very coolly, as if they had met earlier in the afternoon and walked past him into the room. Once inside he sensed that this was to be no ordinary party.

In the first place the room itself did not conform to the classical elegance of the rest of the house. It was low ceilinged, a much taller room having been compartmentalised for the sake of airconditioning which was on full blast making the air quite chill. It was also carpeted to the walls, which were a functional grey colour and decorated with wartime posters by Paul Nash and Henry Moore and a couple of artists unfamiliar to Ferdach. Occupying the centre of the room was a round table with six chairs set about it. Bottles of Scotch and brandy, a soda water syphon and partly filled tumblers, together with ashtrays full of butt ends, suggested that a meeting had been going on for some time. The table was not set for a meal and this irritated Ferdach as, in anticipation of a great Chinese spread, he had hardly eaten that day.

It seemed that Lai Kuan had been deep in conversation with his neighbour Walsingham for both of them turned away from one another and smiled genially at Ferdach, while another man, of rather scholarly appearance, stood up and introduced himself in a soft spoken voice as John Morton. Without further ceremony he, Noel and Coulthwaite sat down leaving Ferdach to take the empty sixth chair that happened to be next to Lai Kuan. It was apparent that they were now in a session of some kind. No mention was made by anyone of what they were there for but a desultory conversation about the riots seemed to be on the point of taking off. By this time Ferdach had little doubt that this was going to be some sort of an interview, another investigation of himself maybe. Noel asked him affably, 'Did you get involved with any of the mobs, Ferdie?'

Certain that those present would take in every word he uttered, and also suspecting that the conversation was being recorded, Ferdach ignored the question, glanced unfavourably at the clutter on the table and, frowning, said, 'I thought we were going to eat. I'm famished.'

Very soon da Souza reappeared, summoned by a bell under the table pressed by Morton who said, 'Mr da Souza, could we possibly have the food now.'

'Some dinner party!' Ferdach whispered to Lai Kuan who grinned and replied equally *sotto voce*, 'Just a ruse to get you here, Ferdie.'

Everyone sat quietly, helping themselves to drinks, until three Indian boys appeared carrying large tiffin carriers containing curried meats and vegetables, a large crab dish, prawns, dhall, rice, papadoms, chutneys and the like. All in all quite a spread and much to Ferdach's taste. Plates and finger bowls were set before them and everyone fell to with gusto. Morton's gentle voice then addressed Ferdach, 'Does this make you feel better, Mr O'Haney? I hope you have an appetite for Indian food.'

'Ferdie has an appetite for many things,' said Noel, with a smirk.

'But especially for information,' Ferdach shot back, looking directly at John Morton whom he took to be the big cheese in the group. 'What's this all about, sir?'

It was Lai Kuan who replied, in his Cambridge voice of course. 'It's aimed more at me than at you, Ferdie. I've told everyone here that I have a high opinion of you. Well that's nothing new to you, I'm sure. But because of that they'd like to talk to you, to assess whether my judgement is to be trusted, you could say. In a nutshell we'd like to have a conversation, a political conversation. All I ask of you is to be honest, as we have always been together.'

Yet before anything resembling a political conversation could develop, John Morton said in a beguiling way, 'Mr O'Haney, you don't fit into the social life of Malaya very easily, so I'm told?'

'Told by whom?' Ferdach asked. 'And what sort of life are you talking about?'

'I suppose he means, told by me,' said Noel, apologetically. 'I merely remarked to John that you're not the sort of person who frequents the clubs, plays golf and tennis or likes bridge. Well it's true Ferdie and there's nothing wrong with it.'

Ferdach had no desire to be irascible this time, especially as he wanted to find out what the meeting was really about. He helped himself to more of the spicy food before saying, 'I've nothing against that way of life, except that it bores me stiff. It's fine, I suppose, for people who were here before the Japs came or for people who want to think that they never came at all. But my youth was in Britain during the war … war the great leveller. I don't want a social life that revolves around my own kith and kin, if I can call the English expatriates that. Why come out here to behave as people do in Surrey or during the Raj? Surely anyone interested in Malaya should mix with its people. So I guess my answer to your question is, no. I don't fit into the old forms of social life. I do my best to relate to Malayans.'

'But,' observed Morton, 'that must make you feel rather uneasy with some of the expatriates, even with other members of the MCS. Mightn't you be thought of as, well, a bit quirky?'

319

Ferdach had leaned forward to catch Morton's words. To make sure that he had got them aright he repeated, 'a bit quirky?' before continuing, as indifferently as he could, 'I certainly hope so. But I don't care a toss. I get the feeling sometimes that the prewar members of the MCS don't think of people like me as real MCS at all. They reminisce about the golden life they had, tennis in the afternoon, shooting in the jungle. Nowadays the new recruit might find himself supervising the construction of latrines in a New Village a week after his arrival and shooting in the jungle doesn't mean wild boar. No, what they think isn't important. So can we please get on? How I do or don't fit into Ipoh social life is hardly a matter of importance.'

'Well that's an opener,' said Walsingham. 'It gives us an idea of what you want for Malaya. I take it that you are very much in favour of early independence?'

'And for the British getting out completely?' asked Sam Coulthwaite, challengingly

Did they suspect him of being a subversive, Ferdach wondered. Had he fallen into some trap set by Lai Kuan and Noel, maybe an investigation aimed at the new intake of officers? He remembered, a little uneasily, his connection with the Communist Party in Liverpool. Had information about that episode been passed on to Singapore? He stared hard at Lai Kuan and said firmly, 'Yes. I do believe we should get out as quickly as possible. I make no secret of my opinion. As a matter of fact, on the Colonial Service course we were told that we were coming out to "work ourselves out of a job". I've never thought of it other than quickly.'

'And would you say,' asked Morton, 'that the present Emergency is likely to speed up or impede that process?'

Since Ferdach was no high policy maker, the question that had been put to him seemed to be supremely academic. Why should he give any answer at all? He was now fully aware of the conflict of interest between Phoenix Park and Malayan intelligence but he decided not involve himself in further discussion on the matter. For the truth was that he saw Malaya more emotionally, in terms of his friendships with Mat Noor, with Lai Kuan, with his platoon, with the others among whom he had worked and with those courageous, determined squatters now being transported willy-nilly into the New Villages. He was quite unlike those seemingly monumental personalities who had shaped the modern identity of Malaya in the early decades of British rule, the brilliant administrators like Swettenham and Hugh Low, and that host of indefatigable English and Scottish compradors who had established a thriving capitalist economy in what had been a land of jungle. Such gigantic beings had no need of ordinary people as participants in their grand scheme of imperial development, except as underlings. Like these present British diplomats and intelligence officers they had thought in terms of overall policies over which they, and their talented successors, would preside. Ferdach felt it was time that such patronising control should be relinquished. He shared Lai Kuan's view, which surely everyone present in the room knew: let the British leave now, and we, the Malayans, whether of Malay, Chinese, Indian or Eurasian blood, will work things out in our own way.

Ferdach rested his hand on Lai Kuan's arm as he replied, 'Obviously it's impeding it. I think my friend here has the right answer. Too many lives are being lost. There's too much suffering. Cut a deal with the communists now. Then the Malayans can sort out their problems without our interference. I'm sure they won't choose communisim.'

Without more ado the topic of the Emergency was dropped. Nor did anyone raise the now passé subject of the Singapore riots. It was as though what had been sought had been found, though Ferdach had no idea what it was. The rest of the meal was accompanied by lighthearted gossip interspersed with questions about Ferdach's contacts in Kuala Lumpur. Naturally he told them of his physically, though not intellectually, uncomfortable sojourn with Gilbert and Hester de Guise in the so-called Cottage that was adjacent to both King's House and Carcosa, the residences of the British High Commisioner and the Chief Secretary in Kuala Lumpur. Being in his cups by now, Ferdach amused himself and his hosts by telling them of the pangs of hunger he had suffered with his almost skeletal hosts who seemed as reluctant to eat nourishing food as a couple of vampires. He also made them laugh by describing the shock the beautiful Hester had given to the very high ranking MCS wives she had met at her first coffee morning in Carcosa by insisting that she would do all her cooking and housework herself.

So that was all there was to the meeting. What a relief it was when the food and the booze had been consumed, and thanks and farewells

52

When he finished his shower and padded into the living room wearing only a sarong, as was his custom, Ferdach was surprised to see that the breakfast table had been laid formally for two. Was Laura, who was already seated, expecting a more distinguished guest? The best silver was out, there were napkins folded like lilies, and a bowl of hibiscus flowers graced the centre of the table. Was it because this was his last day on holiday? Or was Laura celebrating something else? And why was she wearing that extravagant yellow kimono? Her vagaries were so inconsistent that it was better to wait rather than ask for information. Ferdach sat down opposite her and started on a mango.

'What time did your dinner end?' she asked casually.

'About eleven, I guess. I'd lost track of the time by then,' said Ferdach, remembering the kaleidoscopic swirl of lights as the MG sped through the deserted streets of the city and the mild debauch in a Chinese club that followed.

'So it was well before your return at seven this morning?' Laura gave a curious frown at Ferdach's naked chest as though she did not approve of it at the breakfast table.

'With my friend Lai Kuan, evenings out go on indefinitely, yes very indefinitely. Sometimes they make me think I must be getting old.'

'Not with all that wine, women and song. No Ferdie, you're still deplorably young, and immature.' Ferdach was not sure whether Laura was laughing at him or putting him down when she added, 'God, you men are all the same, whatever your race.'

Ferdach refused to be defensive, especially since earlier that morning on his way up Scotts Road to the Goodwood he had glimpsed Norman and Jeff in a taxi on their way down to Orchard Road, no doubt coming from Laura's apartment. 'Well I don't remember any wine. There was certainly a lot of spirits. And there was definitely no song.'

Laura continued with her breakfast, still very coolly. She opened *The Straits Times* on the table and began reading the headlines aloud. 'Riots over. Police confident. Trading brisk. Call for tolerance. Visit of Thai Minister.' Then she said primly, 'Don't expect to go to bed with me when you've been at it with some local tart.'

'Some local tart, just one! There could have been two or more. There's no limit in those Chinese rich men's clubs.' Ferdach projected his sweetest schoolboy smile as he did his best to annoy her. 'In fact there were two, although we had neither. Lai Kuan did try to teach them how to be lesbians but he didn't succeed. It was quite a laugh. I just watched.'

Laura screwed up the newspaper and threw it at him. 'That figures. I can truly believe that. Ferdie the eternal voyeur. You would have had a better time here with me.' She paused and said heavily, 'Well, a more dramatic time.'

'Go and tell that to your marines. Oh yes, I saw them,' Ferdach said airily. 'Sexy yes, uninhibited I'm sure, but dramatic never. Marines are too down-to-earth for drama. Laura dear, why do you always like to represent everything in your life in terms of high drama? I think you should have been an actress you know – in French bedroom farces.'

Of course it was all joking between them. Neither of them really cared a tinker's cuss what the other did in bed but it was fun pretending to be annoyed. It added zest to their relationship. Other people might pretend to be liberated, Ferdach and Laura played at being conventional. Perhaps it was a way of making fun at the outside world; maybe it indicated a yearning for the lost world of respectable behaviour from which they had both escaped. Or almost escaped for out of the blue Laura said, 'It wasn't so farcical last night. Jeff and Norman were hoping you'd be back, and I was too. At about four in the morning we heard a car drawing up and we decided to create a little *tableau d'amour* for your delectation when you entered. But when the door opened and that someone did come in and see us, it wasn't you.' She opened her eyes wide and said, 'Guess who?'

'Oh Jesus,' said Ferdach sensing at last some unlikely reason for the table layout and the flowers. 'Oh my God. Alfred. What did he say?'

'He didn't say anything. He just exploded. Knocking things over. Roaring around like a bull. Yelling. Breaking pots. Kicking the furniture and finally jumping on the bed to punch the marines.'

'That must have been something to watch. What did the guys do?'

'They laughed of course. They were already doubled-up at his antics. He looked like an ape gone berserk. They just pranced about on the bed and tantalised him. Of course the two of them were four times the size of Alfred. There was a bit of a scuffle but in the end Jeff just held him in the air and dropped him on the carpet. Oh their laughter was much more wounding to him than what he'd seen. He could have got over the sex bit. After all, he gets up to all sorts of things himself in addition to Mona Wee. But when he saw two huge naked men mocking him he'd had enough. He just rushed out shouting that it was all over between us; that I've got a week to get out. He's serious Ferdie. I know him. The humiliation was too much for him.'

Ferdach saw at once that there were implications in all this for himself. As though obliged to apologise for the marines he said, 'They shouldn't have made a fool of him. They shouldn't have laughed.'

Laura brushed this aside. 'What else could they do? The fact is, they were very restrained. Some young men would have beaten him up.' She fell silent, abandoned her breakfast and sprawled on the settee. Then she looked up brightly; she even gave a little laugh. 'D'you know. I feel relieved. The nightmare is over. I can begin to live my own life. I'm going to be Madame Butterfly in reverse. Thank God for the marines, heh Ferdie. This breakfast is a celebration you see.' Yet before he could say anything her silent mood returned and she looked at Ferdach then shouted angrily, 'I'll never accept it, Ferdie!'

'Accept what?'

'That it's all right for a man, say you or Lai Kuan, or Alfred or any Tom, Dick or Harry to pick up women and screw them, but if a woman does the same with men, she's a slag, a whore. No. I'll never accept it. But before long the world will have to change its tune. Women will force the change.'

Ferdach said nothing; he had his doubts. Such a change might happen in parts of the Western world but how could it come about here in Malaya where the position of women both under Islam and Hinduism was so remote from Laura's ambitions? What chance of freedom was there for women for ages to come? Of course Laura wanted to be as free as Nina Hamnett, and he sympathised with her. For didn't he often feel stifled in colonial society with its sports, boozing and hearty camaraderie not to mention those moronic clubs and dreary churches. Yet despite the fact that the Malayan Civil Service contained not a few brilliant and civilised men, the establishment went on supporting the stuffy old system. Perhaps it was feared that any relaxation of traditional standards would lose the natives' respect for their masters, even though that respect had already evaporated in the heat of occupation by the Japanese who had done their utmost to humiliate the British in the eyes of their former subjects. What was more, in British Malayan society the English and the Scottish women, of which latter righteous breed there were not a few, played along with the men because their social position in a comfortable, privileged set-up was guaranteed, provided that they also conformed. It was undeniable that things had moved on a bit since the Somerset Maugham days of *The Letter*, but not much. The sort of feelings Ferdach felt for Mat Noor had to be kept well under wraps even though sexuality between males was secretly widespread throughout the country. And so, because Ferdach resented the veil imposed by society on himself, he understood Laura's rage over her own predicament.

Some course of action had to be worked out quickly for Laura. Even if haphazardly a point of no return had been reached. But it was not just what Alfred had witnessed in the early hours of the morning, nor his humiliation, that meant that Laura's marriage was through. Despite Alfred's recent claim that they had designed a wonderfully sophisticated open marriage, the opposite was the reality. The marriage was not just frayed at the edges, it was threadbare through and through. Even if Alfred were to say 'stay' Laura would refuse him.

After her outburst Laura looked vulnerable, not in a physical sense but in her expression there was a tautness that suggested fear, maybe sadness. Whatever it was, it was something that made Ferdach want to respond generously, possibly against his own true interests. He sat beside her and took her in his arms. 'You'll be all right,' he declared. 'You're clever, you're well educated. Alfred's a hindrance. You'll find something to do with your life.'

Just now this was not the best thing to say. Laura did not envisage herself setting forth on a career. Truth be told, she wanted the good life, the comfortable life of a mem, to continue. She disentangled herself from him and said resentfully, 'Oh yes. Maybe you'll send me a brochure of the best courses for women to study. But until then, what am I to do? Go back to England I guess and find a bedsit in Maida Vale.'

He knew the ideal solution for her at that moment, the one she hoped for, would be an offer of marriage. But under the circumstances that would be just as bad as a shotgun wedding leading to a marriage of inconvenience. Ferdach wanted nothing of that yet he was deeply concerned. He could not just abandon her in Singapore and go back to Ipoh, leaving her to fend for herself with such help as Alfred might provide. However, fortunately or unfortunately – he could never decide which – he had been imbued by his mother, who was a fervent believer in character training, with an excessive sense of responsibility; this was an advantage in work but as often as not far from useful in personal relations. Again he put his arms around her and said, 'We have to think carefully about this Laura. Let's just go out tonight and have fun. Tomorrow we'll work something out. I won't let you down.'

'Really Ferdie, really? But you know I don't want to trouble you. No, I'd never dream of forcing you into anything you didn't want. Just a little help. After those riots I'm too nervous to stay in Singapore on my own. Maybe a little time with you in Ipoh until I can figure things out myself.' She kissed him tenderly and ran her fingers over his naked chest. He half expected her to start making love but her next words reminded him that she also lived another sort of social life. 'I've got to go. I'm meeting some friends for tennis at the Tanglin Club. It's ladies singles.'

'You! Ladies singles! After last night I find that difficult to believe.'

Happily Laura could still laugh at Ferdach's wit. She answered, 'You can come if you want but, you being you, I don't think you will. Knowing your highly developed aesthetic sense I can't see you enjoying some of the sights, male and female, if you go near the pool. Not at all like …' Ferdach knew it was on the tip of her tongue to make some barbed remark about Mat Noor and that jungle pool. Wisely she desisted and went on, 'In any case you must get ready for your journey. We'll meet tonight and have a terrific Chinese meal.'

53

Why had Lai Kuan been so insistent that he and Ferdach should meet again before returning to Perak? Ferdach could not imagine any reason for it. Lai Kuan had said they should get together in the Adelphi Hotel that overlooked the grassy square on which St Andrew's Cathedral stood. As there was well over an hour to spare when Ferdach got there, he thought he would look round the cathedral, which might well have been situated in some English country town except for one unusual feature: it was completely white. This accentuated its rather severe gothic beauty and was made more striking by the surrounding greenery of well-tended lawns bordered by wide-spreading trees all under a peerless blue sky. Strolling out of the humid heat and into the building he encountered the coolness of the lofty nave in which some half a dozen women, all Asian, were seated, praying. As he walked towards the choir, halting from time to time to read the memorials to various colonial civil and military dignitaries, he thought how strange it was that a small island on the other side of the Earth had come to dominate and, superficially at least, change the face of this far-off tropical land. It had not been done out of zest for empire in the way that Caesar had conquered Gaul or the French had taken over North Africa. For the most part it had been done in the name of trade when the British traders of the time had demanded protection from a home government that was sometimes reluctant to help them. The administration that had followed had not primarily been established by imperial consuls anxious to spread English culture but by educated gentlemen burdened with that awful sense of responsibility which hung around Ferdach's own neck. They were there to establish law and order and they were seldom corrupt. All the same, Ferdach could not help regretting that the order they had established had led to a further influx of British people out to make money in tin, rubber or in business generally. Such people had not been very enlightened and had, together with the military, brought out with them the snobbish values of the English middle classes. Perhaps their arrogance, and, at worst, their racism had been a defence against the subtle cultures they encountered and failed to understand. Whatever it was, they had created a self-centred white society that did not believe in social or sexual relationships, except furtively, with the local people. Some might think that this great cathedral represented what was best in their society; the club life, beloved by the likes of Laura for its gaiety, was in Ferdach's view among the worst.

One thing that intrigued him was that the memorials in the building had not been damaged by the Japanese. They too respected the past and they too were burdened by a sense of duty but it was of a different order from that of the British. Could one say that their rule was so much worse than that of the Western countries? Of course they were far more ruthless and undeniably cruel, but even the British could, if not to the same degree, be severe enough when it came to putting down revolts against their rule as the forty-seven Indians executed in Singapore following the 1915 Singapore Mutiny proved. The Japanese could, and increasingly did, claim that they had contributed to the liberation of Asian peoples from Western colonialism. No doubt the argument would go on forever for, in reality, all imperialisms had their benefits and their demerits. It was only when he came across a modest memorial commemorating some Chinese residents who had been rounded up and shot by the Japanese without trial for no reason, that Ferdach admitted the really important difference between the British and the Japanese lay in a different approach to law. Arrogant the British might have been but they had established administrative and legal systems which, however imperfect, had taken root in this tropical land and would continue to flourish long after they had gone.

Observing a clergyman taking an interest in his presence, Ferdach beat a hasty retreat from the building and made his way to an antique shop, Red House, which he had noticed not far from the Adelphi. It belonged to the family Kwok, a surname shared by Lai Kuan's family. This implied their membership of the same clan but might there not be some more intimate connection between the families? Inside the shop he moved from cabinet to cabinet looking at expensive jade pieces, patinated bronzes, exquisite simple bowls and less exquisite enormous vessels encrusted with dragons and all the paraphernalia of Chinese mythology. He thought it unlikely that he would ever have enough money to make a collection of such objects, even of the reproductions of which there were many. But the sight of all this luxury and the thought of Lai Kuan's wealthy connections suddenly filled him with inspiration. Lai Kuan must have influence. Might he not be able to find some opening for Laura?

At the Adelphi reception desk he was told to follow a Malay boy with strongly scented hair upstairs to a large room with a deep balcony looking out on the trees surrounding the cathedral. There, recumbent on the tiled floor and wearing only a blue sarong, was Lai Kuan. He had propped himself up on a huge cushion to more comfortably read the newspapers, the corners of which flicked back and forth in the breeze created by the ceiling fan. As Ferdach had removed his shoes on entering the room, Lai Kuan was only aware of his presence when he saw a pair of feet nearby. 'Ah, the pampered feet of a treacherous Irishman who's deserted his people,' he said. 'But sink lower, down to my level won't you?' Ferdach squatted beside him. 'You shouldn't creep up on people like that, Ferdie. You never know what you may find them at.'

'That's very true,' said Ferdach thinking gloomily of the problem that Alfred's unexpected appearance in Laura's bedroom had caused him. However, not wanting to plunge straight in with an appeal for Lai Kuan's help, he decided to talk of something else. 'Well, I see all the headlines are telling us that there's no more trouble in Singapore. Order restored. Everything back to normal. Do you believe it?'

'Things won't be normal in Singapore for a long time to come Ferdie. The place is a seething cauldron. If the British had really wanted to hold on for ages they should have educated all Chinese boys in English as British Christian gentlemen. Too late now. The century of Chinese humiliation is over. I saw a film the other night in a Chinese middle school about the Peoples Liberation Army entering Shanghai in 1948. For Shanghai the students read Singapore. You could hardly distinguish the joy of the crowds in the movie from the joy in the hall. Even I felt moved by all that shouting and cheering and the patriotic songs.'

Ferdach let Lai Kuan thump his arm rythmically while singing a couple of lines in Mandarin from 'The East is Red':

Dongfang hong, taiyang sheng,
Zhongguo chu liao ge Mao Zedong.

The east is red, the sun is rising,
China has brought forth a Mao Zedong.

'But the riots here were about religion,' said Ferdach in a disparaging tone. 'It was the Malays and the Indonesians who got their knives out.'

'And thank your lucky stars the Chinese students saw no reason to join in. Look, the situation here is more dangerous for the British than it is in Malaya. Across the Causeway, you've got the Malays to back you. Here, there aren't so many Malays and you've probably lost even them now. Of course you've got your military and your police. Fortunately for them there's no jungle on the island for a Malayan-type Emergency. No, in the long run, to prevent this place from going communist, you'll have to find some subtle Chinese person to insinuate himself into the Chinese population and do your counter revolutionary work for you.'

'That, Lai Kuan, would be impossible,' Ferdach said heavily, as though the bleak outlook had made him lose interest in the matter completely.

Lai Kuan gave Ferdach a sidelong glance. 'No. That's a method your intelligence people are really good at. They've done it before. They'll do it again.' He paused and scrutinised Ferdach as though he were some weird specimen. 'You really have got a lot to learn about your own countrymen. Do you think people like Morton and Walsingham and the rest are as dull as they seem. They'll already have identified some ambitious young Chinese man to do the job for them. But the brain washing won't have taken place in Singapore; most probably someone is already being indoctrinated at Oxford or Cambridge. You really are an innocent.' He rubbed his hand through Ferdach's hair playfully and then looked at him more directly. 'Ferdie, you're not your usual smiling self today. Is it a hangover? Or is there something on your mind? Yes. I see you're worried. What is it?'

'Be Jaysus, am I so transparent?' Ferdach replied, though truth be told he had deliberately put on a despondent expression while Lai Kuan was expatiating, whether genuinely or in fun it was difficult to say, on the brilliance of British intelligence. 'Well Lai Kuan, I do have a problem, a personal problem. But I don't think it would interest you.'

'I'm interested in everything that concerns my brother,' Lai Kuan said, this time with a quite hard tug on Ferdach's hair. 'How could it be otherwise? Just as you want to know all about me, so I want to learn your secrets. No Ferdie, don't frown. I don't mean your work secrets, I mean what goes on in here.' He patted Ferdach's head. 'And in here.' He lowered his hand to rest over Ferdach's heart.

'There's confusion in both. If you recognised anything in either place, be sure that its opposite is nearby. But my problem at the moment isn't just mine, it concerns someone else, it concerns …'

' Ah, I know … Laura.'

'Well, I suppose it must be obvious. I'm staying with her and there isn't anyone else I know so well in Singapore.'

'Has Alfred had enough of you then? Or is she putting the pressure on you again to take her off? If you're not sure what to do Ferdie, just do nothing. It's easy enough. Leave them to work things out themselves.'

'But I can't. It isn't like either of those things. Well not exactly.' And Ferdach explained the entire circumstances leading up to Alfred telling Laura to get out. He finished by saying quite simply, 'I'm not ready to live with Laura, or any woman. But I have to help her to get a job. She doesn't want to go back to England. How can I help her? I'm not in business. If I can't place her somewhere she'll have to come and stay with me, if only for a while.'

'It wouldn't be for a while.'

'I know that and I'm worried.'

Lai Kuan put his hands behind his head and lay back grinning at Ferdach. 'Two marines – and you too if you'd got back early enough – what a woman! Still, not as good as Princess Shan-yin; her brother King Ts'ang Wu gave her thirty lovers.' Then, seeing that Ferdach raised his eyebrows, he asked, 'Well, brothers should help one another, even more than their sisters, shouldn't they?'

'Yes Lai Kuan, in moderation.'

'So why can't you come out with it and say what you want of me?

In moderation.'

'I felt embarrassed. I don't like asking people for favours.'

'Not very Asian yet are you? But I can solve your problem easily. I can get Laura a job and a place to live in Kuala Lumpur until she wants to move on. You told me she's got a degree in English. Some export firms I know need people to put their documents into good English. She'll be useful and she'll be paid well enough. Is that OK with you?'

Naturally Ferdach thanked him fulsomely; he could not imagine what he would have done without such help. Yes, they were brothers and he, Ferdach, would never forget Lai Kuan's generosity. Naturally too, Lai Kuan disparaged his own help; it was nothing, he was happy that their friendship could be sealed in this way. And yet, even in this moment of brotherhood a tiny worm of doubt was gnawing in the recesses of Ferdach's brain. He knew he was impulsive; he knew that, most likely because of his mother's kind character, he would always be ready to help others. He knew too that his impulsiveness and his kindness were not always in his best interests. Lai Kuan had asked him to come to the Adelphi for some purpose. It would soon, he knew, be revealed to him. But had his acceptance of Lai Kuan's help, made the rejection of some proposal to be put to him, virtually impossible? He did not have long to wait for the answer.

Lai Kuan had resumed his prostrate position. Arms now at his sides, breathing in and out very regularly and deeply, he seemed to be fascinated by the slowly rotating fan as if he sought to be hypnotised by its motion. How immature he seemed for his face was almost hairless and there was a freshness about his skin that suggested youth rather than someone well into his thirties. Yet Ferdach now had to admit to himself that here was a man who, despite appearances, possessed a confidence that he himself lacked, a man capable of taking drastic action and giving ruthless orders that must be obeyed. When Lai Kuan next spoke, it was very softly and Ferdach almost feared to hear his words.

'Ferdie my friend, I have some important things to tell you. I'm going to tell them because I trust you. I will not ask you to promise to keep them secret. Promises are only made to be broken. I'm telling you about them because I know you'll tell no one. No one at all.'

There was no answer to that. Ferdach knew he had been placed on trust in a way that seemed more binding to him than any oath he might take. It was a trust based on the comradeship of one man for another, a form of trust dear to him. All he could say was, 'I'm listening, Lai Kuan.'

'Lie down then, be still, look up at the fan if you want. Or close your eyes. Yes, close your eyes; that's better,' said Lai Kuan, like a psychologist attending a disturbed patient. He waited for Ferdach to do as he had asked before he continued. But he didn't continue immediately. In a melancholy voice, as though the prelude to some sorrowful news, he simply uttered 'Ferdie' and then he fell silent. Ferdach waited a little, then opened his eyes and stared up at the slowly rotating fan that made a strange noise that ebbed and flowed like the groans of a wounded animal. He tried to follow just one of the blades in its circular path but failed. It just slipped through his vision so that, though rotating at a regular speed, it seemed to whizz by quickly at one point and then move slowly at another. Through the balustrade came the sound of cars starting up or stopping as people arrived at or left the hotel. Voices rose and fell, mixed sometimes with the laughter of children. From further afield came cries of street vendors selling *meehoon* and duck feet dumplings, often accompanied by the metallic clash of clappers used to attract customers. But all the external sounds were muted by the monotonous dirge of the fan so that the room seemed filled with somnolence and Ferdach had to make an effort to ward off an unwanted hypnotic sleep. At length he forced himself to say, 'Did you get to Tras, Lai Kuan?'

'To Tras? How did you know I was going there?'

'You told me yourself. Maybe you can't remember. It was so early in the morning, after that long drive.'

'Yes. I remember now. Yes, I did get to Tras. What do you know about the place? You know something, I see.'

'It's a terrorist hotspot I've been told.'

'It's almost a liberated area Ferdie. Some people there have a different definition of terrorism.'

'I know that Lai Kuan. Don't let's argue about semantics. You want to tell me what you did there. No, that's not it.' Ferdach rolled onto his side and propped himself on his elbow looking intently at Lai Kuan whose head had turned so that their eyes met. 'You want to tell me who you met there. That's what it's all about. You met someone important.

Someone who wants you to do something for him.' He paused and drew a deep breath before saying quickly, 'And you want to involve me, don't you?'

Lai Kuan gave a childlike smile; it was disarming. Ferdach stared at his teeth, so regular, so pretty, almost like a girl's, and then again into those dark piercing eyes – the eyes of a demon? He wondered how Lai Kuan saw him. Was it with a similar degree of affection or was he proof against Ferdach's type of love but knew how to play with it for his own ends? As if in a dream he heard Lai Kuan say softly, 'You're making it too easy for me Ferdie. It's as though we both want to be seduced by each other. Very well, let's both surrender. I'll give you what you want. I did meet someone very important in Tras.' There were some moments of silence. 'I met the Secretary General. I met Chin Peng.'

These words set Ferdach's mind racing. They did not exactly surprise him for, from the moment they had left Ipoh together, he had felt sure that Lai Kuan's journey to Tras had some significant aim, some possibly dangerous political aim. And now, bit by bit, it was being revealed. His immediate desire was to ask, what sort of man Chin Peng was, what his current state of mind was, how did he look and so forth, all matters of interest to any intelligent person in Malaya. But at the front of his mind loomed a more ominous question: how did his new knowledge affect himself, an officer in the Malayan Civil Service pledged to loyalty to the Federation government? How could he maintain both that loyalty and his promise to Lai Kuan to keep secret everything he had just been told? An immediate way out of his dilemma suggested itself: he asked, 'Do the people in Phoenix Park know what you've just told me? Do Morton and Walsingham know?'

'Yes. Of course they do.' Lai Kuan asserted. 'They know everything I've told you and a lot more. Do you want to hear it?'

'And the intelligence people in the Federation. Do they know?'

'No, Ferdach. They don't.'

As though a light was flickering on a gloomy horizon Ferdach perceived something significant. 'That means ...' he began and then paused staring searchingly into Lai Kuan's face.

'Yes, Ferdie. Go on.'

'That means that the difference between Phoenix Park and Federation intelligence is irreconcilable.'

'I should say divergence rather than difference.'

Now Lai Kuan turned on his side and pushed Ferdach backwards gently so that their roles seemed to be reversed. 'When I said divergence, I mean exactly that. Both have the furtherance of your fine British interests at heart. The divergence lies in how to further those interests. There wasn't always a divergence. It only became serious once it was clear that Mao had won in China.'

Ferdach decided it was best to let Lai Kuan do the talking, even if it was like listening to his grandmother telling him how to suck eggs. Oh yes, he understood well enough the two major arguments underlying the formulation of Western strategy in Southeast Asia since China had become united again. Either prop up all the dominoes: Thailand, Indo-China, Indonesia and Malaya, or let the dominoes fall quickly without spending a penny on their defence. Let China resume its ancient sway over the area and then stretch out the hand of goodwill towards it. For once its hegemony had been re-established China itself, and all its Southeast Asian minions, would be impelled by circumstances towards economic modernisation. Inevitably the doors to Western trade and investment would be opened and in due course the abrasive edges of communism would be worn away. But while he was waiting for Lai Kuan to persuade him of the merits of this second course, Ferdach was shrewdly laying down his own defence should his knowledge of Lai Kuan's activities become known to Malayan intelligence. Now he could always claim that he was aware of Phoenix Park's complicity in the matter but had never imagined that its Kuala Lumpur opposite number had been kept in the dark.

As if seeking to probe what lay behind Ferdach's silence, Lai Kuan asked, 'Have you ever heard of Lai Teck?'

'Yes, the communist leader before Chin Peng. He vanished from view in '47.'

'You remember me saying that the British will have to find some clever Chinese to subvert the Chinese masses in Singapore to hold back the communists? You remember me saying that they had done that sort of thing before? Well, you probably know the rumours about Lai Teck; that he was a British agent.'

Ferdach endeavoured to be blasé. 'I think most people have heard that by now, Lai Kuan. But what's that to do with Chin Peng?'

In an off-hand way, Lai Kuan retorted, 'Chin Peng was more or less handpicked by Lai Teck. He was his chosen successor. Any spy will choose his successor with circumspection wouldn't you think?'

It seemed that silence had filled the room but it was really the mechanical non-silence stirred around by the ceiling fan. Thump, thump thump it went and Ferdach felt that its rhythm had subdued the beating of his own heart. 'Lai Kuan, you're not trying to tell me that Chin Peng is …' He could not bring himself to complete the sentence. The very idea was too preposterous.

'Ferdie you have yet to learn that in intelligence work no one is either one thing or another. You can't spy on the enemy without understanding his beliefs. But once you understand them, they become part of your own thought processes so an everlasting debate starts up in your mind over which of the conflicting set of beliefs inside you is correct.'

Ferdach got to his feet, walked to the balustrade and turned to look down on Lai Kuan. It made him feel more in control of the situation. 'Yes, I began to learn that when you and Noel Aspinall were argy-bargying away on Pangkor Island. Now don't beat about the bush any more. I don't want to hear about the theory and practice of being a double agent. There's some purpose in all this and it's time you told me about it. I'm to be involved. Why else the put-up meetings with Morton and the rest? And now this lunch with you? You did invite me to lunch, didn't you? Where is it? I'm still a growing boy and my stomach's rumbling. It's OK by me if we eat here. I'll settle for something English but plain and good. Let's say lobster bisque, a sirloin steak à point and a crème caramel, yes and a good French wine. You can choose that.'

Without getting up Lai Kuan wriggled on his belly like a lazy dog towards a low sidetable and picked up the phone. A hint of a smile suggested that he was amused at Ferdach's expense. 'Room service,' he began. Then, obliged to wait, he observed, 'Your definition of English is very malleable Ferdie. But now I remember: you once conquered France as well. Ah, room service?' He placed Ferdach's order, doubled it as an afterthought to include himself, and requested a bottle of Bollinger, the vintage specified being, according to him, a good one.

'So what are we celebrating?' Ferdach asked. 'My recruitment into the Malayan Communist Party?'

'With the right inducement, that would certainly be possible. You have your weaknesses,' Lai Kuan retorted airily. He got up and sat at the table by the balustrade. 'Come. Sit down. We'll admire the square and the trees and look like serious German tourists. Yes, very serious, because I'm going to ask you to do something. No, it's not a favour. It's something you will believe in because I know that you want peace in Malaya and hope for our independence as quickly as possible.' Since Lai Kuan was no longer being facetious Ferdach did as he was told. 'Nor is it anything dangerous or compromising. Just something you can easily do for us.'

'Us being who? The Chinese? The MCP? Or just you and Chin Peng?'

'The last is nearest the mark, Ferdie.' And then out came not the request but, at somewhat tedious length, the reasons for it: the Secretary General and his closest comrades had concluded that a serious tactical error had been made. The Federation government was not going to collapse like a pack of cards. The Malays had become reliable supporters of the British now that the Federation was well established and, with it, the entrenched position of the state governments. If the Party was obliged to wage war year after year its chances of spreading its message among the Malayan masses would be gone: no more infiltration into the trade unions; no more recruitment among the students; no more winning over the intellectuals with promises that they would play a progressive part in the development of democracy; and above all, no participation in the electoral processes, at state and federal level that would lead to independence. In reality the Party's very act of engaging in a prolonged and unsuccessful struggle was likely to prolong independence which, when it came, would witness a Malay dominated country in which the Chinese would be second-class citizens, if that.

Two waiters arrived with the food and the wine and this brought the lecture to a halt. When they had left and the lobster bisque was being ladled out by Lai Kuan, Ferdach said, 'There's one awful thing about Marxists or, even worse, Party members, they become terribly *cheung hei*, long winded. I've heard all the arguments before Lai Kuan. Now tell me, exactly and simply what you are asking me to do?' His voice rose irritably as he spoke. 'If you tell me, then we can enjoy our food.'

Again Lai Kuan's beguiling smile, head tilted a little to one side, again that appealing glance intended to undermine Ferdach's resistance. 'Well Ferdie, we're in need of a postman. Is that exact and simple enough for you?'

Ferdach knew enough about the guerrilla organisation to be jolted into saying, 'You mean, a courier, a runner. What are you thinking of? No, I don't get it.'

Lai Kuan left the table and retreated into the room. Ferdach heard him unlocking a case and fumbling about before he returned with a brown sealed envelope which he handed to Ferdach. On it was written: 'To His Excellency Sir Henry Lovell Goldsworthy Gurney, High Commissioner, Federation of Malaya.' On the reverse side there was a seal with a Chinese character imprinted on it.

'And this is from?'

'The Secretary General of the Party. From Chin Peng.'

Of course there was no longer any doubt in Ferdach's mind. Everything clicked into place. He was to be the postman. A letter from Chin Peng to the High Commisioner was already in his hands. It was absurd. It was impossible. His gut reaction was to say 'No' loudly and emphatically. But it wasn't so simple, there were many aspects to consider: Laura for one, his loyal friendship for Lai Kuan for another, and is some dark recess of Ferdach's brain there stirred a peculiar ambition to play a role, even if only a minor role, in bringing peace to a people he had learned to admire. 'But why me?' he asked tentatively. 'There must be many ways of getting a letter from Chin Peng to Gurney.'

'You don't want to do it,' Lai Kuan said bluntly, a hint of anger coming through.

'I didn't say so. I'd just like to be clear in my mind on the whys and wherefores. Is that too much to ask?' Ferdach paused before adding, 'And then there's the question of how I can do it.'

'Ah, then you are willing to do it.' The anger had gone from Lai Kuan's voice. 'Of course you're right to ask: why you? But the question of how you do it is related to the whys and the wherefores, Ferdie. Yes, there are other ways of getting the letter through, but none of them are suitable. The correspondence must be between Chin Peng and the

High Commisioner only. The Secretary General wants to meet Sir Henry privately, face to face. He wants to be able to make certain proposals to him directly. Naturally those proposals would be referred to London but in the greatest secrecy. Most likely Sir Henry would pay a visit to London to discuss the issues with the Colonial Secretary and the Prime Minister. Only after that, when the go-ahead has been given at the highest level, could the lower echelons of the Federation governement, particularly its intelligence officers and the Malay interests, be informed. Now you must realise that any letter that goes to King's House in the ordinary way, even if marked 'Top Secret', would be seen by some of Gurney's staff, including the intelligence people, in other words by the very people most likely to be absolutely against Chin Peng's proposals.' Lai Kuan paused in his almost breathless exposition to await an assenting nod from Ferdach before he went on, 'Phoenix Park knows about the letter; in fact it is in favour of Chin Peng's proposal for a meeting but again it would be impossible for the letter to go from Phoenix Park to the High Commissioner without the Federation's security services being brought into the picture.'

Ferdach could only stare at Lai Kuan. Yes, he could see the difficulties but would it all be worthwhile? The High Commisioner governed though an executive council. How could he, on his own, change an agreed policy? And yet Sir Henry Gurney's devotion to the people of Malaya and his desire for peace were well known. But what about that other strange thing that Lai Kuan had said about internal treachery in the MCP?

'I don't understand what you were getting at just now,' he said. 'About Lai Teck choosing Chin Peng as his successor. I thought you were implying that ...'

'No. Chin Peng is not in the pay of the British. He's a Malayan patriot and an independent thinker. He learned a lot about the British from Lai Teck. He's not a simple Marxist idealogue. He's a pragmatist. Perhaps that's why Lai Teck favoured him. If he thinks it will advance the Party's interest he'll work with the British again, just as he worked in the jungle with John Davies and Force 136 during the Occupation.'

Ferdach looked down at the envelope, turning it over a couple of times as if he expected to receive a clue on what to do. Lai Kuan took it from his hands and said, 'I could hardly take this to King's House myself because I'd be stopped and searched before I got anywhere near the place. But on the way back to Ipoh you can stay with the de Guises again at Carcosa Cottage. Up there you can easily find your way into HE's presence, maybe on a morning walk, or a saunter around the gardens. You'll have to find a pretext but you're resourceful; you can do it.'

The letter, now inserted into a shiny black leather briefcase, was handed to Ferdach whose failure to make any further protest signalled acceptance of his new role. Indeed, he was thinking, yes, it could be done just as suggested. When out walking with Hester and Gilbert they had often encountered people from King's House and Carcosa, taking constitutionals of an evening along those narrow winding roads but he had never bothered to ask their names. It was only when he started to imagine actually meeting the High Commisioner that he realised that the first question put to him would be, who gave you this letter, or, who is it from. Without hesitation he decided that he would deny all knowledge of the letter's author but would say that it had been handed over to him by a friend who, though not a communist, had, like many neutral Chinese, contacts on both sides of the fence.

Foolishly convinced that he would be doing nothing wrong, perhaps that his action might even be a public good, and more than happy that the immediate problem of Laura was solved, Ferdach was pleased when another bottle of wine was opened. Everything ahead looked rosy. He would be glad to be back at work in Perak and Mat Noor would be glad to see him; all doubts on that score had been swept from his mind, though he said nothing about it to Lai Kuan. Only when he asked Lai Kuan what had happened to handsome Harry Wong did a hint of the fickle nature of his own feelings reveal itself. Lai Kuan looked at him meaningfully and said, 'Oh your friend Harry is alive and kicking. You mightn't believe it but he's never forgotten you. He's the sort of man with whom you could have a deep friendship. He's educated, clever, interested in everything under the sun, a sort of Chinese Ferdie if you can believe in the existence of such a phenonomen. Who knows? You may be meeting him again before long.' Lai Kuan had seen the light that had entered Ferdach's eyes when he mentioned Harry; he fingered the briefcase that lay between them and said, 'Let's hope so, Ferdie. It may all depend on this first little step towards peace.'

54

The idea of travelling to Kuala Lumpur with Ferdach delighted Laura. She did not worry about the danger of ambushes, or of breakdowns on jungle-fringed roads miles from civilisation. She longed to escape from Alfred and indeed from Singapore. Where once she had boasted about the sophistication of the city and the interesting people you could meet there, overnight it had become old hat, dangerous and a place of bitterness.

She now disparaged the young intellectuals, Chinese, Malay and Indian, she had so recently encouraged to come to her apartment. 'Yes,' she told Ferdach, 'some of them are very brilliant but they're totally circumscribed by the atmsphere here. They long for revolution but not one of them has the guts to lead it. They just want to get good degrees and a safe job in the government they affect to despise'.

About the expatriate university staff she was even more contemptuous. What she said about Northcote Parkinson and Patrick Anderson, brilliant men who were to achieve international eminence, and politicians of the left like Devan Nair and John Eber, was less than complementary though it might be interesting to know what they thought of her – not much in all probability. Nevertheless on the evening before her departure many of these newly denigrated people turned up to a party she gave and Ferdach was quite impressed by their solicitude for Laura, the students in particular praising her for the ease with which she had moved in their company without any of the side that made them resent most Europeans.

Ferdach too, was glad to be leaving. So much had happened in a short time. He was leaving with a jumbled impression of a city that swung between revolutionary violence and the careless hedonism of the British who had resumed their prewar attitudes without understanding that they were living over a whirlpool. But more personal issues were fermenting in his mind. By accepting Lai Kuan's brief he had compromised his own loyalty to the Federation Government. As yet this did not bother him greatly. He had earlier in his life loosened other ties when he felt justified. There were elements in communism that still appealed to him; he could never accept the proposition that the wealthy should wield the greatest amount of power in society. Why not the artist, the poet, the musician, all of whom were as capable of leadership as the capitalist? But to make peace now there must be compromise between the extremes. To that end he wanted Sir Henry Gurney to come to an accommodation with Chin Peng. If that happened, his own conflicting loyalties would be reconciled.

It was, therefore, a rather self-satisfied young man who set forth early one Friday morning from the Goodwood Park Hotel, with Laura sitting beside him, to make the journey north. He had an exceedingly important letter in his possession, one that might lead to great things, but possibly, though he refused to think so, to misfortune; he was returning to work that he loved and could do well; he had a sort of proprietary right over a woman he was peculiarly fond of and was happy to enjoy whenever the itch took him without her having any right over him; moreover, he would almost surely have access to the flat in which she was to settle should he choose to visit the capital; and lastly, ahead of him, as in a romantic dream was the image of Mat Noor for whom he longed, despite Laura's words of caution. Yes, he was glad to be on his way. Strangely enough, Ferdach's auspicious departure was witnessed by Alfred himself who had turned up, looking sad, and for a moment tearful, to see the rival knight carrying off his inconstant lady.

Passing through the security checkpoints where the Causeway led into Johore, Ferdach felt that he was coming home, even though Laura had a heated argument with a female customs officer who wanted to examine the entire content of her case and was curious about some contraceptives that Laura at first refused to show her. An incident like that could quickly throw Laura into an irrational temper. 'God,' she said. 'It's like entering the Soviet Union. Hasn't the bloody woman ever seen a Dutch cap before? Oh God, I don't know why I'm leaving Singapore.'

'Shall I turn around then?' Ferdach asked rhetorically, a small part of him actually wondering whether it would be better had she decided not to come.

While Laura was composing herself they passed the enormous vertical secretariat building – intended to affirm Johore's independent status, its Islamic culture and its grandeur – then the horizontal and much more graceful classical Istana until they were skirting the sea. Spanish-style government villas looked out towards Singapore island and some small palm-fringed islets which composed an altogether picturesque scene. 'I'd love to have one of these houses,' gushed Laura who had quite forgotten her argument at the frontier post. 'Do you think you might ever get one Ferdie?'

'I think they're reserved for Johore civil servants, and senior ones at that. They're a different lot from us, from the Malayan civil servants. They're all Malay and fiercely loyal to their Sultan and to Johore. The British have to think twice before they put a foot wrong here Laura. For instance if I saw the Sultan's car and overtook it, I could expect a violent reaction.'

'You mean physically?'

'It's been known. I heard of a British planter who was thumped by the Sultan's driver just for trying to overtake.'

As they drove along the coast road Laura gazed at the glittering seascape for a while before saying, 'That's a good idea. We British might be a lot better out here if we were thumped once in a while, to give us a better sense of perspective.'

Ahead of them on a hill to the right there loomed a huge modern house with grey walls and a high-pitched green-tiled roof. 'That,' stated Ferdach, 'is Bukit Serene, rented at considerable expense by the British taxpayer from the Sultan of Johore for the great proconsul Malcolm Macdonald, the Commissioner for Southeast Asia.'

'Why? Wouldn't he be better living in Singapore?'

'Oh Laura, what a silly question! If your father was Ramsay MacDonald and your friend Mr Attlee was in Downing Street, you would want the best house in the region.'

'So what does a Commissioner for Southeast Asia actually do?'

'Well he's terribly sociable and vulgarly dapper. He mixes with British cabinet ministers and everyone in the UK who matters. Likewise here: he knows the sultans, the rich Chinese and all who count in the neighbouring countries but he's not so popular with the Colonial Service. He entertains a lot, including students, which is a good thing, and he's entertained more. He smiles a lot despite his horrible teeth. He has a way with people and he's an excellent raconteur. In his presence people imagine they're near the source of power, and they're right , if you believe the British still have any power. He's here to preside over the end of empire and to ensure we still come out, if not on top, at least a long way from the bottom. He does it all by charm, though not everyone's charmed. Actually he's just presiding over the inevitable for a fat salary.' While being so scathing Ferdach wondered whether MacDonald knew of the letter. He thought not. The exchange was to be limited, at Chin Peng's insistence, to himself and Gurney. Phoenix Park could not risk a leakage, even in Bukit Serene.

'Oh stop being a bloody know-all, Ferdie. Being a cynic doesn't suit you. At heart you're a woolly romantic. Those marines thought so too; even when you have the grossest sex, you burble of love; at least that's what those guys told me.'

Ferdach did not reply. He was thinking about the long journey to Kuala Lumpur; it would be tiring and Laura's chatter was irritating. Then, immediately ahead of them there was a checkpoint manned by Malay soldiers at whom they both beamed radiant smiles in return for which they were able to proceed without being stopped or searched. 'It's always best to smile at Malays; they're a friendly lot,' said Ferdach knowledgeably.

'I always smile at men, whatever their race, Ferdie. All mankind is a friendly lot too if treated properly. But I bet we'd have been stopped if we'd been Chinese, smiling or not.'

By now they had started to travel through a quieter area: few houses and even those abandoned, few cars and only a few lorries. Such vehicles as they encountered often had their glass windows replaced by steel sheets. Once they saw, advancing on them, a huge lorry on the back of which great tree trunks were precariously held fast by not too thick chains. Ferdach had to slow down on the narrow road to allow the monster to lumber past, remembering as he did so the story of an air force family who had been crushed to death when the chains on such a lorry had snapped, sending the great trees thundering down on them.

Another time a lorry full of British soldiers overtook them. The soldiers, lean young men probably doing their national service, whistled and gestured at Laura who waved back and said sadly to Ferdach how much she pitied their loneliness far from the sort of women they knew and loved. But most of the journey was fairly solitary. The road was straight enough, allowing Ferdach to keep up the best speed a Morris Minor could make; the occasional roadblock, when they passed through a village, provided a little human contact, but the drab rubber trees bordering the road in endless straight lined plantations looked erie and unnatural so that the world seemed to be bleak, despite the hot sun and the cloudlessly blue sky.

'What would you do if we were held up by CTs?' Laura asked, as though the thought of such a danger had only just occurred to her.

Ferdach remembered the same topic arising when he was driving south with Lai Kuan, so long ago it seemed, yet only two weeks had passed by. 'I'd drive straight at them.'

'But they'd shoot.'

'Yes they'd shoot. We might be killed or we might get through. However, if we stopped and surrendered, we would certainly be killed, maybe nastily.'

'Ah well, we'd be dead like Tristan and Isolde with only a gun between us. That would save Albert the trouble of a divorce. So good can sometimes come from violence.' For a moment Laura looked dejected, perhaps at the thought of leaving her old life, or life at all, but she perked up and asked, 'You have got a gun haven't you Ferdie?'

'In the pocket, there, a Browning automatic. Careful, it's loaded.'

Laura took the gun out and held it gingerly. 'I've never held a gun before. Not so heavy, yet so terrible.'

'Then don't fiddle with it. Above all never point a gun at anyone, even if it's not loaded,' Ferdach said sagely, though with an inward tremor as he remembered his near disaster with Waite's weapon.

Laura opened her handbag, took out a floral handkerchief and wrapped the gun up in it. 'It's in disguise now, in my handkerchief. No, I think I'll call it my gunkerchief,' she said with a shrill little laugh. 'I'll keep it on my lap to defend you should the need arise.'

'No. Put it back in the pocket. It's dangerous in your gunkerchief. You can't tell which end is which and you could have an accident.'

Laura sighed and put the gun away. 'I don't know whether I want to live in Malaya again. Blast the Emergency. I'm too flippant for war.'

Ferdach was aware of the despondency beginning to affect Laura's behaviour so, saying he was thirsty, he pulled the car over to the hard shoulder and took a thermos of cold lemonade from the back seat. When they had both had a drink, he put his arm around her and gave her a kiss, first on her cheek and then, much more warmly, on her lips. 'You'll be fine,' he insisted gently. 'In KL you'll make a new life and meet new people and I'll do my best to come to you whenever you need me.' As he spoke a young Chinese man clad in dun-coloured clothes emerged from the rubber estate through which they were passing. He stopped only a few yards away and stared at them curiously, unsmiling.

'Do you think he's a ...' began Laura, but Ferdach was already putting the car into gear to drive off. 'In this part of the world,' he said, 'you never can tell.'

They had already passed through the small towns of Senai, a sad-looking place where the Malayan Communist Party had started life in 1924, and Kulai, a scene of bustle and development beside which a New Village was being established. But nowhere did they stop for Ferdach wanted to eat up as many miles as possible before midday. The further north they went the less populated the state became and they drove, mainly in silence, through vast rubber and pineapple plantations and then across miles of lonely open countryside until Yong Peng, after which the road led northward as straight as a die through dense forest which had been cleared back to create a corridor of tree stumps, intended no doubt to reduce the danger of ambush.

Beyond the cleared zone the jungle trees rose as an immense dark cliff. Because the road lay in an artificial slash through the forest, to Laura the entire scene looked blank, resentful and angry, a landscape that only inspired fear. Nor were Laura's misgivings helped by a turn in the weather. The sky had become dark; there was a distant rumble of thunder. Sporadic bursts of heavy rain stopped and started as if heaven could not make up its mind what to do.

Even though the road was narrow, awash with puddles and slippery,

Ferdach was driving fast, as was a small convoy of three military trucks that they saw approaching. To give the broader military vehicles room to pass he kept to the nearside as much as possible. Laura gasped as the convoy bore down on them much quicker than she had expected. In a flash she drew in her arm which had been resting on the door of the open window. The first two trucks seemed extremely close to the car as they roared by – Laura could feel a blast of air striking her face – but the third, whose driver had had less chance to see what was ahead, was even closer. There was a high-pitched grating noise, rather like the screech of a pig having its throat cut, and Ferdach all but lost control of his stricken car which lurched to a standstill on the laterite shoulder of the road.

Laura was the first to speak. 'Are we alive? Yes we're alive.' She turned towards Ferdach who was white faced and trembling. 'Are you all right, Ferdie?'

Ferdach opened his car door and got out. 'The bastards,' he shouted. 'They've not stopped. We could be hurt and they've not stopped.' In fact the three trucks were well down the road, beyond recall. Then Ferdach became aware that his feet had sunk into the wet laterite. The front wheel of the car was in it even deeper. It seemed that the laterite had both stopped them and also prevented them from careering right off the road. He glanced over the car roof at Laura who had also got out. She was bending down and for an instant he thought she was vomiting.

'The driver must have done his best to pull away,' she called. 'He only hit the mudguard. It's jammed onto the tyre. Maybe we could force it back.' She spoke in a matter-of-fact way. Ferdach had feared she might be hysterical.

He went to look at the damage. 'I don't think we can free it,' he said dolefully. 'We're just stuck here. We'll have to wait until someone comes along to give us a lift.'

'Or shoot us. No. You can be bloody sure that when you want help no one will turn up. It's dangerous here, Ferdie, I feel it. We have to move on. Have you got a wrench or something?'

In fact it wasn't too difficult to push the wrench between the mudguard and the tyre and to lever the metal away from the wheel. 'But how the hell are we going to get out of the laterite? We're well and truly stuck,' said Ferdach.

An unusual Laura had come to life. She was like a girl guide leader faced with a field problem. 'Stones,' she ordered. 'Lots of stones, or wood, anything hard.' She started collecting loose road metal to shove down in front of the wheel until Ferdach thought it time to start the car and attempt to drive out. This only flung up laterite and made the hole deeper but at least a trench had opened up in front of the tyre. Now Laura left the road and stepped into the cleared zone where lots of wood was lying about. Seizing a stout branch she pushed it down in front of the wheel to give it purchase. Ferdach started up again and after many failures he inched forward. It took a frustrating while but at last the car was on the road. He got out and stared at Laura who had done most of the hard work. Indeed they both stared at each other and started to laugh like idiots. They were sweaty and filthy and speckled with blotches of red laterite that had found its way up to the most improbable places, even into Laura's hair.

To add to their misery the rain suddenly came down again. This time not sporadically but with the full fury of a tropical storm. The floodgates of heaven opened. It spewed down on them heavier than the most powerful bathroom shower. To be heard they had to shout, for the noise of the rain on the car was like the rattle of kettle drums, while rough gusts of wind blew leaves and branches from the cleared zone into their path. A fleecy white mist arose from the hot surface of the road when the cold rain from high in the sky bore down upon it. Ferdach knew it would be useless to start driving. When it rained like this, windscreen wipers just lost out. Traffic had to sit still and wait.

That was something Laura had no intention of doing. She was on the road beside the car. First she just looked up into the sky and let the rain wash the muck from her hair. Then she ran her fingers through it until she felt it was clean. That was but the beginning. In the very middle of the highway she started to strip; first her blouse then her skirt and then her underwear until it seemed to Ferdach, who was staring in disbelief at her, that she was doing a sort of dance. No, it could not be a dance; it was just movements dictated by taking off her clothes. But before long the clothes were all screwed up on the top of the car and Laura was indeed dancing. 'Come on Ferdie,' she shouted against the wind. 'This is the only way for us to get clean.'

That was a fact and very quickly Ferdach was as naked as Laura and joined her in prancing hither and thither on the steaming road. They laughed and they jumped and they capered like demons with the rain streaming over their bodies, refreshing them and reviving them. Ferdach knew that in such weather no other vehicle would come along and it made him glad that Laura was now so happy when their accident had portended doom. For an instant he stood still and laughed into her face. She seemed to him to have become lovelier than ever in this natural state, without makeup or clothes or some elaborate hairdo. Yes, he told himself, she is indeed beautiful and she is unusual. He adored her lack of convention that mirrored the content of his own mind. At this moment, with the storm savaging the world about them, he desired her more than ever.

She could see what was in his mind or rather his body. 'Ferdie, you've got a hard-on. Oh Ferdie, the water's all over its little head. It'll catch its death of cold.'

'It isn't a little head and it won't catch cold either,' said Ferdach embracing her and pushing her back over the car bonnet.

They made love, neither long nor very comfortably, but very passionately and very delightfully to judge by their cries which were obscured by the raging storm. Then, after a little more rain bathing they got into the car. They managed to pull out towels and dry clothers from the luggage on the back seat. Ferdach helped Laura to dry her long hair and comb it into some sort of order. He was pleased with the result. 'We'll be able to drive on looking clean and respectable now,' he said. 'No one will guess what a memorable scene they missed on the main road through Johore.'

'But I shall remember it Ferdie, and so shall you.'

55

'Where on earth have you been?' Hester de Guise's greeting to Ferdach when he drew up before Carcosa Cottage was irritated but full of concern. 'You said you'd be here on Monday by six in the evening, today's Wednesday. And honestly Ferdach, when people come up to this part of town, they see that their motor looks better than that.' She gestured at his car which was caked with mud.

'Well I had a bit of an accident in Johore.' Ferdach showed her the battered front mudguard then stroked the top of the offending vehicle. 'You should feel sorry for the poor little thing.'

'Doesn't seem to be much damage to me. You're obviously lying. Anyway, I couldn't care less. You'd better come in, and have a shave as well as a shower. Some people are coming for drinks. Gilbert will be back soon. He's over at King's House.'

'Oh really Hester.' Ferdach felt quite lit up inside by the words 'King's House' and 'people are coming for drinks'. King's House was part of his plans; the 'people' might turn out to be equally so. Then he saw that Hester's face was still stoney. 'Hester dear, I really am sorry. It wasn't just the crack on the mudguard. There was also some internal damage. The water pump. Do you know I asked a Chinese mechanic in Yong Peng to make some ad hoc repairs to it? He made a filter of brown paper. Can you imagine that happening in England? There'd be long faces and, "sorry we'll have to order a new part from the manufacturer". Chinese are so marvellous at improvising. I'm sure the future belongs to them.'

'So you're learning something at last about the East,' said Hester condescendingly, but at the same time somewhat more warmly. 'That's the sort of thing they didn't teach you on that silly Colonial Service training course.'

'And I did try to phone you. Honestly. I just couldn't get through.'

'Well at least I can believe that. Now, put this pile of metal round the back and go and make yourself decent.'

Ferdach obeyed, hoping most sincerely that Hester did not discover that he had been in Kuala Lumpur since the day before and had spent twenty-four hours helping Laura to settle into a flat in a mansion off the oldest and leafiest part of Ampang Road. The finesse of her new accommodation and the beauty of its surrounding garden seemed to have further convinced Laura that she had made the right move. Ferdach had also gone with her to the Kuok Fong Rubber Broker's Office where she was to work, surprisingly on a salary not much less than his own, and left feeling that her reception augured well for her future.

Now, with the letter to the High Commissioner in his possession, the time had come to repay Lai Kuan's kindness, and possibly do something useful for Malaya. The latter however, he was increasingly dubious over. Too many imponderables seemed to be involved and he was in particular baffled by Lai Kuan's hint that Chin Peng might be a plant of the British. Surely if that were so there would be no purpose at all in this letter from him to Sir Henry Gurney; dependable secret channels would be available to them both. Maybe, like so many people who dabbled in politics, Lai Kuan, and even the British intelligence people in Singapore, were amateurs capable of error as much as any Joe Bloggs in the street.

Because of his doubts he had concealed everything concerning the letter from Laura, although he had no doubt that she suspected that the intelligence set-up in Phoenix Park had recruited him for some minor purpose in Malaya. But since he had no desire that Laura should think that her flat was a reward to him for some such activity, which, together with her generous salary, he was now convinced it was, he was at pains to say to her when, early that morning, he left her still ensconced in a bed, 'Lai Kuan is bound to call on you some time Laura. Best to show your gratitude. You know how to do that don't you dear. I won't mind at all.'

'All right, I get it. You don't want me to imagine that you've got any special rights over me Ferdie. I don't belong to you, that's it isn't it? But I'm telling you this: if anything in Southeast Asia belongs to me, it's you, and don't you ever forget it.' That was followed by a well-aimed pillow and the words, 'And if I do screw with Lai Kuan it won't be as a reward for his services. I only screw for fun, except with you. In case you're too thick to see it, that's for love.'

At the back of Carcosa Cottage, Ferdach thought he might find at the very least a *tukang kebun*, a gardener, whom he could tip to wash his car. But the garden of the cottage, falling as it did within the demesne of King's House, was kept immaculate by the Public Works Department (PWD). In fact the servants' quarters were all locked up. To the concern – nay, disbelief – of all, Gilbert and Hester de Guise really did without such help and they seemed happy enough without it.

Indoors, Hester showed him to a room which he had not seen before. With only a single window it was decidedly gloomy but the main guestroom, where he had stayed earlier, was now in use, Hester said, as her painting and photography studio. 'I don't really like people staying with us,' she stated, 'so not having a decent guestroom provides me with a good excuse for turning people down. Of course you're different. You won't mind the gloom.' Ferdach did not ask whether Gilbert too was against having guests. It was difficult to avoid the suspicion that it was Hester of the darkly brooding eyes who made the running in this house. He unpacked his case, took a shower as instructed in the old fashioned PWD bathroom but did not bother to shave; once a day was enough in his view and if Hester could be so relaxed about his accommodation, he would be likewise about his own person. After secreting an ant-proof tin of biscuits in a drawer as a defence against hunger, he surveyed the room. It contained only the older type of PWD furniture: an almeirah, a dressing table, a hard chair, a footstool and a bookcase crammed with Tibetan and English books of an esoteric nature. The large bed, however, was unusual being merely a mattress on a low supporting frame, barely off the floor and without endboards. There was no rug, no curtains, not so much as an ornament (he discounted the black ashtray with 'Stolen from the E&O Hotel' on it) and not even a shade to prettify the bare light bulb. On top of the bookcase however were two Jewish-looking candelabra, each bearing seven candles. The clean white sheet on the bed beckoned him to rest and as he lay under the creaking ceiling fan he became aware in the dim light of several large pictures dominating the room. Right before him, at the foot of the bed, was the terrifying Tibetan God Shindje, Judge of the Dead, his hands and feet grasping the Round

353

of Existence containing six divisions, each replete with gods, men, titans and goodness knows what else, and with some sort of purgatory at the bottom. On a small table in front of the picture, stood a green celadon pot containing burning joss sticks that lent the room the feeling of being in a shrine. To his right was a gentler picture of the Lord Buddha amidst sacred beings, thirty-seven of them Ferdach counted in all, floating ethereally in that sublime form of non-existence, it must be presumed, termed Nirvana, the whole picture a harmonious blend of gold, orange and green. Inscribed below it in large letters were the English words: 'I teach only two things: suffering and release from suffering'.

To his left was a painting by Hester, an icon of remarkable intensity intended to inspire the devotee of Lord Shiva who was dancing within a great nimbus of flames. He grasped the base of his erect lingam with his left hand as a strong sceptre whilst in his right hand he held his trident. His serene face, which had a third eye in its forehead, was both stern and compassionate. Beneath this icon was a poem:

> Be not attached
> That the Great Bliss
> May arise without end.
> Do not cling
> That the Light
> May outshine all barriers.
> Cease not to practice
> Not-making of effort
> To be free beyond striving.

These stilted phrases did not mean much to Ferdach except that 'not-making of effort' was like Waite's advice that he should learn 'not to do anything'. Nor did he give it further thought, for as he rested his head back on the pillow, his eyes were at once taken up by what was on the fourth wall. Behind the bed, impossible not to see from below, was a triptych of paintings of three sculptural compositions, in each of which a male and a female deity with withdrawn expressions, were in an intimate embrace which left no part of their magnificent bodies to the imagination. Curious to learn their provenance, Ferdach looked at the edge of the frame and read that they had been painted by the indubitably talented Hester at one of the Khajuraho temples in India.

As far as Ferdach was concerned, people should be totally free to practise whatever beliefs they held but he could not help suspecting that Gilbert de Guise must be involved in a most delicate balancing act between the syncretic cult suggested by these pictures and his position as Private Secretary to the Chief Secretary. For everything up here on this beautiful eminence overlooking the Lake Gardens, everything on these well-wooded slopes around King's House and Carcosa, was redolent of the Raj, of British authority and of convention. The Private Secretary was expected to adhere to the correct social etiquette, to go to diplomatic receptions, to the races, to accompany His Excellency's party on Sunday morning to the Anglican Church of St Mary if requested. This particular church was located by the *padang* next to the 'Dog', the Selangor Club, in which Somerset Maugham had observed the foibles of his fellow countrymen. Yet up here was a situation that even Maugham had not envisaged: an MCS officer and his half-Indian wife who were adepts in the Tantric form of Buddhism, or was it Shivaism, or a mélange of both, in which sexual congress was said to lead to communion with God. 'Interesting,' Ferdach said aloud. 'Most interesting.' It was inevitable that he found himself wondering whether the low bed on which he lay, was used for ritualistic purposes but, before he could speculate further on this matter, he heard a car drawing up ouside so he got dressed and went to join Hester for the social fray.

The car had brought Peter Molyneux, Hester's first husband. He was a short, balding man with a hunted expression. According to one's point of view he might be described as sensitive in appearance or rat-like. He was acompanied by a fellow officer. Tall, broad of shoulder and heavy jowled, Lieutenant Lionel Smithers, an ex-Gurkha officer, sported a black Adolf Hitler moustache which looked out of place as his face and even his hair were ruddy. Afflicted by shyness he hardly seemed to know where to put himself.

'Do help with the drinks, Ferdie dear,' said Hester, indicating a sidetable on which there was a wide variety of short drinks, some unfamiliar to Ferdach who was not a sophisticated drinker. However, he assumed the role of barman dispensing to Molyneux and Smithers not only whiskey *stengah*s but a firsthand account, suitably embellished, of his experiences in the Singapore riots.

Before he could be questioned too deeply, they heard the sound of a motorbike and then two cars drawing up outside. Before long quite a party had assembled. The motorbike's riders were two RAF men, introduced by Hester as Flight Lieutenant Donald Roxby and his young national service friend Corporal Bill MacGuiness; the cars had brought Eric Maidstone, the Legal Draftsman with his wife Maggie, and Dr Algernon Hebblewhite, with an attractive Mediterranean-looking girl, May da Souza, described as his colleague. Everyone seemed to be well acquainted with one another; they all drank rather quickly or so it seemed to Ferdach for in no time he was pouring seconds and then thirds. To judge by their conversation, which largely revolved around Hester, who presided like the mistress of a salon over them, they formed some sort of 'set'. They were all very liberal and 'postwar', highly critical of both the British and the Malayan governments, especially of some of the 'old hats' in the latter who had recently re-appeared, and distinctly sympathetic to the Chinese. This tendency he gathered from the roar of disapproval that arose when Peter Molyneux told them of some draconian step that was about to be taken against the villagers of the largely Chinese town of Batu Arau in northern Selangor for failing to give information about CT activity.

'My God, how does the government imagine we can win the Chinese over to our side when we treat them unjustly?' fumed Eric Maidstone. No one ventured to suggest that the action might be necessary.

At that moment Gilbert strode in looking elegant in cream slacks, a long sleeved cream shirt with gold cufflinks, and a rather jazzy looking cravat round his neck. His outstanding feature, which everyone remarked on, though not in his presence, were his large plate-like blue eyes. They darted about him so swiftly and intensely that many people formed the impression that he was a bit mad, especially as his face was narrow and ascetic above a tall thin body and a long scraggy neck which perhaps the cravat was intended to soften. This evening he looked more tense than usual, even a little distraught. Hester, who was in a white dress more suited to the tennis court, immediately stubbed out her cigarette and went up to him, seized him by both hands as though to prevent him from using them for some violent purpose and demanded, 'Gilbert, what is it? What did Del Boca say?'

All this was a bit of a mystery to Ferdach except that he knew Del Boca, the Chief Secretary, was Gilbert's boss. Like everyone else there he became all ears.

'Well Hester, we're leaving.'

'Leaving,' said everyone in unison like the courtiers in a comic opera.

'Yes, we're posted out of KL. To Pahang.'

There was general consternation with volleys of 'Why?', 'Oh no' and 'What the blazes'. Ferdach said nothing but felt as concerned as everyone else. He had not decided when to hand over the letter, or how to do it. He wanted to devise a satisfactory way of doing so without attracting attention. He had envisaged heading to KL and returning to the de Guises to carry out his task in a week or so. Now he would have to work quickly.

'It's all rather mad really,' began Gilbert, 'but I'll tell you the whole story. Oh, dear old Ferdie. I didn't see you over there. I've not said hello. I see Hester's turned you into a barman. Well, everyone, top up and listen.'

No one needed further bidding and Ferdach poured the strongest possible measures for he knew that this was the best way of getting a party going.

Gilbert started off with a diatribe against the etablishment office. This surprised Ferdach somewhat as he had always thought that the de Guises had happily profited from the preference shown to them. Gilbert then took some time to tell them what a stupid, limited snob Del Boca was and what a pedantic stickler for form, even if it went against the public, but not his own, interest. He then made it clear, though Ferdach had long suspected it, that he had been chosen by the Chief Secretary himself to be Private Secretary on account of his name, and because they had both been to the same Oxford college, though not at the same time. He now knew too that no effort had been made by Del Boca to ascertain what his real interests were or even that he had got a degree in Tibetan studies. 'Unbelievable, isn't it?' he asked, and everyone shook their heads except Ferdach who thought, no, it's entirely believable.

Among Del Boca's other foibles, Gilbert continued, was his great opinion of himself as a connoiseur of food and drink. He spent a great deal of time building up a cellar of fine wines, much of it paid for out of his entertainment allowance, which was considerable. But mostly Del Boca considered himself to be an expert on whiskey. As proof of his reputation in this regard he would tell people that he was one of some twenty people of eminence worldwide to whom a certain distillery in the fastnesses of Wester Ross presented a very special bottle of their magnificent spirit each year for ceremonial consumption on New Year's Day.

At this piece of information Flight Lieutenant Roxby groaned aloud and said, 'Oh God Bill, I knew it.' He looked anxiously at his friend Corporal McGuiness who replied, 'So vanishes the last place where you and I can relax together Don.'

This was no great shakes to Gilbert who gestured them both to silence and continued, 'Of course, you all remember the party we had in Carcosa on Boxing Day? We all knew I shouldn't have given it there. But the CS and HE were both away and I took the risk and that's it. Well, when I went to look at the bar after you'd all gone, to my horror I saw that Del Boca's presentation bottle had been opened and completely drunk. I guess none of us could distinguish it from a bottle of Black Label.'

Roxby broke in. 'I knew it would happen; it's my fault. I promised Gilbert that we'd fill up the bottle in the mess with the best whiskey we could buy and then seal the top so that no one could tell. But I guess Del Boca must have noticed our repair work.'

'No, he didn't notice it at all because after his New Year dinner with all his special cronies, he asked me to open the bottle and I poured it for the guests. Someone toasted the King and everyone drank the whiskey and told the CS what marvellous stuff it was. Del Boca put his glass to his lips and almost at once put it down. He said nothing. He drank nothing.'

'I know what you're going to tell us Gilbert,' said Hester calmly. She put her arm around Gilbert's narrow waist. It was a protective gesture.

Gilbert kissed his wife, just a peck of a kiss but one that meant something to everyone for he was not given to even mild displays of affection in company. 'This afternoon the CS told me to return to his office after I'd taken an urgent despatch over to King's House. As soon as I went in to see him I noticed the empty bottle on the table on which he keeps his sundowner. He stared at me with that piercing gaze of his and asked quietly, 'Have you ever been to Pahang, Monsieur Gilbert de Guise?' He emphasised the honorific and he pronounced Gilbert in the French way, so I knew at once what was coming but I wouldn't give him the satisfaction of humiliating me. I just looked insolent. He quite lost control and shouted, 'Well, you're going there next week. Now get out of my sight.'

'Christ, how do such people get to the top?' Algernon Hebblewhite looked flushed with anger and was on the verge of starting some great diatribe against everything he did not like when he was cut short by his soft-spoken, almost diminutive, girlfriend May who pointed out that the whiskey had been Del Boca's prize possession. He glared angrily at her and said, 'That's right May, trust you to see the other side of any issue.'

'No. May's quite right. We did drink his whiskey and we did use Carcosa without permission,' said Gilbert.

'Of course,' began Eric Maidstone, in the deliberative tone to be expected of a lawyer. 'But the CS should have a sense of proportion. You've been a first rate PS, everyone says so. You're a young man and it was Christmas, the season of jollity, eh? Damn it, we're all fairly young aren't we? We didn't commit some dreadful sin. Just a silly mistake. No, Del Boca has behaved unreasonably.'

Peter Molyneux seemed to have crumpled up in his chair. There was sadness in his eyes that were constantly bent on his lost goddess Hester. 'You could appeal to him,' he said. 'Gilbert, you could apologise. We could all apologise for making use of Carcosa.'

'None of you will do anything of the sort,' Hester said. 'In any case it would do no good. I believe there's another reason for Del Boca's decision.' She drew Gilbert to the settee and sat down beside him. They turned towards each other and smiled, not broadly nor for more than an instant. Each of their faces looked serene suggesting the mutual possession of a secret source of happiness that would easily transcend any difficulties they might encounter. That done they posed, or so it seemed to Ferdach, like a king and queen quite stiffly as if giving a formal audience to their adoring followers.

'What reason?' asked several people in unison.

'Why, quite simply: me. I am the reason.' Hester spoke quietly and deliberately.

There was an awkward silence as no one wanted to suggest that Hester's being half Indian, could possibly have had any effect on a post Indian independence Chief Secretary, yet that was what she seemed to be implying. And she was indeed but in no ordinary sense. It appeared, so Hester said, that what the Chief Secretary, or rather the Chief Secretary's extremely conventional wife had objected to (and it was she, so it transpired, who was at the root of the problem), was more than the simple fact of Hester's parentage; there was also her divorce from Peter, there was the fact that she had subsequenly had an affair with a Chinese man, a wealthy Chinese man, but wealth had not masked the fact that he was Chinese, and lastly, there were the unacceptable Oriental beliefs to which she and Gilbert were said to be addicted.

Hester now revealed that just before Christmas she had learned from a close friend who worked as a secretary in Carcosa how, when both she and Gilbert were out of town, Mrs Del Boca had paid a visit to the Cottage, ostensibly to check on its furnishings which, she said, were not up to the mark for her husband's PS. She must have had a good look at the room which contained Hester's erotic triptych and the priapic Shiva and no doubt at the volumes, some of which contained even more graphic material, in the bookcase. She had apparently returned from the Cottage looking poker faced and the words 'disgusting'and 'that woman's a bloody witch', had been overheard issuing tartly from her mouth when talking to her husband about her inspection.

Peter Molyneux, somewhat shamefacedly, now confessed that shortly after Mrs del Boca's visitation, the Chief Secretary had asked Special Branch to report on the group of people who were regular visitors to Carcosa Cottage, that is to say everyone in the room except Ferdach. In reality, Peter said, Special Branch's investigation had concentrated on one of their members, Lionel Smithers, whose forthright replies had resulted in it being reported that the de Guise' weekly gathering of rather intellectual men and their wives was innocent of deviant practices but, on the contrary, revolved around their common interest in Indian art and philosophy. When everyone heard this, they looked gratefully at Lional Smithers who, however, was so unnecessarily embarrassed at the revelation of his role that his face became a purplish red that suggested imminent self-combustion. The results of the investigation being innocuous, Peter went on, he had seen no reason to tell the de Guises about it even when the head of Special Branch, who had been surprised by Del Boca's request, had subsequently told him that he, Peter Molyneux, had also been a subject of investigation and cleared. Now, Peter concluded, they could only surmise that it was Mrs Del Boca alone who had suggested to her husband that the de Guise coterie was not in keeping with the values of the little British acropolis formed by King's House and Carcosa, and that it was she who had sown the seeds of doubt in her husband's mind regarding its morality and dependability.

Ferdach now contributed to the nonplussed assembly for the first time. 'So you see my friends, Gilbert's exile isn't the result of a mistake over a mere bottle of Scotch. That was just a pretext, though one that must have given Del Boca a great deal of pleasure. No, as an Irishman I'll tell you: whenever people do some offbeat thing that the establishment doesn't like, they'll be accused of obscenity. Like so many other clever people you've just fallen foul of Anglo-Saxon moral rectitude. Yet you should feel honoured; you've joined the Oscar Wilde Society.'

56

Normally the de Guises were the best of company – intelligent, curious about a wide variety of subjects and excellent talkers – but the news of their imminent departure had turned them in on one another. They seemed overcome by doubt. It was not, so they said, that they minded being sent to Pahang; an active role in the Emergency in a rural district, a role similar to that already played by Ferdach, appealed to both of them in place of the servitor part Gilbert was obliged to play in Carcosa. But Del Boca's reaction to Gilbert's prank had been the last straw in a chain of events that was now making them doubt Gilbert's role in Malaya as a useful Colonial Service officer. They had for some time now begun to see inefficiency and stupidity in every nook and cranny of the government machine. In this they were not alone. In Kuala Lumpur, amongst most of the British who were capable of thought, there was persistent unease. Time was running out: communist China was looming ever more monstrously in the north; the struggle in Vietnam against the communists by the French presaged nothing but doom for the West. And in the background was Indonesia, run by the incalculable Soekarno who might turn in any direction to maintain control of his country. Surely Britain's clinging on here in Malaya was an anachronism fraught with potential disaster. Might it not be better for a young couple like themselves to get out now, while the going was good?

Ferdach listened to them discussing their problem but did not comment as he could not work out what they really wanted nor did he want to be involved. Although he had always enjoyed talking with Gilbert about matters of an intellectual nature, ever since they studied together in London, he had never warmed to him. Gilbert seemed essentially cerebral and, though kind, not exactly a fleshly human being. It was not easy to think of him making love even in the missionary position let alone in one of those erotic Tantric entanglements about which he and Hester had talked in their precise Oxford accents; they might just as well have been describing the mating habits of the frog. To Ferdach this slim, blond, translucent skinned man betrayed an origin on some distant planet where sexuality of an earthly type had been dispensed with, or was that planet some rarefied reaches of English society to which Ferdach had never aspired. Yet passion there must be; the mutual affection of the de Guises strongly suggested it.

Towards Hester, Ferdach felt differently. The longer he stayed with the de Guises the more he was struck by the brooding sensuality of this slight, dark woman. Before long he let his imagination rip: yes, he could easily visualise her as the mistress of rituals, a devoted priestess of Shiva overseeing hidden rites in that sanctum she had created and he found himself regretting her departure. His own fantasies recalled to mind the dictum of the experienced Nina Hamnett's that what went on in an Englishman's bedroom could defy the imagination. Gilbert de Guise was, despite his name, very much an Englishman, pent up and capable of exploding given the right stimulus which was what Hester must have been. As to the other members of the Carcosa Cottage set, Ferdach did not know whether any of them had taken part in any unusual ceremonies, but he certainly could envisage Nina throwing back her head and uttering that gurgling laugh of hers as she shrugged off the de Guises' candlelit erotic rituals as very run of the mill.

Ferdach felt sympathy for his hosts, taken up as they now were with the arrangements of their departure. Though they had to leave him very much to his own devices, Ferdach was in no way deprived of company. The Cottage was in the vicinity of both the High Commissioner's and the Chief Secretary's houses so there was a constant stream of officials, military men, police and public figures flowing in and out of this heaven-borne environment and Ferdach had opportunities for meeting personalities he would not have come across elsewhere.

Whenever he talked to such people, Ferdach found himself listening to political misgivings far stronger than any he had heard in Ipoh. Further north in Ipoh, where the battle with the communists was close and ongoing, morale among the government officers, planters, tin miners and security forces was high, at least outwardly. It had to be for if people actively engaged in a struggle let their own morale drop they were as good as lost.

Kuala Lumpur, on the other hand, was the stage for a political world that was obliged to adopt an overview of the country but it was also the seat of several organs of government and a forum of nascent political activity. Unfortunately this meant that there were a number of overviews, some of them quite conflicting. Strong rivalries existed between government departments, between the police and the military, and between the federal government and the state governments. Wherever there is dissension there is animosity and animosity leads to doubt and so to lack of purpose. At the very core of the problem lay the lack of a single person in command at the helm. Because of a lack of both knowledge and imagination in Whitehall, General Briggs had not been placed in overall control, despite being Director of Operations and a proven commander in the Western Desert and in Burma. Briggs worked as a civilian adviser to High Commissioner Sir Henry Gurney and though the two men got on well together and appreciated each other's qualities, a strange lack of purpose existed at all levels of government and this militated against the successful prosecution of the war against the terrorists.

The day after Del Boca's unhappy decision Ferdach seized the opportunity to pump a man who had firsthand knowledge of Sir Henry Gurney's character during lunch in the Lake Club, the restrictive haven of the great and the white. Staples, the Private Secretary to the High Commisioner, had eulogised his boss's character as modest but firm and burning with a sense of his duty to direct Malaya towards democratic independence. Nor did Ferdach doubt this assessment for Staples himself was the perfect example of the dedicated colonial officer whose honesty was beyond question. At the same time Ferdach wondered how much Sir Henry actually appreciated the reality of the Emergency at grass roots level. He did not travel greatly about the country though he often journeyed with a dangerously small escort in his unarmoured Rolls Royce, bearing the Union Jack, up to his favourite hill station, Fraser's Hill. This was all very courageous but it still left him remote in a lordly sort of way from the people of the country.

Another cause for misgiving arose when Ferdach heard a senior army officer, Brigadier Wildhogge-Partington, a close friend of the de Guises, complain of the forces' reluctance to act as mere supporters of the civil power; how could they be expected to fight effectively with one arm in a sling? Too often, military operations had to be planned on the basis of compromise with the police and with the civil admistration, or rather with a plethora of administrators. The chain of command was so muddied that commanders in the field were constantly prevented from taking dynamic action. No wonder the communists could still operate with impunity. Yet despite all these manifold difficulties which were crying out for reform, it was depressing for Ferdach to hear in the Selangor Club, and at the Swimming Club, to both of which places Hester or Gilbert generously took him, men and women of the old school who were unwilling to accept the fact that the whole system of government was out of date and incapable of dealing with an ever deteriorating crisis. They thought of the Japanese Occupation as a mere hiatus that provided no reason for not resuming the old easy prewar way of life. To such people it was the damned Labour Government, with its ridiculous talk of self-government, even of independence, that was upsetting the natural order of things.

Yet all the time that he was mixing with new people or exploring Kuala Lumpur on his own, Ferdach was perplexed by one problem: what to do with the letter from Chin Peng. Somehow or other it had to be got into Sir Henry Gurney's hands privately without Ferdach himself being implicated in any way that would bring discredit on himself or on Lai Kuan. It was a question of finding the narrow channel between the Scylla of being accused of bypassing the normal government channels and the Charybdis of failing to do anything at all. But another problem perplexed him: suppose Sir Henry responded to the letter; suppose a chain of events was set in motion which led to an early peace. Ferdach himself thought this was desirable but what he had heard from those connected with the police and military in Kuala Lumpur made him fear that any peace which gave communist Chinese a say in government could lead to an even worse situation: a civil war in which race would be the great divide.

One afternoon, sitting on the verandah of the Selangor Club, he fell into conversation with a rich, rotund but retired, businessman Sir Robin Goodall. This man, who did most of the talking, was full of dire prophecies, which he uttered loudly, pompously and with great certainty.

'You government people all assume,' he said, 'that the Chinese are divided in their loyalty to government, with only say ten percent in favour and fifty percent on the fence, which leaves the other forty percent pro-communust, eh? You people assume that the vast majority of the Malays are behind you, that they even like the British. Well, I'll let you know young man, that any such feelings about the British vanished from the Malay soul during the Japanese Occupation. The Malays saw that we have feet, no whole bodies, of clay, and pretty mouldy clay too. And in their heart of hearts they despise us. Now wouldn't you think like that if you were a Malay? But the Malays are so polite, so courteous, they 'll never let you know this. You British officers occupy all your important positions, you mix with one another, you create an unreal British world in which the future of this place seems to rest in your hands. You're in cloud-cuckoo-land which, to the average Briton here, is the Malayan reality. You just don't understand what's happening all around you. Before long you'll all be gone. But you musn't think that in the future the Malays are going to read your history books and believe that since the end of last century the British have laid the foundation of a modern country. Yes, we have done that. But they won't want to admit it because their pride has been hurt. And when we've gone they'll write us out of their past as nothing but a bad dream. In the meantime they'll make use of us to rid the country of the communist threat. But when we've done that, they'll say, politely of course, piss off and then claim that they won the war themselves.'

'Robin!' The voice was hard and piercing and issued from a small but formidable woman who had crept up on them unobserved. 'Talking a load of nonsense as usual. Take no notice of him young man.' Lady Goodall, whose face seemed to be a study in permanent anger, turned again on her husband and bade him come to the dining room at once to meet some friends.

'Yes dear,' he replied in a meek voice, throwing a wistful glance in Ferdach's direction before trailing after her. Ferdach was glad to see them go, he was even more glad that he had not, as he could have done, claimed relationship with them for Goodall was his mother's maiden name and Sir Robin was her distant cousin. How dreadful to have been at the receiving end of their hospitality.

Gloomily he left the club and skirted the *padang* where great thighed, mighty-breasted English women were playing hockey furiously under the prurient gaze of a squatting row of Tamil men. He gazed ahead of him at the beautiful Moorish secretariat building with its delicate domes, its wide verandahs and elegant arches, walked around it and into its back courts which were a foil to a lovely mosque of similar design across the river. Then he returned to the front to look at the statue of Sir Frank Swettenham, one of the greatest of British administrators who had done so much to create modern Malaya and who had done his utmost to understand the Malay character. If Goodall were right, the statue would be lucky to survive for long after independence. Maybe even Mr Spooner, the architect of these beautiful buildings would be transmuted into a Malay. The thought saddened Ferdach, not that he wanted the country to bear a British stamp but because he believed in the desirability of peoples assimilating one another's culture and learning to appreciate the good things each had given the other, which, unlike himself, many of the hate-filled Irish would never do.

Once over the river he walked into the crowded Market Square that was fringed by bustling Chinese and Indian shophouses, all built in a vaguely classical style with Jacobean strap work on their facades. Then, as he did not want to buy anything, though importuned by salesmen at almost every doorway, he recrossed the river to Mountbatten Road and the English department stores of Whiteaway Laidlaws and Robinsons, the ambiance now that of a small English county town. Tired of walking and damp with sweat, Ferdach made his way into the airconditioned comfort of Robinsons' tea room. There, to his surprise, he saw Tengku Mizan, his first Malay friend in Ipoh, sitting at a table with three other young men, all Malays, drinking tea and enjoying what a gothic lettered notice advertised as an English Cream Tea.

There followed an exchange of *selamat*s and courtly introductions and Ferdach was invited to join Tengku Mizan's party. His friends were very different in type. Razali bin Rais, the youngest, was a *penghulu*, a headman, in Gombak, north of Kuala Lumpur. He was light skinned and slim like a champion runner and had refined aquiline features. His profile made Ferdach think of Rudolph Valentino. Mohammed Yusuf was thick set and very muscular, rather like a weight lifter. Through the darkness of his features his radiant smile was like a sunburst. The third young man, Harun bin Isa, was slight and certainly no athlete. His features were sensitive and the length of his face was extended by a wispy beard of the type students affected to identify themselves as intellectuals. His large eyes darted over Ferdach inquisitively and, it seemed, suspiciously. It was he who spoke first to say, 'You see, Tuan Ferdach, how anglicised we are, enjoying scones, strawberry jam and clotted cream.'

'I love Italian food but it doesn't make me a Latin,' Ferdach replied with a smile. 'As for me,' he added to a waiter, 'bring me a curry puff and a coffee.'

'Tuan Ferdach always tries to identify himself with our country,' said Mizan.

'But curry puffs are Indian and coffee, well it's from all over the world, but most of it comes from some place called nescaffee.' Everyone laughed at Mohammed Yusuf's weak joke except Yusuf himself who said baldly, 'I don't think I said anything very funny,' after which he himself exploded with glee.

'Haven't you noticed,' said Harun bin Isa, 'that in Malaya, when people of different races get together, they always start off by being facetious and then when they've got going they start to criticise the race that isn't present. So a Chinese and a Malay will have a go at the Indian or the Englishman, or an Indian and a Chinese will start criticising the Malays.'

'But that happens all over the world,' said Ferdach. 'It's just our tribalism.' Then he too resorted to facetiousness, 'But I myself have never heard anyone criticise the Malays or the British. Surely we are beyond reproach.'

'The British?' asked Mizan. 'Who are they? Do they exist? You have your, "There was an Englishman, a Scotsman, a Welshman and an Irishman jokes" but never "There was a Briton". And why is the Irishman always made to look stupid?'

'Because an Irishman is never British,' said Harun. 'Unless he's from Ulster. And then he's a traitor to one side or the other.'

'A Briton could never be a traitor,' laughed Razali Rais. 'That's a contradiction in terms.'

So it went on. It struck Ferdach that these quick young men were playing *sepak raga*, that game in which *kampung* youths keep on kicking a rattan ball in the air and points are lost when someone lets it hit the ground. He was the ball and it was a little unnerving. 'Isn't it possible to be several things at once?' he asked, putting on a thoughtful air. 'Take me for instance. I'm inevitably Irish by my father, undoubtedly English by upbringing, reluctantly British by citizenship and now peculiarly Malayan because my emotions have been aroused by this country and its people.'

'I am definitely a Malay,' voiced Harun, 'so I like you as far as you've become Malayan. But I don't like the British part of you at all.' He seized Ferdach's hand, stared into his eyes and asked, 'Now tell me good friend of Tengku Mizan, how long will it be before we get our freedom, our *merdeka*? Or is the real British plan to hang on as long as possible?'

Ferdach sidestepped the question. 'Would you like the British to do a deal with Chin Peng and get out tomorrow?'

Harun's expession hardened. 'Today would be better. Once we are free, we Malays will deal with Chin Peng and all the Chinese.' He sounded both adamant and confident.

Tengku Mizan laughed nervously. 'I wonder whether by "deal with" Harun means working with the hammer and sickle or wielding the kris?'

The conversation had taken a darker turn. Either alternative suggested by Mizan implied danger, but the kris, the Malay weapon of death, suggested a bloodbath. Then, quite abruptly, Mohamed Yusuf broke the sombre mood by giving a radiant smile at everyone around the table and saying, 'I agree with Tuan Ferdach: it is possible to have several loyalties. An Arabian sage once said that the good man should be Arabic in faith, Babylonian in education, a Hebrew in astuteness, a disciple of Christ in conduct, a Syrian monk in piety, a Greek in science, an Indian in divining mysteries and a Sufi in spiritual life. Compared to that, Tuan Ferdach's position is simple.'

Everyone fell silent until Razali bin Rais said, 'Then how can a good man ever achieve *merdeka* if he must surrender to so many masters? No. No one is ever really free. So Harun's question means nothing.'

57

Two hours later Ferdach was alone with Tengku Mizan in the Mohammed Kasseem Indian Muslim restaurant on Batu Road. They had not spoken much during their meal which was delicious, most memorable the seafood. Ferdach could not identify the subtle ingredients but he especially enjoyed the *murtabak*, a bread rich with onions, vegetables and spices that subsequently he never seemed able to find.

The restaurant was crowded with parties of men, so that he and the Tengku had to be content with a little window table looking out across the road towards KL's oldest cinema, the Coliseum, a classical building graced with a first-floor colonnade of Ionic columns. It was certainly more pleasing to look at than the drab interior of the restaurant, every corner of which was penetrated by frigid fluorescent light that flattered no one's clothes or complexion. The floor was covered with hideous geometrically patterned oilcloth, while the tables were covered in oilcloth of a bilious shade of green spattered with yellow flowers. In an alcove off the room was a sink with a towel rail on which hung a number of 'Good Morning' towels of the type to be found in cheap Chinese hotels, their purpose to enable customers to wash off the curry and spice stains which inevitably got on one's fingers since everyone ate with their right hand.

But here appearances meant nothing. No one had come to feast his eyes. This was a place where the palate alone mattered for the subtle blend of spices and curries in which the finest and freshest crustaceans taken from the Strait of Malacca had been marinated drew gourmets from many miles around as much as an instrumentalist of surpassing brilliance might draw music lovers to a distant concert. Only the food mattered; all else was functional.

They both belched loudly, smiled at each other and ordered the restaurant's heavy black coffee which they lightened with condensed milk. In fact neither of them drank it. Ferdach asked what Mizan was doing in KL and was told that he had applied for a post in the police force though in the meantime he had got a job on *Utusan Melayu*, the principal Malay-language newspaper. Ferdach saw that Mizan had taken a step in the political direction; indeed, that he might already be in Special Branch with the newspaper job as a cover. Without beating around the bush Ferdach asked directly, 'Harun's view is that the British should go at once; is that also your view? Is that what most Malays are thinking?'

'Are you asking as a government official who'll make a report to intelligence or are you asking me as Ferdie?'

'I'm asking you just as myself. I'm feeling very ill at ease at the moment. To be in charge of anything or rather anybody in a colony saps one's judgement. All the Asians I work with are bound to say they like me, to be polite to me. It goes to one's head. Authority makes young Britishers like me into tin-pot gods. So it's only when one has a true friend like you that I've a chance of knowing the truth.'

'But authority can make anyone into a tin-pot god Ferdie. You should see what tin-pot gods Malayans can be when they're in charge, Harun for instance. They can be even worse than you.'

'If someone else can be worse, you must think I'm tared with the same bad brush. You know how it goes: bad, worse, worst.'

'No Ferdie, you are not so bad ... yet. Some British officers, not the majority, are rotten though. I was thinking of that dictum "power corrupts". Like everyone else you can be corrupted. But you're only here temporarily and you only have little power. Our own politicians, when we're independent may try to become permanent. Then we may have the second part of the dictum: "absolute power corrupts absolutely".'

'You don't seem too enthusiastic about independence, Mizan. You seem to fear your own people.'

'Not in the least. Even if our leaders were no good it would be better than being ordered about by people from thousands of miles away. No, to be serious Ferdie, I don't object to your presence. You must stay until the communists are beaten and then you have my permission to go.'

Ferdach had a great desire to tell Mizan about his secret letter and to ask his opinion of it. As a matter of fact he had had the same desire to talk about it when he was with all the English people he knew in KL, except for Laura. In particular at this moment, he had a strong urge to boast that the document in his possession was one that might lead to the early end of the Emergency and, thereby, to early independence, for he was now convinced that the quicker he, and every other Briton in the country, got out, the better. However, he wisely held his tongue, not an easy feat for Ferdach; Mizan could pass the information to Special Branch like a lightening conductor. So he turned the conversation to the Maria Hertogh case and the riots in Singapore. Mizan, who must have known more about these matters than Ferdach, looked bored but his eyes lit up when he heard that Ferdach and Lai Kuan had met in the city. He asked at once whether they had travelled there from Ipoh together and Ferdach lied that he had not. However, Mizan's interest in the matter was at once dispelled on learning that Laura had deserted her husband and was living in Kuala Lumpur. At this his manner changed completely. He leaned forward and half whispered, as though it were a matter that he did not want to go any further, 'Do you mean to tell me that she's here right now, living somewhere in KL, all on her own.' A frisson of excitement seemed to underlie the last phrase.

Ferdach affected not to know what was happening in the mind, or rather the body, of Mizan whom he had once introduced to Laura in a street in Ipoh. Before doing so he had indiscreetly, and no doubt foolishly, bragged to him, as young men do, of his adulterous affair with her. Now he recalled that during that brief introduction Mizan's eyes had immediately been filled with admiration or more likely simple lust for Laura. A mischievous thought now entered Ferdach's head: why not introduce them to one another in more intimate surroundings, say Laura's new flat, even though it was in the advowson, as it were, of his good friend Lai Kuan. The undeniable, if regrettable, truth was that Ferdach thoroughly enjoyed playing the pander. He resisted the tempting Malay double-entendre 'ada lobang' – a slang expression implying there was a connection or opportunity, in this case to meet Laura, but literally meaning 'there's a hole' – and said instead, 'I'm sure Laura will be at home.' In fact he knew she would be as he had promised to drop round. 'Shall we call on her? It's only half past nine.'

'Will she want to meet me?' asked Mizan, now a little apprehensive.

'How could any woman not want to meet a young man as charming, intelligent and handsome as Tengku Mizan?'

'It's a good job I've learned English so well. I know when people like you are pulling my leg Ferdie.'

'Tengku, you'd probably take it as an insult if I said that, apart from that beautiful skin and hair and face of yours, you could pass for an Englishman.'

A short taxi drive took them to Laura's apartment. She was pleased to see them, asked if they had eaten and, on learning they had, produced a selection of drinks which Mizan, no longer in a Muslim restaurant, sampled both freely and unwisely. It turned out he was friendly with a number of people at the university in Singapore, mostly among the leftwing student population who were also known to Laura, so they had plenty to gossip about. Ferdach also drank heavily, though of little brandy and much dry ginger, and before long affected to be overcome by sleep, leaving an increasingly merry Mizan to go on chatting with Laura who gradually became freer, and was eventually her usual outrageous self in everything she uttered. Now Ferdach really was getting tired though pleased with his little strategem to offset Laura's pressure on him. At one point he nearly laughed aloud when he heard Mizan enquiring whether the marines she had had it off with in Singapore were circumcised. He closed his eyes and began to snore softly when Laura replied, 'God yes. My dear Mizan, I'd never sleep with an uncut guy.' Mizan seemed relieved by her words though Ferdach remembered that, in the case of Jeff, she was telling a lie.

When he observed that Laura and her new friend were in a delicious little huddle on the settee, Ferdach tiptoed downstairs. He could have sworn that neither of them had even noticed him getting up. Then he strolled in the cool starlit night down the short driveway to Ampang Road, hailed a passing taxi and returned happily to sleep alone in that bed designed for amorous ritual in Carcosa Cottage.

58

On his last day in KL Ferdach knew he had to act. He woke up early and lay thinking up strategems to deal with Chin Peng's letter. These might be: taking Gilbert and Hester into his confidence and asking for their help – impossible because given Gilbert's position they would have to refuse; taking the letter to King's House himself that morning and asking for an interview with HE – most likely to result in a brisk refusal as the High Commissioner always had a heavy schedule; and thirdly, giving up the task altogether and telling Lai Kuan he had failed.

By now he was indifferent to any criticism that might later be levelled at him if it became known that he had bypassed the official channels. He did not want to court dismissal from the service but, on the other hand, it did not greatly worry him if he were to leave Malaya as he believed it was only a question of a few years before all British officers would be sent packing and he might as well start a new career before getting older. He even relished the idea of taking Mat Noor, who was never very far from his thoughts, to England with him to begin a new life. Yet firmly in his mind stood his undertaking to do what Lai Kuan had asked him. Loyalty on a personal basis, though never to a political or a religious cause, was rooted in his character. He knew that he must get the letter to HE in person, regardless of cost to himself. Yet having decided to do this, the question still remained, exactly how?

Then, as so often seemed to happen in his life, chance took a hand. Over breakfast, Gilbert and Hester had been talking about the domestic arrangements that had to be made for their transfer to Kuantan where Gilbert was to become an Assistant District Officer. Hester's packing dilemma related largely to her paintings and Gilbert's to his books. The de Guises were not the sort of people who accumulated material things but Hester had many friends and was in a variety of organisations in Kuala Lumpur, ranging from a Bharatya Natya dancing group to the Arts Theatre, now run, Ferdach was intrigued to hear, by his old Ipoh colleague Algernon Broadstairs in a despotic manner that was fast alienating many of the KL thespians. Winding up these social entanglementts was not going to leave her much spare time.

'Look Ferdie,' she said, 'I know it's your last day here, but would you do something for me? It'll only take an hour or so.'

'Certainly. Just tell me what it is.'

'Well, I'd intended to take photographs of this place: King's House, Carcosa, the views over the Lake Gardens, a few shots of this Cottage. I've always made a record of where I've been.'

'Not that they're kept in any order. Just boxes of photos,' said Gilbert.

'In our old age we'll have fun sorting them out and putting them into albums.' Hester looked almost wistfully at Gilbert when she said this, as though she never believed that they would reach old age together.

'But I don't have a camera you know,' said Ferdach.

This was quickly remedied by Hester who produced an expensive Zeiss that was already loaded with film with an extra roll to hand. Immediately it flashed through Ferdach's brain that he would go first to King's House and prowl around, but that might be difficult. Another problem struck him: 'What about security? There are guards around. Won't they arrest me if they see me poking about with a camera? I might be a Russian spy.' This last remark was greeted with derisive laughter.

'In the first case, it's well known that we have you as a house guest. In fact Mrs Del Boca mentioned your name to Lady Gurney. Everyone up here talks about everyone else you know.' Hester then added, 'Actually I phoned the Private Secretary, Mr Staples, a few minutes ago to say that you'd be taking photos. He'll have told the household not to be bothered by your presence.'

'And in the second case,' added Gilbert, 'Sir Henry has never been a stickler for security. He believes in accessibility. He's not the sort of man who goes about worrying about personal danger. Security around King's House is pretty minimal.'

That, Ferdach thought, was an absolute understatement as, sometime later, he sauntered along the well-wooded road that led to King's House. He had done his best to look informal, maybe a bit like a journalist, in slacks and a sports shirt with the camera paraphernalia slung over his shoulder. In one of its leather cases lay the extra roll of film, and the envelope, now folded up and looking somewhat creased, containing the letter from Chin Peng to the High Commissioner.

Just where the road began to run into the lawns of the garden there was a neat little hut where newcomers could 'sign the book'. It doubled as a sentry box. From it emerged a smartly dressed Indian policeman wearing a broad smile that revealed a battery of teeth reddened with betel juice. 'Tuan Hanuman?' he said, obviously apprised of Ferdach's visit by Hester's message. 'Please go in.' Ferdach inclined his head a little, made a gesture that could be interpreted as either a regal wave or a salute and strode on. He chuckled to himself that his name had been transmuted into that of the mischievous Monkey God.

Everything here seemed serene and delightful. The silence was broken only by an eccentric wolf whistle made by some rude but hidden bird, by the brittle sounds of tireless insects, and by the excited whoops of monkeys who had a marvellously protected habitat in this restricted area and who were obviously keeping him under close surveillance. Occasional gaps in the wall of luxuriant trees gave views down to the Lake Gardens, the town's best loved park, providing dulcet glimpses of water and distant pavilions that might have delighted Claude Lorraine. Turning a corner of the drive Ferdach saw four self-satisfied looking cars, one a Rolls Royce, which was being polished to a yet higher sheen by a smartly uniformed driver. But having no wish to photograph such activity, he made for the lawn in front of the house and took some photographs of the high-gabled roof. The whole place gave the impression of a prosperous Victorian mansion though with a larger than usual number of cool balconies and verandahs. He tried his best to make his shots as artistic as possible. Yet he knew he was playing for time, hoping against unlikely hope that the High Commissioner might emerge. And then? Well, one thing might lead to another, but if it did not maybe he could brazen it out at the main door until the High Commissioner went to his car.

As he stood with his back to the building photographing a frangipani tree glorious with white flowers he heard, 'Mr O'Haney', spoken very courteously. He turned and saw a mild, middle-aged man with gentle yet probing eyes coming down a slope on the lawn towards him. 'Now why should you be talking a picture of a frangipani? They are the same wherever they grow. I thought that Hester wanted photos to remind her of the buildings.'

Ferdach stiffened as he might have done when the headmaster of his school bore down on him. 'Yes, sir. You're quite right. But the tree is beautiful. Maybe I wanted to capture it just as it is now.' He hesitated. 'But I'm sure Hester would like a photo of you.' Obligingly Sir Henry straightening his rather casual-looking bush jacket, took up his position in front of the tree and was snapped by Ferdach. 'Thank you, sir. Hester will be very pleased to possess you with a background of flowers.'

'You sound more like a romantic than a civil servant. I've heard your name from Mr Gray. You seem to be working well in Ipoh. How is your Chinese getting on? I'm sure you want to learn the language well.'

Ferdach felt more relaxed now. Of course the High Commissioner saw and discussed the reports on the Emergency from all over the country. Maybe it was not surprising that his own name had been noted. William Nicol Gray, the Commissioner of Police of the Federation was a dynamic man renowned for a memory that seemed to contain endless detail about people and places. But what struck Ferdach most was Sir Henry's question about his Chinese. It was almost as though HE knew that his reason for joining the service had been that promise of learning the language in distant, marvellous China. Boldly he said, 'My Chinese would be better if only the government would reinstate its language training programme in Macau. It's not so easy to learn a language like Chinese working in Malaya.'

Sir Henry prodded an errant leaf trespassing on the lawn with his foot. 'I agree. I agree,' he said. 'We do need more Chinese-speaking officers. The scheme is only suspended you know. We'll have to see whether a few young men like you can be spared again.' With that he glanced at his watch. 'Well now, I must be off.' Ferdach noticed that the last word was pronounced 'orf'. 'Goodbye Mr O'Haney. Nice to meet you. I hope you had a good leave in Singapore.' Without more ado he turned to go.

Now the moment had come. 'No sir. No. Don't go. Don't go yet.'

The High Commissioner turned. He looked surprised to receive an order, quite forcibly spoken, from so junior an officer. 'What?' he asked.

'I've got something for you, sir.' In his anxiety to produce the letter Ferdach began to fumble with the brown leather case that suddenly became reluctant to be opened. Sir Henry stepped back. His right hand ran over his slight grey moustache in an almost protective gesture. Was there a look of alarm in his eyes? At last Ferdach got the letter out.

'Good God young man. I thought you'd got something explosive in there. When I was in Palestine ...' Sir Henry fell silent at some memory or other, then chuckled as though he had never thought any such thing.

Ferdach did his best to make the folded envelope as flat as possible. When he handed it over he could not resist saying, 'It is something explosive, sir.'

Sir Henry took it with both hands, read the address side that merely stated his name and his residence, and turned it over, without venturing to open it. 'Do you know who it's from then?' he asked.

Ferdach spoke quietly, though no one else but Sir Henry was in the offing. 'Yes sir. It's from the Secretary General of the Malayan Communist party. From Chin Peng.' After a pause he added, 'Maybe you shouldn't open it until you are absolutely alone, sir.'

The High Commissioner stood stock-still, his eyes first on Ferdach, then on the letter. At length he said, 'Odd things do happen in life. And I suppose this must be one of them.'

They both stood in silent thought for a little while until Ferdach ventured to say, 'Perhaps the content of the letter won't seem so odd when you've read it. It may even sound very straight and sensible.'

'So you've seen the letter? You know its content?'

'No sir. No to both your questions. But you will want to know how I got it. It's from a member of a family with big commercial interests in Perak, the Kuok family; well, you must know about them. I have a friend in the family, Mr Kuok Lai Kuan. He's not a communist. He's a democrat and he loves this country. But he believes that the Emergency is holding up independence. He believes that some members of the Communist Party have come to the same conclusion. They admit now that they made a mistake going back into the jungle. One way or another Lai Kuan has been in contact with Chin Peng who, it seems, may have come to the same conclusion. Lai Kuan believes this means that the time is ripe for a meeting between you and the Secretary General to talk matters over, in secret. This letter suggests to me that he has been successful in persuading Chin Peng to ask for such a meeting.' Ferdach abruptly fell silent. Maybe he had done the totally absurd. Maybe his guesswork had taken liberties. How could he have been so presumptuous?

Sir Henry had been listening attentively but with a shrewd eye that seemed to rove all over Ferdach's body and, Ferdach felt, into his head. 'Don't stop,' he said. 'No one could say that what you're saying is uninteresting.'

'Well that's all I can say except for one important thing which is really from Lai Kuan. Until you and Chin Peng so agree, the whole matter must be kept between the two of you. Neither the Central Committee on Chin Peng's side, nor any member of your Executive Council should be brought into the picture yet. If the existence of this letter is revealed, the whole matter will be at an end, aborted. Chin Peng will declare the letter to be a scurrilous forgery.' Whether Ferdach feared to look presumptuous or not, when he spoke these words he had unconsciously adopted the authoritative manner Lai Kuan assumed when he wanted to have his own way.

'I see. I see,' said Sir Henry. He spoke gently but kindly as though dealing with a difficult child. 'Well then, as you suggest, I shall read this when I'm on my own.' He put the letter into one of his deep side pockets and fastened its button. 'By the way, you must be aware that you have not followed the usual channels in all this. You could be open to criticism. But maybe you were justified. This is all most unusual.'

Somehow or other Ferdach sensed from the High Commissioner's manner that he had nothing to fear. Nevertheless he decided by way of self-defence, to invent a classical quotation, a ruse he had learned from Nina Hamnet, 'Tacitus wrote somewhere that unusual times require unusual actions.'

'Did he now?' said Sir Henry dubiously. 'But talking of unusual actions, you may have put yourself in an unusual position, or rather maybe your friend Lai Kuan has put you in an unusual position. Do you see your part in all this as … at an end?'

'Of course sir, naturally. I've merely been a postman.'

'But if only Chin Peng and I, and Lai Kuan of course and you, know about this, how am I to reply?'

Ferdach had never thought that this might pose any difficulty. 'Surely you could do so through Lai Kuan.'

'Out of the question. How would I do that without people suspecting something? I can't poke around with a camera into places where I'm not usually expected. Which means Mr O'Haney that if anything were to come of all this, which I very much doubt, somehow or other, you would still have to play the postman.' With that Sir Henry gave Ferdach a gentle smile shook his hand and began to walk back to the house but just before going in he turned and said, ' Perhaps you'd let me have a copy of the photo when I go to Perak next month. I'll be staying with Tuan Albakri. You could bring it to his house.' A few minutes later Ferdach heard a car start up and soon saw the sleek Rolls Royce, with pennant flying, on its way down the hill.

It had not turned out as Ferdach had expected. Willy-nilly he had become involved. He sat down on an iron garden seat and stared up at the grand colonial mansion. A woman was peering down at him curiously over a balcony. He turned away not wanting to catch her eye and perhaps be questioned. What most preoccupied him now was Sir Henry's suggestion that he might still have to be the go-between. He thought hard, particularly of the need for secrecy. Still sitting, he took the film out of the camera and reloaded it with the spare roll. Then he walked about the garden taking more shots of King House before making his way back to the Cottage. Hester and Gilbert were out so he used up most of the remaining film on shots of Carcosa and then of the Cottage, behind which he came across his car, returned earlier than expected by Wearne's after service and repair. Without more ado he drove into town, bought a third role of film and put it in the leather case. When Hester returned home later in the day he gave the camera back to her remarking that he had used up most of her film but not the spare roll which was still in the case. So busy was Hester with last minute paper work for one of her societies that she hardly noticed what he was saying. The Cottage was no longer a place for leisure.

And so, quite suddenly, Ferdach decided that his holiday was at an end. He was to have stayed another night at the de Guises and left the following morning when Wearne's had said his car would be ready. But now it was back and he was free to go. He should have called on Laura to bid her farewell with promises and gentleness and maybe some lovemaking though most likely she was no longer in need of that. He should have thanked people for their hospitality and assured them of a warm welcome should they come to Ipoh, perhaps gone to see Tunku Mizan who was staying with a relative of the Sultan of Selangor. He should have done a hundred things but all he wanted to do was to get away, to get back to his work, especially his fieldwork among the Chinese farmers and workers. No, that was not all he wanted. Up from the depths of his mind came the thought of Mat Noor for whose friendship, and maybe love, he had longed all the time he had been away.

Early in the evening, when darkness had already descended on Kuala Lumpur; when the yellow street lights had come on, and neon lights were stark on bars and cinemas and garlands of bright electric bulbs were lighting up the fairgrounds where you could enjoy Chinese and Malay and Indian food and where you could dance sinuously with Malay *joget* girls or jerkily with Chinese taxi dancers; when the crowds were pouring into the streets to enjoy themselves in the cooler air; when in leafy Kampung Bahru lithesome Malay boys and delectable Malay girls would be sauntering gracefully past kerosene-lit stalls in their richly coloured best and in the mosque old men would be deploring the laxity of the young; when young British servicemen were getting drunk in Nanto's Bar and starting fights which as often as not erupted onto the pavement of Batu Road; when all manner of temptations were stirring into life, Ferdach set out alone, but quite happily, in his car on the darkened road to the north which led through sleeping *kampung*s and little towns each guarded at either end by roadblocks at which he would sometimes have to wait while barriers were raised or gates opened and his identity card examined, because in the north of Perak, in a distant *kampung*, was someone he desired as obsessively as if he were in quest of the Grail.

As for the letter that Lai Kuan had prevailed upon him to forward to the highest British official in the land, it was done and his action was irrevocable. He thought for an instant of the warning labels on fireworks used on Guy Fawkes' night when he was a child: 'Light the blue touch paper and retire'.

59

Ferdach arrived back at Sturrock Road before dawn. There was light in the servants' quarters but none in the house itself. He unlocked the frontdoor quietly and went at once to his room where mail was on his desk. There was quite a pile of it, official documents, some Christmas cards, two airmail letters from his mother, a card from his father addressing him in Irish orthography as Feardach O hÉignigh, but nothing with a postmark from northern Perak. There was, however, one unstamped white envelope bearing the words 'to Ferdie'. He was sure it was from Mat Noor who must have returned to Ipoh. But there was no message from Mat Noor, only the tragic news from Gordon Choo. In the next few minutes Ferdach felt that his world had changed completely.

He read the letter several times; each reading was like a drill piercing his brain. As if refusing to accept Noor's death he screwed the letter up and threw it down; then he picked it up again and read each line over and over, trying to discover something; he did not know what. He longed to piece together the last days, the last hours, of Noor's life, but there was so little to go on. He wanted to search for clues to Noor's death though he knew perfectly well that the heart of it was that the rebellious boy could not reconcile what was expected of him with what he was, and that he, Ferdach, had seemingly blocked his avenue of escape. He dwelt on the lines that said that Noor had not changed his clothes or washed. Was it to remain exactly as he had been when he was still with the person he loved? But why, when he had washed had he decided to kill people in the *kampung*? Was it to express his distaste for a society into which he could not fit, or was it just the wildness of the amok that had seized his tortured young mind? Or had he feared to kill himself because to drown or to stab himself was difficult and uncertain? To be shot would be quicker and easier. Yet perhaps in the mind of the amok the rational and the emotional whirled about in such fractured parts that to assign a motive was impossible. All these questions churned around Ferdach's brain and he let them churn for they seemed to hold the cold fact of Noor's death at bay.

He lay on his bed with his head crushing the letter and started to sob, not loudly for he wanted to keep his grief, like his love, secret from the men he was living with. It would not be done to let Ericson, whose bedroom was immediately above his own, or even Waite, hear him weeping for a young Malay boy. He did not believe they would understand; he even feared their contempt. But the tears flowed copiously and he let them flow for he knew it was the best thing to do. He knew this because he remembered RAF men cry when one of their comrades had died. He remembered men weeping in the darkness of a Nissen hut and the profound silence accorded to their grief by other men lying in the darkness and pretending to sleep. He had never experienced such a loss himself for no one he flew with had been killed. Yet he had wondered how he would react had his pilot, Flight Lieutenant Winterhouse, whom he almost worshipped, or his bomb aimer Flashman Harris of whom he was inordinately fond, been killed. Yes, he had seen grief and known death during the war but he had never experienced it in a personal way. Now death had come into his life harshly and unexpectedly and he was not sure how to bear it.

He was also not sure why his grief was so profound. Despite his hopes for a relationship with Mat Noor a part of him had always recognized the fact that his feelings might not be reciprocated or that mere circumstance might keep them apart. He had half accepted that nothing really lay ahead for them. He also knew that no hint of sexual frustration was saddening him at this moment of grief. Even in that idyllic pool when the two of them were swimming and tentatively touching one another beneath the surface of the water, he had been unsure what he wanted of Noor. Of course it would have been delightful to embrace such beauty, to kiss those lips, those eyes, but what more did he desire? Somehow or other he had known, even then, that the love they had for one another was already absolute and did not need a more physical expression. Or was that a lie? Could it be that he had never dared to imagine what the physical nature of their love might be? He rejected the idea that Noor might be his passive beloved, his eromenos and he the erastes, but neither could he imagine himself submitting to the dominant love of Noor. This was not because he disliked physical love between men, he had indulged in it, but that in this case there was something more powerful between him and Noor that seemed to require equality. And therein lay the source of his deep sadness. Unwittingly he had come not merely to be romantically fond of Noor, he had fallen passionately in love with him in a manner for which he had always had contempt since he did not believe such love existed. In so doing he had released feelings that had been pent up throughout the war years and his university life. It was a first time love and therefore its failure was deeply felt. The sorrow would endure and be bitter.

There was another reason for his sadness. It had always been his desire to understand the Malays, to get to know their culture, to be accepted by them. It had always struck him that this would never be possible if he married an Englishwoman and they lived in the country as a colonial tuan and mem. So many English couples seemed to Ferdach to be deluding themselves that they really did know the country and belonged to it. To belong meant being grafted onto the stem as, in the eighteenth century, many Englishmen had been absorbed into Indian life by marrying Hindu or Muslim women. For Ferdach, as for them, sexual integration had to be a prerequisite to social integration. Yet he had never given any thought to marrying a Malay woman; that would have meant becoming a Muslim which he could never do, not because he was a Christian, indeed far from it, but because his rational atheistical attitude to life would never have allowed him to be silent if he saw his children becoming enmeshed in religion. An intimate relationship with a clever, sensitive Malay man, a man who, unusually for his background, had already, as a communist sympathiser, begun questioning his faith, had seemed the ideal solution to his dilemma. Now that path had been closed because the sort of reciprocal love that he thought he had found in Noor was unlikely to be repeated.

At length his bout of weeping ceased. He could hear Waite and Ericson moving around upstairs while outside his room, across the hall, Cookie and his wife were setting out the usual huge breakfast in the dining room. The delicious smell of fried bacon reached his nostrils recalling him to a sort of earthy reality. He was expected in his office and must go there, even though he had driven most of the night. He shaved and took a shower, waited until he heard Ericson's car speed off and then went, outwardly composed, to join Waite at the breakfast table. Fried eggs and smoked bacon were quietly sizzling on a hot plate on the sidetable. Ferdach gave himself a generous helping and said, 'It's good to be back to Cookie's breakfast. Well Waite, how have things been? Have there been any serious incidents over the past few days?'

'Things are getting worse. And morale isn't too good.'

'It can't be as bad as in KL. Everyone there seems to be pulling in different directions: the police, the military, the civil service. All of them full of clever dicks with different ideas as far as I could gather. And morale hasn't been boosted by what happened in Singapore.' As he spoke Ferdach glimpsed that familiar Browning automatic almost concealed from view behind a packet of breakfast cereal. Did Waite think it was really necessary or did he just love playing soldiers?

There was silence as they both dug into their food. Ferdach noticed a dark look on Waite's face and wondered what was up. Some administrative problem maybe? Some problem with District Officer Bertelli? He was disabused when Waite said softly, 'I was sorry to hear about your friend, about Mat Noor.'

Ferdach's armour was at once penetrated. He had determined that his defences would be invulnerable and now, unexpectedly, an innocent dart had pierced him. Waite must have seen him tremble, certainly saw him put down his knife and fork heavily and could not help seeing the tears that had uncontrollably welled into his eyes. Then Ferdach thought: this was Ipoh where everyone knew everything about everyone else. How could he go out if everyone was watching him and maybe sniggering?

Waite got up, walked next to Ferdach and put his arm around his shoulders. At first the gesture seemed to be stiff but it somehow mutated into gentleness until Ferdach became conscious of the soft touch of fingers stroking the nape of his neck. 'It's OK Ferdie, I'm the only one who knows about the letter. Gordon Choo told me about it. He thought you might need a friend when you read it. It's OK, Ferdie. I swear that I know what it's like for you.'

385

60

During his absence Waite had moved Ferdach's Identity Card Replacement Unit from the district office, where it had been set up, into a building behind the municipal offices so providing Waite with space for more Chinese Affairs officers, young men of great enthusiasm and, Ferdach was told by Gordon Choo, with a ruthless Kuomintang background. The move pleased Ferdach for now he had his own little kingdom of some fifteen clerical staff, who were busy the whole day processing applications for new identity cards. By now the system ran like clockwork and Ferdach knew that he had little to do but preside over its workings which were kept in perfect repair by an elderly but inordinately efficient chief clerk, Mr K. P. Arunasalam, a man with such an eye for detail that it was unlikely that any incorrectly filled form or defective procedure would ever slip through undetected. Since Mr Arunasalam had had a lifetime of working for English gentlemen, as he termed them, in India and in Malaya, he was always careful to refer any matters in doubt to Ferdach together with his recommendation for action which Ferdach never saw fit to contradict. Being based outside the district office, Ferdach was able to avoid being drawn into ad hoc district office activities which were often frenetic and invariably of no purpose other than to enable some government officer to fill in a report as evidence of his scrupulously exercised duty. Indeed, it struck Ferdach that many government officers were much more interested in avoiding adverse criticism than in helping the drive against the communists, such was the poor state of morale at that time.

A part of Ferdach's duties was to go outstation to see that his system, for so he termed it, was working in the field. Mr Arunasalam had always encouraged him to to do this, at the same time directing him to places where there was a good government rest house or a pleasant little Chinese hotel, a stay at which would enable him to avoid the dangers of night driving and, as Mr Arunasalam put it, 'to get to know the country as was his bounden duty'.

He had hardly put foot in the office following his leave when Mr Arunasalam brought him a letter from Mr Barrat, the Chief Registration Officer of the Federation, warmly congratulating him on the excellence with which the system was now working and reminding him that he should be prepared to journey to other states where the communists had started identity card stealing activities, to advise the state government on how to deal with the problem swiftly. In fact this could easily have been prosecuted by letter, or on the phone, or by a visit by Mr Barrat who had little else to do, but why, thought Ferdach, should he argue.

Mr Arunasalam was happy to be left in charge of the office, and Ferdach's spirits were lifted by the fact he now had reason to travel the length and breadth of the country. Everyone in the district office must by now know about his grief for Mat Noor; quite a number of people in Ipoh probably know of it too, but henceforth they would all see much less of Ferdach and in time rumour and gossip would find a new matter on which to batten.

'I believe that Mr Barratt would like you to go first to Pahang, sir. Do you think you could spare some time to do so fairly soon?'

Ferdach looked around the office as though suspecting that there must be important issues to be dealt with. He also looked at his in tray but it was almost empty.

'I took the liberty of opening the mail when you were away and drafted replies for your perusal where necessary, Tuan.' Mr Arunasalam made a self-deprecating gesture with his hands, though both he and Ferdach knew that opening all the mail was the first duty of a chief clerk

Sure enough, in Ferdach's action tray was a substantial pile of letters, overlapping one another like a well-arranged hand of cards, and awaiting his signature. Ferdach never liked to patronise his chief clerk as many Europeans did; sincerely and warmly he put his hand on Mr Arunasalam's arm and said, 'KP, I don't know what I'd do without you.' It was the truth, as they both knew, but its genuine acknowledgement meant much to Mr Arunasalam who beamed at Ferdach with the eyes of a doting father. 'Very well. I'll leave for Pahang next Monday. Perhaps you could book me in at the Gap rest house on the first night.'

'Oh no, sir. It would be most dull to spend the night there, nothing but a roadside stop. I have already taken the liberty of booking you in to a very good hotel on Fraser's Hill for two days. It is much higher than the Gap and very beautiful, almost like an English resort. You will feel that you are back in your Home Counties there. And you will have the opportunity of discussing the security situation in the local pub with the district police and military. They're bound to be able to advise you on what needs to be done. We can certainly justify this as part of your familiarisation with the country.'

'Thank you Mr Arunasalam. You are most thoughtful. Now, more important, how is Mrs Arunasalam? Has her health improved?'

'Oh my goodness, sir. She is still in the very greatest depths of depression. You know that my daughter has had three miscarriages. My wife believes that it is her fault that our only daughter is so afflicted. She has got it into her head that she must have committed an offence in a previous life and we are all being punished in the here and now. I cannot convince her that a child cannot be punished for a parent's sins. We have prayed most devoutly to Sri Krishna but he has not yet vouchsaved his blessing. But I am told that there is a holy man at a temple in Penang who might be able to help. I do not believe in such things myself but my wife … you know she is very devout.'

Ferdach had already advised Mr Arunasalam to take his daughter to a specialist and this he had done with no avail to her condition. But since anything was worth trying he now said, 'Mr Arunasalam, after I return from Pahang you must take some leave and go with your wife and daughter to Penang. Work doesn't always come first, my dear friend. I am giving you an order.'

'Ah Mr Ferdach sir, we will both be thanking you very much.' Mr Arunasalam took Ferdach's hand to express his happiness for such unsought after kindness while two young ladies of the Chinese clerical staff who had been listening to every word without ceasing to work, raised their eyebrows archly at one another and grinned at how these two grown men each thought the other to be a baby in his hands though both girls thought that, by and large, Ferdach was more of a child.

61

Ipoh, or upas tree (*antiaris toxicaria*): a tree so poisonous as to bring death to everything for miles around. What a strange name to give to a town so beautifully situated and so well planned, Ferdach thought. But does its doom extend to everyone who lives here? A superstitious Celtic part of him stirred – at the heart of all beauty a fatal cancer may lie. So perhaps the order he had received to cross the mountains to do some work in a different state was auspicious. Quite irrationally he wanted to get away quickly, despite which, the morning he left Ipoh for Pahang he had to call first at his office to pick up some files prepared for him by Mr Arunasalam.

Unexpectedly he also picked up a young man called Arun who would be 'extremely helpful to you en route and in a state you don't know at all,' Mr Arunasalam said persuasively. 'He's most efficient and I've acquainted him with all our procedures on identity card replacement. Of course he speaks Malay and Tamil but his English is perfect and he knows a bit of Hokkien. You'll find him an excellent secretary especially as you'll want records kept of your meetings.' Although Ferdach knew the names of all his office staff and interested himself in their welfare, he could not remember a linguistic paragon called Arun. It was only when he was alone for a while, sorting things out in his car, that he learned why. Miss Pansy Chong, one of the girls who had overheard his recent conversation with the chief clerk about Mrs Arunasalam's mental depression, slipped out with some stationery he had not asked for, and whispered, 'Mr Arunasalam's nephew will be here soon. He's in the toilet.'

'Mr Arunasalam's who?' Ferdach was perplexed by Miss Chong's secretive manner.

'Arun. The new clerk who's going with you.'

'New?'

'He replaced Willie Chung a week ago, the day before you returned from leave,' said Miss Chong, a girl who observed everything but was surprised by nothing.

Ferdach felt a flush of anger rising in him. He hated being manipulated. Or rather he had begun to hate being manipulated. How subtly he had been manoeuvred politically by Lai Kuan, his friend undoubtably but a businessman for whom manipulation was like wine; how unremittingly Laura persisted in her efforts to manipulate him into marriage. People must think he was easy meat. Now his chief clerk was doing the same thing. Without thinking he said to Miss Chong, 'Wouldn't it be better for some one like you to come with me. Your shorthand is excellent. Can Arun take shorthand?' Then he realised that he had made a stupid suggestion. Miss Chong took a step backward, alarm showing in her eyes. What would everyone think if he were to travel around with a pretty Chinese girl? What hotel arrangements would have to be made? He dropped his voice and murmured, 'Thank you Pansy.'

Arun was a tall dark youth, slim in build and of aristocratic, aquiline appearance. Ferdach was certain that he had a quick brain and was highly sensitive, perhaps irritatingly so. When he came out to the car with his office material he stared at Ferdach with large lustrous eyes, as though he was examining for the first time some new species the safety of which was far from certain. When he spoke, asking where to put the material and his suitcase, his words were velvety and slow, the intonation perfect without the slightest hint of an Indian accent. Though he wore the customary office white trousers and shirt, the material of his clothes was of superior quality and soft, his shirt in particular hanging quite elegantly from his shoulders as though it was reluctant to press too heavily on the slight form within. In his present resentful mood Ferdach immediately thought that the boy was effeminate and had been planted on him by Mr Arunasalam. But for what purpose? To compensate him for the loss of Mat Noor? To spy on him for his uncle? It must be one or the other. In his haste to judge he forgot the possibility of another, more altruistic, reason for Mr Arunasalam's manoeuvre, namely to help his inexperienced master to do his work well.

Arun seemed to drape himself on the seat next to Ferdach, drawing himself as close as possible to the door so leaving a pronounced space between the two of them. Moreover, instead of keeping his eyes ahead of him on the road, he sat sideward so that Ferdach was conscious of those large eyes occasionally sizing him up from one side. This made him drive quickly and nervously, breaking the speed limit as they roared out of Ipoh. Fortunately there were no traffic police to catch him. For a while not a word passed between them. Then, when they were well past the limestone cliffs and cave temples of Gunung Rapat and approaching Kampung Sengat, he asked bluntly and with a hint of contempt in his voice, 'Well Arun, what are your interests? Apart from work of course and your family loyalties.' He half expected the reply to be about fashion design or music.

'I'm interested in martial arts, sir. All my spare time is spent practising tai chi, and also an ancient Indian form of self defence which I think is superior to the Chinese systems.'

'Do you get enough time to do so?' asked Ferdach not a little surprised by Arun's reply.

'It isn't easy with three small children, sir. But my wife is very understanding. She is well educated and believes that men must be prepared to defend themselves. There will be difficult times ahead.'

'Difficult times ahead,' repeated Ferdach. 'Aren't times already difficult enough in this country?'

'My wife has been told by a soothsayer that I myself will experience very difficult times ahead. I do not know what they may be.'

A silence fell between them. This was another of those unpredictable situations in which Ferdach seemed destined to find himself. He was not sure how to deal with the views of soothsayers, who seemed to play a significant role in the Arunasalam family, other than by either bluntly accepting or contradicting their validity; to discuss their merit would strongly suggest that he took them seriously. 'You say that your wife is well educated Arun. What did she study? Has she studied abroad?'

'Indeed sir. She studied under a great Sanskrit scholar in Madras, the renowned Mohan Sundara Rajan. Have you heard of him?'

'I'm afraid not Arun. Can you read the Sanskrit books?'

'Not well, sir. But my wife is teaching me. She exhorts me to strive for the moral purity and goodness of the gods and heroes in the Mahayana and the Ramayana. In the Indian scriptures you will find the highest form of knowledge.'

Ferdach inwardly sighed with relief. Here was a youth who longed for a form of perfection other than that which he himself sought. There would be no problems between them, just a proper working relationship. Still, he could not help wishing that Arun would deport himself in a less languid manner. It would be irritating to labour under a cloud of suspicion without the satisfaction of it being worthwhile.

The road was not new to Ferdach. He had passed this way with Lai Kuan, though in the darkness of night. It had been dark too when he had returned this way to Ipoh from Kuala Lumpur. For the first time now he could see the countryside in broad daylight. Soon they were traversing the district of Sungei Siput with its tin mines and rubber estates. It was on one of these estates that the first communist murders of planters had taken place and precipitated the declaration of the Emergency almost three years ago. The area was still dangerous and there was little civilian traffic on the road. The road ran through a valley between jungle-covered mountains before leading down to a well-wooded landscape interspersed with *padi* fields and made picturesque by innumerable *kampung*s. Each village had a single-storey mosque, often square in shape and surrounded by a broad verandah on which sat elderly Malay men no doubt discussing village affairs, politics and religion.

At Kampung Balun they turned eastward, skirting a rushing river, towards the mountains and the town of Slim where Ferdach took a room in a Chinese hotel while Arun found some relatives with whom to pass the night. This was an aspect of travelling with locals that Ferdach found unsatisfactory. He would inevitably be obliged to stay at a rest house or hotel while they always seemed able to find a relative or a kinsman, or someone they claimed was a kinsman. They had pleasant company whilst Ferdach was left to his own devices or, if it was a rest house, to drink with some Englishmen he rarely wanted to meet again and who probably thought the same of him. In fact on this occasion he found it particularly galling as he had started to enjoy the conversation that Arun had opened on Indian religion and literature. Ferdach was impressed by the young man's knowledge and by the depth of his observations. He remembered being similarly impressed during his first meeting with his friend Tengku Mizan and he reflected once more on how easy it was for Europeans to remain ignorant of Oriental cultures if they viewed their staff and Asian acquaintances from a distance, particularly from a position tinged with even the slightest sense of their own superiority.

Yet with Arun it was impossible for Ferdach to feel any sense of his own superiority. To the contrary, in Arun's presence he felt, or at least he was beginning to feel, decidedly inferior. Was it because Arun had lost no time in telling Ferdach that he was a Brahmin, or was it Arun's consciousness of his own clarity of mind which was filled, if not by knowledge derived from his own experience, then with the philosophy of the mysterious guru in Madras, Mohan Sundara Rajan, at whose feet Arun had sat for a year before coming to Malaya? Whichever direction the conversation veered, it was to his guru that Arun made reference so that Ferdach began to feel the presence of that mysterious teacher who was an apparently limitless source of wisdom.

No sooner had they set off the following morning than Arun began to speak of the ascetic life of his teacher, of his hours spent in meditation, of the simplicity of his diet, of the sacred and most beautiful chants that he gave voice to in the presence of people who came, from far and wide, to see him and seek his blessing.

'And what did you do while all this was going on?' Ferdach asked.

'Why nothing. Well not exactly nothing. I merely sat in the master's presence and drank in his spiritual grace. To be touched by him is to receive blessing.'

Ferdach tried to imagine how full of light Arun must be after so much contact with an infinitely superior being. No wonder the young man moved and talked with such serenity. But Ferdach was curious. Apart from spiritual teachings, did the great guru have any views on the outside world, on politics for instance? 'I suppose,' Ferdach said tentatively, 'that Mohan Sundara Rajah must have been a follower of Mahatma Gandhi and supported his work for independence.'

'Tchik tchik,' said Arun disparagingly. 'Not at all. My master believed that the Mahatma had taken the wrong path. He did not believe in independence. He foresaw years ago that independence would lead to the break up of India and to the deaths of many thousands of people.'

Ferdach was taken aback, indeed quite deeply taken aback. It had never struck him that there could be Indians who were not in favour of Gandhi. 'But think of what the British did to India,' he said heatedly, 'they reduced it to colonial status, destroyed the ancient administration, exploited it economically, ruined the indigenous crafts with Lancashire piece-made goods.' Ferdach went on for some time reciting a list of iniquities, not always with great certainty but to the best of his ability as he tried to remember the words of various leftwing protagonists of colonial independence heard in his earlier years.

Arun no longer seemed to be looking at him. His eyes were on the road before them or he glanced idly around at the passing scene. Without saying a word he seemed to be implying that his boss was talking nonsense. When Ferdach finally dried up there was a silence for at least two miles before Arun said, rather like a teacher addressing a simple-minded child, 'My dear Mr O'Haney, do you know what India was like when you British first arrived? It was a colony, a Muslim colony ruled by emperors who hailed from central Asia. Mongols. What was their marvellous administration? Why, nothing but a tyranny. Yes, their great administration could build forts and palaces, but at whose cost? Do you know that when the Taj Mahal was built there was terrible famine in north India? The administration of the Mogul emperors in no way resembled the British colonial system. As for destroying traditional crafts, those crafts would have been destroyed in any case, by factory goods from other parts of the world and by factory goods made by Indian capitalists. No Mr O'Haney, my guru proved to me that the British created the basis of a modern state in India, they codified the law, and they set up a proper civil service and a modern army. They created a unified transport system and they built dams. They introduced modern medicine and science. All far from perfect but the essential foundations of a modern state.'

'But Arun, what about the way the British behaved in India, segregating themselves, behaving so arrogantly?'

'Of little importance. In any case it did us Brahmins good to have people showing us what it was like to be put a step down. My master's argument rests on the very fact that you did not try to graft yourselves onto India like the Mogul conquerors.'

Ferdach was beginning to feel very hot and extremely flustered. He wanted to drink for his mouth had become as dry as an inch of the Thar Desert. He pulled the car over to the side of the road and asked Arun to reach to the back seat to get a vacuum flask of cold orange juice. When Arun had filled a tumbler and drunk, Ferdach did the same. 'What you are saying Arun, is extraordinary to me. You seem to be defending colonialism. You seem to be saying that the establishment of a modern materialistic state, regardless of by whom, is the supreme good. You seem to be espousing an extreme right wing doctrine.'

Arun smiled indulgently as though Ferdach had not caught up with him and then spoke gently. 'Not at all, sir. I am saying things that I thought you would comprehend. Yes, it is true that my master would have liked to see the Raj continue. He envisaged that, perhaps after many decades, a democratic dominion, rather like Canada or Australia might be the result. But not just because my master was some sort of constitutional gradualist, no, he had a deeper reason.'

'I'm lost, Arun.'

'Well it's quite simple really. Now I ask you: under the Mogul emperors which religion was spreading, eating away at our ancient Hindu beliefs and culture? It is obvious. It was Islam. The initial tolerance of the first Mogul emperors soon faded. The Mogul graft became a cancer. Islam went on pushing back our religion. Fortunately the Mogul dynasty was in decline when the British and the French arrived, but it could easily have revived. The establishment of the British Raj prevented that. And so our ancient religion was protected. That is what mattered. That was why Mohan Sundara Rajan never wanted independence. At least we still have the upper hand in India. But what remains of Hinduism will all but vanish from Pakistan.'

Ferdach thought it best to let Arun have the last word, even if it was an unusual one. He suspected that if the conversation continued he would hear some unflattering remarks about Islam, and since Malaya was an essentially Muslim collection of states, he thought it best to draw the line.

They hardly spoke until they were approaching Kuala Kubu Bahru where Ferdach was to lunch with a colonel in the Scots Guards with whom he had earlier become acquainted in Perak. He looked forward to another meeting with Colonel MacDonald-Bligh, generally just known as Bligh, or sometimes, mysteriously, as Flookey Bligh, who, though a typical guards officer interested in field sports and good living had an atypical but quite passionate interest in medieval Irish history. With his own background Ferdach hoped to get him onto this subject again when they met. Arun would, of course, go off to visit some Indian family with whom he had excellent connections. However, Ferdach felt it might be courteous at least to stop their conversation about India so that when they next set out they could, more profitably, start on a different subject. 'Arun,' he said as they drove into Kuala Kubu Bahru, 'I really do appreciate what you have told me and I think that there is something in what your master says. But we live in the postwar world. Everything is different. Britain is declining. When I joined the service I was told I was going to work myself out of a job. What happened had to happen.'

But Arun still had to have the last, and most definitive words, no longer uttered gently but angrily. 'If you had not dumped Churchill after the war, everything in the Subcontinent would have been different. Churchill would never have set a ludicrous timetable, Churchill would never have bowed to fanatics, Churchill would never have sent a man like Mountbatten out to India. Mohan Sundara Rajan was in New Delhi, working in the Secretariat in those days. He was in a senior post. He was one of the earliest Indian ICS officers. He saw everything that was going on. And he has told me, many times in great sadness, that Mountbatten was nothing but a vainglorious fool.'

Ferdach felt he had to question this contradiction of received history. 'How was he a fool?' he asked. 'Maybe you've got it all wrong.'

'Tuan O'Haney, you British believe nothing but what the establishment tells you. Well here's something it prefers to keep quiet about: there are two ways into Kashmir, the main one from Rawalpindi in the west and the Jammu route from Gurdaspur in the Punjab. Now, Mountbatten switched control of Gurdaspur to India. Remember, Mountbatten's wife was a great friend of the Kashmiri widower Nehru. So Indian troops were able to advance very easily into Kashmir following the illegal deal between its Hindu ruler and the Congress Party. Was Mountbatten's action deliberate or not? My guru couldn't say but I feel certain that when the last Viceroy made it possible for India to take most of Kashmir he must have known that he was bequeathing a poisoned chalice to the Subcontinent as a whole. So maybe Mountbatten was not the vainglorious fool my guru thought him but just a vainglorious scoundrel.' To judge by his tone of voice Arun was in a fury but quite abruptly he fell silent. After breathing deeply several times he said calmly, 'Anyway, please stop opposite that Indian shop over there. It belongs to my uncle's brother-in-law. Pick me up here when you have seen your Colonel Flookey.'

Ferdach stopped as bidden. The day was, of course, hot but the air between him and his clerk felt chilly. Ferdach suspected he was being held responsible for all that had gone wrong in the Subcontinent. But then, just as he was about to drive off, Arun returned to the car and leaned through the window to tell him the best way to the guards camp, after which he put on a sweet smile before disappearing amidst a crowd of little girls and boys who had flowed out of the shop. The smile made Ferdach feel he was forgiven though it was probably no more genuine than Arun's apparent anger.

62

Kuala Kubu Bahru is situated in a hollow at the beginning of the winding road that crosses the central range of mountains forming the backbone of the Malay peninsula. Here the lowland ends and ranges of jungle-covered hills rise in waves northeast towards Fraser's Hill and east towards Gunung Rajah with much of the higher land about five thousand feet high. Today great rolling banks of white cloud were surging around the peaks, often obscuring the dense jungle but at other times brilliant columns of sunlight pierced down to spotlight parts of the landscape as though the whole area was an immense stage prepared for a stupendous drama. In this hollow bowl the heat was sometimes modified by cool breezes that erratically flowed down from the higher altitudes making the place an ideal spot for young men far from England, or at the present time, from Scotland, to be stationed in a well-groomed army base.

There were few officers in the mess for it was late so MacDonald-Bligh and Ferdach were able to eat a large curry tiffin together undisturbed on a broad verandah overlooking a sports field. Ferdach wanted no more than a Tiger beer in the heat of the day but Bligh consumed a good part of a bottle of Scotch as they ate, remarking a couple of times, 'I'm a hedonist Ferdie, a hedonist. It's the only philosophy for life. But it only works if you can see other people having a rotten time.' As if to demonstrate this he turned to gaze at the sports field where two teams were playing seven-a-side rugby. From time to time throughout their subsequent conversation he would interrupt his own remarks or Ferdach's with bull-like roars of 'Tackle him low, Girvan, you lazy bugger!' in a voice like those of the Boanerges, before resuming in his more quietly refined wee Edinburgh tones.

Ferdach told him of Arun's or rather the all-knowing Mohan

Sundara Rajah's opinions on Indian independence which Bligh thought most reasonable. 'It's often religion rather than race that makes a nation,' he observed. 'Look at Ireland: there are parts of the southeast where most of the names and probably the blood is Anglo-Norman but the people are sperm obsessed Roman Catholics so they think of themselves as Celtic Irish nationalists. They've even forgotten that their so-called Irish game of hurley, is Saxon in origin. So Arun is right in saying that had India become Muslim, it would not be India as we know it. Yes, you arrogant English have created some fascinating situations.'

'What do you mean, you English. Whose army are you in?'

'Well, I'd like to say the Scottish army though I have to call it British. Anyway I shouldn't say "you English" either. I'd never have called the Empire the "British Empire", much less the "English Empire". In classical times no one said the "Italian Empire" but only the "Roman Empire". I'd call the Empire we so devotedly serve, the "London Empire". Yes, Rome and London, the seats of moneybags and power brokers. It's London, or rather the small group of people who control it, that runs the Empire. The English are underdogs, peasants, just as much as the people in the colonies.'

Bligh's languid manner made it clear that he himself was not one of the peasants. 'A bit of an exaggeration,' Ferdach said, 'but I get the point.'

'A very important point Ferdie. If the English, Scots, Irish and Welsh all saw themselves as helots under the London establishment, they'd see one another differently. What's more, in the colonies black people would see that Scottish crofters and little English children who worked down the mines were treated as badly as their own ancestors. Just think Ferdie, all sorts of attitudes would change. Most important, the English man in the street wouldn't think that the sun shines out of his arsehole. He'd know he was a coolie like the rest of 'em.'

'I think this is going to lead on to class struggle and Marxism. Well you're in the right area for it. I'm told that some high-ranking communists are in the vicinity of this place. Isn't that so Colonel?'

'There are many communists hereabouts, that's for certain. But you may know more about their ranks than me. I'm just a simple soldier. The MCP is powerful here and over in west Pahang but I only know what our intelligence tells me and I don't think they tell me everything, or know everything. Anyway, I've yet to meet any CTs on either a friendly basis or in a fight.' Bligh turned abruptly towards the sports field and yelled, 'Sergeant Mackintosh, enough is enough. Do you want to kill the poor fuckers? Never more than twelve minutes each way in seven-a-side.' His voice then resumed its normal level or rather below its normal level but still high and precise. 'There's one bloody thing that baffles me Ferdie. We hear all sorts of rumours here; from inside the security forces and from the local population, about Tras being an important CT headquarters. But whenever we suggest a sweep of the area, we are told that some more important objective has come up. Don't you think that's queer?'

It was indeed queer, Ferdach thought, but the word 'queer' had other connotations for him just then. His attention had strayed to the soldiers coming off the sports field, pouring with sweat and smeared with mud, like so many strange mutates evolved in a timeless swamp. He felt sorry for them, some of them no doubt lonely and longing to be in Scotland, and remarked, 'Even a minute is too long in this heat I'd say.'

Bligh said, 'Exhaust the brutes and keep 'em out of trouble,' before shouting at Sergeant Mackintosh, 'Get them to the showers before they stink to high heaven.' Turning to Ferdach he asked, 'And what about nationalism in this country? Can a Malayan nation ever be created? There's no single religion to bind the races into one. There's nothing but work-shy Malays, money-grubbing Chinese, and Indians longing to get enough cash to get back to mother India. Where's the basis for a nation? Still, the place is giving me a good time and that's all I care about.'

'If you are implying that it's impossible to create a nation when there are different racial and religious elements, what about meltingpots like the United States and Brazil?'

'Like my Aunt Fanny's sewing box,' said Bligh derisively. 'With the black buttons all at the bottom. No. They'd need a genius to create a nation here and there isn't one on the horizon. So, Ferdie dear boy, these Asian Johnies will need the British Army until the cows come home to prevent the place from becoming a shambles.'

Ferdach was irritated by Bligh's words. They revealed an aloof disdain for the people of the country. Yet only a short while ago the man had been disparaging English arrogance. Maybe he saw himself as being above arrogance, a praetorian guardian of his 'London Empire' sent out to keep the peasants in order. Probably a completely selfish hedonism really was his philosophy and he didn't care a toss what happened to the people below him, provided they gave no trouble. 'I must go now,' Ferdach said. 'I've got to hit the road to Fraser's.'

'Well don't let anyone know what time you're setting out. Have you got a gun?'

'I've got a Browning automatic and two phosphorescent hand grenades. They're in the glove shelf.'

'Enough to defeat a regiment of CTs,' said Bligh giving a broad red-faced Scottish grin. 'You may be a member of the heaven-born Malayan Civil Service, Ferdie, but for Christ's sake be careful on that road. It isn't Knightsbridge, you know.'

63

Ferdach drove the car to pick up Arun, who was sitting disconsolately in the doorway of his uncle's provision shop, engaged in an argument with another young man of his own age but far less handsome. Even as the car started up the argument continued with both the young men's voices rasping like saws.

'Did you tell your people where we are heading?' asked Ferdach.

'Not my people, my family.'

'Sorry. Your family. Did you tell them?'

'Well, if you start up this road you can only be going to Pahang, can't you?'

Ferdach refused to be rattled. 'Yes my friend, but once in Pahang we could be going to a hundred places. Or we could be going no further than the next village.'

Arun looked glum. 'I told them neither where we are going nor when we intended to leave. The last part was easy, as I didn't know myself. You kept me waiting on my uncle's doorstep.'

'The man you were shouting at just now. Why were you arguing?'

'We weren't arguing. We always talk loudly like that. Anyway, that man is my cousin and a bastard.'

Ferdach decided not to ask further questions which resulted in Arun launching into a detailed account of a rift between various members of his family over some property issue, or was it a dowry issue? Ferdach couldn't quite make it out for the more excited Arun became the more his standard of English declined. Whatever the details, money was obviously at issue. Though admitting that it was probably his own imagination, it seemed to Ferdach that life in a Tamil household must be considerably more fraught with dissent than that in a Malay or Chinese family.

As Arun droned on Ferdach contented himself with nodding his head, as though in sympathy, whilst all the time doing his best to take in the beautiful scenery through which they were passing. Once the neatly terraced flooded *padi* fields with their wallowing water buffalos were behind them, the road began to ascend, passing through Malay-owned rubber smallholdings and patches of secondary jungle. Then the real jungle began. Immensely tall trees seemed to be taller than any forest trees that Ferdach had seen before but this was only an illusion caused by the steep incline of the road.

Occasional *kampung*s nestled near the roadside under overhanging trees – pretty places where the adults, especially the women, moved gracefully, if at all, and only the children seemed full of energy. To Ferdach this appeared to be a peaceful, relaxed area where Malays zealously preserved an age-old courteous culture that seemed infinitely superior to the barbaric industrial blight sweeping the world outside.

Yet was it so peaceful, so secure? As they went on Ferdach got the feeling that they were entering an ominous zone. After a while there were few *kampung*s, only a silent, still forest where anything or rather anybody could be lurking, ready to pounce. Surely there were communists along this road. Surely all movement must be observed and reported back to a nearby command post, particularly when police or military vehicles were involved. This was a road designed to favour the terrorist. Any vehicle could be hit with impunity from the higher slopes and it would be almost impossible to judge where the attack came from. Yet were the communists so weak or limited in numbers that they were unable to throttle this important route across the peninsula or, as was more likely, did they have some ulterior purpose in letting it stay open?

Arun had fallen silent, though Ferdach hadn't noticed when he had stopped complaining about his cousin. But he did hear Arun ask, 'Are you nervous, Mr O'Haney? Yes I can see that you are nervous. I can tell from your silence.'

'Actually Arun, I was enjoying the drive and the countryside.'

'No. You are nervous. But it is nothing to be ashamed of. This area is very dangerous. As for me, I am not nervous. I believe in karma. If it is my destiny to proceed to the next state of existence, I shall accept it. You see, we Asians are much more profound in these matters than you

Western people, Mr O'Haney.'

They had just arrived at a narrow bridge where they stopped for a little while to look down at a gurgling stream that led into a larger river, the Sungei Garachi, flowing on the other side of the road. Ferdach thought how pleasant it would be to help Arun into the next state of his existence by pushing him into the water. It was difficult to resist telling the bumptious young man what to do with himself. But he kept his mouth shut which was probably why he started the car up very roughly so that it shot forward too quickly and nearly hit a Chinese-owned lorry waiting to come across the bridge. It was carrying a load of pigs all squeezed tightly into baskets that rested on top of one another, four deep. It was a cruel spectacle. At that moment a dreadful squeal came from a pig whose front legs were painfully twisted in a pannier directly above the driver's cabin.

'You terrified that pig,' said Arun. 'It must be your nervousness. Perhaps I should drive. I am always a very calm person.'

Ferdach stopped the car, breathed in deeply and said firmly, 'That pig is squealing, Arun, because it's in pain. Can't you see how its legs are twisted? It's in pain.' He shouted the last word loudly.

'Oh you English,' Arun said reprovingly, 'You have such sentimental ideas about animals. Chinese pigs are used to pain. The pig squealed because you frightened it with your driving. To tell you the truth, sir, your driving alarms me too.'

Ferdach drove on in silence wondering whether the young man was trying to provoke him or whether such behaviour was natural to him. Perhaps the heated argument he had just had with his cousin was typical of his relationships with other people. Ferdach did not have to wait long for the next bout. Arun suddenly came out with, 'I don't know how young Englishmen like you have the nerve to come out here to exercise authority over people like me. Could you possibly explain your arrogance to me?' It was said in a cool way, with no feeling of anger and Arun's best English accent had returned.

Ferdach drew up at the side of the road in an area where the thickest jungle abutted either side of them. Then he turned to stare at Arun, who, not abashed, stared back. What was in those intense brown eyes? Was it hatred? Was it real puzzlement? Or was it something else, a kind of test, a probing of this English guy little older than himself to see how he would react, to see how he ticked? For some reason, quite unclear to himself, Ferdach decided that the last was the answer and that it was best to reply quite calmly, as though he was the respondent in some impartial scientific questionnaire.

'Well now, Arun, I can honestly say that I don't believe that I was being arrogant when I joined the Colonial Service. The immediate reason for my coming here was sheer accident, though I don't expect you'll believe that. So I'll take a step back and say that where my horrid domination over you is concerned, it was most likely thoughtlessness, or, if you like, a lack of imagination. Yes. I believed I was coming here to take part in the run-up to independence, a re-run of India in 1947 if you like, but hopefully less disastrous. I was glad to play such a role. But coming down to the nitty gritty, no I never envisaged driving along a dangerous and remote jungle road with a cantankerous young man like you who felt I had no right to be here at all. In fact, I'd be happy if our roles could be reversed, then I could see things from your point of view.'

Arun's face lit up with a radiant smile. 'I think you are a good man Mr O'Haney,' he said. 'That is what my uncle Mr Arunasalam told me about you but I never believed him. He is a real British arse-licker if you'll forgive the expression. So if you were a rotten devil, he would have said the same thing. But now you have said that you'd like our roles to be reversed, why don't you let me take the wheel. I can drive excellently you know. And you can have a rest. No, you can be at the ready with your gun and those phosphorescent hand grenades in case we are ambushed.'

Ferdach did not like the suggestion in the least. The road was now very far from being straight and there were bad patches on its surface. Moreover he did not know how well Arun drove or even whether he had a license. But it was more than he dare do to ask to see it. What torrents of resentment might be released: 'You don't trust me; you look down on me, etc.' So, instead, he said, 'Just wait until we get to Gumut. It's only a few miles. We can have a rest there and a drink and then you can take over.'

This satisfied Arun though it might have been better had he taken the wheel straightaway while the going was only moderately bad. After Gumut the road turned this way and that and was in poor shape. Arun's driving was erratic at best and downright dangerous when another vehicle approached, though fortunately this happened rarely. Worst of all, as the road snaked on, Arun saw no reason to slow down on the bends so that several times Ferdach expected the car to plunge into a ditch or run into the jungle. Seemingly unaware of his errors, Arun sat forward with an excited stare in his eyes, grasping the wheel as though he were in a grand prix, quite oblivious to Ferdach's indrawn breath and gasps whenever they just avoided yet another disaster.

Soon the ascent became steeper. On his left Ferdach could occasionally glimpse the rushing upper stretches of the Selangor River. The road had become straighter and better maintained which encouraged Arun to drive at full speed and even more dangerously. This, he stated, would protect them from ambush, though Ferdach could not see exactly why, since the absence of curves made them visible from miles away. But at least the vagaries of Arun's driving made him forget the greater dangers posed by the area through which they were passing. At length they crossed the Selangor River where it came down from the huge mountain, Gunung Ulu Semangkok, to the east of the road, and then, quite suddenly they saw the rest house at the Gap, nestling amidst trees above the road. It was sturdily built and looked comfortable, rather in the manner of an Alpine hostelry. Ferdach was glad to stop there and order a beer and some sandwiches. But his hope of resting a while was quickly crushed. Arun who had vanished, Ferdach imagined to find a relative, suddenly reappeared and said they must leave at once for since the narrow winding road up to the resort had a one-way system that alternated on the hour. If they did not leave now, it would be dark before upward traffic was again permitted.

Worryingly Arun was in possession of the car keys and ready in the driver's seat when Ferdach left the building. The drive up to Fraser's Hill was more scary than the one up to the Gap but by now Ferdach had become indifferent. He did his best to relax and looked at the changing jungle foliage that was interspersed with huge ferns suggestive of a lost era and fantastic dinosaurs.

Fraser's Hill turned out to be a pretty village that seemed to belong to rural England. There were stone and brick houses with mullioned windows and, of all things, chimney stacks with tall smoking chimney pots. There was a small golf course, gardens with roses and, outside an attractive looking hotel, a notice offering 'Teas with Hovis'. As Ferdach signed the register, the beautiful but rather large Mrs Delphine Osgood, who ran the Balmoral Inn with her husband, asked, 'Is your wife still in the car, Mr O'Haney? Your chief clerk, a Mr Arunasalam, booked a double room.'

'I don't think so. I'm not married.'

'Oh!' Was there a suggestion of alarm and disapproval in Mrs Osgood's voice. 'Perhaps then your fiancée?'

At that point Arun came in, ignored Mrs Osgood and stated in a peremptory way. 'I've parked the car and told the boy to wash it.'

'You've brought your own boy?' observed Mrs Osgood without looking up from the hotel register.

'No,' Arun answered for Ferdach. 'I told one of the hotel boys to wash it.'

Mrs Osgood's face pushed forward, her raised eyebrows suggesting surprise. 'We don't expect other people's servants to give orders to our staff,' she said offhandedly.

'This is Mr Arun Seenivasagam, my companion. My chief clerk booked the room for the two of us. I'm sure he made it clear: twin beds.'

Mrs Osgood picked up the reservation book, glanced at the current page, and said, 'Yes. Of course. A twin-bedded room.'

At that point Mr, or as he liked to term himself, Major Osgood appeared. Florid faced and with a pointed moustache, now quite white, there was a residual air of military ferocity about his features but his body was thin and sagged. Indeed he looked as if life had passed him by whereas his voluptuous wife seemed to have garnered much of what was best in life. Ferdach observed that despite this contrast they looked at, and spoke to, one another in a kindly way that suggested a certain warmth between them. Two Malay porters now carried in Ferdach and Arun's cases which they had taken from the car. 'Room five,' ordered Mrs Osgood. Arun followed the porters. Ferdach brought up the rear and so was able to hear Mrs Osgood say, solicitously, to her husband, 'Now darling, no drinking until sundown. I don't want you making yourself sick again.'

Once he had tipped the porters, which seemed to surprise them, Ferdach saw that Arun had already gone into the bathroom where he stayed an inordinate time bathing and doing whatever else he had to do without thinking that after a long drive Ferdach might have the same needs. But since it was rather pleasant to be relieved of Arun's presence Ferdach did not exhort him to hurry up but found a toilet in another part of the hotel. By the time Arun did appear Ferdach was lying on his bed reading a book of poetry that he had brought along with him.

'I don't think I shall eat in the dining room,' said Arun. 'They might object to you dining with a servant.'

Ferdach put his book down and stared at Arun who was draped in a sarong and was preening himself in the triptych dressingtable mirror turning his head this way and that to see his peerless profile. 'She made a mistake, my friend. After all neither of us looked too smart after that drive. Who could tell who was what?'

'She didn't think that you were my servant. No, I'll just eat some fruit in this room. You can go and enjoy yourself with your jolly roast beef and Yorkshire pudding.'

Ferdach got up abruptly and went to the bathroom where he took a very long shower, hoping that the tedious youth would be in a better mood when he came out. When he did emerge he saw that Arun had been well provided for by his uncle's shop in Kuala Kubu Bahru. On the dressing table was a tiffin carrier with several compartments from which Arun had taken out a variety of curry dishes which smelled most appetising. 'Well Arun, it looks as if you had decided to eat here long before Mrs Osgood irritated you.'

Arun did not bat an eyelid, 'Oh, if Mrs Osgood had not insulted me I would have had dinner with you, just to please you, even though English food is tasteless. No, I'll stay in this room. I know when I'm not wanted. You go and eat with the tuans and mems.'

64

The tuans and mems were already seated when Ferdach entered the dining room. The menu was hardly imaginative but the food was well cooked. Mrs Osgood was determined that nothing second rate should be seen in her establishment. Her eagle eye was everywhere: on the table settings, on the ornamental silver bagpipers at the centre of each of the five tables, but above all on the waiters who were elderly Chinese and Indians, starched and immaculate and mindful of the guests' needs. Probably because he was a single man and Major Osgood was indisposed – in fact he was already drunk – Ferdach found himself seated next to Mrs Osgood. Junoesque she might be but her sexuality, enhanced by an expensive perfume appealed strongly to him. For company they had an Assistant District Officer from Temerloh, and an older, sombre police superintendent from Raub, both, of course, with their lady wives.

Although all the guests were there to have a break from the heat of the lowlying parts of the country and a rest from the arduous duties of the Emergency, it was, all the same, on the Emergency that most of the conversation concentrated. Everyone was intent on hearing the others' assessments of how things were faring in the places they came from, probably because in this way they got a more accurate picture of what was going on than official communiqués and newspaper reports provided.

Ferdach was sorry that he had not been accompanied by someone like Tengku Mizan who could make knowledgeable contributions with a Malayan slant to this kind of conversation but he certainly did not regret the absence of Arun whose unpredictable behaviour could have been embarrassing. Nevertheless Mrs Osgood seemed unwilling to let Arun's name rest. 'How is that young man?' she asked archly. 'The way he darted about, he looked as if he was under some kind of strain. I hope you're not overworking him'

Ferdach was used to dissimilating where questions about young men were concerned. He replied in an abstracted way, 'Oh, you mean my executive officer. Well, he's very efficient and I guess that's his trouble. A glutton for work. A perfectionist. So he tends to boil himself up. And gets terrible migraines. That's why he's stayed in our room. He'll be as right as rain when we set off in the morning.'

'And where are you off to then?' The question, crisply demanded, came from the ADO who was a handsome rather dashing young man with a mane of blond hair and who rejoiced in the name Howard Ponsonby.'

'To Raub and then to Lipis,' replied Ferdach. 'I'm not doing anything spectacular. Just an inspection for the Federation Chief Registration Officer'

'Ah,' broke in Superintendent Smithers. 'I hear you've got things buttoned up in Perak on the identity card stealing front. The system needs some sorting out in Pahang. Some hard, detailed work.' It sounded as if Mr Smithers heartily approved of meticulous endeavour.

'I'll do my best to help,' said Ferdach who, when pressed, briefly told them what he believed the security situation was like in central Perak. He was careful to say nothing critical about District Officer Bertelli's administration nor did he refer to the fall in morale that he had observed since returning from Singapore.

Mrs Ponsonby who might best be described as dainty, or even doll like, piped up in a thin but cutting voice, 'Don't stay too long in Raub. The situation there is extremely bad. The communists have infiltrated the gold mining labour force. If you are stopping there, don't go out at night. The place is a nightmare.'

Mrs Smithers who had been shuffling angrily from one large buttock to another while Mrs Ponsonby was speaking, broke in crossly, 'Really Alice. How can you speak with such authority? You don't live there. Raymond and I do. And I can tell you things are improving. I don't think you help us all by speaking like that.'

'Improving slowly, my dear Kate,' said Mrs Ponsonby in a high drawl. ' Very slowly. The Raub Chinese are mostly on the other side.'

Mr Smithers came to the defence of his frowning wife. 'I don't think that's true Alice. The majority of the Chinese in Raub are fencesitters. They'll rally to us once they feel secure. I can tell you that the Mining Company Defence Force is gradually getting on top of things.'

'Oh yes, I'm sure. The mine guards its own property with its private army but what about all those Chinese squatters outside who smuggle gold out to the terrorists,' said the indefatigable Alice. 'It would be too risky by half to wander among them after dark, or by day. You can judge what things are really like by the fact that every expatriate on the mine has a bulletproof room in his house.'

'Darling, you know how things have been cleared up in Temerloh, Triang and Bentong.' Howard Ponsonby recited the names of other towns and villages further south in Pahang where the Briggs resettlement plan was taking effect with great success. He enthused about well-planned villages and happy settlers that was pleasing to hear, even if it might have been a bit exaggerated before concluding with, 'As the plan moves on, the same will happen around Raub. You mustn't be so negative darling.' Ferdach was glad that he was chiding his wife who, though diminutive, had dominated the table with her high-pitched voice of doom. He had also been struck by how the course of the conversation had been set by the women. Maybe the men were so worn out by their Emergency duties that they were content for it to be so.

As the meal went on the tension between Alice Ponsonby and Kate Smithers intensified. Ferdach observed them with interest. Indeed married people fascinated him. Would it be like this for him if he took the plunge and married Laura? These two women seemed to have their husbands on a line. Perhaps they granted their sexual favours in return for good boy compliance. To Ferdach, who swayed uneasily between two emotional worlds, sex with men was always easy; men were invariably burning to get their rocks off and knew how to please each other; they gave themselves not for a favour but for sheer pleasure so that, in the absence of responsibility, lovemaking was an end in itself, a kind of game. Such, at that time, were Ferdach's strongly held views because he was still good looking and young, factors so important in the world of male love. It did not cross his mind that his desire for Laura, even though it ebbed and flowed inconstantly, revealed that a contrary deep tide was surging in his nature.

The entire conversation at the table seemed to be underscored by the two women's hostility. Not only were they on opposite sides where political matters were concerned, even their choice of food took on an extra dimension. When Mrs Smithers, who was a large and comfortable looking woman, said that she would like Mrs Osgood's quite excellent trifle, Mrs Ponsonby's choice of fresh fruit would be accompanied by some barbed remark about weight watching. This was even carried through to coffee, Mrs Ponsonby opting for black but 'The chocs look delicious, oh do give mine to Kate,' she tinkled. 'She's got such a sweet tooth.'

Ferdach took to Alice; she had the sharpness and the cynicism that he liked in Laura. Mrs Smithers on the other hand, was so obviously worthy and sincere, such a veritable helpmate to her husband that Ferdach instinctively took against her. He was sure she would be judgemental. So he decided to side subtly with Alice, not by supporting her verbally but by following her choice of dishes accompanying his helping with a sly smile thrown in her direction. He even declined the delicious Swiss chocolates, though he was something of a chocoholic himself.

When it was time for everyone to go to the bar Mrs Smithers professed to have a headache and moved to retire. 'You stay with the others Raymond,' she told her husband but he, gallantly, said he would go with her. Bidding everyone goodnight, she added to Ferdach, 'So sorry not to have met your handsome young friend … perhaps tomorrow.' Ferdach said he would be leaving early. He was glad he had sided with Alice at dinner.

'What a bore poor old Kate is,' said Alice, leading Ferdach to a table where her husband Howard was already in conversation and drinking Guinness with two Australians who, he soon learned, worked at the Raub gold mine. This left Ferdach to drink wine and chatter with Mrs Osgood and Alice about the Smithers whom the three of them agreed were very dull. In fact Ferdach was secretly sizing up both Delphine Osgood, who had a sensual presence which her drink-obsessed husband probably no longer appreciated, and Alice Ponsonby who looked to him the sort of woman who might easily find ways of amusing herself when her husband was outstation. Something about the eyes of both women told him that they would be willing; something too suggested that neither would be riled if he were to become the object of both their pleasure. They seemed to be playing with him as if they were the rackets and he the ball. Their playfulness grew as they consumed yet another bottle of the hotel's excellent claret. Openly suggestive remarks were made about his sharing a room with 'young Arun' and did they both 'behave' as Mrs Osgood put it.

'Why should they?' laughed Alice. 'They have to do something if no women are around.'

Ferdach, enjoying the exchange, did his best to look modest.

'You're quite right. Young men of their age are sexually insatiable,' Mrs Osgood enthused so knowledgeably that even Alice raised her eyebrows questioningly. Unfortunately at that juncture a Malay boy appeared and asked Mrs Osgood to come quickly. The Tuan Major had slipped down the verandah steps and was in pain, possibly his ankle was broken. The boy grinned from ear to ear while giving this news. Mrs Osgood glared at him crossly, then apologized effusively as if the accident had been her fault. ' I'd better look after him,' she said. 'He's such a baby over pain though he wasn't like that when he was a soldier.' Ferdach was disappointed. Since Alice's husband was very much around, he had decided to settle for Delphine Osgood but now she was *hors de combat* a night of celibacy loomed ahead.

Before long he was drawn into the men's conversation. The Australians were being cynical about the government's capacity to defeat the communists. 'You limeys,' alleged Bruce, the younger of the two, 'have lost yer bloody nerve.' At this, handsome Howard smiled a patrician smile and said very softly, 'I think you're mistaken Bruce. You should come over and see how we've managed in Temerloh.'

'Aw come off of it cobber,' said Kevin, the older, larger, uglier and more aggressive of the two. 'Yer had a soft target there: Malay communists. Not like the Chinese we have round Raub.'

Bruce concurred with 'Yeah, a soft target for gentlemanly Pommies.'

Howard ordered more beers for the Australians who had quickly downed their own. 'Again you're both mistaken. The communist Malay regiment, the 10th Regiment, was very tough and well organized. It had a lot of Indonesians in it and its leader Wan Ali was considered invulnerable Also it had two ideologies: communist of course, though that was less important than the second, nationalism. Western Pahang has had a strong Malay nationalist movement since before the war. The people there feel they've been neglected by government, especially by their own sultan. But it wasn't just the Briggs plan that won us the day. It was the work of patriotic Malays who didn't want communist or Indonesian domination. It was Pahang Malays who infiltrated the 10th Regiment and led to its destruction. So I tell you guys, never underestimate the Malays, either as friends, or enemies.'

Silence fell around the table. Even Alice said nothing but Ferdach again felt the absence of some Malayans who could add to the discussion. It was as though the expatriates were deeply embroiled in the Emergency but not emotionally involved in it. They imagined they were taking all the decisions, yet at grass roots level all sorts of potentially explosive things were going on. What about those tough Pahang Malays of whom Howard had just spoken? Having defeated the communists, had they just become *kampung* dwellers, praying in the mosque, planting rice, tending their water buffaloes and generally looking picturesque or was something else afoot?

65

Ferdach opened the bedroom door quietly, not wanting to disturb Arun. He need not have worried. Arun's bed was empty though its state suggested that it had been lain in earlier. Without caring where the young man had got to, and feeling a bit drunk, Ferdach peeled off his clothes collapsed on the bed and was asleep in no time. In the small hours of the morning his bladder woke him up but on returning to bed he noticed that Arun's bed was still empty. He must have found some more relatives to natter to, Ferdach thought, and fell back to sleep. Ferdach awoke early in the morning and listened, eyes closed, to the various squeals, howls and grunts that eminated from the surrounding jungle. A faint light had started to creep through the shutters, the harbinger of the morning sun. Thinking that he would like to see the great orb rising above the mountains, he got up and walked over to a window, to open one of the shutters. There was indeed a streak of red light silhouetting an eastern peak but across the lawn, in the annexe house where the Osgoods lived, framed in the colder light of an opening door was another silhouette of two embracing figures. They looked familiar. Ferdach turned and saw that Arun's bed was still empty. So that was why Mr Arunasalam had arranged, or more likely been pressed to arrange, for his nephew to accompany the boss. Ferdach returned to bed quickly, lay down feigning sleep and soon heard Arun return very quietly and slip into bed. But it was quite impossible for Ferdach to sleep. What a charade Mrs Osgood and Arun had put on during the check-in process. He had been completely taken in. After a while he got up and went down, without shaving, to the dining room to take an early breakfast. Looking bleary-eyed and mournful Major Osgood was doing the same thing as if he too were a houseguest, but there was no sign of any physical breakage about his person.

Arun made no effort to be the driver but sat in the passenger seat even before Ferdach got in the car. 'The cool air up here is so good,' he reflected calmly. 'I had a marvellous night's sleep.' He stretched himself out comfortably and then gave Ferdach a beautiful smile. 'I think you did too Tuan, though you got up very early.'

'Yes, and I had a good chat with Major Osgood over breakfast. He must have been so drunk last night that he couldn't remember slipping from the verandah. But no bones were broken. Delphine must have looked after him very well.' Since Arun's face gave nothing away, Ferdach started up the car and off they went down the winding road to the Gap. There they were flagged down by two Malay special constables who asked for a lift to Raub. Ferdach was happy to oblige, not just because the boys had guns but their presence might have the effect of shutting Arun's mouth should he become cantankerous again. However, quite to the contrary, Arun's acerbic manner had vanished and all his remarks to Ferdach were strangely tinged with warmth.

They started the descent down the eastern side of the central range into Pahang. Black clouds pressed down on them and rain was falling. Not a glint of sunlight reached the earth and the gloom was made worse by the sinister jungle on either side. The road grew serpentine, twisting without reason; though its surface was smooth, Ferdach had to grip the wheel tightly and think hard for he could not tell what lay ahead. On his left, within the curves of this highway incised into the mountains, the land fell away, but how deeply he could not tell? Now too he felt that the car was responding unusually due to the weight of the policemen; indeed one of them was really fat. Both were slouched down as far as possible on the rear seats for as they went on to Tras the fear of ambush increased. By now Ferdach was driving much too fast. Worse than that, despite his concentration and his one hundred and eighty degrees grasp on the wheel, he was not over preoccupied with safety; within him stirred more than a hint of irritability with that smooth young man, exuding sexual satisfaction, sitting beside him. Perhaps that had an obscure influence on what followed. As he cornered a sharp bend the car careered to the near side of the road onto the hard shoulder. The policeman behind Ferdach bellowed in his ear *'Mahu mati kah?* Do you want to die?' and Arun shouted 'Let me drive. Slow down!'. Ferdach was unable to do so before there was another bend. He got round it but still too fast. Then, as the car shot forward he saw ahead a road surface shimmering with flowing water. A flooding torrent had made the smooth tar slippery as ice. At once he slammed on the footbrake. Big mistake! The car swerved fiercely to the left to the edge of the road, towards nothingness. Too late now. They were flying through the air, diving into a chasm and their fate.

In that instant, at least in Ferdach's memory, time became extended enough for him to recall that in the glove compartment, were two phosphorescent hand grenades. Time to fear that on impact they might explode and consume them in a fiery death. Time to wonder as the ground rushed up at them, whether the car would hit a jagged boulder.

Ferdach could not remember the impact. He could only remember the darkness from which he slowly emerged, and then the dull pain in his chest and the sharper pain in his forehead. He could not remember anyone crying or moaning. It seemed that the others, like him, had all been stunned. He managed to touch his head; there was a lump over his right temple but no blood. He opened his eyes; the light was dim and against the windscreen there was a dense mass of foliage as if the car had been swallowed up by the jungle. He became aware of a weight on his back; it was the fat Malay Special. He wanted to ask if everyone was all right but no words came from his mouth.

Arun's voice broke the silence speaking in Malay and asking the Specials if they were OK.

'*Baik Tuan*,' they replied in unison.

'Good. Let's get out,' Arun said, first in Malay then in English. It seemed that he had taken command. Ferdach tried to open his door but to the right saw that it was almost against a rock. He then realised the car had been received onto a cushion of jungle between two boulders. It was a miraculous escape. For a moment he had a primitive feeling that all would be well, a feeling almost of elation; they were not intended to die today. Then he tried to move but at once knew that he was still pinioned against the steering wheel that was strangely buckled, the result of his chest driving against it. Painfully turning his head to the left he could see Arun. He looked shocked but unscathed, so unchanged that Ferdach feared that Arun was about to accuse him of being a bad driver and the cause of the crash. But Arun spoke to him gently, asking if he was all right or in pain and promising to get him out of the car. 'We must get out, Tuan. I can smell petrol. It's dangerous with those grenades.'

Easy enough to suggest. It took Arun time enough to force his door open against a thick mass of bushes and struggle out. He could not move fast despite his fear of a fiery death for he was badly bruised and the groans he let out when he moved suggested that he might have suffered internal injury, a fracture perhaps. But at length he did free himself and was able to help the two Malay Specials who had fallen strangely quiet; they looked dazed and were probably concussed. Ferdach was extricated last because he was still jammed between the rear seat and the driving wheel. Yet when the four of them were in the open with only their heads above the vegetation another problem was at once obvious. The cliff over which they had plunged was steep and difficult to climb, especially in their present bruised and battered state. Fortunately its face was covered with a variety of plants the roots of which had intruded tenaciously into crevices in the rocks and shale. They would provide something to grip as they made their way up.

It was only a matter of thirty feet but the climb took an age, each of them sometimes slipping back to the bottom, but little by little desperation and sheer grit got them to the top. The heavily built Malay Special had the greatest difficulty and Arun had to support him on his way up. But at last there they all were safely on the roadside, filthy, scratched, bleeding and worn out. Only then did Ferdach look down at the car. All he could see was the rear window framed by leafy branches. And there across the bottom of the window was the slogan much used by Morris in those days, 'Another Morris'. How bizarre! It made him laugh. The others looked at him thinking he was still in shock until he pointed out the words to them and they all started to laugh wildly, yelling, 'Another Morris, another Morris.' Then their laughter died away as they took stock of their position, stranded and in a highly dangerous area.

'We must wait here,' said Arun in a voice of authority. 'Sooner or later a car, a lorry, something will come. Then we can get up to the Gap or down to Tranum.'

'You mean to Tras,' Ferdach commented. 'That's the next place down the hill.'

'No it isn't,' said Arun. 'Tranum comes first.' He gave the impression of being well acquainted with the area even though he never looked at a map.

'Or we could walk,' said Ferdach.

'We're bruised and aching. The Specials look finished and you look awful. Let's wait here.' Arun was adamant and the Specials, who seemed to understand this English, nodded their heads in agreement.

Just then, from further down the hill, though sounds in the jungle are deceptive, they heard two explosions, perhaps even gunshots. They looked at one another in alarm, everyone wondering whether it might be better to hide in the jungle. A third explosion then, just a hundred yards down the road, a lorry came into view round a bend in the road. It seemed to jog along in fits and starts and then it suddenly stopped dead with another loud fart from its exhaust. It was a run-of-the-mill open-topped vehicle, the sort used to transport livestock. From inside its cabin two men emerged with their hands up. One of them held a white cloth.

'They think we're terrorists!' said Arun. 'They think we're CTs!'

It was not surprising. The four of them were caked with mud from head to toe; from a distance they must look like jungle-dwelling communist terrorists. Arun yelled, telling the driver to drive up the road, '*Mari-lah! Mari sini!*' and not to run away, '*Jangan lari!*' At the same time the Specials pointed their guns at the lorry in a threatening manner.

It turned out that the lorry driver was a Tamil with whom Arun was soon having a lilting conversation in sentences that flowed into one another like the tributaries of a swift-flowing stream. Ferdach had learned that it was better never to interrupt Tamil conversations for a translation. At the end he was always given a single sentence resumé that obviously left out most of what had been said. The driver's assistant was a Chinese man from whom the Specials gathered that the communists had attacked a police vehicle several hours earlier a few miles down the road. There was no question of continuing down the road. Best to go the way the lorry was pointing. So Arun, without telling Ferdach what he had been talking about, climbed in beside the driver while Ferdach, who had just gone through a fit of vomiting, the Specials and the Chinese man lay, much more comfortably, on sacks atop the lorry which toiled up to the Gap in fits and starts. Despite the jerks and snorts Ferdach fell fast asleep.

Subsequently he found it difficult to remember the exact sequence of events that followed. He knew that he had suffered from drowsiness and more vomiting and that he must have been in a disoriented state for days. What he did remember was that an antique Ford 8 taxi had appeared at the Gap rest house from Fraser's Hill and taken him down to the Kuala Kubu Bahru army camp together with Arun who virtually ordered him to go alone into the headquarters to ask for help from his friend Colonel MacDonald-Bligh. What Bligh must have thought of the distraught young man who came into his office asking for assistance as of right, Ferdach never found out for Flookey Bligh was blown up by CTs a few weeks later. Perhaps Ferdach's theatrically commanding manner convinced him it was his duty to help this young MCS officer in distress. More likely it was compassion for the state Ferdach was in. His eyes must have looked a bit crazed and his clothes – well, the less said about them the better.

So it was that in the late afternoon an army lorry with four stalwart but reluctant Scots Guardsmen took Ferdach to the scene of the disaster. The vehicle carried a small crane which quickly lifted 'Another Morris' up to the hard shoulder where the men found that they could not get it onto the road because they had parked the lorry too close to the cliff edge. So the car was lowered back into the ravine and the whole operation had to be repeated. This was almost completed when a police car came up from Tranum and its driver, a Superintendent Griffin, told them to stop the operation as CTs were in the vicinity. He then left at speed. The Scots looked doubtful but were convinced by Ferdach to finish the job with a roll of Malayan dollar notes, money intended for his tour of Pahang.

The grateful Scots took 'Another Morris' to their camp workshop to await its pickup by Wearne's Motors, leaving Ferdach and his luggage at the Gap rest house where he found Arun again making telephone calls. By now it was dark and Ferdach was ready only to shower and then collapse onto one of the comfortable rest house beds. But at five the following morning he was awakened by Arun who forced him into a change of clothes and told him that a taxi was outside to take them to Kuala Lipis. It was a journey of several hours but Ferdach hardly noticed the countryside or the towns they passed through for he slept most of the way until he found himself outside the government offices in Kuala Lipis. There they were interviewed by a proud Malay Assistant

State Secretary about the identity card replacement system. Arun, clearly more resilient than Ferdach, did most of the talking. The Malay officer showed no interest in what either of them told him. In fact he treated Arun with contempt and kept frowning at Ferdach, maybe thinking that this new breed of MCS officer with a bruised unshaven face and a seemingly inebriated manner was a bit *gila* or mad. The interview was a waste of time but it had been conducted, which was what Arun wanted Ferdach to be able to report to Kuala Lumpur. After a bite to eat at a Chinese coffeeshop, Arun took Ferdach back, again by taxi, to the Gap where at last it became possible to relax.

When they had both enjoyed a Chinese meal they went into the rest house garden to enjoy the cool air balmy from flowing down the mountains over the jungle trees. How sweet it was to be safe and fed and clean. Two large glasses of Cognac constituted a sort of coping stone to their pleasure. Yet more was to come. Arun looked closely into Ferdach's eyes before saying, 'You seem better now but not much. That crack on the head really put you out. You'll have to take care of yourself.' He paused, leaned forward so that their faces were close together and went on quietly, 'Tuan, I like you very much. You have been kind to my uncle and to me. You were kind to me even when I was impertinent. I ask your forgiveness not just for the past but for everything I am going to tell you now: in the first case I am not going back to Ipoh. I am staying at Fraser's.'

Words unanticipated even by himself came from Ferdach's mouth, 'To be near Mrs Osgood. To be near Delphine.'

Arun sat up suddenly; his face registered surprise but this gradually mutated to pleasure, as though at the very sound of the word Delphine. 'So you did know. I suspected it. How did you guess?'

'I didn't. I saw you leaving her house early in the morning, after a long kiss in her doorway.' Then Ferdach recalled the depressed-looking Major Osgood at his breakfast. 'But the Major? How about him?'

'My father served the Major in India, in the cantonment at Ahmenabad. As a boy I was in and out of the Osgood's house. Then Major Osgood was wounded in Burma, badly wounded down here.' Arun put his hand for a moment over his crotch. 'After the war they went to Madras for nearly a year while the Major was in and out of hospital. For me, that was a good time because there I met my guru Mohan Sundara Rajan. Later they retired to Malaya and took the hotel at Fraser's. They brought me with them. My father had died, and mother … she died very soon after. I was only thirteen but it had already started, between Delphine and me.' Arun smiled, at some delightful memory no doubt. 'I swear that I was not the one to start it. Of course the Major came to know. Delph told him. But he didn't want to lose her. Uncle Arunasalam does his best to keep me away from Fraser's. He still thinks it's very unseemly of me. That's why I was in Ipoh for a while. But I must stay here. I came to that decision last night. Delph needs me. Even the Major needs me. I am happy with them. They are my family.' He had emphasised the word 'my' but now he paused as though he was too shy to say anything more, which, nevertheless, he did, 'Ferdie, I am the boss there. You can believe it or not.'

It was not at all difficult to believe. It could hardly be otherwise. Arun was a strong character. Ferdach's imagination was much taken up by the thought of that youthful seduction. Oh, the things women were capable of, but lucky Arun all the same. Then he recalled their first conversation together. 'But what about your wife and your three children?'

'I am not married. I wanted to hide my affair with Delph completely.'

'So you were never learning Sanskrit? Now that does disappoint me.'

'But I am, I was, from my cousin, my uncle's daughter; the lady with the three children is my cousin.'

'God Arun, you should have been an actor. I hope you haven't any more secrets.'

'I do have one Tuan Ferdie, one only. It concerns you. I have to confess it to you as a friend. I truly want to stop what I've been doing to you.'

'Doing to me?'

'Yes. Spying on you. It wasn't my uncle who really pushed me into coming with you. I told you: he never wants me to go anywhere near Fraser's. But he was obliged to do so by a Special Branch man, Tenkgu Mizan. Special Branch is very interested in your friendship with Lai Kuan.' Arun drew in his breath and added in a low voice, 'I was told to watch whether you met up with any People's Movement suspects in Pahang, or if any Min Yuen sought you out. That's why I was so nasty to you to begin with. I don't know why but I thought the best way to deal with you was to make myself hostile. But you are a good man. My own heart tells me so. I hated what I had to do.'

Remembering his friendly conversations with Mizan in Kuala Lumpur and his introduction of him to Laura, Ferdach could scarcely believe that the aristocratic Tengku would stoop to dealing with him so deviously. 'This Mizan,' he began dubiously. 'How did he work it?'

Arun sensed Ferdach's disbelief and obviously felt the need to prove his veracity. 'I was a clerk in Special Branch. They transferred me to your office. They can do that sort of thing very easily. But it was convenient to them that my uncle works for you. They could lean on him to teach me about your identity card system quickly.'

Ferdach still felt disappointed with Mizan. 'But the Tengku is a journalist. When I met him in KL he told me so.'

'Yes. He is working as a journalist but it's a cover. He's in intelligence, believe me.' Arun hesitated and looked embarrassed. 'Ferdie, I've more to tell you. There's a file on you in Special Branch. I've seen it. It contains information about you and Lai Kuan and also about you and a boy, Mat Noor. Yes I know he's dead but when he was a Special he was suspected of being a Min Yuen worker. I read a report from Upper Perak that said that you and he were... but I don't believe it.'

Ferdach was shaken but moved by Arun's confession. It merited his own trust in return. He said, 'Well, the one thing that is true is the information you don't believe, about Mat Noor and me. I'm not ashamed of it. I loved Noor.'

'Then be careful, Ferdie, if you're like that. Special Branch could use what it knows about you if it wanted to get rid of you.' Arun then laughed. 'There you go: it's the fault of the bloody British again. If they hadn't introduced the Indian Criminal Code into Malaya there'd be no law about homosexuality at all.'

'That's true,' said Ferdach. 'The bloody British again. Yes, I see that I am at risk. But what about you? Aren't you taking a risk telling me all this?'

'Not at all, not if we both keep our mouths shut. Not that I care about your politics or your sex life. In any case you met no one but the Assistant State Secretary so I won't be lying if I give you a clean bill of health when I'm asked. But I'll only tell them in my letter of resignation. I don't want to spend another day in my uncle's house.'

Ferdach nodded his satisfaction but could not help wondering aloud what the future held for Arun in Fraser's Hill. How would the local expatriates take it? A major's randy wife being screwed – they would see it as no more than that – by a randy young Tamil.

This too Arun took with equanimity. 'Delph says that most English people in Malaya are decent and extremely dull. I'm sure she's right. But all sorts of things do go on here besides the affairs Somerset Maugham wrote about; his were the all-white posh ones. But there are the less respectable ones: the planters and tin miners with their Asian girls, the snooty English mems with their Malay drivers. Sex is like food in Malaya, an exciting ethnic mix. But Delph is right; she says we must conform to the dull proprieties of the majority. Probably everyone in Fraser's knows we sleep together, but outwardly I'll be a hotel employee and no one will say it's otherwise ... in public at least.'

Ferdach could no longer hold back the question that was tickling his curiosity, 'Arun, you say you didn't start the affair with Delphine. May I ask how it happened?'

'May' was hardly necessary. Arun leaned forward, his arms raised and his hands playing an invisible instrument as though his story could be drawn out of thin air. 'Well, you see, my first duty in Ahmenabad, after my morning ablutions, was to carry in morning tea and fruit to the Major and Delphine. After the Major went to Burma I continued to do so. Their bed was inside a large mosquito net. Sometimes Delph was almost naked. I enjoyed that. She had beautiful breasts like pink grapefruits. My eyes would caress them greedily until I spoke her name. Then she'd pull up her sheet but she knew I'd been staring. After a while I was sure she was often really awake when I came in. I'd just stand there looking and looking. I'd get as hard as a rock; I'd fondle myself, wanting but not daring. One day after pretending to wake up, she didn't pull up the sheet. She told me to sit on the bed. She took my hand and slid it over her breasts. Though I was innocent I was on fire for her. Then her fingers crept inside my *dhoti*. I remember her deep sigh. Even then my lingam was in Vatsyayana's horse class; oh don't laugh, it matters. That day Delph made a frontal attack and she's never given up the weapon she seized.' Arun chuckled. 'Yes, I see it interests you.'

'Everything about women interests me. I bet you gave thanks to Lord Krishna and I bet Delph is glad to have a man versed in the Kamasutra.'

Arun warmed to the theme. 'But not then. What I've told you started before Major Osgood was wounded. I quickly learned how much Delph wanted me. To begin with it was just lust; day after day she taught me how to please her. She'd got a copy of the great book though she didn't really need it. Then gradually we fell in love with one another. We still are. It was my first, my only experience of love. I was terrified that the Major would take her from me when he came back. I hate to tell you this but I laughed, yes I laughed aloud and I danced with joy when I heard that a lovely Japanese shell had made a total eunuch of him. Oh Ferdie, his loss saved my life.' Arun paused, ashamed perhaps of both his honesty and his hyperbole. He looked searchingly at Ferdach as though unable to continue.

'How so Arun? You can tell me everything now. It will go no further.'

'I'll admit it then. I was possessed by jealousy. If he had come back as a normal man, I would have killed him and then myself too.' Arun gave a deep-throated cry of pleasure as though the news of Osgood's emasculation had only just reached him.

Ferdach refused to accept his words. He said, 'You could never have done it Arun. You're not a violent man.'

'Oh yes I could. Sex can drive wise men mad. It has a terrible power. It creates and it destroys. That's why Shiva, whose sacred lingam is in all our temples, is both Lord of Creation and Lord of Destruction.'

The memory of a powerful drawing of Lord Shiva, grossly phallic and threatening, crossed Ferdach's mind but he was reluctant just now to embark on a discussion of Indian religion; he would never get away, better to bring Arun's confession to a calm end. So he said, rather glibly, 'Ah well, all's well that ends well.'

'No. Shakespeare was wrong, in my case. I wanted a child by Delphine. Indeed I went at it like a lion and made her pregnant but, without telling me, or Osgood, she ran off to Bombay and got rid of it.' Arun shook his head from side to side, at the memory of his grief. 'Fortunately the child was only a girl. If it had been a boy I think I would have gone mad. Unhappily, Delph can no longer have children.'

425

'Perhaps that's just as well Arun. You can all live together now and, what was it Delph says? Oh yes, conform to the dull proprieties of the majority.'

Arun at once became a stoic. 'It's for the best. Maybe you should follow Delph's advice too, Ferdie. Accept the dull proprieties. I shall. When Delph's tired of sex, maybe before that, I'll get married, have several sons, and settle down in Fraser's.'

I bet you will, probably as a highly successful hotelier, thought Ferdach. Any attempt to dissuade Arun from his decision would be useless: he was a young man who knew where he was going. Anyway, thought Ferdach, why should I try? Then, all at once, his numbed brain had a bout of absolute clarity as he recognised to the full that all the arrangements that had been made since the accident: the taxis, the clothes, the accommodation, the visits to Colonel Bligh and to Lipis, had been master-minded by Arun with his contacts in the area. What a mess things would have been without him; it would have been difficult to cope alone. 'I'm indebted to you Arun, and most grateful. I wish you and Delph and the poor Major happiness. I'll try to persuade Mr Arunasalam that all is for the best, though I think he'll never believe me.'

66

Ferdach returned to Ipoh by a very devious route. He was still shaken by the crash, more than he had expected, and worried to be thought a security risk by the police. Though Arun had arranged for a car to take him to Ipoh, Ferdach travelled in it only as far as Kuala Kubu Bahru, intending to inspect his car there and to thank Flookey Bligh for his help. However, 'Another Morris' had already been picked up by Wearne's Motors and was on its way to Ipoh for repair. This worried him as he had failed to retrieve the Browning automatic and the two phosphorescent hand grenades from it after the crash. He hoped Flookey Bligh might have them but the colonel had left on some operation further south. In the workshop he bumped into two of the Guardsmen who had dragged his car from the gully. They knew nothing about the missing items and could not care less but, remembering his cash incentive, they did ask him to have a drink with them in the NAAFI where he got the impression that though they did their duty as soldiers to the full, they 'didn't care a shit whether the communists took over this fuckin' awful country or not.' They just wanted to get back to Glasgow. Ferdach envied them obscurely. They were harshly honest in their wants and judgements. He half wished he shared their ignorance and could enjoy their comradeship, but he also knew that he was lying to himself and romanticising them. Yet men like them were percipient about men like him. Words were not necessary. They gave him a lift in a lorry to Kuala Kubu Road railway station where he could board the train. When parting, they promised that they would visit him if ever they came to Ipoh where, the eldest of them, a crafty-eyed corporal, said with a wink, they'd both give him the time of his bloody life.

Yet Ferdach felt unable to face Ipoh for a while. He wanted to be

427

with Laura to bask in her sympathy. However, as his brain was not yet working too well, he failed to phone her and when he got to KL was informed by her Chinese office manager that she had gone for a few days to Singapore to see Mr 'Swine Shop'. Ferdach then recalled what she had recently told him; it must be about her legal separation and the financial settlement Albert was to make on her as the 'innocent party', for Albert was anxious to clear the decks for an uncontested divorce so that he could settle down with Mona Wee. Ferdach had never entertained any feelings of guilt on the matter but just now he did feel guilty over his protracted absence from the office and so, to give the impression that he was still hard at work outstation, he phoned Mr Arunasalam to say he proposed visiting Negeri Sembilan to see how its identity card system was faring. Pleased to be left in sole command of the office, disciplinarian Mr Arunasalam welcomed the proposal and even requested that Tuan Ferdach should stop off somewhere outside the state capital to carry out a grass roots level inspection. Ferdach was grateful for the suggestion for he was anxious to disappear completely from the purview of everyone who knew him until his spirits were restored

Ferdach stayed for two nights in the Faai Lok or Happy Hotel at Sepang Road where he got a good meal if not a very comfortable bed. However, the bed's hardness was successfully relieved by the company of a sylphlike Thai girl whom the manager called for him. Since the strain of the past few days had drawn Ferdach's nerves taut it was fortunate that she was enthusiastic and able to give him all the pleasure he wanted. On the second night she said she would like to work for him in Ipoh though it was doubtful whether the hotel manager would want to part with her. At this, Ferdach put on a face redolent of sympathy and said he did not want to make trouble for her. As a consolation he paid her well, leaving her as happy might be, and convincing himself of his own fundamentally good nature. At a less intimate level he always welcomed the chance when in such hotels or in the neighbouring coffeeshops and street markets to talk with local civilians rather than with officials to get some notion of what they thought about the government and the Emergency. In this small place, as elsewhere, his conviction grew that the infrastructure of government, or rather the superstructure of government over the country, was largely irrelevant to the day to day life of the people. Rarely did anyone know even the name of their English District Officer and as long as they were not irritated by restrictive regulations they seemed quite indifferent to the outcome of the Emergency. The tuans and the mems with their nice houses and their hierarchic social life on the estates in the area began to resemble his idea of Roman Britain wherein the life of the villa owners must have been utterly remote from the lives of the subjected Britons. When he visited the Sub District Office near to Sepang Road he was glad to find that the ADO was in Seremban thus enabling him to speak at length to the Malay *penghulu*, the Chinese Affairs officers and the resettlement officers who were inevitably involved when the CTs stole identity cards; he took care to conduct his inspection with a reserved air to make them feel that they were under serious investigation.

By the time he was relaxing in the comfort of an air-conditioned coach on the train to Seremban, he no longer felt the need to wear a cloak of anonymity for the shock of the crash was wearing off and he felt more stable. Whilst half listening to the dire prognostications about the future of Southeast Asia from two French Catholic priests from Vietnam, and enjoying the fine Cognac they produced, he decided to live, in the immediate future at least, more conventionally, until the dangerous suspicions about himself had been dissipated. In this respect he had to admit that it had been a mistake to cut himself off from some English people who could be good friends. This had to change. So he was glad to renew his friendship with Stuart Hills in Seremban, where he decided to stay for a few days. Hills had been with him on the colonial training course in London. A handsome man, attractive to women and a good cricketer, Hills was far from being an academic but he had great personal charm which accorded well with his keen insight into people; perhaps this had been intensified by his wartime experience when he distinguished himself during the invasion of Normandy. After a pleasant dinner together at the Sungei Ujong Club, when they were discussing the strange way in which time seemed to flow at different speeds, Ferdach drew his attention to Proust. To some it might seem a perverse act to introduce such a writer to a sports-loving military hero but Ferdach had always been aware of Hills' sensitivity and felt sure he would, as an indefatigable diarist, respond to the psychological insights of *À la recherche du temps perdu*. And he was right. The introduction was to lead Stuart Hills to research, unlike

429

Ferdach, not the febrile intrigues of a dying colonial era but his own more profound memories of war. Following a daytime visit to the Istana Besar, the elegant royal residence at Sri Menanti, Hills threw a drinks party where Ferdach met Mervyn Sheppard, a scholastic man dedicated to the preservation of Malay culture at its best, and to David Friend, who had studied in Macau and so was able to whet Ferdach's appetite for life in that city. After moving for a few days in Seremban's society, presided over in a courtly way by the state ruler, the Yang di Pertuan Besar and his family, and distinctly more refined than the money-grubbing upper circles of Ipoh, Ferdach felt at ease with himself once more. He was happy in the knowledge that there were many more tolerant people around than he had imagined; he also observed that there were others who had personal quirks to conceal as much as he did, without however being so concerned about them. After all, he was no more than a tiny cog in a huge government machine that had much more to worry about than the peccadilloes of individual officers, for wherever he went, he had seen the machine creaking with weaknesses and inefficiencies in its attempt to curb the CTs. Lest it be thought that he was himself one of those inefficiencies, he decided that he had been away from his office for long enough.

As he returned to Ipoh, changing trains in KL but not leaving the station, he reflected on what he had learned of the situation in the country. It was true that the squatters had largely been resettled and a form of administration established over them, but though General Briggs had insisted that the terrorists must be baffled at every turn in their attempts to dominate the people, how to do this was equally baffling to government. The enormously expanded police force with its thousands of special constables had not been trained to do much more than guard villages and mines and rubber estates. It was not capable of taking offensive action, nor was it trained to play a peacekeeping role among the people. Far from earning their affection, the ill-paid police sometimes battened on the peasants and workers with various methods of petty extortion, an easy thing to do when so many regulations regarding curfews, travelling permits and food carrying had to be applied. Unfortunately, the communists, whose leadership was resilient, had developed new ways of fighting the security forces. To deal with

430

the problem of obtaining supplies of food and weapons they had set up storage dumps in the jungle and devised a variety of ways of intimidating the New Villagers, the remaining squatters and the workers on the mines and estates into providing them through the Min Yuen with everything they needed. All the Chinese and Malay government officers who had spoken to Ferdach privately in Negeri Sembilan insisted that the hidden grasp of the Min Yuen on the masses was as tight as ever. Nor was it only effective in gathering supplies; of equal importance was its role in providing the communist military leadership with vital information on the intentions and movements of the Security Forces. In other words, even though the Government's effort had been toned up and strengthened, so had the effort of the communists. The population, now trapped between two forms of government, was doing the only thing possible, obeying both sides, keeping its head down and waiting for the outcome to become clear before committing itself to either side.

Ferdach's gloom over the situation was reflected in the views of his Sturrock Road housemates, Waite and Ericson. Jimmie Waite, as an Assistant District Officer, was in a particularly awkward situation, as his ideas were in conflict with those of his boss, Harmsworth Bertelli who, from his HQ in Batu Gajah, several miles from Ipoh, was now ruling the district with an increasingly arrogant hand. The issues were those that also worried Ferdach. Resettlement was well on its way to being accomplished in central Perak but Waite knew that, though the people had been physically regrouped, the outlook of the Chinese, who formed the majority of the New Village population, remained much as before. Waite was therefore in favour of a massive effort to win the people over by letting them run their own affairs and by providing them with help to improve their standard of living. He had been a pioneer in establishing New Village councils, as often as not elected at a public meeting, and he took an active interest in village health and education. He strongly emphasised the need for patience. The Chinese were suspicious of government and needed to be convinced of its sincerity. Here the provision of land was all important, for once the people had their own lots they would feel that they had a stake in society. Unfortunately, the Malay states were never very happy to make land available to the Chinese, even on a temporary occupation license basis, nor had Bertelli

431

requested the state government deal with the land issue expeditiously. On the contrary, this inflexible man believed in dangling the land issue over them as a carrot eventually to be eaten if they were good now. He also believed that to turn the people into government supporters as quickly as possible they should be subjected to draconian measures if they were not cooperative. Mr Bertelli was, in fact, in most matters affecting the public administration of his district, totally impatient of patience.

Mrs Thelma Bertelli too had been manifesting impatience, though of a different nature. Only a few days after Ferdach's return he received a formal invitation to a dinner party at the District Officer's house in Batu Gajah. In furtherance of his intended new image he put on his evening dress – white dinner jacket and black bow tie – which he had not worn since setting foot in Malaya but which had been de rigueur on the SS *Canton* coming out. This occasioned great mirth in Ericson when Ferdach went for a fortifying drink in the sitting room. 'God, who'd have thought that only a couple of weeks ago you were airborne in Pahang. Good job you weren't dressed like that.' Ferdach frowned. No one had mentioned that accident since his return. Now it seemed that the whole town must know.

For once Waite supported Ericson's jibe singing, 'He flew through the air with the greatest of ease, that young Irish man on his flying trapeze.'

'By the way Ferdie,' said Ericson, 'there was a call for you from Wearne's. Your trapeze is mended. In fact it's in the garage. So you won't need a taxi to Batu Gajah. But don't fly off the road on the way.'

Ferdach poured out his usual brandy dry and took a deep gulp. 'I suppose I'm a laughing stock,' he began.

'Not at all,' replied Waite. 'Only we know the details, from Arun. He was worried about you. He phoned and asked us to be very kind to you. See, even Ericson is trying. But I'd like to hear the details of the crash again from your own lips.'

Ferdach gave a blow-by-blow account of the crash, not once but twice. As Waite listened he became convulsed with laughter and wanted to hear about the car's flight over the cliff again and in more detail. It was as though danger filled him with delight rather than fear. He made Ferdach describe exactly how he felt hurtling through the air: could he see the rocks ahead? Was he thinking of the grenades? Of being roasted alive? It was as though he envied Ferdach the nasty accident that could have been his death.

'Yes, you'd have ended up like one of Cookie's fry-ups,' said Ericson. 'I suppose you'll never want to see those grenades again.'

Ferdach's expression darkened; he had pushed the missing objects to the back of his mind. 'Oh my God. The gun. The grenades. God, they must be lost, or stolen.'

'As they were police issue it will mean a charge,' said Ericson heavily, casting a ponderous look at Ferdach in the manner of a displeased magistrate. 'A serious offence, I'm obliged to say, in times like these.'

But before the joke could continue Waite reached under the coffee table and from an empty beer crate drew out both the gun and the grenades. 'Ericson went to Wearne's as soon as your car was brought back and found them for you.'

On the road to Batu Gajah, Ferdach drove very carefully – better an ambush than another crash. But he was not worried about either. At that precise moment in time he was happy. Of Waite's friendship he had always been sure, but it felt good that both Arun and Ericson had demonstrated their concern for him.

67

Ferdach had heard that the Bertelli's house was elegant but that seemed an understatement. He drove up to an old building of cream walls and white woodwork, with colonnades and broad verandahs on both storeys, and stepped into a large reception hall. Whereas most MCS officers were content with PWD furniture, mildly enlivened with their own soft furnishings, Thelma Bertelli had imported grand Victorian furniture from Australia and even had earlier pieces of her family's furniture that glowed richly in the light of two chandeliers. There were also expensive ornaments and several oil paintings, mainly of Australian scenes, that revealed her avant-garde taste. Unlike her husband, who at best might be described as just a step above the uncouth, Thelma Bertelli's background was that of a long-established Melbourne family. She was used to moving in affluent circles and perhaps should have remained in them since, after only a few years in Malaya, she heartily regretted marrying Harmsworth Bertelli whom she no longer saw as a dynamic and well-informed expert on Malaya but as pompous, boring and, worst of all, opinionated. Ferdach, on the other hand, seemed to her to be sophisticated, clever and well bred, the ideal partner for her much younger sister Sarah, now on an extended visit to Malaya.

The guest of honour was Tuan Haji Mustapha Albakri whom Ferdach was glad to see once again. Other notable guests included two rising Malay politicians: Dato Nik Hamid, fair skinned and quick witted, from the east Malayan state of Kelantan, and Tengku Ismail, a genial member of the Kedah royal house; an influential Chinese millionaire, Mr Ho Ew Boon, who had assets in Singapore and Indonesia as well as in Malaya; and a brilliant but wily Indian criminal lawyer, Mr D. R. Kuppusamy who was famous for saving the necks of several people, including an

Englishman, who were generally perceived as being guilty. Kuppusamy was renowned for his dictum: 'My clients never plead not guilty; always guilty with extenuating circumstances'. The two Malay politicians were unaccompanied, but the Chinese and the Indian gentlemen had both brought their wives, as had the four European guests: Peter Newton, State Engineer; John Harris, Chief Police Officer, Perak; Enoch Swales, Managing Director of Central Perak Rubber Inc.; and Patrice de Reboul, Président du Conseil d'Administration, French Kinta Tin (the largest of the mining companies operating in the state). On her own was another English woman, the redoubtable Dame Priscilla Mentmore-Smythe of the British Red Cross Society, currently on an inspection tour of her minions in Malaya. The company was brought up to twenty by Miss Sarah Fitzwilliam and Mr Ferdach O'Haney, who were rapidly developing an aversion for one another.

Drinks had gone on for far too long and Ferdach, who drank more than was wise to stave off his pangs of hunger, began to feel over at ease. He was aware that he was at the bottom of the pecking order among these senior people and only one of them, Tuan Albakri, fortunately the most senior, showed any interest in him. Thelma Bertelli had introduced Ferdach to her sister almost at once, saying that they had a lot in common though Ferdach could not think what, except that they had both lived in London. However the nearest Ferdach's London approached that of Sarah's was the Café Royal where the smart of the Mayfair and the Soho worlds could mingle, albeit tentatively. The main reason Ferdach took a dislike to Sarah was not that she was glamorous but that she clearly expected every man she met to admire her. Her clothes were smart, her jewellery expensive, her hair perfectly arranged though how she had managed that in this hot climate Ferdach could not guess. What got up Ferdach's nose was her debutante manner, her primping, the languorous poses she struck, the way she took out a cigarette and expected a male slave to light it for her, and her tinkling laugh, intended to attract men's attention. And attract it did where the three Englishmen were concerned. They would clearly have preferred to be talking to her rather than to each other's wives. But Sarah Fitzwilliam was stuck with Ferdach whose eye was on the slimly built Malay waiter serving drinks and not the glamour puss thrust upon him by his hostess.

The babel of conversation was mainly about the Emergency and its effect on the tin and rubber markets, matters of great concern to most of the guests and so it was quite easy for Sarah and Ferdach to speak home truths to one another without attracting attention.

'God knows why Thelma imagined you'd be interested in me,' said Sarah, blowing a jet of smoke with intended insolence just to the left of Ferdach's head. 'He's very pretty isn't he?'

'I like to dine with the Tories and sleep with Labour,' Ferdach replied with a smile at the waiter from whose tray he took another brandy dry.

'I bet you do.' Sarah stared with curiosity at the hovering Malay waiter whose doe eyes were resting softly on Ferdach and then glanced at the other guests. 'My God, when I look at those expatriates, I think I'd stray in the same direction as you if I lived here for long.' Her manner became noticeably relaxed once she realised that her sophisticated airs cut no ice with Ferdach.

'And God knows why Thelma imagined you'd be interested in me. Look at your clothes, your jewellery. I've heard of the Melbourne Fitzwilliams. You want someone to go with your image, not a junior member of a service that won't exist in a few years time.'

'That's true Ferdie, if I may address you so. And call me Sally. But Thelma's really thinking of herself, rather unrealistically I'd say. You see we've always been close to one another. We were left together a lot, on our own. Parents all over the bloody place and finally divorced. Thelma was like a mother to me all those years. She doesn't like being here without me. She'd love me to find a husband here. That's her motive and it gets stronger the more she becomes fed up with Harmsworth.'

'Then why doesn't she get a divorce? You said divorce is in the family.'

'Thelma's a sticker, and anyway she loves Malaya and what she can do here as an MCS officer's wife. It was Malaya that enthralled her, not Harmsworth; she still seems to think she can make him behave more reasonably. Some hope!'

Ferdach stared across the room to where Thelma – even slimmer it seemed than when he had last seen her, though that might be the effect of her long black dress – was at the centre of a group of guests making them laugh, occasionally coming out with a Malay expression to the amusement of the Malays present and giving every impression of being the queen of the party. Harmsworth on the other hand was holding a secretive looking tête-à-tête near a wall with Mr Ho Ew Boon; the latter was short and fat, the former tall and slim but both had sharp expressions which they focussed on one another suspiciously from their different altitudes as though each suspected that he had met his match from a different planet.

Sarah followed Ferdach's gaze. 'You don't have to bother about your career,' she said confidently. 'There may be no colonial service ahead but you'll find other fields. Look at those businessmen. I tell you most of them are as thick as planks. If you learned their nasty little tricks, you could run rings round them.'

'Would you be interested in me then, if I was like them?'

'I am interested in you in a way Ferdie. Fortunately one doesn't have to marry every man one goes to bed with. Oh don't raise your eyebrows like that. I'm a liberated woman, you know. All the same, don't be completely misled by my manner. Underneath I'm quite a homely bird. I'd like a nice house and children. And I'd like to live with them in Melbourne. I'm gaga about children. I'm sure you never guessed it. Thelma's told me all about you but I don't think she knows you at all. She thinks you'd like to settle down but you're a rover. You'll never make a woman happy in the conventional way. You've got no morality and no self-control. I think you're one of those men who believe that the thing between your legs should go off bang whenever it wants and in whatever direction.' Having delivered that judgement she gave him a peculiarly suggestive glance, almost like a street corner whore, he thought, then added archly, 'And why shouldn't it if the target is up and ready?'

A Chinese gong resounded throughout the house like the prelude to a J. Arthur Rank film. Ferdach took Sally's arm and led her into the dining room where, though happy not to find himself adjacent to her, he was not overjoyed to be sitting next to the great Harmsworth himself.

A fine range of dishes, most of them containing a different Malay curry, extended along the table. A delectable mélange of spicy aromas filled the air and Ferdach knew that gastronomically at least he was about to enjoy himself. He thought it would have been better had the banquet been spread out along one of the sideboards for the guests to help themselves but this might have put paid to Thelma's seating plans. So for a little while reasonable conversation came to an end while a confused exchange of dishes, aided by servants, ensued. During the act of passing a prawn dish Harmsworth whispered crisply in Ferdach's ear, 'I might as well tell you now, my dear Ferdie: I want you in Batu Gajah, in my office. I'm going to make a lot of use of you from now on.'

Wine was being poured by the doe-eyed Malay boy and other drinks offered by a Chinese servant. The Malay guests all plumped for brandy dry in which they were followed by Ferdach, who believed that wine with curry was an abomination. He wondered whether the Malays had convinced themselves that they were not breaking the commands of the Prophet, as brandy, unlike wine, had not been specifically mentioned in the Holy Qur'an. In any case, feeling that the Bertellis had presented him a Morton's Fork – a woman he did not want and a function he was sure to hate – further inebriation seemed the best way of getting through the evening.

As soon as everyone was tucking into the mountain of food, Tuan Albakri said, with the amused glint that often appeared in his eyes, 'Obviously now is the time to discuss how we are going to implement Operation Starvation.' This was the first time Ferdach had heard the term but the laughter and then the nods of the other guests told him that it was nothing new to them. As the conversation proceeded, Ferdach became aware that the operation was to be the second grand phase of General Briggs' plan, the first being characterised by the word 'regrouping', which, however, had not denied the communists the supplies they needed to continue their struggle. Operation Starvation was to be accomplished through a wide range of regulations restricting the sale and carriage of food, obliging shopkeepers to keep accurate records of supplies and sales, enforcing the creation of belts devoid of undergrowth around perimeter fences and so forth. The regulations would be so wide-ranging that, theoretically, no loophole would be left open. The whole population would be called upon to starve out the terrorists and the severity of the punishments would enable the people to give a good excuse to the communists for not helping them.

It was agreed, *faute de mieux*, for who could gainsay the director of operations, that though the plan was excellent in theory, in practice it would be difficult to pursue. These difficulties were pooh-poohed by Harmsworth however. 'Damn it all, the way you get people to obey is by strict punishment,' he maintained.

'You mean put all offenders in jail,' said Sarah lightly. 'A big building programme for the PWD there Mr Newton; and lots of contracts too.' She glanced at Mr Ho Ewe Boon who, among other things, was Chairman of the Chamber of Commerce.

Everyone looked embarrassed and Harmsworth's eyes darted fire, first at his wife and then at his wilful sister-in-law. Tuan Albakri merely smiled gently and commented, 'Out of the mouths of babes and sucklings. No, Sally's quite right. Too many punishments will push the people to the other side. They're already between the devil and the deep blue sea.'

Thelma nodded her approval though directing it towards her husband in such a way as to tell him to keep his mouth shut. Ferdach felt a bit sorry for him. He was under fire from his wife and mocked by his wife's intemperate sister. No wonder he sought refuge for a while in silence. At Tuan Albakri's request, everyone began to put their oar in. Monsieur de Reboul took the lead explaining in rotund phrases that his company, as in Indo-China, would spare no effort in ensuring that its perimeters were tight, well manned and adequately staffed by guards to prevent even a grain of rice from getting outside. Mr Enoch Swales, less forcefully and infinitely more wearily, said that the rubber industry would do likewise though he emphasised that since tappers had to walk many miles through the estates, often in isolation, it would not be easy to oblige them never to help the CTs. He also pointed out that the smaller estates had less financial resources to do what was required of them. Tengku Nik Hamid said that the operation was necessary but cautioned that since most Malay areas were largely free of terrorists – whom the Malays truly hated – the intended regulations need not be so stringently applied to them. Ferdach remembered what Mat Noor had told him about CTs slipping into his *kampung* for food, but wisely held his tongue. Dato Ismail, a more outgoing man, saw the possibility of further employment for many young *kampung* Malays as special constables and security guards. He said he would tour the Malay rural areas if required to speak in favour of any recruitment drive and to heighten morale; everyone knew that such touring would also heighten his own image among the potential electorate. His offer was, however, immediately taken up by the CPO, John Harris, who said that Operation Starvation would never get anywhere without adequate manpower. He repeated several times that his force was undermanned and overstretched. Mr Ho Ew Boon expressed the hope that the regulations would be applied fairly and humanely to the Chinese population which was hovering in its loyalty between government and the communists. His frankness on this matter was applauded by Tuan Haji Albakri who again emphasised that harshness would alienate the people. Here he appealed for support to Mr Kuppusamy who stated in no uncertain terms that he and the legal profession, whilst in support of the operation, would be ready to defend any member of the population who was wrongly accused or treated unjustly. Whilst saying this he directed his gaze at the CPO who, to Ferdach, seemed as mild as a lamb and most unlikely to behave like a German Gauleiter. Finally Dame Priscilla gave them a lecture in a harsh staccato voice on the dangers of malnutrition, not perceiving, it would seem, that the objective of the operation, was only to starve the communists. The European wives exchanged despairing glances, embarrassed by her failure to grasp the situation.

Ferdach had listened to all this with interest. He had heard nothing new but nothing stupid, Dame Priscilla's contribution aside. He even thought it was gratifying that the leaders of Malayan society present were so strongly behind the government. Since he had felt that it was inappropriate that he should say a word he was a little surprised when Albakri turned towards him and asked, 'Now you've been up and down the country recently in your job, O'Haney, is there anything you'd like to add?' Ferdach thought quickly. What had mainly struck him at Tanjong Malim and Slim River and in other smaller places? Yes. He was sure of it, without a qualm of doubt: the great amount of downright administrative inefficiency at all levels. 'Well,' he said reticently, 'I think there's one ingredient which is most important and much neglected.' He was aware of all eyes on him, perhaps even hostile eyes connected to brains which resented his inexperience and junior status. 'I think that much more attention needs to be given to training. New regulations without adequate staff would be useless. But so would staff without really good training.' He went on to outline what he knew of the constabulary who lounged around doing almost nothing or were corrupt; of District Office staff only interested in keeping to office hours, taking home their next wages, and fiddling travel claims; of senior officers still trying to continue the old prewar colonial life. God, he thought, I'd better stop before I'm shot down in flames and stop he did, quite abruptly, sensing that his face had become flushed. To his relief the CPO Perak, mild Mr Harris, sprang at once to support him. 'I agree with O'Haney one hundred percent,' he said, adding with great vehemence, 'A lot of people in this bloody country need to have some lead stuck in their pencils.'

Later in the evening when the hosts had led their guests out of the dining room to lounge on the verandah under Chinese lanterns, Sally smiled at Ferdach and whispered, 'I say, you did yourself proud didn't you. I'm sure you don't need any lead in your pencil, do you dear?'

The start of their affair was not long off, in fact it began immediately after the guests had gone and Harmsworth and Thelma had retired for the night.

'I don't feel in the least sleepy,' Sally said. 'Now that that damned bunch has vamoosed I feel full of life.' They were sitting next to one another on a settee and Ferdach took off his jacket and his bow tie. 'That's better Ferdie. You'll be cooler now. You are going to stay, aren't you?'

'Stay where?'

'Why here of course. With me. Isn't that why you haven't decamped? Golly, I'm feeling very physical. Aren't you?' As though to prove her physicality Sally raised her bare white arms, tugged Ferdach towards her and kissed him not passionately but with the skill that comes from practice. He was conscious of the smell of sweat and the odour of perfume competing for supremacy. The former stirred his lust even though he had not made up his mind whether he really wanted her.

He knew, as Sarah knew, that this was something they both had to do. Thelma had manipulated them into it and puppets cannot move other than directed by the *dalang*. Perhaps that was why neither of them was inclined to play the romantic. 'I guess I'll always feel physical while I have a body,' he said facetiously, 'but after all that talk, well I just don't know.' He paused. He had never turned down an offer of sex if the person offering it was attractive and Sally undoubtedly was, in an Australian lifeguard sort of way. Then he remembered Thelma's intentions for him and stated firmly. 'OK Sally, I'd like to make love to you but with no strings attached. For fun only, because we're in the tropics and the tropics make people randy. And after that spicy food and that booze I guess we're both ready for it.' As an afterthought he gave her a kiss similar to the one he had just received.

'You flatter yourself if you think I'd ever want more from you,' Sarah replied, with an air of indifference that was quite belied by the sly expression that passed over her face and the stagy tone of voice that followed. 'So shall I lead the way to my boudoir darling? You don't know the geography of our stately home.'

'No, not here. I don't want to have breakfast with the Bertellis. Thelma's quite capable of asking for details over the porridge. That would embarrass me because I hate porridge. Let's go to a hotel and get a room there.'

Sally stood up and looked down at Ferdach. 'Jesus, you're so flippant and yet clinical at the same time. Would you behave like that to the Malay waiter you were ogling tonight?'

'I wasn't ogling him. But no, I'd speak to him very differently. I'd woo him. I'd flatter him; tell him how beautiful his eyes are. I might say they were like stars. Men aren't used to such praise whereas women expect it; you certainly adore being the centre of attention.'

'You really are a crude bastard Ferdie. But I like it. I hope you're just as crude in bed.'

Sally pulled Ferdach to his feet and held him close, kissing his face and then his neck until her kisses began to turn into love bites. 'Ow. You must love the taste of flesh,' Ferdach said. 'I'd rather you did that in an air-conditioned room. Bacteria love warmth.' He picked up his jacket and tie and led the way to his car which was parked on the lawn some distance from the house.

He got in, leaving Sally to open her own door. She did not do so. 'I've changed my mind,' she said. 'You're not just crude; you're bloody rude as well. You've got the manners of a pig.'

'Remembering you at the dinner table I'd say you are the expert in bad manners. But come or stay, it's all one to me.'

Sally climbed in and Ferdach drove off at speed. A couple of roadblocks had to be negotiated. At both, the special constables were half asleep. Apart from waking the men up to open the barriers, neither Ferdach nor Sally said much until they got to the outskirts of Ipoh and to a cheap, but discreet, hotel Ferdach had used on previus occasions for purposes like this. The porter, a boy little more than ten, led them up to a room, gave them an enormous old fashioned key and walked off leaving the guests to unlock the door. Ferdach quickly got undressed and lay down on the bed. 'You can see that I can do it very easily with women,' he remarked spreading his body on the bed in the position of da Vinci's man in a circle illustrating proportions, though with less modesty.

Sally switched off the unflattering fluorescent light using the switch by the door. Ferdach immediately switched it on again with the bedside switch.

'I don't like so much light,' Sally complained, less confidently than was her wont.

'I thought you wanted me to be crude. One hundred percent crudity demands maximum light. Get undressed and do what I say.'

Ferdach was in a peculiar mood engendered by alcohol and anger with the Bertellis. He wanted Sally out of fury rather than desire. He was like a rapist rather than a lover. He thought of the war and the behaviour of soldiers in occupied towns. Was he no better than they were, or could all men be like this? Or was he just playing a role, indulging in a fantasy that was not really in accord with his nature? But maybe it was. For some reason he wanted to desecrate this presumptuous woman who professed to want a bourgeois home and a brood of children; this woman who had so impudently told him that he was without morality; this woman who had dared to question his desire for his own sex. So he grappled her to him with all the force he could muster and they rolled about the bed and often on the floor, which was not much harder than the bed, coupling like the beasts they really were, all very noisily with a lot of groaning and moaning and scratching and biting and with Ferdach insisting that love making involved the titillation of every part of their bodies which meant that she must do to him every, for her unusual, thing he had just done to her; he, the archtutor in lust, must be obeyed. Of course, at the end of it all neither knew any more about the other than at the beginning. Nevertheless Sally had become extremely preoccupied with Ferdach.

Indeed the encounter had stimulated an obsessive curiosity in her mind about him.

'What's it like?' she whispered when the battle had ceased and they lay side by side, without touching.

'How can I say when I don't know what you're talking about?'

'What I asked you about before. What would it have been like?'

'Are you doing a grammatical exercise? What would what have been like?'

'Would you have behaved like you've just done if it had been that boy serving the wine at Bertelli's?'

Ferdach was silent. 'Let's rest a while and then I'll take you back before Thelma and Harmsworth are up.' He switched off the light. At once Sally switched it on again, lent over for her handbag and fished out a cigarette.

'Do you have to smoke?' he asked.

Sally began to hammer his chest with her free hand. 'Tell me. Tell me. I want to know. Would it have been different? What's it like between men?'

Ferdach switched off the light again. The woman really irritated him. 'Your question is silly because it's always different with everyone, man or woman. But as you're the sort of person who'll go on and on about it I'll give you a clue as to how it is for me. Just for me you understand.' He paused watching the tip of her cigarette glowing and then dying away and performing little geometrical patterns in the blackness. 'For me, with a man it's much more, well, delicate.' He intended his use of the last word to rile her. 'And with that boy I know for sure it would have been very delicate indeed. But tentative would be a better way of describing it. Before I can give pleasure I have to know how I relate to the other man. Is he alpha or omega or somewhere in between? And whatever he is, how far would he like to go with me. You see it's tentative all the time and so it's best done delicately.' Then Ferdach struck a body blow. 'I guess it's much more beautiful than with a woman on that account.'

Furious at his words Sally recoiled from him, to lie on her side, her head propped up on her hand with her long wavy hair dangling awry along her arm. She stared at him curiously in the morning light that was beginning now to filter through the window shutters. 'Yes, I thought it might be like that,' she said at length. 'You've told me nothing I couldn't guess.' In an attempt to get even she added, 'Sounds ghastly to me, mechanical, like starting up an engine. Yes I guessed it right.'

'Yes, Sally. You can guess everything, except what my heart feels and that eludes you completely. But that's the only thing that matters.'

As the light strengthened, the discoloured walls of the room grew more squalid than ever. Sally shuddered and asked to leave. They dressed rapidly. Ferdach woke up the porter and paid the bill. Neither of them uttered a word all the way to Bertelli's house. The moment Sally got out she slammed the car door violently as though to declare that that was that. Then she hesitated an instant before bending down to look at Ferdach. He couldn't make out whether her dark eyes were angry, or wild, or maybe lustful. It must have been the last for she said urgently, 'I have to see you again Ferdie. Do you understand? I have to.' Then she was gone.

68

Soon all of Ipoh knew that Ferdach was sleeping with the DO's sister-in-law. How Ipoh knew he didn't care; it was what he had hoped for. Nor could he have stopped it for gossip, like magma seeping underground, always found its way up, through endless interstices, into every house in town. But, with misgivings, he learned that Waite had heard it from his driver Yusuf, whose brother Mahmoud was a gardener in Tengku Mizan's house wherein, of course, the news spread like wildfire. Mizan's sister lost no time in phoning her brother in Kuala Lumpur and Mizan, now staying with Laura almost nightly, saw no reason why she should not know of Ferdach's new mistress. In fact he enjoyed telling her, holding up his news until he had just made love to her for the third time and very sweetly, as in his mind knowledge imparted at such a point, was certain to clinch the fact that he, Mizan, was now Laura's one and only lover. Having with a little giggle whispered the good tidings into her ear he fell into a deep sleep. Laura on the other hand remained extremely awake. Generally she liked that black-haired, soft-lipped, long-eyelashed head resting on the adjacent pillow, to be the last thing she saw before being swallowed into the abyss of sleep. But poison had been poured into her ear. This was not how she wanted things at all. Of course she more than liked Mizan; he was amusing, he made love beautifully and subtly, exactly as Malays were supposed to do, but how far could she trust him? She suspected that he told all his courtly Malay friends of his conquest, no doubt with every detail they asked for. But the fate of trophies was to land up on a shelf, a position anathema to her. Mizan was the fill-in, Ferdie was the man she wanted. No man had ever possessed her, body but more especially mind, as he had done. She had no intention of losing him to some antipodean adventuress, one of the annual fishing fleet of husband seekers no doubt, who might carry him off to Australia even before Malaya became independent. Consequently Mizan awoke to find a note on his clothes saying, 'Darling, I didn't want to wake you. I've had an urgent phone message calling me outstation on company business for a couple of days. Love, Laura.' Even though her work did occasionally take her out of KL, she knew that Mizan would not really believe it but, in her view, the nature of their relationship required no more than a brief note by way of explanation.

Yet if Laura's departure by train was precipitate, her arrival in Ipoh several hours later when her eyes and her brain had been stupefied by miles of jungle, rubber estates, and tin tailings, was cautious. The stop at Seremban had given her time to telephone Lai Kuan who sent a car to meet her and take her to one of his family guesthouses. The guesthouse was unoccupied though servants were there to wait on her hand and foot. She had no doubt that Lai Kuan, when he turned up looking extremely smart in a Saigon linen suit, intended staying the night. This did not worry her; there was something exciting about Lai Kuan's hard-faced features. After their first session of love making, which had followed a light meal of tasty small eats and Champagne, she found herself exchanging opinions with Lai Kuan about Ferdach, a topic in which they were both, though for different reasons, deeply interested. Lai Kuan might even have believed her when she claimed she had wanted 'to do this' for a long time but he was not a man to be flattered. Having replied, rather flatly 'me too' – which was true but could also have been said to a clutch of females – he went on, 'So the thought of losing Ferdie to another woman was too much for you Laura. Now what are we to do about it?'

'We? Why we?'

Lai Kuan raised his eyebrows, as though surprised that anyone should fail to understand concern for good friends, then stepped over to a table bearing the drinks and filled his Champagne flute. He looked enquiringly at Laura who was sitting up, like a model sizing up the artist who had been painting her, but in this case a naked artist. With his arm outstretched and holding her wine glass he had unconsciously assumed the stance of an athletic antique statue. He looked good and she told him so, then asked him for a gin and tonic. He brought it over and said, 'Ferdie tells me you're quite a connoisseur of male physique. Do you sleep with many men?'

'Do you sleep with many women?'

'As often and whenever I want.'

'Well that's my answer too,' Laura replied. 'The only difference is that "often" probably doesn't mean as many times as you mean. Women are more choosy. Most men can make love easily with any attractive woman and all most of them want out of it is a quick screw. Nothing wrong in that. They can't help it any more than a dog can stop slavering. It's the way they're made. But if I sleep with a man, he must mean something to me, if only for a while.'

'Ah,' Lai Kuan leaned towards Laura. 'Then what do I mean to you. Maybe no more than being useful to you?'

'Well, my dear boss, wouldn't that be reason enough? Of course I'm grateful to you for helping me; that goes without saying. And I'm glad to make you happy. But that's not what you mean to me really. You're handsome, well built, obviously an experienced lover, like a million other men. Nice of course, but not so important. First comes the fact that you are Ferdie's friend, so there must be something about you that he likes. And if he likes that something I want to know what it is.'

'And have you seen it tonight?'

'I've seen something.'

'Well, what is it?'

Laura paused and then touched Lai Kuan's lips lightly with a finger. A tantalising smile passed over her face, occasioned by a momentary sense of power; not only women were vain, liked to be analysed and made to look more interesting than they were. She enjoyed keeping him waiting. Her hand having stroked his smooth cheeks passed slowly down his body caressed his chest, his hard stomach muscles and then returned to his face. 'So different from hairy Europeans,' she mused. 'You're a real man but your skin is so delicate. In this light it looks porcelain.'

'Come on Laura, you're going to tell me more than that surely? It's almost insulting. You sound like a little girl admiring a doll.'

'What I find interesting in you Lai Kuan is your sadness.'

'My sadness? What sadness?'

He had fallen, as she knew he would, for a ploy she often used. Like many others, she had realised, in her mid-teens, that the process of growing up invariably meant the acceptance of the sadness that is the consequence of self-knowledge. In every adult there was this vein of sadness, hidden by some, recognised by most but not generally flaunted. Men in particular loved to give the impression that all was well. But if she got a man on his own and then confronted him with the fact of his interior grief, Laura always seemed to strike home. It hardly became necessary to tell him wherein his sadness lay, even if she had guessed it. Words would often begin to flow from the man's mouth, relieving him of his own tension as though she was some sort of priestess who might grant him absolution. Lai Kuan looked at her half in admiration, half in surprise. Clearly he was about to speak. All Laura had to do was to open her eyes innocently, to smile sympathetically and to say, very softly, 'Come on, you can tell me, if you want to.'

His story was sad but hardly heart rending. His father had been harsh, a real slave driver who had forced his four elder brothers to learn about tin mining from the bottom up. He could not remember his mother; she had died giving birth to him. He imagined that his father resented him for this but his mother's death had not prevented another wife and more concubines appearing on the scene. What was more, far from treating him as roughly as his brothers, for reasons of state as it were, an expensive education had from the beginning been lavished on him. His increasingly powerful and affluent father required of his youngest son a sophistication entirely lacking in his brothers. Before the war he had had an English teacher, the wife of a missionary and she had taken him to England to attend a prep school. An English public school followed by Cambridge was not the sort of education that subsequently enabled him to identify easily with the rest of his family nor had he experienced the horror of the Japanese occupation with his own people. Lai Kuan felt that he was a foreigner in every world he encountered.

'Yes,' said Laura. 'I can see it must be difficult, but think of the other side. You're obviously on top of the situation. The rest of the Kwok family value you. One might even say that you're pampered. You're the family mascot. As far as I can see you can do what you want. But there's something else isn't there? I guess I know what it is too. Ferdie has told me a lot about you. Although you're the perfect English gent when you want to be, and the Chinese capitalist at other times, you've been bitten by the nationalist bug, the revolutionary bug. You'd really like to be a politician and you don't know how to be one during this Emergency.'

'Ferdie talks too much. He's got no right to analyse me.'

'Oh come off it. We all do that. It's part of being a social animal. But he hasn't told me anything about you in regard to the Emergency, well nothing that could be called a secret.'

At the last word Lai Kuan's eyebrows had shot up. 'Are you sure?' His gaze was piercing, his tone insistent. Something was worrying him.

Laura hesitated. She had not revealed the entire truth. Ferdach had told her, very guardedly, about a document he had delivered for a Chinese friend to Sir Henry Gurney. She had thought he was just name dropping. It was, she had gathered, some sort of survey of Chinese opinion in Perak. But such a document, she told herself, could have nothing to do with Lai Kuan who was no academic researcher. So she said, 'Quite sure.' Yet as soon as she had uttered the words she began to ask herself, yet again, who the friend might be, and what the document contained. Now she quite suddenly suspected that the friend might indeed be Lai Kuan who, she saw, was fishing, somewhat obviously for information. She put her drink to one side, drew him down beside her and said, 'Oh don't let's talk about serious things. Let's forget the bloody Emergency.' Their contact became a warm embrace and led to another bout of love making during which Lai Kuan behaved roughly as if he was angry with Laura. This, for some reason, only stimulated her desire for him.

Yet the deeper motive just now behind Lai Kuan's actions was fear rather than anger. Only that day, early in the morning, one of his field workers had given him a coded message summoning him to a meeting with a communist emissary. It took place in a jungle hideout above the pool to which Ferdach and his platoon had climbed months earlier. It had disturbed him considerably. For just as Ferdach had agonised about handing Chin Peng's letter over to the High Commissioner, so Lai Kuan had experienced great misgivings before he agreed to act as postman. Now he was being questioned exhaustively about every aspect of his relationship with O'Haney, who of course was well in the communists' sights, and particularly on the desirability of using him rather than say Waite for whom the communists had a high regard.

At the meeting Lai Kuan could not help thinking that a good part of his soul had become English. The Party member, who was unknown to him, was cold, unblinking and devoid of humour. Lai Kuan felt contempt mysteriously seeping through the thick glass of the man's wire-rimmed spectacles.

'Are you sure the letter was handed over?' the thin voice demanded, 'Or was it just handed in by your friend to Special Branch?'

'I am certain that O'Haney would do no such thing.'

'Perhaps you are too trusting of this red-haired devil. Comrade Wong Chooi Fong, Henry Wong I think you call him, has reported that you are extremely friendly with him.'

Lai Kuan started. Wong Chooi Fong had not been seen in Ipoh for weeks. Though an active cadre, his Party work allowed him to come out of the jungle from time to time, on missions. His family denied any knowledge of this to the police but to friends they hinted that he had fled to Hong Kong. Lai Kuan did not believe this story. At this moment he felt certain that Wong Chooi Fong had undertaken a duty in which he himself was involved. Quite smoothly he said, 'Comrade Wong was right. We both met O'Haney at the same time. Both of us thought he was a good man, a man with progressive ideas. Not a typical colonialist.'

The Party official, just then addressed as Comrade Lam by a soldier who brought in tea, said, 'British intelligence is subtle. O'Haney is the sort of man they employ. You have been duped. If the letter had really been given to Gurney there would be a reply by now. Don't you understand? The letter was from the General Secretary. It merited a reply without delay.'

Lai Kuan dared not suggest that maybe the High Commissioner did not have the same respect for the Secretary General's seniority in the Party, as did Comrade Lam. He contented himself with replying, 'Yes you are right. But Comrade Lam, perhaps the High Commissioner is still considering the letter.' Then he added, as if he had only just thought of it, 'I know the problem. The High Commissioner will want to keep his reply confidential, no, secret. Perhaps even now he's considering how to get a reply back without a host of people in government, or in his security forces, knowing about it. I guess he'll use O'Haney if he can. We must be patient Comrade Lam. I beg you: let the General Secretary know of the communication difficulties. I will contact O'Haney and sound him out.'

Comrade Lam nodded sagely. Lai Kuan felt relieved; the conversation had ended on a note that gave him something else to do well away from this forbidding hut. In such a place he always wondered whether he would ever leave. He wanted to ask how Harry Wong was. Even more, he wanted to see Harry, to question him but he asked for nothing. With these hard men anything said might be suspect. He could not compromise Harry to slake his own curiosity.

Lying sensuously against Laura's back, lightly kissing her neck and caressing her body, breathing in her expensive perfume, letting his fingers play through her long black hair without awakening her, Lai Kuan contrasted the voluptuous setting of this softly lit room and the beauty of the woman who had given herself so willingly to him with the harsh jungle life which Harry Wong had opted for. The loss of his friend grieved him. Although he understood Harry's motivation for becoming a communist, having been tempted in that direction himself, he found it difficult to believe in Harry's sincerity as a Marxist. Harry had always been light hearted, clever and fun loving. It was mysterious that he should reject the world of women and pleasure, the world epitomised by this very room, to become prey for insects, leeches, disease and bullets, the unremitting diet of a harshly disciplined guerrilla life.

It would have been impossible for Lai Kuan to see Harry Wong just then. Early in the morning Comrade Wong Chooi Fong and a group of guerrillas had attacked the resettlement village of Kampung Tanah Hitam, a well laid out place with good amenities, not far from Chemor. Unfortunately it was close to the jungle which made it possible for them to creep up unobserved and retire safely after their depredations. These involved not only wrecking the school, the clinic and some vehicles but also the punishment of five village leaders who had cooperated with the government. Wong Chooi Fong, as a recent recruit, had been told to prove his uncompromising loyalty by slitting the throats of these men following a kangaroo court which every villager had to attend. In that savage night, lit by the flames of a burning house, Harry knew that the men could not be saved. If not killed by him there were others who would do the job with great cruelty. What he must do he would do quickly. His body moved like a tiger. His pity was suppressed. It was a time of blackness that would remain forever in his mind. But he did it, working from behind the victims who squatted transfixed, arms tied, eyes staring. One of them suddenly screamed like a child. Harry finished him off first. The others made gurgling noises as Harry's *parang* swept across their throats from ear to ear. Then, as the last man sprawled on the ground his legs still kicking, an Englishman ran out of the burning house. It was one of the geologists who had been drafted into Emergency duties on arrival in Malaya without ever touching a rock with a hammer. Harry knew that the boy, for he was little more than that, had lived next door to Waite's house in Sturrock Road. His name was George Carew; words full of fury were bursting from his lips. 'Dirty shit, fucker, bastard,' he screamed as he ran towards the glazed-eyed executioner. The poor fool knew nothing of war or fighting. For the remainder of his life it seemed to Harry that George had deliberately skewered himself on his bloody *parang*. His face, with all manner of foul stuff spurting from his mouth, came right up to Harry's. Their eyes made some mysterious contact before the boy died. Full of hatred for himself and for the world he lived in, Harry followed the other CTs back to the jungle in silence, listening to them joke about the terror of their victims.

69

Kampung Tanah Hitam had been considered a success story, a community Waite had won over by caring administration. His visits there had been regular; not only did he want the people to talk to him directly, he was anxious to dispel the anxiety they felt when they looked beyond the perimeter – two lines of chain-link fencing with barbed wire – towards the hilly jungle. This barrier had been no obstacle to the CTs who had quietly cut their way through it in the dead of night and entered the village.

Waite had never liked the siting of the village and had argued against it with Bertelli from the beginning, but to no avail. Nor would the irascible DO heed Waite's concerns over morale and the availability of farming land. To him the Emergency was a matter of statistics; so many people to be moved in such and such a time, so much land, regardless of its suitability, for vegetable plots, and so much material needed for construction. Bertelli seemed to envisage the resettlement villages as an internment camp where a recalcitrant Chinese population could be kept under control. Waite saw them as places of hope where a secure population could put its roots down and aspire to a reasonable way of life. The failure of the villagers to put up any resistance at Tanah Hitam was proof to Bertelli that the Chinese could never be won over and a justification for his draconian approach to administration. Over breakfast he read to Thelma and Sally a restricted report of the massacre. He did not mention the murder of the geologist whose name was not yet released. Then he asked rhetorically, 'Well, what will that lily livered liberal Waite have to say now?' He seemed almost glad that the atrocity had taken place as he turned his beetling gaze on Sally, 'And I'd like to know what your new boyfriend will say behind my back. Oh, but they'll both find some way of justifying their beloved Chinese. They think the sun shines out of their arseholes.'

'You have such an elegant way of expressing yourself darling,' Thelma said in a withering voice. 'Personally I think Waite is right and you are wrong.'

'So do I,' agreed Sally. 'And so does Ferdie.'

At the word Ferdie, Bertelli paused and stared straight ahead through the double doors of the house onto the expanse of lawn in which he took inordinate pride. Then he helped himself to more toast and marmalade. 'I wonder if one can rely on anyone these days,' he grumbled. 'Tell that blasted *tukang kebun* to mow the lawn this morning. It'll be a jungle if he leaves it another day.'

'Oh, I thought you liked to see jungle near to buildings,' scoffed Thelma. 'Waite told me that you took a risk siting Tanjong Hitam so near to the jungle.'

'Oh bloody well shut up about things you don't understand, the two of you. My God Thelma, why do you have to dress as if you're about to go to a cocktail party at this time in the morning?'

'To keep up my morale in the face of you,' Thelma replied.

Bertelli got up and strode out of the house. His was not a happy home. A large American Ford, which both Thelma and Sally liked to tell him was really vulgar, rolled up at the front door to bear him to the office. He sat on the rear seat fuming over the unfairness of life and the unreasonableness of women. If it had not been for him it might have been Ferdach who was dead and not a geologist. For some time Ferdach had been pestering him to use his influence with the establishment office to post him back to Waite's sub-district office in Ipoh for resettlement duties; surely, Ferdach had argued, this made sense for he was still living in Sturrock Road nor had he been given a specific function at district HQ. In fact Bertelli did not want Ferdach to move residence to Batu Gajah where his affair with Sally would become socially embarrassing and so, since he saw life in terms of power struggle, he refused the request in the form it was made. However, yesterday, as an apparent concession, he had told Ferdach that in order to avoid the sort of cock-up that had happened at Chemor when the CTs had burned a whole convoy of lorries, he should from now on liaise between Waite and himself at district HQ on whose establishment he must remain. By the time he entered his office Bertelli was thus able to flatter himself that he had, to his own ends, applied his rule that subordinates must always be shown exactly who decided their destinies.

Waiting to be taught a similar lesson was the Geological Service, which naturally enough wanted its young geologists back. When a worried chief geologist, who had heard some rumours of the Tanah Hitam incident, phoned later that morning asking him to support their release, Bertelli told him scathingly, 'God man, the damned rocks have been there for millions of years. They'll still be there when you and your men are fossils. The Emergency comes first. So you can wait. We still need your men.' After that his mood improved. It was apparent to all and sundry that the more people Bertelli controlled, the happier he was. He failed, however, to see that he was fast making enemies in high places and that discontented underlings soon find ways of wheedling out of orders. Yet just for now he hoped that, since Ferdach was having an affair with his sister-in-law, he had a stooge who would serve his interests, in particular by informing on Waite who, he imagined, was undermining his influence. It was strange that he could not see that other people's loyalty to *la famiglia* Bertelli was not of the Italian order taken for granted by its imperious head and was unlikely to surmount Ferdach's well-known regard for Waite.

When the Chief Police Officer, Perak, telephoned Sturrock Road with the news of the Tanah Hitam tragedy, Ferdach had not yet left for Batu Gajah. Such a personal call, unannounced by a secretary, was unusual. The moment after Ferdach had stated his phone number, the CPO, in lugubrious tones, said, without any preamble, that George Carew had died a hero's death, that he had died quickly without much suffering, and that he would be grateful if the sad news could be broken to Carew's young wife, Alyson. Before Ferdach could say that Waite was not at home, the CPO rang off.

Married less than a month to George, Alyson was living next door in 'the geologists house', in the absence of suitable married quarters. Ferdach knew he would have to go there at once even though he was only slightly acquainted with her. It would be dreadful were she to hear the news of her husband's death from someone she did not know or over Radio Malaya. Yet how to tell her? She was barely nineteen and seemingly an inexperienced girl who had only recently left a secretarial school in the town where George had taken his degree. Ferdach had thought of her as a child except in one respect: she was totally in love with her husband in whose company she had been so engrossed that she never made the slightest effort to socialise with other women, young or old, in town.

A houseboy showed him to the upstairs flat where Alyson was relaxing on a settee picking at a bowl of fruit that was apparently her breakfast. A Barbara Cartland novel was open on the table. The moment she saw Ferdach a look of alarm passed over her face; her body stiffened. His visit, any visit from a neighbour, at that time was unusual. She must have decided quickly that Ferdach was there regarding some mutual domestic problem; there were sometimes arguments between servants in their two houses, or household dogs had been causing problems. That instant change of mood made Ferdach fearful of telling her what had happened. He sat down beside her even though he was restricted to one end of the settee. She curled her legs to create a space between them. She also gave him a curious look; maybe she knew of his reputation.

Ferdach hung his head, afraid of looking at her directly though maybe that was the right thing to do. 'Alyson,' he said, trying to keep the mournful tone the CPO had used out of his own voice. 'Please forgive me for bringing you some bad news, some very sad news.' Alyson at once sat upright, her body rigid. Ferdach sensed her tautness even though he was only glancing at her. He had never told news like this to a woman. With men in the RAF telling of death was easier because death was part of their life together. But was not death a part of people's life here also? His own affirmative answer hardly helped. He was aware that tears were streaming down his own cheeks. He could not go on.

From far away and very softly, as though she was telling Ferdach the news for the first time, Alyson murmured, 'George is dead. He's not hurt or wounded. He's dead. I think he died very quickly didn't he.'

She had helped Ferdach to accomplish what he had to do. Grateful for the CPO's terse words, Ferdach repeated them, 'George died a hero's death. He died almost instantly. He did not suffer.' Of a sudden they fell into each other's arms, both of them sobbing. Ferdach felt that Alyson, the inexperienced girl, was the one giving most succour.

She did not say 'It's unfair. Why was he killed?' as many people might have done. She did not cry 'No, no, no' or make any other sound. She just seemed to take the news straight into herself as if, young though she was, she understood that the acceptance of suffering was the best way to deal with it. After a minute or so she said, calmly, 'Thank you Mr O'Haney,' and disengaged herself from his arms. Ferdach looked at her fearfully, uncertain what might come next. It was simple enough, 'Please leave me on my own now. I want to be completely on my own.'

Ferdach stood up, 'If there's anything I can do, please—'

'It's all right. I'm sure the authorities will do everything necessary. But you have been very good to me. You had the worst thing to do. But please Mr O'Haney, Ferdach, please leave me alone now.'

Ferdach walked unsurely away from Alyson. At the door he turned towards her again. She was staring at him as though she had heard him asking her a question and said, 'I shall leave as soon as all the arrangements about George have been made. I shall leave Malaya as soon as possible.' Ferdach nodded sagely at her, as if agreeing that such was the only thing to do.

As he drove towards the centre of Ipoh, Ferdach's outrage grew. Alyson had not said that George's death was unfair yet it was so; not unfair as a careless act of some malevolent deity, but unfair because of man. Carew had been recruited as a geologist. All his training had been to that end. He must have mapped out a future career for himself when he had got his degree and decided to join the Colonial Geological Service. No doubt on the basis of an assured future he and Alyson must have planned their marriage and their life in the East together. How unreasonable it was that on arrival in Malaya the new geologists had all been asked to assist in the prosecution of Emergency work as Resettlement Officers. No doubt they had been told that their service would be voluntary but the benefits of their volunteering would have been made clear to them: familiarisation with the country, an easy way to pick up Malay and even a bit of Chinese, and, of course, the fact that their patriotic assistance to the British forces would stand them in good stead with Government. Naturally the excitement of a bit of relatively safe action would have been mentioned. Well, the excitement of action had struck Alyson down with a hammer blow.

Yet the unfairness did not stop there. No longer was there any real need for the geologists to work other than at geology. The resettlement of the squatters was well under way, indeed it was almost completed in Perak. The Emergency was now being dealt with, though not too successfully at present, in different ways. Other men, younger than Ferdach, were now arriving in numbers for administrative duties and many new officers were joining the police force, not a few of them veterans of the chaos of Palestine. Ferdach himself was only marking time at district HQ because Bertelli needed him as some sort of spy on Waite. Handsome young George and pretty Alyson should be alive with the family life they so desired before them. He, Ferdach O'Haney, should have been at Tanah Hitam, not George Carew. By the time he got to the District Office to ask Bertelli what devious job he wanted done today, Ferdach was in a towering rage with the whole system of government and in a mood to throw his career to the winds. It was in his mind to confess everything to Waite: his disillusion with government service, in particular the ridiculous role Bertelli expected him to play, his inability to cope with Malayan society when he was sexually ambivalent, and above all the burden that had been thrust on him as a postman between Gurney and Chin Peng. He would ask Waite to take over that function. Then he considered what he would be asking. Waite would feel bounden to report the matter. Ferdach's own undertaking to both parties to keep his mission secret would be broken. No, he was in a cleft stick. Despite his own inadequacies he must hang on to the task fate or chance had set for him. At least it contained a glimmer of hope for peace.

70

Parties at the Ipoh Club did not appeal to Ferdach. Despite his sensuality and his rejection of religion he was inclined to a certain austerity of outlook, the result of his upbringing which had emphasised the importance of good works and plain living. Nor had the influence in London of his unconventional mentor Nina Hamnett sullied his tastes, for though combining the attributes of an avant-garde artist and a hedonist, Nina was direct and unfettered by fashion. Ferdach had easily identified with her simple, but absolute requirements of life. In consequence, he was well thought of among the liberal expatriates, but those who were more hidebound thought he was a difficult cove.

'But you'll enjoy the company,' protested Thelma in the course of persuading him to partner Sally that night at the Club Ball which she and her husband intended, indeed were obliged, to attend.

'It seems crazy to have such entertainments during the Emergency,' said Ferdach. 'And think of the risk for the planters and miners and the wives who have to drive into town along dangerous roads.'

'That's the whole point of it,' boomed Harmsworth Bertelli from his desk, without turning around to look at the others in the room. 'It's a way of cocking a snoot at the CTs. A way of telling them that British life goes on as usual despite their bloody nonsense.' His fruity voice grew louder as he swivelled round in his chair. 'Really O'Haney. They tell me how smart you are but sometimes you seem to lack common sense. Don't you see that the morale of our kith and kin has to be kept up? The morale of those lady wives who travel in for a dinner and dance at the club is given a boost. They see that their life here is worthwhile, worthwhile despite everything. That's why I, as their District Officer, go along; and why I expect my family to go with me.'

It was on the tip of Ferdach's tongue to observe that the planters' and miners' wives were obliged to keep their morale up willy-nilly otherwise their husbands would be out of a job, but words stuck in his gullet at the implication that he was part of Bertelli's family. Sally, who was standing near a window looking decorative as she sipped a martini, smiled at him, a persuasive smile to which he would have to succumb not out of love but because of his job. He had however made it abundantly and crudely clear that, however exciting their fucking might be, that was the limit of their relationship. Unfortunately she, and even more so, Thelma, had no intention of letting it rest there. The two women were man-hunters, ruthless predators and he was the quarry.

The throng in the club was elegant for the women had gone out of their way to look their best; all wore long dresses though the styles were not particularly modish. For men, black bow ties were de rigueur; some like Ferdach, were in black, others, Bertelli included, were in white jackets. In sartorial contrast, the Filipino band, brought in from Penang, sported garish shirts and dark glasses that made them look like gangsters which they quite possibly were. The music swung between jazz and romantic Filipono love ballads. This created a problem for although many of the women had jitterbugged with American servicemen at home during the war, in the heat of Malaya they preferred to dance, or rather drift hither and thither, to the foxtrot or the waltz rather than to flaccid Manila love songs. As a result, the dancefloor was not crowded.

Ferdach asked Sally to dance even before the dinner was over so that he could get away from Bertelli's guests, twelve in number, who were all the local grandees in rubber, tin, banking and commerce. Compared to their conversations, even the small talk of most government officers was scintillating. Sally liked to dance in close proximity with Ferdach. It amused her to insinuate a leg, whenever possible, between his thighs like a cabaret girl and press against his private parts. Ferdach, of course, did not mind leaving the movers and shakers of Ipoh with the impression that he was a real dog. When their tediously drawn-out waltz had ended, the band suddenly struck up a *paso doble*, a dance the Philippines had inherited from Spain. Because he had learned to do it from Nina Hamnett in a Spanish club they once frequented in Soho, Ferdach told Sally to follow him closely, which she did with aplomb. Unexpectedly they became

461

the only couple on the floor and the cynosure of all eyes, including those of Laura who was at a table on the opposite side of the dancefloor from Bertelli's party, with two women and a military gentlemen, Brigadier Wyldhogge-Smythe, all old friends from her Ipoh tennis playing days.

'That teacher's wife you used to screw is winking at you,' hissed Sally.

'I know. I've just winked back.'

'You know she's screwing that rich Chinese, Lai Kuan. She's moved in with him you know.'

'He's a friend of mine too.' Ferdach said heavily. Momentarily he disregarded the rhythm and kicked Sally's foot quite hard. When she winced he said, 'Oh God, keep in step Sally.'

'I could never sleep with a Chinese. Letting the side down like that.'

'I thought Australians are very liberal.'

'We are, but not to that extent. Do you still like her?'

'Very much indeed Sally. Do you mind?'

Sally drew back and glared at him. 'I'm sick of this bloody dance which you obviously don't know. I want to sit down. My foot's hurting.' She turned abruptly and made for their table leaving Ferdach with his arms outstretched like a stranded statue. He wished that she had asked him whether he liked Laura more than her. Then he could have answered quite honestly, 'Yes, I do.' For an instant he thought of escaping from this ghastly relationship with Sally and the Bertellis and demonstrating his independence by going over to Laura's table right now but the residue in his mind of caution rather than good manners prevailed and he followed his furious partner back to Bertelli's party.

'I liked your demonstration dance,' said Hilary Wilberforce, the wife of the Mercantile Bank manager. 'The way you moved! Really exciting! You looked like a professional–'

'Gigolo,' Thelma cut in, accompanying her words with a silvery laugh intended to suggest that she had said something witty. 'Yes, he looked the real gigolo.' Her *jeu d'esprit* was intended as a back handed complement, nor might Ferdach have minded a remark that boosted his male image if he had taken it in but, thoughtlessly turning his back on Sally, he was acknowledging the smile which Laura was now directing at him right across the room as though no one else was at either of their tables.

'Where did you learn to do it so well?' Hilary persisted. 'I bet it was in Spain or some other Latin place.'

'Yes, as Latin as you can get in Soho,' Sally shouted in piercing tones at the back of Ferdach's head. 'In some seedy joint where he used to hang out with an old hagbag, a so-called artist called Nina Hamnett.'

Ferdach swung round to face her, his eyes darting contempt. 'Woman, your tongue is hinged down the middle and flaps either side so shut your foul mouth,' he burst out in fury. This was the final straw. 'That so-called artist, as you had the cheek to call her, is more of a human being than you'll ever be if you live to a hundred, which I damn well hope you won't. How dare you insult her, you cheap tart?' Some impossibly conciliatory words by Thelma passed him by as he stood up, turned towards Harmsworth Bertelli who was absorbed in conversation at the head of the table, bowed a little from his waist and walked off, but not in the direction of Laura.

As he left the club and went down to the *padang* he wondered why he had let his anger get out of control. In part it was directed at Sally, in part at Laura, not for sleeping with Lai Kuan, he didn't care a toss about that, but for turning up unexpectedly in Ipoh without telling him. She had obviously heard about Sally and was intent on trapping him. What cheek! As if she owned him! Yet even more it was directed at himself for slipping into an impossible relationship with a family he disliked. Then that more constant cause of anger against himself surfaced: why should he bother to dissimulate in this tawdry place about his own nature? It was stupid of him to get involved with women at all. His love for Noor had been less fraught with untruth, it was simple and beautiful, and if it had been tragic, it had been well intentioned, or so he tried to convince himself, until, in the gentle night air beneath the cloudless sky, his abiding acceptance of the sadness of human life slowly began to assert itself once more. All human relationships, whether male or female, whether with parents or children, whether with the wise or the foolish, could become a complicated mess. The best one could hope for was a degree of mutual compassion and good humour. That was the prelude to any deeper understanding and to any serene relationship with any person. Yet it might already be to hand for him: that amused wink Laura had thrown at him in the club, was not jealous, nor angry, it was just amused. She was not trying to trap him. Amusement suggested both toleration and compassion, for the two went together. The thought of Laura was like a balm and soon he was his unruffled self again. Sauntering around the empty playing field, occasionally glancing up at the illuminated club and hearing the distant strains of music, he considered what she had come to mean for him and he concluded that she probably did understand him, that she probably could accept him as he was, and that he probably could accept her. Later, the strains of 'God Save the King' reminded him that she would be coming out of the club soon. Skirting cautiously around the edge of the *padang*, he was careful to return the enquiring grins of some naughty boys loitering on the roadside, no doubt for some nefarious purposes, then walked on quickly. Taking up position beside a spreading hibiscus at the edge of the car park, he kept a wary eye on the club entrance, waiting for a glimpse of Laura.

71

Within a couple of days Ferdach's unidentified role with Bertelli came to an end and he resumed his duties in Ipoh, partly in his own office and partly under Waite, an ad hoc arrangement but it worked. In his move he discerned the hand of Thelma who, he learned, was furious at Sally rather than at him. Bertelli professed to be above such petty domestic discords; if O'Haney was happier working in the field, he said in his lordly way, let him do so. In reality he was glad to see the back of a man who steadfastly refused to dish any dirt on Waite. Ferdach relished the idea of working once more in the New Villages, the organisation of which was going ahead rapidly.

The first priority in each village was to achieve economic viability. Fortunately rubber and tin prices were high, reflecting postwar economic recovery, and the amount of money around was stimulating business. Waite and Ferdach were glad to see that some New Villages were becoming thriving centres in which people were doing well whilst the communists were less welcome.

Despite this, the terrorists were, out of desperation, becoming bolder than ever in their attacks on estates and mines, police posts and convoys. Nor did the capacity of the Min Yuen to extort money and food from the New Villages show signs of waning. Although the Min Yuen and the communist military constituted a sort of alternative government, Ferdach observed that the day-to-day contact of the people with the federal and the state governments was growing. The communists might extort in return for some protection, but it was the government that granted titles to land, issued business licenses, regulated labour conditions, helped set up trade unions and provided education and medical services. The New Villages were weaving the people into the warp and woof of national administration. The increased ferocity of the communists' efforts betrayed their fear that their supporters would be drawn into this web and lose their revolutionary fervour.

Since most of the New Villagers knew little about government, Waite impressed upon Ferdach the need to explain the District Office's functions to them and show how anyone could get help from officialdom. The settlers already knew they were entitled to land for housing and cultivation but they needed to appreciate the work of the District Land Office, in particular that every plot had to be delineated exactly to avoid boundary disputes. Much else needed their acceptance: health and sanitary regulations must be obeyed, forestry law and liquor licensing regulations complied with, and the police seen as friends, not oppressors. But benefit could only come from all these lessons if official corruption was rooted out.

Ferdach quickly learned that it was best to leave the different races to settle their social affairs internally. Among the Malays, disputes would invariably be worked out according to local customary law, or *adat*. This might require the participation of the local chief, the *penghulu*, but for the most part the *ketua kampung*, the village headman, would settle problems relating to village life. Serious cases were referred to the sultan as head of state responsible for land matters and *adat*.

The Chinese too tended to settle their disputes internally, often through their clan associations. If, however, major arguments arose the good offices of the Secretary for Chinese Affairs might be called upon. This never happened as long as Noel Aspinall, now distinctly less friendly to Ferdach than when they were in Singapore, occupied the post in Perak. His policy of 'letting things ride since issues always solved themselves', was well known among the Chinese who accepted it with resignation and courtesy which was more polite than saying he was bone idle.

It was the Indian community that brought most of its domestic problems to the attention of the District Office, a tradition inherited from India where the district commissioner played an important role is resolving disputes. Ferdach did not mind this at all, in fact he rather enjoyed it, even though long hours might be spent on issues of seemingly minor importance. The case of the forbidden privy was a case in point. It began when Ferdach was anticipating a quiet evening doing nothing in particular other than writing overdue letters to his mother and to Nina Hamnett, on the assumption that she was still alive. Just as the office was closing an office boy announced the arrival of a Mrs Sitalakshmi.

She was a small and quite beautiful Tamil lady with refined features and sparkling eyes which flickered first over what she could see of Ferdach, then at everything on his desk and finally over all that surrounded him, the filing cabinets, the almeirah, the coat rack where hung his jacket in case of more formal meetings, the black and white portraits of the King and Queen and, between them, the larger coloured picture of His Royal Highness the Sultan of Perak. He began to feel a bit nervous suspecting that behind that searching gaze there was a mind busily finding fault with something or other; he could only think of peeling paintwork for generally speaking his office was neatly kept.

He returned her gaze politely but not too intently, allowing himself slyly to take in the loveliness of her skin just visible under a diaphanous blue sari bordered with delicate silver thread. Her naked midriff was slender and from her body exuded a musky fragrance that stimulated sensual thoughts in Ferdach's mind, though this was not an unusual occurrence for such thoughts beset him many times throughout the day.

The sweetness of her perfume was almost at once dissipated by thought of the less pleasant smell to which her first sentence gave rise. 'Tuan O'Haney,' she stated firmly as she sat down, 'I have come about my *jamban*.'

Tuan O'Haney knew perfectly well that '*jamban*' was the Malay name for a thunderbox, an unflushable latrine built over a deep hole at the bottom of which the excrement would hopefully decompose quickly. Nevertheless he repeated with some surprise, 'Your *jamban*?'

Mrs Sitalakshmi leaned forward. Her long eyelashes seemed ready to caress Ferdach's cheeks and she placed one bangle rich arm across the desk towards him. 'I know you will understand,' she said in high but slightly lilting English. 'And that is why I have come to beseech your help, if you will condescend to hear me.'

With the greatest affability, Ferdach at once promised to do everything in his power to help, at which Mrs Sitalakshmi proceeded. 'You see, I am from Kampung Pandan New Village which, as you know, has an Indian sector. We of the Tamil community are all highly satisfied with our plots of land and hope to make a success of the place so kindly made available by the District Office. Yes, we are most highly appreciative. Now some of our houses are of the semi-detached variety and well built. Mine is one such. My adjoining neighbour is Mr Ponnusamy.' She shuddered a little as she mentioned the name. 'You see Tuan, when we moved in, Mr Ponnusamy said to me, "My dear Mrs Sitalakshmi, instead of constructing your *jamban* at the end of your own garden, why not build it on my land, adjacent to my *jamban*. Both will be under the trees at the corner of my land and so less unsightly." That is exactly what he said. It was his suggestion.' For an instant Mrs Sitalakshmi sighed deeply and lowered her head before resuming. 'Tuan O'Haney, you must know that Mr Ponnusamy has denied me access to my own privy, to my own *jamban*. Is that not a monstrous thing to do?'

Nonplussed Ferdach replied weakly and with insufficient thought, 'I should say so Mrs Sitalakshmi. Really rotten.' Inwardly he could not help wondering how she was managing in the meantime.

At once she raised her head, shot him a radiant smile and said, 'Ah, I knew that you would help me. I knew that you would call Mr Ponnusamy in without delay and order him to give me access to my privy.'

Playing for time Ferdach answered, 'Well I can't do that right away Mrs Sitalakshmi. The office is already closed. I'll have to ask him to come in.'

'Of course, Tuan. I quite understand. In due course will do for me.' She gave him a subtle smile, her eyes half closed. 'Everything that is really satisfying takes time.'

Ferdach was beguiled, feeling the familiar rush of blood in his loins. The woman's problem could present him with no difficulties. Mr Ponnusamy could be made to see sense. In the meantime there was this gorgeous woman before him, looking friendlier as each minute went by. He had never slept with an Indian woman; the chance might arise when the matter of her privy was solved. The thought of exciting positions as set forth in the *Kamasutra* tantalised his mind. He was not listening to what she was saying very carefully, her melodious tones had a hypnotic quality about them, but it gradually dawned on him that she was telling him, at considerable length, the story of her life. It did not seem out of the ordinary, a middleclass Ipoh girl with an English education at a local convent, an early marriage to a business executive in the famed firm of Jardine Mathieson, unusually no children and, sadly, her doting husband's early death. But this was followed by an even more unusual factor: certainly not suttee which not so long ago in India she might have expected but a pension that would keep her comfortably for life in a somewhat superior New Village house on the outskirts of Ipoh. All of a sudden Mr Ponnusamy's kindly interest in her sanitary arrangements fell into place. As if in telepathic confirmation of his suspicions Mrs Sitalakshmi stated very forcibly, 'Mr Ponnusamy is a very bad man. He has been pestering me ever since our *jamban*s were erected. If I went to relieve myself he would go to his *jamban* at the same time and make suggestions which I did not wish to hear. When I refused him he became angry. You will not be able to observe his nastiness when you speak to him, Tuan O'Haney. But he did something to me, he would never dare to do to you.' There was a long pause ended by Mrs Sitalakshmi of the flashing eyes declaring, 'He made a revelation of himself to me in a most obscene way.'

Ferdach caught on straightaway even though 'revelation' sounded rather biblical. Obviously, even if bizarrely, Mr Ponnusamy must have thought that the display of his private parts, presumably by lifting up his *dhoti*, would convince Mrs Sitalakshmi of his enthusiasm, and no doubt his suitability, to be her spouse. All the same Ferdach temporised, 'Perhaps you were mistaken Mrs Sitalakshmi. Maybe he was just adjusting his *dhoti*.'

Mrs Sitalakshmi's voice became shrill. 'He was in an unbridled state of tumescence. Nothing was left to my imagination. I could see his entire genitalia. I can prove it. There is a wart on one side of his penis. You may see for yourself. Then you could tell him that since you know from me about his bodily parts, you know my allegation is well founded and that I must have unrestricted access to my privy without let or hindrance.' Mrs Sitalakshmi was certainly aware of all the medical and legal terms relevant to her case.

Ferdach's passing lust for this determined woman subsided as soon as he began to suspect that she might be troublesome. If Mr Ponnusamy was equally adamant, this was a situation which he could never resolve. He stood up to indicate that the interview was over, saying that he would do his best for her. As he did so, no longer wishing to maintain eye contact, he glanced sideward through an open window that had not yet been shuttered for the night by the office boy. When doing so he saw a Rolls Royce, with pennant flying, gliding slowly by, with only two police outriders as escort. Obviously Sir Henry Gurney was here. A single question immediately occupied his mind: was it just possible that he had with him a reply to Chin Peng's letter? The more he thought about it, the less he thought it likely but he could not drive speculation from his brain. He became aware of Mrs Sitalakshmi's perfume again. He also became aware of the slightest of touches of her hip against him. Everything suddenly seemed incongruous. He was at one and the same time concerned with a woman's privy in Kampung Pandan and with the possibility of a reply that might affect the future of the country. He heard her repeating something that she must have said already. 'There'll be no taxis or pedicabs around here at this time. Could you give me a lift home Tuan?'

'I'd be glad to do so Mrs Sitalakshmi but I wouldn't like Mr Ponnusamy to see us arriving together. He might question my impartiality when I ask him to come here. Then it might be difficult to help you.'

Mrs Sitalakshmi saw the point and contented herself by saying that it would be fine to drop her in town, say in Hugh Low Street. In fact Ferdach did not do this either for a thousand eyes might see them there. Instead, he went by a circuitous route to a cinema on a side of town not far from Kampung Pandan; there, pedicabs were always waiting outside the ever crowded Mumbai Cinema. Having dropped his passenger whose perfume seemed likely to hover for days inside his little Morris, some instinct made him drive at once to Sturrock Road. A number of cars were parked around the compound and boozy conversation was coming from upstairs. Above the din the voice of Ericson balled through a window. 'Ferdach, that you? A bloke called Staples phoned a minute ago. He wants you to take some photos or other to Albakri's house.'

There was no doubt what it meant in Ferdach's mind. Staples was HE's Private Secretary. Writing letters home would have to wait. Quickly he fished out the photos of HE in the garden of King's House, shoved them into an old Manila envelope, got in his car and, unwashed and rather sweaty, drove rapidly across town to the State Secretary's residence. The

Rolls Royce was parked under the portico.

'That was quick,' said Staples a courteous man of kindly appearance. He must have seen Ferdach's precipitous arrival and was on the steps to meet him. 'No need to have come at once. Sir Henry isn't like Montgomery you know. Tomorrow would have done. I could have given the photos to HE myself but I think he wants to thank you for them.'

Ferdach glanced from the hall into the long reception room where Albakri and his guests were dining. A ceiling fan wafted the delicious aromas of a Malay banquet towards him. Staples saw Ferdach's questioning look. 'HE asked to be excused. He's a bit tired. He's in the study. Please follow me.'

'Oh do go back into dinner, old chap,' Staples was told by Sir Henry as he rose to greet Ferdach. 'Tuan Haji left me in charge here, especially of all this forbidden stuff.' He gestured at a table bearing a wide variety of drinks. 'So I can offer Mr O'Haney a drink myself. Will it be sherry or something stronger?'

'A *stengah*, sir,' replied Ferdach nodding his thanks to Staples who was already at the door. He felt certain that the Private Secretary, though a model of efficiency, had no idea what was afoot. The moment the door was closed, he opened the foolscap-sized Manila envelope in which he had put his run-of-the-mill photos. When he took them out he said, 'They're not much to look at.'

'Of course not. They're of me,' said Sir Henry hardly glancing at the snapshots that Ferdach had placed on the table. 'But that large Manila envelope will be useful.' From his inside pocket he drew out an envelope. Having indicated that it was addressed to Mr Kwok Lai Kuan, Sir Henry slid it into the Manila envelope.

As they sat opposite one another Ferdach hoped that Sir Henry might reveal something, however slight, about his reply to Chin Peng, for though nothing had been spoken, he assumed it was contained in the envelope for Lai Kuan. He was to be disappointed. Yet not entirely so for after a pause during which Ferdach took a deep gulp of a *stengah* that was almost entirely whiskey with only a nod of soda, Sir Henry said, 'When we last met, you reminded me that you were on the Chinese side.'

Without thinking Ferdach protested, 'I hope I'm on both sides, sir. I admire the Malays and the Chinese.' Then, 'And the Indians,' he added, fleetingly remembering Mrs Sitalakshmi's olive midriff. 'But they all have different qualities.'

Sir Henry smiled. 'You misunderstand me; I meant you're still one of the young men assigned to learn Chinese.'

Ferdach hesitated, unsure of what was coming next. 'Ah yes sir. I did. I shouldn't have troubled you about it.' He had all but given up hope of ever learning the language. 'In any case I'm told that the Macau scheme has folded completely.'

'Not exactly. Last year we were so short of staff that many schemes had to fall by the wayside. We needed every man on the Briggs Plan.'

'Including geologists,' popped out of Ferdach's mouth.

'Yes,' said Sir Henry. 'Yes, I know about the young geologist who was killed here. I regret it so much. I feel responsible.'

'It's not your fault, sir,' Ferdach said magnanimously though he could not help feeling that someone, perhaps at not so rarefied a level as Sir Henry, must be.

'Well that's how things go in government. You take a decision and the unexpected always seems to happen.' Abruptly Sir Henry changed tack. 'Would you like to go to Macau for language study? We'll need more Chinese speakers. We can spare some cadets to go there now.'

Unambiguously Ferdach declared, 'Yes, I would. I would indeed, sir.' After all that was why he had joined the bloody service.

'Good. Because as I said, in government the unexpected invariably happens. Now, none of us can be sure how this will turn out.' Sir Henry tapped the envelope that lay on the severely carved ebony table inlaid with yellowing ivory that lay between them. 'It may go wrong and when things go wrong all sorts of people get blamed. What do the Americans say? "The shit hits the fan." Very vulgar, but very good. Blame can land anywhere and everywhere. So I'm glad you want to learn Chinese in Macau.'

Ferdach's thoughts raced at once to HE's envelope. His reply could not be negative or else his remark about people getting hurt when things went wrong would be superfluous. He decided to be bold, 'But if I'm in Macau there'd be no further use for me, as the go-between?'

Sir Henry looked at him shrewdly. 'So that brain of yours has been working out what's in my envelope? Well, let me put it like this:

if the reaction to my message is quick, you may have one more thing to do. If it's slow, I don't see how the matter can remain secret. The intelligence people have ways of sniffing things out, they have moles in the communist camp, and then they'll want to muscle in. Now I've given you a hint why I want you out of the way once your last job is done. If things don't go well, you could easily be accused by your superiors in the service of failing to keep them informed. That's a serious offence. But out of sight, though not foolproof, out of mind.' Sir Henry stared at Ferdach as if waiting for some reaction. As there was none, he continued, 'I take it you'll get the envelope to Lai Kuan without delay.'

'I'll go straight to his house with it.' Ferdach replied, ommitting to say it was a house where their joint mistress was also holed up.

'I suggest you keep it on your person. Locked drawers in houses and offices seem to tempt people, or should I say moles.'

'I'll keep it with me.'

'Good. Until this is all done, you'll be vulnerable.'

Ferdach certainly recognised the risk to himself. Yet the whole business fascinated him. From the daily grind of resettlement work he had been drawn into at least the periphery of an important negotiation that might affect the future of the country, of Southeast Asia even. He could no more turn his back on it than a moth could escape a flame. He prayed that Chin Peng's reply to Sir Henry would be fast.

72

Ferdach was good at getting Laura out of a sulk, such as the one she was in when he reached the Kuok guesthouse where Laura had been staying in Ipoh. He did so by diverting her interest, on this occasion to the problem of Mrs Sitalakshmi and her lavatory which he made to sound extremely bizarre. Before long Laura was hooting with laughter and wondering, without a hint of sympathy, whether Mrs Sitalakshmi had made arrangements to use other people's *jamban*s? Or did she wait until she came into town? Or was she likely to explode? It was all so ribald that Laura quickly forgot the cause of her irritation: Ferdach's unexpected arrival when she had promised herself a quiet evening.

'And you stink to high heaven,' she said. 'When did you last have a shower? And look at your clothes, all soiled and sweaty.' Before long she had peeled off his offending garments, as well as her own, and led him to the sumptuous bathroom with its deep tub and showers where she soaped him all over. This led to an amphibious love session that resulted in water spilling all over the floor and even running into the air-conditioned bedroom.

'This will make Lai Kuan jealous,' said Ferdach looking at the mess when they emerged drying themselves on fleecy white towels, each with a red Chinese character for Kuok embroidered in a corner. 'He'll think that you've been doing all sorts of things with me that you never do with him.' He felt sorry that Lai Kuan had not turned up already and wondered whether he would have joined them in the tub?

'How wrong you are,' was Laura's reply. 'Lai Kuan and I use our imagination. He knows all sorts of clever Chinese tricks. He's very creative where sex is concerned.'

'Tell that to the marines.'

'You mean the marines we had in Singapore?'

'Yes Laura. Do you think Lai Kuan would appreciate it if we told him what you and I got up to with those guys?'

'You don't know him very well Ferdie. I told him the whole story. I gave lurid descriptions, exaggerated of course. He loved them; he's as depraved as you. If Lai Kuan had been given half a chance he'd have joined in.' Laura sat down before a circular actor's dressing room mirror framed with small light bulbs which became a nimbus around her reflection. As she brushed her hair she occasionally glanced in it at Ferdach mooching around the room behind her, his towel draped over his shoulders and his body naked from the waist downward. He put on a popular Japanese record and began to sway his arse to its jerky rhythm. Maybe the sight was meant to tantalise her but she decided that if it was, two could play at the game. 'Ferdie, I told Lai Kuan things about myself that I've never told you.'

'Really, dear,' he replied without ceasing to move his hips. 'Such as what? That you were captain of the school hockey eleven?'

'No, nothing so exciting; just dreary stuff like how I was seduced by my father when I was fourteen.'

Ferdach stopped dancing and came beside her. He looked at her image intently before asking very gently, 'Was it terrible? The experience I mean.'

'Not really. I liked my dad. It seemed natural somehow. He knew how to make love. After a bit I really enjoyed it.'

'Did it go on for long; I mean how many months, or years?'

'Oh for years, until I went to university.'

'But what about your mother? Didn't she ever find out?'

'My mother knew from the beginning and she was glad. It got him off her back. She was a bit of an invalid, by design I think.'

'Wasn't Lai Kuan shocked?'

'Of course not. He said such things take place the world over among poor people, especially in the slums, and among not so poor people too.'

Ferdach sat beside her, put an arm around her waist and said, 'Poor Laura I'm so sorry. It must have had a tremendous effect on you.'

Laura removed his arm. 'I can't comb my hair with you clutching me like that. Do get up and take that record off. What were you saying? A tremendous effect on me? Of course it did. It made me love men, making love with men. It taught me what all men are like, what all men want and it taught me that I too can do what I like without the least bit of shame. Once I'd left my father I began to make my own choices, many choices, and I've never looked back. I seem to remember a smart prostitute in a French film saying something like, '*L'amour est tellement simple pour ceux qui aiment comme nous*'. That's it Ferdie. Love is so simple for those who love like us, like you and me Ferdie. Exactly my philosophy.' Laura chuckled and added, 'Alfred was a mistake of course. I only married him to get to somewhere more exotic than Hackney.' She turned to Ferdach who was gazing at her with a blank expression. 'Why are you staring like that? Have you lost your tongue? Are you shocked or something?'

'No, no, I've always wondered what made you so promiscuous. No, sorry, I'm just trying to take it all in.'

'Yes, promiscuous. The man's way.' Her irritation grew. 'When I told my story to Lai Kuan, he comprehended what I was saying straight away. He didn't say poor Laura. Poor Laura indeed! Lucky Laura I'd say. You know, I really like Lai Kuan. He lives in the world as it is, raw and hard.'

Ferdach went to sprawl on the huge bed and gazed up at the ceiling which had a number of artfully angled mirrors fitted to it so that lovers could get a clear view of their activities. He had suggested that Lai Kuan might be jealous only to find that for the first time, it was he who was feeling jealous, about Lai Kuan. But was it jealousy? Well, not exactly jealousy in a sexual way; Ferdach was always interested in other people's love making rather than jealous of it. It did not take him long to identify his real feeling. It was fear. Lai Kuan was rich enough to offer Laura everything she might dream of and clearly too, he had shown Laura great understanding. 'You're really impertinent,' he said angrily when Laura had at last decided, after fixing her hair, which took at least ten more minutes, to snuggle up against him. 'I'm not depraved. If you use that word about making love it just shows what a lower middleclass puritanical outlook you have on life.' He ranted on in such manner for a few minutes before running dry.

Laura exploded with laughter. 'Who's the puritan then? Preach, preach, preach. It's puritans who preach. Come on Ferdie what's eating you up now?'

Ferdach turned towards her and held her close in his arms almost squeezing her to him. It was best to be honest at this juncture. He had been thinking what she meant to him for some time and he had come to understand his need. Surely he was not too late? 'I don't want to lose you Laura. I don't care how often you make love with Lai Kuan or Tengku Mizan or twenty marines. I'm happy when you do so. But I don't want to lose you to any one of them. And I guess when you told me about the secrets you have with Lai Kuan but not with me, you set the alarm bells ringing.' He looked at her solidly, making direct eye contact that she returned unflinchingly. 'I'm not going to lose you to Lai Kuan for my lack of a crock of gold am I Laura?'

'Oh you silly fool. Not to Lai Kuan. Not even to Mizan.' Immediately she wondered why she had said, 'not even'. She hoped Ferdie had not noticed it and covered up the slip by going on, more vehemently, 'Or to anyone. Are you blind? Can't you see why I've come up here? I feel as you do; I belong to you as completely as you belong to me. I don't mind you going with other women, and I won't worry when you fall for young men. That's your nature; I want you to feel free to explore what you are. All the things we do separately, your activities and mine, should be like buttresses pushing us together because we understand why each of us needs to do them.'

Up till then it had been Ferdach's custom to become facetious or evasive the moment emotional seriousness arose between them. For once, he felt no need to follow custom. As he held Laura in his arms he experienced a wave of assurance rising from deep within his body, or so it seemed, up to his mind. He believed, without any reservations, that he and Laura could trust one another; some insubstantial barrier had been crossed. Now too, for the first time, he felt no need to make love as proof that she meant something to him. It was a contented feeling that banished worry. So serene was the experience that he began to feel drowsy until, distantly, he heard Laura's voice saying, 'You look very tired Ferdie. Let's sleep for a while, a long while. Lai Kuan is only coming back tomorrow afternoon.'

To Laura's surprise, instead of following her bidding, Ferdie opened his eyes wide at the name Lai Kuan. Only back tomorrow, he had echoed, almost wildly she thought. 'But I've got to see him before that. I've got to go outstation tomorrow. I can't get out of it, an important meeting, a corruption case.' He sat up. 'My envelope. I put it down on that table when you were taking off my clothes.'

'Envelope,' exclaimed Laura. 'Why, I thought you didn't want it. It was open at one end. It looked used. I thought you'd done with it.'

Ferdach jumped up. 'Where is it?' he shouted in alarm. The thought of going back to Sir Henry and asking for another copy of such a document was ridiculous. He would look a fool. In fact he would be a fool. 'It must be somewhere.'

'Of course it is, in the waste paper basket in the corner. Go and see.'

Ferdach had already shot across the room like a dart, taken the Manila envelope from the basket and made sure that Sir Henry's envelope was still inside. He slumped down on the floor and let out a long deep sigh. He also, like an idiot, let the cat out of the bag. 'My God Laura. You gave me such a shock. It's from the High Commissioner.'

Sleep was out of the question. Laura would not be satisfied until she knew everything. She was also quick to put two and two together. She remembered him telling her about a message from Chin Peng. ' So you're holding Gurney's reply,' she stated. 'You must know what it says. The envelope has been opened.'

Ferdach squatted naked like an Indian Holy Man on the bed holding the envelope out to her. 'Gurney's reply to Chin Peng is inside this envelope addressed to Lai Kuan. I don't know what's in either. I have to get them to Lai Kuan.' The words tripped out of his mouth without hesitation. He knew that his big mouth had twice hinted enough for her to build an edifice. Yet why should he not tell her? He was certain that she and he were now bound together as one? There need be no secrets for their trust had become absolute.

'And in due course he'll get the one that really matters to Chin Peng.'

'Yes. Somehow or other he'll do that. I don't know how. I'm to be given some other small job. Probably one more reply to King's House. But after that Sir Henry's making sure that I am out of the country, so no one in government can say I've been acting improperly.'

It was Laura's turn to look worried? 'You mean back to the UK? Oh no Ferdie. Not England. It's still so awful. Do you really want to work in the Colonial Office in Great Smith Street? It'll be more rationing and no coal in winter.'

'No, not to England. To Macau. To learn Chinese.'

Laura's face slowly metamorphosed from gloom to delight as she perceived the many implications of the move. Suddenly she cried out, 'How wonderful. I'll come too. We'll start again. Just living together at first to make sure we can do it and then something else if you want. Oh Ferdie, Ferdie, how marvellous.' She flung her arms around him and covered his face with sloppy kisses. They both took to laughing at what might lie ahead for them. Laura rolled around the bed in delight. 'You'll become a Chinese scholar, no a sage and I'll cook the onions.' Then, 'I'll be a sybarite and you'll be a sodomite and I'll be in Cathay afore thee,' she sang gaily. 'Oh Ferdie, we'll try Chinese men and Portuguese, and all the mixtures in between. There are even African soldiers from Mozambique so I'm told. Oh Ferdie, everything's going to be so different once we are out of this country with its bloody Emergency. We'll never come back here again.'

Ferdach slept exceedingly well and when he awoke there were his trousers nicely pressed and some of Lai Kuan's silk underwear and a shirt all laid neatly out for him. A new white envelope was on the coffee table. 'The two letters are inside it,' Laura said. 'It doesn't look so tatty now.'

They started on the breakfast that a pretty Chinese girl, one of Lai Kuan's reserve delicacies, had brought in. Ferdach said, 'I'll give Lai Kuan the letter when I come back to Ipoh.'

Laura poured out strong coffee and then condensed milk into two oversized breakfast cups. 'It's amazing how a vice can grow on one,' she said. 'Do you know I'm beginning to like this foul stuff.' Trippingly she added, as though it was of no consequence, 'Ferdie, I don't think you should carry a letter like that around with you. Supposing you were in an incident, an ambush even.'

'It's most unlikely. I'll risk it.'

'How could you dream of taking a risk with letters like that Ferdie.' Laura sounded genuinely cross but then she added with a look of concern, 'In any case, I'm worried about that extra job HE wants you to do. Lai Kuan's letter may say something about it. Don't be railroaded into doing something dangerous. I'm not going to let you put your neck into a noose

Ferdie.' Without asking his permission she picked up the envelope, put it in a side table drawer and locked it. 'Let me give it to Lai Kuan. I'll find out what I can before you see him.'

Her sudden action took Ferdach aback. For an instant he felt dubious, remembering what he had promised Sir Henry. Then he thought that the letter had, after all, been delivered to Lai Kuan's house and was much safer in that locked drawer than in his own pocket, or his car, or anywhere outstation. In any case, speed was of the essence. Laura could be trusted to hand it to Lai Kuan more quickly than he could, taken up as he was by his duties outside Ipoh.

73

Waite had taken a much-needed break in Penang and Ferdach was under pressure to deal with a number of problems that had arisen in his absence. Several arose from constructional matters in the New Villages where allegations of corruption against contractors had been made. Then more corruption had come to light concerning illegal logging in the forest area near to Kampung Tanah Hitam. Unfortunately, this involved a Scottish ex-Palestine police officer called Aleister Kinloch. It was Waite's policy, in the first instance, to give corrupt building contactors the opportunity of repairing defective work at their own expense but in the case of the illegal logging this was not possible. Great hardwood trees were very valuable and this fact must have tempted a self-proclaimed straightforward Scot into collusion with loggers and, much worse, with CTs. Since the Forestry Service officers were not only overstretched but worked in a dangerous environment, they could not keep a watch on all logging. Some timber firms were willing to pass money over to both the CTs and the police if the safety of their loggers could be guaranteed. After an initial enquiry Ferdach saw that he had no alternative but to refer the matter to police headquarters. It worried him to do this as he knew Mrs Kinloch who was a simple homely woman. But more worrying was the fact that despite phone calls to Laura he could not find out whether she had passed that all important letter to Lai Kuan or indeed where she had disappeared to. He could do nothing but wait to hear from her.

Other issues would have to be dealt with when Waite returned but there was one ongoing matter which could be passed to no one, that of Mrs Sitalakshmi's lavatory. As promised, as soon as Ferdach returned to Ipoh he called in Mr Ponnusamy to ask him to be reasonable and let his neighbour cross his land to her *jamban*. Ferdach was at his most persuasive doing this, offering Mr Ponnusamy a coffee, which he accepted and a cigarette, which he refused. A cold reptilian glint seemed to strengthen in his eyes as he listened to Ferdach's mellifluous words.

A tall hatchet-faced man wearing an impeccably white *dhoti* that he kept adjusting as he sat there, Mr Ponnusamy stayed silent for a little while, as though in deep thought, before replying, 'I can see that you are a very civilised English gentleman Sahib and I am respecting you profoundly. And to demonstrate that I am not unmoved by your words I will endeavour to compromise.' Ferdach beamed on hearing this. Mr Ponnusamy resumed, 'Mrs Sitalakshmi may use her *jamban*, even though it is actually situated on my plot, but I cannot agree to her crossing my land to get there.'

'Why not sir?'

Mr Ponnusamy's head gyrated from side to side, 'I am having to tell you sir, that Mrs Sitalakshmi is a very bad woman. I will not be having my garden defiled.'

'Tell me please; how is she a bad woman?'

'You must ask my son. He is only sixteen years of age.'

Ferdach felt his exasperation growing. 'But I don't see your son here. Do you want to bring him to me?'

'Oh Sahib, I know how valuable your time is. So to be of assistance to you, I shall speak on my son's behalf.' Mr Ponnusamy's face seemed to become narrower and tenser than ever. 'I must confess to you Sahib, with apologies for my immodesty, that Mrs Sitalakshmi placed her hand on my son's privy member. She is a very bad woman.'

Ferdach almost let out a groan. His purview now extended from a meeting between the head of the Malayan Communist Party and the High Commissioner to a sixteen-year-old boy's prick. 'I cannot interfere in such personal matters. But to cut things short Mr Ponnusamy, please suggest to me how Mrs Sitalakshmi is to reach her *jamban*?'

Mr Ponnusamy waved his hands airily, 'Sahib, that will be her business. Oh pardon me sir. I am not making a vulgar joke.' Nevertheless a sly grin passed momentarily over his face before he went on, 'She could go through the garden behind both of our properties.'

At the end of two successive afternoons when Ferdach was feeling jaded there were more interviews with the rival jambanistas. Mrs

Sitalakshmi told him angrily that to use her privy in the manner suggested, would oblige her first to ford a ditch behind her land only to reach a plot that was not merely waterlogged but belonged to Mr Ponnusamy's brother. Discussion with Mr Ponnusamy and his son, who apparently basked in his father's caring protection, resulted in more allegations about Mrs Sitalakshmi's deplorable sexual mores. At this point Ferdach thought it advisable to call on Mr Arunasalam for assistance who said that he would question the son without his father being present. Ferdach then listened to an interminable discussion between Mr Arunasalam and Ponnusamy junior in Tamil which was punctuated from time to time by the older man with the English words 'masturbation' and 'fellatio', no doubt to show Ferdach which way the discussion was heading. Later the word 'congress' occurred so often that it sounded as though the pair had progressed to a discussion on Indian politics. Clerks, typists and office boys paused in their labours to grin at sleek young Ponnusamy who wagged his head to and fro as he spoke and looked mighty pleased with himself all the time. Finally Mr Arunasalam announced his conclusion: on the youth's own admission, full sexual congress had indeed occurred between him and Mrs Sithalakshmi on five occasions and in her house. It was clear that the lad had been not only willing but lucky where his father had not.

At last, one dark and thunderous evening, Ferdach had to confess to the parties his total failure as an arbitrator. Mr Ponnusamy would not give way though he said, with a barely concealed grin revealing teeth stained red with betel, that he had already punished his son with the first of five unmerciful thrashings, intended Ferdach had no doubt, to hurt both of the lovers even more. Mrs Sithalakshmi stared at Ferdach icily, declared that she would take her neighbour to court and swept out of the office after throwing him a glance of supreme contempt. Ferdach was not unused to setback but this failure really got to him. He suspected that his disappointment was, in an obscure way, connected with the sight of Mr Ponnusamy's rat like face and the scented memory of Mrs Sitalakshmi's midriff. Then the roar of the tropical downpour roused him to run after her to drive her home, but she was already gone.

He made a dash for his car using a woman's umbrella left behind by a secretary. By the time he was in the driving seat he was wet through from the waist downwards. On the way to Sturrock Road he found that the downpour was too heavy for the windscreen wipers to cope properly. He had just managed to cross the Kinta River which he could hear surging wildly below against the bridge when he remembered that nearby, just off Hugh Low Street, there was a bar where Lai Kuan and his rich cronies sometimes met. Everyone called it the Snake Pit because though punningly named in both Chinese and English, Baa Baa, the Chinese character used for the two bleats meant a large snake. Ferdach liked the place because he had never seen any other expatriates there. Downstairs it was no more than a well-stocked bar but through a door and upstairs there was a comfortable air-conditioned room available only to habitués. The barman knew him, saw how wet he was and asked him if he would like to go up. It was almost as if he was expected.

As the bar was empty Ferdach took off his trousers and said to the barman, 'Lend me a sarong first and dry these.' Ferdach exchanged wet trousers for a brandy dry and made his way up to the comfort of the air-conditioned room. He never expected to find Lai Kuan in that room, much less Harry Wong. Both of them sprang to their feet and Harry pulled out a revolver.

'How did you know we are here?' Lai Kuan shouted angrily. 'God man. Harry might have shot you. We both thought it was a raid.'

Ferdach was equally shocked but he quickly played it down. 'I don't think the army or the police carry out raids using people in green and red sarongs and wet shirts.' He said sitting down calmly. 'I had no idea you were here. And I've not seen anyone here but you Lai Kuan.' Dubiously the two Chinese men sat down though Harry was reluctant to put away his gun. In fact he just left it on a nearby table within reach. This annoyed Ferdach. 'You may not have noticed but it's raining outside and I'm just seeking shelter,' he added sarcastically. 'Can't you see that I've just come up by chance.'

At the word 'chance' Harry Wong seemed to become his old self. A gleam came into his eyes. 'But chance is always ordered. It's like going into a temple and shaking the bamboo spills until some jump out. Then you look at their numbers and find their meaning in the Book of Changes. There's always a meaning underlying chance.'

At this the more sceptical Lai Kuan, pouring himself a large scotch, said, 'Just listen to the rational Marxist. You'd be bloody clever if you can understand a word that the *I Ching* tells you. The last time my grandmother took me to the family shrine I shook the spills and was told, 'Deliver yourself from the great toe. Then the companion comes and he you can trust.' Now what do think that could mean?'

'You'd need a Confucian scholar to explain it,' said Harry, shaking his head as if some profound mystery had been encountered.

Ferdach was ready, as ever, to play mental games. 'Oh I don't know. It sounds very reasonable to me. Your great toe probably symbolises a claw, holding you to the earth, in a way holding you prisoner. But now comes your companion, Harry of course. You can trust him to free you, or maybe enslave you; my vision goes a bit hazy at that point.'

They looked at one another, as if unsure how the other would take Ferdach's mockery, yet seconds later burst into yells of wild laughter. They had become schoolboys again, playing the fool, capable of laughing at any bit of nonsense hilariously until Harry stood up, took his gun, and put it to Ferdach's lips. 'Suck it Ferdie, suck it. What do you think Lai Kuan? Isn't Ferdie too good for this world. Shall I send him to the next, to frighten the ghosts?' Ferdach kept his calm, for five full seconds, which is a long time under those conditions. Then Harry put the gun down, a great relief to its target, and took to stroking his victim's hair and then mauling his head and shoulders; indeed he seemed on the point of roughing him up as boys do to one another on a playing field when Lai Kuan interrupted his game and said heavily, 'That's enough Harry. Very well, Ferdie says he's here unexpectedly but if so his spirit must have known that we've got important matters to talk about. That's what drew him here. Chance was only hiding an omen of success.'

Inwardly Ferdach was far from calm nor did he agree with, or understand, Lai Kuan's metaphysical view of this chance encounter. Sitting in a room with a known and, so it seemed, a slightly hysterical terrorist one who, according to report, could unconcernedly cut a man's throat, made him apprehensive. Perhaps Harry was going off it. However, the presence of Lai Kuan was at least reassuring and his mind began to dwell on Sir Henry's replies to both Chin Peng and to Lai Kuan. Then the depressing thought struck him that maybe Laura had failed or forgotten or decided not to hand the letters over. Maybe, wanting his safety she had reckoned on his posting to Macau taking place quickly so that the messages could be delivered when the two of them had gone there. But then again, he thought, no, she would never dare to do any such thing.

In the latter supposition he was right for Lai Kuan said, 'I've read the High Commissioner's letter to me, and I know from it that in his reply to the Secretary General he has accepted the idea of a joint meeting, in principal. I don't know what details he's proposing. I'd better say right now that all I've told Laura is that you may still be needed as a courier. I had to since she'd seen the envelopes. Of course, she doesn't want you to get involved but there's no danger in what you'll have to do. As Laura was still worried I told her that you'll be back in KL soon with not much to do except deliver another letter. So she'll have plenty of time to be with you. She went back on the train by herself.' Observing Ferdach's frown, Lai Kuan said, 'She's quite all right, isn't she Harry?' Harry gave one of his beautiful smiles that Ferdach returned though not so convincingly for, despite the sensual stirring that came over him, strongly but unbidden, in the terrorist's presence, he distrusted him completely.

'So Laura's got some idea of what I've got to do. But you still haven't spelt the detail out to me,' said Ferdach glumly. The whole business was starting to depress him. What a fool he had been to let Laura know more than she had guessed. With a sigh he remarked, 'I should have taken more care to conceal that envelope from Laura.' For an instant he thought of asking why Harry should be in on it all either, but he knew better than to question the workings of the Communist Party

'There's no risk where Laura's concerned. She's devoted to you, and she's dependent on me. She's the one person not involved who knows about the letters.' Lai Kuan's assurance made Ferdach recall the High Commissioner's remark that a matter like this could not be kept secret for long. He was right. Everyone had one person to whom he could speak in confidence, or to whom he felt it was his duty to speak, with certainty that the news would go no further. But those trusted recipients always had one person they could trust too so that, intended or not, news and rumour spread like a forest fire.

'So what's the drill now?' Ferdach asked despondently.

'Well it's quite simple. Gurney's letter was taken to Chin Peng the day after Laura handed it to me. It was taken by Harry here.' Ferdach glanced at Harry Wong who once again bent a warm smile on him. 'And Harry has returned and told me that the Secretary General agrees with a stipulation concerning yourself.'

'Stipulation concerning myself? What the hell does that mean?'

'I've told you: it's quite simple. Chin Peng's reply to HE has to be delivered by you to King's House. Now what could be easier than that?'

'Then where is the reply?' asked Ferdach feeling somewhat relieved and inclined to get the whole matter over as quickly as possible. 'I take it Harry has it with him?'

'Well, no. Chin Peng sees it exactly as Gurney sees it. He will only put his reply into your hands, with no other go-between.'

Ferdach's relief had quite dissipated and he started to gabble, 'That means I have to see him, to visit him. I'd be doing something illegal. It's not something I can do without permission. It's too risky. Are you sure you didn't tell this to Laura? You said she was still worried. Was this the reason?'

'Calm down, Ferdie. When I told her you might have to take another letter to King's House, Harry hadn't returned. Even I didn't know about the single go-between stipulation. So how could Laura know that you'd have to see Chin Peng?'

Ferdach decided to dig his feet in. 'No. It's out of the question. I can't do it without official sanction,' he said, certain that this made the task impossible.

'You already have the High Commissioner's permission to do it, no, his orders in writing, here in his letter to me. Obviously the two dealers in this game want to limit the number of intermediaries to one. Isn't that reasonable?' When Ferdach remained obdurate Lai Kuan paused to ask Harry Wong to order some food from the barman below but once Harry had gone down the stairs, he said quietly, 'But there's another reason: in the communist camp as in the government there are people who will oppose the meeting; people who'll do anything to stop it. One can depend on no one: so the fewer the fingers, the better. You see why only a single messenger will do.'

'I do indeed,' replied Ferdach coldly. 'And the reason you've given puts the messenger, puts me, even more at risk. If any one of these mysterious hostile people, whom I'll have no way of recognising, suspects what's going on, they'll want to get their fingers on the message, and on me. You've just said as much yourself.' He stood up, opened the door and peered down the stairway. No one was to be seen. 'And what about Harry? He might be hostile. He's so volatile. I've never met a communist like him. Yes, I like him. Sometimes he looks like beauty itself and sometimes I suspect that he's mad. I admit I'm intrigued by him but he unnerves me.'

'Nothing worthwhile is ever completely without risk,' said Lai Kuan, in a grandly philosophical way. Then he took Ferdach's hands in his own and whispered, as though to a fellow conspirator, 'My good friend, the risk and the job are small. But you'll be doing something to advance the cause of peace in Malaya, which we both long for. You and I believe in that cause. I know you'll do what's required of you.'

By the time Harry Wong returned to tell them that the barman had sent out for food from a Chinese-owned fish and chip shop much patronised by the British soldiery stationed in Ipoh, and increasingly popular with the locals, Ferdach had succumbed and was sitting, quiet as a lamb, smoking ganja with Lai Kuan. Harry looked pleased. 'It's against Party discipline to smoke that stuff,' he said, 'but since I've been ordered to blend into my surroundings you can give me a cigarette.' As Lai Kuan was rolling another ganja cigarette, Harry took to running his fingers through Ferdach's hair again; it seemed to fascinate him. 'Don't worry about anything Ferdie. You'll be very safe with me,' he murmured. 'I'll be the one to guide you to Chin Peng.'

74

'You were pissed out of your mind last night,' said Ericson over breakfast. 'You look ghastly and it's only Wednesday. Who was that noisy Chinese bloke who drove you back?'

'Chinese bloke?' Ferdach tried to focus his mind on Ericson's question. 'What did he look like? Is he still here, this bloke as you call him?' His own question filled Ferdach's mind with anxiety. Now he remembered. Henry Wong, Harry, had taken the wheel of his car to drive him home.

'No, of course not,' put in Waite who had come back earlier than expected from Penang. 'We didn't see him because we didn't go downstairs but we could hear you both talking at the top of your voices. Then Lai Kuan's car came along. He shouted up to us that you'd been stuck in a bar because of the rain. Then he took the bloke off with him.'

'Ah yes I remember now,' said Ferdach affecting to recover his senses. He sighed with relief for there was every possibility that Waite might have recognized Harry from an intelligence photograph. 'The bloke was some crony or other of Lai Kuan. Probably also in tin. I don't know him. My god, those mining people can drink.'

'Which is more than can be said of you,' said Ericson, acerbic as ever.

Ferdach stroked his forehead and smiled weakly, a sort of acknowledgement of his guilt, but inwardly he had started to feel more shattered than his appearance suggested. He had just lied to Waite, the man he trusted above all others in Malaya, and lied about an important matter. Wong Chooi Fong, alias Henry Wong, alias Harry was a terrorist, known to have murdered George Carew. Harbouring a terrorist was itself a criminal offence, an offence of which Lai Kuan was also guilty.

His thoughts then turned to poor Alyson Carew. Wouldn't she want him to report her husband's killer? Ferdach shied away from the thought; Henry Wong had to do what he had done. It was said that George had been killed swiftly, not slowly as communist victims were often dealt with. That suggested a touch of mercy on Harry's part. Moreover, there was now the bigger picture for Ferdach to consider: both Gurney and Chin Peng wanted him as the sole message carrier. The only way he had of getting to the communist leader was to put himself in Harry's hands. What ghastly mess would arise if he were to report his companions at last night's carousing to the police. Far from being able to explain them away, he could only expect a criminal charge to be brought against himself, or, at best, instant dismissal from the Service. The peace negotiation, if such it was to be, would be set back, maybe prevented. Against that the capture of Henry Wong was mere trivia. Justice would have to wait, maybe forever.

Just then he noticed that Ericson's revolver was, unusually for him, to the right of his breakfast cup. Waite's was on the table as usual. 'Why the gun?' he asked. 'Are you expecting some woman's husband to pay a visit?'

'There was a bad incident last night in town,' Waite answered for Ericson. 'An attack on the house of a PWD engineer, Cecil Starkie. No casualties. Cecil and his wife were both upstairs when a grenade was thrown into their hall by a cyclist.'

Ferdach noticed that Waite had pronounced Cecil as Cicil whilst Ericson remarked blithely, 'Says something for the strength of teak floor boards doesn't it. Cecil's house was one of the oldest in town.'

Waite was not in a blithe mood. 'The situation's bad. The CTs are full of confidence. Our morale is slipping. We're not winning the Chinese villagers over.' He paused. 'We're not winning at all.'

'Not surprising given Bertelli's harsh policies,' said Ferdach hoping to suggest that other policies, those of Waite of course, might stem the flood.

'Bugger the policies. There's only one fact: most Chinese are thinking of China, of the rise of China. They think that China's take-over of Southeast Asia, is only a question of time, and they're probably right. Too late now for us to do a bloody thing.' With this depressing prognostication Ericson got up and made for his car.'

'Is he right, Waite?' Ferdach was thinking that if he was, the meeting of Chin Peng and Gurney might at least ensure that the take-over would result in a transition period devoid of bloodshed.

Waite looked perplexed. 'He could be, but it wouldn't be that simple. Even if the whole of Southeast Asia became communist, it wouldn't be Chinese Communism. An elephant can't swallow a whale.'

In the instant before Waite rose to leave for work Ferdach again thought of putting him completely in the picture of his unhappy involvement. He wanted advice badly. Ericson's prophecy and Waite's report of the CT's confidence made him suspect that Chin Peng was knowingly acting from strength. Maybe the cunning communist leader was enticing the High Commissioner into a trap. Perhaps the meeting should be aborted. But before he could speak, his fear of involving more people in his own criminal complicity made him say no more than, 'Cheerio Waite.' Quite clearly now he remembered Lai Kuan telling him, or rather ordering him, that his task as a courier must be undertaken during the coming weekend when no one would be likely to question his decision to visit Laura in Kuala Lumpur.

The dilemma in which he found himself made it difficult for Ferdach to concentrate on routine office work. So he drove out to visit a large New Village near to Chemor, to see if there were any problems involving administrative matters or people, but to his disappointment found none. The three assistant resettlement officers, all clever young men, none over twenty years old, each capable of speaking two or three Chinese dialects, the hearty English Red Cross lady in the well-attended clinic, the slightly arrogant and very handsome *penghulu*, an efficient Chinese Affairs officer and a tubby red faced police lieutenant, he encountered, all seemed to be getting on with their duties happily and confidently. The gloom of the breakfast table conversation was not apparent. It pleased him to observe villagers approaching the government staff with their difficulties without hesitation, and greeting him affably.

The village had matured quickly, maybe because most of the men were employed in tin mining or rubber and could afford to make improvements. The houses were no longer mere huts on raw patches of land; little outhouses had sprouted, palm leaf roofs were being replaced by corrugated zinc sheets which brilliantly reflected the noon sun or made a noise like thunder when struck by a tropical downpour. In this climate vegetation flourished to excess and luxuriant growth had softened the hard outlines of the village's first beginnings. The raw patches had become little gardens with fruit trees, bushes and rows of vegetables. Between the perimeter fences plots of land had been marked out and people were growing vegetables which would find a ready market locally or in Ipoh. The sound and smell of pigs, the crowing of cocks and the clucking of hens seemed to be everywhere, and a couple of placid pools of water, joyful with water lilies, had become the homes of somnolent carp. At first glance the place seemed almost idyllic as if the people had made the transition from living in unprotected clearings into a regularly planned settlement with ease. Of course, they were mainly Chinese and, Ferdach supposed, their industry had made success inevitable. But even the neat and clean Malay section of the village with its houses set high on stilts seemed poised to embark on mild affluence.

By the end of his visit Ferdach had come to the conclusion that both Waite and Ericson had been exaggerating the dangers. However as he was walking back to his car, accompanied by Assistant Chinese Affair Officer Lawrence Chong, Ferdach got a shock. In the depth of a coffeeshop they were passing Ferdach could have sworn that he glimpsed Harry Wong but he walked on without saying a word. This was more than could be said of Lawrence. An olive-skinned Chinese boy with black wavy hair that made him appear more Malay than Chinese and with a fine aquiline nose that made him look like a Rajput, Lawrence was the opposite of what a Chinese youth, at least in Ferdach's opinion, should be. He was irascible, only well mannered when it suited him, and had no respect whatsoever for his father, who was a prosperous contractor, or for family tradition. More than anything he wanted to quit Malaya and get to America which he envisaged as paradise. For almost an hour he had been pestering Ferdach for information about study in America and US immigration procedures. Ferdach knew virtually nothing about either. His one line of defence had been to say that such an ambition would require money, but this, it seemed, was not the problem. The family was rich but Mr Chong was unwilling to let Lawrence go, despite his being the number five son.

'Lawrence, it's a bit difficult to talk about your ambitions walking along in the hot sun. Let's go back to that coffeeshop we've just passed. We can have a couple of cold beers.'

Lawrence at once stopped gabbling about his problems. He frowned a little and then said, as if thinking only of Ferdach's interests, 'Oh I don't want to make you late Tuan. You've been here most of the day. We can talk about me another time. I don't matter.'

'Ah but you do matter,' Ferdach said extravagantly. 'Come on Lawrence, the coffeeshop.'

'Couldn't we go to another place? We could drive to Chemor. There are better eating places there. I know one where you can get very good *meehoon*. I'm sure you're hungry.'

'No. The local coffeeshop first Lawrence,' stated Ferdach, very firmly taking Lawrence's arm and all but spinning him around to walk back the way they had come.'

Lawrence was careful to walk behind Ferdach as they went into the shop whose owner, a swarthy Hainanese, short and muscular with one of the broadest faces imaginable, bustled forward and beckoned them to sit at a table near the entrance. As he went to get the beers Ferdach ordered, Harry Wong and the three men he was sitting with at the back of the shop, affected to be in deep conversation but the very walls seemed to know that they were conscious of Ferdach's presence. Lawrence took a deep gulp of his beer; he was trembling and his marvellous olive skin seemed to have blanched. Ferdach half expected him to dive into the storm drain when the men got up, only to leave by a back door, which was an unusual exit for customers. 'Please Tuan,' Lawrence whispered.'Let's leave now. My beer's not cold.'

'Mine is,' said Ferdach, 'but we'll leave if you want. We'll go back to your father's house in Ipoh. That's where he lives isn't it? But first I'm going to take you for a meal.'

On the way south to Ipoh observing how deeply Lawrence had slumped in his seat, Ferdach said, 'I think it's OK now Lawrence. They're not after us.'

The reply took some time in coming. 'You know who they are then?'

'Not entirely. You are going to tell me aren't you?'

Lawrence was tight lipped and for several miles concentrated on the roadside scenery which was not at all interesting consisting of rubber trees. At length Ferdach said, 'Let's put it like this Lawrence; you want to go to the US. Well, I'll find out everything I can about immigration and scholarships from the US Information Services in KL when I go there. You've got your Senior Cambridge haven't you?'

'Yes Tuan,' replied Lawrence starting to lose interest in the rubber estates.

'What would you want to study?'

'Economics mainly. I'd like to run my own business, in America.'

'And become a tycoon, much richer than your father. You know I've met him several times in connection with the work he's done in the New Villages and I know he's worried about you. He doesn't understand you, he says. He thinks you aren't ready to leave home. But maybe I could persuade him that it might be a good investment to send you abroad.'

'Would you Tuan?' Lawrence revealed his peerless set of teeth in a great smile.

'Yes, I would Lawrence. On one condition.'

'Tuan?'

'You tell me what goes on in your New Village, starting say with those men in the coffeeshop.'

Gradually, in the car and over dinner at the Station Hotel, which communists were not inclined to visit, Lawrence let it all out. The idyllic picture the New Village presented had mysterious shadows. Lawrence did not know Harry Wong, though he suspected that he was from the jungle, but he did know that the men he was talking to were Min Yuen members and important ones too. Part of the prosperity of the village was milked by them to supply the communists in the nearby jungle areas. The tribute, for such it was, comprised money, food, especially rice, medical supplies and, it went without saying, information on the movements of the security forces. In return the village was now left in peace, not only where its Chinese and Malay inhabitants were concerned but also in regard to those government officers whom Ferdach had seen that very day, for the communists admitted that the work they did was beneficial to the people whom they did not want to alienate. The truth was that Lawrence's New Village recognised two authorities: the daytime and the night-time governments, though the time spans of the two tended to overlap, as Ferdach had noticed in the coffeeshop.

In the course of listening to all this Ferdach posed a few oblique questions that enabled him to learn that the collusion to effect this extraordinary modus vivendi extended way beyond the villagers and the communists, to include the Malayan officers working in the village. Indeed Lawrence suspected that both Police Lieutenant Squires and Miss Grimshott, the Red Cross worker, were in the picture. He also wondered how the two New Village missionaries, Father O'Melia and the Seventh Day Adventist, Simon P. Wainright, could travel with impunity in and about the village at all hours with never a thought of peril. They must be at least aware of how things worked.

The next day when speaking to Mr Chong, Ferdach let drop some of the information he had winkled out of his son. Mr Chong grew alarmed fearing that if Ferdach passed it on to the police his son would become a CT target. In fact, Ferdach had no intention of telling anyone anything for he had, perhaps unwisely, brought himself to see in the modus vivendi a pattern for peace: if only the major protagonists could step back, ordinary people would work a still greater miracle. More realistically, when aware that his mild blackmail had decided Mr Chong to pay for his son to leave, he drove home feeling quite pleased with himself though he suspected that the wilful Lawrence, let loose in the United States, might prove a disaster.

The visit to the New Village and what he had learned about it finally clinched Ferdach's intention of doing what was required of him by the High Commissioner and the Secretary General. Suppressing his fear of being branded a traitor, he told himself that if he were, then so was Sir Henry Gurney. What they were both about to do was for peace and the general good of Malaya.

75

As the morning dawned all of Ferdach's misgivings flooded back. He was only a junior officer, still a cadet unconfirmed in the service, and yet he had allowed himself to slip, or rather be manipulated, into such an extraordinary position. Perhaps he had been too arrogant in talking to the intelligence people and the various officers he had met since his arrival, giving the impression that he was capable of acting way beyond his status given half the chance. Then he wondered whether arrogance was not part of the nature of any European who served in the colonies. By what right was he here? Malayans were as capable as the British and as reliable in their judgement. In any case capable and judicious or not, this was their country. Because of little accidents of history the British had managed to entrench themselves in various parts of the world and the slight of hand of those firstcomers had led to the imposition of an enormous confidence trick on vast swathes of the world. He felt himself part of a great hoax which should be brought to an end as soon as possible. All this engendered in his mind a kind of 'what the hell attitude' that resulted in him feeling indifferent to whatever might happen to him. In any case, the worse that could occur would be to be slung out of a position that, in reality, he had no desire to occupy.

He went to work in the District Office which was half occupied and somnolent in mood for it was Friday and all the Malays were at the mosque. Waite was out in the field and Ferdach dealt with some routine problems, a quarrel between two groups of Sikhs over grazing rights; a complaint from Sir Miles Seaborne-Clutterbucke, secretary of the Golf Club about the incursions on the course of cattle belonging to the self same rival Sikhs, and a discussion with some contractors about the specifications of a community centre to be built in a New Village. He longed for Waite to return; he wanted to unburden himself to someone and ask for advice. But Waite did not return and so as midday approached Ferdach decided to phone Secretary for Chinese Affairs, Noel Aspinall, whom he had hardly seen since returning from Singapore.

'Ah young O'Haney,' gushed Noel. 'Ain't seen you for ages. The Churchillian 'ain't' was one of Noel's many affectations. Come to my place for curry tiffin.'

Ferdach then paid his first visit to Noel's bungalow. It was furnished with all manner of bric-a-brac picked up when Noel was learning Cantonese in China: a few pieces were beautiful but most were hideous. In the dining room he saw five guests, all Malay, all male and all unfamiliar to him. This was surprising given Noel's bent towards the Chinese both temperamentally and professionally.

Ferdach knew that Noel was prone to bursts of enthusiasm for whatever new interest he had developed, rather as Toad had become afflicted with enthusiasm for cars to the detriment of his previous hobbies. As Noel led him to the table he whispered loudly enough for the others to hear, 'I'm only just realising how profound Malay culture is. How could I have neglected it before?' Ferdach could not help wondering, given the fact that one of the young Malays present was shy and very handsome, that there might be an emotional undercurrent to Noel's new enthusiasm.

The food was excellent, as was the wine, which all the Malays drank without exception, a couple of them too quickly despite the strictures of the Prophet, Peace be upon his Name. The alcohol soon gave rise to a very warm political debate to which Noel listened with wrapt attention and Ferdach with growing alarm. Except for one older man, the Malays were the sort of upperclass youths who had passed through the Malay Boys College at Kuala Kangsar and they spoke in English out of deference to their host only lapsing into Malay when they got worked up. They were all fiercely nationalist and spoke glowingly of Indonesia in which country, Ferdach gathered, the older man, Rahul Omar, had until recently been a university professor. Their pan-Malay nationalism did not, in itself, perturb Ferdach but what did was the discussion which arose when someone mentioned a rumour that the federal government was already engaged in political discussions with the Malayan Communist Party with a view to ending the Emergency. It was at that very heated point in the argument that Malay predominated.

'They're afraid of being sold down the river by the British,' said Noel quietly to Ferdach. 'And I don't blame them either.'

For an instant Ferdach thought that his secret was out. 'How can they …' he began, when Noel silenced him with a quick movement of his finger to his lips as though he knew what Ferdach was about to ask.

Rahul Omar had also noticed Ferdach's surprise and misunderstood it. 'You were about to ask how can we Malays not want peace. Isn't that so? Tuan O'Haney's not difficult to understand. The MCP has not been defeated and so, if it discusses peace with the federal government it will only do so on the basis of equality. Any peace would be the result of a deal between equals. The British would then have no alternative when they grant independence: they'd expect power to be shared equally by the Malays and the Chinese, the latter by then completely dominated by the Communist Party.' Rahul's speech had grown rapid. His eyes flashed with fury and he raised his hands as if in prayer.

As a result of his association with Lai Kuan, and indeed with Waite, such equality had always seemed a reasonable outcome to Ferdach. He guessed that it was Gurney's belief too and he had a shrewd suspicion it was the point of view of Phoenix Park. He was not sure how to reply to this impassioned speech; he even feared that suspicions might, after all, be harboured about his own role, so he pursed his lips as if expecting more. It came.

'Now the Chinese already run the country economically. If, in addition, they get equal political status with the Malays, the balance will be destroyed. The Malays will lose their own country.' Rahul brought his fist down on the dining table. 'I say this for all patriotic Malays: there can be no end to the Emergency until the Chinese dominated MCP is eliminated.' His companions applauded with racial outbursts that seemed to suggest they meant not just the MCP but the Chinese in general.

Noel too chimed in with, 'Yes, destroyed, eliminated,' which Ferdach found a little odd coming from the Perak Secretary for Chinese Affairs.

Rahul Omar then turned to Noel and Ferdach and all but shouted, 'Tell this to all your British friends: if they want to do anything for the Malays, they must not leave until the MCP is finished off.'

After that the company grew less concerned with politics and more inclined to joke and giggle at anything. The handsome and no longer shy Malay youth, who had drunk glass after glass of excellent Chablis, showed distinct signs of losing control. Noel suggested that he should rest in one of the bedrooms but Rahul Omar who could hold his drink asked for taxis to be called to take all his friends back to his *kampung*.

When they had gone Noel and Ferdach sat for a while on the verandah overlooking the bungalow's great sweep of lawn landscaped with flowering bushes and bordered by lined racks of hanging orchids except where it was separated by a winding stream, directly opposite them, from a rubber estate. Noel had certainly done himself well: a beautiful home, a good position with work only when he felt like doing it, and decided status for there was an indefinable aura about him; it arose from the fact that nobody knew what his duties were in precise terms but believed that they must be highly significant. Just now, however, Noel seemed to be in his cups; his head had lolled to one side, his mouth was opening and closing in response to his heavy breathing giving him a fish like appearance and his eyes seemed fixed on some distant object which nobody else could see. Nevertheless he suddenly pulled himself together and asked Ferdach in a crisp voice, 'Well, what did you think of that?'

'A pleasant group of guys,' replied Ferdach thinking that his reply would please.

'No, not them. That Indonesian-trained bugger Rahul. He's a troublemaker. Soekarno's been sending several like him over you know. They're gaining influence over our impressionable young Malays. We've got to stop it.'

Sensing that Noel was more sober and far more acute than he looked, Ferdach asked, 'That business about negotiations between us and the MCP. Where the hell did it come from?'

The vehemence of Noel's reply reassured Ferdach that he knew nothing. 'A lot of bollocks. Of course you and I know that some of our friends in Phoenix Park would like to cut a deal with the MCP to help Britain cope with China. But you and I also know that the Federation would never countenance it. If Phoenix Park made the slightest move towards the MCP, it would be nipped in the bud by Special Branch and quite rightly so.' Noel's voice became maudlin again. 'No young man, remember the mistake of my generation: 1938. Never appease, never appease.'

Ferdach recognised that this emotional prima donna was not a man to be entrusted with confidences, let alone secrets. He glanced at his watch. In three hours time he had to meet Harry Wong. 'I agree Noel. You're right. Never appease. Never appease. But I must be off. Thanks for the excellent curry and the conversation.' With that he left to start his mission which, after all that had been said, must surely be seen as the start of treacherous appeasement by all patriotic Malays.

Because of that thought he half hoped for some excuse to enable him to backtrack. It actually came in the form of a message, given to him by Cookie, that he must ring a certain Wong Siu Bo in Penang. A call from the first person to help him in the country was a command; their friendship had never fallen off. It turned out that her House of Everlasting Pleasure was experiencing domestic discord. She needed him to advise or rather comfort her as a brother, as he had sometimes done before. Hinting that her own excess kindness was the problem and counselling a firm hand with her girls, he said he could not come just now even though she told him, as a sweetener, that her house had got two pretty new girls whom she wanted him to try out. His imagination was stirred, he longed to go, but knew that duty must come first. For once Ferdach turned his back on an offer of sex. Perhaps it might have been better if he had not.

76

Chin Peng's instructions had been repeated verbally to Ferdach by Lai Kuan, who had made him commit them to memory. They were meticulous as to timing and place and made it clear that any deviation from them would result in the mission being aborted. In the first case Ferdach would leave Ipoh alone and travel down to a certain milestone on the main road south. This was just beyond Gopeng and was distinguished by two gutted shop houses abandoned during resettlement. There he would turn into a laterite rubber-estate track leading eastward. After about two hundred yards he would see Harry, Comrade Wong Chooi Fong, waiting for him at a spot where the track widened and bifurcated. This would enable Ferdach to reverse his car in the darkness and then take to the main road again with Harry as his passenger. At Kampung Dipang, instead of following the main road south through Kampar they must turn eastward up the valley of the Sungei Dipang on the easterly branch of the road south. Just beyond Kampung Sahum they would again leave the road and follow an old track along which they would be met at an unspecified place by Liberation Army soldiers and taken to a hideout where they could sleep. Early the next morning they would resume the journey, the full details of which were known to Harry Wong, who would give Ferdach all necessary directions.

As he took his shower and packed a bag, Ferdach was conscious of his heart pounding and of an inner voice telling him that he was crazy, that he might never be seen alive again, and that even if he were, disgrace would fall upon him. So preoccupied was he with gloomy misgivings that he did not notice Waite come into his room and watch what he was doing. He started when he heard the question, 'Are you OK, matey? You look as if you've seen a ghost or something? Your face is white as a sheet.'

Ferdach pulled his large bath towel more tightly around his body. 'It's the shower. The water's cold as hell. You wouldn't think we're in the tropics.' It was indeed one of those rare days when beneath a heavily overcast rain-filled sky a swift breeze was flowing down from the mountains.

'You've packed your swag. Are you off somewhere Ferdie? You never told me. I thought we were going to see a film and then eat out.'

My first mistake, thought Ferdach. Small mistakes could bugger up the best of plans. Small mistakes could destroy empires. 'Ah, I was going to leave you a note. It's Laura. She's asked me to go to KL for the weekend. I think she's feeling down. Missing her old friends in Singapore or something. I'd better go. I'm sorry Waite.'

'No problem Ferdie.' All the same Waite continued to hover in the room. 'Sure you're OK, Ferdie?'

'Of course I'm OK. I guess I'm worrying a bit, about me and Laura. Marriage during the Emergency isn't for me. I think of Alyson Carew. But carrying on with another officer's wife, well, separated wife; won't it affect my career?'

'Don't be a silly kipper. This is 1951. Nowadays you'd have to commit high treason to be slung out of the Service,' replied Waite with a broad grin. Ferdach shot him a hard glance. Was he joking or was he giving some message? No, it was a joke, Ferdach decided. Waite made to go off, then stopped. 'Oh by the way, your Browning, I had it cleaned in the police armoury. Shall I get it for you? It's upstairs.'

Another of Chin Peng's instructions was no weapons, but Waite knew that when either of them went outstation they always took a gun. 'I don't think I want it,' Ferdach said hesitantly. 'Laura might see it. She hates weapons. Give it to me when I get back.'

'Slain for the love of a woman,' said Waite, but he accepted Ferdach's words and left, bidding him a good journey, '*Selamat jalan.*'

In Ferdach's book, Waite was one of those people he did not lie to. He was a mate, a word which in Australian terms had a nobler connotation than it did in England. One could lie to one's wife, to one's lover, to one's parents, to God if necessary, but not to a mate and now, for the second time, Ferdach had lied to Waite. He was not sure why he had done so. Then he recognised that in some strange way he was elated by the task he was engaged in; he wanted to do it alone. But once he had admitted that, he assuaged his guilt by remembering his undertaking to both Gurney and to Chin Peng that he would be their sole and secret intermediary. Finally he justified his lie by telling himself that he had also been thinking of Waite's interest. If Waite knew, either he would have to remain silent or feel obliged to report the information to his own superiors. No, Ferdach insisted to his conscience, it was best for Waite to remain in ignorance.

Yet was Waite so ignorant? Ferdach had always felt that Waite possessed some extraordinary insight into the people around him without being particularly talented as a conversationalist. Uneasily he recalled those experiments in extrasensory perception he had been subjected to when he first arrived in Ipoh. Moreover, Waite was the sort of person who approached people obliquely. Why had he made that reference to treason if the concept in regard to Ferdach had not been floating in his mind? By the time he was ready to leave the house, Ferdach had thought yet again of going upstairs to make a clean breast of everything to Waite, but just then Ericson arrived at speed in his dirt-covered car, churning up the gravel in the drive and stopping with a screech of brakes. Ferdach shouted, 'Cheerio Ericson. I'm off to KL.'

'For more shagging?' came the reply as Ferdach drove off.

That made Ferdach chuckle and momentarily relieved his stress. These days, though Ericson was friendly with him he could never refrain from making abrasive remarks that really masked a lack of confidence. Ferdach was certain that such a man would never essay the journey that he himself was now on. He would be too hidebound by convention. To get into the sort of morass Ferdach had entered required the subtlety of an eel and an ability to see questions from all angles.

Once through the security checkpoints at Gopeng he anticipated meeting Harry Wong with considerable anxiety. In this young CT he had encountered a mind not unlike his own, for Harry had transmuted himself from being a pampered rich man's son into a well-educated intellectual and then into a Marxist so-called terrorist, a journey opposite to Ferdach's path from the far left to the Colonial Service. How had he done it? For the first time Ferdach considered the fact that he would be alone with the capricious handsome Harry for many hours ahead;

the thought excited him yet he kidded himself that the two of them would merely enjoy exchanging political ideas together. For Ferdach was embarked on that dubious journey in which emotion and politics combine to turn communist spies into agents of the West, and CIA and MI5 men into communists. As these thoughts jostled in his mind he unexpectedly recalled the poet Heath-Stubbs telling him, amidst the babel of the Fitzroy Tavern, about Heracleitus' principle of enantiodramia, the regulatory and self changing function of opposites akin to the Chinese concept of Yin and Yang, whereby male became female, black became white, up became down, and good and bad were equally interchangeable. It came to Ferdach at this moment that his own life was becoming an exemplar of this mysterious process.

The two gutted shophouses that he glimpsed in the headlights looked white and ghostly but driving slowly in complete darkness along the laterite track that lay behind them into a rubber estate was a more eerie experience. Supposing something had gone wrong. Supposing the local CTs knew nothing of the arrangement and saw him as an appetising target. The track was bumpy with many potholes and it would have been easy to slip into a side drain. But then, just as his speed had fallen to less than five miles an hour, up ahead standing all alone at a Y-shaped junction was Harry. He was unusually dressed in a colourful batik shirt and cream trousers, with a camera slung in front of him and carried a smart valise. He gave warning taps on the car to help Ferdach manoeuvre and then he got in.

'Stage one completed,' said Ferdach by way of greeting.

'I had to hide behind the trees twice. Someone went up the track in a jeep and then came back.'

'Police?' asked Ferdach.

'Unmarked. Could have been the police, could have been the estate manager but our people have ways of checking up as well.'

'With jeeps?'

'God knows. With everything you can think of. It makes me shiver sometimes.'

This is an odd way to start a conversation with a CT, thought Ferdach. Is he afraid of his own comrades? He made no comment but drove back carefully the way he had come. Once on the main road, which had been recently resurfaced, the going was good. Harry adjusted his seat to lie back and closed his eyes, having stated, 'I'm an American journalist by the way.' Just then Ferdach noted Harry's rather vulgar two-tone shoes and so felt inclined to accept his assertion.

Occasionally they saw cars heading north – to Ipoh maybe; out of fear all the cars drove fast and never dipped their headlights. No vehicles were travelling south. Commercial vehicles, especially those carrying foodstuffs, could not travel at night lest their contents reach the CTs. The first time Ferdach had to stop was at a checkpoint just before Kampung Dipang. Special constables on duty had a tendency to scrutinise passenger documents and vehicle contents very carefully since they were country lads curious about outsiders and, in any case, night-time duty was very boring and needed variety. When tapped on the shoulder Harry Wong started, gave the police sergeant one of his radiant smiles and produced, not a Malayan identity card but a passport and an American one at that. It must have been the first US passport the policeman had ever seen and he perused every page as if it were a holy relic. Then he returned it, stepped back and gave Harry a smart salute.

'He wouldn't have done that for a British passport,' said Ferdach, as they got on their way through the little town.

'I should think not,' replied Harry.

At the checkpoint at the southern perimeter of the town the same procedure was repeated though this time the salute was replaced by a warm handshake. After that Harry no longer pretended to be asleep and became talkative.

'You know Ferdie I can't understand how a man like you could join the Colonial Service.'

'And I can't understand how a bloke like you, educated at a good school in Hong Kong, and further afield so I'm told, could continue believing that Marxist crap, still less how you could join up with these murderous thugs.'

'Well, you show me yours and I'll show you mine, Ferdie.'

Ferdach felt relieved. How stupid to have called Harry's comrades thugs. He wanted to get through this mission in one piece. Fortunately Harry had suggested the bizarre side of their positions.

At that moment a *pelanduk*, a mousedeer, dashed across the road and into the beam of the car's headlights. Ferdach swerved and for an instant lost control. Harry shouted angrily, 'If you see an animal don't swerve; our lives matter more than a beast's.'

'I didn't want to kill it,' said Ferdach accelerating a little as if to assert his mastery.

'Didn't want to kill it,' scoffed Harry. 'Like a member of the bloody RSPCA. Life has to be taken sometimes.'

'Yes. Like you took George Carew's life,' Ferdach burst out and again regretted what he had said. His emotions were too near the surface. When he got excited something seemed to explode in his brain and he could not control himself until his thought, however bitter, found its way out in words. If they were to carry on like this, they might never get to see Chin Peng. It was, therefore, alarming to feel Harry's arm reaching firmly around his shoulders; he could not tell whether it was a grasp or an embrace until he felt a hand crawling round his neck and stroking his throat softly.

'You believe I cut George just here don't you? That's the report going around, supported by the police.'

'I know you murdered him. Everyone agrees on that. And the five villagers?'

'I did not murder the villagers. I was ordered to execute them as collaborators. I finished them off quickly. I cut their throats. Some of the comrades have worse ways of execution.'

'So you admit that you are executioners.'

'Yes, Ferdie. War is war. And even the saintly British execute traitors. Remember poor old Lord Haw Haw? Killed for opening his mouth. As if an Irishman could ever hold his tongue. You can't hold your tongue, can you Ferdie?'

'Well who did kill George Carew? I was told by the police that he was run through with a long knife, a kris maybe.'

'Yes. I did that Ferdie. He ran at me. It was me or him.' Harry drew in his breath sharply. 'His eyes were right up to mine Ferdie as he died. Maybe we were looking into one another's souls just then. I can't forget his eyes. Maybe he took half of my soul with him. In which case I'm already half dead.'

They were both silent. Harry sat back again staring at the road.

Occasionally as they rounded a bend the eyes of animals glinted brightly in the headlights. It was impossible to say what they were: deer, wild boar, a tiger even. Eyes alone gave away nothing. Ferdach wondered if human eyes glinted in that way. 'Funny you should talk about the soul, you a communist. I don't believe in the soul; only the physical brain acting in a multitude of inexplicable ways, well, inexplicable at present.'

'I was speaking poetically, Ferdie. Communists can be poets. Mao Tse Tung is a good poet.'

'I only know one communist poem; it was about Stalin,' said Ferdach. 'I read it in a Soviet literary review. It was a translation of a Tajik poem:

> Fine of fleece are Ali's sheep
> Woolly, large of size,
> Men of science say he will,
> Win the Stalin Prize.

They both started to laugh like mad, indeed hysterically, so much so that Ferdach had to stop the car at the roadside.

'Let's have a drink,' said Harry, reaching behind him into his valise and producing a bottle of Scotch. Each of them took a swig, repeated three times. 'You know Ferdie, not long ago I was in England but I came back to Malaya to join the Party because I didn't like my life there. And I was fed up with the rationing and the cold. What could I do in England? Become an academic in Chinese Studies at SOAS? My God, what a bore. No, I'd missed the war and I wanted to know what fighting was like, what killing was like. Of course, in fifty years time China will be on its way to dominating the world, communist or not. It's inevitable. But I'll not be around by then. No, I want excitement now and I seem to have got it.'

Ferdach considered for a while and replied, 'Well Harry, it could be the same with me. Yes, I told myself I wanted to learn Chinese, and I guess I do, but not to become a great scholar. I'm too bloody lazy. I just seized the chance of coming to the East, to go to Macau, maybe later to China, to live in an unusual way, an unconventional way. I wanted to throw off the traces, to smoke opium, to drink, to have all sorts of wild sex, to live with people even odder than all those deadbeats in Soho. I knew one of them well, an amazing woman, Nina Hamnett. She could have been a great painter but I think she really thought that living was more important than art. She told me to get out of England. She'd been everywhere, done everything, and been done by some of the greatest artists. I wanted to live the Bohemian life to the extreme like her. But I wanted to be Rimbaud in comfort; hence the Colonial Service. It's the same excitement you want but the opposite side of the coin.'

Ferdach started up the car again and they drove on to their rendezvous with the CTs. As they approached the place beyond Kampung Sahum where they had to turn off the main road into a jungle track, Harry said quietly, as though there were already people nearby who might hear him, 'Ferdie, we understand a lot about one another, but not everything yet. Just one thing, for the time being: when you speak to me in front of the comrades, don't call me Harry. It makes me sound like a capitalist running dog.'

'What then?'

Harry thought for a moment. 'We mustn't look intimate at all. What about Wong *tong bao*? Yes, just Comrade Wong.'

Ferdach knew that the Chinese '*tong bao*' literally meant 'same womb', so with a chuckle he replied, 'OK Comrade Wong. I shall be your womb mate.'

77

A couple of miles up the rough track, driving at a crawl in pitch darkness into a zone of secondary jungle, they saw a slight figure in front of them.

'Switch off your lights and stop,' said Harry.

Ferdach at once obeyed but not before he had seen the hard face of a young Liberation Army soldier under a peaked cap bearing the five-pointed red star of communism. He later told Laura, 'To be frank,I started to tremble; in my imagination the connection with death of that figure was strong.' The next minute the soldier was leaning through the open window of the car and Ferdach was conscious of his warm breath. Simultaneously two older men appeared on Harry Wong's side. A flashlight shone into his own and then Harry's face. The young soldier asked in staccato English, 'You are Hor Hanee?' and Ferdach said he was. 'We get in,' said the soldier. The next moment the three MPLA were in the back of the car and Harry told Ferdach to switch on the lights and drive on. Ferdach wished that everyone would talk about something but they were all silent.

The going was very slow and Ferdach wondered whether his long-suffering little Morris Minor would make it without coming to a halt in the deeply rutted laterite track. But after no more than fifty yards Harry pointed to the right and they turned onto a stony surface that rose up gently before them to a limestone cliff whose base was obscured by bushes. A gap slowly widened in the foliage and Ferdach could see a black hole. Unexpectedly he remembered being taken as a child by his mother to the Empire Theatre in Liverpool and being amazed when the cave door opened at the words 'Open Sesame'. He expected to see bandits of a sort but no treasure. 'Drive in,' said the soldier. Ferdach could hear people behind the car closing up the opening. He obeyed an order to get out and was escorted into a deeper part of the cave that was suddenly lit with an oil lamp. He found himself in the company of five CTs, six if he included Harry.

He was acutely aware of all the men's eyes scrutinising him closely. It was like being in a science fiction story, watched by aliens which, in a sense, the CTs were. Harry made no effort to introduce anyone to him. That would have been a superfluous gesture but after an awkward pause during which he spoke to the young soldier, who it seemed was in charge, Harry told him, 'We'll eat here and then sleep Mr O'Haney but first you and the car must be searched.'

'Naturally, you must take every precaution,' Ferdach replied suavely and stood still, legs and arms apart like a recruit awaiting a medical examination. He understood the suspicious words in Cantonese of one of the men: '*Kui gong mi yea*? What did he say?'. Harry must have reassured the man that no reactionary anti-communist slogan had been uttered. After that three of the men went over to take everything out of the car whilst the officer in charge subjected Ferdach and his clothing to a meticulous search. Though reduced to his underpants Ferdach did not mind this operation; on the contrary it seemed to create a slight degree of human contact between himself and his inspector at whom he smiled very slightly when the man's face passed before him. The contact intensified slightly when he felt the soldier's hand probe inside his remaining garment and search in between his legs.

The inspection over Ferdach suddenly felt that his bowels were on the move. He hoped that he was not going to have an attack of diarrhoea. '*Oi o si*, I want to shit,' he said loudly. One of the soldiers produced a trowel and a can of water and led him through the concealed doorway into the open air and stood watching while Ferdach squatted down some way off, relieved himself and then used the water to wash himself and the trowel to cover his droppings. Fortunately it was not diarrhoea; his nervous reaction to the unusual company he found himself in had made him go in a hurry. Once inside he got dressed and sat down with Harry and the commander to eat a large bowl of boiled rice with vegetables and prawns. The excellent taste surprised him and he said so. The commander then spoke for the first time in a human sort of way, 'Fresh water prawns. Good stream not far off.' Harry Wong then looked severely at the young man as if it had been wrong to engage in trivial talk with a capitalist red-haired devil. The rest of the meal was eaten in silence.

Ferdach did his best not to seem too curious about the location he was in. He hardly moved his head but his eyes were observing the cave and the men as much as possible. He was mainly struck by the order and the discipline that reigned. Everything was neatly stacked away. The men treated one another with a sort of reserve which might arise from mutual consideration or from suspicion. After the meal they occupied themselves with weapons maintenance and later four of them sat down to study books, Marxist no doubt, in the light of the single oil lamp. In fact though he thought of the young man who had given all the orders as the commanding officer, Ferdach had no idea what the ranks of the men were. They were all dressed in the same dun ill-fitting uniform and they talked to one another in an egalitarian sort of way. They did not appear to share any jokes and there was no laughter. Ferdach was reminded of a Quaker meeting he had once attended at Friends House in Bloomsbury; that too was very restrained though the only weapons were those of the spirit. An unusual feature of these men, considering they were Chinese, was that no one spoke raucously; on the contrary they all conversed in low tones, by now no doubt out of habit to avoid attracting unwanted attention. Bit by bit Ferdach began to see them if not as average citizens then as dedicated people who knew what they were about. All the same he knew from security reports that the situation among such men was often far from idyllic and that the rank-and-file CTs were often resentful of the privileges, and the indifference towards them, of their leaders such as those who formed the central committee. Although he would have liked to speak with them he knew that no such opportunity would be given. Soon he was led deeper into the cave where he lay down on a Malay woven mat and fell fast asleep.

He awoke earlier than the others; only soldier on guard stationed near the cave entrance was up. From outside he could hear the cries and calls of animals and birds and the crescendo of insect sounds that greet the onset of dawn in the jungle. He decided not to get up until he was told but lay under the blanket that someone had thrown over him contemplating the strange situation he was in. Supposing there was an attack by the security forces just now. How could he possibly explain his presence? In fact, with the exception of Harry Wong, could any of the others in the cave give a proper reason for him being there? And if these men did know why he was with them, would they be in favour of what was afoot? The more dedicated communists might not want peace at all, feeling sure that time was on their side and that they only had to continue to fight until resurgent China helped them to establish a People's Republic of Malaya. An even greater cause for anxiety was what his own superior officers would think of his actions? Would they brand him as a traitor, a Quisling only worthy of being court marshalled and shot? In the cold atmosphere of this cave he thought he could discern the hand of those intelligence experts in Phoenix Park manipulating Gurney and Chin Peng into making a deal in the interests of London against the wishes of the federal government and the interests of the Malays. The complexities and rivalries in the world of intelligence were hard to fathom; to understand them he must, like Theseus, follow insubstantial strands through a maze as dangerous as the Labyrinth.

The moment he heard the others stirring he closed his eyes and pretended to be still asleep. The senior officer and Harry Wong were talking to one another in Mandarin, which Ferdach could scarcely understand. Then he heard what sounded like heavy objects being pushed, after which the Mandarin voices faded into the distance. To judge by snatches of conversation in Hokkien, the other men were near the front of the cave. The smell of coffee suggested that a meal was in the offing. Certain now that no one was near him Ferdach opened his eyes and glimpsed another opening at the back of the cave revealed by the shoving aside of two crates. In its depths Harry Wong and the commanding officer were looking at boxes with the aid of a torch. Some were already open revealing a top layer of shiny tins. Sacks of what Ferdach presumed to be rice were also there in large quantity. It was clearly a huge food dump. He remained in his false sleep until the two men came out and the sound of the crates being moved told him that the opening was closed. He sat up, yawned and let out a long sigh.

'We must both shave and look decent,' said Harry Wong, who had opened up Ferdach's valise and taken out his toilet bag. 'I've forgotten a razor. I want to be a smart American again.'

'Really Wong *tongbao*, how incredible that someone as efficient as you should forget a thing. I'd begun to think of you as a props manager in a theatre.'

'But I already am, in the theatre of war.'

'I need some coffee before we set out,' said Ferdach. It was brought over by a sharp-featured soldier who gawped at him as if his face contained some secret. The hot black brew disgusted Ferdach but he drank it all down aware that it was certainly a stimulant to action. Such action did not include shaving or putting on a clean shirt as Harry had done.

Within the hour they were once more on the highway to the south. Wong *tongbao*, in the absence of his fellow communists, had quickly resumed his Harry persona and Ferdach was anxious to talk. He started off by saying, 'That was lovely ham we had for breakfast. I think I've had the same stuff from Cold Storage in Singapore; canned in Australia isn't it? And the rice, best basmati I'd say. Only the coffee was the usual Malayan stuff. They might have given us some Colombian.'

Harry Wong looked at Ferdach askance, then laughed, 'So we're not short of food. Despite all your efforts, despite resettlement, we still get all we want.'

'Yes, by terror, but gradually the screw will be turned. Most New Villagers want stricter food control measures,' Ferdach lied. 'They want an excuse for not helping you.'

'But well before that Ferdie, we may be at peace, if the letter you are going to collect does its work.'

Ferdach contented himself by saying that he hoped so. Then, for much of the journey they talked without rancour: about the struggle of the West with world communism, the rise of China, the decline of Britain, all topics that presented no problems. It was also easy to discuss trivialities. They talked about life in England as opposed to life in Malaya, they talked about personalities they both knew. Harry Wong was particularly interested in Waite's character but when Ferdach said 'What a pity we've not got Lai Kuan with us', Harry Wong was evasive, saying that Lai Kuan was a man of high principles, total integrity and so forth, but maybe not sufficiently ruthless for the sort of work a Party member had to do.

'He's a bourgeois liberal; the sort of man the Party often has to make a deal with to win power,' Harry said.

'Ah yes. He's one of those people that Lenin used to refer to as useful idiots.'

Harry said, very seriously, 'I don't agree with everything Lenin said but I'd like to be as ruthless as him. As to Lai Kuan, he may be an idealist but he's no idiot. I still love him as a friend.'

After that exchange Ferdach reverted to innocuous fields of conversation with this fascinating communist who, not long ago, had enjoyed living in Europe or America with plenty of money. He knew the sort of people whose faces grinned from the society pages of fashionable magazines but had never experienced the seamy Soho world of Nina Hamnett and her friends, people who, unlike him, were perpetually short of money. Yet here he was claiming to be as ruthless as Lenin, a claim that Ferdach, in light of Harry's swift despatch of George Carew, had no reason to doubt. Even so, as the hours went by, Ferdach was conscious of a warmth developing between them. They talked easily, sometimes anticipating what the other was going to say. They laughed at the same things. Increasingly Ferdach felt that Harry was, in some indefinable way, the mirror image of himself.

At Slim River they stopped for a meal in the rest house. An English couple from Singapore was in the dining room together with their two small boys. Harry went out of his way to play with the children, giving them piggybacks which they all really enjoyed. The English lady, a youngish woman with sallow skin and a worn-out expression, commented on how good the Chinese were with children – 'unlike some of our species' she added, with a grim glance at her bored-looking husband who, deserting his hot treacle pudding, was already propping up the bar at the other end of the room. 'Are you on your way to KL?' she asked Ferdach who, taken unaware, was for an instant tongue-tied before blurting out, 'Yes, no, well, not exactly. I think my friend wants to go up to Fraser's Hill. He's from San Francisco and it's his first trip to Asia. He's writing a tourist guide and wants to see everything he can.'

'A Chinese on his first visit to Asia! A tourist guide during the Emergency! How absolutely bizarre. Oh well, I guess it's reassuring in a way.'

When they left the rest house Ferdach said, 'I wouldn't mind being told where we are going, in general terms that is. I felt an ass in there when that woman questioned me and I gave a stupid reply.'

'Ah Ferdie you'd be no good in intelligence. Spies are only lost for words when they have to tell the truth.'

'Well Mr Oscar Bloody Wilde Wong, since we may be travelling to the furthest end of Malaya I assume you won't mind if I fill up the tank at that garage over there.'

'Excellent idea Ferdie and when you do, get the car washed as well. I don't like all that laterite on the wheels. It could be a give away. I want us to look smart. And I don't like you looking scruffy, as you do now.'

'Why, Comrade Wong? What does it matter?'

'Because I want everything about us to look good. We'll be in our territory soon. An important mission demands a degree of dignity.' He looked around him as though searching for something while saying quite softly, 'Besides which Ferdie, I like being with you. I like you very much. So it makes me happy to see you looking good.'

78

South of Tanjong Malim they heard a tremendous roll of thunder, one that went on and on as if a celestial drummer had gone berserk, bluish lightening flickered around them rather than piercing the sky and then the storm broke. Heavy raindrops splattered and bounced on the road so fiercely that within minutes the recently washed and polished green Morris looked a dirt-streaked mess as it coursed through the muddy water that overflowed from every hollow in the well-worn tarmac. On each side of the road trees and bushes swayed and writhed as though about to tear themselves up and fly. The car windows had to be closed tight to keep out the driving rain so that soon the heat in the car made the two men sweaty and uncomfortable. 'I think we should stop until the rain clears,' said Ferdach. 'I can hardly see in front of me. You do want us to get there, wherever it is, safely don't you?'

'No, the rain is good. I know soldiers from Kuala Kubu Bahru helped you after your crash. Carry on driving and let's hope it's still pouring when we pass the camp. No one's likely to see you in this downpour.'

Since Kuala Kubu Bahru was on the Pahang road that would shortly branch off the highway to the south, Ferdach said, 'So we're not meeting your great leader anywhere near KL. We're going to Fraser's Hill. Holy Mary Mother of God Harry, you don't need to be so secretive.'

'Orders Ferdie, but I can tell you now, we're not going to Fraser's. Can you imagine keeping Chin Peng's presence secret in such a place? Did you think he'd like to join you over a pint in the Maxwell Arms?'

'Who knows what communist leaders like? Stalin likes to booze, Mao likes to screw girls after chasing them around his billiard table. Chin Peng might enjoy a round of golf in Fraser's. I wonder what his handicap is,' Ferdach replied facetiously though that was not how he felt; fatigue had really got to him. 'Well we'll have to stop somewhere. I don't want to go off the road again. I want a rest before we land up in the middle of Pahang.'

'No need. Keep going. We're stopping in Tras. It's not far.'

'Ah, so it is Tras,' said Ferdach who had already speculated that the suspect place might be their destination. He could not ask any more questions for just then the roar of the rain on the car roof grew so loud that all talk had to end. Driving through such furious weather was difficult but Ferdach had to press on until at last he left the main road, skirted the military camp at Kuala Kubu Bahru and got well up the Pahang Road before the thunder drew away and the storm abated. Abruptly they saw ahead of them the jungle-covered peaks of the central range sharply silhouetted against the blue of the clearing sky. Rolling down the windows they relished the cool air coming from high above. Ferdach soon found the road even more familiar than the main road they had just left since he had been up and down it four times during his last visit to Pahang. What a pity Fraser's Hill was out of the question; it would be good to see Arun again and find out how he was getting on with the amorous Delphine. But Arun would try to worm information out of him; it was in his nature. He would also alert his Indian friends in the places ahead, including Tras, to be on the lookout for his former boss, and watch what he was doing. In his present situation Ferdach suspected even his friends; Arun might still be in contact with his old controller Tengku Mizan.

By now it was dark and Ferdach was relieved when, out of the blue, Harry told him that a room had been booked for them at the Gap rest house. They would go on to Tras early the next morning. 'But no phoning Arun at Fraser's Hill. We don't want any Indian visitor, or his woman.'

The fact that his past was so intimately known to Harry irritated Ferdach yet also intrigued him. The communists' information system must be every bit as efficient as the government's and maybe more perfectly focused on detail. Indeed everything Harry himself did was seemingly performed to perfection. When they were making themselves comfortable in the rest house room they were to share, Ferdach had found himself observing Harry closely. They had showered together, shampood one another's hair and then lain down on the two beds that were pleasantly placed near a window from which there was an expansive view over the jungle-clad hills to which both of them were turned. Harry was nearer the window and Ferdach admired the contours of his back, the subtle curve of his hip, his shapely butt, and his strong thighs. How did he keep in such good shape? He never spoke of playing games or taking exercise. Nature had just done him proud. He was just effortlessly handsome and, it seemed to Ferdach, effortlessly clever, effortlessly well informed, effortlessly efficient. He must have been born with something better than a silver spoon in his mouth, an eighteen carat gold one most likely. And then there was his face, regularly shaped but with that oval roundness around the jaw that was admired in antiquity, despite which his beauty remained distinctly Chinese. Ferdach thought of David Copperfield's admiration for Steerforth as the nearest parallel to his own feelings for the athletic man reclining so gracefully before him. Yet this paragon had become a communist, the British would say a terrorist, and to many people a cruel murderer. Peculiarly though, in his communism there was too facile an acceptance both of its ruthlessness and of its logical but flawed doctrine. It struck Ferdach that Harry was not a communist out of intellectual commitment, or out of some desire to help suffering mankind. At heart he was still an adventurer and an actor and being a communist terrorist was an act of insincerity on a bold scale. From time to time Ferdach sensed in his manner an unease that maybe arose from an inner sadness as though Harry recognised that he was playing false to whatever he really was. This aroused in Ferdach first pity then a rush of affection the intensity of which alarmed him for it was simultaneously accompanied by revulsion at the memory of George Carew's murder; it was as though two strong contrary emotions were struggling for mastery inside him. Perhaps conscious of the scrutiny flowing in his direction Steerforth-Wong suddenly lay back, took a cigarette out of his round tin of State Express 555s, caught Ferdach's eyes and asked, 'Why are you staring at me like that?'

'Like what?'

'As if you are hungry? Yes, you are hungry for me Ferdie.'

'Why do you think that? As a matter of fact I was thinking what a shame it is that you've sacrificed yourself to a false god: communism.'

'Oh what deceivers eyes can be. I thought yours were betraying lust.

Yes, perhaps you really were thinking about communism, the god you would still like to serve.' Harry put down his cigarette, smiled and added softly, 'Love and duty are battling it out in your mind, aren't they Ferdie? Yes, you do want me but thinking about me means thinking about the path I've chosen and where your own duty lies. If you were on my side love and duty would be reconciled.'

Ferdach decided to admit nothing and didn't probe further lest he was worsted. That struggle between love and duty was surely a reflection of the battle raging in Harry's own uncertain mind. Without giving way to the gaze in his would-be seducer's eyes, Ferdach then said, 'I was also thinking how even the beautiful Steerforth turned out to be a rotten apple.'

'Which means?'

'Though the apple is beautiful I'm afraid it might make me sick.'

Harry said not a word, maybe he was annoyed, but when Ferdach glanced at him again those regular features were as serene as ever; occasionally Harry made an O of his lips and, effortlessly of course, puffed little smoke rings into the air whilst his free hand had taken to performing a slow sensual massage of his chest and stomach as if it was his intent to be satisfied one way or another. Ferdach felt himself blushing, with anger and embarrassment; he had been rude to turn down an offer that revealed Harry's affection, and rude in the way he had put it. 'I'm sorry …' he began.

'I don't understand. Is there a problem? Sorry for what?'

It was on the tip of Ferdach's tongue to say brazenly: 'for not wanting to have sex with you', but he held his peace trying to examine the motive for his rejection. For Ferdach knew, and he knew that Harry knew, that men like them often made love, without being in love, at the drop of a hat. They were perfect exemplars of Lenin's dictum that making love was of no more significance than drinking a glass of water. In the shower, their bodies had betrayed that they were stimulated by one another. His refusal must therefore signify something different from physical rejection; embracing might turn out to be less satisfactory than looking. Could it be that Harry's perfection somehow or other awed him and he feared he could not live up to its promise? Or had that intention, which he played with from time to time, of being faithful only to a woman, to Laura in fact, oozed for a moment out of some cranny in his brain? Ferdach found this so unlikely that he almost decided to go back on his quick rejection but he could not; he was afraid to do so. Then, as soon as the concept of fear entered his mind, he thought that it must indeed be fear that had determined his behaviour. Harry wanted more than a bit of sex before dinner. Harry wanted to get him not for himself, but for his cause. Yet could he be sure? What right had he to suspect Harry's motives? Why not be honest enough to admit the longing that was growing in his own mind and racking him fiercely? He went and sat on Harry's bed. 'Maybe I'll feel different later, when we come back from dinner,' he mumbled. It sounded more like an apology than an expression of desire so he let his hand rest lightly on Harry's arm, not intending to remove it too quickly.

'Come back from dinner? We're not leaving this room Ferdie. The food's to be brought up and we're to have a visitor.'

For a moment Ferdach suspected that Harry's talk of going to Tras had been a blind and that the visitor was to be Chin Peng. After all, a room in the Gap rest house would be as safe a place as any to hand over a letter. His immediate thought was that they should both get dressed but before he could move, the door opened without anyone knocking and two men came in, both carrying trays of food and beer. Someone outside closed the door after them. Neither of the newcomers resembled any of the rest house staff Ferdach had seen. They were hard-looking men though neatly dressed in black slacks and flapping white shirts to resemble waiters. As they bent over the table to put down the food Ferdach could see that the heavier one carried a gun in a hip holster. It was even clearer that neither was a waiter when they sat down on two of the four dining chairs, barely glancing at Ferdach and Harry together on the bed. Harry, now Comrade Wong again, spoke rapidly in Mandarin at the same time putting on his sarong while Ferdach did the same. Perhaps he was explaining their nakedness with something like, 'we've just been taking a shower and are resting' but whatever it was the visitors remained poker face and merely said, '*Cheng chor*, please sit down,' so that the meal could begin.

Comrade Wong gestured at Ferdach and spoke his surname as 'Hor Hanee' by way of introduction. Both visitors half rose as they shook Ferdach's hand but their own names were not mentioned. Since he was completely left out of the Mandarin conversation that followed, Ferdach decided to enjoy the rest house food which, tonight comprised lamb chops, boiled potatoes, minted peas, all very well prepared, a large plastic tub of Cold Storage tutti frutti from Singapore and a bowl of delicate little strawberries, presumably from Fraser's Hill. The two visitors obviously liked the ice cream more than the English food to judge by the small amount left in the tub for the two residents. Not that they were impolite to Ferdach. When the food was eaten and the Tiger beers opened, they took out their cigarettes, not the expensive kind smoked by Harry, and offered them round. Before long the room stank to high heaven even though the window was half opened, making Ferdach remember student rooms and idealistic conversations of his past, except that now he played no part to speak of in the exchanges that he suspected were far from idealistic. So after a while he said in Cantonese, 'I'm very tired. I must sleep,' and lay down on his bed. He heard Harry and the visitors leave after a little while and then all was silent until he awoke as dawn was breaking and once again his eyes fell on the half-covered supine form of Comrade Wong, appropriately tinged red from the morning sun.

No lustful feelings stirred this morning in Ferdach's mind which was beset instead by a half-formed memory that he could not quite pinpoint: the face of the heavier visitor last night. Was it of someone he had met, or did it merely resemble someone he had seen? There was an intensity about the man's stare that had several times been directed at him when they were all eating. Then with the freshness of the brain that often comes when sleep has swept the mind clear, it came back to him: in the operations room in Ipoh, as in every important operations room in the Federation, there was an organisational chart showing the structure of Communist Party leadership. Whenever possible each rank would be accompanied by the holder's name and, if available, his photograph. He and Waite were accustomed to studying the chart, which was upgraded regularly, for in their work it was not impossible that they would come across CTs masquerading as ordinary citizens in the New Villages. That was how he had become familiar with the visitor's face. Abruptly, for such is the strange working of the memory, a name popped up from Ferdach's unconscious: Sui Mah. His position on the chart was fairly high though Ferdach could not remember his precise rank.

Leaving Harry Wong to sleep Ferdach went to the bathroom locking the door after him. He did not want to shit, shower and shampoo – as they used to say in the RAF – in the presence of the beauteous one. In fact he felt more wary of him now than earlier on their journey. Though he could understand very little of the previous night's conversation, he could see that Comrade Wong was completely at home with the two CTs. The ease was present in the way they moved, the way they exchanged glances, even in that rare commodity for communists, their laughter; inevitably he had wondered whether any of it had been at his expense. Another cause for misgiving was the ease with which at least three CTs had come into the rest house, and obviously got everything they wanted out of the kitchen staff. It was as though the place was not in the Federation of Malaya, but in what the CTs would like to call a 'liberated area'.

As he looked at himself in the shaving mirror, quite childish thoughts entered his mind: why should I shave for these monsters? Why should I give them an ounce of respect? Then another thought: well I'm really shaving as a representative of the High Commissioner, and a rather weird representative at that. Despite his hope that all would go smoothly, a sneaking fear emerged to tell him that perhaps he was walking into a trap and might end up dead. Don't be an idiot, was the easy answer to that, you are an insignificant little cog in the government machinery, hardly worth anyone wasting a bullet on.

A more real cause of fear was his certain knowledge that the power of the communists lay not just over the Gap rest house, as witnessed last night, but extensively over much of the western part of Pahang where the well organized 6th Regiment of jungle fighters held sway. They were believed to have hundreds of camps, each with accommodation for anything from a handful of men to over five hundred. Was it likely that so many CTs would have an inkling of the reason for his presence? Knowledge of the exchanges between Sir Henry and Chin Peng was restricted to probably five or six people. It was not impossible, therefore, that Harry Wong and himself might be ambushed by mistake.

Harry had sensed the cause of Ferdach's gloom. 'It wasn't very pleasant for you last night,' he said as they started their journey down the eastern side of the mountains, 'just sitting there while we were talking. But we had matters to discuss, in particular your, no, our safety. The men who visited us are in authority around here.'

Ferdach refrained from uttering the name Sui Mah lest it might seem that he had been honing up on the enemy before leaving Ipoh. Trust had to be maintained. So he pretended to be unconcerned. 'A few miles on was where I went off the road,' he said. 'I was nearly killed. I wonder what would have happened if your lot had seen us. Shot us, I suppose.'

'Well you deserved to be punished for rotten driving. But you'll be glad to know that last night we were making sure that your green Morris arrives safely in Tras.'

'Look, there's the place. Where that stream's flowing across the road. The PWD still hasn't cleared the culvert. I'm going to look where we went over.'

It had only been a short time ago but there was no sign of Ferdach's accident. The two boulders between which his car had landed were just about visible but the bushes all about them had grown to a great height. If he and his passengers had died and never been found, the jungle would soon have obscured them from the rest of mankind.

79

After descending the road through the mountains they came to Kampung Tranum where a junction of roads lead south to Bentong and north to Kuala Lipis. There they stopped since Harry said they were a bit too early.

'Too early for what?' Ferdach asked, but was told nothing. Harry looked at his watch and suggested they should go to a roadside stall where they had a drink of mango juice packed with ice ground by a machine that looked like an old-fashioned mangle. Ferdach felt nervous, not at the idea of meeting Chin Peng but because he had lost his freedom to decide anything. Being entirely in the hands of Harry Wong might have been all right except that the whole arrangement seemed to be in a state of flux. Could he be sure that Harry Wong, this Englishman in Chinese clothing and that not always, was trusted by the full-bloodied communists who had visited them last night? He probably wouldn't have felt anxious if Harry had not become nervous too; he no longer talked easily but stared up and down the road, consulting his watch as if the two of them had strayed into uncertain territory. Then, all at once, they heard two shots, one after the other, some distance away and he said, 'Right Ferdach we're off. You're going to meet one of the most remarkable men in the country.' By now Ferdach could think of nothing apposite to the occasion to say but, 'Oh yes?' and that rather dubiously. They drove at a steady twenty miles an hour towards Tras.

It was a small uninspiring place with Chinese shophouses but little business activity in evidence. There was a police post but no sign of security forces. This Ferdach found strange: in most Malayan towns there were roadblocks and security checks manned by Specials. This was a place at peace, or more likely the modus vivendi of Lawrence Chong's

New Village prevailed. In the centre of the town Ferdach was told to turn left into a smaller street. After no more than twenty yards they stopped again. The street was like a film set; there was no one about except for a couple of old men sitting in a doorway some way off. Ferdach was conscious that they were watching him without looking at him. The atmosphere was eerie. It made him think of one of those remote Italian hill towns that hardly ever saw outsiders and viewed them with deep suspicion should they ever turn up. On the other side of the street the row of shophouses was broken by a high brick wall with a solid wooden gate at its centre. As if by magic, this swung open to reveal a dirt track that curved to the right and ended near a modest house raised on brick pillars.

'Drive in there,' said Harry.

Ferdach obeyed, heard the gate close behind him and realised that he had disappeared out of sight of anyone passing through the town.

Without being told Ferdach got out of the car. Harry came round to join him. 'Don't make any moves unless I have first told you,' he said quietly, to which Ferdach replied, 'I hope it's all right if I breathe.'

Harry led him to the front of the house where there was a brick *tangga* or staircase made attractive with coloured tiles set in the treads and a row of flowering potted plants. The house was not large, but the sort of place that might have been just right for the peaceful retirement of a Malay technical officer or a *penghulu*. Above the doorway there was a carved wooden board adorned with lettering in Arabic script, no doubt a quotation from the Holy Qur'an. The back of the house was fairly close to the Chinese shophouses on the street, but on its other three sides there was an extensive open garden with scattered clumps of papaya, banana and palm trees that merged into open country. It might have been expected that such a place would be the scene of movement, especially of children or of women hanging out laundry or just finding a shady place to gossip. But both the house and its surroundings were quiet. After making sure that Ferdach was comfortably seated on the verandah and given tea and cigarettes by a dumpy girl dressed in a black *samfu*, Harry said, 'Wait here until you are called in.' When gazing across the garden Ferdach noticed a couple of men apparently on patrol, and once he turned his head and saw a man peeping at him from an inner doorway.

Left alone it was impossible for Ferdach not to reflect on the ambiguity of the house. It might be behind a wall but it could be no secret to anyone in the town. The ambiance might almost be compared to that of King's House in Kuala Lumpur, a place not completely demarcated from the rest of the town but one to which no one without business would go because they knew that it contained important people. It was also clear that if this was the case then the little town of Tras must be identified with those people, protecting them, succouring them and possibly even defending them if the need arose. Yet a darker thought entered Ferdach's mind: a place so easy to attack could not defend itself if the might of the security forces was turned on it. So why was it not attacked? The answer stared Ferdach coldly in the face: the place must have some sort of tacit protection. This was a 'safe house'. Ferdach then thought of something symbolic. He was fond of looking up Malay words in his Wilkinson's *Malay–English Dictionary*. *Teras*, he recalled, or Tras as the town's name was written, meant the harder portions or the core of a good timber tree. He was now at the hard core of Malayan communism.

It did not surprise him that he should be left alone for almost half an hour. His own association with the Communist Party in Britain had left him familiar with the pedantic nature of its members, always intent on going into every detail before taking action. There was also another concept not unfamiliar in the East that might be operating, that of keeping people waiting before receiving them, the waiting time being related to their relative importance in the scheme of things. However, in the latter assumption Ferdach was wrong.

So preoccupied was he with all these thoughts that he noticed neither the presence of two men who had quietly come onto the verandah and were watching him, nor the return of the dumpy girl who had brought the tea. Indeed he had closed his eyes and begun to drift into sleep. A hand touched his shoulder gently and the girl said in English, 'Please come, Mr Hor Hanee.'

The room he was ushered into was simply furnished. There were no sideboards or cupboards or pictures, only a row of chairs against two of the opposite walls, and an oblong table, at one long side of which a man was seated. Ferdach at once recognised Chin Peng from photos he had seen, but being only mugshots Ferdach was surprised when the Secretary General rose and proved to be a rather slightly built man, of less than medium height with a thick head of hair. He was simply dressed in white slacks and a white shirt with rolled-up sleeves and he might have been mistaken for a Chinese clerk in any office. His face was round and pleasant, an average Chinese face, though with a rather toothy smile which he flashed when he rose and came to shake Ferdach's hand. He then returned to his place at the table and gestured Ferdach to sit opposite him while Harry and the girl who, it turned out, was no mere servant, sat on the two shorter sides.

Chin Peng broke the silence by saying in a soft voice in typical Malayan English, 'I am sorry to keep you waiting Mr Hor Hanee. Comrade Wong was talking to me about you.'

Ferdach kept his eyes glued to this man who, according to Comrade Wong, was one of the most remarkable men in the country. But who could tell whether a man was remarkable just by looking at him. Julius Caesar might have looked no more impressive than one of his foot soldiers, and Ferdach remembered seeing Winston Churchill after the war in Liverpool and thinking what an unimpressive round ball of humanity he was, until the great man had opened his mouth in that ceremony in the Philharmonic Hall and his vibrant voice had stilled to silence even those students intent on mild disruption. So it was with Chin Peng. Certainly his voice was not vibrant but it had a sort of forceful precision. As he spoke he used his eyes, which were kindly, yet had the capacity to pierce into the listener. Or so Ferdach imagined, but he also knew that where charisma is concerned, half of what is invested in any great leader comes from the beholder. Perhaps, Ferdach thought, I am already in a state of autosuggestion because everyone says what a marvellous leader Chin Peng was and still is, and perhaps too, I am overawed by the thought that this mild seeming man is capable, when he considers it expedient, to be ruthless. And so all he could utter in response were the words, 'Thank you,' though they were not at all appropriate. He also smiled blandly as people often do when they encounter a member of the royal family.

'You have not been in my country very long?'

Ferdach did not like the 'my' very much but said, 'Less than a year, sir.' It would be silly for him to address Chin Peng as 'comrade'.

'And you are learning Cantonese. As you know I am a Hakka but we can talk in Cantonese if you like.'

'I am certain that your excellent English is better than my Cantonese will ever be.'

Chin Peng smiled slightly and went on, 'And you were once a communist. Why did you leave us?'

Had Harry told him that? Best not to deny it. And would it signify anything if they saw him as a lost 'one of them'. After a few moments of apparently deep thought Ferdach said, 'Because sir, baring conquest by the Soviets, I would be wasting my time working for a communist revolution in a country like Britain. I didn't want to make the same error of judgement as Marx.' As soon as the words were out of his mouth he realised their implication that he was still to the left at heart.

Chin Peng's face lit up. 'But Malaya is largely a peasant economy, rather like Russia before the revolution. So perhaps you are wasting your time here?'

Though Ferdach had enjoyed this logical reply he did not wish to embark on a conversation about the Emergency and his own slight role in it, so he said, 'If the exchange of letters between yourself and Sir Henry Gurney leads to peace, I certainly won't have wasted my time in Malaya at all.'

'Ah yes, that is so,' said Chin Peng. 'I am sure that the High Commissioner and myself are both grateful to you for what you are doing.' He nodded at the dumpy woman comrade who was making a record of what was said. She immediately took a document from a table drawer and handed it to the Secretary General who stated, somewhat more loudly than he had spoken before, 'This is my reply which I ask you to place in Sir Henry Gurney's own hands without any ...' he seemed lost for a word and the secretary prompted: 'intermediary'. 'Yes, intermediary,' said Chin Peng. For the first time Comrade Wong then spoke. 'The time is 9.40 am.' The girl made a note, presumably of the time, in her record. Ferdach took the letter at the same time reflecting that even the smallest matter in the presence of these people was imbued with superfluous precision.

'Well,' said Chin Peng, 'I think we have finished.' Ferdach rose as the communist leader came round the table towards him to shake hands, but instead of doing so at once he paused, caught Ferdach's eyes and asked, 'Do you know Mr Davis, Mr John Davis?'

'No sir. Unfortunately I haven't met him yet. I would like to. Of course I know how he and Richard Broome and the others in Force 136 worked with you and your people during the occupation. It's a wonderful story.' Ferdach searched his mind for what little he knew about Davis at present. 'Ah yes, he's married now, so I've been told, to a childhood sweetheart.'

Chin Peng had not recognised the last word and looked questioningly at his secretary who whispered, 'Swe hart … *cing yan*.'

'I think I know, I think I know.' Obviously a memory of some sort was racing through Chen Peng's brain. Ferdach thought, well they can't always have talked about killing Japanese when they were together in the jungle. Then, just as he imagined that he could discern a slightly sad, no, a wistful look in Chen Peng's eyes, he heard him continue, 'Of course, you cannot give him my congratulations. You cannot take any message to him. Your mission is secret. But I will tell you, just you Mr Hor Hanee, that John was my good friend. He is a very fine man.'

The interview was over and was followed by an unduly long handshake as though Chin Peng did not wish to let his visitor go. Ferdach wondered for an instant whether he should bow slightly but did not do so, remembering that such a gesture might be a reminder of the ghastly Japanese who had once been their common enemy.

80

At Tranum Harry Wong announced that they must go to Kuala Lumpur by way of Bentong and then over the mountains through the Sempah Pass to Gombak, just north of KL, where they would separate. Citing the strength of the CTs in west Pahang, Ferdach objected to this plan. He was not concerned for his own safety but he wanted to make sure that the letter reached the High Commissioner without mishap. However, Harry's doubts of the previous day seemed to have evaporated and he said they would be safe all the way to the capital. Ferdach knew he was obliged to obey but he rather enjoyed making a show of his independence. In fact he didn't mind taking the Bentong road in the least for he knew the area was considerably safer by now as a result of some important recent defections in communist leadership. He did not reveal this information, which had not yet been made public by government, and which Harry might not know.

Harry Wong was as happy as a schoolboy released for the holidays. His part in the mission had been successfully accomplished. It was a relief for him to be released from the charismatic presence of the Secretary General, but perhaps he too was feeling he had made his mark with the leader; after all he had spent half an hour closeted alone with Chin Peng, a privilege not granted to many Party cadres. Beyond this Ferdach felt certain that Harry was happy to be alone with him. It was a happiness he reciprocated. They drove quickly to Bentong where they stopped to eat and then, at a more leisurely pace, they began the ascent up the Sungei Benus valley towards Genting Sempah. It was a picturesque route, following the river into which a number of tributaries flowed. After a while Harry made Ferdach stop at one of these confluences and they left the car at the roadside to follow the tributary into the forest. Though the path looked little more than a wild boar track it was obvious that Harry knew exactly where he was going. They soon arrived at a wide hollow in the fast-flowing river where it was possible to swim if care was taken to avoid the strong currents that surged between the rocks. They sat on a huge boulder around which water was rushing, drinking beer and eating the rambutans and jambus they had bought in Bentong.

'What are you going to do when you've handed over the letter?' Harry asked. 'Will you stay in KL for a while?'

'I don't know how long it will be before I can see HE so I can't say whether I'll have any time to be social.' This was a lie for, however long it took him, Ferdie had every intention of spending at least a night with Laura. He anticipated talking with her seriously, at long last, about their relationship but could see no reason to tell this to Harry.

'You'll hand it over tonight. Gurney isn't leaving KL until Wednesday. You can easily get up to King's House tonight.'

Ferdach was not unduly surprised that the communists should know where and when the High Commissioner was travelling; it was hardly worth commenting upon. 'Then it will be tonight. I'll use the old photograph ploy: ring up the Private Secretary and say I've got the rest of the photos Sir Henry wants and can I bring them up.'

Harry laughed. 'So simple yet so effective, but simplicity is the last refuge of the complex as your Irish martyr said.'

It was impossible not to be amused by Harry, especially in his lighter mood but also odd to be with a Party cadre who could one moment conduct himself very seriously into the presence of the most senior terrorist in the country, and the next, most flippantly quote Wilde with an appeal to his Irish sentiment. Ferdach watched Harry strip off and slip into the river and he enjoyed the way the rippling water subtly distorted his limbs. Once again Harry was flaunting himself deliberately, which made Ferdach decide that the time had come for a direct question. 'Harry, how do people like you make out in your wonderful liberated new China?'

'What do you mean "people like me"?'

'Tung sing oi yan, homosexuals.'

Harry stood on a submerged rock, visible from his knees upward, as graceful as Aphrodite rising from the waves and, though naked, the image of modesty.

'Ferdie, where did you learn your history? There was no homosexuality in China, before corrupt Westerners took it there.'

'Oh come off it, what about those love poems written by men for other men? Those novels? The emperors with their boys? What about the Manchu court?'

Harry climbed out of the water and sat down with his arm around Ferdach's shoulders dripping water all over him. 'You Europeans can be very thick. Homosexuality as a concept was invented by your head doctors. You love classifying things. You've done it since Aristotle. But once you divide things into categories you falsify them because everything in the universe is connected. Why shouldn't a normal man make love with a friend if they love each other, especially if there are no women around? All animals are like that. Have you never watched monkeys do it? It's all so obvious to any thinking person but there's something strange about Westerners, especially the British, that they can't see it. In the old times, scholars and other educated people in China never worried about such trivia. But you're asking how people like me manage in China with its dose of communist puritanism, which by the way arrived via Marx from Europe. Well, since China is the homeland of the secret society we've developed the art of keeping things under cover. We're good at saying one thing but doing another. What's more, if you don't classify someone as something then you don't have to pry into what he's up to.'

'Then how can you be a Marxist? Dialectical materialism is full of categorical analysis, classifying people this way and that, very Aristotelian really. Without classification you couldn't have class struggle. Now what d'you say to that?'

Harry sat up, gave an exaggerated yawn, pulled his ears out sideways and said in an American drawl, 'My dear, I don't care a damn.' With that he pitched himself roughly into the water making a mighty splash that doused Ferdach. 'Come on in Aristotle. Let's be like boys the world over, from Ireland to China. Come on in. Let's play together.' But having shouted his plea Harry looked suddenly forlorn as if he knew he had expressed a wish that would not be granted.

Ferdach remained seated, contenting himself with the mere sight of Harry circling and then diving down deep in the water sometimes long enough to make him feel alarmed for swift streams have a nasty way of dragging swimmers to their depths. Of course, what Harry had said was near the mark but only partly so. He had exaggerated the Chinese attitude to sexual nonconformity even if his strictures about the Western way of looking at sexual problems had possessed more than a modicum of truth. He had been speaking about a world of cultivated officials, of poets, of people without ignorant prejudices; he was talking as much about Cambridge – and a small clique within Cambridge at that – as he was about sophisticated courtiers. Life as it now was in China might not prove so tolerant. As for those words about his countrymen knowing how to keep secrets, they were true indeed but in this the Chinese were not unique for people of Ferdach's nature the world over were often forced to do the same. Yet Ferdach knew that just for now there was no pressure on them to conform. In this idyllic jungle bowl, where he could hear the cries of beasts but no words of man, where the trees soared to the heavens and the empty blue sky was indifferent to the swift motion of the river, here everything was both transitory and easy. If he slipped into the water and embraced Harry, no one but the fishes would see and all knowledge of what they did together would be washed down to the distant ocean. He must not lose another friend through being hesitant, as in a similar paradise he had lost Mat Noor. All at once he felt more cold water splashed up at him by Harry's flailing hand. With threatening yells he peeled off his clothes and dived towards the aggressor.

The next moment they were in one another's arms in the foaming water. They might have appeared to be wrestling but, as Ferdach recalled later, it seemed that their fierce need just then to possess and be possessed by the other so as to become complete, was exactly that of Plato's divided fragments of the male which, yearning to embrace their lost half, transmute their irresistible desire and pursuit of the whole into love. It was not embracing that might satisfy the prurient; there were no lascivious positions, no drawn-out moans and sighs, no explosive orgasms. It was little more than clinging tightly to one another and trying not to be swept away between the boulders by the swift water. Swirled back and forth they just about managed to bring one another off with their hands without being borne downstream. It was simple and brief yet, with absolute clarity to each of them, their frantic grappling of one another's limbs and, when the sexual act was done, the passion of their lips told them that there was love between them, though each still wondered what he meant to the other. Later they lay side by side, exhausted not by love but by the fight against the current. Ferdach fell asleep on the warm stone. He knew not for how long, but when he awoke the shadows were falling in a different direction. He heard Harry asking, as though what had happened between them was no more than an insignificant explosion of pent-up emotions, 'Did you ever meet that secretary of Del Boca? A man called Gilbert de Guise, married to a woman called Hester?'

Ferdach was surprised both by Harry's cool manner and by the question. He had not heard much talk of the de Guises since their transfer to the east coast. 'Of course I knew them,' he said just as coolly. 'They were my friends. They still are, I suppose.'

'Do you really know what they are like? I mean, what they want out of life in this country?'

There was no need to talk about the de Guises' banishment and still less about their religious sexual practices; it was no one else's business. So Ferdach decided to be facetious. 'You're not going to tell me that they're really communists are you? Anyway they can't be, they went to Oxford not Cambridge.'

'No Ferdie, when you were snoring away I made a decision to tell you something quite different: that I, Comrade Wong Chooi Fong, am not a communist. I am neither a peasant nor a worker; in fact I've never done a real day's work in my life. As you can imagine, that makes me suspect to most Party members. I come from a rich family of delightful idlers: artists, poets, scholars and not a few debauchees. I was brought up on the great classics but I was also taught by masters about Buddhism and Tao. Do you think I could ever give up the riches of our culture and art for Marxist rubbish? My communism is only an expedient but it's also a horrid aberration. In reality my philosophy isn't so different now from that of Gilbert and Hester though I haven't been able to put it into practice like them. I shall do one day. The de Guises are two remarkable people but it was Hester alone who brought me back to the mystic way and it was Hester who led me on to Tantra. It was she who connected me with my earlier beliefs again.' Harry sat up suddenly as if he had to tell the rest of his story from a superior level. 'Maybe you didn't know this but I lived with Hester before she married Gilbert, after she left that boring police officer Molyneux. I'd still be with her but for the Emergency.'

Only then did Ferdach connect Harry's words with what Noel Aspinall had told him on Pangkor Island about a marital scandal two years back in KL. If Hester really was the woman Harry had filched from her policeman husband, Ferdach wanted to know the whys and wherefores of it all. Forthrightly he asked, 'Well then, if it was such a passionate affair, why did you leave Hester? Why did you go into the jungle? I don't believe the Emergency is the explanation. Even Lai Kuan can't make it out. Something must have been wrong.' Ferdach continued to lie there supinely but he cushioned his hands under his head to be more comfortable and stared up into Harry's eyes, like a parent demanding an explanation for naughty behaviour.

'You'll go on at me until you know everything won't you? But don't bother; I want you to know, so you can understand me. But I wish you wouldn't stare at me like that as if I'm the moon. I'll lie beside you and you can just listen, quietly if you're capable of it.' Harry lay down and pressed himself against Ferdach's body. 'You know what Hester's like, she's very ...'

'Intense,' said Ferdach.

'Yes, and if I was superstitious I'd say she was a *wu lei cheng*, a fox fairy.'

'A what?'

'A *wu lei cheng* is a demon that becomes a beautiful woman and drains the life out of a young man with endless sex.'

'You're joking,' said Ferdach, dubiously remembering a Celtic tale of such a being and thinking too that one could never tell what Chinese might believe.

'Well she almost did that to me. If anyone could be a *wu lei cheng* it'd be Hester. There are more things in heaven and earth Ferdie, and it wasn't a Chinese who said that. Well, you've no idea how dominating Hester is. She likes to have her own way in everything but only if there's a challenge. That's why she'd grown tired of Peter well before I came along. He provided her with no stimulus at all. I don't know why she'd married him in the first place, except that marriage enabled her to stay in Malaya;

otherwise it was India in chaos or London in the cold. When Peter found out we were sleeping together, he went crazy; he tried desperately to cling onto her, like a slave who won't be sold. At that time I was still young and even more stupid than I am now so I wanted to rubbish my reputation of not being interested in women. I was also fiercely anti-imperialist and getting a British policeman's wife was a statement to my Malayan friends; it was more important to me than what I felt for Hester. By the time Peter gave up, the rivalry between us had changed her into a trophy but once I win a trophy I lose interest in it. The battle had the opposite effect on Hester, unfortunately. One night when we'd been at it for ages, she told me I belonged to her and her alone. It made me shudder. Ferdach, my nature's the same as yours so you know what I'm saying. I longed for men. But she'd already introduced me to Tantra and she saw me as the faithful lover with whom she would go on and on experiencing sacred bliss. It was too much for me. I felt I was suffocating. I could see what she was aiming at but it had come home to me that for it to work both partners must truly want one another.' For an instant Harry fell silent before asking tentatively, 'I believe it would work for you and me. Don't you, Ferdie?'

Now it was Ferdach's turn to prop himself up on one arm and look down at Harry. 'Maybe it can't work for anyone. It sounds like an impossibility. I distrust these doctrines. I've read about priests having endless bliss with sacred temple women; I bet the stories are all written by men. They're fantasies. We never hear what the women have to say about it.' Ferdach was temporising. He had been asked a question which he was not prepared to answer, neither here in this magical place which might seem to imbue his words with significance nor, more importantly, in the midst of his career during an Emergency which might end soon or could go on for years. If only people would learn to let things ride as Waite had advised: not to do a thing either positively or negatively but not to do anything. Yet he sympathised with Harry for whom he had fallen more deeply than was wise. He let his eyes roam over that upturned face that looked as if it had never known a day of sorrow; he stroked that face like a sincere lover, he smiled and he said. 'You're the sort of man Harry who has to have a doctrine to cling on to. How ironic that Hester's weird beliefs should drive you into the arms of Marxists. Still, after Hester I can see the appeal of all those Spartans braving it in the jungle.'

Harry was disconcerted by Ferdach's cynicism. 'I didn't rush straight into the jungle. It was a slow process. When you first arrived in Ipoh I hadn't made up my mind. In the end I came to believe in the struggle and I was accepted as a Party member.'

'I know you can act well Harry but it still amazes me that you were able to pull the wool over the eyes of astute people like Chin Peng though I guess even he must have been convinced when you murdered George Carew.'

A frown clouded Harry's face. 'Don't go on. It's not the Party I've betrayed, it's myself, my own beliefs. You might say I don't deserve to live but then neither do a lot of other people. Ferdie, you can help me; in loving and being loved I can see some hope for myself.' His manner expressed utter dejection as he looked away from Ferdach who regretted reminding him of his bloody acts, but abruptly he turned his head again. His face had lit up and when he spoke his voice was insinuating. 'I asked you a question. What are you going to do after you've given the letter to Gurney? I'd like us to get together soon. We could have fun together. Rivers aren't good places to make love in. You mightn't realise it but my comrades are often around here. In fact we sometimes use this place as a swimming pool. It's even possible that we are being watched right now. Some of them already think I'm too friendly with you. What we've just done might be the proof they've been looking for.'

'Chin Peng didn't seem to mind our friendship.'

'That's so. He approved. Especially when I told him that you could come over to us.'

'Be realistic Harry. There's no chance of it.'

'Isn't there? Just think of it. If what you're involved in goes well, there could be peace very soon. There might even be a coalition with Chin Peng in the government.'

'Impossible. Why should that happen?'

'Simply because we all know that your side is beaten. Yes, you may keep up nominal control for a while but before long China will be influencing the whole region and your government, no not KL, Whitehall will have to come to an accommodation with it. That's why the Labour Government was so quick to recognise the People's Republic. Soon you'll give up the struggle, like you did in India. Chin Peng won't be negotiating from a position of weakness, but Gurney will be and he'll know it.'

Ferdach listened to all this with amazement. Harry had started to caress him sweetly to arouse his desire. But he was not to be coaxed so easily. 'No Harry. What you're saying is crazy. Recognition was just the gut reaction of Labour when it saw a leftwing government kick out the corrupt KMT.' But insidious thoughts were creeping into Ferdach's mind. 'Anyhow, how could I come over? I wouldn't be with you. What good would I be in the jungle?'

'None whatsoever Ferdie. We're not suggesting that.'

'By "we" you mean …'

'Chin Peng. You wouldn't have to come over openly. But you could keep in contact with us until peace is signed. I would be your contact, in every way Ferdie.'

'You mean be a spy?'

'I mean serve the cause of the people which is what men like you, yes and your friend Waite, really want to do. And when peace is here there'll be need of some expatriates to help run things, to act as a bridge until– '

'You establish the bloody, yes I mean bloody, dictatorship of the proletariat.'

'Yes Ferdie, very true but that could be years away by which time you and I could–'

'Could what, Harry? What do you want of me? Could what?'

'Could have got away from it all. I've told you that I'm not a communist. I despise it. Communism is foul, all that Marxist stuff about quantitative and qualitative change and dialectical leaps forward is nonsense. As a Buddhist, I believe in the unity of all there is. I believe that things flow like a river. They do not leap. To be one with it we must follow the Way, the Tao. I could not travel it with a woman but I could do so with you Ferdie. You and I could find complete fulfilment in Tantra as the de Guises have done. Tantra teaches that the erotic is the threshold to the spiritual.' Harry had noticed Ferdach's dubious expression. 'You still think I'm talking rubbish, but I believe our lives could be joined together. If we lived together, there would be so much for us to explore, my real comrade Ferdie, just you and me.'

Ferdach felt himself recoiling under the urgency of these demands.

Though it was true that something unusual had happened between them, for Ferdach it was all tentative. They now saw each other as lovers, but to what degree? Harry's words about Tantra, of which Ferdach knew as little, disturbed him. He regretted that he had never learned something about Tibetan Buddhism from Gilbert de Guise. He knew that some mystery was pulling him towards its unfamiliar centre but he was not ready to let go and be drawn into it. At this moment the sound of the rushing water seemed to be a part of the mystery but he was also aware that it had a power that was hindering him from thinking rationally. But if he could not think straight, he could feel, so strongly indeed that as he looked into Harry's face he was again moved to wonder by its beauty. Without hesitation, he leaned forward to kiss those willing lips, again and again. 'Harry, I want you even though I think you've taken leave of your senses. Just now, nothing seems to matter except holding you. I don't even want to be told how someone like you can still be a CT.'

Even though their bodies were enfolded in one another's arms, Harry was not willing to let Ferdach's expression of desire divert him from saying what mattered to him. That final statement had shot to the heart of his dilemma. As if he was mouthing words of love he said softly into Ferdach's ear, 'For the same reason as you can still be in the MCS. You hate the British system, its arrogance, its old-boy corruption hiding under all those orders and titles, its selfishness, its exploitation. Yes, for the same reason as you Ferdie, as you as an Irishman. The communists' enemies are my enemies and so I joined them. Aren't they also yours? But when we are in power and the British are gone, I want to leave this country, to live with someone I love, to live for a man I love.' He paused, kissed Ferdach passionately and then declared, 'For you Ferdie.'

Before Harry could kiss him again Ferdach exclaimed, 'But it's too late Harry, even though I love you, even though I want you; yes, I admit it again, I do want you. Don't you understand me, Harry? I'm truly a man divided. I like women; I like men. But loving men is too difficult in our society. I've set my mind against living like that. I think I'd be happier if I got married and had children. Maybe in the future, who knows? What's more there's already a woman in my life. I intend to marry her.'

Harry drew away but still gazed steadfastly at Ferdach. His voice was dull when he said, 'Come out with her name Ferdie. You mean

Laura. Lai Kuan has told me about her.'

Ferdach stretched his arms out again towards Harry in a futile sort of gesture, as if to say 'we can still be friends' or some equally mundane rubbish though his words were to the contrary, 'Yes, with Laura. I've more than hinted, no, I guess that one way or another I've admitted to her that I want to live with her, that I shall live with her in the end. That end is almost here Harry. But it doesn't mean that you and I can't have a good time together. Why, you yourself said just now that we could have fun together when we get to KL.'

Harry uttered a loud and very angry 'Hah!' followed by a Chinese expression '*hei yau chi lei*', which literally meant 'where is there a principle in all this' – a quite justifiable sentiment in the light of Ferdach's insensitivity to his feelings. He scrambled out of Ferdach's reach and began to put on his American clothes. Everything he said, every movement that he made spoke of his mounting fury. 'Come on O'Haney. Let's go. We won't make love again, ever again. I don't want to be just a good time, just fun, no more than that girl Wong Siu Bo you shagged the first night you were in Ipoh, a thing to be chucked aside when finished with.'

'I've never lost contact with Siu Bo. We write. I go to Penang to see her. She means a lot to me,' Ferdach said defensively, but to no avail.

'We write! I go to Penang to see her!' Harry's regular features were transformed; it was as though some wild mocking creature had taken over. 'So she means a lot to you does she? Liar! You think of nothing but your own cock, O'Haney. That's all love means to you. Yes, you are a man divided, but a man who knows how to satisfy both sides of your nature without trouble. You visit Siu Bo's place to fuck her girls. I know and the Party knows everything about you. You've been watched. But those girls don't matter to you any more than I do. You see me only as an object to gratify you but it's the shell you want, not me. And to think that I would have given up everything for you. Oh yes, I see why you didn't tell me what you'll be doing after you've seen Gurney. It's Laura, Laura, Laura. Hah! But what a stupid way to tell Laura that you want her: hinted at, admitted, will live together in the end, while you still get up to your tricks with whatever bit of flesh takes your eye.' His voice quivered with total contempt. 'I know what it's all about. You imagine that she'll be useful to you, don't you? You don't love her; you're just using her to become a "normal" officer, a career man who puts his job first for quick promotion. Oh Ferdie, Ferdie, what are you doing? What have you done?' Harry fell silent after uttering his grief. There was no sound then but that of the surging water that drowned even the shrill cries of the jungle. He stared at Ferdach not so much in anger now as with pity and said, 'One day, not so far off, I shall show you what living for someone really means.'

81

Laura's apartment had been transformed since Ferdach had last seen it. While she was pouring drinks and popping in and out of the kitchen to talk to a servant, Ferdach poked around a bit. Where before it had been simply furnished with rattan chairs and settees and had an unpleasantly cheap 1930s look about it, it had now been redecorated in a style that reflected Laura's taste for rich colour and the opulent. There were Indian carpets, antique tables and cupboards picked up from the dusty so-called 'junk' shops of Malacca, comfortable chairs and settees with richly coloured batik cushions on which to loll and Javanese lamps that gleamed their silvery light over a variety of wood carvings and pictures to create the impression of an Aladdin's cave. In a spacious extension to the main sitting room stood a new piano; not the upright Ferdach had heard her play in Ipoh but a very handsome baby grand. He tinkled on the keys to test the tone which was excellent. On it and scattered about on the chairs and the floor were music scores and books of poetry by the likes of Donne, Marvell and Milton. A mock up of a programme on the music stand suggested that Laura was involved as a pianist in a recital of baroque chamber music and poetry. It all looked rather precious to Ferdach who was not in the least surprised to read that it had been organized by Algernon Broadstairs, Ipoh resettlement officer now metamorphosed into concert director; well, who else could put on such a concert in Malaya. The memory of the long line of burned-out lorries outside that New Village in Perak – Broadstair's last major production – crossed Ferdach's mind and he chuckled out loud before sprawling on a long settee. Yes, this was a delightful place to relax in even if, by Public Works Department standards, it was a sophisticated riot. Every bit of it seemed imbued with Laura's character. A smell of some heavy perfume gave Ferdach the feeling that he had entered a Middle Eastern brothel. It was not easy for him to repress the notion that Laura had found an Asian gentlemen of even greater wealth than Lai Kuan, who had set her up in the luxury that she had always desired. Laura noticed which way his thoughts were turning and preluding her words with that throaty laugh which she had recently been cultivating, stated, 'No Ferdie, I bought it all myself. Alfred has agreed to be the guilty party when the divorce goes ahead. He really has come up trumps and he's been generous already. I had quite a tearful parting from him and sweet little Mona Wee. I told him to keep everything we had together, apart from a few silver bits and pieces and some of the books I'm really attached to. Oh the piano's on HP. With two incomes I thought I might as well pamper myself and set up a nice home where I can entertain in style.'

Ferdach was certainly glad that he would not have to help Laura out with any money but he did feel obscurely worried about her new set-up. However, as he was very hungry he concentrated on the food that was produced, rather surprisingly, by a young Malay maid. 'What's happened to Ah Yong, the girl Lai Kuan got for you? You used to say how efficient she was.'

'Oh she went off to get married,' Laura replied airily, which made Ferdach look up with surprise as Ah Yong, despite her efficiency, was far from pretty.

'How did she get a husband? She's got no money and she isn't pretty. Surely she was better off with you.'

'Oh I didn't mean married as a first wife. I think she's really going to be wife number two, or a concubine or something. She'll really be more like a servant.'

This was more believable but the account bore an uncommon resemblance to a story Ferdach had himself told Laura some months back. Being cute, however, he accepted it at face value and went on eating. Then for the first time he really took in the fact that Laura's clothes were quite different from her usual style. She was wearing a Malay sarong and *kebaya* and the material of which they were made was rich and beautiful. Her hair too had changed; it no longer fell over her shoulders but was piled up and held by a silver and horn comb at the back of her head. Ferdach did not really like the change though he had to admit to himself that she looked extremely sophisticated. It was not his custom to say much about the appearance of women; he just expected them to look good but tonight he actually commented on the changes fulsomely to which she replied, a bit testily, 'Oh I was wondering when you were going to notice anything different. So you really like me like this?'

'Of course I do Laura, but I was as hungry as a hunter and tired when I got here and so I guess my eyes were only brought to life when the food arrived.'

'So all went well, did it Ferdie? Are you free to tell me about it?'

At that moment Ferdach was feeling very sure of himself. He had willy-nilly made a break with Harry in favour of Laura, he had accomplished a useful mission for the High Commissioner and he saw no reason why he should not enjoy a modicum of praise from the person with whom he was going to spend the rest of his life, so he had no qualms about saying, 'Yes Laura. It went perfectly. And as it's almost over I guess I can tell you, especially as Lai Kuan said that you know half of it already. But first you must make a solemn promise not to let it go further. It could be harmful to me if you told anyone.'

'Of course I promise.'

'A solemn promise.'

'Oh Ferdie, of course I give you my solemn promise. In any case who could I tell? But before you say a word I bet you were taken to see a very important communist leader.' As she spoke the last words Laura gave a funny downward glance and flickered her eyelids like a vamp in an old time silent spy movie manifesting her commitment to secrecy even under torture.

'As a matter of fact, I did. He put his letter in my hand for personal delivery to HE. That was how both parties wanted it.' Ferdach laughed, squeezed Laura's hand and said, 'There. I've rubbed off some of his charisma on you.'

Laura did not press him even though she wanted to hear everything he could tell about Chin Peng, but since it would come in due course she asked nonchalently, 'And Harry Wong. Where is he now?'

'I dropped him off at Gombak. Oh, by the way, I've brought something for you.' Ferdach went to the hall to get his travelling bag from which he took out a charming Indian god, Krishna playing his flute.

His skin was blue and his pantaloons bright yellow. His eyes were large, staring and very beautiful. 'Be careful,' he said, 'the god has tremendous power.'

Laura gasped, 'Ah it's so lovely. But where did it come from?'

'Well, when we got near to Gombak Harry told me to stop. We went a little way into an abandoned rubber plantation. Harry had to change his clothes. He'd been a sort of American up to then. You won't believe this Laura but out of his hold-all came a CT uniform, five pointed star cap and all, oh and a revolver. I don't know where he'd concealed them in the car. Nearby, amidst some overgrown bushes, there was an abandoned Indian temple, the sort Indians build near their labour lines on estates. Harry knew the way into it. There were a lot of smashed plaster gods and demons lying around but this one had been carefully placed against a wall. Harry picked it up and told me to take it.' Laura must have got the impression that Ferdach and Harry had parted in a friendly way and that the Krishna was a parting gift, a warm gesture of friendship from Harry. But if it had been so, the friendship was deeply hidden for the idol had been thrust into Ferdach's hands by a silent resentful Harry who had said no more than, 'Get the letter up to King's House as quickly as possible. If it leads to anything, we may meet again. If it doesn't this will be goodbye.' And with that he had gone.

Laura made it sound as if she was more curious about Harry Wong than the famed communist leader. 'How could a clever man like that go into the jungle? What a tragedy for his parents. And sad for you too Ferdie. You once told me he was one hundred percent your type.'

'Nonsense. You seem to think I'm after every handsome guy I meet. Everyone isn't like randy Laura, you know.'

Laura smiled and snuggled up close to him, 'Your lips can lie Ferdie, but never your eyes.' She stroked his hair affectionately, 'Oh Ferdie, I still love you, so much.'

'Why "still"?'

'Oh, well, with us being apart so much. I never know what new interest you may have developed. There's that Wong Siu Bo you see in Penang and her bevy of beauties, or maybe Mat Noor's got a successor.'

Ferdach knew that Laura was upping the ante. He finished off his meal in silence while Laura went off for a while to make coffee in the kitchen. He shouted after her, 'Can't that new Malay girl make good coffee? Ah Yong could.' But Laura had gone. He stood up and took a turn about the room mainly to see what books Laura was reading for she invariably had an interesting selection of novels and magazines on the go. Displayed on the shelves of one of her antique acquisitions, a rosewood bookcase, he saw not only Laura's favourite books but also the 'few silver bits and pieces' Alfred had let her keep; they were the best items Ferdach had seen in the Schweinsnoep's Singapore apartment. Alfred had certainly been ready to cough up for his freedom to be with Mona Wee. Then, in an alcove Laura had set up as a home office, he saw some files relating to the Kwok Company, which was not surprising but what did surprise him was the number of publications on Malaya, its customs and its language. A cursory glance at an open edition of an early Malay autobiography, *Hikayat Abdullah*, a Malay–English dictionary and a well-used notebook revealed that Laura was in the throes of learning Malay. When he heard women's voices coming from the kitchen, he hovered near the doorway and was flabbergasted to hear Laura and the maid chatting away in Malay that was well above his own standard. By the time Laura returned, Ferdach was back on the settee reading *The Straits Times*. Laura sat beside him, looked at him as if she had only just realised he was there and told him how wonderful it was to be with him again. 'Fatimah will bring the coffee in a minute. And what about a Cognac?'

'No Cognac, thanks Laura. Hadn't I better tell you about King's House before we forget about everything else in our absolutely incredible joy at being together again?'

Laura gave him an odd look but she was genuinely interested in what he had to say which was that having driven into KL, he had gone to the Selangor Club and phoned HE's Private Secretary Donald Staples. Quite casually he said he had come up for the weekend and had with him some photos additional to the ones he had already given to Sir Henry and could he drop them at the Private Secretary's house. Staples had immediately replied that HE had mentioned the possibility of O'Haney calling and had asked that the photos should be brought to him personally unless, of course, he was out of KL on tour. When he had heard this ready reply, Ferdach could not help wondering whether

Sir Henry had any other sources of information regarding his visit to Chin Peng, but it was pointless to speculate. He had driven straight up to King's House, been admitted past the sentry box and had soon been shown into Sir Henry's study.

'And what did Sir Henry say?' asked Laura.

'Nothing out of the way. He held the letter in his hands a little while and turned it over a couple of times before putting it in his desk. Then he looked hard at me and thanked me. He thought I had taken quite a risk. Of course I described the house in Tras but he was more interested in what impression I'd gained of Chin Peng. I said very intelligent and with a calculating mind, which is what I really think about him. Then Sir Henry told me something interesting, very interesting. It affects you Laura.'

Laura turned towards Ferdach open eyed, 'Affects me?'

'Of course. Sir Henry told me that two cadets, Hills and Alabaster, are already on their way to Macau to learn Chinese. Language training there has started up again.'

'How does that affect me, Ferdie?'

'Have you forgotten what you said? It's the opportunity we've always wanted Laura. We can get away together. We can get married. You can learn Chinese too. Who knows, we may never come back to Malaya at all. We can leave all this behind.' Ferdach gestured at Laura's new possessions as if they were mere baubles.

Laura did not exactly jump for joy which, Ferdach knew, she would have done only a short while ago. 'But what about your work in Ipoh? You've got such a good reputation. Why must you go now? It isn't as if anyone else knows about your meeting with Chin Peng. Or is there?'

Ferdach scrutinised Laura carefully. 'No,' he replied, 'No. The only people who know about it apart from HE are Lai Kuan, Harry Wong and of course you and me.' Ferdach paused, thinking to himself that this was already quite a bunch. 'And of course Chin Peng and some of his close staff.'

'What about the people up at King's House. Staples must know. And what about Lady Gurney?'

'Only HE knows. He's the sort of man who can keep things to himself.' Ferdach nearly added, 'Not like me.'

'Then it's safe for you to stay in Malaya.'

At that moment Fatimah came in with the coffee. She could not put the tray on the table before them because Sri Krishna was reclining there, so she placed it on another table further away. Then she waited in silence. 'Oh,' said Laura, '*minta ma'af*, excuse me, Fatimah.' She picked up the idol and put it elsewhere. 'Muslim susceptibilities,' she whispered to Ferdach as Fatimah glided silently away.

Pennies began to drop rapidly in Ferdach's brain; the new Muslim décor, the Malay maidservant, the study of the language, the sensitivity to Islamic beliefs. Taking the bull by the horns he asked outright, 'Are you seeing much of Tengku Mizan?'

It was not Laura's custom to be subjected to questioning. 'Look here Ferdie, you know I want to be with you. I do love you very much. I guess we will be together in the end.' Ferdach recognised the words with which Harry had mocked him. 'But is it convenient just now? I'm involved in all sorts of things in KL, especially music. But more important is our work. Yours is more important than mine I know, but I have made myself useful to the Kwok business and–'

'I'm seeing Tengku Mizan very regularly and he's very good at fucking,' Ferdach burst out angrily.

Laura sat back and shook her head sadly. 'Men, men men,' she said. 'Even intelligent men like you Ferdie, how weird you are. How you enjoyed telling me all about Nina Hamnett and her boxers and sailors. And how liberal you were in praising her. Don't you remember complaining that when her Tenby compatriot Augustus John carried on with all and sundry, that was regarded as a sign of his virility, but when she did the same, it was oh what a slut, except of course to liberal-minded Ferdie. And now, when you think I'm doing a Nina on you, your amour proper is wounded and you become just like the men who put her down.'

Ferdach recognised the truth of Laura's words and was crestfallen. All he could say was, 'I don't want to lose you Laura and I had always thought that you ...'

'You needn't lose me Ferdie. Yes, I am having a good time with Mizan. And yes he does make love very well, much better than you Ferdie because your heart is always in another place when you make love with a woman. Don't ask me to change my life just now Ferdie. Mizan doesn't want me as a wife. His family wouldn't allow it. Anyway, he's already got a wife and I'd never want to be one of four or divorced when he felt like saying 'I divorce you' three times. No Ferdie, let me keep this freedom. I like my job and I've been given a lot of responsibility. I'm learning how to trade in tin and rubber. Never in my life have I had such independence. Soon I'll be able to make money on my own bat. In the end that could profit you as well. You go to Macau and in a few months time, maybe a year, I'll follow you, if you still want me. And who knows who you might meet in Macau? You've always found the Chinese very beautiful, men and women. You'll become involved in another world. See, I'm glad you'll have the freedom to find out about yourself You could say that for a while we'll both be doing the same course of study but in different places.'

At first Ferdach thought he would argue with Laura and press her to go with him but at the back of his mind a certain excitement was beginning to burn about living in Macau. What a place in which to be completely free. Perhaps Harry might be able to join him there too, for a while. Laura could be right in suggesting a delay in their plans. With a slight play of reluctance, a deep sigh, a fond look, a few blinks as though to hold back tears, he said at length, 'Very well Laura I accept what you say. I accept it because I know that in the end we will be together. Dear Laura, just think how much we'll have to talk about in our old age.'

They sat down side by side and embraced one another conscious of the fact that there was something between them that should not be lost, but what it was neither of them knew for sure. Then the tenderness turned to passion and they went to the bedroom where they made love. Unfortunately Ferdach could not help remembering Laura saying that Mizan was better at making love than he was and Laura sensed his inner fear; she could not help lying half inert so that Ferdach, though conjuring up Harry's image in his brain, and especially its most virile part, had in the end to pretend, for the first time with Laura, that he was coming, which did not fool her in the least.

Afterwards when they lay together listening to the sounds of the night, Ferdach asked what sort of work Tengku Mizan was now doing and was somewhat shaken to learn that he was now in Bluff Road, the nerve centre of Malayan intelligence, 'But I don't know exactly what branch he's in,' Laura added.

Ferdach looked piercingly into her eyes. His concern was obvious. 'Remember your solemn promise. You're to say nothing to Mizan, nor to anyone about the letters. It's Sir Henry's wish, no his command.'

'I do understand that,' said Laura reassuringly, then all at once asked, 'So what do you guess will happen next?'

Ferdach did not think too carefully before answering, 'I haven't seen the letters and I don't know what's in them but I guess Gurney will want to meet Chin Peng somehow, somewhere and on his own.'

'On his own? Without any protection?' Laura looked perplexed. 'Ferdie, you've kept everything secret so far, I mean about about the role you played and the letters. But isn't your duty different now? Surely Special Branch should know, for Gurney's protection.'

'Gurney said no one else in government must know about the role I played. That's why he wants me out of the way. If anything went wrong I could get some of the blame and he wants to protect me from that. He really is that British ideal Laura, an officer and a gentleman. No, no one else must hear of it and you just keep your promise to keep everything secret.' Ferdach spoke vehemently but inwardly it was only now that he asked himself Laura's question: how would any meeting be arranged. 'In any case,' he exclaimed as though full of confidence, 'HE will know how to set up a meeting safely. He's had that sort of experience in Palestine where things were much trickier.'

Laura put her head on Ferdach's chest, 'Then we'll not think any more about it. What you told me is just between the two of us.'

Fortunately Tengku Mizan did not turn up unexpectedly that night, which was something he often did for he was in love with Laura, probably not deeply but certainly in a sexually possessive way, so that the next morning neither of Laura's paramours was ruffled by any jealous encounter. Ferdach was thus able to devour, in complete peace, a large English breakfast, though with beef sausages instead of bacon, cooked by Fatimah, with the delightful prospect of Macau growing ever stronger in his mind.

When they had exchanged promises to write regularly throughout the year or so during which they would be in different worlds, Ferdach and Laura kissed each other very tenderly and with a certain reluctance to break apart as though they feared that uncertainty was too powerful an element in their lives and that the happiness they had once anticipated might never be theirs. As soon as Ferdach was in the driving seat, Laura called, 'Wait a minute.' She ran up the carport steps and came back with a cardboard box. 'I can't help thinking that Harry Wong must have meant you to keep Sri Krishna,' she said. 'When it's on the wall of our place in Macau we can say that Harry gave it to us as our first wedding present.'

Ferdach drove off not quite sure what pleased him most: Laura's stated intention to join him in Macau but not too soon, or that Harry's potent gift was back in his possession.

82

Early one morning a few weeks later the steamship *Tai Loy* tied up at the quay in Macau bearing Ferdach O'Haney. He was met by the two cadets who had preceded him. Both had been on the same training course as himself in London. Stuart Hills he had of course last talked to most pleasurably in Seremban but Adrian Alabaster he had not met since disembarking at Penang. An Englishman of the traditional kind at its best, Adrian was always there, over the months to come, with sensible advice for Ferdach even if he did not always take it. Adrian and Stuart helped him to settle down in a flat overlooking a broad inlet of the Pearl River estuary between Macau and China and also introduced him to a number of language teachers. After that he was on his own and became engrossed in his studies. The vast cultural world of China then opened before him simultaneously with the opportunity to participate in a small inward-looking Portuguese colonial society, an eighteenth-century time capsule, run by a conservative but permissive regime. For Macau contained a world of tolerated pleasures, some might say vices, which Ferdach started to explore with gusto. Like other young men sent to learn Chinese he enjoyed a number of women who ensured that his contact with their language was both pleasurable and unceasing but, being Ferdach, they were not the only people whose company he sought. Little over a year back Nina Hamnett had advised him to experiment with pleasure and this he did, savouring all the diversions that Macau offered, the sensual and often secret pleasures of the opium houses, the invariably disappointing excitement of the casino, and the everlasting round of parties, banquets and balls which took place in the Portuguese palaces and clubs of the beautiful city in the company of its Chinese and Portuguese grandees. On occasion, he even took part in its sports, though not often. However, he would not have been himself if he had not also scrutinised with compassion the way in which the majority of the colony's population lived or often merely existed. But not being a saint and holding that saints invariably intervene in intractable situations for their own indulgence, and then to little avail, he never thought of doing a thing about it.

Not surprisingly therefore he felt his ties with Malaya and with Laura if not exactly breaking then placed on the back burners of his brain. Macau was where he had wanted to come from the day his mother had read that advertisement in *The Times*. He felt lucky to be in such a place, to study with such excellent Chinese scholars, and to be free to move in a world of behavioural freedom such as even Nina Hamnett had never known. His sojourn in Macau was something separate from his life in Malaya, though not entirely divorced from it. For towards the end of 1951 the news from Kuala Lumpur brought him two shocks.

The first came on October 8th; it was Sunday morning, when he was listening to the radio news from Hong Kong. A brief announcement stated that the British High Commissioner in Malaya, Sir Henry Gurney, had been ambushed and killed in the early afternoon of the preceding day on his way to Fraser's Hill. Comment on the announcement concentrated on the shocked reaction of all sections of the Malayan community whose morale, it was suggested, had reached rock bottom. By Monday the Hong Kong newspapers had arrived and Ferdach devoured every detail of the murder that he could find. It seemed that the whole world was wondering how the High Commissioner, riding sedately along in his Rolls Royce with his pennant flying and with such small military protection, could have been caught unaware. It looked as if Sir Henry had been contemptuous of danger. There were other sad details, of how Sir Henry, to protect his wife, had got out of the car to draw the CT's fire while his private secretary, Mr Staples, had bravely covered Lady Gurney with his own body. Many journalists had begun to speculate on whether this disaster was the final nail in the coffin of British colonialism in Malaya and the termination of a guerrilla war that was now ending in a communist victory. Strangely enough, to begin with, Ferdach in no way connected his job as a go-between with the assassination. It was not that he had forgotten the part he had played, it was just that it now seemed a minor, if somewhat extraordinary, role that had come to nothing and was best forgotten. But after a while certain circumstances associated with Sir Henry's death began to attract his attention and suspicious thoughts began to float about in his head; these suspicions were to increase when, over the next couple of weeks, he read how peculiarly the Malayan authorities had reacted to the loss of someone who, it was generally accepted, had been courageous, liberal and far sighted, indeed a man who, had he lived, might have been classed with Sir Stamford Raffles and Sir Frank Swettenham for his contribution to the development of the Malayan peninsula.

By Monday evening however, Ferdach had started to seek connections and once his mind had begun to travel along that path he picked on the information that Sir Henry had invited the Attorney-General, Mr M. J. Hogan, a close personal friend, to accompany him on his journey. Would not an acute legal mind be useful to the High Commissioner if he were, in fact, to be involved in discussions with Chin Peng? It was true that Sir Henry had said that the exchange of letters was to be exclusively between himself and Chin Peng but might he not have decided that this secrecy would need to be extended to a legal colleague if only immediatly before any negotiations took place.

It was well known that Sir Henry regularly travelled about Malaya with only a small escort; indeed it had crossed Ferdach's mind that there might well be an unwritten agreement between government and the CTs on this matter. After all the safety in which Chin Peng lived in Tras suggested some hidden agreement in regard to the communist leader's safety. It was as if the two kings on the board were to be kept well away from the skirmishing. Ferdach next noted that there was much speculation on how the CTs might have known that Sir Henry was on his way to the mountain resort; it was even suggested that the cook at King's House was a Min Yuen member and had telephoned someone he knew in Fraser's Hill or at the Gap with the information. But most disturbing to Ferdach was the news that came in later that Sir Henry's escort, such as it was, had been fatally weakened shortly after leaving Kuala Lumpur when the radio van which normally accompanied him had broken down and fallen behind, together with Mr Hogan and a police scout car. This had meant that Sir Henry had gone ahead with only a land rover, manned by six Malay policemen, as escort, and with no means of communication with the outside world. The fact that there were rival schools of thought at the highest level in regard to the further prosecution of the anti-CT campaign now returned in full force to Ferdach's mind; could the assassination have been the result not only of communist activity but of sabotage at police headquarters? The thought alarmed him thoroughly. A visit by the High Commissioner to Fraser's Hill would be nothing out of the ordinary as far as the Special Branch was concerned but a visit to see Chin Peng would. If sabotage had been involved was there some channel that might have provided the information about such a meeting to someone at police headquarters?

Gradually Ferdach's concern died away. Life in Macau preoccupied him and he was content to let himself believe that what had happened was just another of those mysteries of history that periodically resulted from the ineptitude of those allegedly in control. All the same there was further strange news that momentarily revived his interest and then gave rise to his scorn. The ambush had been followed up by great air raids and artillery bombardments on the areas of jungle adjacent to the ambush spot. Any idiot could see that such action was useless and was designed to give the impression that the authorities were doing their utmost to get the assassins. The one action that might have caught them, the use of Emergency Regulation 17D against Tras, was not taken until well into November, a most suspicious delay for under that regulation an entire population could be cordoned off and arrested. Of course, by then, all the CTs in Tras, both high and low ranking, had cleared off.

Yet what disturbed Ferdach most was a letter he received from Laura just before Christmas. Its content was different from their usual exchanges and pushed to one side what he had come to regard as his pointless speculations about the assassination of Sir Henry Gurney.

83

My dearest Ferdie,

Maybe you will think I have no right to say my dearest when you have read this letter. But whatever you may think, to me you remain my dearest friend and the person with whom I have got on best in the entire world. And because you are so dear to me I know it is my duty to be totally honest with you and to tell you what has happened to me without further delay. Only if you have the knowledge that I shall give you will you understand the decision I have made about our relationship.

You know that I have been having an affair with Tengku Mizan. Both you and I initially imagined that it was no more than a passing pleasure but it has not turned out to be so at all. It is no longer an affair; it is a love affair. Yes Ferdie, I have to tell you that I am in love with Mizan who has brought to my life a joy that I have never known before. Ours is a complete love; we have no secrets, absolutely no secrets at all, from one another. Because of that, I know that we will not marry or spend a lifetime with one another but as long as our love lasts I wish to be with him. It would be quite impossible for me to tell him that I want to break with him just because you and I are great friends and once had an arrangement to settle down together. All the same, I know the time will come when Mizan will move on, especially as he rises in the political world and will need more important connections. You too will have moved on by then but, dare I say this, I would not rule out the possibility, even if years ahead, of our being together once again just as we once were, for in some strange way that baffles me, I *still feel more akin to you than to any one I know.*

Yes, between us there is a wonderfully close emotional and mental bond, but though we are at ease making love together, I have never felt that there was, in our love making, what for a better word, I can only call a feeling of magic, the sort of magic you felt with Mat Noor and Henry Wong and I now feel with Mizan. It takes the inner desire of both partners to produce this magic. For you Ferdie, my inner desire has always been there but the magic is still born because nothing is returned by you. The cold truth is that you probably cannot experience the magic of love with any woman, and that makes you derogate such love against the love of men.

What I have just written must sound hard but it is the truth. Unfortunately being truthful does not always make one happy and there is always the fear, at the back of ones mind, that one may have been wrong despite all the thought that lies behind ones words. More than that, I am sad, fearing I will hurt you. As for me, I shall remain your loving friend for as long as you want me to be.

Your loving Laura

With rising anger Ferdach read the letter twice, screwed it up and threw it at his cat who saw in the sudden movement an invitation to play and chased the paper ball hither and thither, skidding as he went, across the polished tiled floor. Ferdach retrieved the scratched paper from under a chair, spread it out and read it for a third time. Tears sprang to his eyes but they soon stopped flowing for it annoyed him greatly that Laura, who had once mocked what she termed his romantic, adolescent obsession with Mat Noor, should prate of magic with someone who was already a married man with a brood of children. 'I hope he drops you and leaves you in the bloody lurch,' he shouted aloud, yet he realised that his words not only signalled a childish wish that she should be punished for telling him the stark truth, which he already knew, but suggested that he was still hoping that in the end, even if the end was a long way off, she might come back to him.

Yet even though he possessed a degree of the male arrogance that can afflict men who have a woman in many ports yet resent the infidelity of any one of them, Ferdach had no intention of suffering on Laura's account. How could anyone suffer in Macau? It was a modern Sybaris as far as he and the other Malayan Civil Service officers studying there were concerned. They were lotus-eaters, enjoying themselves to the full while learning a language whose acquisition was more rewarding than finding a treasure. He could, therefore, like Jane Austen's Mr Bennett, say of his displeasure, 'It will pass,' but not out of mental laziness as out of the countervailing security of a happiness that was both intellectual and hedonistic. On that account his concern over the loss of Laura, like that over the murder of Sir Henry, withdrew to the back of his mind.

When the period of his language study was drawing to an end, Ferdach was full of regret that he must leave Macau, giving up, out of necessity rather than out of Buddhist abnegation, his attachment to the persons and things and places that had given him so much delight. At the same time he felt refreshed and anticipated with excitement a new period of involvement in Malaya, fortified by his greater understanding of the Chinese people and their remarkable culture that the often far-sighted, and occasionally remarkably wise, old colonial service had enabled him to acquire.

compound was in a beautiful though still dangerous situation.

Ferdach's social life was much constrained by work though Templer's approval of what he was doing had led to a couple of invitations to King's House. Such invitations were no longer issued for reasons of status but because of the recipient's merit in the eyes of Sir Gerald and his equally dynamic wife. Otherwise he had developed few relationships outside the working friendships of the District Office. Indeed it was in the company of Jimmy Waite and his wife Jessica that he found the most solace and reassurance. He had thought it best to keep well away from Laura. On a couple of occasions he had seen her driving around town in a large car but it was impossible to tell from such brief glimpses how she was nor did he want to find out when he had so much on his plate. Then, towards the end of his tour of duty he met her early one afternoon in the café inside Whiteway Laidlaw's store. She was leaving as he was going in. They caught one another's eyes but each was silent. He thought that she looked taut and nervous; he must have looked gaunt and ill to her. Quite unexpectedly she put her hand out and seized his arm, drawing him towards a table where they sat down looking almost stupidly at one another. He asked her how she was but she did not answer. A waiter came and Ferdach ordered two coffees. For almost a minute Laura just stared down at the table and tears began to form in her eyes. He asked her what was wrong but she seemed unable to reply and then what came out was a peculiar sound, almost like a sob or a groan. 'Forgive me Ferdie. Forgive me. I've wanted to tell you since you came back, but I daren't, I just couldn't. Now we've met, just by accident I know, I can't hold it back any more.' Her eyes darted around the café, but it was almost empty and no one was near them. As Ferdach looked at her he felt moved and knew that deep inside he still cared for her. Again he asked her what was wrong. Her reply was rapid but disjointed and almost whispered so that Ferdach had to lean forward to hear her. 'About Sir Henry. It was all my fault. I thought it was the right thing to do, to protect him. I told Mizan that those letters might lead to a meeting; that Gurney might be in danger. But I was telling the wrong person. I didn't know that I was telling the wrong person. I swear it Ferdie.' Ferdach tried to convince her that she could not take any blame, that as the only one to read the letters, no one but Sir Henry knew the date of his journey up to Fraser's, that there could therefore be no link between Mizan and Sir Henry's murder, above all that she had jumped to conclusions. But she brushed his words aside. 'I just know it's my fault. I asked Mizan what he knew but he refused to reply. I could see he was angry with me for suspecting him. Still I pressed him for an answer. He said that women had no right to interfere in men's work. I disagreed with him vehemently and that made him more angry. In the end he shouted several times that he'd only tell me when water turned to stone.' Then he walked out of my apartment. Laura hesitated. Her eyes had grown tearful as she remembered the miserable scene. Almost in a whisper she uttered Mizan's final words again but now in Malay, '*Sukat air menjadi batu*. But it was Mizan's heart that turned to stone, towards me Ferdie. So now you know that I am on my own again. I wrecked the trust between Mizan and me. Just as I seem to wreck the trust with all the men I meet. Once wrecked trust can't be mended. Maybe with Alfred and Mizan it wasn't all my fault so in time I won't let it matter but what I did to you does. I know you'll never forgive me for breaking my promise. Oh Ferdie, I can't ask you to forgive me. That wouldn't change what happened.' Her voice choked and almost at once she rose to leave. Ferdach looked up at her dumbfounded, unsure that he had heard what he had heard. He closed his eyes to muster his thoughts but when he opened them she was gone. He went to the door but she had vanished through the store. An hour later he phoned her office but was told that she had left for Hong Kong and would not be back for three weeks, well after his leave had started. The brief incident shook Ferdach but such was the pressure on him, that he did not try to contact Laura in any way or even to think very much about her words. In fact to begin with it struck him that she had been behaving hysterically; perhaps the break-up with Mizan was at the heart of it. But that night when piecing together bits of the past he could not help regretting that he had lost her, pitying her for assuming more feelings of guilt than she merited, and wanting her back as much as ever.

Two days later he spent a very full day at work. The fever was clearing and though still tired he worked late catching up on a mass of correspondence. It was getting on to midnight when he left the secretariat building in which the District Office was situated and started to drive back to Ampang. Soon he was well beyond the town centre and the suburban houses into an open area of scrub and trees from which at last he turned off the main road, very slowly as was necessary, into the narrow drive that ran to his house. Then, very unusually, for there was a curfew, he was alarmed to see someone sitting on a tree stump beside the compound gate. The figure lurched towards to the car and Ferdach found himself looking into the barrel of a gun. A familiar voice said, 'Take me back to your house.' Without more ado Harry Wong, in CT uniform, got in the car behind Ferdach who knew there was nothing for it but to drive up the sloping track that was overlooked by three other occupied Pacific Tin houses, to park at the back of his own bungalow. His Malay servant Minah had gone to bed but had left on the outside light, between her quarters and the kitchen, in case of burglars. 'Go in. Switch off the light. I don't want to be seen, but don't think of raising the alarm,' said Harry, or was he Wong Chooi Fong? What else could Ferdach do? He had no gun; Harry could have been after him like a shot and in any case, even had he shouted aloud the late-working, or otherwise boozed-up, tin mining engineers would be unlikely to hear him.

Once in the kitchen Harry opened the fridge and helped himself to a cold chicken. Ferdach noticed that he was dirty as if he had just had a long jungle trek and that his face was tense and grim. Things did not bode well Ferdach thought as he opened two bottles of beer and said as calmly as he could, 'Well Harry, to what do I owe this honour?' His eyes fell on the revolver that Harry had put in front of him on the kitchen table. 'Is that to threaten me with?' Then he remembered the fate of George Carew and half in jest but more in apprehension asked, 'Or to shoot me with?'

Harry began to devour the chicken and then took some cold rice out of the fridge leaving Ferdie to eye him like a mesmerised rabbit. 'Do sit down Ferdie, you look tired out and ill. Are you ill?'

'I've had dengue but it's nearly gone. I keep going with codeine. Anyway, I'm off on leave soon.'

'Going on leave? Back to the good old United Kingdom?' Harry paused as if remembering something that was bothering him. 'But not with Laura. You don't see her any more do you? She's no longer part of your life is she?'

Harry's last question was one Ferdach sometimes asked himself without coming to a conclusion so why should he deny Laura merely to satisfy a man who seemed intent on tantalising him, harming him perhaps? 'Laura will always be part of my life Harry and one day I shall see her again, if I survive.' Ferdach eyed Harry narrowly uncertain whether that peculiar noise that had just come from those well-formed lips of his was a chuckle or the result of eating too quickly. Very precisely he asked, 'Am I going to survive or is something unpleasant going to happen to me?'

'Is your bedroom air-conditioned?'

Though still uncertain of his fate, Ferdach replied quite casually, 'Yes it is; one of the advantages of a US company house. Why do you ask?'

'We'll go in there to talk. If there's a light burning, people will only think you've gone to bed. We don't want callers, do we? But bring along something stronger to drink, yes, that Cognac. Still your favourite, eh?'

Once in the bedroom Harry locked the door and put the large key in his pocket. He looked around the room which was simply furnished and smiled at Krishna who was on the wall next to a steel gun safe in which Ferdach might have kept a rifle but never had. Harry opened it and said, 'No weapons, Ferdie? Only Krishna?'

'No Harry. I'm at your mercy. Are you merciful? Like Krishna?'

'That door over there?'

'Just a cupboard. The other one's the bathroom.'

'Good. We're both sweaty and dirty and I stink. We'll wash together. The first time we met was in a shower. Do you remember? The Carefree Hotel in Ipoh.'

Ferdach still wanted to know Harry's intentions. Was it possible to make a jump at him and fight? Maybe it was but in his present weakened state he was unlikely to win. All the same he must somehow prepare himself. Looking as determined as he could he said, 'Harry, that's sounds ominous. If the Carefree was the first time we showered together, is this going to be my last?'

Harry started to get undressed though still keeping the revolver near him. He laughed outright. 'It may be our last Ferdach but not because I'm going to murder you. Well, I guess you might as well know it. I was sent here to kill you but I'm not going to obey orders.'

Ferdach was dumbfounded. 'How do I know you're telling the

truth? Am I some sort of hostage then?'

'You're some sort of silly ass really. If I was going to kill you, wouldn't I have done it by the gate? You were a sitting duck.'

'Why are you keeping that revolver by you all the time then?'

'Because you might get the wrong idea and try to jump me. You've already shown how suspicious you are.'

Ferdach decided to take the bull by the horns. He went up to Harry and put his arms around him. A host of memories and regrets was passing through his mind. That surge of pleasure he used to feel in Harry's company was beginning to stir if only slightly. From out of his mouth, unbidden it seemed, came the words, 'I could never kill you Harry. I never wanted to see you captured. I've never forgotten you. I like, no, I still love you too much. So much for my loyalty to King and country.'

Harry looked Ferdach straight in the eyes, then cupped his face in his hands, drew him forward and kissed him. 'And did you imagine that I could forget you? I feel exactly as I did when we were last together. What a fool I was, refusing to accept you as a divided man. We can only be what we are. Ferdie, I could never hurt you, never kill you. I am Chinese. When I'm committed, I don't back out. There's been no change in me. I love you too much to obey mad orders. So much for my loyalty to the Party.'

With that exchange of words their old trust seemed to have been re-established. Harry put the revolver in the gun safe and they both forgot about it. In the bathroom they enjoyed a shower under icy cold water drawn from the stream that gushed down from a reservoir that nestled higher up in the foothills. Once the mud and grime was gone Harry's body appeared to be unchanged though perhaps leaner but there were two bullet wound scars on his left thigh. When Ferdach saw them he knelt down and kissed them one after another. Tears came into his eyes at the thought of his friend suffering. He looked up and noticed how tenderly Harry was gazing down on him. Then they stood together embracing each other and sometimes laughing with joy as the water streamed over them bringing them to life just as the rain makes the parched desert bloom once more. Once dry they went inside the huge mosquito net that hung from the ceiling like a baroque fantasy about a bed designed no doubt for some exceedingly large American male and his equally voluminous wife. Ferdach switched off the light and they lay side by side, though not in the darkness for through the green glazed windows came the glow of the compound perimeter lighting that made Ferdach imagine sometimes that he was a sea creature in a strange tank of translucent water; yet now his situation was no less bizarre. Harry had once told him how clever the Chinese were at keeping things under cover. He remembered those words of his: we are good at saying one thing and intending another. Despite his loving words he could still have turned up tonight for murder. Yet perhaps it was indeed for love; some remnant of passion still existed between them but if that was all Harry had come for where could it lead to at this stage in their lives? Ferdach found it difficult to believe what was happening. He felt that he was an observer outside both the present and the past. Everything that had happened to him before he had left for China was remote. His once romantic yearning for Mat Noor had become nothing but a sad and fractured memory. In Macau, that unreal city, a new strata of experiences had been laid down only to become quickly petrified. His passion for Laura still burned in him but only deep down now; on the surface he deliberately made her loss worth only a shrug of the shoulders. His adoration of Harry Wong had retreated to the depth of his mind like a plant affected by the winter cold. Could he believe that life was really stirring in its frozen root? And in the light of his own cool doubts could he believe that Harry Wong's feelings for him were still vibrant?

He was still unsure what Harry expected of him. It could hardly be about his part as a go-between. That matter was as dead as a doornail. Was Harry lonely and in need of affection? It must be pretty foul to live with people whose political ideology he no longer shared and in jungle camps where sensuality, let alone love, must be at a discount. Should he put an arm around Harry, say something comforting? Again he did not know. He could only think of one thing to ask, 'Why were you ordered to kill me? I think that's what you said. Who ordered you? Is it because of the work I'm doing among the squatters in KL?'

Harry asked rather condescendingly, 'What are you doing among the squatters?'

'Well I'm carrying out an investigation and a census to give us all the details of their lives, age, sex, occupation, schooling, wages, race, dialect group, you name it.' Ferdach's voice gained in enthusiasm. Nervously he gabbled on, 'I work under Jimmy Waite ... you remember him from Ipoh. We report directly to Templer who wants a solution to the KL squatter problem. We're going to suggest two ways of dealing with it: resettlement in suburban New Villages and regularisation in their existing settlements. The regularised areas would then be provided with basic services and the people in them given temporary occupation licenses.'

'And you and Waite really imagine that measures like that will win them over to your side?' Harry's voice in the half-light sounded sepulchral yet slightly amused like that of a ghost having fun in a haunted house.

'Maybe. At least it would make them feel more secure. It will have more than a chance of success if Templer supports us.'

The old well-informed Harry was resurrected. He stated, 'Soon Templer will be gone and the state government won't want to grant squatters in the capital even a temporary occupation license. Too much land and hard cash are involved just when the country's moving into recession. There'll not be enough money to fund your ideas. And if there are fewer incidents in the squatter areas there'll be no emergency funds for your schemes either. Poor Ferdie, you'll see. No, I've not been told to kill you because of anything you've done at all. The Party doesn't think it's threatened by what you and Waite are doing. The one they see as a threat is me.'

'I don't understand. What do you mean?' Only then did Ferdach turn on his side and place his arm across Harry's chest in a gesture that might seem either one of tenderness, or just the result of needing somewhere to rest his arm.

'It goes back to the assassination of Gurney. It was a mistake. It had nothing to do with Chin Peng. He can be ruthless when necessary but he keeps his word. Well, there's an anti-peace group in Bluff Road that doesn't want an agreement with the Party. It's mainly British and Malay but there's one important Chinese intelligence officer among them, a man with close connections with the KMT in Taiwan. He's influential and completely ruthless. He'd murder to get his way. I suspect he's even got tentacles in the Party. These men want the war to continue as long as need be. Communism, which means Chinese power in Malaya, must be eliminated. Somehow they found out what Gurney was planning.'

Ferdach listened intently but still with disbelief. Suppressed fears were forcing themselves up in his mind. He began to tremble. He was not sure whether this came from the dengue or from somewhere else. 'Found out? How could they find out? We kept it all secret and I'm sure Sir Henry did,' he protested nervously. But now his feverish brain was busily connecting words and phrases: Bluff Road, intelligence work, Tengku Mizan, the anti-peace group, and above all Laura's confession that she had talked to Mizan out of fear for Gurney's safety. Inevitably Ferdach slipped into a fearful speculation: if told by Mizan of the letters and a possible meeting, the anti-peace group would quickly surmise the purpose of a peculiarly unscheduled journey that HE and Attorney-General Hogan were about to make to Fraser's. The group must then have decided on sabotage by damaging the escort vehicles; this, they may have thought, would probably suffice to abort HE's journey. Even though Laura's mind may not have followed this path exactly, Ferdach could see why she had quickly made a connection between her failure to keep her solemn promise and Gurney's death that had so soon followed her lapse.

He did his best to suppress the thoughts racketing about in his head as mere speculation but then Harry gave the knockout blow. It came slowly as though intended as a communiqué. 'Someone in Bluff Road, maybe no more than one fanatic who wanted to make a hundred percent sure of stopping the meeting, leaked the details of a trip some top officials would be making up to Fraser's to a Min Yuen member in Kuala Kubu Bahru. The news quickly got to Sui Mah, the local CT commander who had no knowledge of the arrangement between Chin Peng and Gurney. He immediately deployed his men for action. And so the ambush was carried out but for days even the Party leaders didn't know precisely what had been done, or exactly who had been killed.'

Ferdach's horror of killing and of his part in killing, engendered in him during the war, loomed in his mind like a foul miasma to mortify him. He began to see connections he would rather ignore. How deeply he could sympathise with Laura's pain. Her sense of guilt, her break-up with Mizan and her failure to keep her promise must be taking a heavy toll on her. But as he visualised her misery he began at last to face up to the reality of what he had done, which meant fully accepting his own error. He had let Laura find out more than she should. Lai Kuan had been slightly involved in the error but not crucially. What Laura had subsequently done had been well intentioned. What Mizan had probably done must have seemed to be in the Malay interest. But Ferdach saw that what he himself had done was just plain stupid. He had blabbed and that was at the root of the whole tragedy right up to the slaying of Sir Henry Gurney. However, because there was no point in retailing this to Harry, he stated roundly but perhaps too vehemently, 'At least the Party can't suspect you Harry.' His grip on his lover's body tightened as if he wanted to protect him from any unpleasant reality.

Harry did not ask what was meant by 'at least' but went on: 'Sui Mah apologised to Chin Peng who ordered him to find out where the information about Gurney's journey had come from. This was not difficult; through the Min Yuen agent he traced it back to Bluff Road but he never identified the man who had leaked the details. I suspect a certain person who is neither British nor Malay but I have no proof. Chin Peng asked me if I thought you had told Special Branch about the letters. I said no, never. But some Party people suspected me of treachery. You and I had been seen together in that pool on the way up to Genting Sempah. They said I was too friendly with you; in fact they said we were not only traitors but *kai dai*, homos, and couldn't be trusted since we'd always put one another first.' Harry laughed, 'At least that was true.'

Ferdach was now wondering how British intelligence in Singapore had taken the disruption of a plan that had ultimately stemmed from them. He asked, 'And Chin Peng? Why hasn't he tried for peace again despite the accident of Gurney's death? I know it would be difficult but ...'

'He felt he'd been betrayed, though not by Gurney. He likes to warn us that treachery can lurk anywhere, even in the marriage bed, but he keeps his own feelings and his intentions to himself. He's as tight as a clam and never admits to anything. And then something very interesting happened; Chin Peng lost all interest in peace.' Harry paused, eyed Ferdach cautiously and went on in a low voice, even though there was no one to hear him, 'I've been told by Lai Kuan, yes I see him from time to time, that Phoenix Park has changed its tune. Because of the Korean War any British deal with China is out of the question at present. The British now think it's better to win the war against the CTs here; ultimately an anti-communist Malaya in Southeast Asia will be valuable to the West when problems arise in Vietnam and Indonesia.'

Comrade Wong Chooi Fong never suggested that Chin Peng might be acting at the behest of the British or that he was, like his predecessor Lai Teck, a British agent. He knew that speculation on this question would be sterile. But Ferdach had firmly concluded that, in one respect, Chin Peng had got it right: the good leader should be as tight as a clam and never admit to anything. He also added, and give hell to fools like himself for the mistakes they make, intended or not. But for now, to escape from his own confusion, all Ferdach wanted was for Harry to give a final answer to his question: 'Why were you ordered to kill me?'

'I thought I'd made that clear. They suspect our friendship. They suspect me. They are testing me. To prove my loyalty I have to kill you.'

Ferdach was thinking rapidly. He must get Harry out of Malaya. He hugged him as if to hang on to him forever. Their kisses told them that their feelings for one another were far from dead. Yet more than that Ferdach was stunned by the thought that in his arms there was someone who, out of love for him, would risk his own life rather than kill him. Laura's words about hoping he would find someone whom he could love profoundly began to have a resonance in this mind. 'Harry, when I go on leave I'm sailing from Penang and Colombo is the first port of call. You must get to Penang and find a boat, any boat, to Colombo. You can ask my friend Siu Bo to hide you in Penang. She will, I'm sure. I'll give you all the money I've got in the house and you can borrow more from Siu Bo. Have you still got that US Passport?'

'Yes,' said Harry, but then he started to laugh obviously seeing Ferdach as a child with no feeling for reality. 'Ferdie you've no idea of the danger. I'll try to get away, for your sake. But I'm not worried about myself. I'm detached from everything now except you, even though only one half of you wants me. But I'd be happy with that and Laura could have the rest if it were possible. As for getting away, I'll tell you, every track to this house is watched by CTs. They'll easily catch me.'

'If they catch you, say that I'm dead, that you cut my throat. That's why there was no gunshot. You're clever Harry. I know you'll find a way through.' Ferdach sat up and looked down at his lover. 'But there's another way too. I could phone the police now and tell them that I've got a CT who's just surrendered. They'll come and take you away. The CTs couldn't get you then. At least you'd be safe.'

Harry pulled Ferdach down to him. 'Do you mean to say you'd actually phone them now? Now? Oh Ferdie tomorrow morning please. We're alone together in this comfortable room. I want you much more than a ride in a police van.' He stopped Ferdach from replying to his facetious remark and went on, seriously. 'No. That way's impossible. Remember Ferdie, I'm not just a guerrilla soldier, I'm a man who committed atrocities. Remember those men whose throats I cut. Think of George Carew. His name never quits my mind. What would I face? A life sentence or the hangman? I'd prefer the latter; I deserve it. But don't worry. I'll do my best to avoid capture by the British and the CTs. I'll aim for Penang. I'll go in the morning when it's light. I'll keep to public places. There's just a chance.'

Ferdach did his best to be positive. 'You'll do it Harry, I'm sure. Once we're both in Penang there'll be no problem getting away. I can afford everything.' As if they were playing a childish game Ferdach took to thumping Harry. 'Just obey my orders and you'll get through. Once we are in London I'll resign from the Colonial Service. I'll get a job and we'll live together. We'll be what we really are. Think of that Harry. Have faith in me. There'll be no problem.'

Harry drew Ferdach close to him and whispered, 'It'll be what we've dreamed of, but let's have fights from time to time. Tomorrow I'll do what you've ordered for until you resign you're still the colonial master. If I fail, what will it matter, so long as you don't forget me? But tonight Ferdie, nothing must snatch this little bit of happiness from us, not even your fever. I want you to moan with pleasure, not pain, so take some of your precious codeine and we'll make it a night to last a lifetime.'

85

Two days later Ferdach returned to work having called the office the day before to say he was too feverish to come in. He hoped that no one had seen him in his house though he had to admit that the greatest proof to any observing CT that he was not dead lay in the tranquillity of the compound, no police, no ambulances, even Minah hanging out the washing in the sun. All he could do was to pray that Harry was already in Penang. He hoped for a phone call from Wong Siu Bo but none came.

At nine o'clock he went to a security briefing at police headquarters. The usual reports of incidents, mainly minor today, were made. All at once an intelligence officer entered the room and reported that a body had been found in peculiar circumstances by a ruined temple in the Gombak area. It looked like a CT execution, he said. Photographs were produced and passed around. 'Oh God, what a ghastly sight,' Ferdach heard Waite say. Others echoed his words. Ferdach knew what to expect; he tightened his stomach muscles. Two photos, one a close up, were put in his hand and he stared. A man was bound to a tree with barbed wire, his body had been cut open, great gashes told of torture, even that beautiful face had been ripped apart. Ferdach stared again, uncomprehendingly; that face he had gazed at with such love, that body he had desired so tenderly. On that last night together Harry must have thought that this was inevitable and yet he did not care, he had put their love above fear. Ferdach's expression remained completely impassive but in his head a dreadful sound arose, a drawn-out howl. Was it Harry's agony or his own rage that gave birth to such a sound that would unite their brief love in his memory for the rest of his life?

'He doesn't look well. Maybe it's still the dengue. It takes ages to clear up. Take him home Ahmad.' Having spoken to his driver Waite leaned over Ferdach, who was lying on the ops room table, and addressed him in a fatherly way, indeed his voice was full of concern for Ferdach looked as white as a corpse. 'Come on matey. Come on Ferdie. I don't want you flaking out on me. We're sending you back home to have a good rest. Jessica and I will come and see you as soon as we can. You're too ill and tired to be here. You shouldn't have come. You shouldn't have come at all.'

Waite's words were still echoing in Ferdach's mind a few days later as he made his way slowly, under the sad gaze of Wong Siu Bo and two of her pretty girls, up the gangway of the P&O liner *Corfu*: 'You shouldn't have come. You shouldn't have come at all.' But I did come, he told himself. And I don't regret a thing. He turned and waved at the little trio on the Penang wharf. When my leave is over and I'm well, I'll be back. My Malayan life isn't over. I'm coming back.